THE BROADMOOR LEGACY

www.traciepeterson.com

www.judithmccoymiller.com

THE BROADMOOR LEGACY

THREE NOVELS IN ONE VOLUME
A DAUGHTER'S INHERITANCE
AN UNEXPECTED LOVE
A SURRENDERED HEART

TRACIE PETERSON
AND JUDITH MILLER

BETHANYHOUSE
a division of Baker Publishing Group
Minneapolis, Minnesota

© 2008, 2009 by Tracie Peterson and Judith Miller

Previously published in three separate volumes:
  A Daughter's Inheritance © 2008
  An Unexpected Love © 2008
  A Surrendered Heart © 2009

Published by Bethany House Publishers
11400 Hampshire Avenue South
Bloomington, Minnesota 55438
www.bethanyhouse.com

Bethany House Publishers is a division of
Baker Publishing Group, Grand Rapids, Michigan

Printed in the United States of America

Library of Congress Cataloging-in-Publication Data is available for this title.

This is a work of historical reconstruction; the appearances of certain historical figures are therefore inevitable. All other characters are products of the author's imagination, and any resemblance to actual persons, living or dead, is coincidental.

Scripture quotations are from the King James Version of the Bible.

Cover design by John Hamilton Design
Cover photography of 1000 Islands: Reprinted with permission from Ian Coristine's book *1000 Islands*, his fourth book of photography of the region.
www.1000islandsphotoart.com

12 13 14 15 16 17 18   7 6 5 4 3 2 1

A DAUGHTER'S INHERITANCE

ℬroadmoor Family Tree

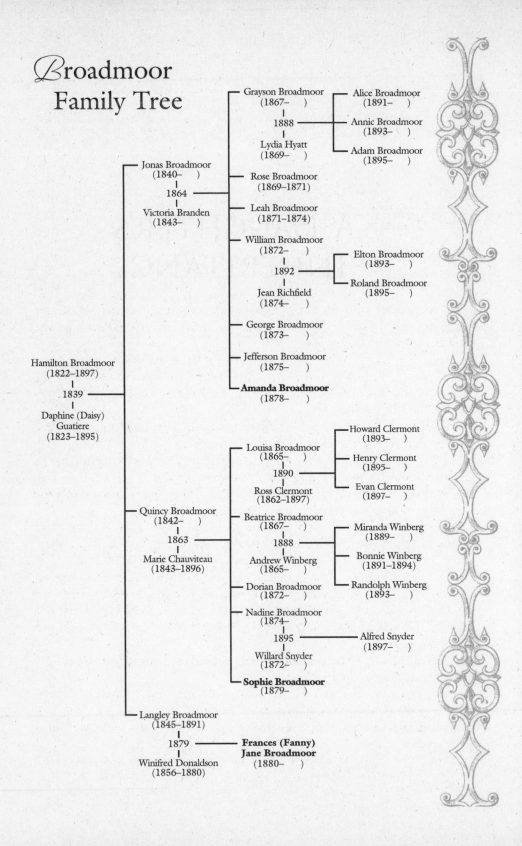

Hamilton Broadmoor
(1822–1897)
|
1839
|
Daphine (Daisy)
Guatiere
(1823–1895)

Jonas Broadmoor
(1840–   )
|
1864
|
Victoria Branden
(1843–   )

Grayson Broadmoor
(1867–   )
|
1888
|
Lydia Hyatt
(1869–   )

Alice Broadmoor
(1891–   )

Annie Broadmoor
(1893–   )

Adam Broadmoor
(1895–   )

Rose Broadmoor
(1869–1871)

Leah Broadmoor
(1871–1874)

William Broadmoor
(1872–   )
|
1892
|
Jean Richfield
(1874–   )

Elton Broadmoor
(1893–   )

Roland Broadmoor
(1895–   )

George Broadmoor
(1873–   )

Jefferson Broadmoor
(1875–   )

Amanda Broadmoor
(1878–   )

Quincy Broadmoor
(1842–   )
|
1863
|
Marie Chauviteau
(1843–1896)

Louisa Broadmoor
(1865–   )
|
1890
|
Ross Clermont
(1862–1897)

Howard Clermont
(1893–   )

Henry Clermont
(1895–   )

Evan Clermont
(1897–   )

Beatrice Broadmoor
(1867–   )
|
1888
|
Andrew Winberg
(1865–   )

Miranda Winberg
(1889–   )

Bonnie Winberg
(1891–1894)

Randolph Winberg
(1893–   )

Dorian Broadmoor
(1872–   )

Nadine Broadmoor
(1874–   )
|
1895
|
Willard Snyder
(1872–   )

Alfred Snyder
(1897–   )

Sophie Broadmoor
(1879–   )

Langley Broadmoor
(1845–1891)
|
1879
|
Winifred Donaldson
(1856–1880)

**Frances (Fanny)
Jane Broadmoor**
(1880–   )

CHAPTER 1

The warm summer air rang with laughter as eleven-year-old Fanny Broadmoor made her way up from the river's edge. The day had been perfect, and she couldn't help but be pleased.

Her companion gave a tug on her pigtail. "What are you giggling about now?" fifteen-year-old Michael Atwell asked. Michael lived year-round on the island with his parents, the primary caretakers for the Broadmoor family castle and island estate.

"Do I have to have a reason?" Fanny questioned. "I'm just happy. We caught a great many fish. Your mother will be pleased."

"I think your grandmother will be less excited to see you've spent a day in the sun. You've got at least a hundred more freckles."

Fanny touched her hand to her face and shrugged. "Papa says it goes with my red hair, and he thinks they are quite delightful."

Michael shifted the string of fish and waved them in the air. "I think these are far more delightful. When my mother gets through frying them up, you'll think so, too."

Fanny gave him an adoring smile. She practically worshiped the ground he walked on. He was dashing and adventurous and never failed to treat her kindly. Other servants passed her over as nothing more than a child, but not Michael. He was always good to listen to her and never too busy to stop and see to her needs.

"You're lagging," Michael said as they reached the back of the house. "It's probably due to all that giggling."

Fanny caught up and put aside the fishing poles she'd been carrying. "Grand-mère says that being of good cheer is the secret to a long life."

Michael opened the back door and grinned. "Then you ought to live to be a hundred."

"There you are," Mrs. Atwell said as they stepped into the kitchen. "I

7

thought I'd have to send your father out to find you." She spied the string of fish. "I see 'twas a very productive day."

"The very best," Fanny agreed. "I caught the first fish, and then Michael caught the next two. After that I lost track."

Mrs. Atwell laughed. "Well, I can see I'll have my work cut out for me. Just put them over there in the sink." She motioned to her son. "I suppose you're both ready for a bit of refreshment."

"We are. We ate everything you sent in the basket, but now we're famished."

"I'm not surprised." Mrs. Atwell affectionately tousled her son's wavy brown hair. "I'll bring you refreshments on the porch, but first I need to fetch Fanny's father. I was just on my way when you arrived. Your grandmother wants to speak with him."

"I can get him," Fanny told her. "Where has he gone?"

"To your special place," Mrs. Atwell said with a sympathetic smile. "The place he always took your mother—and now you."

Fanny nodded with great enthusiasm. "I'll go. It's not so very far."

"I'll go with her," Michael said. "It's farther than a young lady should go by herself."

"The island is hardly that big," Fanny declared, "and I am eleven years old."

Michael laughed. "And very opinionated."

"All right, you two. Get on with you now. Miss Fanny, it would be the better part of wisdom to allow Michael to join you. Besides that, if I remember right, your father took a picnic basket with him. Michael can fetch that back for me."

Fanny didn't really mind Michael's company. She simply didn't want him to think of her as a helpless child who needed to be watched over.

They made their way across the well-kept lawn and headed for the northerly side of the island, where the trees thinned out and gave way to rocky outcroppings. Fanny knew where she would find her father. Langley Broadmoor had often regaled her with stories of how he'd courted her mother on this island—how they would love to steal quiet moments in a very secluded place during their whirlwind romance. Fanny loved coming here each year. The island caused her to feel a sense of her mother's presence just in knowing how much she had cherished this place.

The family always tried to spend some time on the island during the warm summer months. The Thousand Islands of the St. Lawrence River were popular gathering retreats for the very wealthy, and this popularity had only increased in the years since Grandfather had purchased the island. The opulent way of life had increased, as well. What had once been a modest summer retreat was now a palatial estate with a six-story castle that held over fifty rooms.

"I found some fossils over this way," Michael told her. "Maybe we can go hunt for more tomorrow."

"That would be grand," Fanny replied and then frowned. "Oh, but I cannot. Your father is taking us to some birthday party on one of the other islands. Amanda and Sophie insist I come."

"Your cousins can be rather bossy, but I'm sure a party will be far more fun than scouting about in the dirt with me."

Fanny thought to deny that idea but spied her father down the path a ways. He was leaning up against a tree, the basket beside him. Apparently he'd fallen asleep while watching the river.

"Papa!" Fanny hurried down the path, barely righting herself as she tripped on the loose rocks.

"Slow down, you goose!" Michael called from behind her. "You don't want to fall and tear your dress."

Fanny checked her step and slowed only marginally. "Papa, wake up. Grandmère wishes to see you." She reached her father's side and knelt beside him. Reaching out, she gave him a shake, but he didn't open his eyes.

"Papa?"

She shook him again, and this time his body slumped away from her. His hand fell to the side, revealing a small framed photograph of her mother.

"Michael, something's wrong." She looked to where Michael had come to stop. "He's . . . he's sick. He's not waking up." Fanny shook him harder, but he only slumped closer to the ground. "Papa!"

In less than a second, Michael was at her side. "Mr. Broadmoor. Wake up, sir." He gently reached out to touch the man, then pulled away. "Fanny, I think you should go get my father. Maybe get your uncle Jonas, too."

"But why? What's wrong?"

"Just go now. Hurry."

Fanny straightened and, seeing the grave expression on Michael's face, did exactly as he told her. She fairly flew up the path, and despite knowing how much her grandmother would disapprove, she ran as fast as she could to get help.

The men were easy to find. Fanny let them know the situation in breathless gasps that left little doubt to the serious nature of the moment. The men headed out, demanding she stay behind, but Fanny wasn't about to be left out of the matter. She allowed them to leave without her then followed behind, ignoring her cousins as they bade her to come and play.

Something inside Fanny's chest felt tight. She couldn't help the sense of dread that washed over her. Papa was very sick, otherwise he would have awakened. What would happen now? Would they remain on the island while he recovered, or would they head back to Rochester early? Deep inside, a most terrible thought tried to force its way through the maze of fearful considerations. What if he wasn't sick? What if he had . . .

She couldn't even breathe the word. Fanny couldn't imagine life without her beloved father. She'd already endured the horrible loneliness of being without a mother. Her mother had died giving birth to Fanny, and all she had of her were a few trinkets.

Edging up quietly to where she'd left Michael with her father, Fanny watched the men as they dealt with the situation at hand.

"This is just great," her Uncle Jonas declared. "Langley always did have a flair for the dramatic."

"Jonas, that's uncalled for," Uncle Quincy countered. "You know he's been lost in grief ever since Winifred died."

"He was a weakling. He couldn't even end his life like a man. What reasonable man would take poison?"

Fanny shook her head and flew at them. "No! My papa isn't dead!" She pushed past Uncle Quincy and reached for her father. It was Michael, however, who stopped her. He pulled her away quickly.

"Get her out of here," Uncle Jonas growled. "Take her away at once, Michael."

Michael pulled Fanny along, but she fought him. "No! I want to be with my papa. He needs me."

"He's beyond need now, Fanny." Michael's soft, gentle words caused her to halt her fighting.

"But . . . he . . . he . . . cannot be . . ." She looked back to where her uncles and Michael's father stood and then braved a glance down to her father's silent form. Tears poured and blinded her eyes as she looked up to Michael.

"Come on."

Fanny gripped Michael's hand tightly and closed her eyes as he led her up the path. Her father was dead. It seemed impossible—horribly wrong. How could it have happened? Uncle Jonas said it was poison. Her father had taken something to end his life.

"Why did he . . . do this?" Fanny barely whispered the words. "Was it my fault?"

Michael dropped to his knees and pulled Fanny against his shoulder. She sobbed quietly for several minutes, just standing there against him.

"This wasn't your fault," Michael finally said as she calmed. "Your father was just too sad. He couldn't bear the pain of being without your mother."

"But he had me," Fanny said, pulling away. "He had me, and now I have no one."

Michael reached up and gently brushed back her tears. He offered a hint of a smile. "You have me, Fanny. You'll always have me."

CHAPTER 2

TUESDAY, JUNE 1, 1897
ROCHESTER, NEW YORK

"Fiddlesticks. Where are they?"

The heels of Frances Jane Broadmoor's shoes tapped a rhythmic click on the Italian marble tile as she paced the length of the entrance hall. Thus far, the technique had failed to control her impatience. At seventeen Fanny was usually not given to such displays, but this occasion merited her frustration.

"Amanda is never late. Sophie would be late to her own funeral, but not Amanda." She went to the window and pulled back the sheer fabric. One glance told her the same thing she'd known for over fifteen minutes. Her cousins had not yet arrived.

They hadn't seen each other since last Christmas, when Fanny was home from finishing school. Amanda had gone away shortly after that to take a grand tour of Europe, while Sophie remained at home. The separation had been absolute misery for the girls. They were closer than most sisters.

"Why must they torture me like this?" She dropped the sheer and began to pace again. Passing by her grandfather's study, she peered inside at the ornamental frame that held her grandmother's likeness. Grand-mère. Fanny smiled at the French word. Her grand-mère's aristocratic French ancestors would be appalled at the English use of Grandmother.

There were those who thought Fanny resembled her grandmère, but the young woman couldn't see it for herself. Fanny had a ghastly collection of dark auburn curls, while Daphine Broadmoor had hair the color of ripe wheat. At least when she'd been younger. Even as an older woman with a snow white crown, her grandmother's beauty surpassed all rivals.

Fanny heard a noise from outside and rushed back to the window. Frowning, she let out a rather unladylike sigh. It was only Mr. Pritchard, the gardener. He offered a smile and waved. Earlier in the day they had worked the garden together, one of Fanny's greatest pleasures. She waved but then quickly walked away from the window.

Had she known both of her cousins would be late, she could have allowed herself additional time in the garden. Mr. Pritchard would have been pleased for another half hour of her help. Though the gardener could be cranky, Fanny had convinced herself years ago that the man enjoyed her assistance. Hamilton Broadmoor hadn't been quite so certain, but her grandfather's assessment hadn't quelled Fanny's desire to learn from Mr. Pritchard.

With no more than the fleeting thought of her grandfather, Fanny glanced up the mammoth stairway. Sunlight spilled from the circular skylight and cast dancing prisms across the palatial landing above the first flight of stairs. She should go upstairs and see if he was awake, but she'd ascended no more than a few steps when the front door burst open.

Amanda rushed inside, holding her straw hat with one hand while lifting her skirts with the other. "I am terribly sorry, Fanny. As usual, Sophie has made us late. Goodness, but what happened to your hair?"

Instinctively Fanny pressed a palm to her unruly curls. No matter how she brushed and pinned the tresses, they popped loose and circled her face like unfettered coils. "I'm afraid my pacing has undone my grooming." She tried to force the pins back into place while scanning the entryway for some sign of Sophie. Giving up on her hair, Fanny descended the steps and hurried to embrace Amanda.

"And where is Sophie? Still in the carriage?"

"Absolutely not! I finally departed without her. Next time she'll believe me when I say I'm not waiting any longer." Amanda pulled away, removed her hat, and twisted a blond tress around her finger to ensure proper placement.

Fanny smiled at the gesture. Amanda's hair was just like Grand-mère's—the same golden shade and never disheveled in the least. "Exactly where did you leave poor Sophie?"

"Poor *Sophie*? Don't you *dare* feel sorry for her. I arrived with the carriage at exactly one-thirty. The time we had both agreed upon, by the way. When she still hadn't gotten into the carriage by two o'clock, I warned her and then departed." Amanda frowned and shook her head. "Some fellow I've never seen before was sitting in the parlor visiting with her when I arrived. Even though he clearly knew of our plans, he made no move to leave. Certainly no gentleman, wouldn't you agree?"

"Well, I . . ."

"When I issued my ultimatum, he grinned and the two of them continued their private conversation. I decided I'd wait no longer. I knew you would be worried about us." Amanda's high cheekbones bore a distinct flush; her usually gentle brown eyes flashed with anger.

"'Tis true I wondered at the lateness of your arrival. In fact, I'd decided to go upstairs for a brief visit with Grandfather, though I wasn't certain he'd be awake." She lowered her voice. "The doctor gives him a great deal of medicine, and he sleeps almost constantly. Hazel and I take turns sitting with him."

Amanda bobbed her head. "Oh, how I've missed you. It seems we've been apart for years instead of months."

"I know. I was thinking the same thing." Fanny's voice was barely audible.

"Why are you whispering?"

Fanny shrugged. "Habit, I suppose. I've become accustomed to keeping my voice low when someone is sick. I guess it's silly."

The girls looped arms and walked into the parlor. "Not so silly. You've been around more sickness and death than most of us."

That fact was certainly true, although Fanny tried not to dwell on it. It just made her all the more lonely to think about what she'd lost in her young life. She couldn't remember her mother, but her father was a different story. Memories of their years together only served to make the loss seem new all over again. She had thought they'd been happy together—that they would always have each other to hold fast to. Remembering him dead only made her loneliness more acute.

After her father's funeral, Fanny hadn't had to make any adjustment to her living arrangements. At her grandmother's insistence, Fanny and her father had been living with Grand-mère and Grandfather at Broadmoor Mansion since the day after Winifred's death and Fanny's birth. But once her father had died, there had been subtle changes in her life. People talked about her father in hushed whispers. After all, it was quite unacceptable to take one's life. Fanny felt as though she'd been hidden away from society while the gossip died down. Still, she'd been fortunate, for her grandparents had easily slipped into the role of both legal and emotional guardians of their youngest granddaughter.

But now Grand-mère, too, was gone, and Grandfather seemed destined to follow. Fanny had suffered greatly when the older woman had taken ill and died two years ago. Her grandparents had insisted she remain at finishing school, and there had been no time for final good-byes with Grand-mère. A situation Fanny continued to regret. She'd had no control over that decision or anything else in her life, for that matter. With Grandfather hovering on the brink of death, she now feared losing him, as well. The two of them had become inordinately close throughout the years, but even more so since Grand-mère's death.

Amanda grasped Fanny's hand and pulled her toward the divan. "Now look what I've done with my dreary talk of illness and death. You've turned gloomy. I can see it in your eyes. Do promise you'll cheer up. I want to hear all about what's happened during your final session at Greatbriar. I know you must be delighted to have completed your education at that distant place. I do wish Grandfather would have permitted you to remain at home and attend finishing school here in Rochester."

Still clasping hands, the girls dropped onto the floral upholstered divan. Greatbriar Manor for Young Ladies of Exceptional Quality, located in Montreal, Canada, had been Grand-mère's choice. Her father had never acquiesced, but after his death, Grand-mère had insisted Fanny would love the school. She hadn't.

"He was following Grand-mère's instructions. She thought it best I finish my schooling at Greatbriar, but who knows what will happen now that I've completed my final year. Grand-mère said after my grand tour of Europe, I could consider attending Vassar." Fanny scooted into a corner of the divan. "From what you tell me about Sophie and this young man, it sounds as though she's adjusted."

Amanda cocked an eyebrow. "To her mother's death, you mean?"

Fanny nodded. It seemed all of their conversation this day would center upon the topic of death. "Yes. She appeared terribly downcast when I saw her during the Christmas holidays. She wouldn't even accept my invitation to come and spend time with Grandfather and me. I didn't take offense, of course. I knew she must be missing her mother terribly."

"You are a sweet girl, Fanny, but I don't believe Aunt Marie's death—"

Before Amanda could complete her response, footsteps clattered across the marble floor tiles. "Forevermore, where is everyone? Fanny? Amanda? Doesn't the butler answer the door anymore?"

Fanny jumped to her feet and hurried toward the parlor doorway. "We're in here, Sophie." She touched her index finger to her lips.

"Why am I supposed to be quiet? And where are the servants? No one answered the door when I arrived. Ever since grandfather has taken ill, the servants take advantage. As head housekeeper, you'd think Mrs. O'Malley would issue some reprimands."

"Grandfather is resting, and the servants are attending to their duties." Fanny frowned. "I didn't hear the doorbell."

The girls exchanged a brief embrace before Sophie shrugged and crossed the room. "You were very rude to my guest, Amanda. And I absolutely could not believe my eyes when I saw your carriage departing without me. I should think you'd have acquired better manners while traveling abroad these past six months."

Amanda squared her shoulders. "My manners have always been impeccable, Sophie. If either of us has disregarded proper etiquette, it is you. I arrived at the assigned time and gave you fair warning before I departed. You failed to heed my word."

Their long-awaited reunion was quickly turning into a disastrous affair. Fanny clapped her hands together. "I have a wonderful idea. Why don't we go out and visit in the garden? It will be just like old times, when we were little girls. Besides, I want both of you to see my lilacs."

"No need to go to the garden for that. I saw a vase of your lilacs sitting on the pier table in the front hall when I arrived. Do you like my new dress?" Sophie cast a glance at the billowing leg-of-mutton sleeves that made her waist appear even narrower than the fashionable handspan.

Fanny assessed Sophie's latest purchase and nodded. It certainly wasn't a dress she would have chosen for herself, but it suited her cousin. Intricate dark brown embroidery embellished the entire length of each sleeve and decorated the pale pink yoke before flowing downward into a simple gored skirt. The deep brown embroidered stitches were a near match to Sophie's coffee-colored tresses, and the pale pink shade of the gown emphasized her skin tone to perfection.

Amanda shifted forward and stood. "I think we should go outdoors and enjoy the garden." She ran a finger along the embroidered sleeve of Sophie's dress. "Only last week you were lamenting the fact that Uncle Quincy was pouring all of his funds into helping the homeless. It appears as if you've managed to redirect his thinking. I'm certain you paid a dear price for this dress."

"The price was fair," Sophie defended. "And after a bit of cajoling, Father agreed. How could he refuse? The dress had been custom made for me."

They all three understood that Quincy Broadmoor could have refused to pay for the gown. Likely he'd been overcome by the need to please his daughter, or Sophie had simply worn him down. Fanny suspected the latter was correct. When Sophie wanted something, she wasn't easily deterred. Fanny waved her cousins toward the entrance hall. "Come along. I promise the lilacs I want to show you are different from the ones you've already seen." She tilted her head. "They are like nothing you've ever before observed."

"If you had a hand in raising them, I'm certain they are absolutely gorgeous." Dimples creased Sophie's cheeks, and her brown eyes sparkled as she walked alongside Fanny through the conservatory and into the garden. "I used the services of the same dressmaker to design and sew my gown for the Summer's Eve Ball."

Amanda slowed her step. "Truly? Then you ought not complain in the least about Uncle Quincy being tightfisted with you."

"Easy enough for you to say, Amanda. Unlike Fanny and me, you have a mother who delights in shopping and purchasing the latest fashions for you. You live in elegance and beauty, while our home has been all but stripped of such amenities in order to finance Father's home for the friendless. He only lets us keep a housekeeper because I refuse to do the work and need someone to lace me up in the morning and help me dress."

"Perhaps it wouldn't hurt you to help him with his endeavors," Amanda countered. "At least your father cares about the impoverished."

"I'd rather he care about our place in society, like your father does. Besides, I don't see you down there volunteering your time."

Fanny could barely keep pace with the flying barbs. Where had all this animosity come from? The three of them had always been dear friends. Cousins who shared everything. Even their secrets—at least most of them. Now it seemed each comment was followed either by an angry rebuttal or injured feelings.

"Has your mother completed arrangements for the ball?" Fanny stepped between her cousins, hoping to ease the banter.

Before Amanda could respond, Sophie bent forward and peeked around Fanny. "Personally, I am surprised your mother is hosting the event this year, Amanda. There are other prominent families here in Rochester who could have stepped in to host the event for one year. Did she not consider Grandfather's medical condition?"

Amanda exhaled a loud sigh. "Grandfather specifically requested that the annual ball take place here in Rochester. And he even said he expects the family to depart for Broadmoor Island as scheduled."

"*What?* But that's impossible." Fanny yanked on Amanda's arm. "Grandfather can't possibly ride a train to Clayton and then take a boat out to the island. He's unable to even come downstairs to eat his meals."

"I don't think he was implying that he would join us, Fanny. Merely that he expected the family to maintain the annual tradition. He promised Grand-mère."

Fanny loosened her hold on Amanda's arm. "I'm eager to return to the island, but—"

Sophie held up a hand and interrupted her cousin. "As far as I know, you're the only one who wants to return."

"You enjoy our summers together at Broadmoor Island." Fanny looked back and forth, waiting for one of her cousins to agree. "You do, don't you?" The Broadmoor family had been summering on their private island located in the heart of the Thousand Islands in the St. Lawrence River for as long as Fanny could remember.

"Of course we do, dear girl," Amanda said. "Now, let's go and look at those lilacs you promised to show us."

But instead of her earlier excitement, Fanny's thoughts piled atop one another in a jumble of confusion. All these years she'd believed her cousins had enjoyed the endless summer hours whiled away on their grandparents' private island.

Her grandfather had purchased the island on a whim, an anniversary gift to Grand-mère, because the land was located in close proximity to Brockville, her Canadian home—or so he said. Grand-mère's version of the story differed. She said George Pullman had convinced Grandfather that the seaway islands and small communities of Clayton and Alexandria Bay were destined to become the summer playground of the wealthy, and Grandfather wanted a hand in the matter.

Fanny didn't know which story was correct, but time had proved Mr. Pullman's assessment correct. Each summer the number of vacationers flocking to the hotels and resorts that dotted the seaway increased in number. And each summer the excitement and merriment increased, also—at least that's what Fanny had thought until today.

The three cousins silently marched toward the far end of the garden. The profusion of pale purple, deep lavender, and milky white blooms swayed in the spring breeze and filled the air with their perfume. Unlike the sweet fragrance and silent beauty of the lilacs, their conversation had been a mishmash of fragmented comments and angry retorts. Before her cousins left this afternoon, Fanny hoped they would regain their former unity of spirit.

Moments after Amanda and Sophie had departed, Fanny raced upstairs. She slowed her pace in the upper hallway and tiptoed to the door of her grandfather's bedroom. Hazel sat near his bedside reading from the newspaper an update on the Cuban war. From what Fanny could hear, the paper reported that Spanish officers stated they were receiving a higher rate of pay than their counterparts in Spain and had declared their willingness to indefinitely remain and fight for Spain on Cuban soil. Silly men! Why would anyone want to go and fight in another country? For that matter, why would anyone want to participate in war at all? Thoughts of dying young men clouded her mind. She was pleased when Hazel folded the paper.

Fanny quietly approached and touched her grandfather's veined hand. "How are you feeling this afternoon?"

His color remained pale, but his eyes were clear. He motioned her toward the chair. "Sit and take Hazel's place. You can read to me."

Hazel handed Fanny the newspaper. "If you're going to be here for a while, I'll go up to the third floor and complete my chores."

"Yes, of course. Take all the time you need." Fanny glanced down the page, hoping to find something to read other than war reports.

"Well, are you going to read?"

Her grandfather had never been a patient man, and his illness hadn't changed that particular trait. "Let's see," she murmured. Tracing her forefinger down the page, Fanny scanned the report of a body being found in the river, the description of a steamer collision, the account of a bank president who had killed himself, and a tale of destruction due to an earthquake in Montana. Was there nothing cheery or uplifting in the news these days? She snapped the pages and refolded the paper.

With an air of authority, she placed the paper on the bedside table and folded her hands in her lap. "Let's visit instead."

Her grandfather cast a longing glance at the paper. He did enjoy his newspaper, but he didn't object. "What shall we talk about? The war in Cuba, perhaps?"

She giggled. "You can save that conversation for Uncle Jonas. Did Hazel tell you that Amanda and Sophie came to visit this afternoon?"

He nodded. "When I asked where you were, she mentioned your cousins were expected."

"If I had known you were awake, we would have all come upstairs for a few minutes."

Wisps of white hair circled his head like a lopsided halo. "I've been awake only a short time. You can tell me all about your visit with the girls. I'll see them the next time they come." A convulsive cough followed the rasping words.

Fanny jumped up and poured water from the cut-glass pitcher sitting on the table near his bedside. She offered the glass. He coughed again and then swallowed a gulp of the liquid. "Better?" She waited until he nodded and then returned the glass. Grandfather was adamant: they were not to make a fuss over his coughing spells. And though it was difficult, Fanny adhered to his wishes. "Let's see. Where shall I begin?"

He grinned at her and winked. "At the beginning."

She and Grandfather had exchanged those same words many times over the years. It had become their own private joke, and she was pleased he remembered. Scooting her chair closer to the side of his bed, she recounted the afternoon's events—at least a goodly portion of them. She didn't mention the barbs that had been exchanged early in the afternoon, for Grand-father didn't need to be bothered with their childish discord. He appeared pleased when Fanny mentioned Sophie's fine appearance and her beautiful gown. "She was absolutely radiant in her pink dress."

Hamilton patted his granddaughter's hand. "I'm pleased to hear Quincy purchased Sophie a new gown. I'd be happier if he'd devote a bit of time to her, though. From what I've been told, Quincy has been spending all of his time and money on the Home for the Friendless, which he's determined to make successful."

His response surprised Fanny. She considered her grandfather a generous man, someone who was willing to aid the less fortunate. Not with his time, of course, but certainly with his money. "You contribute to many charities, Grandfather."

"Of course I do. But Quincy isn't using wise judgment right now. He's allowing his emotions to rule his good sense. Marie kept Quincy on an even keel. Since her death, he seems intent upon forging ahead with these plans for the less fortunate."

"Perhaps it's his way of dealing with his grief. If my father had had such a project, he might still be with us." She frowned and looked away.

"You are right, of course. I'm sorry. I didn't mean to cause you distress."

"It's just that losing loved ones is so very hard."

"Your grandmother and I always tried to ease your pain."

Fanny nodded. "And you did. I could not have asked for a better home or more love. Still. . ." She let the words trail off.

"Still, it would have been better to have grown up with a mother and father at your side. I know that full well, Fanny dear. We never hoped to replace them in your life but rather to comfort you—ourselves, as well, for we had lost a son most dear."

"Of course. I sometimes forget that," Fanny admitted. She forced a smile. "I'm sure that Uncle Quincy will not succumb to sadness as did my father."

"He needs to think more objectively about the use of his time and energy. He needs to think about business and family." Grandfather turned loose of her hand and rubbed his cheek. "Why am I discussing this with you? Tell me more about your visit with Amanda and Sophie."

"Amanda said you insisted upon Aunt Victoria and Uncle Jonas hosting the annual Summer's Eve Ball and that you expect the family to depart in July for Broadmoor Island in spite of your illness." She leaned forward and pressed closer. "I won't leave you here alone, Grandfather. You know Grand-mère insisted I return to school when she was ill." Her forehead scrunched into a frown, and she wagged her finger. "As much as I love Broadmoor Island, I won't leave you."

Her grandfather brushed an auburn curl from her forehead and smiled. "Never fear. You won't be required to leave me behind, dear Fanny."

CHAPTER 3

SATURDAY, JUNE 12, 1897

The upstairs maid carried Fanny's silk taffeta gown into the bedroom and waited for Fanny's approval.

"Thank you, Hazel. The dress looks wonderful." Fanny beamed with pleasure. The color was perfect, the precise shade of the lilac blooms from the first bush she had planted many years ago with Mr. Pritchard's help—exactly two weeks after her father's death. At Grandfather's insistence, the dress had been fashioned by a local dressmaker for the Summer's Eve Ball. Outsized caps of lilac taffeta topped the full ruffled lace sleeves, and a thin ruffle edged the neckline. Crystal beads in an iris motif embellished the bodice and skirt. Had she designed the dress, she would have used a lilac motif instead.

Hazel fastened the gown and handed Fanny a pair of long white gloves. "You look lovely, miss. That shade is perfect with your hair."

Fanny bent forward and pecked Hazel on the cheek. "You're always so kind, Hazel. What would I do without you?" She took one final peek in mirror. "I'm going to go and tell Grandfather good-night before I depart."

Hazel fluffed the hemline of the skirt and gave an approving nod. "He said to waken him if he's asleep. He wants to see you in your dress."

Fanny hurried out the door and down the hallway. When she neared her grandfather's room, she slowed her step. After a gentle tap on the door, she entered. "Are you asleep?"

He opened his eyes and waved her forward. "Come. Stand by the window and let me see you."

Fanny followed his instruction and took her place in front of the window. He waved his forefinger in a circle, and she compliantly turned slowly for inspection.

"Lovely. Simply lovely."

"Thank you, Grandfather." She leaned down and kissed his pale weathered cheek. "I promise to tell you all the details tomorrow morning."

He nodded. "I love you very much, Fanny. Now off with you and have a wonderful time."

Fanny promised to enjoy herself, and she would make every attempt. But a formal dinner followed by dancing with the eligible bachelors of Rochester, New York, didn't rank high on her list of pleasant pastimes. She would much prefer dipping her toes off the dock at Broadmoor Island or stealing away for an afternoon of fishing with Michael Atwell. He knew the waters of the St. Lawrence Seaway and could navigate her grandfather's skiff into the finest fishing spots along the river. Grandfather enjoyed referring to the young man as his boatswain. Michael had been charged with maintaining the Broadmoor boats and equipment for the past five years—since the summer he had turned sixteen. Through the years, the size and number of Grandfather's boats had increased, and so had Michael's ability. Without Michael, life on Broadmoor Island wouldn't be nearly so pleasant. This year, however, Fanny doubted whether she'd be seeing Michael or fishing at Broadmoor Island.

She stepped into the carriage, sat down, and smoothed the folds of her skirt before resting her back against the leather-upholstered seat. It was strange the way things occurred. Her cousins would be delighted to forego the annual summer visit at the island. In fact, except for the youngest children of Fanny's cousins, the entire family would prefer to remain in Rochester for the summer—or at least choose a hiatus away from one another along the New Jersey shore or touring abroad. There was little doubt that time on the island would be less stressful if the entire family weren't there at the same time. Though the house on Broadmoor Island far surpassed the Rochester mansion in size, there had been no structure created that would peacefully house all members of the Broadmoor family. The possibility remained an enigma, but that hadn't stopped Grand-mère from insisting upon the family coming together each summer for what she had called "reunion and refreshment." Other members of the family had created their own special names for the summer get-togethers, designations that weren't nearly as lovely as the one chosen by Grand-mère.

"I don't understand why they all hate each other and the island," Fanny murmured to herself. "They don't understand how blessed they are to have one another. I would love to have brothers and sisters. I would give anything to have my mother and father alive and well. How can they be so flippant about the blessing of family?"

She couldn't reason the matter in her mind. The extended Broadmoor family seemed worse than strangers. At least with strangers a modicum of manners remained in place. With family, however, the Broadmoors seemed to have a penchant for insult and upheaval. They were masters at taking offense for the silliest things. Fanny could recall a time when much of the family had been in a complete tizzy when Grand-mère had had the audacity to serve roasted lamb at the evening meal on what was clearly a beef day.

"They're all a bunch of ninnies," Fanny said, shaking her head. With the exception of Sophie and Amanda, she couldn't even pretend that any of them cared one whit for her.

Much too soon the carriage came to a halt in the driveway of Jonas and Victoria Broadmoor's impressive home and abruptly ended Fanny's musings. Soft music, played by string musicians, wafted on the warm evening breeze to greet the arriving guests—pleasant melodies that were intended to delight even the most severe critic. And there were many among the social set who would judge not only the music but every aspect of the party. Each one eager to discover any faux pas or indiscretion that would fuel local gossip.

Fanny would have preferred to enter by a rear door and mingle without fanfare, but her aunt would be scandalized by such an arrival. Aunt Victoria had obviously taken great pains to ensure an illustrious review in the society column of the newspaper. Her niece would be expected to enter through the front door and stand before the gathered assemblage for her introduction. How she longed for Grandfather's presence and his strong arm to lean upon at this moment. She didn't realize how much she had depended upon his support at these ghastly social affairs.

She followed the servant's instructions and stepped to the entrance of the oversized parlor. "Miss Frances Jane Broadmoor." His voice bellowed above the twittering guests, who momentarily ceased their chitchat and stared in her direction. With her chin lifted to what she hoped was the proper height, Fanny entered the parlor. She could only hope she wouldn't trip and embarrass herself. With a quick glance, she scanned the area for an out-of-the way spot where she could gain her bearings before commencing the required rigors of mingling with the other guests.

"*There* you are!" Amanda pulled her cousin into an embrace and then stepped back, her gaze traveling up and down the length of Fanny's gown. "Your dress is lovely. You didn't mention it when we were at the house." She touched Fanny's shoulder. "Turn around and permit me a view of the back."

Feeling somewhat foolish, Fanny completed a quick pirouette. Her appearance couldn't begin to compare to that of Amanda. Though the attention was offered in kindness, the close scrutiny only caused Fanny further discomfort. Although Hazel had maintained it would take an explosion for even one hair to escape the nest of curls she'd created atop Fanny's head, the hairpins had already begun to pop loose. The maid truly lacked a full understanding of Fanny's unmanageable tresses. She forced a curl back into place and glanced about the room. "I haven't seen Sophie. Has she arrived?"

Amanda nodded toward a far corner. "Over there, surrounded by that flock of young men. No matter where she leads, they follow."

Moments later the group of men separated and Sophie walked toward them. The scene was somewhat akin to the parting of the Red Sea, Fanny decided. Amanda beckoned to their cousin and she approached, her entourage following close on her heels. When she stopped in front of her cousins, the young men clustered into a tight knot directly behind her. It seemed that each one longed to escort the vivacious young woman to the supper table.

"All my friends are wondering who will sit next to me at dinner, but I've told them I had no say in the decision." She batted her lashes at the assembled group standing behind her.

Anticipation glazed their eyes as they awaited Sophie's further attention. Amanda pointed her fan toward the distant doorway and then looked at the huddled group of bedazzled followers. "You may inquire of my mother if you desire."

None of them moved. It appeared as if the young admirers feared leaving Sophie for even a minute. And Sophie seemed to enjoy the suffocating attention. Before Fanny could contemplate the situation further, one of the servants announced dinner.

Amanda looped arms with Fanny, and they followed Sophie's formally attired devotees toward the massive dining room located on the third floor. The rooms were used only for large parties, and the servants were aided by the dumbwaiters in the dining hall. Otherwise they'd not survive such ordeals. Amanda giggled when they neared the doorway.

"Each year the young men become increasingly smitten with our cousin."

"And with you, also. If you didn't shoo them away, you'd have a large assemblage following you," Fanny replied. While Sophie's vivacious personality attracted the men, it was Amanda's natural beauty that wooed them. Fanny decided it was Amanda's regal deportment that set her apart, along with her perfect blond hair and striking features.

They parted at the table in search of their place cards. This was yet another scheme Aunt Victoria utilized at her dinner parties. She insisted that her guests delight in the process of locating their assigned seats. "Utter chaos," Fanny muttered while she circled the table in search of her name.

"Over here, Fanny." Lydia Broadmoor, Grayson's wife, waved her forward. "You're on the other side of Grayson."

Although Aunt Victoria enjoyed the unconventional method of requiring her guests to search for their place cards, she continued to insist upon a traditional male-female seating arrangement. Accordingly, Fanny knew she would be flanked by men. Sitting next to Amanda's oldest brother wouldn't have been Fanny's first choice, but at least he was a relative. After rounding the table, she glanced at the place card to her left. Mr. Snodgrass. So she would have Amanda's older brother on one side and old Mr. Snodgrass, Uncle Jonas's favorite banker, on the other. This would be a long dinner!

She exchanged pleasantries with Grayson and Lydia and politely inquired after the health of their three children. Fanny hadn't seen any of them since Christmas. "Are the children looking forward to the summer on Broadmoor Island?"

Lydia silently waited for her husband's response. "They enjoy their time at the island, but our plans remain indefinite."

"How is that possible? Nothing has changed."

Grayson looked at her as though she'd lost her senses. "*Grandfather?* You do realize the gravity of his illness, do you not?"

"Yes, of course, but that changes nothing. He still expects—"

"It changes *everything*, dear Fanny. While the youngsters and one or two older members of the family enjoy summering on the island, the rest of us will be relieved and, dare I say, delighted to end that compulsory tradition."

Fanny's jaw went slack. How could they find anything objectionable with that lovely island? She felt as though she'd been jabbed in the stomach by a sharp elbow.

"Appears as though Victoria surrounded me with both beauty and youth this evening." Fanny turned to see Mr. Snodgrass smiling down at her. The lanky old man towered above her; he looked to be at least six feet tall. Beatrice, one of Sophie's older sisters, had been positioned on the other side of the banker. Though Fanny wouldn't have described Beatrice as either young or beautiful, she couldn't fault Mr. Snodgrass. Fanny didn't consider herself pretty, either—young, but certainly not pretty.

Fanny nodded and returned a smile. "Good evening, Mr. Snodgrass." She leaned forward. "How are you, Beatrice?" Most of the time, Beatrice seemed to be either in pain or sad. Fanny couldn't decide which it might be this evening. Even when Beatrice smiled, her lips drooped at the corners.

"I'm well, thank you, Fanny. When did you return to Rochester?"

"I've been home nearly two weeks now." She scoured her thoughts for some tidbit that might keep the conversation flowing. "How is Miranda?"

"Fine. She seems to think she's all grown up; she was insulted that she wasn't invited to the ball this evening." Beatrice forced her drooping lips upward. "I explained that eight-year-olds aren't considered adults, but she would hear none of that."

"I'm certain she's looking forward to spending July and August at the island."

"Island?" Mr. Snodgrass pointed a bony finger at Fanny. "You mark my words: this country will have men in Cuba before the end of the year. With the newspapers pushing for intervention, Congress will follow suit. We'll march onto that island, even if it's not the intelligent thing to do. And you can quote me on that!" Everyone at the table was now staring at them.

"We weren't discussing Cuba, Mr. Snodgrass," Fanny shouted. She disliked speaking so loudly, but she didn't want the old man to misinterpret anything else she said.

"Well, even if you weren't, you *should* be. This country is going to find itself in a real mess. Folks need to wake up before we're in the middle of someone else's war. I say, let those Spaniards and Cubans fight it out for themselves."

Aunt Victoria nudged Uncle Jonas into action.

"No talk of war or fighting at the dinner table, William. Victoria insists it ruins the digestion."

Wisps of white hair appeared to be waving at the guests as Mr. Snodgrass enthusiastically nodded. "The whole matter is more than I can digest, too, Jonas. That's why I say we need to stay out of it. What do you young fellows say? You don't want to see this country involved in war, do you? Why, you'd likely go over there and get yourselves killed."

Aunt Victoria visibly paled. From all appearances she was about to faint. Lydia signaled across the room, and one of the servants soon arrived with a cool cloth for Victoria. Mr. Snodgrass appeared not to notice, for he continued to solicit comments from several of the young men. If he received an answer that didn't suit, he immediately shouted an angry rebuttal and then turned to the next fellow.

Although a hint of color returned to Aunt Victoria's cheeks, her displeasure remained evident. Uncle Jonas tapped his water goblet with a spoon until the room turned silent. "My wife does not wish to hear any talk of fighting or war at the dinner table, William." He shouted loud enough that Fanny was certain anyone within a two-block radius could hear the admonition.

Mr. Snodgrass appeared unperturbed by the comeuppance. "Fine. We can discuss it over a glass of port and a good cigar later in the evening," he muttered.

Throughout the meal, which progressed at the usual snail's pace, Fanny did her best to talk with Grayson and Mr. Snodgrass. The extravagant floral centerpiece prohibited much visiting with guests seated across the table, though it mattered little. Fanny doubted she could interest them in discussing fishing at Broadmoor Island.

Several servants returned to the dining room and started to remove the dinner plates. When one of the servers approached Fanny, Mr. Snodgrass shook his head and turned a stern eye on Fanny. "You've eaten only a few bites of your food, young lady. Do you realize what food costs nowadays?" Before Fanny could respond, he cast a look of doom at the guests seated around him and proclaimed the country would be hard-pressed to recover from this latest depression. "I'm a banker, you know. I understand economics, and even though you all think this country is on the mend, we've a long way to go. Best think about that when you're agreeing to this war, too."

Thankfully, the servant ignored the conversation and removed Fanny's dinner plate while Mr. Snodgrass predicated the country would soon lapse into complete ruination.

Uncle Jonas cleared his throat. "William . . ."

Mr. Snodgrass waved at Jonas with a quivering hand mottled with liver spots. "I know, I know. No talk of war, no talk of financial ruin, no talk of anything other than the weather and the ladies' gowns." He dipped his head closer to Fanny. A strand of white hair dropped across his forehead. "Do none of you young ladies have interest in anything other than frippery?"

"William!" Uncle Jonas shook his head. Mr. Snodgrass failed to take into account that his whispers could be heard by everyone in attendance.

"Fine, Jonas!" Mr. Snodgrass turned toward Fanny and cocked an eyebrow. "Tell me, Miss Broadmoor, who fashions your gowns for you? And what color do you call that particular shade of purple? Did you bead the gown yourself?"

The old man's voice dripped with sarcasm, and several of the other men snickered until their wives disarmed them with icy stares. While one of the servants placed a dish of lemon ice in front of Fanny, she leaned close to Mr. Snodgrass. "The color of my gown is referred to as lilac, Mr. Snodgrass."

He grinned. "Makes sense. Same shade as Rochester's famous blooms, right?"

"Yes. My favorite flower, too."

"Well, I find lilacs quite lovely myself. What about you, Jonas? You prefer roses over lilacs?" The old man winked at Fanny.

Her uncle was clearly annoyed. "Neither. I prefer deep purple irises."

Mr. Snodgrass swiveled toward Fanny and arched his bushy brows. "Your uncle dislikes the color of your dress, Miss Broadmoor. This bit of news will likely render you unable to digest your supper. I'm certain you're wishing you had purchased a deeper shade of purple." Mr. Snodgrass tipped his head back and laughed. "Shall we discuss the beading on your gown, or perhaps I could ask Mrs. Winberg if she prefers lilac over purple."

Unless Uncle Jonas vehemently objected, Mr. Snodgrass's name would likely be permanently removed from Aunt Victoria's guest list. Perhaps he would depart early this evening, for he'd evidently not read his invitation. Dinner guests were expected to retire to the ballroom immediately after the evening meal. For this auspicious annual occasion, Aunt Victoria always invited fifty guests to partake of dinner prior to the dance. However, many more guests had been invited for the ball—a veritable array of New York society. Instead of enjoying a cigar and glass of port, Mr. Snodgrass would be expected to locate a dance partner. Fanny wondered if the man's legs would support him for an entire waltz.

She'd never been so pleased to conclude the evening repast.

Amanda stood on tiptoe and waved her fan in the air until she captured Fanny's attention. Weaving her way through the crowd would take a bit of effort on Fanny's part. Within moments, Amanda lost sight of her cousin amidst the throng of guests. She had hoped to visit with Fanny before the promenade, but it didn't appear that would occur.

The musicians had gathered in their appointed places. The grand promenade was a tradition that had begun years ago at the very first Summer's Eve Ball. At least that's what Amanda's mother insisted when anyone suggested eliminating the ritual.

Instead of Fanny, Sophie arrived at Amanda's side, her entourage in tow. "Is your mother angry that Father didn't make an appearance this evening? Or has she even missed him?"

"Of course she misses him, Sophie. We all miss him. Mother mentioned last week that he hadn't responded to his invitation." She shrugged. "You know Mother. She detests any breach of etiquette. Uncle Quincy will be in for one of her lectures the next time they see each other."

"He's so consumed with expanding his charity shelter that he thinks of nothing else." She jutted her chin in the air. "He doesn't consider that his own children consider themselves parentless."

Amanda offered her cousin a sympathetic smile. Sophie tended to exaggerate from time to time, but her cousin's feelings of abandonment were genuine. Ever since the death of Sophie's mother's last year, her father had been consumed by his work with the homeless. "Well, I doubt you can speak for your brother and sisters, Sophie."

Sophie shrugged. "I suppose you're right. They all have their own lives now. I'm the one who deserves at least a bit of my father's time and attention."

That much was certainly true. Sophie's eldest sister, Louisa Clermont, who had been widowed five months ago, lived in Cincinnati with her three children. Nadine, who had been the youngest sister until Sophie's birth, lived in Rochester with her husband, Willard Snyder. They had welcomed their first child, Alfred, only a few days ago, and no one had expected them to attend tonight's festivities. Nor did anyone expect Dorian, Sophie's only brother, to be in attendance. Dorian had departed Rochester three years ago to explore Canada. He'd written only once since he left, and none of them had the vaguest idea how to contact him. He didn't even know his mother had died a year ago. Of course Beatrice and her husband, Andrew Winberg, were in attendance this evening. Beatrice might not be enjoying herself tonight, but she would never breach social etiquette or disappoint her relatives—especially those of higher social standing. Beatrice had married a Winberg—a Rochester family but certainly not of the same social standing as that of the Broadmoors, not by any stretch of the imagination.

Not that Amanda cared a whit about making the "proper" marriage. Personally, she wasn't interested in marriage at all. At least not now. Jonas and Victoria Broadmoor desired proper marriages for all of their children, but they had conceded to the choices made by both of their sons. Grayson and William had each married a young lady of lower social standing. The Broadmoor social status had, of course, assured that their wives would be accepted into all of the proper circles. Neither Jefferson nor George, Amanda's two other brothers, had chosen a wife. They were no more interested in marriage than was their sister. Yet when the time came for Amanda to choose a husband, her parents would expect a wise choice. For when a daughter married beneath herself socially, remaining a member of the higher class wasn't guaranteed.

The musicians struck the first chords of the promenade march while Amanda's parents took their places at the far end of the ballroom, the guests' signal to find their partners and position themselves in line.

Sophie grasped the arm of one of her many admirers, leaving each of the others to locate an unescorted young lady. "Come on, Amanda. We need to get in line." Sophie glanced over her shoulder while her escort preened like a peacock.

Before one of Sophie's rejected suitors had an opportunity to ask Amanda, her brother Jefferson swooped her into his arms. "I've decided to escort my beautiful sister in the promenade," he said.

She grinned and grasped his arm, thankful he'd saved her from a member of Sophie's entourage. "All the unmarried young ladies will be wondering why you chose your sister instead of favoring one of them with your attention."

His boisterous laugh caused several couples to turn and stare at them. "I would tell them that I chose my sister because she is the most beautiful woman in the room."

"And would you also tell them that dancing with your sister prevents any expectations from your dance partner?" She leaned into his arm. "An invitation to escort one of those girls onto the dance floor is not tantamount to a marriage proposal, Jefferson."

"I'll favor several of them with my attention later in the evening. But you know how everyone watches to see the couples in the promenade. They all make assumptions. You know that is true, dear sister."

"Oh, dear me, I hope not." She stopped and clasped her hand to her bodice. "Do look at who is escorting Fanny. If people make assumptions, our Fanny is doomed."

Standing near the middle of the line, old Mr. Snodgrass was clinging to Fanny's arm.

Fanny turned away and hoped her cousins wouldn't notice she was now standing beside Mr. Snodgrass. If she had possessed more gumption, she would have loudly refused when he clasped her arm and insisted upon escorting her in the promenade. Instead, she'd mumbled a polite rebuff that he'd misinterpreted as an acceptance.

"Fanny! This is my first opportunity to visit with you this evening." Jefferson's eyes twinkled as he leaned down and kissed her cheek. "How are you, dear girl? And welcome to you, Mr. Snodgrass." Jefferson extended his hand to the older man. The hearty handshake was enough to cause Mr. Snodgrass to wobble even closer to Fanny's side.

She cringed and took a sideways step. She longed to wipe the grin from Jefferson's face. "I am fine. Thank you for your concern, Jefferson." She stabbed him with an icy glare. "I'm certain we'll have time for a chat later this evening."

"I'd be delighted, but I certainly don't want Mr. Snodgrass to think I'm attempting to steal his girl." Jefferson's lips curved into a devilish grin. "Are you planning to keep Fanny all to yourself this evening, Mr. Snodgrass? I've never been one to come between a happy couple."

Mr. Snodgrass scratched the white fluff of hair that barely covered his balding pate. "Couple? Oh, we're not married yet," he shouted.

Silence reigned. All eyes turned on Fanny. At least that's what she felt. There may have been one or two folks near the back of the room who weren't staring at her, but she couldn't imagine why not. Mr. Snodgrass had shouted his remark loudly enough for everyone in town to hear him. If she could have found a hole, she'd have crawled inside and pulled it in after her.

"Nor will we ever be—married, that is." Everyone continued to watch. Why had she bothered to justify the old man's remark with a response? Coupled with Mr. Snodgrass's statement, her response appeared to affirm they were romantically involved yet not planning to wed. Forevermore! How did she get herself into these situations? She should have screamed her refusal. Well, it was too late now.

The orchestra began to play the promenade music while Jefferson and Amanda retreated to the rear of the line. Fanny lifted her chin and continued to step forward, with Mr. Snodgrass resting heavily on her arm. Could the man even dance? she wondered.

Jefferson had thoroughly enjoyed her embarrassment. Well, turnabout was fair play. She'd have her chance to return the favor once they were at the island. Fanny grinned, relishing the thought. But her smile soon vanished. Instead of spending her summer at the island playing jokes on her cousin, she'd be caring for Grandfather in Rochester.

When the final chords of the promenade waltz finished, Fanny freed herself of Mr. Snodgrass. She helped him to a chair, fetched him a glass of punch, and promptly escaped to the other side of the room before he could shout a marriage proposal in her direction. Kindness was one thing, but dealing with Mr. Snodgrass for the remainder of the evening went above and beyond what she could endure. The waltz itself had been sufficient torment. Dancing with Mr. Snodgrass had been comparable to attempting a waltz with one of her young nephews, only worse. Much worse.

Fanny didn't need to concern herself with Mr. Snodgrass throughout the remainder of the evening. As soon as he'd consumed his liquid refreshment, he fell asleep in his chair. Once some of their guests began departing, Uncle Jonas called for the old man's carriage. After a final shouted warning about the war in Cuba and the state of the economy, Mr. Snodgrass bade the remaining guests farewell.

Jefferson stepped to Fanny's side. "I think you should have accompanied Mr. Snodgrass to his carriage, Cousin. He obviously is smitten with you."

Fanny jutted her chin. "I believe I'll ignore your silly remark."

"You're letting a good catch get away, dear Fanny. Mr. Snodgrass is quite wealthy. All the widowed dowagers would love to get their claws into him. Didn't you see the evil looks Widow Martin cast in your direction while you were dancing with him?" Jefferson folded his arms across his broad chest and grinned like a Cheshire cat.

Without further thought, Fanny stomped on his foot. He yelped and danced about, though Fanny knew she'd not hurt him in the least. He'd probably felt no more than a slight thump. Jefferson continued to hop about until his mother walked toward them with a solemn look on her face. Fanny wasn't certain whether she or Jefferson would be upbraided for their unseemly behavior.

"All of the family needs to go to the parlor immediately." That said, Jefferson's mother continued to seek out their other relatives.

Amanda grasped Fanny's hand. "What do you suppose this is all about?"

Jefferson fell in behind them. Soon Sophie caught up with the trio, clearly annoyed. "Why have we been summoned to the parlor?"

"None of us know," Fanny replied. "I doubt we'll be detained for long."

"I hope not. I promised John Milleson he could accompany me home."

Jefferson exhaled a low whistle. "Does your father know about John?"

"My father wouldn't care even if he did know, so you can't use that bit of information against me, Jefferson." She chucked him beneath the chin as though he were a little boy rather than a young man four years her senior.

Jonas Broadmoor stood in the center of the room, watching as each of the family members filed into the parlor. When they'd all assembled, he nodded for one of the servants to close the pocket doors. "I received word from one of the servants at Broadmoor mansion that my father died a short time ago."

Grandfather dead? It was Fanny's last thought before she fainted.

CHAPTER 4

Friday, June 18, 1897

The day dawned bright and warm, a glorious summer day that Grandfather would have enjoyed. Fanny could easily picture him sitting on the balcony outside his bedroom on a day such as this. But Grandfather wouldn't be sitting on the balcony this day or any other. Instead, he would be buried in the huge family plot next to Grand-mère in Mount Hope Cemetery.

Relatives had been arriving at the mansion—crawling out of the woodwork, as Grandfather used to say. There had been no reason to inquire as to the length of their stay: the reading of the will would take place three days hence. None would depart until hearing the terms of Grandfather's will—not even the most distant relative. Once the mansion had been filled to capacity, additional relatives had been sent to Uncle Jonas's home and then to Uncle Quincy's. A rare few had opted to stay at a hotel once they reached Quincy's abode, for he had sold his mansion shortly after Aunt Marie's death and purchased a small house in a less affluent section of Rochester.

All of this had been done against Sophie's strenuous objections, but Uncle Quincy refused to hear her protests. Shortly thereafter he poured all the profits gained from the sale of the family home into his fledgling charity. While Grandfather and Jonas shook their heads and warned against such a disproportionate contribution, Uncle Quincy chided them for their selfish nature.

Fanny didn't know about Uncle Jonas, but she certainly didn't consider her Grandfather tightfisted. He regularly contributed to the church and charitable organizations. He'd even given a tidy sum to Uncle Quincy's Home for the Friendless. But after Quincy had gone off on a tangent, which was the term Grandfather used when he referred to her uncle's behavior, all gifts to the charity had ceased. Grandfather had thought it would bring Uncle Quincy to his senses, but it seemed to have had the opposite effect. Instead of kowtowing to his father, Quincy had disposed of his other assets and contributed much of the money to his charity. Only the small house remained. Until now. With Grandfather's death, both of her uncles would inherit a vast sum of money. At least that was the assumption of most family members. Still, the majority held out hope that they, too, would be remembered in the will.

Sophie, Amanda, and Fanny sat side by side at the funeral service. At first Aunt Victoria had opposed the arrangement, but when Uncle Quincy stated he had no objection, her aunt conceded. Sitting through the funeral service would be difficult enough for Fanny, but sitting by herself would prove unbearable. Her cousins would provide the added strength she needed to make it through this day.

Too soon Fanny's future would be decided by someone other than her grandfather—but by whom? If only she had reached her age of majority prior to his death. Then she wouldn't need to concern herself with worries over a guardian. She suspected Uncle Jonas would be appointed, but what if Grandfather had decided upon some lawyer or banker? Someone like Mr. Snodgrass? She shivered at the thought. Surely Grandfather wouldn't do such a thing.

A half hour before the service, the church had already filled to capacity. Fanny didn't realize her grandfather knew so many people. It appeared as if all of Rochester had turned out to honor him. Once the preacher began to speak, Fanny plugged her ears. Not in the literal sense, of course, but she quit listening. If she listened, she would cry, and she considered her grief a private matter.

"Fanny? Fanny, are you all right?" Amanda asked. She gave Fanny's shoulder a bit of a shake.

Fanny realized Amanda had been speaking to her. The funeral was over and people were already filing out. She straightened and squared her shoulders. "I'm fine. So sorry to give you worry."

Sophie and Amanda exchanged a look before each one took hold of Fanny. Fanny thought it strange that they should fuss over her so, but ever since she'd fainted the night of Grandfather's death, her cousins treated her as though she might break apart should any further bad news come her way.

"I thought it was a very nice service," Amanda began. She moved the trio out to follow the others.

"It was quite nice," Sophie agreed. "Grandfather would have loved the kind words said about his business capabilities and the importance of the Broadmoor family to the community."

Fanny nodded. She didn't have the heart to explain how she'd kept herself from hearing a single word of the eulogy. In her mind she remembered the last time she'd seen Grandfather alive. She was to have told him all about the party. But of course that would never happen now.

She couldn't help but wonder how this event would alter the family. Jonas would now be the head of the Broadmoor clan. As eldest brother he would no doubt be the one who would decide her fate. She supposed it didn't matter, but she'd never been all that close to the man. He had opposed the idea of her living with her grandparents, believing it would have been better for her to have been sent away to live with distant relatives who were closer to the ages of her deceased parents. Grandfather had refused the idea, however, and Fanny had blessed his name ever since.

But he's gone, she thought. *Who will protect me now? Who will encourage me and show me such tenderness?*

"Well, I hope this puts an end to our miserable summer routine," Beatrice said rather haughtily. "If I have to spend one more summer listening to Lydia criticize our family, I might very well take to violent behavior."

Louisa, Sophie's oldest sister, nodded. "I hate that woman. Just because she married into the Broadmoor family doesn't make her a true Broadmoor."

"I know. There is certainly no love lost between the cousins, as far as I'm concerned." She looked up, as if seeing Fanny and the girls for the first time. "Well, I suppose there are exceptions."

"I should say so," Amanda replied coolly. "It would probably behoove you to stick to talking about what you know, rather than speaking in generalities." She pushed Fanny away from the two women.

"You two are really quite the pair," Sophie threw out. "If you've no love for this family, then be gone and have nothing more to do with it, but leave the rest of us alone."

"No one cares about this family—at least not in the way Grand-mère had hoped," Louisa said.

Fanny stopped and turned to face Sophie's sisters. "Perhaps that is because no one tried to care. Everyone seems so caught up in their own troubles and issues, they've forgotten the blessing of family. You all have one another now, but I have no one."

"That isn't true, Fanny," Amanda said, hugging her close. "You will always have Sophie and me. We are your sisters in every way."

"Better sisters than my own are to me," Sophie said, coming to stand in support of Fanny. "Of that you can be sure."

Fanny was touched by her cousins' support. Their words reminded her of what Michael had told her so many years ago when her father had died. He'd remained a dear friend, and yet Fanny knew that their time was no doubt coming to an end. He was four years older and surely had begun looking for a wife. No woman in her right mind would understand her husband slipping off to go fishing with his employer's daughter.

Sometimes promises simply could not be kept forever. The thought saddened her more than she could express.

The three days after the funeral had been the longest of Fanny's life. She'd been surrounded by people, but except for the short periods of time when Sophie and Amanda had come by the mansion, she had felt completely alone. Soon it would all be over and the expectant relatives would return to their homes. She'd come to think of them as vultures, each one waiting to prey upon Grandfather's estate. Where had they been when he was alive? Most of them had been invisible, except on those occasions when they had wanted something.

The extended family was looked down upon by the immediate relatives, who knew they stood to gain much from Grandfather's passing. The three Broadmoor sons—Jonas, Quincy, and Langley—had always been the foundation for Hamilton Broadmoor's estate. That didn't keep second and third cousins from showing up to see how they might benefit, however.

Fanny had been appalled to actually find a collection of women she barely knew rummaging through the house, declaring which pieces they intended to ask for.

"I don't understand why we have to be here," Fanny said to her cousins. They sat on either side of her and waited, along with the rest of the family, for the reading of Grandfather's will.

"I don't, either," Amanda said, looking around. "I suppose it's some formality, but Father said that everyone was to be present."

"They just want to pick apart Grandfather's possessions and get what they can for themselves," Fanny said sadly. "They were never here for him or for anyone else. They hate one another and treat one another abominably. The only reason they came to the island each summer was to get what they could."

Sophie squeezed her hand. "Ignore them. They are undeserving of your concern. Grandfather was no fool."

"It's true," Amanda whispered. "He didn't brook nonsense, and there's nothing to suggest he will now."

"But he's dead. He has no say over anything anymore." Fanny fought back her tears. She couldn't help but wonder if this loss would signal the final demise of family as she knew it.

"If I know Grandfather," Sophie said, leaning close enough for them both to hear, "he will control this family long after he's in the ground. You mark my words."

"Is everyone present?" Mortimer Fillmore stood in the center of the library and looked around the room. Extra chairs had been carried into the room to provide seating for the family.

Uncle Jonas nodded. "I believe everyone was notified of the time and place for the reading. You may begin."

Fanny stared at the lawyer and decided he was probably close to the same age as old Mr. Snodgrass. She tentatively lifted her hand.

"This isn't a classroom, Fanny," Jonas said. "You need not raise your hand before speaking."

"Where is Grandfather's lawyer? Shouldn't he be reading the will?"

Mr. Fillmore's complexion paled. She hadn't meant to offend the man, but Mr. Rosenblume had been her grandfather's lawyer for many years. It seemed only proper that a member of the Rosenblume Law Office would be present today.

Her uncle frowned. "Since I am to be executor of the will, I have requested that my personal attorney handle the estate."

Fanny ignored the other relatives, who had by now begun to fidget in their chairs. "Did Grandfather inform you of your selection as executor before he died?"

"Yes, Fanny, he did. Now if you have no further questions, I believe the rest of us would like to proceed."

A hum of agreement filled the room. If she asked anything else, the shoe-string relatives would likely toss her out on her ear. All eyes were fixed on the old lawyer. He walked to Grandfather's desk and sat down before he unsealed the thick, cream-colored envelope. He pressed the pages with his palm and faced the relatives one final time before he began. In a clear, crisp voice that belied his age, Mr. Fillmore first read a brief note to the family.

"I do not want or expect my family to mourn my death. I am at peace with my heavenly Father, and I do not desire any family members to drape their houses with black bunting and wreaths or to wear the mourning clothes dictated by society. Those we love should be honored and loved while alive. Few of you honored or loved me while I was alive, and I don't want the pretense of mourning now that I'm dead. You've all gathered to divide my money—not because you held me in high esteem; of that much I am certain. I have, however, placed a stipulation upon specific family members who will receive a portion of my estate. It is my specific direction—"

Mr. Fillmore coughed, cleared his throat, and poured a few inches of water from the glass pitcher. They waited with bated breath while he consumed the liquid.

"See, I told you. Grandfather was no fool," Sophie said, elbowing Fanny.

Fanny scooted forward on her chair, eager to hear her grandfather's stipulation. The money wasn't important. She expected her uncles to divide the lion's share of Grandfather's estate, while a few specific gifts would be distributed among close friends, loyal staff, and favorite charities.

"All of my family members who were expected to spend their summers on Broadmoor Island in the past shall continue to do so until the summer following Frances Jane Broadmoor's eighteenth birthday."

Angry stares were immediately directed at Fanny, and she slouched low in her chair.

Mr. Fillmore drummed his fingers across the wooden desk. "Please! If I may have your attention?" Thankfully, the relatives turned to face the lawyer.

"The usual exceptions will be allowed for illness, including childbirth. Once recovered, however, I will expect that person to rejoin the rest of the family. There is also the work provision for the men. They may come and go as needed but will spend at least a portion of the summer in residence on the Broadmoor Island. In their absence, their families will remain on the island."

The announcement was followed by several loud sighs. Uncle Jonas could be counted among those who thought the edict repugnant. "Let me see that." He walked around the desk and grabbed the letter from Mr. Fillmore's hand. "I should have known he'd find some way to torture us," he muttered, tossing the letter back across the desk.

Sophie giggled. "I told you Grandfather would continue to control this family."

"It is rather amusing," Amanda agreed, leaning across Fanny. "I've never seen my father turn that shade before. This most assuredly is a kick in the knickers for him."

Sophie's sister Beatrice waved her handkerchief toward Mr. Fillmore. "Does this mean that if we don't go to Broadmoor Island, we won't receive our inheritance?"

Amanda's eldest brother, Grayson, jumped up from his chair. "Exactly what makes you think *you're* going to receive an inheritance, Beatrice?"

"I'm merely inquiring how it's supposed to work, Grayson. You need not become defensive. I don't know any more about Grandfather's will than the rest of you do." She folded her arms across her chest and tightened her downcast lips into an angry frown.

"Beatrice plays the innocent, but I know from overhearing her that she's already making plans to add on to her house with her share of the inheritance," Sophie said, leaning closer to her cousins.

"But why should any of us expect that kind of thing?" Fanny whispered. "There are sons to receive their father's wealth. It seems pretentious that the grandchildren and distant relatives should expect something, as well."

"I think it's nonsense to have the island imposed upon us," someone behind Fanny muttered. Several other voices rose in agreement.

The reading wasn't going at all as Fanny had expected. The relatives continued to fire angry barbs while Mr. Fillmore rested his chin in his palm and stared across the desk. At this rate she wondered if they'd ever hear the remaining portions of Grandfather's will. Finally Uncle Jonas shouted above the din, and an uncomfortable silence fell across the room.

Mr. Fillmore picked up the letter. "If you'll remain silent, I'll continue." The last paragraph of Grandfather's letter explained that he intended for the family to continue the summer tradition of gathering at Broadmoor Island until Fanny's eighteenth birthday, where annual monetary distributions would be disbursed, a custom that had begun after Fanny's birth.

Grand-mère had wanted Fanny to spend time with her relatives each summer. In order to accomplish that feat, she convinced her husband to distribute an annual bonus from company profits each summer, but only to those who came to the island with their families. Fanny hadn't been privy to that bit of family information until two summers ago, when Jean, her cousin William's wife, had told her. In retrospect Fanny realized Jean had been angry and blamed Fanny that they must spend their summers on the island. Jean had wanted to go to the New Jersey coast with her own family, but William insisted she come to Broadmoor Island instead. She had been willing to forgo the bonus, but William wouldn't hear of it. Although Jean later apologized, Fanny remained uncomfortable in her presence, especially on Broadmoor Island.

Jonas gasped at Mr. Fillmore's revelation. "My father's *entire* estate will be divided into summer distributions? For how long?"

Mr. Fillmore shook his head. "Please, Jonas. If you would permit me to read the will, your questions will be answered."

The lawyer unfolded the document while Jonas dropped into a chair alongside the desk and waited. In a monotone voice, Mr. Fillmore read her grandfather's dying wishes. As Fanny anticipated, her grandfather had made a number of small bequests. Mr. Fillmore continued:

> "Other than the specific bequests, my entire estate shall be divided among my three sons, Jonas, Quincy, and Langley, as set forth below."

Mortimer continued to read the details necessary to obtain the distribution. Fanny could see that Uncle Jonas was not at all pleased. He had hoped, as had most, that the requirements would be abolished with the death of the family patriarch. And although seventy percent of the estate would be distributed as soon as possible to the beneficiaries, their remaining thirty percent would be received in yearly allotments—at Broadmoor Island—a plan they'd not anticipated. It appeared even Uncle Quincy wished it might have been otherwise.

When the chatter ceased, Mr. Fillmore read the next stipulation.

> "My granddaughter Frances Jane Broadmoor shall be entitled to receive my son Langley Broadmoor's one-third share in its entirety."

"What?" Jonas jumped to his feet and sent his chair crashing to the floor. "Whatever was my father thinking? How could he possibly have done such a thing?" Fanny's uncle turned his full attention upon her. "She's not even an adult!" He directed his rage at Mr. Fillmore, but his anger was meant for Fanny. Anger that he'd be required to share his father's fortune—anger that she'd ever been born.

"There's more, Jonas. Please!" Mr. Fillmore pointed to the overturned chair.

> "In the event my granddaughter Frances has not reached her age of majority at the time of my death, I hereby appoint my son Jonas Broadmoor to act as her guardian and trustee. Once Frances has reached her majority, she may elect to maintain Jonas as her advisor or select another person of her choosing."

Fanny gulped a deep breath. *Not Uncle Jonas.* She had figured as much but wished it could be otherwise. She knew Grandfather would choose his eldest son to handle any and all unpleasant details—herself included. Admittedly her uncle was a better choice than someone such as old Mr. Snodgrass, but Fanny would have preferred Uncle Quincy or even Grandfather's lawyer, Mr. Rosenblume. Uncle Jonas had never respected her father, especially not after he'd taken his own life. Fanny had heard more than one tirade about Langley

Broadmoor's lack of spirit, strength, and admirable qualities. In fact, Jonas barely acknowledged Fanny in the aftermath of his brother's death. He'd wanted to send her away—remove her from sight. And now he would be in charge. He'd be a wretched substitute for her father and grandparents.

When Mr. Fillmore concluded, he carefully refolded the pages and looked up. He scanned the room. "Any questions?"

Shouted inquiries rang from every corner of the room and the many spaces in between. Mr. Fillmore waved the folded document overhead until the relatives quieted. "I'm unable to hear your questions with all of you talking at once. All necessary paper work will be filed with the court. I will contact you by letter, advising each beneficiary when you may expect payment. Unless you have questions beyond what I've told you, please feel free to depart."

Fanny turned to Amanda and then to Sophie. It suddenly began to dawn on her that they, too, might be offended at the provision Grandfather had made for her.

"I don't know what to say." She shook her head. "Please tell me that you don't hate me like the others do."

"Of course not, silly," Amanda declared.

"No. I was rather pleased. Now I have a wealthy cousin who will come of age in March and then treat us all to a very wonderful party."

"Sophie!" Amanda rebuked in a stilted tone. She glanced around her. "Don't speak in such a way here. Most of the family is fit to be tied. Your sister Beatrice looks as though she'd like to wring Fanny's neck."

Fanny met Beatrice's hateful stare and felt her strength wither. "Oh, I have a feeling Grandfather has managed to put me in a very difficult situation."

"Don't worry about Bea," Sophie said, offering her sister a smirk. "She complains the loudest, but she has no backbone. I can deal with her."

One by one family members got to their feet. The grumbling continued even as chairs scraped across the oak floors that surrounded the imported Turkish carpet her grandfather had always thought quite lovely. Fanny thought it rather ugly, but she'd never told him. And since it had been placed in Grandfather's library, she was certain Grand-mère also considered it un- attractive. Otherwise she would have placed it in the center of the grand entry hall for visitors to admire. Today, however, the rug seemed different, not nearly as ugly as the character exhibited by the Broadmoor relatives.

While many of the family members scattered from the room, Uncle Jonas and Mr. Fillmore turned their backs. With their heads close together, they spoke in hushed tones.

"We might as well leave," Amanda said, getting to her feet.

"You two go ahead without me. I need to ask some questions," Fanny replied.

Amanda nodded. "Very well. We'll wait for you upstairs."

Fanny's mind whirled with the uncertainty of concerns that seemed to have no answers. The death of Grandfather had turned her entire world upside down. She wasn't even certain where she would live now. When the shuffles and murmurs ceased and the room was once again quiet, Uncle Jonas lifted his head.

His jowls sagged when he caught sight of her. "What is it you want, Fanny?"

"I have questions."

"*You?* Why, you're not even of legal age, Fanny. What questions could you possibly have that are important enough to detain Mr. Fillmore? I'm your guardian now, and I can see to any matter necessary."

Either her uncle's tone of voice or an interest in Fanny's questions brought several members of the immediate family scurrying back into the library like mice after a morsel of cheese. They folded their arms across their chests or sat on the edges of their chairs, their eyes shining with anticipation.

Fanny drew in a deep breath. "I'm wondering about my personal living arrangements. Not immediately, of course, for I realize the family will soon depart for the Thousand Islands. But afterward. With my schooling complete . . ."

"I don't know that I consider your schooling complete. There is college to consider. And I believe my father planned for you to begin your grand tour of Europe after summering at the islands. It is much too soon to make such determinations. Once decisions are completed regarding your future, you'll be advised."

An auburn curl escaped from her hairpins and curved alongside her cheek. "But I don't want to go on a grand tour. Grandfather said he would reconsider my wishes later this summer."

"She's an ungrateful orphan who doesn't deserve a third of the Broadmoor estate," Beatrice twittered.

Stunned, Fanny remained silent. Soon other family members added their angry opinions. To Fanny's amazement, most of them sided with Beatrice.

Fanny jumped to her feet and scanned the group, her gaze finally coming to rest upon Beatrice. "You act as though I've taken something that belonged to you, when in fact it belonged to none of us. Grandfather's wealth was his to distribute as he saw fit. I didn't ask to receive my father's share of the estate. And from what Mr. Fillmore has told us, there is ample money for distribution. I don't believe any family member is going to be forced into poverty. I don't see arguing over money as a way of honoring Grandfather."

Beatrice pinned her with an icy stare. "We could cease this squabbling, and you could honor Grandfather by giving up your inheritance, Fanny. I don't see why you think you should be entitled to an entire one-third of the estate."

Mr. Fillmore waved the bulky envelope containing her grandfather's will overhead. "People! There is no use arguing over distribution and who gets what. This will is valid, and its terms complete. If one of you attempts to have it set aside, I predict you will meet with utter and resounding failure." He peered over the glasses perched on the tip of his nose. "In addition, such legal action will delay any partial distributions of the estate—which is not something the majority of the beneficiaries will take lightly."

A clamor of voices echoed the lawyer's assessment while several family members glared at Fanny as though everything that had occurred were her fault. She startled when a hand touched her shoulder.

Her Aunt Victoria offered an encouraging smile. "You need to pack a few things, Fanny. You'll come home with us this evening."

"But I'll be fine here until we depart for the island. The servants will be here. There's truly no reason for me to—"

Uncle Jonas stepped to his wife's side, his brows knit together in an angry frown. "Must you argue about everything? This day has proved most stressful for the family, and you continue to add to the strife with your incessant questions and lack of cooperation."

"But I wasn't attempting to be obstinate. I merely thought it would be less disruptive if I remained here until we all depart for Broadmoor Island." Her shoulders slumped in defeat. "If you truly want me to pack and come to your house this evening, I'll go upstairs and put together the items I'll need for the night. I can return tomorrow and—"

"Please don't prattle on like a senile old woman, Fanny. Do as your aunt instructs." Her uncle turned on his heel and strode across the room toward Mr. Fillmore.

"Don't let him frighten you, dear. He's more bark than bite. What with the added responsibilities since your grandfather's death, he's become more abrupt." Her aunt grasped Fanny's elbow. "Do you need help?"

"Amanda and Sophie are waiting upstairs for me. They can assist me in packing."

Aunt Victoria nodded. "Try not to be too long. I'll send someone up to help you with your trunks."

Fanny made her way upstairs to the bedroom she had known for most of her life. It seemed strange to imagine that this house would no longer be her home. She entered the room to find Sophie and Amanda in a deep discussion.

"Oh good. You're here," Sophie said as she straightened.

"Not for long. Aunt Victoria has sent me up here to pack. Uncle Jonas insists that I come to live with them immediately."

"How grand," Amanda said. "You know we will have great fun. Just like at the island."

"But this is my home." Fanny sank to the bed. "Every memory I have is of this place."

"My comment was thoughtless," Amanda said in apology.

"But still, you don't want to just ramble around this big place alone," Sophie put in. "It might be very frightening—especially at night."

"I don't think I would ever be afraid here." Fanny looked around the room and felt tears come to her eyes once again. "Leaving here will be like leaving them all. Father. Grand-mère, and Grandfather. I don't know how I will bear it."

"We will bear it together," Amanda said softly. "Won't we, Sophie?"

"Absolutely. We've always been there for one another. Nothing is going to change now that you're far richer than the rest of us." She grinned.

"Sophie!"

Fanny actually smiled. "It's all right. I don't mind her teasing. It's the anger of the others that hurts me."

"Forget about them," Amanda said, getting to her feet. "Come on. Let's get you packed. There's nothing to be gained by standing here shedding tears. It won't change the fact that Grandfather is gone. We will all miss him, but perhaps none of us will miss him as much as you, dear Fanny."

Jonas leaned against his father's desk and waited until Victoria and his niece were well out of earshot. "We need to talk, Mortimer. My father's bequest to Fanny came as a shock."

The lawyer dropped into a chair opposite Jonas. "Obviously! Your behavior nearly set off a storm among the family. I must say I've never seen you lose control of your emotions at such a critical moment. You usually play your cards close to the vest, Jonas. Such restraint would have better served you today, also."

"I know. I know. But something must be done in regard to my father's bequest to Fanny. He blindsided me." Jonas attempted to hold his irritation in check.

Mortimer settled back in his chair. "How so?"

Several relatives gathered in the entrance hall, and Jonas couldn't be certain if they were bidding each other farewell or attempting to overhear his conversation with the lawyer. "Just one moment, Mortimer." He strode to the library door and waved to the gathered relatives before sliding the pocket door closed. He returned to his chair. "I'll be glad when they've all departed."

The lawyer retrieved his pocket watch and, after a glance, shoved it back into his vest. "You said your father had blindsided you."

"Yes. He called me to his bedside last week and advised me that he'd made me executor of the will and Fanny's guardian and trustee until she reached her age of majority. Of course I agreed. The old man has been dying for years. I didn't count on him actually up and completing the process before Fanny's next birthday. I also didn't think to question how much of an inheritance he had left her. I assumed he would leave a small bequest—enough for her to make her grand tour and keep up appearances until she made a proper marriage. He certainly gave no indication she would receive a full third of his estate or that we'd be required to return to Broadmoor Island in order to receive final distribution. An abomination, as far as I'm concerned. The girl knows nothing about handling money. Is there no way my father's bequest can be set aside?"

"I'm afraid not, Jonas." Mr. Fillmore shook his head. "And have you considered the effect such behavior would cause throughout the community? You would appear an ogre who is attempting to take advantage of a poor defenseless young woman. There are other ways to overcome this bit of difficulty. We need only to plan a strategy and work within the purview of your father's will."

"What do you have in mind?"

"You know the girl much better than I. Does she trust you? Will she comply with your decisions? If not, we'll need to rely upon a more cunning method."

Jonas edged forward on his chair. "I have no doubt she'll be difficult. My father mentioned she'd likely object to the grand tour. Knowing Fanny, she'd much prefer to spend the remainder of her days living on Broadmoor Island. It's the place where she's most content—at least according to my father." Jonas tugged on his vest. "Unlike most young ladies, she's always enjoyed fishing and being outdoors. She knows every inch of Broadmoor Island like the back of her hand."

"If she goes on her grand tour, she'll be out of the way and you'll have full authority over her funds. We mustn't lose sight of the fact that an accounting to the court will be necessary. Good judgment in how we manage matters will be key." Mortimer massaged his forehead. "I believe you have several choices for your niece's future. With both of us considering all options, we'll arrive at the perfect solution. I'm confident of that."

For the first time since hearing the contents of his father's will, Jonas held out hope he could gain control of Fanny's bequest. Money that rightfully should be his! Money he needed to cover some rather bad investments. His irritation mounted at the remembrance that his father had given Fanny the same bequest that he, the eldest son of the family, had received. Never would he have believed his father would do such a thing. The girl obviously had a way about her if she'd enticed his father to leave her such an inheritance.

Then again, had he preceded his father in death, Jonas would have expected his father to divide his share of the estate among his family members. But this was different. His brother Langley hadn't been of much use during his lifetime, especially after his wife's death. And Jonas thought his parents had already done more than their share for Langley's daughter. They'd reared and educated Fanny since she was an infant, even though Langley had lived until Fanny turned eleven.

Langley was the one who had turned the girl's fancy toward the outdoors and encouraged her to try new things, even if they weren't considered completely appropriate for young ladies. Fanny had been threading worms onto fishing hooks from the age of five. When Jonas's wife had objected, Langley had simply brushed her comments aside. He professed a theory of permitting children the opportunity to explore the wonders of nature. Jonas considered his brother's theory no more than an excuse for lackadaisical child rearing. But then, Langley had remained apathetic about all important matters of life. He had cared little about money, power, or position; yet his daughter had received a full share in the estate. But not for long. Not if Jonas had his way in the matter.

Mortimer shoved the will inside his leather case. "Well, my friend, what do you think? Shall we banish the girl to Europe or to Broadmoor Island?"

"Let me think on it. Once we've transported the family to Broadmoor Island, I'll be better able to consider the best path to follow." Jonas leaned forward and rested his chin atop his tented fingers. "This situation seems entirely unfair. In all probability, Quincy will pour every cent of his inheritance into that charity of his. I don't know which problem is more irritating."

Mr. Fillmore raked his fingers through his thinning white hair. "I do understand your frustration, but I'm certain your father understood Quincy would donate his share toward the home. If he'd objected, your father could have easily placed conditions on the money or even written Quincy out of the will if he'd so desired. As Fanny's guardian and trustee of her estate, you'll have a much easier time if you concentrate on her and put aside any ill feelings toward Quincy. In fact, you might consider making him an ally."

Jonas leaned back in his chair and shook his head. "I'll see what I can do, though I doubt I'll have success with that tack."

Mr. Fillmore rested one hand on the desk and pushed himself upright. "Well, remember what they say, my boy. Nothing ventured, nothing gained. In this case, there is much to be gained if you play your cards correctly."

Jonas shook hands with Mortimer and walked him to the front door, thankful the house was finally quiet and the guests had departed.

CHAPTER 5

Thus far, being at her aunt and uncle's home hadn't been nearly as uncomfortable as Fanny had anticipated. After Uncle Jonas's behavior during the reading of the will, she'd expected to be the object of his anger. Surprisingly, he'd proved most amiable during supper, even inquiring if she'd taken an interest in any young men. This was a topic that had made her the recipient of much teasing from both Jefferson and George throughout the remainder of the evening—at least until she and Amanda escaped upstairs.

The two girls curled into the comfortable chairs situated at the far end of Amanda's bedroom. Victoria Broadmoor had objected to the easy chairs, stating they were far too masculine for a young lady's sitting room. But Amanda had successfully argued that once upholstered in rose and beige silk damask, they would be perfect. Fanny was glad her cousin had won the argument, for the chairs were far more comfortable than the straight-back, open-arm chairs in her own rooms at Broadmoor Mansion.

"I'm pleased you agreed to come and stay with us until we leave for the island. I find it a great comfort. It's so terribly sad to lose the people we love," Amanda said with a sigh.

"I'm glad I didn't remain at the mansion, too. I know I would have been lonely." Fanny tucked her legs beneath her and rearranged her skirts. Aunt Victoria would certainly disapprove of the unladylike position. "I'm thankful your father was more pleasant at supper. He nearly frightened me to death when he knocked over his chair at the reading of the will this afternoon."

"His reaction *was* startling. I asked Mother about it, and she said he sometimes acts strange when he's caught off guard. She attributed his offensive behavior to grief over Grandfather's death and the unexpected contents of the will."

Fanny didn't argue. Perhaps Aunt Victoria was correct and her uncle was suffering from grief. If so, he'd quickly recovered, for he'd been all smiles at the supper table while quizzing her about any beaus and the possibility of her grand tour. Neither topic interested Fanny in the least. "I was pleased your father at least mentioned my love of Broadmoor Island. He didn't seem overly put off when I suggested remaining there year-round. Do you think he might agree?"

"Oh, Fanny, don't be silly. He didn't argue at the supper table, but I don't believe either of my parents would agree to such an arrangement. And why would you want to live on the island during the winter? There's nobody there except the help. What would you do with yourself once the cold weather set in?"

"The Atwells are there, and Michael would take me ice fishing. I could help him with the chores. I'm certain I could find plenty to keep me busy."

"You? Doing chores? Will you milk the cows or perhaps feed the chickens?" Amanda's lilting laughter filled the room.

Fanny folded her arms across her chest. "I can do those things. You forget I've spent much more time on the island than the rest of you. I could milk a cow years ago, and I learned to gather eggs without being pecked by the hens, too."

"Well, those are accomplishments all young ladies of society want to list among their credentials. *Really*, Fanny. I do understand that you're not interested in the social life of the family, but milking cows is carrying the matter too far."

"And what do you think you'll be required to do if you truly want to work with the less fortunate? Or have you changed your mind since traveling abroad?"

Amanda shook her head. Fanny was mystified when her cousin's blond tresses remained perfectly in place. Why wouldn't her hair cooperate like Amanda's?

"I haven't changed my mind in the least, but I don't consider charitable work on the same level as milking cows and feeding chickens." Amanda patted her head. "And why are you staring at my hair? Does it need to be brushed and refashioned?"

"Quite the contrary. There's not a strand out of place." Fanny cupped her chin in her hand. "Tell me what you've planned for your future. I'm interested to hear about the work you're thinking about."

"Nothing is laid out just yet. Mother has agreed she'll talk to some of her friends who are involved in several of her charitable causes. Of course everything will hinge on what Father says. He's permitted Mother to have her freedom working with her ladies' aid groups and the like, but now that I've returned from my grand tour, he seems determined I should wed." Amanda shivered. "And most of the men he's suggested are either simpletons or bores."

"Likely sons of his wealthy business associates," Fanny said. "Did you tell him of your dream to perform charitable work?"

"Yes, but he says there's plenty of time for that after I wed. He pointed to Mother as a prime example, saying she's been involved in more good works than most unmarried women."

"Have you ever considered the fact that your mother is more suited to Uncle Quincy than to your father?"

Amanda jolted upright in her chair. "*What?* No. I can't even imagine such a thing!"

"Well, it's true. They both believe in giving of their time and money to aid those less fortunate, while your father is interested only in his business success and accumulating a vast fortune. He disdains those of lesser social position and wealth. He never exhibited love for my father, and he holds Uncle Quincy in low esteem. I think the reason he permits your mother to perform her charity work is because he can take credit for her good works. His name is automatically attached to the many hours she devotes to working with the underprivileged."

Amanda frowned. "You make him sound simply dreadful. He can be caustic, but he is esteemed in the community. And he donates money to charity," she defended.

"I suppose I was a bit harsh, but I've given you points that could bolster your argument. Explain that your good works would bring additional prestige to the family name, but that prestige would go to your husband if you were to wed—along with a sizable dowry, I'd venture. If all else fails, you could insist you'd prefer college over wedding plans."

Amanda sighed. "I do wish Father would put forth as much effort finding wives for Jefferson and George. After all, they're older than I."

"But they act like young hooligans, what with their silly pranks and constant teasing. It seems they've become even more immature since they've been away at college. I would think your father would tire of their unruly behavior."

Amanda shrugged. "He hears little of their antics. He's gone most of the time, and Mother says she doesn't want to upset him with such trivial matters. She insists he has more important issues weighing on his mind."

"When Mrs. Donaldson discovers your brothers are the ones who have frightened her young sons by donning sheets and pretending to be ghosts, I doubt she'll consider their behavior trivial."

"Are you certain my brothers were involved?"

Fanny bobbed her head. "I heard them talking with some of their friends after the funeral service the other day. They're planning a return to the Donaldsons' tomorrow evening. All of them think it's great sport scaring those little fellows. I wish we could think of some way to turn the tables on them."

Amanda tapped her chin. "With a little thought, perhaps we can."

"Fanny! Wake up! I've come up with a plan." Sunlight poured through the east window of Amanda's second-floor bedroom.

Fanny rubbed her eyes and sat up on the edge of the bed. "Plan for what?"

"My brothers. How we can even the score for the Donaldson children." Amanda waved her forward. "Come and look."

Fanny shoved her feet into her slippers and padded to the window. She peered into the garden and then looked at her cousin. "What am I supposed to be looking at?"

"Do you see old Henry whitewashing that fence out near the far flower garden?"

Fanny nodded. She wished her cousin would come to the point. Her brain was still fuzzy from lack of sleep. They'd stayed up last night talking and giggling until the wee hours of the morning. Now Amanda wanted her to wake up and immediately solve some silly puzzle about one of the servants whitewashing the fence.

"I'm going to have Henry give me some of that whitewash. After my brothers sneak out of the house tonight, I'll convince Marvin to help us rig it up above the back door. When they return home, they won't need sheets to turn them into ghosts." Her eyes sparkled. "What do you think?"

The plan delighted Fanny, but she doubted whether Marvin, the butler, would be inclined to help them. The man was as rigid as the bristles on a brand-new scrub brush. "I like your plan, but what if Marvin won't help? We could be the ones who end up doused in whitewash."

"Don't fret. Marvin will help us. Now let's get dressed and go tell Henry to make certain he has plenty of that whitewash left over for us."

The entire day had been filled with the excitement evoked by a mixture of fear and anticipation. As Amanda had predicted, Marvin agreed to lend his help and meet them in the kitchen at exactly ten o'clock. Thankfully Aunt Victoria and Uncle Jonas had retired to their rooms earlier in the evening. Now that the designated hour had arrived, the girls silently picked their way down the back stairs. Fanny struggled to stifle the laughter bubbling deep in her throat. She clung to Amanda's hand until they finally reached the kitchen, where Marvin stood at the ready.

"Well, ladies, are you prepared for this bit of folly?" His shoulders were stretched into formal alignment as he addressed them. "Not rethinking your decision, are you?"

The girls shook their heads in unison. Amanda pointed to the bucket of whitewash. "My brothers deserve to receive their comeuppance. Frightening small children isn't humorous in the least. The next time they consider such a plan, I believe they'll remember what happened to them tonight."

Marvin nodded and pulled a ladder near the back door. "As you wish, Miss Amanda. Once I've secured the ropes and this board to the transom, you can hand me the bucket." The two girls craned their necks and watched as Marvin fitted a board between the knotted sling he'd created with the ropes and secured them above the doorway. He stepped down and tested the device several times before making his final ascent on the ladder. After retrieving the bucket from Amanda, he placed the pail of whitewash strategically atop the board.

After descending the ladder, he tipped his head back for one final look and then gave a firm nod. "I believe that will serve your purpose quite nicely, miss."

Amanda agreed. "Now all we must do is wait."

"Which is sometimes the most difficult thing of all," Marvin said. "If you'll excuse me, I believe I'll turn in for the night and permit you ladies to maintain your watch."

"Yes, of course," Amanda said. "And thank you for your help, Marvin. We couldn't have done it without you."

Marvin grinned. "Let's make that our little secret, shall we? I wouldn't want to incur the wrath of your father for aiding in this tomfoolery."

Amanda glanced at her cousin. "Our lips are sealed."

"Absolutely," Fanny agreed and touched her index finger to her lips.

After a final instruction that they should turn out the lights, Marvin retreated up the stairs, and the girls began their vigil in earnest. The minutes ticked by slowly as they listened for any unusual sounds near the back of the house.

"You don't think they'll return and use the front door of the house, do you? Or perhaps they've devised some way of crawling through an upstairs window and we'll end up sitting on these steps all night." Fanny grimaced. "The joke would surely be on us if that occurred."

Amanda shifted on the hard wooden step. "No. They'll come in this way. I'm certain of it."

Though she wished they could see a clock from their vantage point, Fanny was certain at least two hours had passed since Marvin's departure. Her backside ached, and she wanted to go up to bed. Her cousins were likely spending the night with some of their friends. Just as she opened her mouth to suggest they call off their prank, Amanda nudged her.

"Listen! I hear voices. It's them." Fanny clutched Amanda's hand in a death grip.

Amanda squeezed back until Fanny thought the bones in her hand would break. "That's my *father's* voice. He's with them." Amanda's gaze fastened on the door, her eyes now as big as saucers. "What are we going to do?"

"Maybe it's not—"

Amanda wagged her head. "It *is* him. I know my own father's voice. Do you think we have time to stop them?"

"Let's pray the boys walk in the door—"

Before she could complete the sentence, the back door opened. Just as Marvin had predicted, the whitewash descended like a milky shower from heaven. Only instead of dousing her cousins, Uncle Jonas was the surprised recipient. He sputtered and gasped, his arms flailing while the whitewash poured over him.

The girls considered running up the stairs, but Jefferson had already spotted them. "Look what you've done, Amanda and Fanny," he chided in a loud voice. He stood behind his father, grinning like a silly schoolboy, obviously delighted by their plight.

Amanda jumped to her feet. "I'm so sorry, Father. It was a silly attempt to put Jefferson and George in their place. I thought you had retired for the night, and we heard the boys talk about frightening the Donaldson children, and . . ."

Her father yanked his spectacles from the bridge of his nose. "Do cease your prattling and fetch me a towel, Amanda."

Once he'd removed his jacket and wiped off a portion of the whitewash, Uncle Jonas pointed the girls to the table. "Sit down and explain." He turned toward his sons. "And you two sit down at that end of the table."

One look at Uncle Jonas was enough to deduce that if their scheme had gone according to plan, they would have achieved perfection. Fanny's older cousins would have turned into ghosts. Instead, her uncle was glowering at the two of them and awaiting a full explanation.

"I'll let you tell him," Fanny whispered to her cousin. After all, the plan *had* been Amanda's idea, and Uncle Jonas was unhappy enough with Fanny already.

All of them focused on Amanda while she explained how the entire scheme had been formulated in order to teach Jefferson and George a lesson and force them to quit harassing the young Donaldson boys. "How were we to know you would be with Jefferson and George? If only one of them had entered the door first."

"Well, they didn't. And what makes you think that you need to take charge of supervising your brothers and their behavior? I am well equipped to manage such matters without your intervention. Your brothers had already been strongly chastised before our return home."

"But how did you know what they were up to?"

"Mrs. Donaldson spoke to me before she departed the other day. She apprised me of your brothers' pranks, and I had gone to confront them in the midst of their frivolity this evening. All had been resolved, until this." Uncle Jonas gestured toward the dripping whitewash.

"What on earth is all the commotion down here? Oh, dear me, Jonas! You look like a ghost." Aunt Victoria clapped a hand to her mouth and shook her head. "What has happened to you? I thought you went out to put a stop to all these pranks, and now I find you've joined in. I never would have believed my husband—"

"Oh, forevermore, Victoria. I've been caught in a prank set up by your daughter and niece. I'll explain when we get upstairs. For now, I suggest we all get a few hours of sleep before the kitchen staff comes downstairs to prepare breakfast. I don't want them to find me sitting here with this painted face."

Aunt Victoria removed several dishcloths from one of the drawers and dampened them with water. "You children run along to bed. I'm going to help your father."

Amanda and Fanny didn't hesitate. They raced up the back stairs at breakneck speed, with Jefferson and George not far behind, both of the young men chuckling over the girls' blunder. When Amanda reached her bedroom door, she turned around and pointed her finger at her brothers. "Don't think you've had the last laugh. We have two months at the island, you know."

Jefferson chortled. "I believe these girls are throwing down the gauntlet and offering us a challenge, George." He offered a mock salute. "To an exciting and entertaining summer, dear ladies."

Fanny and Amanda watched them swagger down the hallway. This would, indeed, be a summer of challenges.

Fanny twirled in front of her cousin. "I think this dress will do just fine."

Amanda pointed to the pink sash that surrounded the waist of her own pastel foulard dress. "If you don't mind wearing last year's frock, who am I to object? Would you tie my sash?"

While Amanda watched in the mirror, Fanny tied the sash in a proper bow. "I don't see why a new frock is needed to attend church and the Independence Day festivities."

"I think the celebration is a perfect excuse for purchasing a new dress. You merely dislike going for fittings, so you're willing to wear your old dresses. Grand-mère would be most unhappy with you," Amanda said. "She didn't approve of appearing at a public function in the same gown."

"No one remembers what I wore last year. You wouldn't have known if I hadn't told you. I do wish your father would let us attend some of the other celebrations in town after the parade. I don't know why the family always insists upon immediately returning to East Avenue. I hear the celebration at Brown Square is great fun. Sophie said some of her friends are going there. She plans to sneak off and join them. I wish we could, too."

"We'd be found out for certain. Sophie doesn't have to worry about getting into trouble because Uncle Quincy seldom knows where she is. Sometimes I don't think he even cares. On the other hand, my mother and father won't let me out of their sight for a moment. There should be some sort of balance, don't you think?"

Fanny agreed. She would love just a taste of the freedom Sophie enjoyed. Not that she wanted to run amok and stay out late, but she would like to see some of the things Sophie had mentioned—like all of the girls removing their stockings and dipping their feet in the wading pool that Sophie referred to as the mud pit. Hearing the German musicians play their accordions and seeing them dressed in their lederhosen while celebrating the independence of the United States would be great fun. Sophie had enthusiastically told Fanny of the beer drinking, singing, and laughter that continued until well after midnight. Perhaps she and Amanda could steal away for just a little while during the early evening hours. Then again, she knew they wouldn't be brave enough to do anything so daring.

Aunt Victoria stood at the foot of the staircase, wearing a pale green corded silk dress with a square yoke of white chiffon. White ospreys and pale green ribbons adorned the fancy straw hat—a perfect match for her gown. "Come along, girls. We're going to be late for church. The carriage is waiting." She stopped midstep and inspected Fanny's dress. "Isn't that last year's frock? I thought you told me you had a dress for today's festivities."

Fanny shrugged. "It's perfectly fine. No one will know I wore it last year."

Her aunt frowned. "*I* knew. The dress is out of fashion. I don't want people thinking your Uncle Jonas isn't treating you well."

"If you hear any of the local gossips prattling, you may send them my way and I will set things aright."

Aunt Victoria tapped her index finger on her chin. "Amanda has another new gown. Perhaps we have time for you to change." She glanced at the grandfather clock.

"Mother! You can't give away my new gown." Amanda folded her arms across her chest. "Besides, it wouldn't fit. Fanny is shorter, and the dress would drag on the ground."

Her aunt waved them toward the door. "I suppose there's nothing to do then but hold our heads up and pretend that all is well."

"All *is* well, Aunt Victoria. We need not pretend," Fanny replied as she looped arms with her aunt and proceeded down the front steps. "Will Sophie and Uncle Quincy be meeting us?"

"I invited them, but Quincy didn't respond to my note. That man is in a world of his own. And who knows where Sophie will be. Certainly not her father. You girls keep an eye out for Sophie at church this morning. If you see her, tell her she's expected at the family festivities this evening. Uncle Jonas has arranged for a spectacular fireworks display."

"That's what he said last year," Amanda commented.

Her mother held her finger to her lips. "Shh. It wasn't your father's fault that the fireworks didn't arrive. There was some mistake in the order or some such thing, but he's told me the fireworks arrived last week, and he's arranged for them to be discharged once it turns dark. It's going to be great fun."

"They have fireworks and Japanese lanterns and music at Brown Square. And the children play in the wading pool, too," Fanny said.

Her aunt regarded her with a stern expression. "Very unsanitary, Fanny. And who's been telling you about the activities at Brown Square?"

"Some of the servants were discussing the festivities," Amanda replied.

"The servants need to cease their chattering and tend to their duties. They have more than enough to keep them busy, what with preparing food for the picnic and guests this evening."

"And packing our belongings to depart for the island. I can hardly wait. I do wish I could go with the servants on Tuesday." Fanny sighed.

Her uncle assisted the three women into the carriage. "I thought you ladies were never going to join me. At this rate we're going to be late for church, and you know how I dislike making an entrance. Where are Jefferson and George?"

"Don't fret, dear. They departed earlier and said they'd meet us at church."

"Likely story. Those boys are going to be the death of me."

While the coach traversed the short distance to the church, Uncle Jonas continued muttering to his wife about the behavior of his two youngest sons. If Jefferson and George weren't at church, there was little doubt they would incur their father's wrath.

Fanny thought that would be a delightful turn of events, considering the whitewash episode two weeks earlier.

"Uncle Jonas certainly seems pleased with himself," Fanny murmured as she scooted closer to Amanda on the garden settee.

A burst of silver shot up overhead and sprayed out against the black skies. The little children clapped and cheered while the adults oohed and ahhed. The fireworks had truly been amazing, and now as the evening's festivities were nearly over, Fanny was sorry for it all to end.

"Everything has gone off as scheduled," Amanda replied. He's always pleased when he has charge of everything." She leaned back and sighed. "It has been a very pleasant day, to be sure."

"I agree. I prefer celebrating the Fourth at the island, but this was quite grand," Fanny admitted. "I ate too much, however."

"It's hard not to when there are so many delightful delicacies to choose from."

"Especially the iced creams. Goodness, but I had to sample a bit of each one," Fanny said rather shamefully.

Amanda laughed. "As did I."

A yelp from Jefferson caused everyone to take note. One of the lit fireworks had fallen over, and when it erupted, it sent sparks into the few remaining fireworks near Jefferson's feet. It was only a moment before everything was firing off at once and flames were burning up the paper wrappings.

"Grab a bucket of water," Amanda ordered Fanny, "and follow me."

There were many well-placed buckets around the gathering, and everyone raced for them at once. They knew that keeping the fire under control was critical, and plenty of water had been made available for just such a purpose.

Jefferson grabbed a bucket offered by his mother and put out the bulk of the flames right away. George followed suit, dousing much of the remaining fire, while their father, too, cast a bucket of water.

Amanda came up behind Jefferson, who already had another bucket in hand. She motioned to Fanny and pointed at George. Grinning, she nodded and Fanny immediately figured out her game.

Without warning, the girls tossed the water, drenching George and Jefferson. The young men gave such loud cries of protest that Victoria immediately worried they were injured.

"Have you been burned?" she called out.

Jefferson turned to face his sister. Water dripped down the side of his face. "Not burned, but nearly drowned."

"I'm so sorry, brother dear. I was attempting to cast water onto the flames," Amanda said innocently.

"Yes, we were just trying to be helpful," Fanny agreed.

"Of course," George said, narrowing his eyes ever so slightly. "Just like we're going to be helpful in return."

"Boys, get inside and change those clothes before you catch your death," Victoria instructed. Fanny thought she detected a hint of a smile on her aunt's lips. "Girls, I suggest you avoid trying to help with the fire next time."

Amanda and Fanny grinned. "But of course, Mother," Amanda replied as she looped her arm with Fanny's. "At least until our aim improves."

"I'd say your aim was just fine," her mother said with a wink.

CHAPTER 6

MONDAY, JULY 5, 1897
BROADMOOR ISLAND

Even though there were many duties that required Michael Atwell's attention, the hours couldn't pass quickly enough for him. He would work day and night to complete the necessary tasks if it would hasten Fanny's arrival at the island. While most of the island staff dreaded the return of the Broadmoor family, Michael counted the minutes until their return—at least until Fanny arrived. The influx of the family meant added work for all of the staff, but Michael knew he would find ample time to spend with Fanny.

From her early years, Fanny had been different from the rest of the Broadmoor family. She hadn't cared that Michael was the son of the hired help or that his status could never match that of the Broadmoors. She had taken to Michael and then to his parents, treating them as though they were family and exhibiting a fondness for Frank and Maggie Atwell that amazed Michael.

"There you are!" Michael's mother stood in the doorway of the kitchen.

"There's no time for daydreaming. The family will be arriving this week and there's much to be done. Come in and help me rearrange some of this furniture." Michael strode toward her, his mass of wavy brown hair tucked beneath his cap. "And take off that cap when you cross the threshold, young man."

He grinned and doffed the flat-billed cap. "I'm twenty-one years old, Ma. I know to remove my hat when coming indoors."

"Then why is it I find you sitting at my table drinking coffee with your cap atop your head from time to time?" She didn't wait for his answer. He knew she didn't expect one. His mother was more concerned with all the work that must be accomplished in a short time.

Though Michael and his parents remained on the island year-round, the remaining servants who would care for the needs of the Broadmoor family would arrive either a day in advance or with the members of the family. The servants' quarters would easily accommodate the twenty staff members, but for Michael, the added staff created an air of discomfort. Even as a child, he'd considered the separate servants' quarters to be his home. And now that he was older and in charge of the Broadmoor vessels, he'd developed a sense of ownership over the boathouse, along with the skiffs, canoes, and steam launch housed within its confines.

The granite and wood-framed servants' quarters didn't begin to compare with the six-story, fifty-room stone castle where the family resided during their visits, but Michael possessed no feelings of ownership for the castle. Unlike the servants' quarters, he found Broadmoor Castle cold and uninviting—overindulgent, like most of those who would inhabit the rooms throughout the summer months. Like Mr. Broadmoor, the castle loomed large. A huge flag bearing the family coat of arms flew from the castle's turret and could be distinguished among the islands that had become known to tourists and locals alike as the Thousand Islands. In truth, the copious islands varied in size and shape and numbered far more than a thousand. So numerous were the land masses that began at the river's mouth and continued downriver for nearly fifty miles, even the locals couldn't always be counted upon to distinguish the international boundary line between New York State and Ontario, Canada.

While most of the servants, including his mother, spent long hours in the castle, the bulk of his father's time was committed to the grounds and the separate stone edifice that housed the coal-fired, steam-powered electric generator. An addition to Broadmoor Island that allowed for even greater elegance, the generator fully electrified both the castle and the servants' quarters, something not many in the islands could boast. But the permanent residents of the area hadn't failed to note that most were beginning to follow Mr. Broadmoor's lead to electrify. Likely anxious to keep both their image of wealth intact and their complaining wives happy, Michael suspected. It seemed it was either one or the other that caused these wealthy island owners to continue in their attempts to outdo their peers. If one purchased a larger launch or hired additional servants, others followed suit by the summer's end.

He'd found only Fanny to be different from the rest. Though she dressed in the same fine clothes and attended the required parties and social gatherings of the elite, she much preferred donning a pair of ill-fitting trousers, tucking her hair beneath an old cap, and fishing for hours in one of the boats. His blood raced as he contemplated seeing her once again.

"Michael!" His mother's voice echoed in the vast room. "Quit your daydreaming and help me move this divan. We don't have time to lollygag. There are supplies that need to be brought over from Clayton once we finish with this furniture."

Michael would be glad to escape the confines of the island and pick up supplies. Though he routinely visited Clayton, the flourishing village situated on the New York shoreline, he'd been relegated to the island for the past week, helping with the myriad preparations. The thought of taking the launch to Clayton was enough to keep him following his mother's directions at a steady pace for the remainder of the morning.

His mother surveyed the rooms and then returned to the entry hall. "We'll eat dinner, and then you can go over to Clayton. And don't plan on spending the afternoon visiting with the locals or the fishermen. I need those supplies back here so I can begin preparations."

Michael followed his mother out the front door of the castle. "If you would have sent me this morning, I'd already be back."

She shook her head. "And I'd still have all that furniture to uncover and move into place when you returned." She looped arms with her son and held his gaze with her hazel eyes. "I know you're anxious for Fanny's return, but you need to remember that she's all but a grown woman now. The two of you can't continue to go off by yourselves, fishing and reading books and the like. It's not proper. You didn't heed my counsel last summer, and I can already see the glimmer in your eyes every time her name is mentioned. She's not yours for the having, Michael. Those people are in a different class from us. You'll have no more than a broken heart when all is said and done."

His mother's words stung, and he turned away. "Fanny and I have been friends for years. She's not like the rest of them. You know that."

"She's a sweet, kind girl. I'll not disagree on that account, but she's still not available to the likes of a caretaker's son. I don't want any trouble."

Michael kicked a small rock. "There won't be any trouble, but I'll not agree to ignoring Fanny, either. She's a friend, and I look forward to seeing her again."

His mother sighed and waved him inside. He was thankful she didn't argue further. He didn't want a windy discussion to ensue, for it would delay his trip to Clayton.

Michael steered the steam launch into the bay and docked at the Fry Steam Launch Company pier. After securing the boat, he peeked inside, offered a quick hello to Bill Fry, and headed off toward Warnoll's Meat Market. He'd leave his list and come back to pick up the cuts his mother had ordered once he'd completed the remainder of the shopping. He nodded and spoke to several acquaintances as he made his way to the market.

"Morning, Albert," Michael said while he ambled toward the large counter. He shoved the list in Albert's direction.

Albert took the paper and glanced at the order. "Guess this means the Broadmoors are coming after all. Right?"

Michael frowned. "Why wouldn't they be coming?"

"With old Mr. Broadmoor dying, folks was speculating whether the family would return this summer. None of them seemed particularly fond of the island. We just thought maybe—"

"Wait! What did you say about Mr. Broadmoor?"

Mr. Warnoll arched his brows. "That he's dead?" He studied Michael for a moment. "You mean you folks didn't know?"

Michael shook his head. "When did this happen, and how come nobody let us know?" Word traveled quickly from island to island, and Michael didn't understand how this important bit of news could have bypassed them.

"Everyone figured the family had advised the staff. When we didn't see any of you in the village, we thought you might be observing your own period of mourning or some such thing. We didn't want to intrude."

Michael wasn't certain why Albert thought they'd be in mourning out on the island, but the fact that everyone else knew Mr. Broadmoor was dead and the servants on his island hadn't been advised was baffling. Why hadn't the family sent word? Since they hadn't contacted the island staff, did that mean they were coming as scheduled, or had they assumed word would somehow reach the island and the staff would realize they wouldn't arrive? Michael was nonplussed by the odd behavior.

"Do you still want me to fill the order, Michael?"

"I suppose so. I'll assume they're still coming since we haven't had any word advising us to the contrary. They'll expect the larder to be stocked if they arrive."

The man nodded. "And empty if they don't. I'll get busy on your order. Should have it ready for you in an hour."

"I'll be back then. I've got to fill an order at the general store and pick up some items at the drugstore." Michael pulled his folded cap from his back pocket and headed out the door. "And cut those chops nice and thick the way my ma likes them," he called over his shoulder.

Mr. Warnoll's hearty chuckle filled the room. "I'll see to it. I don't want your mother coming in here and giving me a lecture on how to cut a proper lamb chop."

Michael waved to Mr. Hungerford as he passed the plumbing and tinware store and offered greetings to several men visiting outside the Hub Café with Mr. Grapotte, the owner.

"My condolences to you folks. I'm sure things will be different now that Mr. Broadmoor's passed on." Mr. Grapotte stroked his whiskers and shook his head.

"I suppose they will," Michael replied. He didn't intend to tell others that today was the first he'd known of Mr. Broadmoor's death. He still didn't know exactly when his employer had died.

"Family still arriving?"

"Far as we know. Got to keep moving. I've got a list a mile long." He waved the piece of paper and hurried onward.

By the time he'd filled the lists and the launch had been loaded, Michael was exhausted. Not from the work itself but from fielding the many questions and comments from the village residents. He knew they meant well. The death of someone such as Mr. Broadmoor was no small thing in this village. He had been, after all, one of the wealthiest men in all of New York State and an elite member of the Thousand Islands community. Before making his final visit to Mr. Warnoll's, Michael stopped by the newspaper office and purchased a copy of *On the St. Lawrence,* the edition that had announced Mr. Broadmoor's death. Michael felt the need to have tangible proof before he carried such shocking news home to his parents.

He attempted to formulate some simple yet straightforward way to break the news to them as he crossed the water in the *Daisy-Bee,* the name Mr. Broadmoor had christened the launch—in memory of his wife, he'd announced after purchasing the boat last summer. Several of the family members had been offended, but Mr. Broadmoor had insisted his wife would have enjoyed the tribute. With great fanfare, he'd had the name painted in large gold and black letters across both sides of the hull and then commanded the presence of the entire family and staff when he broke a bottle of champagne across the boat's prow and formally christened his steamer the *DaisyBee.* Michael didn't care what Mr. Broadmoor named the boat as long as he was the one who would have the pleasure of guiding her over the waters of the St. Lawrence River. Against his better judgment, Michael had been forced on occasion to hand over the helm to some of the younger male members of the Broadmoor family, who then insisted upon showing their prowess to young female passengers on the boat. Infrequent as those instances had been, Michael always dreaded having Jefferson and George Broadmoor aboard—especially when they were imbibing.

He guided the steamer past Calumet Island, where Charles Emery's castle-like home, constructed of Potsdam sandstone, sat directly opposite the village of Clayton. Folks said Mr. Emery, one of the partners who had formed the American Tobacco Company, decided to build his new house on Calumet Island and provide a view for Clayton residents that would rival George Pullman's Castle Rest on Pullman Island. Some thought Mr. Emery had succeeded, for his was the first large castle-type home that ships would see as they headed downriver from Lake Ontario. Michael wasn't so sure a winner could be declared, for the castled structures hadn't yet ceased to rise out of the water. Inspired by Pullman, other giants of industry had purchased islands and established magnificent homes for themselves in what they now dubbed their summer playground. George Boldt of Waldorf-Astoria fame, Frederick Bourne, president of the Singer Sewing Machine Company, Andrew Schuler, owner of Schuler's Potato Chips, and many other wealthy capitalists now descended upon the Thousand Islands every summer. Life on these islands continued to change—a transformation in progress.

Once downriver, Michael turned toward Broadmoor Island, the island that had been his home since birth. He knew every inch of this two-mile-long island like the back of his hand. Since his early years, he'd explored the dog bone–shaped island with its sloping lawns that led to the docks and its craggy ten-foot-high seawall that protected Broadmoor Castle as it towered toward the heavens. Now he wondered if his days on this island were numbered. With Mr. Broadmoor's death, the family would possibly sell the island. Few of them enjoyed this magnificent treasure, and Michael knew wealthy men would be willing to pay a generous sum for the palatial summer home of Hamilton Broadmoor.

He docked the boat and glanced toward the house. His mother had been watching for him, for she was already picking her way down the path to the boathouse. Moving with haste, he lifted the bundles of food and dry goods onto the dock, where he would transfer them into a cart for transport to the residence. It would take several trips, but the cart would be easier than attempting to carry all of the items in cumbersome baskets.

"I was beginning to worry," his mother called out when she neared the boat.

He bit his tongue. No need to remind her how many items she'd requested or how long it took Mr. Warnoll to fill her massive order for roasts and chops.

"Did you pick up the mail?"

"I did, though that reminder wasn't on your list." He pecked her cheek with a fleeting kiss.

His mother extended her arm, and he handed her the bundle of mail. If she was looking for a letter from Broadmoor Mansion, she'd find nothing there. He'd already checked. She riffled through the mail while he loaded the cart, always careful to keep the newspaper hidden from view.

By the time he had unloaded the final cart of goods, his mother was already scurrying about the kitchen, arranging the new supplies in their proper locations and checking to make certain he'd purchased every item in the quantity requested.

"So far I haven't found any mistakes." She lifted her chin and gave him a smile.

Without fanfare he spread the paper across the table in front of his mother and pointed to the picture of Hamilton Broadmoor. She gasped and dropped into a nearby chair.

CHAPTER 7

TUESDAY, JULY 6, 1897

They didn't need to worry long. Early the next morning, Mr. Simmons from the telegraph office arrived by boat with a message that servants from the Rochester mansion would begin arriving that afternoon. Michael was instructed to meet the train and transport the servants and the family's trunks to the island. Unlike some of the summer residents, who transported their riding horses and milking cows to their homes each summer, the Broadmoors' two riding horses as well as the farm stock were kept at the island year-round, expediting the process of moving their goods to the island. With the arrival of the servants several days in advance, the family's clothing would be pressed and hung in their wardrobes, menus would be planned, and the individual needs and desires of each family member would be met prior to their coming.

Michael was waiting outside the Clayton station when the train from Rochester hissed and jolted to a stop. He would have no difficulty recognizing at least some of the Broadmoor staff. Each year several new servants arrived with those stalwart members of the staff who were expected to spend each summer at the island, regardless of their families back home. Michael's mother always looked forward to reuniting with some of them. No doubt his mother's favorite, Kate O'Malley, would be among those arriving. As head housekeeper at Broadmoor Mansion, Mrs. O'Malley's presence was expected. Maggie Atwell and Kate had become good friends over the years. Yet not good enough friends that Kate had written to inform them of Mr. Broadmoor's death, he thought while watching the housekeeper detrain.

He waved his cap and headed across the tracks. "Welcome, Mrs. O'Malley. The launch is in its usual place. I'll see to the baggage if you want to direct your staff."

"Good afternoon, Michael. It's good to see you." She waved the other members of the party together. "I trust your parents are well."

"We would have sent word if anything were amiss." He had hoped to gain a reaction, but Mrs. O'Malley merely offered a curt nod and led the group toward the launch. As expected, there were some new faces, but there were fewer servants this year. Was this decrease in staff an ominous sign? His mother had said they must maintain their faith, for their future was in God's hands. Michael knew that much was true. However, he feared their future also lay in the hands of the Broadmoor family, a family that wasn't fond of the Thousand Islands.

His mother stood on the dock awaiting their return. She waved and greeted the new arrivals with the same enthusiasm she offered to her own family.

The moment Kate stepped off the boat, the women hugged and exchanged pleasantries. Kate turned and beckoned a dark-haired, blue-eyed young woman forward. "This is my daughter Theresa—the youngest. I was pleased to be able to have her come with us this year. Miss Victoria wanted her along—says Theresa is the best at styling hair and choosing gowns and the like." Kate tipped her head closer. "I didn't argue. Theresa is getting to an age where I don't like leaving her at the main house for the summer, if you know what I mean," Kate said with an exaggerated wink.

Michael pressed by the women with one of the trunks in his cart. He didn't care to hear any more of this discussion. He had started up the path when Theresa caught up with him.

"Can I help you with that heavy load?"

Michael shook his head and continued pushing. "No. It's easier for one person to push, but thanks. There might be some other items down there you could carry."

She ignored his suggestion and continued alongside him. "How long have you lived here, Michael?"

"All my life."

"How can you stand it? I mean growing up all alone on this island with no one to talk to or play with?"

Michael laughed. "I was never bored. Besides, I had two older brothers to keep me company while I was young. Now one of them lives in Canada and the other in Delaware. They were anxious to leave, but I love this island. I have no desire to live elsewhere."

Theresa's dark unbound tresses blew about her face, and she brushed the strands behind her ears. "Well, I suppose that's a good thing for the Broadmoors. They don't have to worry about finding a replacement for you."

Perhaps Theresa could answer some of his burning questions. He wondered if he should broach the topic of Mr. Broadmoor's death. "How long have you worked for the family, Theresa?"

She shrugged. "It seems like I've always worked for them in some capacity. Mother was working for Mr. Jonas and his wife when I was born. My father died when I was five years old. The Broadmoors didn't want to lose Mother, so they permitted her to move into the house and me along with her. As you heard, she was delighted when Miss Victoria listed me as one of the servants to come here this year." She lowered her voice. "I truly was surprised. I thought with Mr. Broadmoor's death they'd all be wearing their mourning clothes and not care about parties and the like."

Michael raised his brows. "And?"

"Mr. Broadmoor said in his will that he didn't want them mourning him." She stepped closer. "He said they hadn't cared about him while he was alive, so they didn't need to mourn his death."

"He said that?"

"Well, something along that line. The servants weren't invited into the library to hear the reading of the will and such. But Treadwell, he's the head butler at Broadmoor Mansion, was close enough to the doors to hear most everything that was said."

While Theresa held the door open, Michael hoisted the trunk and carried it inside. Theresa pointed to the trunk. "That one belongs to Miss Fanny. You can put it in whichever room is hers."

Throughout the remainder of the unloading, Theresa remained by Michael's side. She carried an occasional basket or pretended to help him with a trunk. It was a charade to avoid helping her mother in the kitchen, he decided. He didn't object, for Theresa seemed to enjoy talking more than most anything else. His simple questions were answered with lengthy, informative replies. Theresa was a virtual fount of details. He'd learned more about Mr. Broadmoor's death and the family's reaction to it in the past hour than the other servants would have divulged over the next two months.

"Since this is my first time on the island, why don't you take me for a tour, Michael? Once the family arrives, I doubt I'll have much free time for exploration."

Theresa's interest in the island pleased him, and he agreed to meet her once he'd completed his chores. When he returned to the house a short time later, she was waiting outside.

She formed her lips into a tiny moue. "I thought you'd forgotten me. It's been nearly an hour."

He laughed and shook his head. "I needed to complete my chores and secure the boat in the boathouse. But I have enough time that we should be able to walk a good portion of the island. Does your mother know you're going with me?"

"She's busy preparing menus with your mother. They won't miss us." She skipped ahead of him. "Tell me what it's like living here. I'm amazed that this house is even bigger than the mansion in Rochester."

"It was built that way because the entire family comes here every summer. Each family is accustomed to being in their own home, so Mr. Broadmoor wanted to be certain there would be adequate space when they gathered under one roof. That's what my mother told me when I was a little boy." He grinned. "I can't imagine they truly need all this space, but the men who build these houses aren't happy unless they are huge."

"Status. They all want to outdo one another," Theresa said. "They act the same way in Rochester. One after another, they build their enormous houses along East Avenue. Perhaps I would do the same if I possessed their wealth."

Michael led Theresa to an outcropping of rocks that overlooked the water and assisted her as she sat down. "Not me. If I had enough money, I'd buy my own island." He pointed toward the diverse plots of land that dotted the river like a hodgepodge of stepping-stones. "I'd be happiest with even the smallest piece of land out there. No big house or steam launch needed. I'd settle for a tent and a canoe or skiff—at least until winter set in. Then I might build something a little more substantial."

Theresa laughed. "You must want more out of life than a small island and a tent."

"A woman to love me and children someday." At the mention of marriage and children, he pictured Fanny. She would make the perfect wife for him—if only . . .

Theresa tickled his ear with a wild violet. "And who might you be thinking of as a mother for those children you hope to have one day?" She tucked her knees beneath her chin and batted her lashes.

"That's not yet been decided. Most of the girls who live on the islands or in the villages can't wait to move to a large city, and the girls who come here to vacation are wealthy socialites. I may never find the perfect woman." He glanced toward the sun. "I need to get back. There will be things needing my attention with the family soon arriving."

Theresa took his outstretched hand and jumped up from the rock. With a sharp cry, she clenched his hand. Michael attempted to grab her other hand as she toppled to the ground. "I've twisted my ankle." She lifted the hem of her skirt.

The ankle hadn't yet begun to swell. Michael carefully removed her shoe and gently moved her foot until she yelped in pain. "I doubt it's broken, but I can't be certain. Let's see if you can sustain any weight on it." He complimented Theresa on her brave attempts, but from her anguished cries, he didn't think she could walk back to the house.

She tilted her head to the side and looked up at him. "Perhaps you could carry me—if I don't weigh too much."

Michael surveyed her form and laughed. "I doubt I'll have much trouble. You're no bigger than a minute. Since the terrain is rough, maybe it would be best if I carried you on my back. I won't be able to see as well with you in my arms."

She gave him a momentary pout, but then agreed. Though riding on his back would not prove the most ladylike position, Michael didn't want to chance a further injury. He was afraid Mrs. O'Malley wouldn't be pleased when her daughter returned with a swollen ankle. And if Theresa wasn't up and about by tomorrow, he imagined the Broadmoor women would be displeased, also.

Theresa's hands were clasped around his neck, and he could feel her breath on his ear as they continued toward the house. She was good company—not like Fanny but nice. "We'll need to get ice on your ankle."

"You're panting. I'm heavier than you thought, aren't I?" She giggled. "You can say so. I promise I won't be angry."

He shook his head and rounded the corner of the house. "I'd never admit—" At the sound of laughter and voices, he glanced up, straightened, and nearly dropped Theresa to the ground. "Fanny! When did all of you arrive? I mean, how did you get to the island?" The entire Broadmoor family stood in the path before him. One glance at the river and Michael knew they had ferried from Clayton on the *Little Mac*.

Theresa wiggled and then whispered in his ear. "You can put me down, Michael."

He lowered her onto the steps leading to the rear of the house while the family continued onward. "I thought you weren't to arrive until tomorrow. Mrs. O'Malley said . . ."

Jonas Broadmoor looked over the top of his glasses. "And I decided we would arrive today." He turned a cold stare on Theresa. "Don't the two of you have duties to perform? I'm not paying you to play about in the woods."

"Yes, sir. I mean, no, sir, we weren't playing about. Theresa fell, and . . ."

Mr. Broadmoor continued walking, obviously not interested in an explanation, but Michael didn't fail to see the look of betrayal in Fanny's eyes. He must talk to her. Goodness, but she was more beautiful than ever.

"Michael!"

His mother was calling from the kitchen, Theresa was injured, Mr. Broadmoor was angry, and he'd obviously caused Fanny pain. On his way up the steps he promised to return with ice for Theresa's ankle. So far it was a glorious beginning to the summer.

Mrs. O'Malley was down the steps in a flash, without the ice. Michael and his mother followed close behind.

"So you're already thinking to get out of some work, are you?" Mrs. O'Malley was standing on the step below her daughter. "Let me see that foot." She lifted Theresa's skirt, wiggled the ankle, and pointed a finger under the girl's nose. "Put your shoe on and get upstairs. There's nothing wrong with your foot."

Theresa didn't attempt to argue. She shoved her foot into the shoe, laced it up, and followed her mother up the stairs. With a grin and a shrug, she strode past Michael.

"There's no time for romancing Theresa O'Malley." His mother's brows knit together in a frown. "We've enough problems with the family arriving unexpectedly, Michael. You know better."

Without giving him an opportunity to explain, his mother marched back up the steps to begin meal preparations for the unexpected family members. He sat down on the steps and rested his head in his hands.

"I see you and Theresa have become fast friends."

He startled and lifted his head at the sound of Fanny's voice. "Fanny! I'm so glad you've come outdoors. Would you let me explain?"

"There's nothing to explain, Michael. Theresa injured herself and you were kind enough to assist her."

"Well, that's what I thought until Mrs. O'Malley chided Theresa and declared the injury a hoax. After watching her scurry up the stairs, I realized I'd been duped. I wanted to explain so you wouldn't think I'm courting her."

Fanny smiled. "I've known Theresa for many years. Further explanation isn't necessary. She's a nice girl who is anxious to wed and begin a life of her own."

Michael changed the subject. "I was sorry to hear about your grandfather. We didn't know he had died until I went into town yesterday to pick up supplies. One of the shop owners told me."

"Uncle Jonas didn't send word?"

"No, but that's not what's important now. How are you doing, Fanny? I can hardly believe my eyes. You're all grown up."

"For all the good it's done me," she declared. "My life seems to constantly be in the hands of others to order about."

He listened while she told him she'd been forced to move from the mansion and that her uncle Jonas had been appointed her guardian and the trustee of her estate. "He wants me to go on a grand tour of Europe, but I truly want to remain here—on the island."

"Would your uncle agree to such an arrangement?"

Fanny tucked a curl behind her ear. "Not without proper supervision. Even then, I'm not sure he'd agree. He's angry that I inherited my father's share of the estate, and I think he's determined to force me to bend to his will until I've reached my majority."

Michael rubbed his jaw. "It's lonely out here on the island once all the summer people return home."

"I know what it's like, Michael. Don't you recall the many summers when my grandparents and I would arrive well ahead of the family and remain at least a month after they'd all departed? I enjoy the solitude and beauty of these islands as much as you do."

He didn't dare tell her he remembered every minute of every day that she'd spent on this island with him. When they were young, he'd been like an older brother to her. Sitting under the trees with a picnic lunch and reading books together, teaching her how to thread a worm onto her fishing hook and then how to remove the fish, exploring the river in her grandfather's skiff and finding caves beneath the rock outcroppings—he remembered it all.

"Do you think your parents might agree to take on the responsibility of providing proper supervision?" she asked. "We could talk to them, and if they thought it was a feasible plan, perhaps they could help convince Uncle Jonas. After all, I'll be eighteen in March."

"We've nothing to lose by asking them, but I think we should wait a few days. Your family wasn't expected until tomorrow, and Mother won't want to think about anything except food preparations."

"Thank you, Michael." She glanced toward the house. "I better go back inside before I'm missed, but I'm looking forward to a picnic very soon."

He nodded his agreement and then watched her return to the house, his thoughts jumbled. Fanny was now an heiress with a vast amount of money. To some, that might be exciting news. To Michael, it meant only one thing: the chasm between them had grown even wider. Unless he could find some way to bridge that gulf, she would be lost to him forever.

CHAPTER 8

WEDNESDAY, JULY 7, 1897

Jonas sat beside Quincy in one of the outlook rooms in the castle turret. He'd been anxious to speak with his brother privately, but since his father's death, either they were surrounded by other members of the family or Quincy would sneak off and return to his Home for the Friendless, which remained a matter of contention between the brothers. But Jonas was determined to present a magnanimous spirit this day. He wanted his brother as an ally.

Jonas settled into one of the heavy leather chairs and puffed on his cigar. "It's only early July, and already this has proved to be a summer of difficulties. Let's hope our troubles will soon ease."

Quincy fixed his gaze on a freighter moving downriver. "I won't be able to spend much time on the island, Jonas. I know the provisions of Father's will require the men of the family to devote as much time as possible to the family during the summer, but I'm sure you understand that if I'm to keep the shelter afloat, I must be absent a great deal during the week."

"Yes—Father's will left us all in a bit of a bind, didn't it?" He took a long draw on the cigar and blew a smoke ring into the air above his head. "I completely understand your need to oversee your work, Quincy. Just as I must oversee mine. For a man who made his own fortune, Father seemed to remember very little about how time-consuming it could be."

"I do hope Victoria is willing to supervise Sophie during my absence. My daughter can be a handful at times."

"I'm certain Victoria won't mind. The three girls will spend all of their time together anyway." Jonas flicked the ash from his cigar. "I've wanted to talk to you about other provisions in Father's will."

Quincy turned back toward the river. "The terms of his will were very precise. What is there to talk about?"

"Fanny's inheritance. Surely you don't think she's entitled to the same inheritance you and I will receive. It's not as though Langley ever contributed anything to the family."

"He was our *brother*, Jonas!"

"I don't deny that, but think about it—what did his life amount to? Langley was completely useless after Winifred's death. He may have talked about his journalism career, but he never put pen to paper, and you know it. And how many grown men do you know who would have moved back home with a child after the death of their wife?"

"Mother insisted. You know that. She wanted Fanny to have a woman's influence in her life. You can't fault Langley for giving in to her. To be honest, if Marie had died when our children were young, I might have done the same. It's been difficult enough raising Sophie for the past year by myself. And she was seventeen when Marie died." Quincy tented his fingers beneath his chin. "Left with an infant, I think I would have succumbed to Mother's wishes, also. Langley and I never were as strong as you. Perhaps it has something to do with your being the eldest son."

"Don't sell yourself short," Jonas said. "You were quite successful while working for the company. Father couldn't have run the milling business or his later investments without your astute business acumen. And if you'd give up that idea of spending all your time and money on your Home for the Friendless, I could terminate Henry Foster. He can't hold a candle to you when it comes to accounting and investments."

"I'm not interested in the business. I feel God's calling to do this work, and if you've brought me up here to convince me otherwise, you'll not succeed."

Jonas silently chided himself. He didn't want to put his brother on the defensive. He needed him as an ally if he was going to succeed in gaining Fanny's share of his father's estate. Though some of the other relatives agreed with him, it was Quincy who would prove most beneficial. With Quincy on his side, he could present a unified front to any dissenting family members and to the court, if necessary.

"I think we should contest Fanny's inheritance."

Quincy stood and walked to the window. "I don't think that's wise. Didn't you hear what Mr. Fillmore said? I don't want the funds tied up because we contest the will. I need cash to keep the shelter operational. Besides, Fanny is entitled to Langley's share. It's what our father wanted."

"And what if I could find some method other than contesting the will? Would you side with me then, dear brother?"

A wave of Quincy's dark brown hair streaked with strands of gray fell across his forehead. "I think she's entitled to her father's share. Unless you can show me a reason other than what you've spoken of this afternoon, I don't think I could agree. Of course, she's much too young to handle such a large sum, but Father placed you in charge of her funds. I trust you will handle her money with the same care with which you handle your own."

Jonas's lips curved in a slow smile. "You may rest assured."

"If there's nothing else, I believe I'll go downstairs. The architect delivered his most recent renderings for expansion of the shelter before we departed. I brought them along and want to examine them."

Jonas waved his cigar. "As you wish. I'm going to remain up here awhile longer." He didn't add that he needed to gather his thoughts and suffuse the anger that burned in his heart. Quincy's offhanded dismissal galled him. Now he'd be forced to develop another plan. And develop one he would. He had to. The investments he'd made earlier in the year had not played out well. Added to that, his own company was failing to make the same level of profits it had the year before. None of that by itself would have been damaging, but Jonas had spent large amounts of money on expanding his house and gardens, as well as purchasing a team of matched horses that had cost him a pretty penny. And the bills from Amanda's trip abroad had been far more extensive than he'd originally thought they'd be. He wasn't destitute, but his finances were greatly strained. Dangerously so.

One way or the other, he'd have Langley's share for himself, and Quincy need not think he'd share in it, either. He'd given Quincy his chance. At the very least, with a bit of finagling, he'd mange to skim and pilfer a goodly portion of her inheritance with no one becoming the wiser.

After stubbing out the cigar, Jonas pulled his chair near the window and stared down below. Amanda, Sophie, and Fanny were gathered together on the front lawn enjoying a game of croquet, while Jefferson and George, along with several of the younger children, shouted instructions from the sidelines. Fanny waved and Jonas watched as Michael Atwell approached from the far end of the lawn.

Fanny touched his arm and then perched on tiptoe to whisper into Michael's ear. The young man laughed and nodded while Amanda and Sophie continued knocking the croquet balls toward the metal hoops. Michael withdrew something from his pocket and then held out the object for Fanny to examine. Jonas leaned forward, his forehead touching the glass. What did Michael hold in his hand? Whatever it was, the object had captured Fanny's interest. It appeared the young man had a way with the girls—first Theresa and now Fanny. If the young boatswain continued his amorous behavior, one of the local girls would have him at the altar before long.

Jonas continued to stare at the young couple. He paced back and forth, his gaze flickering down toward the lawn each time he passed the windows until he recalled his conversation with Mortimer Fillmore. They had discussed the possibility of an arranged marriage for Fanny.

He stopped. Fanny had placed her croquet mallet in the stand and was strolling toward the boathouse with Michael. He'd have to find additional work to keep that young man busy! Fanny tucked her hand into the crook of Michael's arm. From all appearances, she was encouraging the young man's advances. Surely young Atwell didn't think he could woo one of the Broadmoor girls. Jonas would never permit such a liaison. If anyone thought Hamilton Broadmoor's granddaughter was being courted by the hired help, she'd be blacklisted from ever making a proper marriage.

Jonas massaged his forehead. An arranged marriage was exactly what he needed for Fanny. And it looked like he needed to move swiftly. He would begin to prepare a list of possibilities. With a word to his business associates, he could surely locate the names of a number of possible candidates with the proper lineage and little intelligence. That was precisely what he needed. Unless he could arrive at some other solution, he must find the perfect marriage partner for his niece.

"I missed you," Fanny told Michael as they walked along the island path to her special place. She had brought a bouquet of flowers to put there in memory of her father, just as she did every year.

"I missed you, too, although I have been quite busy. We built a new boathouse that kept us occupied."

"I saw it. I thought it looked grand." She gathered her skirt and climbed down the rocky trail to where she used to sit with her father.

The tree where she'd found him dead still stood as a reminder. Fanny could almost see him there. She bit her lip and forced back tears. How could it still hurt so much after all these years?

"I don't know if it's a good idea for you to keep coming back here," Michael said as he came alongside her. "It seems to only make you sad."

"It's not just sadness," Fanny told him. "It's the wondering about what might have been. I miss him so much. I miss my mother, too, but I suppose that seems silly."

"Never. Everyone longs for a mother's love."

His voice was soothing and very compassionate. Fanny couldn't help but look up into his eyes. No one in the world mattered more to her now. "I'm glad you understand."

"I do. I can still remember that day—finding Mr. Broadmoor here. It seems like just yesterday."

"I know," Fanny agreed. "I always wished Papa would have left me a letter or something to show that he was thinking of me—that he loved me."

"His actions showed that every day," Michael whispered.

"Every day but the last," she countered. "If he had loved me that day, he would never have left me."

Michael reached out and gently touched her shoulder. "He loved you that day, too, Fanny. His pain caused his actions, but it couldn't take away his love for you."

"I suppose you're right." She placed the flowers at the trunk of the tree and then straightened. "I'm so glad to be back here—on the island—with you."

He smiled and the look he gave her caused Fanny's heart to skip a beat. If possible, he was even more handsome than he'd been the year before.

"It always seems to take forever before the winter and spring pass and you return. I always fear this will be the year you won't come back."

Fanny laughed. "I'll always come back, Michael. This is my home. I love it here more than anywhere else on earth. I'll never leave it . . . or you . . . for good."

CHAPTER 9

Later the same afternoon, the three girls sauntered across the lawn until they reached their favorite spot beneath one of the large fir trees that dotted the lower half of the grassy expanse. They carefully positioned their blankets to gain a view of the river—watching the water flow by was one of Fanny's favorite pastimes on warm afternoons such as this.

Sophie tucked her dress around her legs and leaned against the trunk of the ancient conifer while Amanda settled between her two younger cousins. Sophie had promised to give them a full account of the Independence Day party she had attended at Brown Square. Though Amanda and Fanny had been much too frightened to sneak off with Sophie that day, they both were eager to hear the details now.

Fanny brushed a persistent fly from the sleeve of her striped shirtwaist. "Well? Did you have as much fun as you expected?"

Sophie bobbed her head. "Of course. In fact, even more. I met two wonderful young men who were ever so sad to hear I would be leaving Rochester for the summer. They've promised to come calling the minute I return to town. Both of them were quite handsome, too." She giggled and tucked a curl behind her ear. "Promise you won't tell a soul, but I permitted one of them to remove my shoes so I could get my feet wet."

Amanda gasped and clutched her bodice. "Please tell me that's *all* you let him remove."

"If you're worried about my stockings, fear not, Amanda. I would have preferred to remove them, but it didn't seem prudent at the time. Instead, I waded in with them on. The men thought me a good sport." Sophie leaned forward and sighed. "They were both so attentive all evening. I think they were competing to see which one would have the privilege of escorting me home. The boys offered to buy me some of the German beer that was for sale in the park, but I told them I didn't like the taste. Do you know what Wilhelm did then?"

Amanda quirked her brows. "I can only imagine."

"He went and got me a large cup of fruit punch." Sophie glanced over her shoulder. "And then he removed a silver flask from inside his jacket and poured some whiskey into the punch. It was wonderful."

Amanda's eyes grew wide. "That's disgraceful, Sophie. Those boys were likely hoping to get you drunk in order to take advantage of you." She grasped Sophie's hand. "Please tell me that didn't occur."

Sophie laughed. "You need not worry, Amanda. It would have taken more than that to render me defenseless."

"You're accustomed to imbibing alcoholic drinks?" Fanny's mouth gaped.

"I've had more than my share, I suppose. Oh, do close your mouth, Fanny. There are far worse things than alcohol. I could tell you about them, but I fear both of you would faint—and how could I possibly explain that to the family?" Sophie pointed toward a launch filled with summer visitors. "I'd guess they're on their way to the party at Hopewell Hall. I do wish your mother would have given permission for us to attend. I'd love to sneak off to that party, but this isn't like being at home. Here, I have your mother watching after my comings and goings."

There was little doubt Sophie was unhappy. She'd been pouting ever since discovering Aunt Victoria had sent regrets to the Browning residence on Farwell Island. Several of William Browning's grandsons were hosting a party at their grandfather's island, and all three of the girls had hoped to attend. Even Fanny enjoyed the occasional gatherings hosted at the home of the man who had spawned his fortune making uniforms for the Union Army during the American Civil War. Hopewell Hall provided a spectacular view from its perch high above the river, and though Fanny didn't care about mingling with the elite, she did enjoy exploring every island she visited and watching the variety of boats and barges that consistently dotted the waterway.

Amanda patted Sophie's folded hands. "There will be parties all summer long, dear Sophie. Mother wanted us all in attendance to welcome your sister. After all, this has been a trying time for Louisa and her children."

Sophie shrugged. "My entire life has been trying."

Fanny giggled.

"Don't you dare laugh at me, Fanny. You have no idea of the difficulties I've been forced to endure."

Fanny leaned forward and peeked around Amanda. "You are so dramatic, dear Cousin. I fear I haven't noted the many tragedies you've suffered. Do tell us of all your horrid life experiences so we may commiserate with you."

Ever melodramatic, Sophie gazed heavenward and exhaled deeply. "How could you possibly fail to notice, Fanny? While my mother was alive, she was always consumed with my brother and sisters. Even when they were gone from home, she didn't have time for me. She was either worried about Dorian being forever lost to her in the Canadian backcountry or worried about my sisters' marriages and the births of her grandchildren. There was never time for me."

"You may be exaggerating just a wee bit," Amanda said.

"And how would you know, Amanda? Your mother is constantly at your beck and call. You don't know what it's like to be ignored by your mother. While Mother was alive, my father spent all his time working for Grandfather and was seldom home. As for me, I don't miss either of them."

"Sophie Broadmoor! How can you say you don't miss your mother?" Amanda clucked her tongue.

"You can't miss what you never had." Sophie's rebuttal dripped with sarcasm.

"That's not true," Fanny declared. "I never knew my mother, but I feel a deep longing in the pit of my stomach at the very thought of her. You were fortunate to have your mother for so many years. One day you'll agree with me. And you should make an effort to spend time with your father, too. If something should happen to him, you'll regret not having made the effort."

Sophie groaned. "Haven't you become the idealistic soul! My father is so consumed with his Home for the Friendless that I could disappear from the face of the earth and months would pass before he even realized I was gone."

"You do have a flare for the dramatic," Amanda said with a chuckle. "And if your father is so uncaring, why does he provide aid to the homeless and why does he make an appearance on the island during the middle of the week? My father seldom arrives until Saturday afternoon and departs on Sunday evening or Monday morning. He's rarely on the island, yet I don't condemn him as heartless."

"I suppose that's because you're a better person than I am. And don't think my father is here because he's interested in my welfare. Do you see that young man he met at the dock only a few minutes ago?"

Fanny and Amanda strained forward and watched their uncle crossing the lawn with a young man they'd never before seen. Fanny cupped her hand over her eyes and squinted. "Who is he? I don't believe I've met him."

"You haven't. He's Paul Medford, father's new protégé and a recent graduate of Bangor Theological Seminary. You'll notice Father has scads of time for Paul. He clings to every word young Mr. Medford utters."

"He works for your father? Doing what?" Amanda asked.

Sophie turned her back on the two men as they continued toward the house. "Father advertised in the newspaper and contacted several divinity schools, stating he planned to hire a man to live at the shelter—someone who had a heart for ministering to the less fortunate and was willing to reside on the grounds with all those *friendless* people he takes in." Sophie wrinkled her nose. "According to Father, Paul is a gift from God, a man who seeks nothing more from life than helping his fellow man. The man is a true bore. He thinks of nothing but God and those wretched people who live at the shelter."

"I think he's quite handsome," Fanny remarked.

"I find him somewhat plain," Amanda observed, "but I'm sure he must be very kind."

"I suppose because I am rather plain, I attempt to find beauty in the simple," Fanny said.

Amanda chuckled. "You are far from plain. With your beautiful skin, those auburn curls, and beautiful brown eyes, you are a beauty."

Fanny didn't argue with her cousin. If the conversation continued, they would think she was begging for compliments, but compared to her cousins, she was very ordinary.

Sophie leaned close to Amanda. "Paul would be perfect for you, Amanda. Just like you, he thinks people should spend all their time serving mankind through charitable works."

Fanny leaned against the tree while her cousins argued about Paul Medford and Amanda's aspirations to perform charitable work. They all three realized the one who would have the final say in Amanda's future would be Uncle Jonas. They also understood that he wouldn't agree to his daughter's seeking a career. He would expect Amanda to wed. He would insist her husband be a man of wealth and position, regardless of Amanda's personal desires or the physical appearance of her intended. Amanda was his only daughter, and Uncle Jonas would not permit her to marry some beggarly fellow who didn't meet his expectations. For years, Amanda had worked alongside her mother performing charity work, and her mother knew of her desire to continue with such endeavors. But her father had also made his desires known: she could perform her charity work as a married woman, just as her mother had done before her.

A passing launch drew close to the water's edge, and several of their friends waved and hollered greetings. "They're likely on their way to Hopewell Hall. I do wish my sister would have chosen some other day for her arrival. You might know that she had to select the day when the Brownings are hosting their party." Sophie pulled a handful of grass and tossed it into the air.

"We'll be attending parties, dances, and picnics all summer long, Sophie. You may as well cheer up. Your continued pouting hurts no one except yourself." Amanda waved to the group as they continued down the river. "And I'd think you'd want to offer a show of support for Louisa. Life can't be easy for her with three little children and so recently a widow, too."

"Louisa should have no difficulty. Her husband left her with a handsome inheritance. She had best keep her purse strings tied or Father will be seeking a large contribution for his Home for the Friendless."

"Sophie! What a terrible thing to say." Amanda frowned at her cousin. "You've become quite disparaging of late, and it doesn't suit you well."

"Say what you will. I know my father. He had Paul arrive today so it would coincide with Louisa's arrival. Oh, what if he's planning some wild matchmaking scheme between the two of them? Now wouldn't *that* make for an interesting summer!"

Fanny couldn't believe Sophie's flippant attitude. "Louisa's husband has been dead for less than a year. Your father would never consider such a thing."

Sophie pulled her hair off her neck and bunched it together atop her head. "You must admit it's a delicious idea. If Amanda has no interest in Paul, I shall mention him as a possibility to Louisa myself."

"You wouldn't! Promise me you'll do no such thing." Fanny reached across Amanda and grasped Sophie's arm. "If you're angry with your father, then talk to him, but don't add to your sister's pain and bereavement with such irresponsible antics."

"Oh, I suppose you're correct. Louisa isn't to blame for our father's behavior."

Fanny gave a sigh of relief. She couldn't believe her cousin would entertain such a foolish idea. Then again, after hearing of Sophie's behavior at the Independence Day party, Fanny knew she shouldn't be surprised. Obviously, the breach between Sophie and her father had widened considerably during the past year. It seemed Sophie hoped to gain her father's attention with her outlandish behavior. Instead, he seemed even more distant and aloof.

"It appears your sister has arrived while we've been discussing her future." Amanda pointed toward the dock. Louisa was holding a child by each hand as the *Little Mac* slowly moved away from the dock.

Sophie shaded her eyes and looked. "I suppose we should go down and see if she needs our help."

When Sophie made no move to get up, Fanny jumped to her feet. She extended her hand and helped Amanda up from the grassy slope. "Come on, Sophie. Let me help you up."

"There's no rush. And where are the servants? Don't they see her down there with her luggage and the children?" Sophie slowly got to her feet. Before heading off with her cousins, she stopped to fold the blankets and stack them beneath the tree.

The wails of the little boys were carried on a rush of wind as they walked alongside their mother. Louisa bent down to pick up one of the boys, and the other immediately ran from her side. The child fell as he reached the graveled path, and the nanny hurried to lend aid to Louisa and the injured child.

"Hurry, Sophie. Louisa needs our help with the children and her baggage," Fanny shouted. A sudden wind whipped at the girls' skirts, and whitecaps crested the breaking waves. "There's a storm moving in. We'd better get the luggage before it begins to rain."

They hurried toward the dock as another gale of wind swooped down from the sloping path. Slowly but then beginning to gather a trace of speed, the unattended baby carriage rolled down the dock. Fear clawed at Fanny's throat. "Is the baby in there?" She gasped for air. "Did the nanny have the baby in her arms?"

Amanda's blond tresses whipped about her face. She clawed at the hair and held it from her eyes. "I don't think so. *Hurry!*"

Fanny sprinted at full speed with Amanda and Sophie on her heels. A roar of wind muted their urgent screams for help. Fanny squinted. Surely her eyes deceived her. The buggy had picked up speed. Without slowing her pace,

Fanny uttered an urgent prayer for the child who might be lying in the buggy. Her shoes clattered and echoed on the dock's wood planks. Her screams continued. If she could only lengthen her stride, she would reach the buggy before it plunged into the water.

She stretched in a mighty leap, but the toe of her shoe caught between the planks as she landed. She hurtled forward, unable to gain her balance. A keening wail escaped her lips, and she could do nothing more than watch the carriage topple into the dark water below.

CHAPTER 10

Michael was in the boathouse when he heard the first scream. More screams followed and sent him running from the shelter up the path toward the house, where he saw several people yelling and pointing at the river.

Fanny was lying prone on the dock, her arms stretched toward the end of the structure. He turned and saw what appeared to be a carriage dropping off the end of the pier and into the water. Horrified, he raced to the dock's edge and jumped into the water. The buggy had tipped sideways in the water, and the hazy sun cast an eerie shadow across a pale blue blanket. Michael fought his way through a surging wave and grasped the object. He lifted the bundle into the air and was greeted by a howling cry. Jumping to avoid a wave that threatened to toss him off his feet and the baby into the chest-high water, Michael struggled to maintain his balance while holding the infant. He leaned forward and fought against the current that pummeled and pushed him toward the wood pilings supporting the dock.

"Michael! Can you move this way so I can reach the baby?" With her cousins holding her legs, Fanny lay flat on the dock and stretched her arms over the edge.

Easing his foothold, Michael allowed the current to move him toward the dock. The wind briefly abated and he lifted the baby high into Fanny's hands before ducking beneath the deck and grabbing hold of a wood piling on the other side. He worked his way forward into the shallows and then hefted himself onto the dock. Keeping his wits about him, Michael spotted the buggy, now wedged in a stand of rocks not far from the dock. After retrieving a pole from alongside the pier, he freed the soggy carriage from the rocky crevice.

The wind snatched Mrs. Clermont's flower-bedecked hat and bounced it across the lawn as she raced toward the dock. From the terror reflected in her eyes, it was obvious she'd observed the frightening scene. "Evan! Is he all right?" Her scream pierced the air.

Several family members followed behind carrying blankets while Mrs. Clermont shouted commands and clutched the infant to her chest. She grabbed one of the blankets and wrapped it around the wet child.

Michael sat hunched on the edge of the dock. Mrs. Clermont slowed her pace and stepped to his side. "Thank you for saving my child. Once the baby is cared for and asleep, I shall speak with you."

The staff and family members who had continued to scurry to the dock during the incident now gathered around Mrs. Clermont. While the group walked toward the house as one huddled mass of humanity, Michael was left to consider the woman's final comment. She had thanked him, but did she expect some explanation of what had occurred? If so, he surely couldn't tell her. He'd not observed anything until the carriage careened into the water. Surely she didn't hold him responsible. After all, she *had* thanked him for saving the baby. He forced himself upright. Right now there wasn't time to dwell on the matter.

The storm clouds and rough gales had continued to build with surprising ferocity, and unless the wind turned, the water would soon be rising. Though he longed to change out of his wet clothes, he couldn't spare the time. He must secure the boats.

While the nanny rushed off to unpack dry clothing for the infant, Louisa fiercely rubbed his tiny limbs with a soft towel. With each wail, the baby's lower lip quivered, but the bluish purple shade had now vanished from his lips. His rosy complexion had been restored—due either to Louisa's robust toweling or to the fact that his body temperature had returned to normal. Fanny couldn't be certain where to assign credit.

Sophie held her fingers to her ears. "That baby certainly has healthy lungs, doesn't he?"

Louisa glanced up at her sister. "Yes, and his name is Evan—not *that baby*."

"I don't need your criticism, Louisa." Sophie glared at her sister. "If it weren't for the three of us, he'd have drowned in the river."

"I believe it was that young man on the dock who saved Evan, not you."

"But it was our screams . . ."

Fanny tugged on Sophie's sleeve and tipped her head close. "Not now, Sophie. Your sister is quite upset. She's likely blaming herself for leaving the baby unattended."

Dinah Hertzel, the baby's nanny, hurried into the parlor with a fresh diaper and soft gown for little Evan. "You sit down and rest, ma'am. I'll dress the lad." She took in the gathered throng. "Perhaps one of you could fetch a cup of tea for Mrs. Clermont."

One of the servants hurried to the kitchen, and Louisa sat down beside her father. "I believe the young man who saved Evan's life should be rewarded. Once the storm abates, I'm going to visit him at the boathouse. I need to properly thank him and give him five dollars for his heroic act."

Quincy rubbed his hand along his cheek. "I doubt the young man expects any remuneration for his action, but I agree he should receive a reward. I do think it should be ten dollars rather than the five you've proposed."

"I would think the life of a baby would fetch a much higher price," Sophie muttered.

Louisa folded her arms across her waist and glowered at her sister. "If he were an educated man accustomed to receiving large sums of money, I might agree. However, to someone of his class, five or ten dollars is a handsome sum. He'll be pleased with whatever he receives."

William Broadmoor nodded. "I heartily agree. He's young and uneducated. If you give him any more than that, he'll squander it all on a good time."

Victoria Broadmoor tapped her son on the shoulder. "Are you suggesting that educated men don't squander their money on a good time? I believe I recall several educated young men—members of this family, in fact—who have misspent money on many a frivolous activity."

"Based upon the fact that the water was no higher than his chest, his risk was limited, and he's not entitled to any more than ten dollars," Jefferson declared.

"Well, where were you, Jefferson?" Sophie demanded of her cousin. "I didn't see you out there in the water! And the waves were exceedingly strong. He could have been pulled under and the baby along with him."

"George and I were playing a game of billiards in the game room. Besides, we were sufficiently doused on the Fourth of July, if you remember."

"I agree with Jefferson," George said. "I think his risk was minimal, at best, and ten dollars is sufficient."

"Of course you agree. You agree with everything your brother says," Sophie rebutted.

Fanny could barely keep up with the continuing battle. Rather than celebrating Evan's safety, they were entrenched in a silly dispute over money. It was an inconsequential sum to a wealthy family yet still deemed worthy of an argument.

She walked outside, anxious to be away from her family's nonsensical disagreement. The glimmer of sunshine peeking from behind a bank of clouds brought a smile to her lips. The wind had shifted, and the storm appeared to be moving to the south. She was relieved they wouldn't suffer a night of pounding rain and lightning.

From the far end of the lower veranda, she noticed the side door to the boathouse remained ajar. She wandered to the dock, anxious to speak with

Michael and thank him for rescuing her youngest relative. After lightly rapping on the door, she peered inside. "Michael? Are you in here?"

"Over here!"

She spotted his mass of dark curls on the far side of the boathouse. "I'm pleased to see the storm has passed."

"Be careful you don't trip and fall on those boards," he called.

She gathered her skirts and picked her way across the expanse. "I wanted to make certain you were all right."

"I'm fine. Once I hoisted the boats out of the water, I was able to get into some dry clothes. How's the baby?"

"He's fine, thanks to you. I can't tell you how much I admire your bravery. You jumped into the water with no thought for your own well-being. Little Evan is alive, thanks to your heroic action."

He shook his head. "You're making far too much of what happened. By hanging over the edge of the dock, you placed yourself in greater danger than I faced in the water. And if you hadn't screamed, I wouldn't have known anything was amiss. Mrs. Clermont has you to thank for saving her child."

"No, Michael. You're the hero. Please don't say otherwise. Not to me or to anyone else in this family. You've performed a brave deed this day, and you shouldn't discount saving a life."

He wrapped his callused hands around the handle of the boat pulley.

Fanny looked up and noted the straps that had been secured around the *DaisyBee*. "You're preparing to lower her back into the water?"

He nodded. "The storm has moved on. No reason to keep her out of the water. Someone may want to take a boat ride later this evening."

"That sounds like a wonderful idea. Was that an invitation?"

"Not unless you have a chaperone. I don't want to lose my job. I'd be forced to leave this island that I love, and I'd miss my mother's cooking, too."

She giggled. "I couldn't bear to be the cause of such horrid consequences."

He turned the pulley handle, and Fanny watched as he lifted the boat high enough to remove the wood planks. He then lowered each one, careful to keep it from falling into the water in the slip below. His muscles rippled as he fought to control each of the heavy timbers. His strength and agility to handle the task on his own amazed her. Through the years, he had developed a system that served him well.

"If you're going to remain down here for a while, you might as well sit down," he shouted over the squeals of the pulley. "I think I better oil this thing. After the launch is back in the water, I'm going to take care of the skiffs and canoes." He held the handle of the pulley with one hand and pointed to the nearby corner. "There's a chair over there. It looks a mess, but it's clean."

Michael's assessment was correct. The chair had seen better days. Layers of white had been applied years ago, but in the dampness of the boathouse, the paint had peeled away to leave a jagged design of wood splotches. Fanny hiked the skirt of her pale green lawn dress and perched her straw bonnet on the chair's curved finial. There was a peace to this place: the hypnotic rhythm of the water lapping against the timbered boat slips, the musty smell of wet wood—she felt as though she could drink in the sights and smells forever. This island offered a sense of security and well-being that she experienced nowhere else. Michael was fortunate to live here. She could only hope to convince Uncle Jonas that this would be the perfect place for her, too.

The boat slowly settled into the water, and she applauded. "Good job."

He leaned forward in a deep bow. "Thank you, dear lady. Your kind words are a pleasurable reward for my difficult labors."

"You are most welcome, sir," she said with a grin. "As for rewards, I do believe Cousin Louisa will be offering you a monetary gift for saving little Evan."

"That's not necessary. In fact, receiving money for meeting the need of another would cause me great discomfort. I don't want or expect to be paid for doing what is right."

He lifted one of the canoes from its place of safety overhead. Fanny rested her elbow on one knee and cupped her chin. Michael's attitude continued to astonish her. Through the years they'd occasionally discussed their faith in God. Like Michael, she had gone to church with her family. They filled several rows each Sunday morning and were frequently lauded for their monetary gifts to the church. But her family didn't live their faith—not as Michael and his parents did.

While her family argued over both important and trivial matters, she'd never witnessed such behavior in Michael's family. Instead of arguing, they always talked and worked together to find a resolution to their problems. His family appeared to find joy in simple pleasures, while her family constantly moved from one obsession to another, always searching for something that would make them happy. Even with a household of servants and the most modern conveniences life could offer, they bickered and argued in a gloomy state of existence. Rather than love and affection, the family money was the glue that held the Broadmoors together. The bribery required to bring them together each summer was evidence enough to support Fanny's bleak assessment. Uncle Jonas didn't hide his obsession, and although Uncle Quincy used a great deal of his money to help the homeless, he'd become obsessed with his mission, placing it above God and family. He willingly offered support to the impoverished while ignoring the needs of his own children, especially Sophie. The Broadmoors gave and spent their money only where it would garner accolades and respect among their peers.

With an involuntary shiver, Fanny understood that money had replaced even the God they self-righteously claimed to serve.

"I miss the days when we were free to wander at will and enjoy ourselves," Fanny said with a sigh. "My favorite memories are of this island—and of you."

Michael looked up, and his expression seemed pained. He quickly refocused on his work. "Nothing ever stays the same."

"I suppose not. I feel that my life has come quite undone—once again. Every time I lose someone, I feel as though a part of me has died, as well."

Michael stopped and came to her. "I'm truly sorry, Fanny. I know how close you were to your grandfather."

"It's not just that." She felt tears form in her eyes and blinked hard. "I never realized just how much the Broadmoor family hates one another, and this island."

"I thought you knew."

"I knew they bickered and that often the summer was spent with one group or another secluded away from everyone else because of some riff. But honestly, no. I didn't realize how much hatred existed among them until I saw them fighting and backstabbing at Grandfather's funeral."

"I'm sorry."

"The reading of the will was even worse. They are so jealous—so worried that someone will get more than they will. They're like a pack of wolves picking over a dead man's bones."

"Greed and money make people do strange things."

"I suppose my desire for a family simply caused me to overlook the truth. I thought everyone was as eager to come here as I. I thought they loved it as much as I did. It's the only place I've ever been truly happy, despite it being where Papa . . . where he . . . died. I was confident that the others longed for this respite just like I did."

Michael knelt down beside her. "No. Your love of this place is special. Few share your heart in that matter. But I know how you feel. I love it, too. Just as I . . ." He fell silent as if embarrassed and then jumped quickly to his feet. "Fanny, you should go back to the house. You're a grown woman, and it's not seemly for you to be here alone with me."

Fanny looked at him for a moment before rising. "I suppose I shall lose you, as well. Nothing ever stays the same."

Michael watched her walk slowly back toward the house. He longed to go after her and convince her that she was wrong, but his mother's warning rang in his ears. He wasn't ever going to be allowed to court a Broadmoor.

Fanny faded from view as she topped the hill. Michael felt her absence like an intense pain that would not abate.

"You'll never lose me, Fanny" he whispered. "But I know I shall lose you, and that will be my undoing."

CHAPTER 11

SATURDAY, JULY 10, 1897

Fanny fidgeted in her chair. The evening meal was progressing particularly slowly, either by Aunt Victoria's design or due to some unknown difficulty in the kitchen. The servants didn't appear flustered during their appearances in the dining room, so Fanny eventually concluded the pace had been set by her aunt.

Aunt Victoria delighted in entertaining, especially when the local newspaper could report Edward and Elizabeth Oosterman had accepted her invitation for a private supper party. Mr. and Mrs. Oosterman topped the list of prestigious and influential people who summered in the Thousand Islands. Their attendance at any social gathering of the wealthy ensured success—and newspaper coverage. Fanny wasn't certain who had given the Oostermans their ostentatious designation, but topping the list was assuredly tied to their wealth. Money spoke volumes among the summer people.

Mr. Oosterman sat to Uncle Jonas's right. At the opposite end of the table, Mrs. Oosterman was seated beside Aunt Victoria. With Mrs. Oosterman on one side and Louisa on the other, Fanny had quickly grown bored. Rather than George and Jefferson, she wished Sophie and Amanda had been seated across from her. Instead, her female cousins were at the other end of the table. Thus far the dinner conversation had consisted of wearisome discussions about guest lists, menus, and themes for summer parties.

Mrs. Oosterman suggested a masked ball be considered a possibility for the summer agenda of frivolity. "I would even consider hosting the ball myself. What do you think, Victoria?"

Fanny sighed. She wished the women would discuss something other than parties—she didn't know what, but anything would be more interesting than what they'd been covering. She glanced to her right. "How is Evan faring, Louisa? I haven't seen him since Wednesday. I hope he hasn't developed a cold or the croup since the accident."

"He's well," Louisa whispered.

Mrs. Oosterman choked on a spoonful of clam chowder. "What's this about an accident? You never mentioned any accident to me, Victoria. Was someone injured? I didn't see anything in the newspaper." She cast a disparaging look at her hostess.

Aunt Victoria frowned. "A minor incident. It was really nothing, Elizabeth." A forced smile replaced the frown.

"*Nothing?*" Fanny exclaimed. "Evan's carriage blew off the pier, and he nearly drowned, and you say it was *nothing?*"

"*Whaaat?*" Mrs. Oosterman clasped a hand to her chest. "I heard nothing about this tragedy? How is that possible?"

Victoria shook her head. "It isn't a tragedy. The baby is fine. You know the old saying, Elizabeth. 'All's well that ends well.' Louisa preferred the incident to remain quiet. We'd been very successful—until this evening." The frown returned.

"Dear me, this is shocking. I trust you discharged the child's nanny. I daresay, decent help is impossible to find nowadays. Don't you think?"

Fanny now realized why there had been no mention of the accident. The family was embarrassed someone might discover Louisa had left her child unaccompanied on the dock. Now the incident would be discussed over luncheons, after-dinner drinks, and dinner parties, with each guest adding an additional twist to the story. Though gossiping about other families was commonplace at the Broadmoor dinner table, being the topic of discussion held little appeal. Fanny hadn't intended to stir up a hornet's nest. She would surely receive a rebuke once their guests departed.

Aunt Victoria made a valiant attempt to change the subject, but Mrs. Oosterman wouldn't be deterred. She wanted every detail. With her diamond and ruby necklace draped across her dinner plate like a swinging pendulum, the old dowager leaned forward to gain a better view of Louisa. "I know you must be mortified, dear Louisa, but we all make mistakes. This was simply an accident. Personally, I believe it would be beneficial if others knew of what happened. You might prevent another such tragedy if others learn what occurred."

"I'll give your suggestion some thought, but I was hoping for a quiet summer. I came only to spend time with my family."

"*And* because Grandfather's will required it," Jefferson added with a chuckle.

Mrs. Oosterman perked to attention. "Truly? His will required a summer visit to the island?"

"Ouch!" Jefferson quickly leaned down and rubbed his shin.

"Please forgive my son's rude behavior. He ofttimes forgets indelicate matters are not to be discussed at the dinner table. Teaching him good manners has been a genuine struggle."

The spotlight moved away from Fanny and Louisa and now shone on Jefferson and his remark. Anxious for more details, Mrs. Oosterman immediately pardoned Jefferson's faux pas and pressed on. "Edward and I consider ourselves more than mere summer acquaintances, Victoria. We count you and Jonas among our dearest friends. You're like family to us."

The compliment worked. In hushed tones Aunt Victoria confided in Mrs. Oosterman. The older woman soaked up each detail like a dying plant in need of water. Fanny doubted Mrs. Oosterman's sincerity and thought Aunt

Victoria's trust badly placed, but she didn't interfere. In fact, she didn't utter another word throughout the remainder of the meal.

Once they'd completed their lemon cream pie, Jonas pushed away from the table and suggested they all gather on the upper veranda, where the men could enjoy a cigar and a glass of port along with a view of the river and the early evening breeze. He didn't wait for a response before leading the group away from the dining room.

"What was all the whispering at your end of the table?" Jonas asked Mrs. Oosterman as she walked alongside her host. "Edward and I thought you two women might be plotting a huge party or a shopping excursion in Brockville."

"Quite the contrary. Victoria and I were discussing some of the conditions contained in your father's will." She tapped a finger along the side of her elaborately styled hair. "That Hamilton always was one step ahead of the rest of us, wasn't he?"

Fanny remained in the shadows, listening to her uncle's response regarding the distribution of the Broadmoor estate.

"My father didn't always use the best judgment, I fear, but there's nothing we can't live with. We will, of course, abide by Father's wishes and vacation on the island each summer. Though the time away from Rochester interferes with my work schedule from time to time, I do count it one of life's pleasures that I can spend time on the island, especially with fine friends such as you."

Fanny nearly laughed aloud. She knew Uncle Jonas would have done most anything to avoid coming to Broadmoor Island—anything except forfeit a portion of his inheritance. She thought his false bravado annoying and slowly inched her way toward the far end of the veranda. No one would miss her if she slipped away for a walk. Sophie and Amanda had already returned indoors. If the others came looking for her, they would assume she had joined her cousins. Yes, fresh air and exercise would prove a perfect cure for her unkind thoughts of Uncle Jonas.

Choosing the well-worn path that led to the special place she'd shared with her father, Fanny inhaled a deep breath. Her perch provided an excellent view of the beauty these islands provided. At every angle the miniature islands offered a resplendent picture of God's creation, each island as unique as the people who inhabited it. From verdant fields to wooded shores, from rocky promontories to stately groves or dense thickets, the islets peeked out of the tranquil waters and beckoned her to explore.

She could almost hear her father's voice, smell his cologne. "You've been gone for so long now," she whispered, "and yet it feels like just yesterday."

Glancing at the place where she'd found him, Fanny remembered every detail of that day. He had seemed so peaceful, so content. He had simply gone to sleep. Fanny walked to the place where he'd died and sat down as she had often done in the past. Somehow, sitting here was comforting. She imagined herself on her father's lap, safe and protected.

"Papa, why must things change? Why must people die and leave us sad and alone? Grandfather is gone now, and Uncle Jonas will control my life. He has no heart for me—no love of the things and people I adore."

The wind blew gently, rustling the brush and grass around her. Fanny closed her eyes and tried to let go of her anxious thoughts.

Life would be much simpler if Uncle Jonas would agree to her plan and grant permission for her to remain on the island when the rest of the family departed for their respective homes. She loved Sophie and Amanda, but she wouldn't fit into either of their families. Not that Uncle Quincy would ever make such an offer. He remained far too involved with his good works to provide a proper home for Sophie, much less for his orphaned niece.

She tucked her knees beneath her chin and opened her eyes to watch the sun descend in a glowing display of blazing pink, mottled with hues of orange and lavender. Much too soon the setting sun was swallowed into the distant horizon, and she longed for the ability to request another performance.

"Another beautiful sunset in the glorious Thousand Islands."

She recognized Michael's voice and twisted around. "Oh yes. Weren't the pinks especially beautiful this evening? I only wish it could have lasted longer."

In four well-placed giant steps, he was beside her. "You need only wait until tomorrow evening for a return appearance. Who knows? You may see an even finer vision in twenty-four hours." He plopped down and offered a grin. "I'm sorry for being so short with you earlier. I never want to cause you pain."

"You weren't short with me. I was just keenly feeling my losses. I came here to feel some sense of peace again."

He nodded. "I knew I would find you here. Mother said she was cooking for a dinner party tonight. Did you have the good fortune of being excluded?"

Compared to the stuffy social set who attended the round of parties each summer, Michael was a breath of fresh air. He was a constant reliable friend who never changed. Perhaps it was because he grew up on this island with his parents' steady hand in his life; she couldn't be certain. But Michael was never envious or impressed by the wealth and pomposity that invaded the islands each summer.

"I wasn't excluded from the evening meal, but I did manage to sneak away while some of the family gathered on the veranda. I had tired of their party planning and gossip long before I escaped." She pointed toward a fish that broke the water and then splashed back into the river. "Uncle Jonas was complaining that my grandfather hadn't distributed his assets in accordance with my uncle's wishes."

"It was your grandfather's property. I'd say he could do whatever he wanted with it."

"Those are my sentiments, also, but money is the all-important commodity in the Broadmoor family. Uncle Jonas wants the power that he thinks money gives him; Uncle Quincy wants his share in order to perform good works for others, although he consistently forgets his own daughters need his time and attention; many of the others simply want the things the money will buy and the social status they are afforded by virtue of wealth. I dislike their superficial nature."

"Don't become disheartened. You may be overreacting to some of the things they say and do."

Fanny gave him a sidelong glance. "You may be correct. It is truly a gift to know I will always have a roof over my head and a warm meal when I'm hungry. Granted, it may not be the exact roof I want or the food I desire, but wealth does offer a certain security and comfort."

"But our genuine comfort and security should come from the Lord and not from our earthly possessions, don't you think?"

"You're absolutely correct; it's the things that money cannot buy that I love the most." She spread her arms. "This island and the river, for instance. God's creation abounds out here, yet no one in my family can see it. They view this island as an obligation they must endure. How can that be possible?"

"They've never taken time to consider this island a privilege to be savored and enjoyed. Consequently they don't see what you do, Fanny. Perhaps they never will." He stood and offered her his hand. "It's getting dark. I'll walk you back to the house."

She enjoyed the warmth of Michael's hand and wished he hadn't withdrawn it once she'd stepped down from the rocks. "Have you mentioned our earlier conversation to your mother and father?"

His dark eyes shone in the waning light. "About remaining here on the island?"

"Yes. Have they indicated if they would be willing to have me move to the island? I know they may find it difficult to approach Uncle Jonas, but I could pave the way once I know if they'd be willing to speak with him."

Michael pulled a leaf from a tree branch and folded it between his fingers. "I'm sorry, Fanny. I haven't spoken to either of them just yet. I thought it might be best to wait until everyone is more settled." He flipped the leaf to the ground. "It's always hectic during the first few weeks, what with the new routines, added people, and the like."

She was thankful for the evening shadows. Otherwise, he'd surely detect her disappointment. "I understand. Whenever you think best," she said, feigning her best lighthearted tone. "And if they refuse, please tell them I will understand. I don't want my request to cause them discomfort."

"I don't know what their reaction will be, but I believe they'll agree unless your uncle Jonas opposes the idea. In that case I doubt they'd be willing to offer much argument." He directed her away from the path. "This is a shorter route back to the house."

Fanny wasn't interested in locating a shorter direction. If she had her way, she'd remain in Michael's company awhile longer. But what could she say? *Please don't take me back to the house? I prefer to spend my time with you?* She couldn't possibly behave in such a forward manner. Michael had already gone against protocol by coming here to be alone with her. Two or three years earlier it wouldn't have mattered, but now that she was considered a young woman of marriageable age, the rules were different. And so she followed along, the thick grass folding beneath her feet in a soft, silent cushion.

Once they were alone on the veranda, Jonas and Mr. Oosterman settled in chairs overlooking the vast lawn. For well over a half hour, Jonas had attempted to steer their conversation toward financial investments. Each time he thought he'd neared success, Mr. Oosterman changed directions. Jonas hoped to learn a few tips from the wealthy investor, tips that might rescue him from the mistakes he'd already made. However, Mr. Oosterman was more interested in discussing his latest flare-up of gout, an ongoing medical problem that caused him severe pain from time to time.

"The doctor keeps telling me that if I'll give up rich food and alcohol, I'll see great improvement. Now I ask you, Jonas, what good is having money if I can't enjoy a fine meal followed by a good glass of port?"

"I suppose you must evaluate the options and decide for yourself. Are the food and drink important enough to you to make enduring the possible pain worth it?" Jonas shifted in his chair. "Much like deciding upon the proper investment, don't you think?"

"How so?"

"If you're willing to endure a loss, you take greater risks with your investments. Isn't that how you've managed to increase your fortune? By taking risks?"

Mr. Oosterman's barrel chest heaved up and down in time with his laughter. "I pay other people to make those decisions for me. Don't tell anyone, but I've never enjoyed devising plans for multiplying my money. It takes away from the time I have to spend it." Once again, his chest heaved up and down.

Jonas sighed. Either Mr. Oosterman was telling the truth or he played his cards close to his vest. Jonas couldn't decide which. One thing had become obvious: Edward wasn't going to give away any secrets this evening.

Mr. Oosterman reached for the bottle of port sitting on the nearby table and poured himself another glass. Jonas stared across the landscape and then narrowed his eyes. He couldn't quite make out the faces of the man and woman who were approaching the house. Then a shaft of light danced off her hair and he recognized Fanny, but that wasn't Jefferson or George walking with her. He strained to the side; then he recognized the man. *Michael!* Those two were spending far too much time together. Even with the added duties he'd assigned the young man and Fanny's social obligations this evening, the two of them had made time to wander off together. Unacceptable! He would speak to Michael.

Though he had hoped to return to Rochester immediately following Sunday dinner, Jonas knew that the Sunday evening vesper service would provide another opportunity for Michael and Fanny to enjoy each other's company. And he did not dare suggest the family miss the service. They'd think he'd turned heathen. The only time they missed the service at Half Moon Bay was when the weather threatened their safety. He would leave first thing Monday morning.

No one seemed exactly certain how the services had first begun, but Jonas surmised they'd been started years ago when religious camps and revivals operated on the islands. Though the camps had lost popularity, they still maintained a presence on some of the larger islands.

And the boat services had never lost their appeal. Folks would load into their skiffs, canoes, or launches and arrive at the bay each Sunday evening. Preacher Halsted's pulpit was a permanent fixture perched on a hillock near the water's edge. The ladies in their Sunday finery and the gentlemen in their summer suits would sit in boats that were anchored close enough so that the occupants could shake hands with one another. Boats would arrive each Sunday evening and fill the entire bay. Reverend Halsted used a speaking trumpet for important announcements, though he refused to shout his message through the cumbersome horn. Those at a great distance might not hear all of the preacher's words, but they joined to sing God's praises on the preacher's cue.

If necessary, Jonas could have navigated the launch, but questions would have arisen if he dismissed Michael from the chore. So Jonas had remained. He accompanied the entire family to the launch but shook his head when Fanny attempted to board. "Wait until Louisa is situated with the children." With practiced ease, he directed Quincy's daughter and her children to the location near Michael and continued directing the other family members to their seats. Fanny would be sitting between Amanda and his wife. Pleased with the arrangement, he sat down beside his wife and hoped the services would be short this evening. He wanted to speak with Michael upon their return.

Jonas didn't notice exactly when Mr. and Mrs. Oosterman arrived, but their boat was soon wedged beside the Broadmoor launch. Mrs. Oosterman waved and smiled; then she pointed to Louisa and nodded.

Louisa offered a faint smile. "Why is she pointing at me?"

"I'm sure I don't know, my dear. Just smile and wave," her aunt instructed.

There was no time to contemplate Mrs. Oosterman's behavior, for Reverend Halsted had already raised his speaking trumpet to his lips. "Announcements for the week are as follows: Eliza Preston will entertain all young ladies between the ages of fourteen and twenty at her parents' cottage on Tuesday for an afternoon of Bible study, followed by tea and a nature walk."

The preacher continued to read the remainder of the week's activities before turning the speaking trumpet in the direction of the Broadmoor launch. "I am told that we've had nothing short of a miracle occur already this summer. The infant grandson of Quincy Broadmoor was snatched from the very depths of the river and brought back to life by our own Michael Atwell."

"Praise God!" one of the attendees called out from his boat. Jubilation followed from all quarters, and soon one of the men burst forth in a chorus of praise.

The preacher waved toward the *DaisyBee*. "Would one of you like to say a few words?"

Folks were straining in the direction of the Broadmoor launch. Quincy was suffering from a stomach ailment and hadn't accompanied the family to the vesper service. The responsibility to acknowledge God's blessing would fall to Jonas. He stood and cupped his hands around his mouth. "We're all pleased to say that little Evan is doing just fine, and we're glad to have him right here with us." He motioned to Louisa to hold the boy in the air.

"Hallelujah!"

"Praise God!"

"You did a fine thing, Michael."

The shouts surrounded Jonas, and he dropped into his seat and shook his head. "*Right*. Praise God," he muttered. "I had the pleasure of paying the ten-dollar reward."

CHAPTER 12

THURSDAY, JULY 15, 1897

Sophie spotted her cousins sitting beneath a distant stand of trees that shaded the water's edge. Without thought to proper etiquette, she hurtled down the sloping hill at breakneck speed. Had Amanda remained in place, Sophie would have plowed her over. Sophie stretched out her arms and headed for one of the large fir trees to break her run. A whoosh of air escaped her lungs as she collided with the ancient conifer.

Fanny jumped to her feet and hurried to her cousin's side. "Are you injured, Sophie?"

She grunted and rubbed her arms. "That didn't go quite as I had intended." She examined the bloody scratches that lined her hands and sat down.

Amanda returned to her previous spot on the blanket and dropped down between the other two girls. "Whatever were you thinking, Sophie? Or were you? Don't you realize you could have seriously injured one of us or yourself? Sometimes I think you give little thought to your behavior! You're no longer five years old, you know."

Sophie wrinkled her nose and deftly extricated a piece of tree bark from her flowing tresses. "I may not be five, but I'm not an old woman, either, Amanda. If I want to have fun, I will. And why did the two of you leave me when you knew I planned to join you?"

Amanda stiffened. "Are you implying that I act like an old woman?"

"Most of the time you act older than your own mother. You're so intent upon acting proper that you're afraid ever to have fun. I know you want to please everyone, Amanda, but you need to please yourself on occasion, too."

"I don't need you to tell me how to behave, Sophie. At least I don't embarrass the family by making a spectacle of myself."

Before Sophie could offer a rejoinder, Fanny clapped her hands together. "Please don't argue. We're supposed to be enjoying our time together." She examined Sophie's hands and then pulled a handkerchief from her pocket. "You were having a private conversation with Paul, and we didn't want to interrupt. That is the only reason we came ahead without you."

"I wish you would have interrupted. Paul Medford has become an albatross around my neck. He seems to view me as a part of his assigned duties."

"How so?" Fanny poured a trickle of water from the jug they'd carried from the house and wet her handkerchief. Thankfully they'd not chosen lemonade to accompany their picnic lunch. She daubed Sophie's hand with the damp hankie.

Sophie took the cloth from Fanny and began wiping dirt from her arms. "He said he came to the island in order to bring Father some reports regarding his charity shelter, but I know that's not true. My father is planning to return to Rochester later in the week, and I'm certain the paper work could have waited until his return."

"What has any of that to do with your belief that you've become an assignment of sorts?"

"If you'd just wait a minute, I'm getting to that part." Sophie frowned at Amanda. "Paul whispered that he needed to speak to me alone about a matter of importance. I joined him outside." She glanced at Fanny. "That's when you two saw me with him. He told me that he had heard some unsettling gossip about me from several sources in Rochester."

Amanda arched her brows. "Unsettling in what way?"

"That my behavior is occasionally viewed as inappropriate for someone of my social standing." She giggled. "As though I have any social standing."

"You *do* have social standing, Sophie. You are a Broadmoor. Your behavior reflects on the entire family." Amanda retrieved a glass from the picnic basket and picked up the water jug. "You act with wild abandon, and the whole family must suffer the consequences. Exactly what has he heard about you?"

Sophie shrugged. "I don't know. I didn't ask him to go into detail, for I truly don't care." She handed Fanny the handkerchief. "Unlike you, Amanda, I don't live my life to please others."

"Perhaps you should give it a try. Paul is obviously attempting to help."

"Help? He thinks I'm immature and take dangerous risks. *He's* the one who needs help. The man is twenty-five years old, yet he talks and acts like an old man. As I said the first time he visited the island, he'd make a perfect match for you, Amanda. You both think there's nothing more important than charity work and meeting the expectations of others." Sophie winked at Fanny. "And you're both averse to having fun."

"I am *not* averse to having fun. It's simply a matter of defining fun. You and I have completely different views."

"That's at least one thing we can agree upon, Amanda." Sophie reached into the basket and removed the tablecloth and napkins. "Are we going to eat our picnic lunch?"

Fanny shook her head. "Why don't we see if Michael will take us to Boar Head Island on the launch? We can eat there and then explore. Besides, we'll be all alone, and that makes it even better. No one will be able to bother us."

"I'm not so fond of being alone, although I'd like to get off of this island. I'd like it better if we'd go to Round Island. We could visit at the New Frontenac Hotel there. There are certain to be more guests arriving by the day."

Amanda gave Sophie a sidelong glance. "If you dislike socializing with prominent families, I don't know why you'd want to visit Round Island or the Frontenac."

Sophie locked her arms across her chest. No matter what she suggested, Amanda would find fault. "I'll defer to Fanny, and we'll have our picnic on Boar Head Island. I can visit the Frontenac this evening. I plan to attend the dance even if the two of you decide to remain at home."

They gathered their blanket and basket and sauntered toward the boathouse.

Amanda circled around Fanny and came alongside Sophie. "I'd like to know exactly what rumors are circulating in Rochester, Sophie. How can we dispel such talk if we don't know what's being said?"

"I told Paul I didn't want to hear any of the small-minded tittle-tattle and walked off before he could tell me. I'm certain it has to do with the Independence Day celebration over at Brown Square." She giggled. "I believe I may have been a bit tipsy by the time the evening ended. I was singing with the German musicians. I didn't know the words, but I made up my own. You two should have come along. We had great fun."

Amanda gasped. "I love you dearly, Sophie, but I do wish you'd find some other method to gain your father's attention. In the end, you're hurting yourself more than Uncle Quincy."

They neared the boathouse, and Sophie decided she'd carry the conversation no further. Arguing with Amanda always proved useless. Her cousin would never change her idealistic attitudes, and Sophie didn't plan to change, either—not for Amanda, not for Paul, and certainly not for the sake of the beloved Broadmoor name! She and Amanda stood inside the doorway of the boathouse while Fanny talked to Michael. Strange how animated Fanny became while visiting with him—her smile widened, her eyes sparkled, and her laughter rippled with a delightful lilt that Sophie had never before heard in her younger cousin's voice.

Fanny beamed and waved her cousins forward. "Michael says he's willing to take us over to the island, and he'll come back and pick us up at four o'clock. Does that suit?"

Sophie wrinkled her nose. "Nearly four hours is a long time, don't you think?"

"Boar Head is a large island," Michael said. "You'll find plenty to keep you occupied. If you want to take some fishing poles along, there's a great ledge where you'll be able to sit and fish." He curled his fingers into a fist and pointed his thumb at Fanny. "Your cousin can bait your hooks, and if you catch a fish, she'll be able to help you out with that, too. Fanny's an expert when it comes to fishing."

Sophie saw the way Michael looked at Fanny. Were these two interested in each other? She glanced at Amanda and wondered if her cousin noticed the attraction, but she appeared oblivious.

"I thought I heard voices down here." Theresa O'Malley entered through the side door, glanced around, and immediately flashed a pouting smile at Michael. "Are you all going on a picnic?"

Michael shook his head. "I'm merely providing boat service for these ladies. I won't be gone long. If anyone is looking for me, you can tell them I've gone to Boar Head Island."

Theresa tucked her hand beneath his arm. "Oh, may I ride along with you? I've completed my chores, and Mother said I didn't need to return to the house for an hour."

Sophie didn't fail to note the way Theresa gazed into Michael's eyes—and that demure smile. Theresa had set her cap for him!

"I promise I'll be good company on the return trip," Theresa cooed.

"I don't know," Michael mumbled.

Sophie felt pity for the girl. Like Sophie, Theresa was obviously bored to tears on this island. "Oh, do let her ride along, Michael. What difference does it make?"

But one look at Fanny told her that it did make a difference. Fanny's earlier sparkle had been replaced by a brooding stare. So there *was* something between these two. Fanny was jealous of Theresa. And from the possessive hold Theresa maintained on Michael's arm, Theresa was jealous of Fanny. Little Fanny was hiding a secret. Uncle Jonas and Aunt Victoria would not approve! This picnic might turn out to be more interesting than she'd anticipated.

Fanny's eyes met Michael's as he helped her into the boat. She read the apologetic look—at least that's what she wanted to believe. Having Theresa accompany them wasn't his fault. After Sophie's comment, what else could he do? Of course he could have discouraged her from remaining so close to his side throughout the excursion. Fanny peeked from beneath the brim of her straw hat and watched Theresa talking to him. He seemed engrossed in what she was saying. Fanny looked away when Theresa placed a possessive hold on Michael's arm. Perhaps he enjoyed her company. A picture of Michael carrying Theresa out of the woods on the day of her arrival paraded through Fanny's mind, and she turned away. And he'd been unusually distant since Sunday, when they'd gone to vespers. In fact, he'd avoided her on several occasions since then. She could feel tears beginning to form in the corners of her eyes. She'd be unable to explain if someone should notice.

Theresa continued to cling to Michael's arm. By the time they arrived at the island, Fanny was pleased to disembark. Having Theresa along had diminished her pleasure. The three of them waited while Michael unloaded their belongings.

He touched Fanny's sleeve as he handed her the fishing poles. "I'll return at four o'clock." He set a can of worms on a rock near her feet. "I'm sorry," he whispered before returning to the launch.

Fanny remained near the shoreline and watched as the boat churned through the murky water before picking up speed. Theresa's enthusiastic waves continued until they were nearly out of sight.

"I think she's quite taken with Michael, don't you?" Sophie leaned forward and picked up the can of worms.

"It would appear that way." Fanny swallowed hard and pushed back the lump in her throat.

"But I don't think she loves him as much as you do."

Fanny twisted around to face Sophie. She rubbed her fingers along the nape of her neck in an attempt to relieve the dull ache that was working its way up her skull and toward her temples. "I have no idea what you're talking about. Michael and I are friends. You know we've spent many hours together since we were young children. I believe you're permitting your fanciful imagination to run wild."

Amanda giggled. "How could you even say such a thing, Sophie? When Fanny is interested in a young man, she'll be looking for someone of her own social class. Not that Michael isn't a fine man," she quickly added. "But someone of his class could hardly ask my father for Fanny's hand."

Though Fanny did not dare object to Amanda's remarks, she wanted to tell her cousin she was guilty of snobbery in the extreme. Amanda had pledged to spend her future helping the less fortunate, yet she possessed her father's view regarding class and status. Did she not understand her attitude would spill over to those whom she attempted to serve in the future? Her cousins were at opposing ends of the spectrum. Sophie wanted the world to know she had no use for class or society, although she enjoyed the pleasures wealth could buy. On the other hand, Amanda thought social status of import. She viewed the family social status as a way of opening doors to aid charitable causes.

Strange that she could clearly articulate her cousins' beliefs, but when it came to her own convictions, Fanny experienced difficulty. Perhaps because she disliked confrontation, she had never clearly decided what she believed. Fearful of being ridiculed or appearing foolish, she typically kept her thoughts to herself. Only when she talked to Michael did she feel she could freely express herself. From all appearances, Theresa felt entirely comfortable in his presence, also.

Sophie wiggled the can of worms beneath Fanny's nose. "Are we going to fish or explore the island? This is your outing of choice, so you lead the way."

"Let's spread our blanket. We can decide after we've eaten lunch." Without waiting for her cousins' consent, Fanny flipped the blanket into the air and spread it on a well-shaded spot not far from the water's edge.

While Amanda and Fanny unpacked the basket, Sophie reclined on the blanket and eyed each selection. "You could have requested something other than sandwiches, Fanny. Rather boring fare, don't you think?"

"I did the best I could. Mrs. O'Malley and Mrs. Atwell were busy planning the week's menus. I didn't want to interfere, so I prepared our lunch on my own."

"Do tell! Aren't you becoming quite the domesticated young woman! No need for servants to do your bidding? I believe you *would* fit into Michael Atwell's life without much difficulty." Sophie removed several grapes from a large cluster and tossed one into her mouth.

"Make yourself useful and pour our drinks, Sophie." Amanda flashed a sour look across the blanket.

"Oh, all right, but I do wish you'd quit your bossing, Amanda. It's very unbecoming, you know." Sophie placed her hands on the ground and pushed herself up. "Ouch! What was that?" She examined her palm. "Now, look. What with my earlier scratches and now this cut, I'm truly injured. Where's your handkerchief, Fanny?"

While Sophie blotted the cut with the handkerchief, Fanny lifted the corner of the blanket and brushed her fingers over the ground. There! Something sharp protruded through the grass. Probably just a rock, but she yanked the grass and weeds surrounding the object. "Hand me one of those spoons, Amanda."

"You're going to dig in the dirt with the good silver?"

"Forevermore, Amanda, just give me the spoon. It isn't the good silver— I promise." Fanny grabbed the utensil from her cousin's hand; soon she'd excavated the sharp object. After removing the traces of dirt with one of the napkins, she extended her palm. "Look."

Sophie shrugged. "A flat piece of rock. So what?"

"No. It's an Iroquois arrowhead," she said with an air of authority.

"How would you know? I agree with Sophie. It looks like a pointed flat stone."

"No." Fanny shook her head. "Michael had several in his pocket, and he showed them to me. He's been collecting them since he was a little boy. He has some that he has discovered are Iroquois and a few that are Mississauga. Both tribes inhabited the islands years ago." While her cousins helped themselves to the chicken sandwiches, Fanny used her napkin to continue polishing the arrowhead. "This is ever so exciting. I wonder if we can find some others."

Amanda glanced heavenward. "Please, Fanny. Let's not make this some archaeological expedition. You're not another Sir Austen Henry Layard."

"Who's *that*?" Sophie asked before taking another bite of her sandwich.

"He's the famous archaeologist that grandfather met in England a long time ago. He died a few years past. Surely you remember. He discovered the remains of the Assyrian regal monuments and cuneiform inscriptions and concluded they were the visible remains of Nineveh. He wrote a book about his second expedition. Grandfather told us about it several times."

"Isn't Nineveh in the Bible or something?"

"Yes, it's in the Bible, but this is—oh, never mind." Amanda tossed a grape seed toward the water. "You're not even listening."

"Wouldn't it be wonderful to discover some ancient ruin?" Fanny tucked the arrowhead into the pocket of her dress.

Sophie sighed and leaned against the trunk of an ancient white spruce. "It would be more exciting to discover some nice fellows. I'm bored. I haven't met even one new man who strikes my fancy. I'm ready to go home."

"Well, *that's* not going to occur. We're here for the duration of the summer, so you might as well decide to enjoy yourself." Amanda repacked the picnic basket and closed the lid with a decisive thump. "Are we fishing or exploring, Fanny?"

"We'll explore first, and then we'll fish. That way we'll see Michael when he returns."

"And I'll wager you're hoping he'll return without Theresa. Am I right?" Sophie nudged her cousin and giggled.

Fanny pretended she didn't hear.

CHAPTER 13

MONDAY, JULY 19, 1897

Jonas had planned to catch the early train, but his plans had gone awry when Victoria insisted upon accompanying him to Clayton in order to visit one of her favorite dressmakers. He'd missed the early train, so the first day of the workweek would be a complete loss. She ignored his grumbles and told him it was summertime and he should relax. Women! They didn't understand the complexity of operating a business and acquiring assets. They did, however, possess the ability to spend money without difficulty.

During their short boat ride from the island, Victoria regaled him with details of the fabric and the dress she was having fashioned for one of their upcoming parties. When he thought a response was expected, he offered no more than a grunt or a nod. The two of them had been married long enough that she should realize he cared not a whit about chiffon and muslin or whether a dress was pleated, tucked, or puffed. He reminded himself that a woman's brain could be easily occupied with matters of little import, whereas a man's mind required the meaty issues of life.

He offered his hand to Victoria and assisted her onto the boat dock that bordered the Clayton train tracks. She tucked her hand beneath his arm. They appeared the perfect couple.

When they'd safely traversed the tracks and reached the platform, Victoria pecked Jonas on the cheek. "I do wish you'd make an effort to return on Thursday evening rather than Friday. The family could enjoy a nice long weekend together. Promise you'll do your best."

Jonas touched the brim of his hat. "I'll try, but with my late departure today, I doubt I can return before Friday. You do remember that I may have guests with me."

She stopped midstep. "Guests?"

A train whistle wailed in the distance, and Jonas glanced down the tracks. "I told you that I plan to use my free time each evening deciding upon eligible suitors for Amanda and Fanny. I told you I'd be bringing the young men to visit at the island."

"But I didn't think you meant so soon. I wanted to discuss the matter further, Jonas. I've already told you that I'm opposed to this matchmaking idea. I want the girls to marry for love, not because they've been forced into an arranged marriage."

He craned his neck and peered down the tracks. Why didn't the train arrive? He was tired of explaining the same thing over and over to his wife. Why couldn't women merely accept that their husbands knew what was best!

"As I've already told you, it is much too risky to allow them to make such weighty decisions. Besides, it's time the girls accepted a few of the responsibilities that accompany the wealth they've enjoyed all these years. Marrying well is expected, and young women can't be trusted to make wise choices."

A breeze played at the hem of Victoria's pale blue muslin gown. "And I say they are intelligent young ladies who should have a say in choosing a husband."

Jonas sighed. "Why do you argue with me? We didn't marry for love. Surely our marriage is proof enough that love can grow."

"Speak for yourself, Jonas Broadmoor." With a stomp of her leather slipper, she turned and strode off without a backward glance.

"Don't forget to alert the staff there will be additional guests arriving for the weekend," he called.

His wife didn't acknowledge him, but Jonas knew she'd heard the reminder. In time he'd win Victoria over to his way of thinking. If necessary, he'd tell her Fanny's interest in Michael was proof enough that the girl couldn't be trusted to marry a man of worth. Even if Victoria didn't come around to his idea, she would accept his decision. She had no choice.

Once settled on the train, Jonas searched his mind for potential candidates, primarily for Fanny. He would concentrate on her first. Finding the proper man for Fanny was urgent. There were plenty of young men who would prove acceptable for his own daughter. But the man for Fanny must be very carefully selected. He'd need a man of social position. Yet the proper candidate must be willing to adhere to Jonas's commands. Someone with an eye toward attaining the wealth and power associated with the Broadmoor name, a man who would not otherwise be considered.

Suddenly he was struck by a thought of brilliance. This would not be so difficult after all! Many powerful families in New York had suffered through the depression and still remained in a state of economic instability. Others would never recover. For the present, they all maintained their social standing within the ranks of New York society. Fanny's group of suitors would be the sons of such men! Any of them had much to gain by marrying young Frances Jane Broadmoor and would be easily managed.

Indeed, he would speak to his lawyer as soon as possible. Mortimer would surely know of some suitable young men—and if he didn't, his younger son, John, would prove helpful. Still unmarried, John Fillmore enjoyed the social life; he was certain to know any such eligible men. Of course Jonas wouldn't confide in John. He'd rely upon Mortimer to extract the information from his son. While Jonas trusted both the lawyer and his older son, Vincent, implicitly, he thought John exceedingly lazy. Somewhat akin to his own sons Jefferson and George.

"Must be this generation," Jonas muttered hours later as he stepped down from the train. Weary from his journey, he departed the station and signaled for a cab. There would be little accomplished at this late hour. He'd go directly to the house. First thing tomorrow, he'd set his plan in motion.

Jonas signaled Mortimer toward his table at the Revere Hotel. Over a lunch of thick open-faced beef sandwiches and strong coffee, the lawyer placed his stamp of approval upon Jonas's plan and agreed to provide a list of candidates posthaste, even a name or two by the end of the day. Then the men departed for their respective offices.

Jonas paced in front of his wide office window that offered a view of Main Street and inhaled a deep breath. His office clock chimed five but still no word from Mortimer. Neither anger nor irritation would serve him well. He wanted to schedule private meetings with each of the men tomorrow. If Mortimer didn't furnish names, Jonas would be delayed.

While still contemplating his departure for home, the telephone rang. "Jonas! I'm glad to find you still in the office." Mortimer's voice crackled through the line. "I have some names for you if you'd like to jot them down."

Though Jonas still didn't like telephones, it was at times such as these that he appreciated the contraptions. He knew telephone usage would continue, but Jonas had little respect for the telephone company. He'd been unimpressed when the company had imposed continuing increases that had eventually compelled the subscribers to form a users' strike that had continued for two full years. Not until the Rochester Common Council had ordered the telephone company to remove its unused poles from the streets of Rochester was a compromise finally reached and telephone usage resumed.

The company immediately expanded to the more affluent neighborhoods of Rochester and even began to offer reliable long-distance service. Much to his wife's dismay, Jonas refused to have the jangling piece of equipment in his home. But work was another matter. One must keep pace with the competition and be accessible. He'd learned that lesson long ago.

"Just the names and nothing more. I don't like discussing private concerns on the telephone," Jonas said.

Mortimer grunted his agreement and offered four names. "I'm not so sure about that last one. John recommended him, but don't set up an appointment with him until you hear from me tomorrow."

"Three provide a sufficient beginning. You're certain these men meet our criteria?" He recognized only one of the names.

"Two of them are from New York City but are currently in Rochester seeking new opportunities. I know their fathers. I can stop by the house this evening if you'd like further information before contacting them."

Jonas hesitated. "I don't even know *where* to contact them."

Mortimer laughed. "One is staying at the Regent Hotel, and the other has a room at the Exeter."

Jonas heard a click on the telephone line and hesitated. "I'd prefer discussing this in person." Someone had picked up another phone and was listening to their conversation. Annoying contraption! "On second thought, why don't you come over around eight o'clock and have a brandy. We can speak privately."

"Good enough."

Jonas continued to hold the receiver to his ear. Two clicks followed Mortimer's farewell. Someone *had* been listening. Little wonder he seldom used a telephone. He'd learned early in life that people were nosy and enjoyed gossip. His wife and daughter were prime examples. They constantly discussed every tidbit that came their way, while men tucked away useful bits of information and discarded the remainder as nonsensical prattle.

Donning his hat, Jonas departed for home. There was much to accomplish this evening. The moment he entered the house, he instructed the housekeeper to serve his dinner in the library, a practice he often employed when the family was away. Tonight, the solitude would permit him time to consider his plan in broader detail.

After a brief time upstairs to refresh himself, Jonas returned to the library and set to work. He had made little progress when the maid entered with his tray. Nodding, he signaled her to place the tray near the doors leading into the garden. Jonas didn't particularly enjoy gardens or flowers, but he appreciated what the flower industry had done for Rochester. Visitors were continually amazed at the city's resilience and adaptation to change. Both his grandfather and father had realized the need to follow that same example.

For a time, the numerous flour mills in the area earned Rochester the nickname Flour City, but the flour industry eventually moved west to accommodate the wheat farmers, and Rochester lost its prominence in flour production. The city had already become acclaimed, however, for its beautiful flowers and the production and shipping of flower seeds. The city's nickname switched from Flour City to Flower City, and the Broadmoor family purchased an interest in the flower industry. Thereafter, Hamilton and Jonas invested large portions of the family wealth in the Eastman Dry Plate and Film Company and Bausch and Lomb, two other local businesses. Thus far, the investments had proven themselves valuable, and Jonas remained certain he would reap huge financial rewards for years to come. At least those investments had proven sound. If only they would produce enough profit to cover the mess his failures had caused.

After wiping his mouth, Jonas pushed his tray to the side, returned to his desk, and awaited Mortimer's arrival. As expected, his trusted attorney arrived precisely on time. Their discussion led to drafting an outline for a speech Jonas would give to each of the young men. They'd briefly considered bringing them all together for a dinner meeting but soon decided upon individual appointments. In a private meeting Jonas would be better able to evaluate the pliability of each man and determine if an invitation to the island should be extended. Groundwork would be clearly established with each man at the initial meeting. Together, Jonas and Mortimer drafted a letter including an appointed time to meet with Jonas on Thursday. The men agreed an hour would be allocated for each candidate. When Mortimer departed at eleven o'clock, Jonas was confident he would find the perfect husband for Fanny.

On Thursday morning Jonas arose early and stepped onto his bedroom balcony. Like an emperor inspecting his kingdom, he surveyed the perfectly manicured gardens below. Jonas performed the daily ritual except during foul weather. And Rochester had its share of foul weather. Not as dire as Buffalo. But what city's weather could compare to that of Buffalo—or wanted to, for that matter. He inhaled a vigorous breath of fresh air and promptly returned indoors.

Giving special attention to his attire, he chose a pinstripe suit with matching vest. The suit had been delivered by his tailor only three weeks earlier. These were young men who should recognize quality and detail at every quarter, and Jonas wouldn't disappoint them. After his usual breakfast of coddled eggs and fresh biscuits, he stepped into his carriage. As was his custom, Jonas entered his office at precisely eight o'clock and was greeted by Mr. Fryer, his office clerk for the past fifteen years.

By now Mr. Fryer knew Jonas's preferences, and few words were necessary between them. A fresh pitcher of water and glasses had been placed on the table, the mail had been opened and arranged in order of importance, and a neatly written list of the day's appointments rested atop the mail. Behind the closed door, Jonas perused his mail and silently practiced the speech he would give to each of the young men.

At exactly nine o'clock, a knock sounded on his door. "Yes?"

"Mr. Frank Colgan to see you, sir."

"Please show him in."

Jonas stood behind his desk and extended his hand to the young man who followed Mr. Fryer into the office. "Jonas Broadmoor," he said while evaluating the strength of Mr. Colgan's grasp.

"Frank Colgan. Pleased to make your acquaintance, Mr. Broadmoor. I hear good things about you."

"Do you?" Jonas signaled for the man to sit. "Such as?"

Colgan's eyes widened. "Excuse me?"

"You said you hear good things about me. I wondered exactly what you've been told."

The young man stammered, "That you're an influential member of the community, and ah—"

"A free bit of advice for you, Mr. Colgan: I don't appreciate hollow flattery."

Mr. Colgan's complexion paled. "I do apologize."

"Accepted. Now, let's move on. I'm sure you're wondering exactly why I've asked you to come to my office. I'll come right to the point."

Jonas explained his plan to find the perfect husband for his niece: a man willing to follow direction and refrain from gossip, an intelligent man of good social standing, a man willing to live a life of ease with his niece, a man willing to grant Jonas permission to continue handling his niece's inheritance. "Does my proposal interest you, Mr. Colgan?"

Frank squirmed in his chair. "Is she quite homely or disfigured? Is that the reason for this arrangement, Mr. Broadmoor?"

Jonas laughed. "On the contrary, she is a lovely girl, but I suppose there are those who might consider her somewhat plain. A bit strong-willed perhaps but well educated, a fine figure, and capable of running a household."

"In that case, when shall we be wed?"

"Not so fast. If you agree to all of the terms, you will be one of several young men who will vie for my niece's affections. You see, this arrangement between us is to be kept secret. Once Fanny makes her choice—whether she chooses you or not—you will be paid a handsome sum . . . if and only if you play by all of the rules I've set forth. In the event you mention this arrangement to *anyone,* I will deny any knowledge of having met with you, and you will receive nothing from me." Jonas leaned across his desk. "And should you betray me, you will face great difficulty being accepted in proper social circles or securing meaningful employment."

Frank rubbed his jaw. "And you're making this proposal to all of the men who will meet your niece?"

"I didn't say that, Mr. Colgan. You may be the only person to whom I make this offer. On the other hand, I may have this conversation with all of the men who court my niece. You won't know. But if another suitor should mention he has spoken to me, it would behoove you to report his conduct to me. That man will be removed as a possibility." Jonas leaned back in his chair. "Well? What say you, Mr. Colgan? Are you interested in competing for a life of luxury?"

"It appears I have nothing to lose. Even if your niece chooses someone else, I'll be paid a handsome sum."

"Exactly right."

This young man would make a perfect candidate. If he didn't think he had anything to lose by participating in this venture, Frank Colgan would be easily manipulated. Jonas extended an invitation for a weekend visit to Broadmoor Island, and Mr. Colgan readily accepted.

Jonas closed his office door and walked to the window. He removed his pocket watch and checked the time: exactly one hour had passed from the time Frank had entered his office until Jonas watched him hail a cab. Tucking the watch into his pocket, he returned to his desk. One interview completed and three to go. If the remainder of the appointments went as smoothly as this one, he would be most pleased.

CHAPTER 14

FRIDAY, JULY 23, 1897
BROADMOOR ISLAND

Fanny pulled a brush through Amanda's thick blond hair. Amanda's golden mane fanned across her shoulders like a luxurious cape. Though Fanny tried her best not to envy her cousins, she couldn't help but compare her own bushy auburn curls to Sophie's shining tresses or Amanda's flawless locks. Fanny pinned a loop of her cousin's blond hair into place.

"I don't like the way you placed that curl." Sprawled across the bed in a most unladylike position, Sophie pointed to the side of Amanda's head. "It should be lower, over on the side."

Initially Fanny followed Sophie's instruction but then moved the curl back to its previous position. "You're wrong. It looks better here."

Sophie flopped onto her side and rested her chin in her palm. "Hairstyles have changed, Fanny." She watched a moment longer and then jumped up from the bed. "Let me do it."

Fanny willingly relinquished the brush and walked to the bedroom window. From her vantage point, she could see Michael leaning over the skiff pulling a string of fish from inside the boat. A successful day of fishing! She wished she could have been with him.

"What do you see down there?" Sophie asked.

Fanny didn't want to turn away from the window for fear Michael would disappear. "Nothing."

"You're far too intrigued for there to be nothing down there." Fanny didn't hear Sophie approach. "I see! It's Michael you're watching. Whether you want to admit it to us or not, I know you have feelings for him."

"You're right, Sophie. I am fond of him." Why should she continue to deny what she'd known was true since seeing Michael carry Theresa out of the woods the day they had arrived? Besides, Sophie would hound her until she made an admission.

"I knew it!" Sophie danced around Fanny, wielding the hairbrush overhead. "You see, Amanda? I told you, but you said I was wrong. You should never doubt me in matters of the heart. I'm always right."

Amanda frowned. "Remember what I told you the other day, Fanny. You're a Broadmoor. Father will never permit such an arrangement. Think what Grand-mère would say if she were alive. You know she would be disappointed at the very idea."

"I don't think so. She and Grandfather loved and respected the Atwells. I think she would have approved."

Amanda joined her cousins at the window. "You're dreaming, Fanny. They may have respected the Atwells, but they wouldn't have blessed your marriage to Michael."

"I said I was fond of him. It's the two of you who are discussing marriage." Fanny folded her arms across her waist and wished she could escape this conversation. Her cousins had ruined her earlier pleasure over seeing Michael.

"Well, once Fanny reaches her majority, she can marry whomever she chooses," Sophie said, toying with the brush. "She will be quite wealthy, after all, and no one will be able to tell her what to do."

"Money won't keep people from telling a woman what to do," Amanda replied. "Especially when it comes to matrimony. No, if anything, Fanny will have it much harder now. She will be scrutinized and watched at every turn."

"Do you truly suppose so?" Fanny asked.

Amanda nodded. "No one, especially my father, is going to allow you to take such an important matter into your own hands."

"All the more reason Fanny should take charge now," Sophie said firmly. "Honestly, you'd think you two were chained to Uncle Jonas's arm. He cannot be everywhere at one time. You should think long and hard about what you want out of life and make it happen for yourselves, rather than wait for someone else to dictate it."

"But wisely choosing a mate is the most important thing in the world," Amanda said. "Especially when you are a part of a more privileged class of people. The wealthy make so many decisions that affect the lives of the poor."

"There you go again worrying about the poor," Sophie said in a tone that clearly betrayed her exasperation. "You are such a ninny sometimes."

Amanda retrieved the hairbrush from Sophie and returned to the dressing table. "We'd best finish our hair if we're going to be dressed by the time Father arrives from Rochester. Mother said he might be bringing some additional guests for the weekend, and she appeared none too pleased."

"Oh? Who? I do hope it's none of Uncle Jonas's business associates. We'll be forced to remain at home all evening. They'll expect us to join them for a game of whist or charades. I was in hopes we could go to the hotel in Clayton. There's a dance tonight." Sophie's dark eyes sparkled, and she winked at Fanny. "Maybe Michael would agree to take us in the skiff."

Fanny smiled, but in truth she was still caught up in Amanda's comments. "I don't know. Let's wait and see."

The three girls were on the upper veranda when they spotted the launch nearing the dock. Amanda cupped her hand over her eyes and squinted. There were additional passengers in the boat. "I can't see well enough to determine who Father has brought with him."

Sophie leaned over the railing and continued to watch until the boat neared the pier. "I can't see one woman among the passengers." She glanced over her shoulder. "Strange, don't you think?"

"I just hope he hasn't brought old Mr. Snodgrass with him. I don't think I could bear an entire weekend of his attention," Fanny said.

"Perhaps Uncle Jonas is thinking Mr. Snodgrass would be a good match for you, Fanny." Sophie doubled over in a gale of laughter.

Fanny shook her head emphatically. "I would run away first!"

"I don't think you need worry. Unless my eyes deceive me, the men with Uncle Jonas are all young and quite good-looking."

"I recognize only a few of those men," Amanda said.

"Let's go downstairs and meet the rest. For once Uncle Jonas was thinking about someone other than himself when he chose guests to visit the island," Sophie said as she pushed away from the railing and hurried indoors. "We may not need to go to Clayton after all."

Amanda reached out to stop Fanny as she followed after her cousin. "Wait. I want to say something."

Fanny turned in surprise. "What?"

Amanda frowned, then seemed to recompose her feelings. "I didn't mean to upset you earlier. It's just that I've overheard my father and mother talk on so many occasions about the responsibility of seeing me properly wed. I know how my father feels about such matters, and I know that the fact you've inherited your father's share of Grandfather's estate will create problems for you that you may not have expected."

"But why? I don't see how that should change anything."

"I know. But mark my words, it will. With Father being put in charge as your guardian, he will endeavor to do whatever is necessary to safeguard your fortune and his reputation. The idea of you with Michael is something he would never consent to. I know without a doubt he would do whatever was necessary to keep you apart."

"Does he not care at all about true love?" Fanny asked in disbelief. "Wouldn't he want you, or even me, for that matter, to be happy?"

Amanda sighed and looped her arm through Fanny's. "Father will want whatever benefits him the most, unfortunately. Just guard your heart. Otherwise, I fear the results will not be to your liking."

Jonas didn't fail to note the covetous looks of several of the young men as the launch approached Broadmoor Island. He enjoyed seeing a good plan come to fruition, and if this first step was any gauge, he and Mortimer had developed an excellent strategy. Careful to make a mental note of those who appeared most impressed with their surroundings, he sauntered toward the house with his entourage. Together with the candidates he'd interviewed, Jonas had invited three bachelors from Rochester who were acquainted with his wife and family.

That idea had been one of Mortimer's suggestions. *"The ladies of your household may question why you've brought all these strangers and become suspicious. You must also take a few eligible men with whom they're acquainted.*" Using all the resources at his disposal, Mortimer had suggested several, and three of them were willing to travel to the island with him that weekend. There had been insufficient time to properly interview the final choices, but Jonas would remain vigilant throughout the weekend. If Fanny demonstrated an interest in one of the added candidates, Jonas would take the proper steps to meet with the young man next week.

Jonas hadn't felt so alive in a long time. He enjoyed nothing more than a good challenge. "I do hope all of you are going to enjoy your weekend here at Broadmoor Castle."

His delight increased twofold when the three girls stepped into view and the men murmured words of approval. A good sign. He waved the girls forward but was disappointed when it was Sophie who immediately broke away from the other two and rushed forward while Amanda and Fanny waited at a distance.

His pleasure diminished when he caught sight of his wife. She rounded the edge of the porch with a determined step and a firm set to her jaw. The moment he drew near, Jonas forced a broad smile. "I am so pleased to be back on the island," he said before kissing her cheek.

Victoria backed away from his grasp and surveyed the bevy of young men. "I suppose you should make introductions, Jonas. I don't believe I've met several of these young men."

Forcing an air of joviality, he waved the men forward. "I know how you young ladies prefer a variety of escorts and thought I should assist in that regard." As though showcasing a new product, he extended his arm with a flourish and introduced each of the men.

"Could you assist us by adding a few young ladies to the mix next weekend?" Jefferson hollered from the veranda.

Jonas ignored his son's remark. He didn't want to be forced into a more detailed explanation regarding the visitors. At the moment, he was counting on his wife's impeccable manners and etiquette to help him survive the evening. Once they were alone, he'd be the object of her wrath. Until then, he knew she would play the perfect hostess. All of these young men would believe she was delighted they had accompanied him to the island.

While Jonas was making the introductions, he'd been doing his best to gauge Fanny's reaction. *Indifference.* Not a spark of interest in even one of the men. In fact, if Jonas hadn't grasped her hand, she would have disappeared.

Before leading Victoria into the house, Jonas insisted the young people engage in a game of croquet. "I'll hear no excuses. I expect every one of you to participate." He glanced at his younger niece and called from the front porch, "Frank, you make certain Fanny doesn't make an escape. She likes to wander off into the woods."

Frank smiled at Fanny. "I'll be pleased to keep her company, Mr. Broadmoor."
Victoria yanked on his sleeve. "What are you doing, Jonas?"

"Offering opportunities, my dear. Shall we go inside?" He didn't await a
response, but the hurried click of her heels on the stone porch revealed both
her submission and her anger.

The moment Victoria cleared the threshold, she yanked on his arm. "I told
you I wanted to discuss this matter further, Jonas. I had hoped that just this
once you might abide by my wishes."

"This isn't the time or the place, Victoria. There are tasks to accomplish
before the evening meal. I have already decided upon a seating arrangement."
He removed a paper from his jacket pocket. "This is a list of names and a
diagram. You'll need to prepare the name cards."

Victoria quickly perused the page. "I see that you plan to position Fanny
between Frank Colgan and Benjamin Wolgast. And you've seated Fred Portman and Daniel Irwin across from her. I believe she'd prefer to have Amanda
or Sophie nearby, and both of them are at the other end of the table." Victoria
picked up a pencil and quickly sketched a different arrangement. "Besides,
you know how I feel about having the seating arranged man, woman, man,
woman, and so forth."

Before she had time to complete her idea, Jonas withdrew the pencil
from her hand. "We will use my diagram, Victoria. This is not open to
discussion despite your traditional seating arrangement. There is nothing
wrong with having several men or women seated side by side. Please advise
Mrs. O'Malley to make room assignments for the young men. I trust you
had already instructed Mrs. Atwell we would be entertaining dinner guests
this evening."

"I told her the possibility existed, but I certainly didn't expect you to arrive
with *seven* young men. We can only hope that she prepared enough extra."

Jonas shrugged. "Mrs. Atwell is accustomed to cooking for large groups.
She'll adjust. Incidentally, when is Mrs. Oosterman hosting her masked ball?
Is that next Saturday evening?"

"Yes. Why do you ask?"

"I'll likely want you to secure invitations for at least some of the young men
I've brought with me this weekend. I'm certain Mrs. Oosterman won't object
to the addition of eligible young bachelors at the party."

"Such a request goes against every rule of proper etiquette, Jonas. I'll not
ask her to enlarge her guest list on my account—especially at this late date."

"Then you may do so on *my* account." He patted her shoulder. "Place the
blame on me, but do not fail to secure the invitations. I'll give you the names
before I depart on Sunday evening."

Victoria stormed from the room without another word.

Fanny had endured the game of croquet, but her spirits plummeted when she entered the dining room and noted the seating arrangement. Aunt Victoria had placed her near the head of the table, where she would be surrounded by Uncle Jonas and several of his unexpected guests. Glancing over her shoulder, she picked up her name card and switched places with Sophie before slipping out of the room. No one but Aunt Victoria would be the wiser, and her gregarious cousin would doubtless be delighted to entertain the young men.

"There you are, Fanny. We were beginning to wonder what had happened to you." Her uncle beckoned her forward with a broad smile.

Fanny wondered if he'd had an extra glass of port, for he was behaving in a far friendlier manner than normal. Unless issuing a command, Uncle Jonas barely spoke to her. She longed to join Amanda on the other side of the veranda, but she dared not ignore her uncle's order.

"I understand you and Frank were declared winners of the croquet game."

The blond-haired man she'd been paired with for the game of croquet flanked Uncle Jonas on his right. Mr. Colgan had been friendly enough—in fact, more friendly than she preferred, but she'd rather talk to Amanda or Sophie. "The win is due to Mr. Colgan's ability. He appears to have quite a knack for the game."

"Don't sell yourself short, Fanny. I've challenged the others to a rematch and have already insisted that you'll remain my partner."

"I don't know, I—"

"That sounds like a splendid idea. I believe you're sitting next to each other at dinner. The two of you can discuss your strategy then." Uncle Jonas winked at Frank. "Unless Benjamin succeeds in occupying Fanny's attention. If memory serves me correctly, he's going to occupy the chair to Fanny's left."

Fanny gulped. How did Uncle Jonas know the seating arrangement? Had he already been in the dining room? For that matter, Fanny wondered if all of the other guests had been in the dining room before she came downstairs. What if everyone discovered what she had done with the place cards?

"I don't believe so, Uncle Jonas. Aunt Victoria knows I always request a chair near Amanda or Sophie." She pointed to the lake. "Do you fish, Mr. Colgan?" Perhaps if she changed the topic, Uncle Jonas would forget the seating arrangement.

Frank shook his head. "Do *you* fish, Miss Broadmoor?"

From his grin, Fanny knew her answer would surprise. "Indeed I do, Mr. Colgan. Fishing is one of my favorite pastimes."

"Then I hope you'll agree to take me fishing during my visit this weekend, Miss Broadmoor. I would be delighted to have you act as my instructor."

Now what? Her plan to change the conversation from the seating arrangement had turned into an afternoon of fishing with Mr. Colgan. She didn't have time to object before Uncle Jonas was offering to have Mrs. Atwell pack a picnic lunch for their proposed outing.

"I suggest you take a canoe and row over to one of the far islands, where the fishermen usually meet with great success," Uncle Jonas proposed. "Early morning is best. Why don't the two of you plan on going out tomorrow? I'll see to the arrangements for the canoe. No need for you to go down to the boathouse, Fanny. I'll have Michael tie one of the canoes to the small dock, since it's closer to the house and will be more convenient."

The family seldom used the small dock. It had been constructed years ago, before completion of the new boathouse. Her grandfather had considered having it dismantled, but Grand-mère had objected, citing its proximity to the house. Grandfather had bowed to her wishes, though Fanny didn't recall Grand-mère ever using the small dock.

"No need adding to Michael's workload, Uncle Jonas. Surely Mr. Colgan doesn't consider a walk to the boathouse taxing." If luck was with her, Fanny would have a few minutes alone with Michael. She'd make certain of it!

"That's why I pay the staff, Fanny dear. You need not worry about Michael Atwell's workload. The canoe will await you and Frank at the small dock in the morning."

The maid announced supper before Fanny could offer further argument. Not that she could change her uncle's mind. From the set of his jaw, he appeared resolute, and her thoughts had already returned to the exchanged place cards. Following Aunt Victoria's usual custom, the guests circled the table searching for their names. When Fanny stopped at the chair next to Amanda, she didn't fail to note her aunt's surprise.

Uncle Jonas signaled his wife. "I'm not certain we're all in the proper seats, are we? After all, Amanda and Fanny are seated next to each other."

"I do believe we all know how to read, Jonas. I daresay, the name cards are clearly printed with each guest's name." Aunt Victoria offered an apologetic smile to the group. "Would you please check your name card to ensure you're at the proper chair?" Murmurs and nods followed the request. When no one made a move, their hostess shook her head. "I'm sorry, Jonas. It appears that you're mistaken. After all, there is nothing wrong with having two young women seated side by side."

CHAPTER 15

SATURDAY, JULY 24, 1897

Late the next morning Fanny spotted Amanda sitting beneath a stand of white spruce not far from the little dock and waved from the canoe. She was pleased to be returning home. Fishing with Frank had been an exercise in futility. Though she'd done her best to teach him the proper technique for baiting his hook, he'd been as inept as a young child. He'd bloodied his fingers not once but on three separate occasions. And all had been in vain, for he'd accomplished nothing other than to feed his worms to the fish.

And he wouldn't be quiet! She had explained that fishing was a silent sport, but Frank had ignored her requests to cease his incessant talking. When she finally confronted him, he actually admitted fishing didn't interest him in the least. The fishing trip had been a ploy to gain her full attention—at least that's what he'd said. And that was when Fanny decided they would immediately return to Broadmoor Island.

Frank had argued they should remain until after their picnic lunch, but Fanny refused. Seeing Amanda confirmed her decision. Perhaps the two of them could take the picnic lunch Mrs. Atwell had packed and retreat to the far side of the island by themselves for the remainder of the afternoon. The thought prompted her to hurry Frank in his attempt to guide the canoe alongside the dock. She didn't fault him for his clumsiness, for he'd had little experience paddling a canoe. However, her irritation continued to mount when he steadfastly failed to follow her instructions.

Fanny glanced over her shoulder and pointed at the paddle. "Turn the paddle in the other direction or we'll head back into the current, Frank."

She hoped he would listen, for this outing had gone on long enough and she had no desire to have to paddle back upstream.

"I think I can use my—" The canoe lurched back and forth.

"Sit down, Frank! You're going to cause us to—"

Before she could complete her sentence, Fanny was immersed in the St. Lawrence River. She flapped her arms and sputtered, her gown and petticoats quickly soaking up water like a parched flower bed. Her new straw hat bobbed toward shore, and remnants of Mrs. Atwell's carefully packed sandwiches were already providing sustenance for a hungry duck. She need not worry about Frank, for he had remained with the now overturned canoe and was trying his best to climb atop it. Using his arms and legs for support, he wrapped himself around the canoe like a bear clinging to a tree trunk, only to fall back into the water again and again.

After two wide arcing strokes, Fanny forced her torso down and into a standing position. Fighting against the weight of her drenched clothing, she pushed through the water with determined strides and maneuvered toward the dock.

Amanda stood grinning at the water's edge. "We have a bathtub, Fanny. You need not bathe in the river."

Fanny held out a hand for her cousin to help her onto dry land. "If you weren't wearing that lovely gown, I'd be tempted to pull you in here with me."

The two of them giggled, and Amanda glanced toward Frank, who continued to cling to the canoe, even though he couldn't seem to climb atop. The river's motion was gently bringing him toward the dock and shallower water.

"When are you going to tell him he can touch bottom?"

"I thought I'd wait a few minutes longer." She turned toward the dock and shaded her eyes. "Can you swim, Frank?"

"No! Would you send someone to help? I don't have strength enough to lift my weight onto the canoe. If I turn loose, I'm going to go under."

"I'd attempt to save you myself, but I believe I'd pull us both under, what with all this water weighing down my dress. Amanda can swim, but I don't want her to ruin her new dress. You do understand, of course."

"Yes, of course!" he hollered. "Send one of the other men or the fellow over at the boathouse."

His hands were beginning to slip, and Fanny could see him fighting to gain control. She tipped her head toward Amanda. "Oh, I don't suppose I should torture him much longer, should I?"

"I suppose not. He does look rather frightened—and you do need to get out of those wet clothes."

The two girls headed toward the path. When they'd neared the house, Fanny turned around and cupped her hands to her mouth. "Frank! You can touch bottom if you'll put your feet down."

The two girls watched for a moment, but Frank continued to clutch the canoe as it bobbed against the dock. Amanda shook her head. "He doesn't follow instructions very well, does he?"

"That, my dear cousin, is exactly why we ended up in the river! When he grows weary enough, he'll discover I've told him the truth." Fanny opened the door for her cousin. "Shall we go inside?"

Jonas couldn't believe his eyes—or his ears, for that matter. Considering the number of guests visiting for the weekend, the house had seemed unusually quiet, and he had walked outdoors expecting to see the young people engaged in a game of croquet. Instead, he was greeted by a call for help and immediately ran toward the river.

There, beside the dock, he caught sight of young Frank Colgan clinging to one of the Broadmoor canoes. "Let go and stand down, Frank. The water is less than six foot."

"I can't swim," Frank shouted.

Jonas wiped the beads of perspiration from his forehead and attempted to restrain his irritation. "You don't *need* to swim! You can walk. Put your feet down!" He could see the hesitation as Frank finally dropped his legs and then loosened his hold.

"I *can* touch the bottom." Relief flooded the young man's voice, although he continued to remain close to the dock's edge while wading out of the river.

"What happened? And where is my niece?" Jonas took several backward steps as Frank stepped onto dry ground and then shook like a wet retriever.

"Oh, sorry, sir. I didn't mean to get you wet." He slicked his hair back with one hand. "Fanny and Amanda are inside."

"Then would you care to explain what you're doing pretending to be drowning?"

Frank's eyes opened wide and he trembled. "I wasn't pretending, Mr. Broadmoor. I truly believed I was going to die."

How cruel of the girls to walk off and leave a man to think he might die. The very thought! "Are you telling me that my niece and daughter were aware of your dilemma and didn't advise you there was no need for concern?"

"Fanny told me, but I was afraid to let loose. What if she hadn't been telling the truth?"

Jonas massaged his forehead. Clearly this young man was foolish enough to serve the purpose for which he had been brought here, yet if he wouldn't follow a simple direction that could save his own life, Jonas wondered if Frank would prove a wise choice. Without prompting, the young man would likely forget to come in out of the rain. Jonas wanted a man he could control, but he didn't want a dolt. Maybe Benjamin or Fred would prove a superior selection.

Jonas sent for Michael to retrieve the canoe and then directed Frank upstairs to change into a dry suit. After dealing with Frank, Jonas needed to solidify his plan. Just when he had thought his strategy was moving forward with ease, Frank had dashed his hopes.

He returned to the veranda and a short time later heard Amanda and Fanny giggling. "You girls come out here immediately."

"Yes, Father?"

He ignored his daughter and beckoned to Fanny. "I discovered Frank in the river a short time ago." He wagged his head back and forth. "He's upstairs changing clothes. I suggest you go and join our other guests."

Fanny arched her brows and glanced toward the lawn. "I have no idea where your guests have gone, Uncle Jonas. Besides, Amanda and I are going to enjoy a late lunch at the far end of the island. If we can convince Mrs. Atwell to supply us with a few sandwiches, that is. Our picnic basket is at the bottom of the river."

Fanny grasped Amanda's hand and the two girls marched inside. The fishing excursion with Frank had been a misstep, but Jonas would not permit one mistake to foil his plan. He couldn't permit the entire afternoon to pass by without the remaining prospective grooms vying for Fanny's attentions.

He'd nearly given up hope when the two girls returned with their picnic basket a short time later.

Then, as if in answer to his plight, Jonas heard the sounds of excited chatter and laughter. "The others are returning, and it would be rude if you two ran off by yourselves—a breach of etiquette."

"They weren't expecting me to return until this afternoon—remember? I'm supposed to be fishing with Frank."

The note of triumph in Fanny's voice struck a nerve, and Jonas strengthened his resolve. With a flap of his hand, he signaled the girls to sit down and walked to the far end of the veranda. He would not be manipulated by a seventeen-year-old female. Fanny Broadmoor would *not* ruin his plans for her future inheritance.

The sight that greeted him at the far end of the lawn had a more disquieting effect on him. Sophie paraded toward the house, surrounded by the entourage. They swarmed around her like bees seeking their queen. What were those young men thinking? They'd obviously forgotten the reason he'd brought them here. Jonas waited until Benjamin looked in his direction and motioned the group to hurry along.

Jonas detected the pout on Sophie's lips. Quincy needed to gain control of his daughter before she acquired a tawdry reputation. Jonas had recently heard remarks about her behavior, and he made a mental note to speak with his brother. Though he cared little about Sophie, Jonas didn't want any scandal tarnishing the family name.

"Where have you been?" Jonas clenched his jaw.

Sophie flicked an errant strand of hair over her shoulder. "Jefferson, George, and I have been giving our visitors a tour of the island. We're famished and returned for some lunch and a game of croquet."

"Good. I'm certain you'll want Fanny to join you. She returned from her fishing excursion earlier than expected."

The young men offered their hearty agreement while Sophie continued to pout. But as long as Jonas achieved the desired result, he cared little whether he pleased or angered Sophie. He escorted the group around the veranda while hoping Fanny hadn't decided to disappear in his absence. The girl was proving more headstrong than he'd suspected and certainly more difficult to handle than his own daughter. Both Sophie and Fanny had lacked proper rearing. Had they received appropriate instruction early on, they would have adopted the compliant nature of a true lady. But all of that would now change—at least for Fanny. His strong hand would be directing her behavior and her future.

One by one, Jonas pulled aside Daniel, Fred, and Benjamin for a private discussion and a reminder that Fanny should be the object of their affection. Only Benjamin argued.

He tugged on his stiff shirt collar and fidgeted like a schoolboy. "I like Sophie a lot, Mr. Broadmoor. And Fanny doesn't appear to be interested in having me around. If it's okay with you, I'd rather take my chances at winning Sophie's heart."

"This has nothing to do with love or winning a young woman's heart, Benjamin. Have you so quickly forgotten this is about money—a large inheritance?"

Benjamin winked. "But Sophie is a Broadmoor. One day she'll inherit, too."

The young man's sly grin took Jonas by surprise. Benjamin was plotting to have his cake and eat it, too! Perhaps this young fellow wouldn't prove as tractable as Jonas had thought. "Don't expect Sophie to come into a large sum of money. Her father will pour his inheritance into his Home for the Friendless. Even if there should be some small remainder, Sophie has four siblings who would share in such funds. You would reap little financial gain from such a marriage, and even that would not occur for years." Jonas squeezed Benjamin's shoulder. "This is your decision, but I expect you to remember our agreement." The boy's shoulder quivered beneath his grasp, and Jonas smiled. Benjamin had understood his warning.

Jonas ordered Amanda to the kitchen with instructions for Mrs. Atwell to prepare a picnic lunch large enough to feed all of their guests. But when Fanny attempted to join Amanda on her errand, Jonas blocked her path. "Amanda doesn't need your assistance, Fanny; she knows her way to the kitchen. You can help Daniel gather the mallets and balls for the croquet game. He doesn't know where they're located."

Daniel hastened to Fanny's side. "I'd be most pleased to have your assistance."

"I'll help, too," Benjamin said. "We can set up the wickets now and begin our game as soon as we've eaten our lunch."

Soon all of the young men were following Fanny's bidding as she directed placement of the wickets—all except George and Jefferson, who were lounging on the lower veranda, watching in amusement.

Sophie paced in front of them until George begged her to sit down. "I realize you're angry because you've lost your admirers to Fanny, but do take heart. She's not at all interested in any of them. Watch her! She's merely tolerating their attention. And the men are out there because Father insisted. To ignore his request would have been rude. Bide your time, Cousin. They'll soon be fawning over you again."

Amanda rounded the corner, and both of her brothers jumped to their feet. "I do hope you've come to announce lunch. We're starving," George said.

"I'm afraid not, though you may as well help yourself to the lunch Mrs. Atwell packed for Fanny and me. It's over near the front door. Don't eat it all, or you'll ruin your appetite."

Jefferson laughed. "Don't worry. I doubt your dainty sandwiches will be sufficient to ruin my dinner."

Amanda dropped onto one of the chairs. "They appear to be having a gay time."

Sophie glanced over her shoulder and then joined her cousin. "They all are quite nice and very attentive. At least they were until your father turned their attention toward Fanny."

"In truth, I thought Father had decided upon those young men as possible suitors for me. Silly, but I actually believed he'd been thinking of me while he was in Rochester last week. He'd recently mentioned finding a young man who would prove a perfect match." Amanda rested her chin in her palm. "Not that I desire a husband anytime in the near future, but my father is seemingly more interested in Fanny's future than that of his own daughter."

"And that surprises you?" Sophie groaned. "In case you haven't noticed, none of the Broadmoor men have ever taken an interest in their daughters—unless it offered some advantage."

"I suppose that's true enough," Amanda agreed. Her father had never doted upon her. In fact, he'd shown her very little attention throughout the years. It was one reason she'd been stirred to seek fulfillment in charity work rather than a marriage to someone who would likely treat her as impersonally as had her father throughout the years. "Why, then, do I feel betrayed that this group of men wasn't invited for my benefit? I knew Father would concern himself with finding Fanny a proper husband. He is, after all, her guardian."

"Not only that, she's become exceedingly wealthy," Sophie added.

"Still, I thought he would give her time. She is only seventeen, and I'm nineteen."

"But you're completely dependent upon your father's money and therefore the situation is not quite so urgent. Uncle Jonas is your father, but he's devoted his time and thought to Fanny and her future rather than yours." Sophie turned her gaze back toward the group of men knocking the croquet balls across the lawn. "I believe your father has chosen one of those fellows as Fanny's husband. I think he's going to force her into an arranged marriage. Something I would rail against. You should count yourself fortunate."

"What makes you think that's what he's doing? Grandfather just died. Surely Father would not expect Fanny to consider matrimony just yet."

"Do open your eyes, dear girl. He sent her out with Frank this morning, and now that she's returned, he's busy arranging for her to spend time with the others. Maybe he hasn't selected the exact one yet, but I'd guess he's trying to choose a favorite. If you watch closely, you'll see that he keeps maneuvering several of the men toward her."

Amanda sighed. "You may be right. I had mentioned that very possibility to Fanny but hadn't expected it this soon. I know Father will worry about undesirables trying to woo her now that she has a fortune. Still, none of us will have the final say in the person we wed. The women in our family are expected to marry a person of their own social standing."

"Did I hear the two of you discussing the possibility of prospective husbands?" Both girls swiveled toward the sound of Beatrice's voice, and she laughed. "It appears I surprised both of you."

Sophie glared at her sister. "You were eavesdropping—not a particularly admirable behavior."

"And you would certainly know about admirable behavior, dear Sophie. Have you decided to marry one of those fops Uncle Jonas brought with him for the weekend, Amanda?"

"Quite the contrary. Sophie thinks my father has brought them as possible suitors for Fanny. I haven't decided if that's the case, but she may be correct."

"I don't care whether she finds a suitable husband or not. I still can't believe Grandfather left a third of his estate to that little snippet. It's completely unfair! And she has no brother or sisters—no one with whom she'll have to share." Beatrice's lips drooped more than usual.

"Would you like all of us to apologize for being born, Beatrice?" Sophie asked. "Your greed is even more unbecoming than your eavesdropping."

Beatrice wagged her finger. "One day you'll care. Then it will be too late."

Sophie chuckled. "Too late? I have no control over how the family money is divided, and neither do you. More to the point, I don't care if Fanny receives a greater share of the estate. Just as your future was decided by the men in this family, mine will also be determined by their whims." Sophie smoothed the bodice of her gown as Fanny and the men sauntered toward the lower veranda. "For now, dear Beatrice, I intend to assert my own will and have more fun than proper society permits."

CHAPTER 16

SATURDAY, JULY 31, 1897

Fanny buttoned Sophie's dress and then bade her cousin turn around. "I do fear your father won't be pleased with the gown you've chosen."

"My father won't even notice. He seldom is aware of me, even when I'm in the same room." The topaz necklace that circled Sophie's neck sparkled in the soft light. "Beatrice will swoon when she sees I've pirated our mother's necklace and brought it along." Sadness shone in her eyes as she touched a finger to the jewels. "I always thought Mother looked beautiful when she wore this necklace."

"And so do you," Fanny said. "She would be pleased that you've chosen to wear her necklace."

Sophie brightened. "In any case, I doubt Father will attend this evening. He dislikes parties and dancing. He'd much rather be in Rochester working alongside Paul than out here on the island with his family." She shrugged. "But then, I'd rather be in Rochester, too."

Fanny arranged a lace insert in the décolletage of her emerald green gown. "I thought you were excited about the ball."

"I am, but the ball lasts for only one night." With a giggle, Sophie leaned forward and attempted to remove the insert from Fanny's dress. "You're old enough to wear your gown without an insert."

Fanny swooped to one side and warded off Sophie's maneuver. "Perhaps, but I prefer to use it. And remember, you're the one who says we should be free to make our own choices. I didn't attempt to force you to add an insert to your dress, did I?"

"You're correct. I'll permit you to make your own choice, but I truly believe it's Aunt Victoria's decision rather than your own," Sophie replied. "And speaking of Aunt Victoria, where has she secreted Amanda? I haven't seen her since we came upstairs to prepare for the party."

"I imagine she's in her rooms. I think she wants to surprise us with her dress. Aunt Victoria had it designed especially for the ball. Show me your mask," Fanny requested.

Sophie held a half-mask of shimmering gold to her eyes. In an effort to further camouflage the wearer's identity, filmy lace and feathers had been attached to the edges of the mask. Yet anyone who'd ever met Sophie would identify her behind the mask. With or without a mask, her beauty shone like the sparkling gems in her necklace.

While Sophie had expressed excitement when Uncle Jonas returned with several of the young men who had visited the previous weekend, Fanny cared little. None of them had captivated her interest, though she was surprised when Sophie pointed out the fact that Frank Colgan wasn't among the returning men.

"I thought him rather good looking," Sophie remarked as they exited the bedroom.

"Perhaps, but not very bright. If his arms would have provided him with the necessary strength, he'd likely still be in the water hanging on to the canoe." Fanny looped arms with her cousin, and the two of them descended the stairs.

The young men had departed for the Oosterman mansion fifteen minutes earlier. Once Michael had delivered them, he would return for the ladies. At Mrs. Oosterman's request, Aunt Victoria insisted every effort be made to keep the guests' identities secret until the unmasking at midnight. While Sophie preened in front of the hallway mirror, Fanny stepped onto the upper veranda. A full moon shone overhead, and Fanny strained forward, unsure if the distant lights were stars glistening on the black water or the flickering oil lamps of the *DaisyBee*. Her heart tripped as she caught sight of the tangerine glow from beneath the boiler and heard the distinct hissing of the engine.

Not much longer before she would see Michael. He'd been uncharacteristically absent from the boathouse every time she'd gone to see him during the week. Even Mrs. Atwell hadn't seemed forthcoming when Fanny had inquired about Michael's whereabouts. She merely shrugged and mumbled that she hadn't seen him and then excused herself to complete chores somewhere else in the house. It was as if both mother and son were attempting to avoid her, yet she couldn't imagine why. She could recall nothing she'd done to offend either of them.

Fanny was still on the veranda when the rest of the Broadmoor women arrived downstairs. With Aunt Victoria taking the lead, they all walked the short distance to the boathouse, where Michael awaited them. One by one he assisted each of the ladies into the boat. Finally it was Fanny's turn. Seizing the opportunity, she gave his hand a squeeze, but her spirits wilted when he ignored the affectionate gesture. She claimed one of the few remaining seats, all of them located at a distance from Michael. There would be no opportunity to speak to him during the boat ride.

Aunt Victoria remained in charge of the group, issuing instructions throughout the journey. They were to keep their masks in place at all times, they were to make every attempt to disguise themselves from their dance partners, and they weren't to withhold their dance cards from any gentleman in deference to another. Her aunt cast a stern look at Sophie when she issued that particular directive. "All female guests are to enter by the side door, and we will gather in the parlor. Mrs. Oosterman has arranged for each of us to be individually escorted into the ballroom." Aunt Victoria appeared delighted by the idea. "Her method will aid in keeping our identities secret. Each of the male guests will be assigned an identifying number that will be used to sign your dance cards."

Sophie poked Fanny in the side. "Why is Aunt Victoria so anxious to please Mrs. Oosterman?"

"Uncle Jonas has instructed Aunt Victoria to cultivate a friendship with Mrs. Oosterman. Their wealth supposedly exceeds our family's fortune. At least that's what Amanda told me," Fanny whispered. "Sounds like something Uncle Jonas would say. Money is always at the top of his list."

"Money and control," Sophie murmured. "Did you hear Beatrice upbraid me before we left the house this evening? The minute she spotted Mother's necklace, she lit into me. Had it not been for Aunt Victoria's intervention, I believe Beatrice would have ripped it from around my throat."

"You should have told her you were wearing it with your father's permission."

Sophie's even white teeth shone beneath the boat's lantern light. "Oh, but I'm not. He doesn't even know I removed it from the safe." She chuckled as Michael steered the boat alongside the Oosterman's dock.

Servants awaited them on the dock, holding brightly lit brass lanterns. The Broadmoor ladies were escorted to the parlor with a formality befitting royalty. Though Fanny considered the decorum overdone in the extreme, Aunt Victoria and Beatrice extolled the pomp and ceremony.

Sophie nodded toward her sister. "Beatrice *is* full of herself this evening, isn't she? Did you see her fawning over Mrs. Oosterman? Who would ever think we were blood sisters? After being around my family, I'm more and more convinced that I must be adopted."

Fanny laughed at her cousin's remark, but before she could respond, Sophie was the next to be whisked away. Fanny was one of the final guests to be escorted into the ballroom. Not that she minded. Less time in the ballroom meant fewer hours tolerating the fanfare and grand gestures that pervaded these gatherings—and less time socializing with the masked male guests. Though the women invested much more time in their costumes and masks, the men were always more difficult to recognize. They all tended to wear their black formal wear, disguise their voices, and wear simple black masks. One or two of the rotund or bald male guests could be easily discerned, but in recent years the men had begun the practice of donning old-fashioned powdered wigs to disguise themselves. Fanny noted most had employed the practice this evening.

She spied the shimmering golden hue of Sophie's gown. A group of male guests surrounded her cousin, all of them vying to scribble their assigned numbers on her dance card. Fanny backed toward a narrow cove alongside the doors leading to the wide veranda. If all went well, she could fade into her surroundings and then escape outdoors once the dancing began. Unfortunately, her aunt had stationed herself with a clear view of all the exits while she talked to Uncle Jonas. The two of them ceased their conversation and glanced around the room.

Her aunt spotted her and signaled Uncle Jonas. Fanny watched in dismay as her uncle grasped a young man by the arm and directed him toward her. She wanted to run, but her limbs wouldn't budge. She remained paralyzed as the man approached and bade her good evening.

When she didn't respond, he grinned. "Is it that you don't want me to recognize your voice, or has the cat got your tongue?" He grasped her dance card between his thumb and forefinger. "It appears that I'll have the privilege of being the first to sign your card. Perhaps I should fill every dance with my number. Would that displease you?"

"I don't believe that's permissible." She stared into his eyes, hoping to gain some clue. "I have no idea who you are. Rendering any further opinion in regard to my displeasure is, therefore, impossible."

He signed his number on several lines before returning her card. "Since you appear to desire a man who plays by the rules, I'll abide by your instruction." He tipped his head a bit closer. "I've signed your card for four dances. I hope you won't believe me overly presumptuous when I tell you that I secured both the first and last dances of the evening as well as the two that precede the short interludes prior to dining. With any good fortune, perhaps I'll discover our hostess has seated us side by side for at least one of the evening's repasts."

"Since you have no idea who I am, you may soon discover you've made an ill-conceived decision." Fanny glanced over the man's shoulder and noted that her uncle continued to keep her in his line of vision. "Unless someone has already revealed my identity."

"Now why would you think such a thing?"

His words rang false to her, and she knew this must be one of Uncle Jonas's weekend visitors. It truly didn't matter which one, for she had no interest in any of these men. "You'd best locate some other dance partners before the music begins. Otherwise you'll be required to join the old men discussing politics in the den."

"Or join you on the veranda for a cup of punch."

The man had effectively blocked her into the alcove from which she longed to escape—but escape she must. If not, she'd be forced to spend the entire evening in his company. "I do believe that gentleman on the far side of the room beckoned to you," she said.

When he stepped aside in order to gain a better view, Fanny edged free. "If you'll excuse me, I must speak to someone in private." Before he could object, she hurried away to the ladies' parlor for a brief reprieve. How she disliked these parties!

By Sophie's standards, the evening had thus far proved a success. She'd been one of the first to make an entrance into the ballroom and *the* first to be surrounded by a host of men. Just what she preferred. One man in particular intrigued her. Though he'd been among the first to surround her, he hadn't immediately fought to place his number on her dance card. Not until she'd coyly pressed the card into his hand did he succumb and poise a pencil above the lines.

She grasped his hand with her lace-gloved fingers. "Not there. Write your name on the line that precedes the supper repast. We'll have additional time to visit." With a flick of her hand, her lace fan spread open and she brushed it beneath his chin. "You would like to visit with me, wouldn't you?"

He nodded his head. "Until then."

His hasty departure surprised her. Unlike the other men, who couldn't seem to get enough of her, this one seemed distant and aloof. She spotted her uncle Jonas across the room visiting with a circle of friends and excused herself from the gathered men. Though she would have preferred to speak to her father, she'd not yet located him among the crowd.

She waited while the men completed their boring discussion. She half-listened to their talk of rumors circulating in the English newspapers that Japan would go to war with the United States if the Senate ratified a treaty to annex the Hawaiian Islands. Why did men enjoy discussing war? she wondered. Whether the debate was about Cuba or Japan, they seemed to revel in it. If there wasn't a current conflict to discuss, they thrashed out the possibilities of all imminent prospects.

When the men dispersed a short time later, Sophie tapped her uncle Jonas on the arm. Confusion registered in his expression, and she finally said, "It's me, Sophie."

His jaw tightened. "I can see that it's you. I recognize the jewelry. Does your father know you're wearing that necklace? That is a family heirloom that belonged to my mother."

Sophie ignored the question. "And it was a wedding gift to my mother from Grand-mère. Have you seen my father?"

"He's not here. I believe he sent a note to your aunt saying he had urgent business in Rochester. Quite frankly, I believe he simply wanted an excuse to avoid tonight's party. I can't imagine any matter of urgency in regard to a homeless shelter."

"Perhaps there was a fire and a sudden influx of starving children arrived, Uncle Jonas. Would you consider *that* an emergency?" She shook her head. "Probably not, for those children wouldn't be of any use to your financial empire, would they?"

"You had best withhold your caustic remarks, young lady. If I recall, you hold no greater fondness for that homeless shelter than the rest of the family." His lips tightened into a frown.

She offered an apology, but not because she was sorry. She wanted information about that mysterious man, and her father wasn't available to help. Uncle Jonas was her only remaining choice. "I wonder if you know that young man standing to the left of the double doors leading to the dining hall."

Her uncle took a step forward and peered. "No, I don't believe I do. It's difficult to be certain at this distance and with these ridiculous wigs and masks, but he's no one I easily recognize. He's not one of the men who arrived with me. And I don't recall seeing him when the men gathered prior to the party. As I said, though, it's nearly impossible to be sure." His scowl returned. "Is his behavior boorish? If so, I'll seek Mr. Oosterman's assistance and have him thrown out on his ear."

Sophie placed her hand on his arm. "No, nothing like that. In fact, quite the opposite. He was most genteel."

Her uncle's frown disappeared and he offered an affirmative growl. "You let me know if you have trouble with any of these young fellows."

Sophie stifled a giggle as she hurried off. Jonas would be aghast to know the number of fellows she'd been able to handle without any assistance over the past several years.

During the next hour Sophie charmed her dance partners while keeping a lookout for the stranger who had captured her interest. He had remained near the doors until moments ago, when she noticed him seeking out a dance partner. She was surprised to see him circle the floor with Fanny. Perhaps he *was* a friend of the family.

She rushed to Fanny's side the moment the young man escorted her back to the edge of the floor. Sophie's next dance partner approached, but she waved him away and grasped Fanny's hand. "Who was that fellow you were dancing with?"

Fanny shrugged. "I don't know. We didn't talk much."

"Tell me everything he said," Sophie persisted. "I'm attempting to discover who he is, but even Uncle Jonas doesn't know."

"I fear I'll be little help. Our exchange was no more than polite conversation regarding weather and the like. Oh, he did mention he had recently moved to Rochester."

"You see? You discovered more than you thought. Did he say why or exactly when he moved?"

"I didn't inquire, but your dance partner awaits you."

"Very well, but if you think of anything else, be certain to inform me after this dance."

Sophie couldn't believe her cousin had shared an entire dance with the dashing young man and hadn't gained further information. Of course, he'd not been particularly forthcoming when she talked with him, either. Once they were together on the dance floor, she'd discover who he was. She wished the time would pass more quickly and his number would be the next on her card.

Several of her dance partners remarked upon her detached demeanor, but Sophie offered no apology. They had merely filled the time until this moment arrived. Her partner escorted her to the edge of the dance floor, and she waited for the stranger to approach. Unlike the other men, he didn't hurry to claim her. She wondered if he had forgotten he had claimed this dance.

Not until the musicians took up their instruments did he casually stroll along the edge of the dance floor and stop in front of her. He offered his hand. "I believe I have this dance?"

Sophie offered a comely smile. "The music's already begun. I thought perhaps you'd forgotten." She had expected him to tell her that he could never forget a dance with someone so lovely. Instead, he silently led her onto the dance floor without apology or compliment. "You've piqued my curiosity. While I've been able to identify most of the men in this room, you remain a mystery. Have we ever met?"

He grasped her waist and they joined the dancing couples on the floor. "My dear lady, you're in disguise, yet you believe I know who you are. You assume too much. Tell me, are you summering in the islands, or have you come here only for this party?"

"I make my home in Rochester, but my family has summered in the Thousand Islands for many years." She tipped her head back and gazed into his eyes. "Now you must tell me something about yourself."

"Why?" he asked, expertly guiding her across the floor between two other couples.

"Because I told you something about myself. That's only fair."

"Fair? Is that what you expect? Everything in life to be fair?"

"I do, but generally I'm disappointed," she admitted.

"It's good you've come to that realization. There's little equality this side of heaven. The rich continue to amass wealth while the poor remain hungry."

She detected pain in his gentle laugh and wondered if he had experienced the hunger of which he spoke. Surely not, for the people invited to these parties had been reared in wealth. Who *was* this man?

"You bewilder me, kind sir. I can place neither your voice nor the dark brooding eyes behind your mask. Yet somewhere deep inside, I believe I know you. Will you give me no hint at all?"

"Tell me of your dreams, miss. How do you plan to spend the remainder of your life? How will you bring joy to the lives of others?"

The music stopped; they stood facing one another. She tapped her folded fan lightly against his chest. "Your questions are intriguing. Most men ask how they can make *me* happy."

"Do they? And is that because most men believe you're unhappy or because they realize you'll permit their attentions only if they attempt to meet your every expectation?"

Her jaw dropped at the unexpected question. The two of them remained face-to-face, but Sophie found herself at a loss for words.

Mr. Oosterman signaled for quiet while his wife stepped forward. The men and women were instructed to form separate lines. Their hostess patiently waited until two distinct rows had been created. She then explained that each man's number had been written on a small piece of paper, folded, and placed in Mr. Oosterman's top hat. She stepped in front of the first woman, dipped her veined hand into the top hat, and read a number. The diamonds that decorated her fingers sparkled in the dim lights as she waved the man forward. One by one, each man was randomly assigned to escort the next woman in line to dinner.

Sophie held her breath when Mrs. Oosterman stood before her. The mysterious man's number had not yet been drawn. She longed to hear his number. Instead, the number belonged to her cousin Jefferson. Even with their masks in place, she could recognize both George and Jefferson from across the room. He hurried to her side when Mrs. Oosterman called his number.

"Aren't you the lucky one?" he whispered.

"Oh, do stop, Jefferson. It's me—Sophie. Don't you recognize your own cousin?"

His shoulders sagged. "With all of these ladies here, why'd I have to get stuck with one of my own relatives?"

"*Stuck?*" Sophie jabbed him with her elbow. "You could have been partnered with old Mrs. Beauchamp. Think about shouting into her ear trumpet for the next ninety minutes. Cousin or not, that thought alone should make you happy to be paired with me."

Jefferson mumbled his apology, but Sophie had already returned her attention to the mystery man. His number must now be at the very bottom of the hat, for Mrs. Oosterman was nearing the end of the line and his number still hadn't been picked. She tilted her head toward Jefferson. "Who's the third man from the left? Do you know him?"

Her cousin glanced down the line at the few remaining men. "No, I don't believe I've ever seen him before. I've talked to nearly all of the men this evening, but I don't even recall seeing him when the men gathered in the ballroom before any of the women arrived. Despite the masks, I can pick out nearly every man in this room—except him."

Jefferson's intrigue nearly matched her own, and both of them gasped when Mrs. Oosterman finally called the stranger's number. *Fanny!* He'd been paired with their younger cousin. Fanny wouldn't extract any information from her dinner partner. In fact, she'd likely remain silent throughout the meal.

Sophie tapped her fan on Jefferson's arm. "We must do something. I want to know who he is."

Jefferson's eyes gleamed from behind his black mask. "I'll help, but you must promise to tell me if you discover his identity."

Sophie clutched his arm. "Oh yes. I promise. Do you have a plan?"

He chuckled and patted her hand. "You'll see. Wait here."

The paired guests had already begun the slow march into the dining room when the stranger suddenly stepped into line beside Sophie. "I hope you won't object to a change in partners."

Sophie didn't know how Jefferson had managed this, but she would be forever in his debt. Throughout the meal she teased and cajoled the masked stranger, all to no avail. When dinner had ended and she'd made no progress, Sophie expressed her dismay. "What must I do to discover who you are?"

He pondered the question for several moments. "Walk with me before the dancing resumes, and perhaps then I will tell you."

She didn't hesitate—not even for a moment. Before Mrs. Oosterman had completed her instructions for the remainder of the evening, Sophie was tugging on the stranger's arm. After she took a possessive hold on his arm, they strolled outside toward the Oostermans' huge pier and boathouse.

Moonlight and starlight commingled to adorn the dark water with bright dancing prisms and beckoned them onward. When they reached the end of the pier, Sophie released his arm. "You've still not even given me a clue." She tightened her lips into a tiny pout to entice him.

He laughed and softly grasped her shoulders. For a moment, she thought he might lean down and kiss her. She hoped he would. Instead, he gently turned her toward the water. "You may turn around when I tell you."

She remained still and looked down at the water, her excitement mounting with each shallow breath.

"You may turn around."

Ever so slowly, she made the half-turn. Shock, anger, frustration—her emotions mounted inside her like a bubbling volcano and then exploded with one unwitting backward step. *"Paul!"*

Paul Medford's name was all that Sophie screamed before falling into the water. The skirt of her golden gown floated up to surround her like a misplaced halo.

CHAPTER 17

Sophie's shrill scream echoed in the stillness.

At Jefferson's insistence, Fanny had walked outdoors following the evening meal. Not that she disliked being away from the hubbub of the mingling guests, but she hadn't particularly desired company. She much preferred being alone with her thoughts. Besides, Jefferson had appeared more interested in following after Sophie than enjoying a stroll through the lighted gardens. And though the possibility of seeing Michael near the Oostermans' boathouse had appealed to her, Fanny knew she'd dare not visit with him in Jefferson's presence.

The two of them raced toward the pier. Fanny's shoes slid on the grassy slope, and a mental picture of her body sprawled on the lawn in some ungainly position with her skirts arranged in an unladylike fashion flashed before her. She grasped Jefferson's arm in a death grip. His objection served no purpose, for she tightened her grip even more.

"What do you think has happened?" she panted. The moon outlined a huddle of men—likely the skippers of the guests' boats. Several appeared to be holding poles.

"Looks like someone's in the water. Let's hope it's not Sophie." The cadence of Jefferson's reply synchronized with their pounding feet.

Fanny was certain her cousin had screamed the name Paul, but she couldn't imagine why. The only Paul any of them knew was Paul Medford, Uncle Quincy's assistant, and he hadn't even been invited to the party. And why would he be? Fanny considered Paul quite nice, but Mrs. Oosterman wouldn't consider someone such as Paul an acceptable addition to her guest list.

One of the launches equipped with a small searchlight aimed a beacon toward the pier, and Fanny gasped at the sight. Two burly men had hauled a drenched and wilted Sophie from the river. Her sopping gown was ruined, her beautifully coiffed hair hung in dripping ringlets, her mask was tipped sideways atop her head, and greenish-brown weeds poked between the topaz stones of her mother's cherished necklace. She continued to clutch her beaded reticule in one hand while she gestured to Fanny with the other.

Fanny gasped in surprise when her cousin's knees buckled under the weight of the gown. Sophie had angled herself forward but lost her balance and tipped in the opposite direction. Without a moment's hesitation, Paul grasped her by the arm and managed to hold her upright. Had he faltered, Sophie would have been underwater for the second time in one evening.

"Don't you touch me!" She slapped Paul's hand from her arm, and both Fanny and Jefferson hurried to her side.

"What's he done to you?" Jefferson asked.

Sophie glared at her cousin. "What does it *look* like, Jefferson?"

Jefferson's jaw sagged. "He pushed you into the river? Why, I . . ." He balled his fists and positioned himself in a fighting stance near the end of the pier.

"Oh, forevermore, Jefferson, do put your arms down. Next they'll be fishing you out of the river," Sophie exclaimed.

"I didn't push her into the river. She accidentally stepped backward and fell in." Paul glowered at Jefferson. "I can't believe you'd think I'd do such a thing."

Michael stepped forward and offered two blankets he'd retrieved from the *DaisyBee*. "Wrap these around her. Do you want me to bring the boat around and take you back to Broadmoor Island?"

Fanny draped one of the blankets around her cousin's shoulders and nodded. "You must get out of these clothes, Sophie."

She pulled the blanket tighter and turned around to thank Fanny but instead her jaw dropped in horror. Word had obviously spread, and a group of guests was hurrying toward the pier. "Hurry! Get me into the boat before they all come down here and see me looking like this." She grabbed Fanny's hand. "Please say you'll come with me."

"Yes, of course." Fanny motioned toward the crowd. "Head them off, Jefferson. Tell them the excitement is over and all is well."

Jefferson headed off to do her bidding. Once Michael had departed to retrieve the launch, Paul approached. "I'm terribly sorry, Sophie. I didn't intend to startle you, and the last thing I wanted was to have you fall in the water." He took a step closer. "You do believe me, don't you?"

Sophie clenched her jaw. "I believe you're a fraud, Paul Medford. What are you doing here, anyway? You say you disdain the ways of the wealthy, yet you mingle with us when you can hide behind a mask. What are you doing here, and how did you obtain an invitation to permit your entry?"

"Your father gave me his and suggested I use it."

"My father? But why?"

"He knew I wouldn't be recognized. He suggested I speak with some of the guests about the possibility of donating to the shelter." Paul shrugged. "I told him it was a bad idea, but he persisted. Eventually I yielded to his request—and here I am."

"Yes, here you are," Sophie said. "And I thought you were someone special."

Fanny poked her cousin in the side. "Sophie!"

Paul smiled. "It's quite all right, Fanny. I know I'm someone special. Perhaps not in your eyes, Sophie, but in God's eyes, I'm extremely special—and so are you." He glanced toward the approaching boat. "I believe that would be your ride."

Michael held out his hand to assist them into the boat and then waved at Paul. "Do you want a ride over to Broadmoor with us?"

"No, but thanks for the offer."

"You shouldn't be offering him a ride," Sophie hissed. "It's his fault I'm soaking wet!"

Michael eased the boat away from the pier and headed out into the water. "I thought you said it was an accident."

After a good deal of prodding, Fanny managed to elicit the truth from her cousin. Though Jefferson hadn't betrayed Sophie's confidence, his explanation of why he needed to change dinner partners had never been fully explained until now. "You truly shouldn't involve others in your deceit, Sophie."

"Well, it's not as though I've tainted him. Jefferson is far more cunning than you can imagine, dear Fanny. He was pleased to act as my accomplice. I still can't believe it was Paul beneath that mask."

Michael steered the boat alongside the pier near the boathouse. "The water is too shallow or I'd take you over to the little pier, where you'd be closer to the house."

"This is fine. I'm going into the boathouse to remove my gown and petticoats. I can wrap the blanket around me. You can take Fanny back to the party. I'll be fine."

"Oh, but I don't want to go back."

Sophie shook her head. "You must. Uncle Jonas will be angry if you don't return," she said and headed to the boathouse.

Fanny's heart pounded an erratic beat. The boat ride would permit her time alone with Michael, but one look at his face was enough to reveal he didn't relish the idea. Nevertheless, she didn't want to anger her uncle.

Careful to keep his distance, Michael set about his duties without a word, pushing the craft away from the pier. Fanny got up and moved to his side.

"You should sit down. If we hit rough water, you might lose your footing. I don't want you to fall."

She folded her arms across the waist of her taffeta gown. "What is wrong with you, Michael? What have I done that you're treating me like a complete stranger? I've been to the boathouse every day this week, and the minute I come near, you mysteriously vanish."

"I don't know what you're talking about. I've been busy all week. Your uncle has assigned me some additional chores. Unlike you, I must work in order to earn my keep and live on Broadmoor Island."

Fanny reeled at his response. What had happened to her friend—the man she believed cared for her, the man she thought she loved. Silence hung between them like a thick early morning fog. She longed for the words that would touch his heart but doubted her ability to melt his frosty demeanor. He stood with his shoulders squared and his jaw taut until they reached the Oostermans' pier.

He stepped out of the boat and then offered his hand. She grasped hold, and when he attempted to withdraw, she refused to turn loose. "Tell me what I've done, Michael. I truly have no idea why you're angry."

He wiped a tear from her cheek with the pad of his thumb. "I'm sorry, Fanny. I don't want to hurt you, but these feelings . . . we can't . . ."

She closed the gap between them. "Please, Michael. You're my best friend. Please don't do this."

"Victoria! Take Fanny back to the house." Uncle Jonas's voice boomed through the evening silence. He took a menacing step toward Michael. "And you!" He pointed his index finger beneath Michael's nose. "Over here. We need to have another talk."

Fanny pulled against her aunt's grasp. She didn't want to go back to the Oosterman party. She wanted to remain and hear what Uncle Jonas said to Michael. Why was he so angry?

"Didn't Jefferson explain what happened? I returned to Broadmoor Island with Sophie—she asked me to ride along with her, but then she insisted I return to the party. Why is Uncle Jonas angry with Michael? He was merely performing his duties."

"Come along, Fanny. You'll only make matters worse if you don't do as your uncle asked."

"You mean commanded," Fanny muttered. She glanced over her shoulder. Uncle Jonas and Michael stood toe to toe. There was little doubt Michael was receiving a stern lecture.

Her aunt ignored the remark. Once they'd reached the decorative stone wall that circled the Oosterman mansion, the older woman slowed her pace. "You'll be pleased to know that Mrs. Oosterman has changed her plans for the unmasking. Rather than waiting until the end of the evening, we played a delightful little game in which we removed our masks. I am so sorry you missed it, but I'm sure Amanda will give you all the details."

Fanny wasn't certain why that information should please her, except that she wouldn't be required to wear a mask for the remainder of the evening. Unlike Sophie, she hadn't cared who was behind the masks.

"I believe your uncle Jonas told me there are a number of gentlemen inquiring about your whereabouts. Is your dance card full?"

Fanny wanted to fib, but she shook her head. "No. There are some empty spaces."

"Let me see." Her aunt stood watch while Fanny opened her lozenge-shaped reticule and retrieved the card. "Oh, dear me!" She clutched a hand to her bodice. "You've hardly any dance partners at all." Victoria turned the card over and slowly wagged her head. "This is very sad."

"It's fine. I don't enjoy dancing."

"You were intentionally avoiding dance partners?"

"I wasn't hiding, but I didn't flirt, either. You know I dislike these parties, Aunt Victoria. I prefer exploring the island or fishing with—" She stopped short of uttering Michael's name and waved toward the mansion. "I don't like all of this."

The older woman patted her lace-gloved hand atop Fanny's arm. "You must adapt, Fanny. I understand you enjoy outdoor activities, but if you are to find the proper man to love and marry, you must attend the functions where you will meet him."

The two continued toward the sweeping veranda. Music drifted through the open ballroom doors. Fanny dared not tell her aunt she'd already located the man she wanted to marry, for neither her aunt nor any other member of the Broadmoor family would consider Michael proper—not for Frances Jane Broadmoor.

Jonas couldn't sleep. When he could take no more of the tossing and turning, he rolled out of bed and shoved his arms into his dressing gown. Though it wasn't yet six o'clock, the sun was already breaking the horizon in a blaze of bright tangerine and gold. He opened the French doors that led from the bedroom and stepped onto the covered balcony. Lapping water and twittering birds were the only sounds that greeted him. Peaceful. Perhaps that's why his parents had loved this place. It provided the peace and quiet that eluded them in the city.

He leaned on the pink granite ledge that surrounded the balcony and knew it wasn't the tranquil setting that had drawn them to this island each summer. Quite the contrary. It had been his mother's incessant desire to create a family circle for Fanny that had been the motivation for the family gatherings at Broadmoor Island. Fanny! Always Fanny. And it had been Fanny who had caused his sleeplessness last night.

Thus far she'd shown no interest in any of the young men he'd brought to the island. Even with the promised incentive of a future of wealth, none of the men had been able to capture her interest. Young men nowadays certainly didn't have the ambition required to succeed. Look at his youngest sons! As far as Jonas was concerned, the two of them lacked enough enthusiasm to perform a decent day's work and enough intelligence to make a sound decision.

His thoughts were interrupted by the sound of a woman's soft lilting laughter, and he stepped along the balcony until he reached the south end. Theresa O'Malley had followed Michael out of the rear of the house. She was fawning over him like a woman in love. Jonas rubbed the dark stubble that lined his jaw and considered the young woman. If he handled the matter properly, perhaps Theresa would prove helpful.

Jonas waited until midafternoon, when few family members and guests remained on the island. His wife had announced plans during the noonday meal to travel to Round Island for the annual picnic hosted at the Frontenac Hotel. Jonas thought the family could find sufficient entertainment on their own island, but Victoria had insisted. And he'd relented, as long as he didn't have to accompany them and endure the mindless conversation of weekend guests visiting the hotel or the endless games of badminton and croquet that had become favorite summer pastimes of his family.

He pushed away from the desk in the mansion's cherry-paneled library and made his way down several hallways to the rear of the house.

Mrs. Atwell looked up from her piecrust and stopped midroll. "Is there something wrong, Mr. Broadmoor?"

Jonas understood the concern he detected in her questioning expression. His visits to the kitchen were rare, and entering Mrs. Atwell's domain naturally gave rise to apprehension. He glanced about the kitchen. Theresa was nowhere in sight. "I thought you might have a pitcher of lemonade." He touched a finger to his throat. "I'm feeling a bit parched."

Mrs. Atwell wiped her hands on her apron. "I can bring a tray to the library or the veranda if you'd like."

"I don't want to interrupt your work. Where's Mrs. O'Malley's daughter? Perhaps she could bring the tray."

"She should return in a few minutes. She was helping her mother press linens, but I don't mind stopping to prepare a cool drink for you."

He waved her back to the worktable. "I wouldn't think of it. Just have Theresa bring it to the veranda when she returns. There's no hurry." He didn't wait for the older woman to object before leaving. He knew his servants well enough to realize Mrs. Atwell would prepare the tray, and if Theresa hadn't returned to the kitchen in short order, Mrs. Atwell would go and find her. He'd made his wishes known; he expected them to be met.

He stopped in the library long enough to retrieve a book from the shelf. He didn't want to read, merely present the appearance of a man relaxing with a book and anxious for a glass of lemonade. He chose a chair near the distant railing, where he could see if anyone approached.

Though he'd already checked his watch three times, only twenty minutes passed before Theresa approached with a pitcher of lemonade, a tall glass, and a small plate of dainty cookies.

She placed the tray on the glass-topped wicker table. "Would you like me to pour your lemonade, Mr. Broadmoor?"

"Yes. Then please sit down," he said, indicating the chair directly beside him. The fact that Theresa's hand shook when she lifted the pitcher didn't surprise Jonas. In varying degrees, he had an unsettling effect upon all of the Broadmoor servants. It was a fact that pleased him. He waited in silence until she poured his drink. He took a sip and nodded his approval.

"Is there something else I can fetch for you, sir?"

"No. However, I was wondering if you would be interested in making a bit of extra money."

She gasped and touched her hand to her heart. "I am not *that* kind of girl, Mr. Broadmoor."

"Of course you're not, Theresa, but I think you're a young lady who would be willing to help me play a trick on someone." He watched her and could see she was weighing the possibilities. "Would you like to hear more?"

She inched forward on her chair. "Yes."

"First, you must promise that our little talk be kept a secret. If you should tell anyone, it could mean that both you and your mother would find yourselves unemployed. Do I make myself clear?"

She gave him a somber nod.

"I want you to devise a plan by which Fanny will see you and Michael sharing an intimate moment—a kiss or embrace, whatever you prefer."

Theresa bent forward and rested her arms across her thighs. "You want Fanny to think Michael and I are in love with each other?"

"Something like that. Are you interested?"

She rubbed her hands together and giggled. "This sounds as though it could prove to be a great deal of fun! And I believe I am just the person to help you—if the price is right."

Jonas frowned. Moments ago, the girl's hand had been shaking while she poured his lemonade, and now she was going to attempt to haggle over her price. She had best not get greedy or he'd have her off the island by nightfall and her mother along with her!

"Why don't you tell me what price you believe is right, Theresa." He waited, pleased when she appeared baffled. Exactly what Jonas had hoped for.

"Fifty cents?" Her voice quivered.

He nodded. The silly girl would have gotten much more had she kept her mouth shut. He'd been prepared to give her a dollar. "We have a bargain. Now, off with you to the kitchen before your mother or Mrs. Atwell comes looking for you. And remember, not a word of this to anyone, Theresa."

CHAPTER 18

MONDAY, AUGUST 2, 1897

Mortimer Fillmore looked old. Had there been a mirror close at hand, Jonas would have checked his own appearance. Mortimer was only a few years older than Jonas, but the man appeared ancient. A light breeze drifted from off the water, and wisps of white hair splayed about the lawyer's head like arthritic fingers. He relied upon a hand-carved walking stick to aid in his climb up the sloping grass embankment from the boathouse. The sight of his decrepit lawyer was enough to make Jonas consider his own mortality.

Mortimer had ascended half the distance to the house when Jonas spotted the man's older son and partner, Vincent, hurrying after his father. He pointed to his arm and the older man leaned heavily upon his son. Jonas doubted whether his own sons would ever show him such compassion or concern.

He stood and waved to the two men. "Welcome! I'm pleased you were willing to come out here and keep me company for an afternoon."

Mortimer's chest heaved, and he gasped for air as he dropped into the wicker settee on the lower veranda. "I need to rest a few minutes." He signaled for his son to sit down while he continued inhaling great gulps of air.

Vincent offered Jonas an apologetic look. "I attempted to convince him he didn't need to come out here. He's been ill this past week. I told him you would understand and that I could relay any information to him later today, but he insisted."

"Quit talking about me as though I'm still in Rochester, Vincent." Mortimer glanced at Jonas. "The doctor says it's my lungs, but what do doctors know? They take my money, but their guess usually isn't any better than my own."

Jonas laughed and agreed, but there was little doubt Mortimer was suffering from some debilitating illness. "I won't ask you to make any further trips to the island until you're feeling better, Mortimer. You need to get well, my friend." He patted the older lawyer's shoulder. "Why don't we go into the library, where you'll be more comfortable, and I'll have one of the servants bring some refreshments. Are you hungry?"

The men followed him into the library. When they'd finished their refreshments and Theresa had cleared away the trays, Jonas closed the doors. "Let me tell you why I've brought you here." Both men came to attention, the younger of the two pulling out a pencil and paper, poised to jot down notes. Jonas appreciated Vincent's attention to detail, but he shook his head. "Don't make notations, Vincent. I don't want this conversation committed to writing."

Vincent immediately returned the paper and pencil to his leather case. "I didn't want to forget anything you might want completed upon our return to Rochester."

"Quite all right, Vincent, but you won't forget today's conversation, for I've brought you here to gain your ideas rather than assign any specific tasks." Jonas leaned back into the thick padding of his leather chair and explained that the family had left for a trip to Brockville.

"Off to spend your money shopping for new gowns and baubles, I suppose," Mortimer said.

"And to visit a few of the familiar sights they used to visit when my mother was alive. She instilled a love of the town in most of them. I didn't object, for I wanted to meet privately with you, and I had promised Victoria I would spend at least one entire week on the island." He chuckled. "She was unhappy with me when she discovered I'd chosen the week they would be in Brockville. I believe she may return early, just because I'm here."

"Women! Who can figure them out?" Mortimer coughed and wheezed, finally taking a drink of water before settling back in his chair. "What kind of ideas do you want to discuss, Jonas?"

"I continue to feel an enormous sense of discomfort concerning my niece's inheritance. I've developed a plan whereby I'll be able to appropriate a portion of her money by simply falsifying paper work to show poor investments. However, it's the bulk of her estate that concerns me. Although I'm attempting to find her a malleable husband who will give me authority over the money, Fanny has been less than cooperative. Thus far she's shown no interest whatsoever in any of the young men I've brought here."

Mortimer offered his son a sideways glance. "Too bad Vincent is married. Otherwise, this could be easily remedied. I'm sure he'd be able to sweep the girl off her feet."

Vincent tugged at his collar and glowered at his father. "No need to discuss *that* idea any further."

"Then let's discuss some ideas of how I can gain control of her funds once she reaches legal age. She's an obstinate girl. There's no way of knowing if I'll convince her to marry." Jonas lifted the lid of his humidor. "Cigar?"

Mortimer reached toward the desk, only to have Vincent grasp his hand. "No cigars, Father."

Jonas removed one of the fat cigars and lovingly passed it beneath his nose. He inhaled the scent and offered an appreciative sigh.

Vincent massaged his forehead. "More important, you need to consider what would happen to all of that money if Fanny should attain legal age and remain unmarried. Who would ultimately receive her estate? Is she intelligent enough to seek legal advice and prepare a will once she's attained the age of majority? Depending upon her social mores, she could elect to bequeath her estate to a church or a charitable group."

Mortimer inched forward in his chair and pointed at Jonas. "That's not so farfetched, considering the fact that Quincy has nearly bankrupted himself with his Home for the Friendless. Fanny might decide to leave her money to such an institution. They tell me this sort of thing runs in families."

Mouth agape, Vincent stared at his father. "Don't be ridiculous, Father. We're talking about bequeathing money to a charity, not some mental disease."

"Nearly the same thing, don't you agree, Jonas?" Mortimer cackled.

"In most cases. Of course there are rare occasions when money to the proper charity can yield great benefit. However, this would not be one of those instances. My brother has squandered far too much of the Broadmoor fortune."

Mortimer rubbed his arthritic hands together. "Let's hope you have more control over that girl than you do over your brother. He's a disgrace, Jonas."

Vincent momentarily buried his face in his hands. "I'm beginning to think you're suffering from a lack of oxygen to your brain, Father. Your insults are uncalled for. What has come over you?"

Mortimer shrugged. "Merely speaking the truth and attempting to help Jonas with a plan. What do you propose?"

Vincent rubbed his forehead again. "It's truly a conundrum. I could prepare a will for her, but she's not of legal age to sign such a document—it wouldn't be binding in the court."

Jonas perked to attention. "But it would show clear intent that Fanny had planned for the estate to come to me, and you or your father could obtain the services of one of those *friendly* judges. That process might lead to an agreeable outcome."

Mortimer frowned. "I suppose it could work, but we'll probably all be dead before the girl—you had best continue working toward arranging a proper marriage partner."

Jonas nodded slowly. "You're absolutely correct, Mortimer."

Mortimer thumped his cane on the floor. "Well, of course I am."

"Please, Father, Jonas and I need to discuss the idea of a will in further detail. If Fanny should predecease you, do you think your brother or other family members would protest the document and attempt to have the document set aside, based upon Fanny's tender years?"

Jonas considered the matter for several minutes. He knew there would be a hue and cry if he were to receive the share allocated to Fanny. Most of the family coveted her money as much as he did. Money had set the relatives against each other for years. Jonas found it rather entertaining. "What if the will provides a clause in which Fanny acknowledges her tender years? It could further state that she fully understands the terms, and it is her desire to name me as her sole heir. Perhaps a judge would then be willing to overrule any protests."

Vincent jumped up from his chair and paced in front of the windows. "Yes, I like that idea. And we could have a clause specifically stating that even though the document has been drawn and signed while in her tender years, she desires for it to remain her final declaration until set aside in writing."

"Yes! I believe we're on to something. How soon could you have the document delivered to me?"

Vincent glanced at his father. Mortimer had nodded off. "I want to be certain nothing is overlooked. Would next weekend suffice?"

"Yes, but have it delivered by a courier. With the family here, another visit might give rise to questions."

"Tell me, Jonas, how will you persuade her to sign the document? If she's as bright as you indicate, won't she insist upon reading the contents?"

"I'll be giving that matter thought. In the interim we need to consider every possible method to have the girl disinherited. Then my father's bequest to her could be easily set aside. Surely we can think of something."

Vincent shook his head. "I don't see how she could possibly be disinherited, Jonas."

Mortimer jerked to attention. "Nothing's impossible where money's involved. Right, Jonas?"

"You are entirely correct, Mortimer."

Theresa descended the stairs, her feet striking each step with a heavy thud. Since reaching her agreement with Jonas Broadmoor, she had done her utmost to capture Michael's interest. She'd been to the boathouse more times than she cared to think about, and she'd attempted to use her feminine wiles on each occasion. Although Michael had answered her questions and was cordial during her visits, he always shied away from her advances.

The previous day she'd even attempted to lure him away from his work under the guise of a fishing expedition. After packing what she considered a delightful picnic lunch and securing her mother's permission to be gone for the afternoon, Theresa had gone to the boathouse filled with anticipation. With Fanny and the other women away for their shopping excursion in Canada, she'd decided the time alone would give her an opportunity to begin her seduction. But Michael had steadfastly refused. His excuses were as numerous as legs on a centipede.

After an hour of cajoling, she'd finally dumped the contents of the picnic basket into the water. Seeing their lunch enter the murky water had been the only thing that had evoked any emotion from the man. He'd been aghast to see the traces of crusty chicken sandwiches floating on the water, but he hadn't even noticed that he'd wounded her feelings. She'd never faced such difficulty luring a man. His constant refusals were taking their toll on her ego. If she was going to succeed with Michael, she needed help—a desperate thought.

Theresa plodded down the hallway toward the kitchen. Her mother would be going over the day's schedule with Mrs. Atwell and would expect to see her. The voices of the two women drifted into the hallway, and Theresa quickened her step. The older women might offer some insight, especially Michael's mother.

Entering the kitchen, she forced a bright smile. "Good morning," she said in her cheeriest voice.

A hint of suspicion immediately shone in her mother's eyes. "Is that *my* daughter? Cheerful so early in the morning?"

Theresa frowned. "I'm usually cheerful in the morning."

Her mother laughed, shook her head, and immediately returned to her discussion with Mrs. Atwell. Theresa quietly listened while the two women prepared a lengthy shopping list for the following week.

Mrs. Atwell ran the tip of her pencil down the list and gave an affirmative nod. "I believe we've thought of everything. I'll give Michael our list and send him to Clayton tomorrow morning."

Theresa stepped closer and reviewed the menus the two ladies had prepared for the following week. "Which one of these meals is Michael's favorite?"

Mrs. Atwell appeared confused. "None of them. Michael prefers the more common fare I've been serving this week while the family's been in Brockville. Thus far, Mr. Jonas hasn't voiced an objection," she said with a grin. "I think Mr. Jonas prefers butter-browned fresh fish and fried potatoes more than the fancy dishes we serve when the missus is in the house."

"And what about dessert? Does Michael prefer your pies or one of your lovely cakes?"

Mrs. Atwell dipped out a cup of flour and sifted it into a crock. "Why all this interest in what Michael enjoys for his meals? Are you planning on assuming my kitchen duties?" She pointed toward the crock. "If so, you can begin by mixing up the dough for this evening's dinner rolls."

Theresa laughed. "I don't think you want me making the rolls, Mrs. Atwell. They'd likely come out of the oven as flat as pancakes."

"Then why the interest in what Michael likes to eat?"

Theresa plunged forward. "Well, don't tell him I said so, but I think your son is most interesting." She pressed her fingers to her dark tresses. "Although most men tell me I'm quite pretty and seemingly enjoy my company, Michael completely ignores me. I don't know what I've done that has caused him to behave in such a standoffish manner."

The older woman brushed the flour from her hands. "Michael's behavior has nothing to do with you or your fine looks, Theresa. Michael has eyes for only one woman. And after all these years, I doubt he'll be tempted by the sway of your hips or a fashionable hairstyle."

Theresa's mother clucked her tongue. "You had better encourage him to keep on looking, Maggie. We both know he's never going to have that one."

Mrs. Atwell finished mixing the dough and plopped it onto the wooden worktable. She plunged her fingers into the heavy dough. "What's a mother to do? He's a grown man, and he knows she's out of his reach, but it doesn't change his feelings."

Theresa turned and exited through the kitchen door leading to the back lawn. Let the two women argue about Michael. They weren't going to offer any help to her predicament. She circled the house, her thoughts a jumble of confusion. If she failed Mr. Broadmoor, he'd likely fire her. Worse yet, he might discharge her mother, too.

"Theresa!"

Mr. Broadmoor stood on the upper veranda with his arms folded across his chest. He pointed toward the ground. "Meet me on the lower veranda."

Theresa sighed. Mr. Broadmoor was going to expect a report on her progress. No doubt he'd find her excuses unacceptable. Perspiration dampened her palms. Theresa swiped her hands down her skirt and prepared to be chastised. She forced a smile as Mr. Broadmoor stepped onto the porch. His white shirt appeared nearly as stiff as the set of his shoulders.

He didn't waste time with idle chitchat. "How are matters progressing between you and Michael?"

She remained standing, though Mr. Broadmoor had settled into one of the cushioned wicker chairs. "Not as smoothly as I had hoped—though it's not from my lack of trying," she hastened to add. The older man remained attentive while she proceeded through the litany of difficulties she'd experienced. She was certain he was unhappy with her. He rubbed his jaw and stared into the distance.

When she could no longer bear the silence, Theresa sat down beside him. "I even spoke to his mother and inquired how I might win his affections."

Jonas arched his brows. "And?"

"Mrs. Atwell said he had eyes for only one woman, and she didn't think I'd be successful."

"Hmm. So even his mother realizes he's smitten with my niece." Jonas studied the vessel slowly moving downriver. The steamer whistled two short blasts, and Captain Visegar waved his hat high in the air. The aging captain conducted fifty-mile cruises through the islands twice a day in his *New Island Wanderer*. Visitors came armed with the captain's brochure that described the different islands, the beautiful mansions, and résumés of the various owners. "I have an idea that Michael won't be able to refuse."

Theresa leaned forward, anxious for details. Her excitement mounted as Mr. Broadmoor described the harbor lights cruise that was conducted every Saturday night. "Perhaps you've heard some of the family or guests mention it?"

"I haven't, but it sounds like great fun. However, I doubt Michael would invite me."

"I'll take care of that. My wife and I will host all of our guests on the tour this Saturday night. I'll purchase tickets for you and Michael. I'll tell him that I mistakenly purchased the incorrect number of tickets and ask that he act as your escort, since this is your first summer on the island and you've not been on the tour."

"What a wonderful plan."

"Indeed. And I'll expect you to make good use of your time on the cruise. Make Fanny believe that Michael is romantically interested in you." He leaned forward in his chair. "May I count on you to do your very best?"

She gave an enthusiastic nod. "Trust me. You won't be disappointed, Mr. Broadmoor."

CHAPTER 19

SATURDAY, AUGUST 7, 1897

Fanny slumped in her chair. "I don't want to be included in the searchlight excursion this evening. I truly cannot believe your father purchased tickets and expects all of us to attend." She rested her chin in her palm. "The entire outing is unlike him. He detests socializing with anyone other than his equals and discourages the rest of us from doing so, too."

Amanda giggled. "With the entire family and all of our guests, he's likely assumed there will be no space for any other passengers."

Sophie wrinkled her nose. "I hope that isn't true. I want to mingle with some other people—we've been with family all week long. I think I'll send Michael to Castle Rest and have him deliver an invitation to Georgie and Sanger Pullman. They're always enjoyable company."

Amanda turned from her dressing table. "You'd best not send out any invitations without Father's approval."

Sophie had already retrieved a piece of writing paper from Amanda's desk and didn't hesitate while dipping her cousin's pen into the bottle of ink. "I'm not sending an invitation. I'm merely telling them we'll be on the steamer and they should join us if they have no other plans for the evening." The minute she'd completed the note, Sophie jumped up from the writing desk.

"I'll go with you. I've a need of fresh air," Fanny said.

Sophie playfully grasped her cousin's arm. "Would you feel the need for fresh air if I wasn't going to search for Michael Atwell?"

Fanny ignored the question. Sophie already knew the answer. Though they invited Amanda to join them, she declined. The two cousins hastened toward the boathouse, their laughter drifting overhead on the warm afternoon breeze. The clatter of their shoes on the wooden dock surrounding the boathouse eliminated any element of surprise. Michael was watching the door when they entered.

He continued to sand one of the small skiffs. "What can I do for you ladies?"

Sophie held out the envelope. "I was hoping you'd have time to deliver this note to Castle Rest within the hour. Is that possible?"

Michael stroked his palm along the black walnut gunwale of the skiff. "So long as Mr. Broadmoor has no objection." He stepped closer and retrieved the envelope.

"If Uncle Jonas should ask, I'll tell him you made the delivery at Sophie's instruction," Fanny replied.

He nodded. "Good day then, ladies." Michael tucked the envelope into his pocket and picked up the sandpaper.

Sophie stared at him when he didn't budge. "When are you going to depart?"

Michael shrugged. "In a half hour or so. It doesn't take long to get to Pullman Island."

She waved toward Michael's pocket. "That's a note asking the Pullman brothers to join us for the spotlight tour of the islands this evening. The sooner it's delivered, the better."

The sandpaper dropped from Michael's hand and fluttered to the floor. "You're going on the cruise, too?"

"What do you mean, *too*? Are you going?" Sophie shot a grin in Fanny's direction. "As much as you're around boats, I wouldn't think you'd be interested in a cruise on someone else's vessel."

Fanny pinched her cousin. If Michael was going to be on the boat, that changed everything. The idea of a late-evening cruise now held appeal, and she didn't want Sophie to influence Michael otherwise.

"He's taking *me* on the cruise, aren't you, Michael?" Theresa sashayed to Michael's side and grasped his arm in a possessive hold.

Fanny wilted at the sight.

Michael wrenched free of Theresa's grasp. "I'll deliver your note immediately."

Theresa hurried behind him. "Oh, may I go with you? I've completed my chores and—"

"No. Against the rules," he curtly replied before jumping into the launch. "Am I to wait for a reply or merely leave this with one of the servants, Miss Sophie?"

She pondered for a moment. "No need to wait for a reply, but ask that it be immediately delivered to either Sanger or Georgie."

Michael touched two fingers to the brim of his cap and saluted. Had Sophie not yanked on her sleeve, Fanny would have remained to watch his departure. Truth be told, she would have waited until he returned. She couldn't believe he had invited Theresa to accompany him on a cruise that was touted as the islands' most romantic tour. Yet he hadn't denied the assertion. And her pride wouldn't permit her to question Theresa.

Fanny plodded back toward the house with Sophie at her side. "Can you believe Michael asked her? I think it was probably the other way around. Theresa purchased the tickets and asked him. Or his mother's forcing him to go as a favor. She and Mrs. O'Malley are friends. I'd wager that's what happened." She tipped her head to the side and arched her brows. "Don't you think, Sophie? I mean Michael absolutely wouldn't have taken it upon himself to do such a thing. I don't believe it—not for a minute!"

Sophie stopped in her tracks. "Do you want me to answer, or have you already sufficiently answered the question for yourself?"

"I'm not certain. I want you to respond but only if you say what I want to hear."

Sophie giggled. "At least you're honest. I think Theresa played a large part in arranging the evening with Michael, but you must remember that Michael is a grown man. He has the ability to say no—and he obviously didn't." She grabbed Fanny's hand and continued up the hill. "You need to make him jealous. Michael needs to see that you can attract other men. Perhaps we should ask Sanger or Georgie to help us with our plan. One of them would be willing to play the part of an amorous admirer. That would be great fun."

"No. I don't want to involve anyone else. The twins would ask questions, and soon everyone would know of my feelings for Michael."

"Then simply act interested in one of those young men in Uncle Jonas's entourage. Problem resolved."

Fanny didn't agree, but she didn't argue with her cousin. Unlike Sophie, she had never learned the finer points of flirting. What's more, she had no desire to cultivate her cousin's womanly wiles.

Fanny's excuses failed. Uncle Jonas had turned a deaf ear to her every attempt. She'd even resorted to going behind his back and seeking her aunt's permission to remain at home, but that too had proved futile. In the end there had been no escape. Along with their weekend guests and other members of the household, Fanny donned her finery and boarded the *DaisyBee* for their ride to Clayton. They were packed into the launch like sardines in a can, with Fanny squeezed between Daniel Irwin and Benjamin Wolgast. Theresa had positioned herself as close to Michael as humanly possible—or so it seemed to Fanny. At least they wouldn't be sandwiched together in close quarters once they boarded the *Wanderer*. Hopefully she could escape Daniel and Benjamin as well as their tiresome anecdotes.

"Which one have you chosen?" Sophie whispered as they disembarked in Clayton.

"Neither," Fanny hissed.

Sophie grabbed her by the hand and pulled her away from the crowd. "If you're going to gain Michael's attention, you must do as I say. I'll be required to sic Georgie or Sanger on you if you don't choose someone and begin to flirt."

"Don't you dare, Sophie!"

Sophie cast a triumphant look over her shoulder. "Then do as I say, Cousin."

Fanny surveyed the men and then noticed that Michael and Theresa had distanced themselves from the Broadmoors and their guests. Obviously they were uncomfortable. She experienced a twinge of pity and then shoved the feeling aside. Michael should have known better. Did he care so much for Theresa that he would subject himself to this awkward and humiliating situation? Perhaps he did. The thought was sobering.

"Come along now. We don't want to detain the captain or the other passengers." Uncle Jonas stood at the edge of the pier while waving them forward.

As predicted, her uncle had assumed there wouldn't be space on the *Wanderer* for anyone other than his guests. He'd been wrong—and he was unhappy. Her uncle had attempted to persuade the captain to send the additional passengers over to ride on the *St. Lawrence*. Citing the fact that angry customers made for bad publicity, the captain hadn't yielded to Uncle Jonas. The captain was bright enough to understand that a rare excursion by Jonas Broadmoor and his family didn't hold enough sway to offset the possibility of a bad reputation among the hordes of vacationers who arrived daily and didn't hesitate to spend their hard-earned cash for an outing on his boat.

Her uncle did his best to arrange their seating in a segregated manner, waving Jefferson, George, and both of the Pullman twins toward the rear of the boat when they attempted to mingle with the tourists. Unexpectedly, he directed Michael and Theresa toward the rear of the boat, also.

With a smug smile, Theresa squeezed onto the seat and forced Fanny closer to Daniel, who immediately assumed she was seeking his attention. When he fumbled for her hand Fanny yanked away and accidentally elbowed Theresa in the ribs. Theresa yelped in pain while Aunt Victoria shook her head and clucked her tongue. "Please don't cause us any embarrassment, Fanny."

Fanny glared at Daniel. "Keep your hands to yourself and there won't be any further problems."

Daniel grinned and casually draped his arm across the back of the seat. "That should give you a little more room." He tipped his head closer and winked. "You need not be coy with me. I can always tell when a lady is captivated by my charm."

"Can you? Then I'm certain you realize I find you a total boor," she whispered before turning her attention to her aunt. "Did you tell Uncle Jonas we visited Mrs. Comstock while we were in Brockville, Aunt Victoria?"

"Thank you for the reminder, Fanny," she said and then addressed Jonas. "Mrs. Comstock mentioned that her husband wants to visit with you in the near future regarding some investments."

Jonas rubbed his hands together. "I'd wager he's concerned about George Fulford infringing on his patent medicine business. Did you invite them to come to the island for a visit?"

Victoria nodded. "I did. She was going to check with her husband, but they may visit in late August if their schedule permits."

The boat continued slowly downriver while the captain pointed out the colored gaslights that lit numerous islands, including their own. When Theresa and Michael moved from their seat toward the rail, Fanny edged away from Daniel. He immediately closed the gap.

"What other news was circulating in Brockville? Was there much talk of the gold strike in the Yukon?"

At the mention of the gold strike, the young men's excitement escalated. Daniel finally shook his head in disgust. "Only a fool would waste his time running off in search of gold. The men return broken and destitute."

"You'd best not make such a comment in front of our father," Sanger told him. "It's Colorado gold that helped him on his way."

Daniel laughed. "You'll not fool me with that story. It was his luxurious railroad cars that made the Pullman money—not gold."

"Sanger's speaking the truth," Georgie said. "Of course not all of those men were as fortunate as our father, but for those who were . . ." His voice trailed off on the breeze. "I'm just glad I don't have to concern myself with making money. There's far too much time and energy involved in the process, and I wouldn't want to rob my father of the pleasure. Besides, I much prefer the spending process, don't you, Sanger?"

Fanny noted Michael's obvious interest as he leaned forward to listen to the conversation. Gold—and lots of it, one of the fellows reported. Ready for any man willing to head north. Fanny experienced a sense of satisfaction when Theresa's attempt to lure Michael into a conversation failed. Like the rest of the men, he was far more interested in the Yukon gold than the colorful island lights or the moonlight dancing on the water.

Fanny yanked the thick-bristled brush through her unmanageable curls. "Did you see how Theresa behaved this evening? She draped herself across Michael like a wool shawl on a cold night!"

Amanda giggled. "I do think that's an exaggeration, dear girl. And I don't believe I saw Michael object to her attentions."

Sophie slipped into her nainsook nightgown and tied the pale blue ribbons. "I'm not so sure. He attempted to withdraw from her several times, but she followed after him like a puppy dog longing for affection. Do you think she loves him?"

"How could she love him? She barely knows him," Fanny protested.

"No need to take your anger out on me," Sophie said.

Amanda unpinned her hair and let it fall around her shoulders. "I thought you had released all your anger when you poked Theresa in the side. I heard her complaining to Michael when we returned home. He had to nearly lift her off the *DaisyBee.*"

Fanny slapped the hairbrush onto her dressing table. "Oh, pshaw! She wasn't hurt in the least. Can't you see that she's nothing more than a flirt and a fraud? She wasn't injured, and she doesn't truly care for Michael. He's simply a diversion, another conquest."

"Sounds as though you're describing Sophie," Amanda said with a grin.

Sophie tapped her finger to her chin. "Hmm. I suppose it does." She immediately brightened. "If she's truly like me, then she doesn't care about Michael and you need not worry yourself, Fanny. I think you should confront Michael and ask him if he has feelings for Theresa. The two of you have been friends for years. If he's half the man you profess, he shouldn't object to giving you an honest answer."

Amanda immediately warned against Sophie's suggestion. Such a confrontation would be foolhardy, she advised. So by the time Fanny departed for her own bedroom, her thoughts were a jumble and she'd arrived at only one conclusion: she wanted Michael for herself.

Fanny's sleep was fraught with dreams of Theresa and Michael. Theresa in a beautiful wedding gown while Mrs. Atwell held a wedding cake high in the air for inspection; Theresa's name inscribed on the cake in large black letters; a happy Michael retrieving a wedding ring from his pocket to show her and then turning to place it on Theresa's finger. At the sound of wedding bells, Fanny awakened with a start. Her forehead was damp with perspiration, and the ringing bell that had awakened her was a boat on the river. The wedding had been a dream—or a nightmare.

Fanny's decision was clear when she descended the stairs. The rest of the family hadn't yet come down for breakfast. Michael would be at the boat-house, and Theresa would be helping with breakfast preparations. Fanny and Michael could talk without fear of interruption—if he didn't find another excuse to avoid her.

The river cooled the August breeze, and Fanny longed to be out in the skiff fishing with Michael. He'd refused her every request, citing his increased duties, yet he seemed to have time for Theresa. Her decisiveness waned as she opened the boathouse door. What if he said he loved Theresa? What would she do?

Michael turned as she opened the door. Surprise shone in his eyes, but he didn't move. She hurried toward him, anxious to close the distance that sepa-rated them. "We need to talk, Michael." He glanced over his shoulder toward the rear exit, and she touched his arm. "Please don't make excuses and run off. I thought you cared for me, that you were my friend. Yet every time I come near, you flee. What have I done?" When he didn't answer, she forced herself to ask the question that burned in her heart. "Is it Theresa? Do you love her?"

"What?" He grasped her shoulders and looked into her eyes. "How could you ever think such a thing? I love you!" He shook his head. "Forgive me. I shouldn't have said that."

She touched her palm to his cheek. "I love you, too. If it is true, why should your words remain unspoken?"

"Because it only deepens my pain. We live in different worlds, Fanny. You know that as well as I do. Your uncle will never grant me permission to marry you."

"And that's why you've been avoiding me?"

He nodded toward the door. "Let's take a walk."

Together they strolled up the slope and then turned and walked toward a wooded area offering a magnificent view of the river. Her heart had soared at Michael's declaration of love. Surely they could devise some reasonable method and overcome her uncle's objections.

Michael held her hand while she sat down on one of the outcroppings that overlooked the river. He dropped down beside her and stared across the water. "Life seems so simple when we're out here alone, doesn't it?"

"But it can be, Michael. Once I'm of legal age, Uncle Jonas can't prohibit our marriage. We need only wait until then."

"You underestimate his power. He knows we care for each other—why do you think he's been forcing me to spend time with Theresa?"

Her jaw went slack. "So that's why you've been unwilling to go fishing or spend time with me. And all along I thought—"

"That you'd done something to anger me?" He shook his head. "You've done nothing. But your uncle insists I mustn't spend time with you. I'm required to follow his orders, Fanny. If I disobey his wishes, it could be disastrous—not only for me, but for my parents, also. I've been praying for a solution, but I'm not certain whether what has recently come to mind is actually God's answer or if I'm grasping at straws." A branch crackled and Michael jumped to his feet.

Fanny giggled and pointed to a squirrel that skittered toward them and up a nearby tree. "It's only a squirrel."

"We had better return. You'll be missed if you don't appear at the breakfast table."

He grasped her hand firmly and tugged her to her feet. Her heel caught in the hem of her skirt, and she lurched forward against Michael's chest. He gathered her in his arms and held her close. She gazed up into his eyes. He lowered his head and their lips lightly touched.

Thick grass muffled the sound of approaching footsteps.

"What is the meaning of this!" Her uncle's words reverberated through the early morning calm like a roaring clap of thunder.

CHAPTER 20

"I object!"

"*You* object? You have no voice in this matter." Jonas paced the library. Only hours ago he'd caught his niece in the arms of a servant. "I am your legal guardian. You will sit down and listen." Jonas turned and glared at Michael. "I thought I had made myself perfectly clear. This situation that you've created must come to a halt." He clenched his jaw. "Must I discharge your entire family in order to make you believe that I will not tolerate your behavior?"

"That's not fair, Uncle Jonas," Fanny challenged. "They've done nothing wrong. Are you so cruel that you would make others pay for something they didn't have any say in?"

"I told you to listen," Jonas said, glaring at his niece. "Unless you want to find yourself relieved of any future freedoms, I would suggest you obey me."

"Please. I beg you," Michael appealed. "My parents would be devastated if they were forced off the island. This is their home—and mine, too. They would be heartbroken."

"If you're truly concerned about your parents, why have you continued to disregard my orders?" Jonas drummed his fingers on his desk. "Well?"

"I've made every attempt, sir. What you saw this morning was innocent.

Fanny tripped and I caught her in my arms." He wiped his palm across his forehead. "The kiss and the words of endearment weren't planned. And I did tell her we could never entertain thoughts of a future together."

"You tell her you can't have a future together and then you kiss her? What does that ungentlemanly behavior tell her—or me, for that matter?"

"What I wanted her to know is that I truly love her, but you do not consider me a possible suitor or marriage partner."

Jonas chortled. "And do you consider yourself worthy of my niece, Michael?"

He shook his head. "Even if I had as much wealth as you, I would not consider myself worthy of someone so sweet and kind."

"Oh, do stop with your gibberish. Love isn't what's important. Social standing and wealth must always be the first consideration when choosing a husband for any of the Broadmoor girls." Jonas tucked his thumb into the pocket of his vest. "With the money that Fanny will inherit, I feel an even greater responsibility to protect her future with the proper man."

"And am I have to have no say on this subject?" Fanny asked.

Jonas saw the fire in her eyes. He thought to answer angrily but calmed himself and drew a couple of deep breaths. He needed to find a way to win Fanny's cooperation—or at least her understanding.

"Fanny, long ago your father told me that he only wanted the very best for you. He felt you deserved to be well cared for and provided for. You were the reason he gave up his own home and moved in with our parents. You were the most important person in his life, and he wanted you safe."

"I believe he also wanted me loved," Fanny protested.

"Absolutely. And who better to love you than family. He always told me that if anything happened to him, he would want me to step in and be a father to you. Of course when he did pass on, your grandmother wanted to direct your schooling and such. I decided not to protest because it helped her through her grief over losing your father. Now there is no one else to challenge—now I can fulfill my promise to your father."

"If you care about me," Fanny said, meeting his gaze, "you'll understand that I love Michael. It doesn't matter to me that he's not rich."

"But in time it will, Fanny. In time you will resent that he cannot provide for you in this manner and style."

"If I were wealthy, would you consider me a proper choice for Fanny?"

Jonas leaned back in his chair and studied Michael. The boy had courage and didn't easily back down. He was a hard worker and a talented boatswain. But a suitable match for a Broadmoor? He knew his answer would hold little sway, since Michael would never accumulate any wealth.

"I would give you consideration," he said.

"No. I would like your word as a gentleman that if I become wealthy, you will grant me permission to marry Fanny."

Jonas frowned. "How do you propose to make this money? If you have no plan, I see no reason to continue this discussion."

"The Yukon."

"The Yukon?" Fanny questioned, her eyes wide in surprise.

"You want to go off in search of gold?" Jonas asked doubtfully. "It takes money to purchase the necessities to enter into such a venture."

"I have money saved that I'm willing to use."

Jonas could see the young man's excitement mounting as he continued to talk about his plan to travel north. Though the idea hadn't previously occurred to him, having Michael leave for the Yukon would be ideal. With him out of the way, Fanny would soon be more easily managed. And once Michael was in the Yukon, who could say if they'd ever see him again. After all, his nephew Dorian had taken off for Canada three years ago, and other than one letter shortly after his departure, they'd heard nothing from him.

If and when Michael returned to the Thousand Islands, Fanny would be married to a man of Jonas's choosing, and her money would be controlled by her uncle. Indeed, Michael's idea of a trek into the Yukon held promise. Jonas furrowed his brow, as though contemplating the matter. He didn't want to appear overly excited by the proposal. "Have you discussed this with your parents? I'm certain they'd object to your plan. Your father has come to rely on you a great deal."

"My parents would point out the possible pitfalls of such a decision, but they wouldn't stop me from doing what I believe is an answer to prayer."

"Prayer? You think God wants you to go into the goldfields, Michael?" Jonas chuckled.

"I prayed for you to grant me permission to marry Fanny. You've done that."

Jonas held up his hand. "Not exactly. Here is my agreement. You go to the Yukon and search for gold. I will even agree to loan you enough money to purchase the necessary supplies for your venture. However, Fanny must agree to accept the invitations of other gentlemen during your absence. She is young and has experienced very little of life. She believes she loves you, but she is very young. I don't want her to make a mistake."

"But I don't want to see other men. I'm willing to wait until Michael returns," Fanny argued. "I know I won't change my mind."

Jonas tented his fingers beneath his chin. "You are too young to know anything with certainty. If you won't agree to my terms . . ."

"Please, Fanny. It's the only way," Michael whispered.

She searched his face, a slight frown wrinkling her brow. "If you're truly certain you want me to agree."

He nodded.

"I'll agree." She fingered the pearl button at her neckline. "But the invitations you accept on my behalf shall not outnumber those you accept for Amanda." She settled back in her chair. "I believe that's a fair agreement."

Jonas slapped his hands on the desk. "I'm setting the terms of the agreement—not you. Amanda's future is not under discussion."

"Perhaps not, but won't it appear strange and hurtful if I'm living in your home and you are more involved in my future than that of your own daughter?" She leaned forward as if to press home her point.

Though he was loath to admit it, Fanny was likely correct. Victoria had already expressed her displeasure over arranged marriages. If he was going to maintain control of Fanny's future, he must show the same care regarding his own daughter. Otherwise, there would be far too many of Victoria's incessant questions and bothersome discussions.

"Since Amanda is older than you, I'm certain you won't be surprised to hear that I am planning a full social calendar when the family returns to Rochester." He folded his hands across his midsection. Fanny may have thought she'd outwitted him, but he'd bargained with some of the most powerful men in the country. This girl had no idea what lay in store for her.

Michael edged forward on his chair. "If there's nothing further, Mr. Broadmoor, I believe we have reached a final agreement."

"One more thing, Michael. I don't know when you plan to depart for the Yukon, but the clandestine meetings at the boathouse and out in the woods must cease immediately. I don't want Fanny's reputation ruined."

"Nor do I, Mr. Broadmoor. I can assure you that I would never take advantage of—"

Jonas waved his hand. "I, too, was a young man, Michael. Most young men intend to conduct themselves in an honorable manner with young ladies, but—well, we need not say any more regarding this topic, especially when a woman is present in the room."

Anger clouded Fanny's eyes. "You are insinuating that we . . . that Michael and I . . . that . . ."

"Exactly. You say you are in love and have asked that I believe you. I know passions run deep when young people are in love. Consequently, I must insist the two of you adhere to my decision."

Michael's agreement was enough to please Jonas. With a final admonition for them to heed his restrictions, he dismissed them.

Fanny tugged on Michael's sleeve once they stepped outside. "We need to talk." She pointed to the far end of the veranda.

"You heard your uncle. We're not supposed to be alone. Do you want him to withdraw his agreement so soon, Fanny?"

"We are standing in full view of anyone who might pass by the open windows or walk outdoors. I hardly see how he could object." Fanny ignored his protest. Keeping an ear attuned for the sound of his footfalls, she strolled toward the cluster of wicker chairs.

She nodded toward one of the chairs, but Michael remained standing. "Please, Fanny."

"I do wish you would have mentioned your thoughts about the Yukon to me prior to striking an agreement with Uncle Jonas." When she reached for his hand, he took a backward step. "I don't believe that your going off in search of gold is the answer to our dilemma. And who can even guess the dangers you'll encounter or how long you'll be gone."

He squatted down and leaned against the stone rail that circled the porch. "We'll have to trust God to keep me safe. I truly believe this is our answer. I'll write to you every chance I get."

Fanny's gaze settled on his scuffed work boots. "We both know letters will be scarce. And what about the mail service in a place such as the Yukon?"

"In the end, I believe our gain will be worth the sacrifice. Not the money, but the fact that I will have received your uncle's blessing. I don't want to come between you and your family or make any decisions that either of us will later regret." Michael bowed his head until he looked into her eyes. "I do love you, so don't you fall in love with one of those dandies that come knocking on your uncle's door."

She attempted a smile, but a tear trickled down her cheek. "I don't want to spend time with any man but you. How soon will you plan to leave?"

"Please don't cry." He wiped away her tear with his thumb. "I should head out as soon as possible. If arrangements can be made, probably within a week."

She gasped. "So soon? I thought you would at least wait until the family departed at the end of summer."

He shook his head. "The sooner I leave, the sooner I'll return. My father can look after the boats and pick up supplies in Clayton for the few remaining weeks your family will be here. And if I can't spend time with you on the island, there's no need for me to stick around, is there?"

She didn't want to offer an affirmative answer, for she had already contrived a plan to have Sophie help her arrange secret meetings with Michael. Yet she wondered if he would agree. He seemed determined to abide by his agreement with her uncle.

"You would never leave without telling me good-bye, would you?" She met his gaze and saw the love in his eyes. He didn't need to say a word. His answer was as clear as the blue sky overhead.

"Fanny!" Her uncle stood in the doorway, his face as red as the tip on his cigar.

With a fleeting good-bye to Michael, she hastened toward the front entrance. Let him bluster—they hadn't broken their agreement. "You shouldn't be smoking that smelly cigar, Uncle. I doubt that it's good for your health."

"What's bad for my health is a niece who doesn't do as she's told." He stubbed out the cigar and followed her into the house. "Breakfast is waiting. You'll be delighted to hear my announcement."

She doubted that she'd be delighted. Her uncle sounded far too pleased with himself. Most of the family and their guests had already gathered around the breakfast table by the time Uncle Jonas took his place at the head of the table. They'd hardly begun their fruit compote when he signaled and asked for quiet.

"I've an announcement that I believe you'll all find most pleasant." All eyes turned in his direction. "The Thousand Island Club will be hosting the annual polo matches in two weeks. And I know that you ladies will be anxious to show off your latest fashions. I have made arrangements for all of us to attend."

Aunt Victoria frowned. The weekend of the polo matches had always been a weekend free of guests. "It's difficult managing during that weekend, Jonas. There are so many activities, and we must be coming and going at different times. I truly don't know . . ."

He glanced around the table with a look of expectancy. "Our guests won't expect you to look after their every need. We have a houseful of servants who can assist them if you're busy, my dear."

Sophie forked a piece of melon. "I agree with Uncle Jonas. The more the merrier. I'm sure these fellows can find their way to the kitchen or ring for a servant if need be."

The young men nodded their heads and murmured their agreement. "Very kind of you to include us, Mr. Broadmoor," Daniel said. "I look forward to additional time with your family." He glanced across the table at Fanny and winked.

She curled her lip and turned away. What a rude man! Did he believe she would think his bold behavior endearing?

"May I request your permission to escort Fanny to the polo matches and ball, Mr. Broadmoor?" Daniel inquired.

Fanny smiled demurely. "I'm sorry, but I've already accepted another invitation, Daniel."

Her uncle glowered. "Without my permission? I think not."

"You object to Sanger Pullman?" She tipped her head to the side and waited for his response.

Sophie giggled. "I'm sure Mr. Pullman wouldn't be pleased to hear that you find one of his sons an unacceptable suitor."

"I never said any such thing, Sophie, and don't you consider repeating such a comment. I was merely surprised by Fanny's announcement. Naturally, I have no objection. However, in the future, I would appreciate it if you would speak to me *before* making any arrangements, Fanny."

Fanny politely agreed. She didn't participate in the remainder of the breakfast conversation, for her thoughts were awhirl. Plans had to be made and expedited as soon as possible. She signaled for Sophie and Amanda to meet her outside the minute they'd finished breakfast. Fanny led her cousins across the front lawn to a spot that afforded a clear view of anyone who might approach.

"Sit down over here by this tree." Fanny glanced over her shoulder to make certain none of the young men had followed. "I am in dire need of your help."

Sophie straightened the delicate edging on the sleeve of her dress. "There's no doubt about that!"

Fanny ignored the remark and hastily explained Michael was departing for the Yukon and that he'd made an agreement with Amanda's father. "Please promise you'll not tell anyone about this. Not even your mother, Amanda."

"I promise, but I find all of this most unsettling. I don't understand why my father believes he must be so involved with your future. I understand he's your legal guardian, but he's taking those duties more to heart than parenting his own children."

"No need to become so dramatic, Amanda. You should be thankful it's Fanny he wants to control. Remember, you're the one who keeps telling us you're intent upon discovering your true calling in life rather than merely finding a man and exchanging marriage vows."

"I never meant that I didn't want to wed some day, and Father should care about the plans for my future, too."

Sophie snapped open her fan with a flick of her wrist. "Oh, do enjoy your freedom, you silly goose."

The men had been gathered on the porch but were now strolling toward them. Fanny grasped Sophie's hand. "I need you to speak with Sanger about the polo matches and the ball. Ask him if he'll act as my escort."

Sophie chortled. "You treacherous girl! I wondered when Sanger had invited you."

"You mean—" Amanda gasped.

"That's exactly what she means, Amanda." Sophie snapped her fan together. "I truly didn't think you had a devious bone in your body, Fanny, but it appears that Uncle Jonas's desire to control your life has turned you from the straight and narrow."

Fanny ignored the remark. "Will you help me?"

"Of course I will. I'll have Michael deliver a note this very morning."

Amanda tied a ribbon around her hair and walked to the window. "Here comes Sophie, and she has an envelope in her hand. Do you think she's already received word back from Sanger?"

Fanny joined her cousin near the window. "Let's hope so. This has been a most worrisome day. If your father discovers my misdeed, he'll force me to accept Daniel's offer. And that's an invitation I find most distasteful."

Waving the envelope overhead, Sophie rushed into the room and dropped onto the side of the bed. "Bad news, I fear."

Fanny stepped forward. "What do you mean?"

"Martha Benson has already accepted Sanger's invitation to the polo matches and dance."

CHAPTER 21

SATURDAY, AUGUST 14, 1897

Amanda and Sophie stood on the veranda and watched as the *Little Mac* docked and two men disembarked and trudged up the path toward the house. Sophie shaded her eyes. With a scowl, she turned away and folded her arms across her waist. "Oh, forevermore! I do wish Father wouldn't bring Paul with him every time he makes an appearance on the island."

"Paul seems very nice, except when his surprises cause you to fall into the river." Amanda giggled.

"I don't find your comment humorous. And if you think he's so nice, you may entertain him during his visit. I grow weary of his chiding comments." Sophie ran down the path and greeted her father with a kiss on the cheek.

Except for a curt greeting, Sophie appeared to ignore Paul until they arrived at the veranda. With a mischievous grin, she pulled Amanda forward and then turned her attention to Paul. "Amanda tells me she would like to visit with you about her interest in charity work. If you're very nice, I'm certain she'd be glad to offer you a glass of lemonade, wouldn't you, Amanda?"

Amanda glared at her cousin. She didn't want to participate in this silly charade, but she wouldn't be rude or embarrass Paul. "Yes, of course. I'd be delighted to fetch a pitcher of lemonade."

Paul hurried behind her and opened the door. "May I help?"

"You young people shouldn't be interested in spending your day indoors. It's much too pretty a day," her mother said as she walked down the front stairway. Light spilled through the door and Victoria squinted. "Ah, Paul. I didn't realize you were here. May I assume Quincy has finally arrived?"

"Yes, Mrs. Broadmoor. We were detained in Rochester. Problems arose that needed immediate attention."

Mrs. Broadmoor instructed one of the servants to bring lemonade to the veranda as she grasped Paul's arm. "Do come outdoors and tell us all about what's been happening." With a quick look around the porch, she turned to Paul. "And where is Quincy? Has he gone off in search of Jonas? I'd think he would want to spend some time visiting with Sophie."

"He spoke with Sophie upon our arrival, but I believe she hurried off to play croquet with some of the gentlemen who are visiting." Paul's gaze drifted toward the sounds of boisterous laughter beyond the house. "Mr. Broadmoor had a matter of great import to discuss with your husband."

"Regarding your delayed arrival? We expected Quincy to arrive Friday evening and here it is Saturday afternoon." Mrs. Broadmoor motioned the approaching servant to place the lemonade on a nearby table. "Why don't you pour us each a glass, Amanda?"

"I know he disliked the delay, Mrs. Broadmoor. There was a fire in a tenement building that left many with nothing but the clothes on their backs. A number came to us seeking food and shelter. We couldn't turn them away in their hour of need." Paul shook his head. "We don't have adequate space for them all, but they have nowhere to go. Some of the churches are collecting clothes and donating what they can to help defray our additional expenses, but the budget of the Home for the Friendless is already stretched beyond its limits."

Victoria wiped the beads of condensation from her lemonade glass with a linen napkin. "Dear me, this is unfortunate. The timing couldn't be worse, what with so many of us out of the city for the summer."

"Financial donations have been limited for that very reason. We have willing hands, but we need funds with which to purchase food and help these people reestablish a place to live."

"No doubt you are in dire need of the organizational skills of the Ladies' League. I do wish I could offer assistance, but we won't be returning to Rochester until early September." Victoria set her glass on the table. "That's not so far off. Could you make do until then?"

"What about me, Mother?" Amanda chimed in. "I could return with Uncle Quincy and help. You know I desire to devote my energies to charitable work. This would permit me a grand opportunity to test my skills."

"Oh dear, Amanda. Neither your father nor I would agree to such an idea. I am surprised you would even suggest such an arrangement."

"There are servants at the house. I wouldn't be alone. Perhaps some of those homeless people could come and stay at Broadmoor Mansion or at our house until they . . ."

Victoria paled and shook her head. "*That* is not even a possibility. While we are called to help the less fortunate, sound and rational judgment is necessary. The fact that you would even make such a foolhardy suggestion demonstrates your inexperience."

Amanda frowned. "If we have an empty house, servants, and food, why is my suggestion inappropriate?"

"I greatly appreciate your offer to help," Paul interjected, "but I must agree with your mother. Though I commend your charitable spirit, an unescorted return to Rochester would be highly inappropriate."

Amanda rested her arm on the chair. "I can't go into the mission field unless I am married, and I am in need of an escort if I'm to be of assistance in the city. How am I ever to fulfill my desire to make a difference in the world?"

"Forgive me for being so bold, but I am surprised you're not making marriage plans, Miss Broadmoor. I'm certain you have no lack of eligible suitors."

Amanda tapped her fan in her palm. "I do plan to wed and have children one day. But before that time arrives, I want to explore other possibilities. It would appear, however, that society will not permit me to do so without my good name being ruined."

Paul laughed. "I believe you can discover a way to help others while still meeting the proper rules of society. I'm certain the Ladies' League would be pleased to add your name to their membership roster and assign you a myriad of duties upon your return to Rochester."

Victoria took a sip of her lemonade. "But that is neither here nor there at this moment. I'm curious about Quincy's discussion with my husband. If it is financial aid he is seeking, I doubt Quincy will meet with much success."

"I have prayed your husband will look upon the plight of these people with sympathy and be anxious to share his resources," Paul said.

"You obviously have much to learn about my father, Paul." Amanda pointed her fan at Sophie and the group of young men. "Shall we join the others in their croquet game?"

He had gained Mr. Broadmoor's permission to bid Fanny good-bye, yet Michael knew his time with her would be brief. Along with Paul Medford and Messrs. Jonas and Quincy Broadmoor, Michael would board the Monday morning train to Rochester. Following his employer's instructions, Michael arrived on the veranda at precisely six-thirty. Mrs. Broadmoor escorted Fanny outdoors to meet him for their final farewell.

The older woman bade him good morning and then strolled to the far end of the veranda, where she could keep watch over them. Michael had hoped for a few minutes alone, but Mr. Broadmoor obviously wanted to ensure the opposite.

Fanny grasped his rough hands between her own. "I wasn't told until last evening that you were leaving this morning. I've been awake all night."

Dark circles rimmed her deep brown eyes. Her sorrow reflected his own, though he forced himself to smile. "I slept little myself. Please don't be sad, Fanny. I know this is what I am supposed to do. Your uncle's agreement to loan me the money for my necessary supplies is truly a blessing. If all goes well, I'll still have time to get to the Yukon before winter sets in. Then I can work all winter and spring and return before summer's end next year. You'll have had little time to miss me."

"I already miss you, Michael. I've missed you since the moment you made your decision to leave." She squeezed his hand. "You must remember that even though my uncle will force me to accept these silly invitations and attend social functions, my heart and my thoughts are only for you."

"And mine are only for you and our future together. You'll write to me once I've sent word, won't you?"

"You know I will."

Her lips quivered, and pushing aside all thoughts of propriety, he pulled her into an embrace. "Please don't be sad, my love. One day soon we'll be able to build a wonderful future together. I promise you."

She tipped her head back and looked into his eyes. "And if you don't strike gold? What then, Michael? Will you give me your word you won't let that stand in the way of our future together? I must know that when you return, we will be married—even if it requires disobeying my uncle's wishes."

He looked up and saw Mrs. Broadmoor's disapproving signal. He released his hold and nodded. "You have my word. Rich or poor, upon my return we will be married if you haven't changed your mind."

"I won't change my mind, Michael. I would marry you this minute if only my uncle would agree. By the time you return, I shall be old enough to marry without his permission."

A loose strand of hair flew into her eyes in the early morning breeze, and Michael's heart ached with the thought of leaving her behind. Now that they had declared their love for each other, it seemed unfair to be parted, yet this was the only way. "You must keep me constantly in your prayers, dear Fanny, and I will do the same." Before Mrs. Broadmoor could object, he pulled her into his arms and softly kissed her lips. "I love you with all my heart, and I shall return to you at the earliest opportunity."

Mrs. Broadmoor's heels clicked on the veranda as she hurried toward them. "Michael! Your behavior is completely inappropriate." She grasped Fanny's arm. "As is yours, young lady. What would your uncle say if he walked out here and saw the two of you embracing?" She creased her forehead in an angry frown. "He would be outraged. And not merely at the two of you. I would receive my comeuppance for failing to chaperone properly."

"Don't be overly harsh, Aunt Victoria. Surely you can understand our feelings. You were young and in love at one time, weren't you?"

With a faraway look, she said, "I was once young, Fanny. Now come along. I hear your uncle. We'll walk down to the dock and you may wave good-bye."

Jonas rubbed his forehead and contemplated the happenings of the last few days. None of it good. He'd angered Quincy with a refusal to assist the latest batch of homeless victims with a monetary contribution. After returning to Rochester, he had lined Michael's pockets with sufficient funds for his travel and supplies. He had bade him farewell and offered hollow wishes for success. Until last evening, Jonas suspected the young man couldn't possibly meet with success. Now he wasn't so certain.

After spending several hours at his gentlemen's club and hearing reports of the vast amount of gold already brought out of the Yukon, his concerns had begun to mount. Like many others, Jonas had read newspaper accounts and listened to what he considered exaggerated stories, but now those reports had been verified. At an early morning meeting with his banker, William Snodgrass, Jonas had heard more of the same: *"Biggest strike ever to be discovered—gold just lying around for the taking."*

He thought he'd sent Michael off on a fool's errand, but now it seemed he was the one who would be made the fool. In all likelihood the young man would return in short order with a burgeoning bank account and firm plans to wed Fanny. Although Vincent Fillmore had delivered the will, Jonas had not yet developed a plan to secure Fanny's signature. He massaged his temples as the pain behind his eyes continued to mount. Never before had he experienced such difficulty in formulating a plan. And never before had the stakes been so high. There was little doubt Fanny would continue to balk at any talk of marriage. Disinheritance seemed the only avenue he'd not thoroughly explored.

Jonas removed a sheet of paper from his desk drawer and wrote Fanny's name and birth date across the top of the page. Along with her parents' names, he listed every detail of her life—at least all of those he could recall. None of it was of any assistance. He shoved the paper into his desk and removed a packet of headache powders.

Without a defined plan to secure Fanny's fortune, returning to the island and a weekend of polo matches, balls, and firework displays caused the unbearable throbbing in his head to worsen. He poured a glass of water. He would think of something—he always did.

CHAPTER 22

SATURDAY, AUGUST 21, 1897
BROADMOOR ISLAND

Mr. Atwell stood on the pier and welcomed the family members and guests as they stepped aboard the *DaisyBee*. Daniel had attempted to position himself near Fanny, but she had immediately surrounded herself with Louisa's children. The sight of the baby in her arms had obviously been enough to stave off his advances, for he'd stepped to the other side of the launch. She'd not yet decided how she would keep him at bay once they arrived at their destination. There was little doubt her uncle would be keeping a close watch on her. Once he discovered Sanger in the company of another woman, she would likely be expected to answer difficult questions.

"Any ideas yet?" Sophie inched forward and whispered into Fanny's ear.

She shook her head. "No, but I'm certain something will come to me once we arrive."

Sophie giggled. "If it doesn't, you can be sure Daniel will step in to act as your escort. He's been watching your every move even more closely than Uncle Jonas has."

Their approach to Wellesley Island was slowed by the numerous vessels arriving for the day's festivities, but once they docked and disembarked, Sophie grasped Fanny's hand. "Come along and stay close to me. I spotted Sanger and Georgie. I'll see if we can join them. That way, Uncle Jonas may not notice you're actually unaccompanied." She glanced over her shoulder and motioned to Amanda, who hastened to come alongside them. "Has your father paired you with a beau for the day?"

"In his concern over Fanny's escort, he didn't worry over me," Amanda told them. "Several of those fellows he brings with him each weekend asked to accompany me, but I declined. For the life of me, I cannot understand why it is considered such a necessity to have an escort to all social functions."

"Because we're supposed to be looking for a husband." Sophie chuckled. "Just look at the three of us. I'm having far too much fun to settle upon one man; Fanny doesn't want anyone but Michael; and you, dear Amanda, would rather care for the needy than find the proper husband. We certainly don't fit into the mold of proper young ladies."

Sophie waved and called out to Sanger and Georgie.

"Sophie! That's most unladylike," Amanda chided.

"I care little, so long as I gain Sanger's attention. If we stay close to the Pullmans throughout the afternoon, your father won't realize Fanny is without an escort. At least that's my hope."

The ladies paraded across the grounds, anxious to flaunt their fashionable gowns and parasols. Though the gowns they would wear to this evening's ball would be more elaborate, wearing lovely dresses, hats, and parasols to the polo matches had become a ritual not to be outdone by any other. While the men admired the horseflesh that had been transported to the island by barges earlier in the day, the women assessed the gowns worn by their social counterparts.

When the first half of the match ended, the spectators flooded onto the field in a sea of dark suits and beautifully colored gowns and parasols for the stomping of the divots, which was the only enjoyable portion of the polo match as far as Fanny and her cousins were concerned. In her venture onto the field, Fanny didn't consider Sanger's whereabouts. She had stomped several clumps of dirt into the ground when she suddenly came face-to-face with her uncle.

He grasped her elbow and nodded toward Sanger Pullman. "Would you care to explain why Sanger is with that young lady instead of with you? If I didn't know better, I would guess he was her escort rather than yours."

"Martha Benson?" Fanny balled her hands into tight fists and squeezed until her fingernails were cutting into the palms of her hands. "The Benson family is visiting with the Pullmans for the weekend. It seems Mrs. Pullman had arranged for Sanger to escort Martha without his knowledge. He was most apologetic, but since neither of us wanted to cause Martha unnecessary embarrassment, we agreed simply to make do. The arrangement is working out nicely, but I do thank you for your concern, Uncle."

Her uncle stared across the grassy expanse toward Sanger and Martha for a moment. "Your arrangement will prove impossible at this evening's ball. Sanger can hardly act as an escort for two young ladies. Whom would he choose for the grand march? I'll speak with him and then have Daniel join your group."

Fanny clenched her jaw. "No need. I wouldn't want to run the risk of Martha overhearing your conversation. You may send Daniel to join me if it pleases you."

"It pleases me very much."

The memory of her uncle's smug smile lingered in Fanny's mind long after he had walked away. While continuing to stomp on divots, Fanny strolled off in the opposite direction. She didn't plan to stand there and wait for Daniel Irwin to join her.

Fanny looped arms with Sophie and, using the toe of her shoe, pushed a clod of dirt into a hole on the playing field. "I'm sorry that our plan has failed." She tromped the lump with the heel of her shoe.

Sophie quickly stepped back. "I'm glad my foot wasn't beneath your heel, Fanny. I'd be injured for life. Tell me what has happened to cause a change of plans."

Fanny lowered her voice to a whisper and quickly explained. When she looked up, Daniel was loping across the field toward her. She sighed. "After my earlier refusal, I had hoped he would decline Uncle Jonas's suggestion."

"You never know what could happen between now and the ball. Perhaps a word or two in the proper ear and Daniel will lose interest in you." Sophie tapped her index finger to her pursed lips. "I may have an idea that will annoy our dear uncle and free you from Daniel."

Jonas had watched Daniel and Fanny in earnest for the remainder of the polo match. Although Daniel had been welcomed into the group of young people, Fanny had seldom been near his side. Not once had he succeeded in separating her from the crowd. Jonas had had a long chat with the young man when they returned home to prepare for the ball, and he now hoped he'd made his point. At least the group of young people would be required to break into couples for the dances.

He coached Daniel before they departed for the ball and hoped the young man would heed his advice. Although the men he'd brought to the island were malleable enough, none seemed particularly skilled as suitors. Or perhaps they were unaccustomed to such a headstrong girl as Fanny.

Jonas's spirits flagged when they boarded the *DaisyBee* and Fanny immediately managed to separate herself from Daniel. Instead of attempting to reestablish his position, Daniel stood near the rail, obviously content to watch the passing scenery.

Jonas grasped Daniel's arm. "You need to sit beside Fanny or bring her over here to stand beside you."

Daniel glanced over his shoulder. "There's no space near her, and I doubt she wants to stand."

Jonas glowered. The young man had no resolve. Perhaps Fred Portman would have been a better choice for Fanny. First the difficulties with Frank, and now Daniel appeared to have little pluck. If Daniel didn't step up and take command, Jonas would soon cross him from the list of possible candidates.

When the boat docked at Round Island, Jonas barred Fanny's escape. "You don't want to appear uncultured, Fanny. You need to wait for Daniel to assist you off the boat and escort you."

"I'm perfectly capable of walking without assistance, and I'm sure no one cares if I enter the lobby of the hotel without an escort."

Jonas touched her arm and shook his head. "Please remember our agreement, Fanny. I don't think you want to cause me problems so early on, do you? I believe Michael would prefer to hear that you are behaving in a cooperative manner and honoring the terms of our agreement." She clearly abhorred his interference, but he cared little.

Jonas waved Daniel forward. "I trust you will have no further problems this evening," he whispered.

Although Jonas hadn't been thrilled with the news, the Broadmoor women had been delighted that Charles Emery's New Frontenac Hotel had been selected as the site for this year's ball. The hotel had been remodeled and enlarged by Emery seven years earlier and now stood seven stories tall and boasted over four hundred rooms, each with its own electricity and bath. Many of the guests who attended the polo matches took rooms for the entire week preceding the games and would remain at the hotel until the festivities concluded.

Jonas viewed the size of the edifice as a detriment to keeping an eye on Fanny and Daniel. The girl would likely seize every opportunity to distance herself from her suitor. And there were ample places where she could conceal herself in a structure of this magnitude.

Colored lights shone upon the path, and banners and flags welcomed the guests. Those who weren't attending the ball sat on the huge porch and watched the beautifully gowned women and the accompanying men in their formal attire as they ascended the steps to enter the center hallway. The pleasant sounds of a string quartet welcomed the guests, although dancing would not begin until after the grand march. Until then, Jonas hoped Daniel would keep Fanny at his side. He had wanted to help keep the girl in line, but his wife was intent upon greeting every person in the room—to discover who was wearing the most elaborate gown, he surmised.

Fortunately, their delay at the dock permitted Victoria only time enough to speak to a small number of the guests. The full orchestra soon took to the stage, and Charles Emery stepped forward and announced that the couples should prepare for the grand march.

Jonas craned his neck and finally spotted Fanny and Daniel. They were among the same group that had formed together earlier in the day. He did wish Daniel would force her out of that crowd. At this rate the man would never make any progress winning Fanny's affections.

Arm in arm the couples slowly began the promenade. When Jonas and Victoria reached the front of the line, they stopped and faced the next couple moving down the row. The number of couples was daunting, and the promenade would likely take longer than he wished. He took a modicum of comfort from the realization that the misery of his counterparts equaled his own.

His smile disappeared when he looked down the line and saw Martha Benson clinging to Daniel's arm. What was he doing with Martha? The fool was grinning like a Cheshire cat. Directly behind them, Fanny walked alongside Sanger Pullman. She beamed at her uncle as she walked past him. Well, he would see to her the minute the promenade ended.

"A word with you, Jonas."

Jonas sucked in a deep breath and turned to greet George and Hattie Pullman. "Good evening. Good to see both of you."

"Hattie had some concerns about the young man who escorted Martha Benson during the promenade," Mr. Pullman stated. "I assured her there was no need for concern. Sanger told me the young man was your guest, and I knew he would be of reputable character and position if you welcomed him into your home." He chuckled. "I'm right, aren't I, Jonas?"

Jonas cleared his throat. "He's a nice enough fellow . . ."

When her husband faltered in his response, Victoria added the words Hattie Pullman wanted to hear. "Rest assured that he is a fine young man or my husband wouldn't consider him a possible suitor for any of the unmarried Broadmoor girls."

Hattie nodded. "I didn't want to insult you in any manner, but Emily Benson and I are dear friends, and I assured her I would confirm the young man's credentials. We don't want our daughters selecting young men who can't keep them in the manner to which they've been accustomed. Don't you agree, Victoria?"

"To a degree, though I think love can overcome many obstacles."

Jonas laughed. "If you ever had to do without money, I believe you'd soon change your mind, my dear."

George slapped Jonas on the shoulder and agreed with his assessment before leading his wife off to assuage Mrs. Benson's fears. Fanny's ploy to disobey him could cause more problems than even Jonas could handle.

He must develop another plan.

CHAPTER 23

WEDNESDAY, AUGUST 25, 1897
ROCHESTER, NEW YORK

With his eyes closed, Jonas leaned back in his chair, determined to arrive at a solution that did not require Fanny's cooperation. He'd accomplished nothing of substance since returning from the island. The weekend had been a complete disaster, and though he had originally planned to remain until Thursday, he departed Tuesday morning. He needed the solace of his office in order to arrive at some logical solution.

What to do? What to do? The question flashed through his mind the next morning like a beacon in a lighthouse. He opened his eyes and pulled a sheet of paper from his desk drawer. He stared at what he'd written. Notes regarding Fanny, along with a few comments about Winifred and his brother—nothing that seemed to help. Jonas had never liked Winifred. She'd been a poor choice for his brother. He'd married beneath himself. She was nothing more than a companion to a very wealthy friend of his mother's. A companion! Nothing more. And when she died in childbirth, Langley professed he could never love another. Had it not been for Winifred, Langley would still be alive. *Love!* His brother had taken his own life because he thought he couldn't live without that woman. *Nonsense!* And it appeared their daughter was going to follow in their footsteps. Just like her parents, Fanny was determined to marry for love. Winifred had demonstrated the havoc a poor bloodline could wreak in a family.

His brother's brief marriage had caused a myriad of difficulties. Jonas rubbed his cheek and attempted to remember exactly when they had wed. Victoria would remember, but he had no penchant for tracking such dates. He did recall Fanny's birth had been premature. That's right! His mother had been angered over the gossip that followed Winifred's death. There had been whispered remarks that she had been pregnant prior to the wedding. His mother had countered the remarks, but rumors had persisted that perhaps this had been God's punishment upon the young couple.

Langley had cared little what anyone said. Throughout the weeks and months following Winifred's death, he could be found sitting beside her grave or with the infant. Jonas had been certain his brother would blame Fanny for Winifred's death, but Langley had proved him wrong and loved Fanny. However, the child had never been enough to counter the depth of his grief.

Now Jonas wondered if those rumors and Fanny's premature birth could work to his advantage. He smiled and folded the sheet of paper. If he could prove Fanny wasn't Langley's child, his problem would be solved. He would no longer need to worry about brokering a marriage and the possibility of a husband who might later turn obstinate, for Fanny wouldn't be entitled to share in the Broadmoor estate. He rubbed his hands together and pushed up from his chair. Suddenly he was hungry.

There was a spring to Jonas's step when he entered his men's club for lunch. He greeted his fellow businessmen with an affable smile and cheerful hello. Both the conversation and companionship during the noonday meal bolstered his spirits. It wasn't until he was preparing to depart that he spotted Harold Morrison at a distant table. The man had defaulted on his loan and had been avoiding Jonas.

Though not prone to loaning money, when Morrison had first approached him, Jonas had considered the loan to be a sound investment opportunity. Harold had promised a six-percent return on the money and prompt monthly payments. And although Jonas should have checked in to Harold's assets more carefully, he'd thought there was little risk. The man had inherited his father's burgeoning lumber business in Syracuse ten years prior and had planned to expand into Rochester and Buffalo.

The expansion had caused Morrison to become overextended, and he sought a large yet short-term loan. Jonas hadn't asked to see his books or required any verification from Harold's banker to ensure the man's assets were secure. Pity that hadn't been the case, and his failings were just one more issue that was slowly eroding Jonas's financial security.

Recently Jonas had heard rumors that Harold could be found at the gaming tables at all hours. "Rather early in the day for whiskey, isn't it?"

Harold started and turned. "Jonas! I've been meaning to stop by your office and speak with you."

"Good! Let's walk over there right now."

Morrison glanced at the clock. "I have another meeting in a few minutes."

"It will have to be delayed. I've been waiting three months for your payments. You haven't responded to my correspondence or my calls. I don't want to make a scene here in the club, Harold."

With a look of resignation, Morrison pushed away from the table. "I suppose I can spare you a few minutes."

They were silent during the brief walk to Jonas's office. There was no need for small talk. Money would solve their problem, not idle chatter. And from all appearances, Jonas doubted he would receive any money from Harold—at least not anytime soon.

Once inside his office, Jonas pointed to a chair. "Sit down." Jonas walked to the other side of his desk and dropped into his chair. He leaned back and fixed his eyes on the nervous man across the broad desk. "When you needed money, I couldn't keep you away from my office door. Now that your payments are due, I can't locate you. Explain yourself, Harold. You owe me at least that much."

Harold stared at the floor. "I've come upon hard times. I can't make the payments. I'm sure you've heard the rumors."

"Look at me!" He waited until Harold met his gaze. "I want to know *why* you can't make the payments and what you're going to do about it. Repayment of my money has nothing do with rumors. You had no difficulty articulating your wishes when you approached me for the loan. Tell me exactly what has placed you in this precarious situation."

"I didn't lie to you, Jonas. I wanted to expand the business, but I had already amassed gambling debts when I borrowed from you. I used part of your money to pay off those debts and thought I could win back that amount with what I had left."

"So my money was never invested in your business? Is that what you're telling me?"

"If you'd loan me a few thousand, I could make it all back."

"You're pathetic, Harold. To knowingly jeopardize a business that has been in your family for years is abhorrent. I would think your father is rolling over in his grave."

"I know." Harold raked his fingers through his thinning hair. "I would do anything to extract myself from this situation, Jonas. Anything! I will be completely ruined if I can't find someone to help me."

"I would say your options are limited. No banker will lend you funds to pay off gaming debts, especially when you've already mortgaged your business beyond its worth. And me? Well, I'd be a fool to do such a thing, wouldn't I? If those men you owe gambling debts don't do you harm, I can have you thrown in jail for nonpayment of your liability to me."

Harold slumped and buried his face in his hands. "Is there no help for me then? No way you can see your way clear to assist me?"

"You say you'll do anything?"

Harold looked up. The man's eyes shone with expectancy. Jonas had hooked him with far greater ease than he could reel in a muskellunge from the St. Lawrence Seaway. Fortunately for Jonas, Harold didn't have the fighting spirit of large game fish.

"Yes, anything. I can't bear to bring any further shame upon my poor wife. If I can dispel the rumors and pay off my outstanding debts, my wife will be able to maintain her place in proper society. I owe her that much."

Jonas didn't hide his contempt for the man. "You owe *me* much more. If I have your word that you will do exactly what I tell you, I am willing to wipe the slate clean. I will return your note marked paid in full. In addition, I'll give you a sum that should pay off your gambling debts. You will remain away from the gaming tables until our business is complete—no drinking, either. You'll need a clear head if you're to work for me."

"Whatever you say, Jonas."

The man would be like putty in his hands for the moment, but Jonas wondered if he would be so compliant once he learned what was expected of him. "I want you to visit our family on Broadmoor Island this weekend."

"Oh, my wife will be delight—"

"Hear me out. This won't be a social visit. You may recall that my brother Langley died a number of years ago. The two of you would be the same age."

Harold nodded his head. "I met him at social functions on several occasions. Nice fellow, as I recall."

"My brother's wife, Winifred, died in childbirth. Their only child, Fanny, was under the care of my parents after Langley died. With my father's recent death, Fanny has become my ward. As my brother's only heir, Fanny will inherit a full share of the Broadmoor estate when she reaches her majority." Jonas leaned across his desk. "Needless to say, I do not want that to occur."

Harold nodded again. "She'd have no idea how to handle such wealth."

"Exactly. But the girl is headstrong, and I know she won't take my counsel. Consequently, I see no other way to protect my father's holdings than to take control of her share."

"Good. Good. You can invest it for her, and when she's older and wiser, you can turn it over to her."

Jonas didn't comment on the man's assessment. "The only way I can gain Fanny's share is to have her disinherited."

"But how can you do that?"

"Oh, *I* won't. Having Fanny disinherited is how *you* will repay your debt to me. Sit back and listen while I explain." Jonas savored his good fortune for a moment. "When you visit us at Broadmoor Island, it will be for the purpose of identifying yourself as Fanny's father."

Harold's jaw went slack. "What? But I—"

"I know you've been married less than ten years, Harold. You were a single man back when Fanny was born. I'm certain your wife realized that you had *befriended* a few women before you married."

"But you would cause this young woman to think her mother had been . . . well, less than virtuous. I doubt that's something you want to do. Investing her estate and keeping her future financially intact doesn't seem worth the pain she'll suffer." He rubbed his forehead. "And what are my wife and I to do with her? Would she come and live with us? Would you rip her from the only family she's ever known? This is more than I can even fathom."

The man was a greater fool than Jonas had imagined, for he truly believed Jonas was merely attempting to protect Fanny's estate. "I didn't ask or expect you to understand. Only I know the depth of Fanny's future needs. She is a young woman accustomed to wealth. Her inheritance must be protected. As for her living arrangements, once we've established you are her father, I can generously step forward and suggest she remain under my roof."

"This is all so difficult to comprehend. How will I be able to prove any of this, and how can I answer any of her questions? I know *nothing* of her mother."

"Relax, Harold. We have the remainder of the week, and you will learn all that you must know. As for proof that you are Fanny's father, we will need nothing more than a letter from Winifred telling you of her plight but that she has accepted Langley's marriage proposal." Jonas drummed his fingers atop his desk. "I will take care of those details."

"I don't know, Jonas. This isn't at all what I expected."

"What *did* you expect, Harold? That I would erase your debt and require only some simple task of you?" Jonas shook his head. "You have asked much of me. I expect the same in return. Well? Have we reached an agreement?"

Harold nodded, but his enthusiasm had disappeared.

"I want you here in my office at nine o'clock in the morning. I will develop your entire story this afternoon, commit it to paper for you to study here in my office, and gather some photographs that will assist you in your endeavor."

Harold grasped the chair's armrests and pushed himself up. "Nine o'clock. I'll be here." The words lacked any fervor.

"I expected a bit of enthusiasm—and your thanks. I've saved you from ruination, yet you look as though you've lost your last friend."

"I'm afraid I've suffered a much greater loss. My dignity." He departed without another word.

Jonas smiled. He had no pity for men like Harold Morrison: they were weak and easy prey for the powerful. They deserved to fail. Survival of the fittest prevailed—among both man and beast.

CHAPTER 24

FRIDAY, AUGUST 27, 1897
BROADMOOR ISLAND

Preparations for the first family picnic and treasure hunt were in full swing by Friday afternoon. In a surprising announcement, Uncle Jonas had suggested the family develop a new tradition that could become an annual event. Though the family had been surprised by his uncharacteristic interest in family and fun, they all contributed ideas and had finally agreed upon the picnic and treasure hunt as a tradition that all of the family members could enjoy.

Fanny, Sophie, and Amanda had requested permission to take charge of the treasure hunt. Throughout the week they had developed two separate hunts—one for the older children and adults and one for the younger children. The three of them had agreed they would assist the small children so that their parents could enjoy the festivities. They had scoured the island, seeking easy locations to hide their clues and treasure for the children and more difficult sites for the adult set.

"All that's left is to hide the clues first thing in the morning," Amanda said.

"I see no reason to wait. Why not go ahead and be done with it today? There's not a cloud in sight, Amanda. You worry far too much," Sophie chided.

Fanny folded the handwritten notes. "It's not merely the weather that's worrying Amanda. If we hide the clues ahead of time, the older children are sure to sneak off and find them. They'll ruin the fun for the others. I agree with Amanda. We should wait."

Sophie frowned. "The two of you fret overmuch. We need not tell any of them."

"We dare not do it. One of them would track us. Have you not noticed that they've been watching us the entire morning?"

"I'll merely explain that they will be ruining their own fun if they choose to do so," Sophie rebutted.

Amanda shook her head. "And does that stop you from sneaking about and discovering your Christmas gifts each year, Sophie?"

"No, but it does ruin the excitement on Christmas morning. I can explain how disappointed I've been each year."

"And how will you explain that you still continue the practice?" Fanny strengthened her resolve. "We must wait until tomorrow morning. If you don't want to get out of bed, then Amanda and I will hide the notes."

"Better yet, we could hide them tonight after everyone has gone to bed. I'm certain I could locate a few fellows who would like to help us." Sophie's eyes sparkled with excitement. "What do you say? We could have great fun."

Fanny and Amanda both rejected the idea with an emphatic *no*.

"The two of you are less fun than two old spinsters."

Amanda giggled. "I'm not old, but there are those who already consider me a spinster."

"Apparently not your father, for he spends far more time worrying about Fanny's gentleman callers than yours." Sophie gathered up the clues and tucked them inside a bag.

"Earlier this summer, it truly bothered me when Father seemed intent upon finding the proper husband for Fanny. However, the truth is I don't want a husband right now—perhaps ever. So there was no reason for my jealousy. Besides, Fanny and I have talked. She has never desired Father's matchmaking efforts." Amanda stood and walked toward the doors leading to the veranda. "Now that we've completed our task, we should join the others in a game of lawn tennis."

Sophie wrinkled her nose.

"Or the three of us could go fishing," Fanny suggested.

"Lawn tennis it is," Sophie said. "I truly do not know how you can enjoy fishing. If you aren't out in one of the canoes or a skiff, you're sitting on the dock with your fishing pole. Honestly, Fanny, you should live on this island."

"I couldn't agree more. It's Uncle Jonas who disapproves. I could have great fun out here in the middle of winter."

Sophie grinned. "Yes, I know. You'd be carving a hole in the ice so you could continue with your fishing."

"Or joining the locals for sleighing or the annual ice races. I don't think I'd be bored for a minute. Of course I'd miss the two of you, but you could come visit me."

They all three knew their discussion was nothing more than idle chatter. Fanny would never be permitted to remain on Broadmoor Island. She would be expected to continue to see the parade of men her uncle marched through the front doors—but only until Michael returned. That was the thought that warmed her heart.

As Sophie predicted, the morning dawned bright and clear. The three young women were up and out of the house before the others arose. With the clues in hand, they followed their preplanned course, and soon all of the papers were hidden. A treasure box filled with candy was hidden for the young children, while the treasure chest for the adults contained a note entitling the winner to either a new fishing pole, which had been Fanny's idea, or a small piece of jewelry from Crossman's Jewelers, Sophie's suggestion.

"If we hurry, we may be able to return for another hour of sleep," Sophie said as they rounded the corner of the house on their return. But her hope proved incorrect. The excitement of the upcoming day had been enough for the children to arise far earlier than usual.

"This is as wearisome as Christmas Day," Beatrice's husband, Andrew, lamented as he chased after his young son. "The children thought they were going on the treasure hunt before breakfast."

Amanda laughed. "Anticipation is half the fun."

"Not for the parents," Andrew growled. He scooped his son up into his arms and headed toward the dining room.

As the breakfast hour wore on, they agreed the meal had been an effort in futility, at least as far as the younger children were concerned. None of them wanted to eat. All were excited for the day of fun and festivities to begin, especially when Uncle Jonas announced he'd arranged for a huge fireworks display after dark. By ten o'clock the children were gathered on the front lawn awaiting the adults with growing anticipation.

Uncle Jonas stood on the top step of the veranda with the family gathered around. "You must listen closely to your instructions, and there will be no pushing, shoving, or cheating." With a flourishing gesture, he motioned Amanda, Fanny, and Sophie to the veranda. "You may now give your instructions for the treasure hunt."

The girls took their place at his side while Amanda explained the rules. With a clear view of the waterway, Fanny shaded her eyes and watched as the *Little Mac* approached and docked. A man stepped off of the boat, and she glanced at her uncle. "We're about to begin. Were you expecting additional guests?"

He shook his head. "No, but we can wait a few minutes more."

The children were running around the lawn playing tag, and their parents unsuccessfully attempted to maintain control. The rest of the family murmured and guessed who the visitor might be.

Aunt Victoria soon approached her uncle. "Who in the world is that? Did you invite a business associate without advising me?"

"No. But I believe I recognize him. I think it may be Harold Morrison. What in the world is *he* doing here?"

Her aunt arched her brows. "How would *I* know? He's certainly not here to see me."

"No offense intended, Victoria. I didn't mean to insinuate he was here to see you."

The man removed his hat and waved it overhead. Her uncle nodded. "That's Harold Morrison, all right. Haven't seen him in ages."

"He owns the lumberyards over in Syracuse," Andrew said.

"You know him?" Jonas asked.

"No. I heard he was going to expand his business into Rochester six or nine months ago, but I've heard nothing more. Maybe it was Buffalo. I can't remember."

Fanny remained on the porch with her cousins as Uncle Jonas stepped forward and greeted Mr. Morrison. He was a kind-appearing man with thinning dark hair and a rather long angular face. Not handsome but not unattractive, Fanny guessed him to be a few years younger than Uncle Jonas. Keeping a downward gaze, he nervously pressed the brim of his hat between his fingers while he spoke to her uncle.

"Mr. Morrison would like to speak to you, Fanny. Of course a private conversation would be completely inappropriate. I've told him I must be present if he wishes to speak to you."

Fanny narrowed her eyes and stared at the stranger. "I have no idea why you want to speak to me, Mr. Morrison, but if we are to have a conversation, I prefer that my Aunt Victoria act as my chaperone."

Jonas nodded. "We can both—"

"I'm certain one chaperone is more than sufficient, Uncle Jonas. You must take charge of the day's festivities. The children are anxious to begin the treasure hunt. I'll remain behind, and when Mr. Morrison has spoken to me, we will join the family."

Uncle Jonas's complexion flushed deep red, and Fanny knew it wasn't from the heat. Her choice had angered him, for Uncle Jonas disliked confident women. Not that Fanny was feeling self-assured. In truth, she was frightened to hear what this stranger had to say.

Her uncle shook his head. "If it's a matter of business he wishes to discuss . . ."

Aunt Victoria waved aside the comment. "Why would a stranger wish to discuss business with a mere girl?"

He tipped his head closer. "Because she will soon inherit a great deal of money?"

Aunt Victoria lowered her parasol. "Fanny hasn't come of age, so her money is not yet an issue. I'm certain Mr. Morrison doesn't have anything to say that I can't handle. And if he does, he'll need to speak with you after the treasure hunt or make an appointment to call on you at your office next week." She grasped Fanny's hand. "Come along, dear."

"Why don't we all wait for Fanny? The children can play a game of croquet," Amanda suggested. "Fanny worked very hard on the clues, and I don't want her to miss the fun."

Mr. Morrison removed a handkerchief from his pocket and wiped his forehead. "I've obviously come at a bad time for all of you." He glanced at Fanny. "I don't want to ruin your festivities, but I fear I'll lose courage if I don't speak to you today."

"If it will help, you may tell me right this moment. There's nothing you can't say in front of my family."

The children had scattered, but the adults had fixed their attention upon Harold Morrison. A daunting group, to be sure. Fanny stepped closer and offered an encouraging smile. She couldn't help but take pity on him.

He bowed his head and mumbled something she couldn't quite make out, all the while pressing his hat brim between his fingers.

She couldn't be certain what he'd said, and she leaned to one side in an effort to make eye contact. "I'm sorry. I don't believe I heard you correctly. Could you speak up, sir?"

Mr. Morrison straightened his shoulders and looked at her. There was a sorrowful look in his eyes. "You are my daughter, Frances. My name is Harold Morrison, and I am your father."

Her legs felt weak and shaky, and she grasped the railing. She didn't want to faint. Questions flooded her mind, yet the words stuck in her throat. Mouth agape, she stared at him as though he had two heads. Aunt Victoria held her around the waist, and Jefferson hurried forward with one of the wicker chairs from the far end of the veranda.

Fanny dropped into the cushioned seat and cleared her throat. "I believe I must have misunderstood you, Mr. Morrison." She looked into his eyes. "I thought you said you are my father." She watched him nod his head in agreement. "That's impossible, sir. As you can see, I am surrounded by my true family. I am the daughter of Winifred and Langley Broadmoor."

Mr. Morrison glanced over his shoulder. The entire family had drawn near, eager to hear every word that passed between the two of them. Even the children had returned to their parents' sides and grown quiet.

Mr. Morrison turned back to face her. "Perhaps we should go indoors with your aunt and speak privately." He touched his fingers to his jacket pocket. "I have a letter from your mother."

Victoria glowered. "And I have a number of questions for you, Mr. Morrison." She leaned forward and grasped Fanny's hand. "Come along, dear, and we shall see this matter settled."

"I can't believe this stranger would declare such a thing, Aunt Victoria," Fanny whispered. "Must we truly discuss this any further?"

"I think it best we hear him out and put the subject to rest." She patted Fanny's hand. "Mr. Morrison's assertion is momentous. I believe it's probably best that your uncles come inside with us."

Her aunt was likely correct. Fanny's thoughts were no more than an incoherent muddle. She would need clearheaded people to guide her through this maze. The five of them entered the parlor. Uncle Quincy and Uncle Jonas stood at either end of the fireplace, while Mr. Morrison sat down opposite Fanny and her aunt. Instead of heading off for the treasure hunt, the remainder of the family had gathered on the front porch, where the open windows provided access to the ongoing discussion.

Fanny inhaled a deep breath. "Well, Mr. Morrison. I believe you mentioned a letter?"

Mr. Morrison withdrew the missive from his pocket. "Please understand that I hold the memory of your deceased mother in deepest respect."

Her uncle Jonas cleared his throat. "I imagine she's more interested in seeing that letter than hearing of your respect for her mother."

"Yes, of course." Mr. Morrison blushed, and the letter trembled in his fingers. "Years ago your mother and I were friends—more than friends. We had a short-lived but passionate romance. She was a fine woman, and I don't wish to disparage her in any way, Miss Broadmoor."

"Oh, do get on with it, man," Jonas commanded.

"I loved your mother. I believe she loved me. It was through that love that you were conceived."

A chorus of gasps fluttered through the open windows, and Fanny captured a fleeting glimpse of her cousins. Like her, they appeared stunned into silence. Fanny extended her hand and took the letter. She withdrew the missive from the envelope and slowly read the words.

"Anyone could have written this letter, Mr. Morrison. I have a birth certificate and baptismal record that list my parents—my real parents."

"May I?" Her aunt nodded toward the missive. Fanny handed her the paper and watched her aunt scan the contents. "As well as I can recall, this does resemble your mother's script, and the dates and personal information appear correct."

Harold withdrew a photograph from his pocket. "This is a picture she gave to me."

Fanny had seen a similar picture of her mother wearing the same dress—in a photo album at her grandparents' house. She stared at this stranger who claimed to be her father. Her stomach churned, and she feared she might expel its contents. She swallowed hard and shook her head.

"Why, after all these years, have you come forward? This makes no sense."

He massaged his forehead. "I could no longer live this lie. I've developed a weak heart over the past year, and I couldn't bear the thought of going to my grave without speaking the truth. Whether you choose to believe me or not, I knew I must make an effort to do the right thing."

"Still, I don't know what good purpose you think is served by bringing me this message. Did you never speak to my mother again? And what of my father? Did he know?"

Mr. Morrison folded his hands and rested them on his knees. "Your mother and I did not see each other again. As you read in her letter, she requested that I never contact her, and I honored her wish. I thought it best for all of you. But now, with Winifred and Langley deceased and my poor health—I thought you deserved to hear the truth."

"I believe you cared more about clearing your own conscience before you met the Almighty, Mr. Morrison." Her aunt pointed at the man's chest. "You gave little thought to the damage your careless actions would cause this young woman."

"That's not true, Mrs. Broadmoor. I want nothing but the very best for Frances. It was for that reason I never interfered in her life until now. I stand to gain nothing by divulging the truth, and surely one more person to love her is not a bad thing."

Jonas stepped away from the fireplace. "We all need time to digest this information, Mr. Morrison. May I suggest the New Frontenac Hotel on Round Island if you wish accommodations for the remainder of the weekend?"

Mr. Morrison stood. "If you care to discuss the matter further—any of you, I will remain at the hotel until the first of the week." He smiled at Fanny. "I am very pleased to have made your acquaintance. You are a lovely young lady."

CHAPTER 25

The remainder of the day was chaotic: a mixture of pitying stares, curious children, and unanswered questions.

When nightfall arrived, Fanny was pleased for the cover of darkness that could hide her tears. There had been little time to think on her situation, but now that the family had picnicked, searched for treasure, and watched the fireworks, there would be ample time. She watched as children were herded off toward the house and wondered if she'd ever again spend a summer on this island. A tear trickled down her cheek, and she brushed it away.

"*There* you are! Sophie and I have been looking everywhere. Why are you off by yourself?" Amanda asked as she settled on the grass beside her.

"I'm attempting to sift through what has happened to me. One minute I was surrounded by a huge family of people I love, and the next minute I was told that none of you are even related to me." She pulled her handkerchief from her pocket. "Can you even begin to imagine how that must feel? I've been set adrift. To think that the two of you are not my cousins is impossible."

Amanda enveloped her in a warm embrace. "That letter doesn't change our love for you. We shall always be the dearest of cousins. Do you think that after all these years of love and friendship, Sophie and I could simply walk away from you?"

Sophie plopped down beside them. "Personally, I'm quite hurt that you would even consider such a thing, Fanny." She giggled. "After all, it takes both of you to keep me on the right path."

"And even then we fail," Amanda remarked. "You know we'll never allow anything to come between us and ruin our friendship, don't you?"

"I know you'll try your best. But our lives are bound to change. I just don't know how much, and I'm frightened."

"Then maybe you need to face your fears head on and find out." Sophie pointed toward the boathouse. "The three of us could have Mr. Atwell take us over to the hotel and you could talk to Mr. Morrison. It's not too late. Sitting here in the dark and worrying isn't going to resolve anything. We need to take some positive action."

"I'm not certain that's the correct manner to handle this. I think you should wait until morning when you've had a night of rest and can think more clearly," Amanda said.

"Don't be silly, Amanda. She's not going to sleep when her thoughts are stirring like a paddle churning cream."

"That's what I love about you two. You couldn't be further apart in how you think."

"And you're our balance, Fanny. You always bring us back and center our thoughts." Amanda squeezed her shoulder. "However, this time I'm correct. I don't think we should do anything until morning."

"I'm not sure I agree with you, Amanda. Come morning, the entire family will be offering their ideas of what I should do. Sophie's correct: I need to gather more information from Mr. Morrison." She stood and smiled down at them. "Either of you want to come along?"

Jonas puffed on his cigar. "The family seemed to enjoy the day of festivities, don't you think?"

Quincy nodded. "Had it not been for Mr. Morrison's unexpected news, the day would have been a grand event. His visit certainly put a damper on things."

Jonas flicked the ash from his cigar. "True, but the family seemed to recover by afternoon's end. They were in high spirits during the fireworks display. And I don't believe the treasure hunt could have been any more fun for the youngsters."

"I'm having difficulty digesting the truth of what Morrison revealed. It's difficult to believe that Winifred would have gone to her grave with such a secret. She and Langley were such a devoted couple."

"Who knows? She may have told him. If you'll recall, our brother wasn't prone to confiding in either one of us. He adored Fanny. Even if he knew, he wouldn't have wanted to cause the girl embarrassment—losing her good name and social position."

Quincy frowned. "I hadn't thought of that issue. Indeed, she will suffer if people no longer consider her a Broadmoor. Fanny's name will be crossed off every dowager's social directory, and her situation will become the latest item of gossip at their parties."

"Sad but true. To be accepted, it takes both name and money."

"Hmm. And what about the money?" Quincy asked. "What does all of this mean in regard to Father's estate? It would seem that Fanny will be excluded from receiving Langley's one-third portion, does it not?"

"I hadn't even thought about the inheritance issue." The lie crossed his lips with ease. "I'll check into the matter with Mortimer or Vincent after we return to Rochester. I'm certain they can offer sagacious advice on how we must proceed. The girl is already suffering dearly."

"Oh, of course, of course," Quincy agreed. "I wasn't suggesting we immediately inform her of the dismal future that may await her. Sad that she may be solely reliant upon Mr. Morrison for her well-being."

Jonas snuffed out his cigar and nodded. "Very sad, indeed."

"Then again, the two of us could offer her aid. She has, after all, been reared as a member of this family her entire life. If you thought it best, I believe I could see my way clear to help her when I receive my inheritance." Quincy leaned forward and rested his arms across his thighs. "It would be the charitable thing to do. Of course I couldn't let my children know. Other than Sophie, they would be livid—especially since I plan to invest most of the money in the Home for the Friendless."

Jonas shook his head. "*That* is not an investment. You will never see any return on your money, so quit referring to it as such. As for continuing to financially support the girl, I'm not so sure. There might be legal ramifications involved with that idea. We had best rely upon Mortimer and Vincent. We wouldn't want to act in haste and then be required to withdraw our offer. Such behavior would only cause the girl further distress. If they approve, then we will discuss the matter further."

"Very thoughtful, Jonas. I wouldn't want to cause her any additional anguish. I'm certain both Father and Mother would have wanted us to do something to help. They did, after all, consider her more a daughter than a grandchild."

Quincy had taken the conversation into another realm, one that Jonas didn't want to explore with his brother. He had merely wanted to draw Quincy's attention to the fact that Fanny would no longer inherit. Now his brother wanted to support the girl. If he didn't turn the conversation, Quincy would likely suggest they simply forget Harold Morrison's arrival and give her one-third of the estate.

"You are most thoughtful, but let's remember that Fanny has already received more direct monetary aid from Mother and Father than any of our children. And remember that Father was a strong believer in the Broadmoor bloodline."

"True enough." Quincy pressed his hands on his thighs and stood. "I believe I'll retire to my room. I have some paper work that needs my attention before going to bed. I'll rely upon you to speak with the lawyers and settle these troubling issues."

"Rest assured that I will take care of everything." Jonas smiled and bid his brother good-night.

Mortimer Fillmore would be surprised to hear how easily Jonas's plan had come together. There might be a few legal issues to overcome, but that's why Jonas retained a wily lawyer. Mortimer and Vincent should easily prevail in any possible legal battles. He walked to the edge of the veranda and inhaled the clear evening air. This had been an excellent day. He would sleep well tonight.

Michael's father didn't question the girls. It wasn't proper for an employee to question family members regarding their decisions. But Fanny had seen the question in his eyes when she asked him to take her to Round Island. He'd appeared even more concerned when he saw Sophie was to be her companion. Amanda had declined, although before Sophie and Fanny departed, she agreed to conceal their whereabouts if someone should discover they weren't in their rooms.

"Just say that Fanny convinced me to go night fishing with her," Sophie had instructed.

Fanny didn't know if anyone would believe that lie. Sophie wouldn't even go fishing during the daylight hours. They could only hope no one would realize they'd left the island.

"What if he's already gone to bed for the night?" Fanny whispered as the boat slid across the dark water. A knot the size of a grapefruit had taken up residence in her stomach. One part of her wanted to ask Mr. Morrison questions, but the other part wanted to hurry back to Broadmoor Island, rush upstairs to her room, and bury her head beneath the covers. Perhaps she would awaken and discover this had all been a nightmare.

"Don't borrow trouble, Fanny. He's staying at the liveliest hotel on the islands. You'll probably find him sitting on the veranda with a glass of port and a cigar, considering all that has occurred today."

Mr. Atwell docked the boat a short time later and assisted them onto the pier. "Shall I wait for you ladies?"

Fanny blinked. "Yes, of course. We should return within an hour." She waited until they were out of hearing distance. "Why did he ask if he should wait, Sophie? Do you sometimes spend the night over here?"

"On one or two occasions I stayed with the parents of friends from school who were staying at the hotel." Sophie made no apology for her behavior. She seldom judged others and didn't seem to care what others thought of her. There evidently was nothing that frightened Sophie.

They walked side by side toward the bright lights of the hotel. "What if this had happened to you, Sophie? How would you feel?"

"I don't know. I would feel betrayed, naturally, but at least Uncle Jonas won't be able to tell you what to do in the future." She grinned. "Then again, Mr. Morrison may be even worse."

Fanny shuddered. She hadn't considered that Mr. Morrison might be a cruel or unkind man. He had seemed quite nice when they talked earlier in the day. But anyone could appear gentle and kind for short periods. Perhaps she could remain with the family until her birthday; then she'd have her inheritance and could move out on her own. Or could she? Nothing had been said about whether she would be entitled to the money her grandfather had bequeathed to her. But he wasn't really her grandfather anymore, so what would that mean now?

No need asking Sophie, for she wouldn't know, either. If her talk with Mr. Morrison went well, perhaps she would ask him. Uncle Jonas had mentioned Mr. Morrison was a businessman. Surely he would have some idea how such matters were settled.

"There he is!" Sophie elbowed Fanny and then pointed toward the open-air seating. "Over in the courtyard with the woman in the rose and beige gown."

Mr. Morrison had spotted them. He briefly spoke to the woman and then rose from his chair. Sophie tapped her foot as music began to play in the other room. She edged toward the entertaining sounds. "I'll be in there when you're ready to go home." Fanny wanted to grab her hand and beg her to remain, but Sophie no doubt sensed the conversation with Mr. Morrison should be private.

The woman didn't turn around. Was she Mrs. Morrison? He hadn't revealed if he had a wife or children. *Children.* She might have sisters and brothers she had never met. The thought was both exciting and disagreeable. What if they disliked her? And what of his wife? What did she think of all of this—if that was, indeed, his wife. She would inquire.

"Frances. This is a surprise. I had hoped for time alone in a neutral setting where we might speak freely, but I hadn't expected you this evening." He looked through the archway at the huge clock in the lobby. "I'm surprised you are out so late."

His look was filled with concern, but he didn't chastise her imprudent behavior.

"Shall we sit over here where it is a bit less noisy?"

She evaluated his every feature and nuance, searching for something recognizable, some connection to herself. But nothing about this man's appearance was familiar—not the tilt of his head, the curve of his lips, or the slant of his eyes. And though his mannerisms were those of a sophisticated, well-educated gentleman, they were dissimilar to a Broadmoor's. She hadn't arrived with high expectations, but she had hoped to discover some connection to this man who claimed to be her father.

They sat side by side. Father and daughter. Perfect strangers. The thought overwhelmed her. She grasped the arm of the settee. This would seem no more than an illusion if she didn't hold on to something tangible.

"The woman you were sitting with when I arrived—is she your wife?"

"Yes. I thought it would be better if the two of us became better acquainted before you meet her. She is a forgiving woman. Although I don't deserve her kindness, she came along to offer me moral support." He folded his hands in his lap. "You may be surprised to hear that this has been very difficult for me also." His smile was gentle. "Nothing in comparison to your experience, of course."

"Has she always known? Your wife, I mean. Did you tell her about my mother and you before the two of you married?"

"No. We've had this discussion only recently." He stared at the floor. "She knew nothing of your existence." He looked up at her. "I hope it doesn't hurt you to hear me say that. I fear I've already caused you a great deal of pain."

"I believe the act of clearing one's conscience can be a very selfish act. While it helps the offender, it often inflicts pain on others. I have a married friend back in Rochester. After a year of marriage her husband made admissions regarding his missteps outside their marriage vows. He felt cleansed and ready to begin anew, but his confession cut her to the depth of her soul. I doubt whether she'll ever recover."

"So you think it would have been better if he continued to live a lie and had never told her?"

Fanny shrugged. "Who am I to say? I do know that his confession didn't help their marriage. My friend is most unhappy. If her husband had asked for God's forgiveness, changed his ways, and lived with his secrets, I believe their marriage could have survived. Right now, I'm not certain what will happen. It's most unfortunate that his struggle with conscience didn't occur until after he had stepped outside of his marriage vows."

"From what you've said, I can only assume you wish I hadn't cleansed my conscience."

"What purpose does all of this serve, Mr. Morrison? Your revelation has injured your wife, besmirched my mother's name, and I've not yet counted all the consequences I will endure. Was revealing your secret so important at this late date?"

His eyes revealed the pain she'd inflicted with her words. She hadn't meant to hurt him, but she wasn't going to tell him she was pleased to have him waltz into her life and turn it upside down after seventeen years.

"My plan was ill-conceived. I truly regret having come forward—I shouldn't have even considered such an idea. The damage I've caused you is irreparable, and I do apologize."

She reached forward and touched his hand. "I didn't mean to wound you, Mr. Morrison. Please . . . tell me about yourself. Do you have children? I mean other than . . ." She couldn't complete the sentence. This man could not so easily supplant her father or his memory.

"No. Unfortunately my wife and I have no children. We had always hoped to have a child. My wife would have been an excellent mother. Why don't you tell me about your life, Frances?"

"Fanny. No one uses my formal name—except in school, where the teachers always insist upon using my given name."

"Then if you have no objection, I shall address you as Fanny, also. You had a happy childhood?"

"Oh yes." Since Mr. Morrison had inquired, Fanny didn't hesitate to tell him of the close bond she'd shared with her father—their love of fishing and nature and the many hours they'd spent together on Broadmoor Island and in the gardens at Rochester. She spoke of her beloved grandparents and the affection they'd showered upon her throughout the years. Mr. Morrison listened intently when she told him about her love for flower gardening and her special lilacs.

"My wife is an avid gardener, too," he said. "I'm certain she would enjoy showing you her flowers someday."

His offer was gentle, but Fanny didn't want to see anyone else's flowers. She wanted to return home and enjoy the Broadmoor gardens. "What can you tell me about my mother, Mr. Morrison? My father found it painful to speak about her, and my grandparents discouraged such questions. Consequently I know little of my mother."

"Like you, she was very attractive, gentle spoken, and attempted to please others. She found it difficult to refuse my advances, for she disliked quarrels and arguments. I knew that and used it to my advantage. What occurred was totally my fault. I would never want you to think less of your mother. She was a truly wonderful woman."

Like everyone else in her life, Mr. Morrison seemed reticent to reveal many details. Perhaps after all these years, he'd forgotten. "How long did you know my mother before she married?"

"Less than a year. She was wise to select your father over me. He loved her and provided well for both of you."

"He was devastated by her death. It has always been difficult to think that my birth was the cause of her death. As a child, I wondered if my father would have preferred it the other way."

"I'm sure you brought him much joy."

She may have provided him with occasional joy, but Fanny wondered if her father might still be alive if she had died at birth. No need to dwell on the thought. She couldn't have changed it then, and she couldn't change it now. Life-and-death matters were beyond her control. At present the clock was ticking, and she needed to find out what Mr. Morrison expected from her and if he'd given thought to the future—specifically, to her future.

Throughout the remainder of their visit and almost against her will, Fanny discovered herself drawn to Mr. Morrison. His gentle character and honesty remained prevalent throughout their discussion. He didn't shy away from her questions, though she wished he remembered more of the past. But after seventeen years of attempting to forget his past, she couldn't expect him to recall the minute details.

They parted with an agreement that Mr. Morrison would return to Syracuse and give Fanny and the Broadmoors time to consider her future. Mr. Morrison didn't want to dictate Fanny's choices, but he did offer her a home in Syracuse with him and his wife. He explained that he owned a large lumberyard in Syracuse and his attempts to expand the business had caused him to fall upon hard times. Fanny would be required to adjust to a meager lifestyle if she moved to Syracuse. She thought that somewhat surprising, since the Morrisons had rented accommodations at the New Frontenac Hotel.

Not that she begrudged them the fine accommodations, but it seemed a man of limited means would choose a small hotel or a boardinghouse in Clayton or Alexandria Bay. Then again, perhaps he believed it was the least he could do for his wife, considering the pain he'd caused. Who could know what Mr. Morrison had been thinking. Fanny could barely manage to keep her own thoughts in order.

Mr. Atwell was patiently waiting when the two girls returned a short time later. As the boat cut through the water and headed toward Broadmoor Island, Fanny stared down into the water. Sophie had recognized her need for silent comfort and hadn't assailed her with questions. If only Michael were here with her now. If only he'd waited just a brief time longer before departing for the Yukon. If only Mr. Morrison hadn't made an appearance. *If, if, if.*

Hopeful the morning light would provide some clarity on decisions that must be made, Fanny thanked Mr. Atwell for delivering them safely home. He grasped her hand and assisted her onto the dock. "If you need to talk, we're here, Fanny."

Had the Broadmoors already spread word among the staff? She had wanted to tell Michael's parents herself. "I'd like that. I'll come and talk with both of you tomorrow."

She also wanted to be the one who would write and tell Michael of the changes in her life. But until she received word from him, she had no idea where to write. And he'd already warned her that mail could pose a problem once winter set in—and winter arrived early in the Yukon. Fanny hoped a letter would arrive before that time. She wondered how he was dealing with the changes in his life, for the thought of moving just to Syracuse was nearly more than she could bear. She could only pray the family would want her to return with them to Rochester.

CHAPTER 26

Wednesday, September 1, 1897

Fanny hurried downstairs to the kitchen. This would be her last opportunity to have a few minutes alone with Michael's mother before returning to Rochester. Her uncle had refused Fanny's request to remain on the island with Mr. and Mrs. Atwell. Until everything was settled and a final determination made in regard to her future, he declared she would live with his family in Rochester. He didn't say how long that might take, but Aunt Victoria had assured Fanny there was no need for concern. Fanny wasn't so certain. Uncle Jonas had never offered such encouragement. Rather, he frowned whenever Aunt Victoria claimed nothing would change.

A frayed cotton apron covered Mrs. Atwell's dress. She looked up from the mound of bread dough and greeted Fanny with a broad smile. "You'll write to me the minute they've decided what's to happen, won't you? I don't want to send my letters to the house in Rochester and discover you've moved to Syracuse." She wiped her hands on the corner of her apron. "This is all going to work out according to God's plan, my dear. You must keep your spirits high and not lose faith in the Almighty."

"I'll do my best, and I'll write to you every week. Maybe more often. I do wish I knew what was going to happen. I've never before been so uncertain about where I belong."

"You belong to God, child, and that's what you must keep at the forefront of your mind. Mr. Broadmoor and Mr. Morrison may shift you around from pillar to post, but your Father in heaven has you in the palm of His hand." She wrapped Fanny in a warm embrace. "Fretting will serve no purpose. When you feel insecure, talk to Him. And search your Bible for verses that will sustain you."

For as long as Fanny had known Mrs. Atwell, the woman had been offering living proof of her faith in God. Trust in Him came so naturally to the older woman that it always found a place in their conversations. Now, however, it was more important than ever, and Fanny cherished the advice. "I'll try, but I won't deny that I'm frightened."

Mrs. Atwell kissed Fanny's cheek. "I know you are, but you're going to be just fine. Before you know it, you and Michael will be married, and you'll look back on this day and wonder why you ever worried."

"I wish I would have discovered this before he left. If I'm not a Broadmoor, there is nothing to stand in the way of our marrying. Uncle Jonas would have no reason to protest."

"But your father might," Mrs. Atwell replied. "I wouldn't borrow trouble, child. I'm positive you've nothing to worry about. The entire matter will soon be behind you."

Fanny didn't argue, but she wasn't convinced Mrs. Atwell was correct. Somehow she feared the forthcoming days would be the most difficult she would ever face. She must believe God would be at her side. Otherwise, she would be completely on her own.

Forcing a brave smile, she said, "I wish we could remain until the weekend, but everyone else wants to return to Rochester for the Labor Day parade."

"I'm sure you'll have a good time if you just give yourself permission to forget your worries." Mrs. Atwell squeezed Fanny's shoulder. "I do wish I could visit longer, but I'm running behind schedule with breakfast. Mr. Jonas will be acting like a wildcat with a sore paw if he misses the train because the family didn't have their morning meal on time."

After a final peck on the cheek, Fanny hurried back upstairs. The entire family would depart for Rochester today, but most of the servants would remain behind to pack their belongings and help Mrs. Atwell clean and then close the main portion of the house before taking their leave. They likely enjoyed being alone in the house without members of the family ordering them around. She could picture the servants laughing and joking while they cleaned and covered the furnishings, washed the windows and removed the screens. Once the family had left, did they pretend they were the masters of the house? Did they eat their evening meal at the formal dining table with the good silver or sit on the veranda sipping lemonade? She wondered if Mrs. O'Malley would permit such behavior.

Fanny placed a few remaining items in her valise and carried it downstairs to the veranda. She wandered off toward the boathouse. In summers past she and Michael had spent much of their time fishing for bass and pike and enjoying a shore dinner over an open fire. She could picture him squatted down with a large skillet, browning slabs of buttered bread or frying perfectly browned potatoes to accompany their catch of the day. Her heart ached at the remembrance, and she hurried back to the house for one last look. What if she never again could return to this place she so loved?

Although they'd had more than sufficient time, Uncle Jonas had hurried the family onto the *DaisyBee*. Once they'd arrived in Clayton, he'd marched up and down the platform, watching with obvious anticipation for the arrival of the train. They were then herded into the Pullman car that had been rented for the family's journey. Her uncle Jonas dropped into his seat beside Aunt Victoria as though he'd performed a hard day's labor.

"Much more pleasant traveling by myself," he muttered.

"Excuse me?" Aunt Victoria rose to attention in apparent offense.

"Trying to maintain a proper head count of the family is enough to cause a headache. My comment was not meant as a reflection upon you, my dear. I am always pleased to have you with me."

"Do you think she believes him?" Sophie whispered to Fanny and giggled.

"I doubt it, but at least she put him on notice that she'll not tolerate such comments. Aunt Victoria is about the only one who can put him in his place."

"What are you two whispering about?" Amanda asked. She moved from her seat across the aisle and joined them.

"Just commenting that your father had better watch his step or he'll be sleeping in the guest room tonight," Sophie replied.

"Sophie Broadmoor! I can't believe you said that. Where my father sleeps isn't a proper topic of discussion for young ladies." One by one Amanda tugged on the fingers of her gloves. "You should be thankful Mother didn't hear you."

"That much is certainly true." Mischief danced in Sophie's eyes. "She'd likely swoon at the mention of sleeping with your father, don't you think?"

All three girls glanced across the aisle and were met by Victoria's questioning gaze. "Is something amiss?"

"No, Mother, nothing at all," Amanda replied.

"I've been thinking that since you did so well in finishing school, you might enjoy a year or two of higher education while Michael is away, Fanny. There's no telling how long he may be in the Yukon, and education is never wasted. What do you think? Does the idea hold appeal?"

Jonas cleared his throat. "Higher education is expensive, my dear. You're forgetting that until we unravel Fanny's situation with the lawyers, we don't know if Fanny will have the finances available to attend school."

Victoria clasped a hand to the frilly collar of her blouse. "Jonas! We can't wait around for lawyers and judges. They are prone to dragging things on for insufferable periods of time. I made application for Fanny at several schools before we departed for Broadmoor Island. If we've received an affirmative response, and if Fanny wants to attend, I'm quite sure you can afford to pay the fees."

"I don't believe this is a discussion we should be having at the moment."

Fanny didn't miss the warning in her uncle's eyes. The look successfully quelled any further discussion of her future but didn't dampen Sophie's spirited disposition.

"What about new gowns for the Labor Day festivities, Uncle Jonas? Do you think there's enough in the coffers to purchase a new gown or two?" She pursed her lips and shook her head. "Then again, such an expenditure might cause the Broadmoor fortune to teeter on the brink of financial disaster."

Her uncle leaned forward and glared across the aisle. "Your father needs to have a conversation with you about your impudent behavior, Sophie. You are a disrespectful young lady. Your lack of regard for your elders is most unbecoming. It seems my brother should be concentrating his efforts on your manners rather than worrying over the homeless and poverty stricken."

"Perhaps it is a good thing my father continues to maintain the charity. If you continue in your efforts to cast Fanny aside, she may need a place to live."

It wasn't difficult to assess the impact of Sophie's comment. Aunt Victoria paled, Uncle Jonas's complexion turned the shade of a boiled beet, Amanda remained bug-eyed, and Fanny's stomach roiled. She gave thanks that she hadn't eaten any breakfast. The grain of truth in Sophie's remark had been sufficient to create a stark reaction. If nothing else, Sophie had become an expert at causing a stir.

Beatrice leaned over the back of the train seat. "She has a father she can go and live with, Sophie." Cruelty shone in her eyes. "I heard Grayson tell Andrew that Mr. Morrison is an extremely poor businessman who may lose the family business if he doesn't cease his—"

"That's entirely enough, Beatrice." Her uncle pointed toward the rear of the car. "I believe I hear one of your youngsters calling you."

Beatrice remained firmly planted and glared at her uncle. "You agreed heartily enough that she shouldn't inherit a full third of Grandfather's estate. I don't know why you think it improper for me to discuss the topic now."

Her aunt Victoria scooted to the edge of her seat. "Your behavior nearly matches that of your sister, Beatrice. This is neither the time nor the place for your comments. If your mother were alive, she'd be quite disappointed. Your greedy attitude is most unbecoming."

"*My* greedy attitude? There isn't a person in this family who doesn't long for the power and influence associated with wealth. Your children can well afford to appear pious and appalled by the mention of receiving a fair share of Grandfather's inheritance." Beatrice's lips tightened into an unattractive snarl. "They know you will protect their position and they will be cared for. Our father, however, is more interested in giving his money to the homeless. He doesn't consider the fact that his philanthropy will likely force a life of destitution upon his own family."

Jonas appeared to regain his composure. "You are off on a tangent that makes little sense, Beatrice. What happens to Fanny's inheritance will have no impact upon what your father chooses to do with his share of the estate. That is something best discussed with him in private." With a dismissive wave, Jonas snapped open his newspaper.

"You can't hide behind your newspaper forever, Uncle Jonas. This matter will be settled, and I see no difference whether it's on a railcar or in the parlor of your East Avenue mansion." Beatrice turned and tromped back down the aisle.

Sophie grinned. "Beatrice is in rare form today, don't you think?"

"You'd think Andrew would attempt to control her," Amanda whispered.

"She'd snap his head off if he tried. He ignores her because it makes his life easier. No different from the way my father ignores me. Neither one of us is able to gain the attention of the men in our lives."

Fanny rested against the seat and closed her eyes. She had hoped to enjoy the journey home with her cousins. Instead, her joy had been replaced by a feeling of gloom and foreboding. Even if she remained in Rochester, her life would never be the same. Obviously Beatrice and the like-minded society dowagers of East Avenue would make certain of that. Though she could easily live without the fancy dresses and parties, there was much of her old life Fanny would sorely miss.

Jonas studied the paper work. During a visit to Broadmoor Island by Mr. and Mrs. William Comstock, Jonas had agreed to further invest in Comstock's patent medicine company. He didn't mention, however, that he was in the process of planning an even larger investment in George Fulford's expanding patent medicine company. For that, Jonas planned to use a large portion of the money his father had bequeathed to Fanny. If by some fluke the court found her entitled to receive a share of the estate, he could allege he'd merely been acting as guardian of her estate. If the investment turned sour, he would make every attempt to force that portion of the estate upon his brother Quincy. Of course, should it prove to be as sound an investment as Fulford projected, Jonas would claim it as his own. Either way, he would protect himself—or his lawyers would.

He placed the papers on Mortimer's desk and picked up a pen. "You're recommending I move forward, are you not?"

"Indeed. As a matter of fact, I'm investing some of my own money in Fulford's Pink Pills for Pale People. Business has soared, and I think we'll see a fine return."

Jonas nodded and scribbled his signature on the designated line. He returned the pen to its holder and pushed the paper across the desk. "Now, let's discuss my niece and the demise of her bequest from my father."

Mortimer rubbed his arthritic hands together and shuffled to the office door. "We had better have Vincent join us for this conversation. As you're well aware, my days of standing in a courtroom have come to an end. With my supervision and assistance, Vincent will be in charge of any conflict arising from the estate."

Moments later Vincent entered the room with his pencil and notebook. No clerk would be included in these meetings. Jonas wanted to be certain no one else knew what was discussed among the three of them. "No memos or notes, Vincent. I want nothing committed to paper regarding our meetings." He leaned forward and arched his brows. "Do I make myself clear?"

"Very clear, Mr. Broadmoor." He placed the paper and pencil on his father's desk. "Why don't you tell us what has transpired since we last met."

Without need of further encouragement, Jonas launched into the details. Mortimer appeared mesmerized by the tale, but there was little doubt Vincent was much less than enthusiastic. "This is, quite frankly, beyond anything I'd bargained for, Mr. Broadmoor. Although preparation of Miss Broadmoor's will was improper, I was relieved when you told me you'd been unable to gain her signature. As for this latest scheme, I am at a loss." Vincent sighed. "Do you realize both the legal and moral implications of what you've done? You are denying this girl more than her inheritance: you are denying her the memory of a father she loved, and you've besmirched the reputation of her mother."

Mortimer thumped his cane on the floor. "Do you realize how much money is in the balance? You had best throw off that cloak of self-righteousness and change your attitude."

Vincent's nervous laughter didn't offer the level of accord Jonas expected.

"Since when is your law firm worried about ethics and morality?" Jonas demanded as he stood and turned to face Mortimer. "Should I be seeking another lawyer to handle my business?"

"Of course not, Jonas." The old lawyer motioned toward the chair. "Sit down. We're going to get this resolved to your satisfaction." He pinned his son with an angry glare. "Aren't we, Vincent."

"Yes, but I do believe we should make every attempt to cause the least harm possible to the girl."

Jonas groaned. "I don't believe this is going to work, Mortimer."

Mortimer poked Vincent with the tip of his cane. "You listen to me, young man. This *is* going to work, and *you* are going to make it work. Do I make myself clear?"

Jonas clearly understood the veiled threat. So did Vincent, for he quickly offered his assistance. "If you're planning to send the girl to visit Mr. Morrison in Syracuse, I'm willing to accompany her in order to observe what transpires."

"No need. I plan to have her visit for an extended period of time. How long do you think it will take before we can have the court declare she's not a blood relative and is not entitled to any share of the estate?"

Vincent picked up the pencil and nervously tapped it atop the desk. "I surmise that none of the family will protest the process. Still, there are statutes we must follow, and the court's docket must be considered, too. I would guess six to nine months until all is said and done. Of course, if the girl hires counsel to represent her in the proceedings, it could take much longer."

Jonas jumped up from his chair. "Six to nine months is far too long!" He paced back and forth like a caged animal. "She doesn't have money to hire a lawyer."

"But Mr. Morrison may be able to find a counselor who would handle the case on a contingency basis. And if Morrison can prove he isn't Fanny's father and that his assertion was made under duress . . ."

The comment brought Jonas's pacing to a halt. "You think a lawyer might be willing to risk such a thing?"

"I can't say with absolute authority, but an argument could certainly be made that your father may have known of Fanny's parentage. Who's to say? Her attorney might find a witness who would testify your father knew Langley wasn't Fanny's father."

Had this man gone completely daft? "The three of us realize that isn't possible, since Langley *was* her father. Are you forgetting this plan is based upon a lie of my own making?"

"No. But you're obviously forgetting there could be others willing to perjure themselves for a price. In somewhat the same manner as you've convinced Mr. Morrison to succumb to your scheme, a wily lawyer could hire a witness. One who would testify your father was aware of the truth regarding Fanny's lineage."

This was becoming more complicated by the minute. He had hired lawyers to achieve his desired goals, not to speak of failure. Working with Mortimer had been much less difficult when he'd been in practice by himself. However, with Mortimer's failing health, Jonas couldn't depend solely upon the old lawyer. Had he realized Vincent possessed so many scruples, he would have taken his legal business elsewhere.

"And you're concerned we might not be able to convince Mr. Morrison that he should dissuade Fanny from seeking legal counsel?" Jonas asked.

Vincent shrugged. "I don't know your niece or Mr. Morrison. If the girl is not easily swayed, I have no doubt she could find someone to assist her. The contingency fee would be quite handsome—certainly worthy of a hard-fought battle, don't you think?"

"Any other obstacles you'd like to throw in the pathway to our success?"

"If you're truly interested."

Now what? Was there no end to this man's desire to fail? "I prefer men who possess a positive attitude, Vincent. Is failure your objective?"

"Not at all. My objective is always to win. That's why I always consider the flaws in a case before I step into the courtroom. I want to be prepared."

"I'm pleased at least to hear you want to succeed," Jonas muttered.

Vincent once again began tapping his pencil. "Let's remember that Mr. Morrison has a long history as a gambler. After thought and consideration, he may view this entire matter as a gamble."

Jonas leaned forward. "How so? If he wants to free himself of debt, he must do my bidding."

"Not necessarily. Once he and Miss Broadmoor develop more of a relationship, he may decide that the two of them could strike a deal. One that would be of greater financial benefit to him. What if he tells your niece the truth and the two of them enter into an agreement that once she receives her inheritance, she will pay off his debt and perhaps even give him additional funds? Even if she pays him no more than you've offered, he's freed himself from the criminal act of perjury. In addition, he can assuage any feelings of guilt with thoughts that he hasn't permanently injured the girl's future or reputation. Of course the same couldn't be said for you if that should occur."

With an unexpected rush, the warmth of the afternoon overpowered Jonas and beads of perspiration lined his brow. He withdrew a fine linen handkerchief from his pocket and swiped it across his forehead. Was Harold Morrison cunning enough to create and carry out such a plan? He recalled Morrison's distaste when he'd heard the particulars. Surely the man wouldn't go to such lengths when Jonas had already offered him a simple method to extricate himself from his financial difficulties.

Jonas studied Vincent for a moment. He couldn't decide if the young lawyer was truly attempting to help him or if he was hoping to create an avenue of disentanglement for himself. Either way, he had presented Jonas with food for thought. He should have talked to the lawyers before arranging Fanny's visit with the Morrisons in Syracuse.

CHAPTER 27

STEPHEN'S PASSAGE, ALASKA

"Headin' for gold, eh?" an older man asked Michael.

Standing on the deck of the steamer *Newport*, Michael nodded and gave the man his hand. "That I am. Michael Atwell's the name."

The man exchanged a shake and smiled. "The name's Zebulon Stanley, but you can call me Zeb."

"Glad to meet you, Zeb." Michael looked out at the passing collection of islands. "This sure reminds me of home." Although it was the first week of September, the air had a chilled promise of colder days to come.

"Where you from?"

"The Thousand Islands. Are you familiar with the area?"

"Can't say that I am." The older man scratched his beard and shrugged. "No, I can't say that I've ever heard of such a place."

"It's in the St. Lawrence River between New York and Ontario. There are thousands of little islands similar to these. But instead of being barren of homes, many of our islands have huge castlelike estates. The very wealthy own them and usually spend their summers in leisure there."

"Oh, so you're already very wealthy?"

Michael laughed. "Not me. Not my parents, either. We worked as island staff for the Broadmoor family. I'm quite handy with boats."

"Do say. So what brought you up this way?"

"Well, of course the gold rush," Michael admitted. "Sounds like it's quite the adventure."

"Oh, it is, quite the adventure," Zeb repeated. "'Course I was up here awhile before gold was discovered, so it's less so for me."

Michael noted the man's unkempt appearance. He was, as Michael's mother might have noted, rather scruffy around the collar. Still, he was a companionable enough soul, and Michael figured he might well learn something about the frozen north.

"So you're already familiar with the Yukon?"

"I am. Been up here nearly five years now. I'm what they call an old sourdough."

"What's it like? I've heard all sorts of stories."

"Most of 'em are probably true. 'Cept for maybe the ones about picking up gold nuggets the size of babies' heads."

"What about how the gold is just lying there waiting to be picked up?"

The man laughed. "Well, the gold is there, that much is true. But it's hardly lying around. You have to work for it."

"I don't know anything about gold mining. What kind of thing is required? Do you go digging into the ground like you do for coal?"

"Seems all mining is about digging. The only problem with the Klondike is that the ground is frozen most all of the time. We have to light fires to warm up the dirt and melt the frozen ground. Then we dig that up and sluice it, using water from the creek or river," Zeb replied. "It's quite the process. You put the dirt in these rocker boxes and go to work. The goal is to wash away the dirt and rocks. The gold sinks 'cause it's heavier. Of course some folks don't want that kind of setup. They prefer panning for gold."

"How is that done?"

"You take a round pan and basically do the same thing as the sluicing but on a much smaller scale." He pretended to hold a pan. "You put it in the creek and get some soil from the bed. Then you rinse it like this." He made a motion as if shaking a pan gently back and forth. "You keep rinsing it with the water until the debris is gone and the gold sinks to the bottom."

"And you can do this in any river or creek?"

"Not all of them have anything to offer. And there are claims that have to be filed with the authorities. A lot of the good ones have already been taken."

"Do you have a claim?"

The man nodded. "Me and my brother Sherman have a small one. He's up there right now keepin' it safe from intruders."

"Did you come down to get supplies?"

"Yeah. The winters are mighty long up north. Dark, too. We figure to work through as best we can, but we need equipment." Zeb looked around. "You come north with someone?"

"No," Michael told him. "My employer did loan me the money, but I'm traveling on my own."

"So you have a grubstake," Zeb said. "That's good. Too many folks try to come north without supplies, and they die. The wilderness ain't that forgiving."

Michael nodded. "I know that well enough."

"I doubt most of these folks do," Zeb said, tipping his head toward the throngs of passengers. "They haven't got any idea what's in store for them. They don't know about anything but the glory stories of gold." He looked at Michael. "What about the gold caused you to leave your home?"

Michael leaned back against the railing. "A beautiful young woman."

Zeb grinned. "A woman? Like I said, me and my brother have been up there for a long while. I don't recall a woman being a part of the deal."

"My employer has a niece, and . . . well, we're in love. We want to marry, but he doesn't believe me worthy. We struck a bargain that I'd come north and make my fortune, and then he would allow us to marry."

Zeb rubbed his chin thoughtfully. "And if you don't make your fortune?"

"I can't even begin to think that way," Michael replied. "Fanny means everything to me. If we can't be together . . . nothing would be the same."

"I had me a gal once," Zeb began. "She was a pretty little thing. Sweet and gentle, and boy, could that girl cook."

"What happened?"

"She passed on. We'd been married about six years when she died in child-birth. Baby died, too."

"I'm sorry. Fanny's mother died in childbirth," Michael offered, but he wasn't really sure why.

"It was only the good Lord that kept me from following them both into the grave," Zeb admitted. "That and Sherman. Neither one would leave me for even a minute for fear of what I'd do to myself."

Michael could imagine how he might feel if Fanny died. Would he want to go on living? The thought caused him a moment of panic. What if she died while he was gone? What if she took sick and needed him?

"Are you a God-fearin' man?" Zeb asked.

"Most certainly." Michael smiled. "I learned Bible stories at my mother's knee. My father's, too, for that matter. Working with the boats and transporting the wealthy back and forth on the river gave me a lot of time to pray and to listen."

Zeb nodded. "I knew there was something about you. Just felt like when I saw you that I ought to come and talk with you. I have an idea if you want to hear it."

"Sure. What do you have in mind?"

The steamer blew its whistle, and only then did Michael notice that they were heading in toward land. "Is this Skagway?"

"No. Juneau. It's a fair-sized settlement—another gold camp. I heard it said that prices are actually cheaper here than in Seattle. Once the stampede was on, everybody in Seattle tripled their prices. I was fortunate. I secured my stock when I first got into town, before the word got out."

"So you came down with the *Portland* and *Excelsior*?" Michael asked, knowing those two ships had changed the lives of many across the nation.

"I did. Me and a million dollars worth of gold."

Michael's jaw dropped. "You found a million dollars in gold?"

"No. I found plenty, but not that much. No. The whole ship carried some sixty passengers out of the north, and together we had over a million in gold."

"I can't even imagine what that would look like." Michael strained to see the small settlement of Juneau from the ship.

"Well, maybe you will once you work the claims for a while. That's what my idea is. Why don't you come work for Sherman and me? We'll see to it that you get a fair cut. You won't have to worry about filing your own claim, and we're already set up and working. Most of these folks won't see gold until next summer, but we'll be working through the winter."

"Do you think I could make myself a fortune by this time next year?"

"I do. Our claim is a good one."

Michael suddenly grew suspicious. "Why would you do this for me?"

Zeb laughed. "It might sound strange, but you remind me of myself, and Sherman and I can use the extra hand. We're not young anymore. You have your supplies, so it's not like we'd be hard off having you there. And what might sound even crazier still, I think God put us together for a purpose. That seems as likely a reason as any I can think of."

Michael grinned. "God does work in mysterious ways. But what about Sherman?"

"He'll be glad for the help. We talked about hiring on someone. We even talked about a third man coming in as a partner. You're younger and in better shape than either of us, so I know we'll get a fair amount of work out of you. Say, why don't we talk about it over some grub. I know a little place here in Juneau where we can get a decent meal. The ship will be here for hours, so we have plenty of time."

"Sounds good," Michael said, returning his gaze to the town. The mountains rose up behind the settlement, displaying white crowns of snow. Michael had to admit the beauty was startling. Everything seemed so massive—so impressive. If only Fanny were here to share it.

They were delayed leaving Juneau due to a storm, but when they finally arrived in Skagway, Michael felt a new sense of direction. He and Zeb had struck a good friendship as well as a solid agreement. Michael would work for the Stanley brothers through the winter and net twenty percent of what he found. Of course Sherman would first have to agree to the arrangement, but Zeb felt confident his brother would be willing to part with ten percent of his share in order to accumulate that much more gold. And based on what Zeb had told him they'd made from last year's work, Michael stood to make thousands of dollars. The thought pleased him immensely.

"Well, we're here," Zeb said, slapping Michael on the back. "Now the hard work begins. You'll have to face the Chilkoot."

"Is that the mountain pass you were telling me about?"

He nodded. "There are two ways north from Skagway. One goes straight up from the town. It's a vicious trail, though. I prefer the route out of Dyea. It's a little town to the west of here. It's too shallow to take a steamer in to dock, so we dock here and then hire a boat to take our supplies over. There's a lot of Tlingits looking to make a few dollars."

"Klinkets?" Michael questioned. "What's that?"

"Local natives. They're good folks. Peaceable types unless you cheat them."

"Sounds reasonable. I tend to be the same way myself," Michael said with a grin.

Zeb leaned closer. "We're not going to hole up in Skagway tonight. We'll get a boat to take us right over to Dyea. Most folks will stay here. They don't know what they're doing. We'll get on over and hire us some help. You did say you had some cash to your name, didn't you?"

"Some. Not a whole lot."

"Given the fact that you'll be making upwards to a hundred trips up and down that mountain without help, you'll be happy to pay some of the natives to pack the goods for you."

"You mean there are no wagons to take the stuff? No boats?" Michael realized he knew just about as little as the rest of the newcomers.

Zeb shook his head. "It's hard terrain. Not at all kind. Like I said, this is a most unforgiving land. If you have any doubt about that, you'd best put it aside now. You'll be walking most of the way. Boat ride comes after you get up and over the Chilkoot Trail."

"And we have to carry everything?"

"Afraid so. Some of it can be hauled a ways by horse or mule. Not a whole lot of 'em available, though. You can sometimes pull a load. The Tlingits can make some great sledges, but they only work until you get to the pass itself."

"I see. Well, I suppose there's nothing to be done about it," Michael said, squaring his shoulders. "I'll have to trust you on this one."

Zeb met his gaze and smiled. "Nah. Don't go putting your trust in me. The good Lord is the only one who deserves that. It's not going to be easy, but with a little hard work and a whole lot of prayer, I'll get you to the gold fields ahead of this stampede. And the sooner we get there, the sooner you can get back to your little gal."

Michael looked at the daunting mountain peaks already topped with snow. He couldn't imagine how a man could ever manage such an arduous feat. The terrain looked jagged and severe. Zeb's words about the land being unforgiving were gradually beginning to make sense.

I can do this, Michael told himself. *For Fanny and for our future, I can endure whatever I must.* He gazed heavenward, past the craggy peaks and snow. *I can do all things through Christ which stengtheneth me.* The verse from Philippians had never seemed so comforting as it did at this moment, for Michael was sure there was no possible hope that his own strength could see him through the challenges to come.

CHAPTER 28

WEDNESDAY, SEPTEMBER 8, 1897
SYRACUSE, NEW YORK

In a crisp tone the conductor announced the upcoming stop before continuing on to the next railcar. Fanny's heart beat in quick step when the train lurched and hissed to a halt a few minutes later. *Syracuse.* She'd been filled with a mixture of anticipation and dread ever since bidding Amanda, Sophie, and Aunt Victoria farewell at the Rochester train station. In truth, she'd been suffering from a bout of nerves since Uncle Jonas announced she would make the journey.

Her fingers trembled as she pulled on a pair of lightweight summer gloves.

She told herself this could be no worse than listening to the murmurs when she attended a social function with her cousins or hearing the rumors passed on by *thoughtful* acquaintances who always began their sentences with the same verbiage: *"I thought you'd like to know what I heard."* Their proclamation was immediately followed by a ghastly report of her mother's illicit behavior or a mean-spirited comment regarding Fanny's parentage. And they always smiled and offered pitying looks while they delivered the painful tidbit. Fanny didn't know which was worse: hearing the comments or knowing that the messenger took pleasure in the delivery.

Hat in hand, Mr. Morrison stood near the terminal doorway. Fanny spotted him the minute she stepped off the train. He waved his hat, and when he stepped forward to greet her, she surveyed the area. He seemed to be alone. Mrs. Morrison had apparently chosen to remain at home; Fanny hoped the woman's failure to come wasn't an indication that she would be unwelcome in their home. Mr. Morrison's letter of invitation to come for an extended visit had spoken of his wife's desire to meet Fanny. She wondered if he'd spoken the truth.

His gaze traveled to the small valise in her hand. "You have other baggage, I assume?"

"Yes, my trunks were loaded into the baggage car." She looked over her shoulder. Two burly men were unloading them and placing them at the far end of the platform. She'd not had the luxury of a Pullman car on this excursion. If all she'd heard about Mr. Morrison was true, she doubted whether she'd ever have such a luxury again.

She waited while Mr. Morrison made arrangements for her trunks to be placed in an old horse-drawn wagon. She had expected a carriage, but she supposed a wagon would prove reliable, and there'd be no need to pay extra for the delivery of her trunks. Mr. Morrison assisted her up onto the wagon but offered no apology or explanation for their transportation. With a click of his tongue and a snap of the reins, the horses stepped out.

When they'd traversed only a short distance, Mr. Morrison said, "My wife would have come to meet you, but she wanted to have a fine meal prepared for your arrival. She decided a good meal after your journey was more important than waiting at the train station." He gave her a sidelong glance. "I hope you agree, for she would never intentionally offend anyone."

A breeze that carried the scent of approaching fall weather rippled through the air and tugged the first of summer's dying leaves from nearby trees. A desire to be at home, where she could help the gardener prune the bushes and prepare the gardens for winter, created a dull ache in Fanny's bones. The ache deepened when she considered the truth: she had no place to claim as her home.

Since Grandfather's death, Fanny could no longer consider Broadmoor

Mansion home. Uncle Jonas had moved her under his roof, but neither he nor Fanny considered his house to be her home, either. Like the leaves that fluttered along the street, she had been discarded and set adrift.

Now she would be immersed in a situation for which she felt ill prepared. Then again, she didn't think any amount of education or training would have prepared her to live in the same house with a long-lost father and his wife of many years. She realized dignity and grace would be required, but days filled with forced smiles and uncomfortable conversation held little appeal.

The conveyance made a final turn, and Mr. Morrison pulled back on the reins. The wagon came to rest in front of a modest white frame house with a pleasant enough yard and large front porch. Lilac bushes had been planted to advantage, and Fanny imagined a spring breeze carrying their sweet scent through open windows to perfume the interior. Mr. Morrison jumped down from the wagon and circled around to assist her.

A thin woman with chestnut brown hair stepped onto the porch and shaded her eyes. Although she waved, her right hand remained affixed to the handle of the front door. She conveyed an anxiety that matched Fanny's own. Fanny understood, for she would have taken flight if there had been someplace for her to run.

Mr. Morrison held on to her hand and gently drew her forward. "Come along and I'll introduce you to my wife. I can return for your baggage after you're settled inside."

Settled? Fanny doubted she would ever again feel settled until Michael returned to claim her as his bride. She didn't withdraw from Mr. Morrison's grasp. Without the strength emanating from his hand, she would surely sink to the ground in an embarrassing heap.

With a sweeping gesture, he motioned his wife forward. "My dear, let me introduce you to Miss Frances Jane Broadmoor." He gently squeezed Fanny's hand. "However, she tells me she prefers to be addressed as Fanny."

Mrs. Morrison released the door handle. "I'm pleased to meet you, Fanny. And you may call me Ruth—or Mrs. Morrison—whichever you decide is more comfortable."

"For now, Mrs. Morrison seems appropriate."

The older woman opened the door and ushered Fanny inside. "If you wish to reconsider your choice at any time, please don't feel the need to request permission."

Once they'd been introduced, the woman's earlier trepidation appeared to melt away. She asked her husband to retrieve Fanny's trunks and proceeded, with neither apology nor embarrassment, to point out the few amenities their home offered, explaining that they'd fallen upon hard times.

"Many people suffered greater losses through the depression, and we've had a few setbacks along the way. But even if we're never restored to our previous financial status, I still consider myself fortunate." Mrs. Morrison glanced toward the street, where Mr. Morrison was removing Fanny's trunks from the wagon bed. "I've been blessed with a wonderful husband, we've never gone hungry, and we have a roof over our heads. God has been faithful to answer my prayers."

Perhaps Mrs. Morrison didn't know that, rather than the economic downturn, her husband's gambling was rumored to be the cause of their financial woes. Fanny doubted whether the woman's praises for her husband would ring forth with such conviction if she'd heard those tales. Then again, Fanny couldn't be certain the gossip was true. Who could believe her cousin Beatrice? True or false, Beatrice repeated every morsel of tittle-tattle with great delight. And Mr. Morrison did seem a nice enough man.

"I do hope you'll find your room comfortable. I know you're accustomed to much finer accommodations. Harold said I shouldn't worry. He said you knew you wouldn't be coming to a huge mansion with servants and the like." She tucked a strand of hair behind her ear. "Come along and I'll show you to your room."

Fanny couldn't help but notice the faded print and worn cuffs of Mrs. Morrison's gown. Although she'd clearly done her best to control the fraying cuffs with a thread and fine stitches, the dress had surely seen better days. Once again, Fanny wondered how a couple with such meager means had afforded a stay at the New Frontenac Hotel. Mrs. Morrison didn't appear the type who would squander money on such an extravagance. When they became better acquainted, Fanny would broach the subject.

The room was very small, and Fanny doubted her clothes would fit into the wardrobe, but she didn't mention her concerns. Instead, she simply accepted Mrs. Morrison's invitation to unpack her belongings. "I'll join you downstairs once I've finished."

"Supper should be ready by then. I do hope you don't mind simple fare. There was a time when Harold and I—" She stopped short. "I'll be serving chicken this evening, and I hope you'll find it to your liking."

"I'm certain it will be most enjoyable. Thank you."

Fanny unlatched her trunk and shook out her dresses. She'd hang her best gowns, and the others could remain in her trunk until she discovered an alternative. The bedroom offered a view of the backyard. She surveyed Mrs. Morrison's garden from the window. Though the spring and summer blooms had disappeared, the older woman clearly enjoyed flowers. Mr. Morrison had spoken the truth: if nothing else, she and Mrs. Morrison had gardening in common.

Supper had been preceded by a prayer, offered by Mrs. Morrison at her husband's request. An odd occurrence as far as Fanny was concerned. She was accustomed to the men in the family performing the ritual. Apparently Mr. Morrison had detected Fanny's surprise, for he had quietly remarked his wife's prayers were more likely to reach the ears of the Almighty than his own unworthy utterances. Fanny didn't comment because until then she'd never given thought to God having a preference of whom He heard from. Perhaps He did. If so, she thought Mr. Morrison's assessment was incorrect. The world considered women's thoughts of little value. Wouldn't God then prefer to hear from men? She would write that question in her diary tonight so she could ask . . . Whom would she ask? Mrs. Atwell! Michael's mother frequently spoke of her faith in God. She could pen Mrs. Atwell a letter this evening and ask. Moreover, she wanted to advise the older woman of her change in address.

Fanny insisted upon clearing the table and drying the dishes. It seemed strange to work in the kitchen yet not uncomfortable. Mrs. Morrison chatted while she washed the dishes and asked Fanny simple questions about her childhood. "Did Harold drive you past the house where we lived before moving here?"

"He didn't mention it if he did. Is it on the way from the train station?"

She dipped a saucer into a pan of rinse water and handed it to Fanny. "It would depend on the route he took. Our old house had belonged to Harold's parents. Originally it was constructed by his grandparents after they became wealthy. The lumberyard was a thriving business for many years."

"I heard it mentioned that he had planned to expand his business to Rochester and Buffalo."

Mrs. Morrison arched her perfectly shaped brows. "Truly? Harold never mentioned expanding the business in my presence."

"Then perhaps I misunderstood." Fanny couldn't remember who had spoken of the expansion. It may have been her uncle Jonas; then again, it could have been Beatrice's gossip. She wished she hadn't remembered the information or at least had kept it to herself. Mrs. Morrison appeared alarmed.

"When did you hear talk of this proposed expansion, Fanny?" Mrs. Morrison stared into the soapy pot and continued to scrub.

"I don't recall. In all likelihood I overheard some of my uncle's business associates and completely misunderstood." She shrugged her shoulders. "Who knows? They may have been discussing the Bancroft Lumberyard."

Mrs. Morrison frowned. "But that closed two years ago."

Fanny wanted to kick herself. She should have remembered it had closed! Lydia Bancroft's father had died unexpectedly, and when Lydia's brother refused to return to Rochester and take over the business, Mrs. Bancroft had sold off the existing stock and closed the doors. Mrs. Bancroft later sold the building, and against Lydia's protests, the two of them had moved to New York City.

"Then perhaps it wasn't even a lumberyard they were speaking of, Mrs. Morrison. I can't be certain." Fanny nodded toward the backyard. "I see you enjoy gardening. I'm fond of flowers myself."

Thankfully Mrs. Morrison was more interested in discussing her annuals and perennials, so no further mention was made of her husband's business plans. When the conversation lulled, Fanny spoke of her childhood and the lilac bush she'd planted after her father's death. She hesitated and looked at Mrs. Morrison from beneath hooded eyelids. "I know what that letter says, but I don't think I'll ever be able to think of another man as my father."

Mrs. Morrison wiped her wet hands on the corner of her apron. "I don't believe either of us would ever expect you to do so, Fanny. From what you've told me, Mr. Broadmoor was a fine father, and you must revere his memory."

Fanny hung the dish towel to dry. "How long have you known about me?"

"Not long. My husband told me only a few days before we went to the Thousand Islands." She stared into the distance. "Those islands are the most beautiful place I've ever visited. I should like to return there one day—under more pleasant circumstances." Her comment seemed to jar her back to the present. "Not that anything about you is unpleasant . . . I didn't mean to imply . . ."

"I know, Mrs. Morrison. You need not apologize. I know this must be very difficult for you, also."

The older woman sank onto one of the wooden chairs. "Yes. It was such a surprise, you know, after all these years." She reached for Fanny's hand. "I always wanted a child, but we were never able . . ." She inhaled a ragged breath. "Knowing that you are Harold's child is a good thing. I am not saddened by the news, merely surprised that he never told me. I thought I knew everything about Harold." At the sound of Mr. Morrison's footsteps, she released Fanny's hand. "We should join my husband before he thinks we've deserted him."

While they sat on the front porch making small talk, Fanny wondered how the Morrisons would explain her to their friends and neighbors. "Am I to be introduced as a visiting relative or friend of the family? I don't want to say or do anything that would cause either of you embarrassment."

Mr. Morrison gestured for his wife to answer.

"What is your preference, Fanny? We are happy to concede to your wishes."

"If we say I'm a relative visiting from Rochester, they will expect further explanation and wonder why they've never before seen me in your home, don't you agree?"

"Why don't we say you are a relative who has come to visit for the very first time? We need not say anything further unless questioned." Mrs. Morrison offered a kind smile. "Our friends don't delve into our private affairs, and acquaintances have no right to do so. If the need arises, I believe I can discourage further questions." Mrs. Morrison's response reflected a quiet conviction that dispelled Fanny's concerns. Should questions arise, she would direct them to the older woman.

Mr. Morrison knocked the bowl of his pipe against the porch rail. "How were you received in Rochester after your return from Broadmoor Island?"

Fanny watched the charred tobacco flutter to the ground below. "It was more difficult than I anticipated."

He tamped fresh tobacco into the pipe. "The social set was ready to discard you like last year's fashions, I suppose?"

"They continued to invite me to the parties, but I was not treated in the same manner. In fact, I doubt they would have invited me at all had I not been residing under my uncle Jonas's roof. Until the matter is settled in court, they'll simply continue to twitter and gossip. If the judge declares I'm not a Broadmoor, I doubt I'll see any of them again—except for Sophie and Amanda." She glanced at Mrs. Morrison. "They're two of my cousins, and we're as close as sisters. They would never abandon me."

"I'm sure they wouldn't. And they are always welcome in our home." Mrs. Morrison reached for her mending basket and then decided against the idea. "I believe it's soon going to be too dark to accomplish any sewing out here on the porch."

A red glow shone from the bowl of Mr. Morrison's pipe, and Fanny studied his profile as a curl of smoke wafted above his head. He was a fine-looking man, but she could see no resemblance. Blood or not, she much more closely resembled the Broadmoors.

CHAPTER 29

TUESDAY, SEPTEMBER 14, 1897
ROCHESTER, NEW YORK

Jonas stared heavenward. Why must he listen to yet another of Victoria's verbal onslaughts? His wife questioned the validity of Mr. Morrison's claim of fatherhood as well as Jonas's decision to send the girl for a lengthy visit. And since Fanny's departure, there'd been no escaping her scolding arguments.

"Are you listening to me, Jonas? You cannot hide behind a newspaper." Victoria flicked the paper with her fingers. "In addition, I might point out that your behavior is beyond rude. I am attempting to have a discussion with you, and you're behaving like a child."

Jonas sighed and refolded the paper. A man couldn't even enjoy an evening of quiet in his own home. There was no escape. His wife wanted to have yet another *discussion*. Either he'd participate or Victoria would continue to carp at him for the remainder of the night.

"We've already gone over all of this, Victoria. Must we do this every evening? I grow weary of rehashing the same thing over and over."

"How can we be rehashing something we've never discussed? I talk, you ignore me, and we go to bed. There has been no discussion, only avoidance. I don't believe Mr. Morrison is Fanny's father, and I want to bring her back home."

"On the other hand, I believe Mr. Morrison *is* her father, and I agreed she could remain in their home." He reached for his newspaper, but Victoria slapped her hand atop his.

"Not so quick, Jonas. I want to know why you, a man who constantly questions everything, would so easily accept a letter supposedly written by Winifred years ago as substantial proof. We can't be certain that letter is authentic. I fear you are doing Fanny a grave injustice." She sat down in the chair opposite and clung to his hand, as though he might attempt an escape. "Even if Mr. Morrison is Fanny's father, I believe Langley would have known before he married Winifred. Langley and Winifred were devoted to each other, and he remained devoted to Fanny after Winifred's death. I simply cannot accept this."

"Have you considered that the question of Fanny's parentage is what drove him to take his own life?"

"Jonas!" Victoria withdrew her hand. "What an awful thing to say—and it makes no sense. If he was burdened by the child's lineage, he would have refused her at birth—immediately after Winifred's death."

"Since he didn't do that, I can only assume Winifred didn't tell him. Let us remember the child was born when they had been married only eight months."

"She was premature, Jonas. She was so tiny that she nearly died. Many babies are born early—do you not remember Amanda's birth?"

Jonas shook his head. "But she wasn't our first child. If she *had* been . . ."

"You would have accused *me* of impropriety?" Anger flared in his wife's eyes.

"This conversation has nothing to do with us, Victoria. Let's get back to the topic at hand. Winifred's letter is substantiation enough for any court, and it's enough for me."

"How do you know what the court will require? And who can truly verify that Winifred wrote that letter? Even if she did write it, who can attest that Langley and your parents didn't know?"

Jonas massaged his temples. "My father would have told me."

"*Pshaw!* Your father adored Langley. If asked, he would have protected Langley's secret. His will was drawn with specificity, and I believe he wanted Fanny to have Langley's share of his inheritance. Even if all of this is true, Langley and your parents considered Fanny a member of this family."

"With all due respect, my dear, you're forgetting that Mr. Morrison is the one who stepped forward to claim Fanny as his child. We'll let the court decide."

Victoria folded her hands. "The court can decide whatever it wants, but Fanny is still a member of this family. Mr. and Mrs. Morrison should let Fanny decide where she wants to live, and no matter what any judge rules, you and Quincy should see that Fanny receives her inheritance."

Jonas gulped and choked until Victoria finally clapped him on the back. Give the inheritance to Fanny? Had Victoria taken leave of her senses? He attempted to clear his throat as tears rolled down his cheeks.

His wife offered a fleeting look of concern. "Are you all right?"

He nodded. "Yes," he croaked. "I totally disagree with your thinking. For all concerned, it's best we follow the dictates of the court. We both know that there are members of the family who would strenuously object to your plan, particularly in regard to the inheritance."

"And you are one of those family members, aren't you, Jonas? You said as much at the reading of the will, before any of this business with Mr. Morrison came to light. Do the right thing, Jonas. If you'll pray about your decision, I believe you'll change your mind."

Jonas squirmed under his wife's watchful scrutiny. She'd changed her tactics. She had departed from her earlier theory of a bogus letter and was now attempting to sway him with religious conviction. It seemed there was no end to what she would attempt in order to win her argument. However, there was too much at stake for him to relent now.

"I'll consider what you've said, but don't expect me to change my mind."

"At a minimum, I want Fanny back under our roof. I'll not see this family abandon her."

"We have not abandoned her. She is no more a Broadmoor than a stranger walking down the street. She is likely quite happy with her new family."

"Father! I cannot believe what you said." Amanda stared wide-eyed at her father as she walked into the room. "Fanny is my dear cousin and best friend. How can you cast her aside and speak of her as a stranger? Are you so heartless? Is it because you want her money?" Amanda curled her lip in disgust.

"Her money? It is not hers, Amanda. She is not a Broadmoor. This is a private conversation between your mother and me. And you'd do well to remember that you enjoy the pleasure of new gowns and jewelry—all the fine things money can buy."

"I'll give up my jewelry and fine gowns if you'll permit Fanny to return home to live with us." Amanda sat down beside her mother. "Please say you'll agree, Father."

Jonas shook his head. "It isn't my decision. Mr. Morrison has the final say in where Fanny will live. For the present, he has chosen to have her in his home." Jonas rose from his chair. "I'm not going to discuss this any further."

He'd not satisfied the wishes of his wife or daughter, of that he was certain. However, he had to escape or he'd soon be ensnared by the two of them. Handling Victoria's questions was difficult enough, but when she worked in tandem with Amanda, he knew flight was the only answer. A visit to his men's club would provide a needed respite.

With his mind set upon peace and quiet for the remainder of the evening, Jonas stepped down from his carriage and approached the front steps of the men's club—a place where he could enjoy a good cigar, read his paper, and visit with fellow businessmen about the latest fluctuations in the business world, or at least in Rochester.

He started as a man approached from the shadows. "I hoped I might find you here. I didn't want to come to your house."

"Morrison! What are you doing in Rochester?" Jonas looked about, half expecting to see Fanny somewhere nearby.

"I'm by myself. We need to talk."

"Not here," Jonas said. There had been enough rumor-mongering since Fanny's departure. He didn't want to fuel the gossip by appearing inside the club with Harold Morrison at his side. They needed to be on their way. One of the members could arrive or depart at any moment. The thought caused his palms to perspire. "We can go to my office." After giving the driver instructions, Jonas and Harold climbed into the carriage.

"I wanted to tell you . . ."

Jonas held up his hand to stave off the conversation. "Not until we are inside my office."

"Who is going to hear? The carriage driver? You don't trust your own driver?" he whispered.

"I trust very few people, and my hired help aren't counted among that small number."

Save for the creaking of the carriage and the sound of the horses' hooves clopping down the macadam street, the remainder of the carriage ride was made in silence, which allowed Jonas time to gather his thoughts. Seeing Harold Morrison had been far from his mind when he'd arrived at the club. Pieces of his conversation with Mortimer Fillmore came to mind, and he wondered if Fanny and Mr. Morrison had already been scheming. Had Morrison arrived with a plan to bilk him out of more money? The thought alone made him edgy.

"After you," Jonas said when the carriage came to a halt in front of his office building. Stepping down from the carriage, he instructed the driver to wait in front of the building. "We shouldn't be long. I'll want to return to the men's club."

Jonas led the way, unlocking doors and turning on lights until they were inside his office. Harold didn't wait for an invitation to sit. "I want to discuss Fanny's future with you."

"I do wish you would have sent word that you wanted to speak to me. I prefer my business appointments during office hours. And I prefer they be scheduled in advance."

Harold leaned back in the chair. "I consider Fanny's welfare more of a family concern than a business matter. One that shouldn't require an appointment."

"If you've come here thinking I'm going to up the ante, you're sadly mistaken, Harold."

"On the contrary. I've come here because I believe what we are doing is completely unconscionable. Fanny is a sweet young lady who deserves much better. I have come here hoping you will be of the same mind and we may come to a gentleman's agreement."

Jonas grunted. "When did *you* develop a conscience?"

"After observing the pain the two of us have caused that young girl. You with your greed and me looking for an easy way out of the mess I've created with my gambling."

"I have no problem seeing you in jail for nonpayment of your debt. I think before we jump to any rash conclusions about the handling of this matter, we need to explore all of the ramifications, as well as the possibilities." Jonas leaned across his desk. "Remember, your wife will be left to her own devices if you are in jail. Can she support herself?" Jonas didn't wait for an answer. "Go home, Harold. You'll hear from me by the end of the week."

Fortunately Harold didn't argue. The driver delivered Jonas to his men's club. After bidding Morrison good-bye, Jonas issued his driver instructions to deliver Harold to the train station. He added whispered instructions to his driver to remain at the station to see that Harold boarded the ten-o'clock train to Syracuse. The last thing Jonas desired was another surprise visit from Harold Morrison.

CHAPTER 30

THURSDAY, SEPTEMBER 16, 1897
SYRACUSE, NEW YORK

Fanny wiped her hands on an old towel and leaned back on her haunches. She'd spent the morning planting tulip bulbs that would add early color to Mrs. Morrison's flower garden come spring. In spite of all the changes forced upon her, Fanny was thankful for the kindness of Mr. and Mrs. Morrison and for this flower garden. Mrs. Morrison had given her free rein to garden in both the front yard and the back. Working in the dirt provided a connection between her former life in Rochester and the present, although she remained uncertain what this new life held in store for her. She patted the dirt that covered the bulbs. The cold earth would hold them snug until spring, when they would force their green sprouts through the hardened ground and eventually bloom into a low-lying canopy of yellow, red, pink, and white.

And what of herself come spring? she wondered. Would she remain dormant through the winter months and burst forth with a life of promise, or would she be one of the bulbs that didn't have the strength to survive the harsh winter? Maybe her life would resemble those occasional blooms that made the effort to push through the ground but failed to ever bloom. That's how she felt right now—as though she'd never have the energy to bloom again.

A tear trickled down her cheek and surprised her. She swiped it away with her sleeve, annoyed that she'd permitted her feelings to erupt into tears. The back door slammed, and she glanced over her shoulder.

Mrs. Morrison waved a letter overhead. "Mail for you, Fanny."

The sadness disappeared, and her heart pounded in quick time. *Michael! Please let it be from Michael,* she silently prayed while pushing up from the ground. If she knew that he was safe and that he continued to keep her in his thoughts, she could withstand the changes that swirled around her. She ran to Mrs. Morrison's side. One glance at the flourishing script on the envelope was enough to send her spirits plummeting back to the depths of despair.

Mrs. Morrison smiled as she handed her the missive. "Mr. Morrison and I received one, too."

Fanny opened the seal and removed the piece of thick stationery. An invitation. She perused the printed words and shoved it back into the envelope. A ball would be held at the home of Jonas and Victoria Broadmoor on the second of October, and she was cordially invited to attend. She nearly laughed at the paradox. For seventeen years she'd been a Broadmoor; she still carried the name. But now she received an engraved invitation, as if she were any other social acquaintance. Not even an additional word of greeting. The gesture stung.

"We'll need to send our acceptance or regrets," Mrs. Morrison said.

Fanny heard the question in her statement. "I would enjoy seeing my cousins, but I will leave the decision to you and Mr. Morrison. There is, of course, expense involved if we should attend."

Mrs. Morrison glanced at the frayed sleeve of her gown. "I have nothing appropriate to wear to a formal ball, but you could go."

Surely the Morrisons had attended formal functions in the past—before they had fallen on such difficult circumstances. Though they'd never attained the same social standing as the Broadmoors, they would have been invited to balls and parties in Syracuse. "Perhaps we could update one of your old gowns?"

A faint smile traced Mrs. Morrison's lips. "I was fortunate enough to sell all of my gowns when we were in desperate need of money. The funds helped for a short time."

Fanny thought they were still in desperate need of money, but she refrained from saying so. Since her arrival, Mrs. Morrison had been nothing but kind. Such a comment would sting. "What about the dresses you wore when you and Mr. Morrison were in the Islands earlier this summer?"

"My last two. I sold them so we would have the funds—" She stopped short. "We needed the money. Let's wait and see what my husband has to say about the invitation."

Fanny wondered if the funds had been used to furnish her bedroom or cover the expenses of the additional food she consumed each day. The thought saddened her. She returned to her gardening. She pushed the small spade into the ground and turned the dirt. If the Morrisons wanted to attend, she would find a way to pay their expenses.

Mr. Morrison mentioned the cost of train tickets during the evening meal but added he would find some method to cover the expense if the two ladies wished to be present at the ball. The thought of a reunion with Amanda and Sophie outweighed Fanny's trepidation at having to face the local gossips. Mr. Morrison hadn't mentioned the cost of a hotel room, although he surely realized they'd not be able to return to Syracuse after the ball. Though Fanny was sure she would be welcome to stay with Amanda, there was still the cost of a room for the Morrisons.

She penned a letter to Amanda setting forth her concerns. There was little doubt Uncle Jonas would be of no assistance, but perhaps Aunt Victoria would help with a solution. Fanny would post the letter and the two acceptance cards the following day. There had been no further mention of attire for the ball, but Fanny had come upon the perfect solution.

On Friday morning, after Mr. Morrison departed the house, she located his wife in the parlor working on her embroidery. "I have an idea for your gown. To wear to the ball," she quickly added.

Mrs. Morrison looked up from her sewing. "Then you are much more innovative than I, for although I gave the matter great thought last night, I've been unable to reach an appropriate solution. I shouldn't have agreed to attend."

"On the contrary, I should have thought of my solution earlier. You and I are approximately the same height, although you are considerably thinner. There is no reason we cannot alter one of my gowns to fit you. There is sufficient time, and you are adept with a needle." Fanny's enthusiasm mounted. "My rose-colored gown would be the perfect shade for you." She grasped Mrs. Morrison's hand. "Come upstairs and let's take a look at what would be best."

Mrs. Morrison didn't budge. "I wouldn't consider such an idea. Your gown would be ruined." She patted Fanny's hand. "And you have no idea if and when you will ever have sufficient funds to purchase new dresses. You must take good care of what you have in your wardrobe."

"I will not accept your refusal. I insist. Otherwise I will be forced to remain here in Syracuse, for I won't attend the ball without the two of you. I know you wouldn't want me to miss this opportunity for a visit with my cousins. I've longed to see them again." Fanny hoped her added comment would be enough to sway the woman.

For a brief time Mrs. Morrison appeared lost in her own thoughts, but finally she gave an affirmative nod. "I won't be responsible for spoiling your chance to visit Rochester. I know it is important." She tucked her sewing into the basket and held Fanny's hand. "Let's go upstairs and look at your gowns."

Fanny had been correct. The rose color was perfect against Mrs. Morrison's pale complexion. It added color to her cheeks, and though the dress hung on her, she now appeared years younger. With the gown turned inside out, Fanny pinned the sides to conform with Mrs. Morrison's form.

Mrs. Morrison removed the dress, careful not to stick herself with the pins. "If we leave the extra fabric in the seam allowance, I can remove the stitching once we return home. After the gown is pressed, no one will suspect it was ever altered."

Fanny giggled as she held the bunched up fabric in her hand. "If you leave this inside the dress, you'll look as though you have some sort of deformity. You must trim away the extra fabric. Otherwise the dress will fit improperly. I insist." Fanny waved toward her wardrobe. "As you can see, I have plenty of others, and there are more in my trunks. In fact, I didn't bring all of my clothing because I didn't know how long I would be staying here."

"If you insist, then I shall do as you've asked. You are a very kind young lady, Fanny, and I'm thankful you've come into my life." She gathered up the dress and hung it across her arm. "I only wish all of this hadn't caused you so much pain."

Fanny wished the same. Beside the fact that she'd been yanked from her home and from every person she'd ever considered family, she'd said good-bye to Michael. If she had received this news of her parentage before Michael's departure for the Yukon, there would have been no reason for him to leave. Jonas Broadmoor would have had no reason to object to the marriage of Harold Morrison's daughter to his boatswain on Broadmoor Island.

And though they'd not yet received any final determination from the court, Fanny was convinced she would be disinherited. Uncle Jonas would make certain she was stripped of both the family name and her inheritance. Likely that would please many of the greedy family members who had objected to the bequest. But she refused to dwell on the thought. If she continued to reflect upon such matters, she would become as bitter and unkind as Sophie's sister Beatrice.

Late the next week a reply arrived from Amanda. The letter contained sufficient funds to cover the cost of train travel and hotel expenses for the Morrisons, along with an invitation for Fanny to stay at the Broadmoor home for the duration of her visit. Amanda had secured the funds from her mother, and from the tenor of the letter, it seemed Aunt Victoria was eager for Fanny's visit. She doubted Uncle Jonas would be nearly as pleased. In fact, Fanny wondered if he knew they would be in attendance. Surely her aunt hadn't extended their invitations without his knowledge. Then again, when Aunt Victoria set her mind to something, she didn't worry about Uncle Jonas or the possible consequences.

Mrs. Morrison had been feverishly working on her dress, and when Fanny presented her with the funds for the train tickets and hotel accommodations, her eyes welled with tears. "I truly do not think I should be taking this money from you. I'm not certain my husband would approve. Especially for something as frivolous as attending a ball."

"I believe it will prove to be money well spent. Mr. Morrison agreed we could attend. Please tell him it is my desire to have the money spent to cover the costs. I only hope we will all have an enjoyable evening."

Fanny didn't mention her cousin had sent the money; thankfully, Mrs. Morrison didn't inquire. Mrs. Morrison probably thought the Broadmoors had given her substantial funds before her departure. The older woman tended to believe others possessed her same thoughtful nature. Fanny wished that were true.

The weekend of the ball approached more rapidly than Fanny had expected. Mrs. Morrison had completed the alterations on her gown two days ago. Once pressed, the dress looked as though it had been custom made for the older woman. Mrs. Morrison had added a layer of fine ecru lace to the sleeves and neckline, the final touches that gave the gown a fresh appearance. Fanny doubted that even her cousins would recognize it. However, they were certain to recall the one that she would wear.

The thought evoked a remembrance of Sophie's complaints throughout the past years—her cousin's anger when her father hadn't purchased her a new gown for a special party. Fanny wondered if Uncle Quincy had succumbed to Sophie's desire this time and if Fanny would be the only one wearing an old frock. She pushed aside the idea. In the future she wouldn't have need of such finery.

When Michael returned, they would use his gold to purchase their own island and build a home. One for his parents, too, if they should so desire—she hoped they would. And though she might find use for one or two gowns for annual parties held at the New Frontenac, she wouldn't be distraught if she couldn't attend. Parties held little appeal. It was Michael and the possibility of living on the islands that filled Fanny with joy.

She had sent a note to Amanda advising they would arrive on the three o'clock train. When the train pulled into the station, she hoped it would be her cousin or Aunt Victoria waiting to greet her and not Uncle Jonas. "Please not Uncle Jonas," she murmured.

Mrs. Morrison stopped in the middle of the aisle. "What, dear? I couldn't hear you over the train's noise."

"Nothing important," she said.

As she stepped off the train, Fanny surveyed the waiting crowd for some sign of her cousin or aunt. Moments later she heard Amanda's voice calling to her and caught sight of her parasol waving in the air. "Over here, Fanny!"

When Amanda finally reached her side, her hat was askew and she was out of breath.

"I am so sorry I'm late. I thought I had more than enough time, but the street was blocked with fire equipment." She gazed heavenward. "Of all days, there has to be a fire today."

"Dear me, I do hope nobody was injured." Mrs. Morrison clasped a hand to her bodice.

Amanda's cheeks tinged pink. "My remark was rather insensitive, wasn't it?"

"Yes, but we'll forgive you. Did your mother or father come along?"

"Mother sends her regrets. She wanted be here, but she's overseeing preparations at the house. You know Mother: she believes everything will fall apart if she isn't there to supervise."

Once Mr. Morrison gathered their luggage and joined them, the driver delivered Mr. and Mrs. Morrison to the hotel. Fanny bid them good-bye and said she would await their arrival at the ball. She squeezed Mrs. Morrison's hand. "I don't want the two of you to feel alone or out of place when you arrive."

"That's very kind of you, Fanny. We'll look forward to seeing you tomorrow evening. I hope you girls have a lovely visit."

Once the carriage lurched forward, Amanda leaned closer. "Has it been absolutely terrible for you, Fanny?"

"They are very nice people, but I could never think of Mr. Morrison as my father. I am fond of his wife, though."

Throughout the remainder of their carriage ride, Amanda pressed for additional details. Fanny answered her questions honestly, but she didn't elaborate. Somehow she felt a need to protect the privacy of the Morrisons. They'd suffered enough embarrassment. There was no need for every detail of their lives to be scrutinized and dissected by Rochester's social set.

"Do tell me more about what you've been doing. You mentioned several young men in your latest letter to me. It seems your father has redirected his matchmaking efforts. I can honestly say that I don't miss that aspect of my life." Fanny giggled. "I hope he hasn't decided upon any of those young men who were at the island this summer. They were a miserable lot. Not one of them would make you happy."

"No. He's found several others, but I've told him that I've made up my mind to remain single for the time being. He doesn't believe me, but he'll soon learn that I'm serious about a career." She tipped her head close. "I've decided I want to begin college and then attend medical school."

Fanny didn't say so, but she knew Uncle Jonas would never agree to Amanda's plan. And if Uncle Jonas didn't agree, he would simply refuse to pay. *Money.* As far as Uncle Jonas was concerned, money was the answer to everything.

CHAPTER 31

SATURDAY, OCTOBER 2, 1897

The guests had come dressed in their finery, the women wearing the latest fashions they'd purchased in Europe or creations their dressmakers in New York City or Rochester had stitched to exacting measurements. The array of colors and fabrics decorated the rooms like a bouquet of spring flowers. The women in those gowns, however, weren't nearly as sweet as the scent of fragrant blooms. Fanny couldn't help but hear the murmurs of women hiding their lips behind opened fans while they ridiculed or envied the guests clustered in yet another group. Some things never changed. She didn't miss the petty gossip fueled by insecurity and jealousy. At every social gathering the women took inventory of one another, each one always fearful she'd be found lacking.

Fanny kept a vigilant watch on the front door, and the moment she saw Mr. and Mrs. Morrison approach, she hurried across the foyer. They were every bit as elegant as any of the other guests. Indeed, Fanny thought Mrs. Morrison outshone most of the women in attendance. A deep flush colored her cheeks, probably from nerves, but it added to the older woman's natural beauty. Although Mr. Morrison's cutaway wasn't new, it was stylish. Together they made a striking couple.

"I'm so glad you're here. I was becoming concerned."

Mrs. Morrison handed her wrap to the servant. When her husband stepped away to hand his hat to the butler, she whispered, "Mr. Morrison isn't feeling well. I wanted to remain at the hotel, but he insisted we couldn't disappoint you."

He did appear pale. This party was taking more of a toll on the couple than Fanny had anticipated. They should have remained in Syracuse. Other than permitting Uncle Jonas an opportunity to publicly display that she was no longer a member of the Broadmoor family, this final social appearance served no purpose. She hadn't given the matter sufficient thought before sending their acceptance.

Fanny touched Mr. Morrison's arm. "I'm so sorry you're feeling unwell. There's no reason to remain. I can have a carriage take you back to the hotel, and we can depart first thing in the morning."

"I'll not hear of it. We've come to attend a ball, and that's what we're going to do. My wife looks beautiful, as do you, Fanny. We are going to hold our heads up and act like we belong, even if we don't."

The butler edged around them, and with Fanny clasping Mr. Morrison's right arm and Mrs. Morrison clutching his left, they were announced to the staring throng of guests. "Mr. and Mrs. Harold Morrison and Miss Frances . . ." The butler stopped. He'd known Fanny since she was a tiny girl and appeared confused. He cleared his throat. "And Miss Frances Broadmoor."

Murmurs filled the vast flower-scented room. The butler hurried away, obviously uncertain if he'd properly announced the threesome. If Uncle Jonas had wanted Fanny introduced as a Morrison, he should have told the servant. And though her uncle seemed anxious to erase her name from the family tree, the court had not yet rendered a decision.

Since her arrival the day before, Jonas had done his best to avoid her. He'd excused himself immediately after the evening meal, citing work that needed his attention before morning. Not that Fanny had expected him to welcome her back into the fold, but she had hoped to hear the latest news regarding the court proceedings. When she had asked at supper, her uncle told her that in polite society such topics were not discussed at the dinner table. His gibe that she'd forgotten proper etiquette in such a short time had nearly caused her to come undone. She'd wanted to lash out and tell him that although the Morrisons might not have money, they had far more refinement than he'd shown since her return. But she'd remained silent. She was, after all, a guest in his home.

The three of them entered the room and clustered in a far corner. Fanny was determined to remain close at hand and keep any of the nosy dowagers at bay. She doubted whether Mrs. Morrison could hold her own against them—especially if they approached in twos or threes.

"Would you like something to drink, Mr. Morrison? A glass of punch or water? Do you think that might help?"

"I think the only thing that would help get me through this would be a stiff shot of whiskey and a determination to match." He offered a faint smile. "I already have the determination, but I don't think it would be wise to request the whiskey." His lack of color was disconcerting.

Mrs. Morrison remained close by his side. "He's having chest pains again. With rest, they usually subside within a few hours."

Fanny looked up in time to see her aunt swooping across the room, her gown flowing behind her in a sea of green silk. She descended upon them, her bejeweled neckline shimmering in the pale light cast by the crystal chandelier. "Mr. and Mrs. Morrison, I am so pleased you could join us this evening. I have truly enjoyed having Fanny back with us. I hope you'll permit her to remain a few extra days to visit with all of the family."

The stiffness in Mrs. Morrison's shoulders relaxed. "Whatever Fanny desires will be agreeable with us."

Her aunt took a step closer to Fanny, but her focus remained fixed upon Mrs. Morrison. "Your gown is quite lovely." Victoria turned toward Fanny. "I seem to remember you owned a gown of that same shade." She stared a moment longer. "Or perhaps it was a shade or two lighter. Do you recall the one I'm thinking of?"

Fanny nodded. "I remember. Rather plain. Unlike Mrs. Morrison's dress, mine lacked embellishment."

"You're absolutely correct. I never did think the dressmaker did that gown justice. In any case, I do hope you're all ready to partake of a fine meal." She tipped her head as though confiding a deep secret. "We have an utterly marvelous group of musicians for the dancing that will follow."

Mrs. Morrison responded politely. At the mention of food, Mr. Morrison's pale complexion turned slightly gray, and Fanny wondered if he'd be able to remain for the entire evening. Fortunately they were soon ushered into the dining room, where they were seated side by side. Fanny was pleasantly surprised to see Amanda and Sophie draw near.

Sophie winked as she led Amanda to the chairs directly opposite Fanny and Mrs. Morrison. She picked up the name card and smiled. "You see? I told you we were seated near Fanny."

Fanny giggled. "Up to your old tricks, Sophie?"

"Of course. Until people cease their attempts to seat me next to some of their stodgy old guests, I'll move my place card and sit where I please."

Amanda nudged her cousin. "That is completely improper behavior, Sophie."

"In that case I suppose I could return yours from where it came. You'll be seated beside your father's old banker, Mr. Snodgrass." Sophie grinned across the table. "Fanny can tell you how much fun you'll have."

Fanny's curls bobbed. "And he'll expect to remain your escort and dance partner for the remainder of the evening. You do remember my embarrassment, I assume?"

Amanda turned contrite at the mention of Mr. Snodgrass. "I suppose it doesn't matter. There are enough guests that Mother won't remember where we're supposed to be seated."

"You're truly the fortunate one, Fanny," Sophie said. "Even though you have no money, you're no longer under Uncle Jonas's thumb."

Mrs. Morrison unfolded her napkin and placed it across her lap. "I believe Fanny misses all of you very much. She's such a well-mannered young lady that I doubt she ever had difficulty following her uncle's rules."

Fanny shot an annoyed look at Sophie. Once in a while Sophie needed to think before she said whatever popped into her mind. At least she seemed to realize she had caused Mr. and Mrs. Morrison discomfort with her offhand remark and said little throughout the meal. As their apricot pudding was served, Fanny inquired how Paul Medford was adjusting to his career at the Home for the Friendless.

"I don't know how he has sufficient time to perform his duties. He's too busy attempting to intervene in my life." Sophie dipped her spoon into her creamy dessert. "He says Father is preoccupied and doesn't realize I need supervision. What do you think of that, Mrs. Morrison?"

Mrs. Morrison sipped her coffee. "Perhaps your father has granted this young man permission to act as a surrogate parent during his absences."

"Ha!" Sophie pointed her spoon in Paul's direction. "Do you see that young man sitting beside Amanda's mother?"

"Yes."

"That's Paul Medford. He's not that much older than me, so I don't think he's capable of acting as a parent, surrogate or otherwise."

Mrs. Morrison leaned to see around her husband. "Rather a nice-looking young man. Have you considered that he may be romantically interested and that's why he's attempting to look after your best interests?"

Sophie jerked to attention. "*Paul?* Interested in *me?* I think *not!* We're as different as day and night. Never in a thousand years would I be interested in someone like Paul."

"Opposites can sometimes be a good thing. You each bring different strengths to the marriage," Mrs. Morrison said.

"That might be true for some people, but Paul and I can't move beyond our disagreements." Sophie looked down toward the other end of the table. "And I don't see why everyone says he is nice appearing. I find him rather plain."

Mr. Morrison laughed. "If he were the most handsome man in the room, I believe you'd find him unappealing, for he represents authority. And I would surmise that is something you dislike."

"You're correct. I detest authority. However, I control my life—not Paul Medford. I merely want him to take heed of that fact."

The sound of the musicians tuning their instruments signaled the end of the meal, and soon the guests were all gathered in the ballroom adjacent to the dining room on the third floor. No one seemed to think of the hardship these parties placed on the staff. Truth be told, it wasn't until Fanny saw the work Mrs. Atwell performed at Broadmoor Island that she'd realized the life of a servant was far removed from those they served. When she and Michael were married, they would be more cognizant of such inequities.

Sophie pulled on Fanny's hand. "Come along. Let's see if there are some eligible men looking for dance partners."

Fanny withdrew her hand. "I promised my first dance to Mr. Morrison. I'll join you later."

Sophie nodded. "I'm spending the night here at the house with you and Amanda, so we shall have plenty of time to discuss the men tonight."

Fanny watched Sophie weave through the crowd with grace and agility. No doubt she was making her way toward a cluster of young men at the south end of the hall. Fanny stifled a giggle when she saw Paul following after her. He'd likely attempt to curtail her fun.

The musicians struck their first chords, and Fanny insisted Mr. and Mrs. Morrison dance the first dance of the evening together. "I promise to wait and dance the next waltz with you, Mr. Morrison." She watched as they took to the floor. They made a lovely couple, and there was little doubt of their devotion to each other. Still, Fanny saw no resemblance between herself and the man who was circling the floor with his gentle wife. Sad that they'd never had any children of their own. She thought they would have been excellent parents. Given the opportunity, she thought Michael would be a wonderful father. She hoped one day she could give him a child.

"Daydreaming?"

Fanny turned at the sound of her uncle's voice. "Thinking how sad it is that I didn't discover my lineage before Michael departed for the Yukon. We could have been married and . . ." She hesitated.

"And *what*, Fanny? Live on Broadmoor Island as a servant? Your lineage aside, if Michael is the man you choose to marry, I've done you a service. If he returns a wealthy man, you'll have a life of ease and prosperity rather than a life of menial work. Either way, you should thank me."

Fanny clenched her jaw. "You equate happiness with money, yet you don't appear particularly happy or content. If you'll excuse me, I've promised this dance." She turned and walked toward Mr. Morrison.

He proved to be an excellent dancer as he led her around the floor. "You don't need to remain much longer. You've made an appearance. Uncle Jonas can assert he's a generous and proper gentleman who has deigned to entertain us in his home."

Mr. Morrison took a backward step and pivoted to the left. "You deserve so much more than I can ever give you, Fanny. I can no longer pretend—"

He gasped and clutched at his chest. His color turned sallow, and he stared at her with surprise in his eyes. Slowly he dropped to the dance floor, still clinging to her by one hand. Fanny quickly kneeled down beside him, her gown spread around them like a protective shield. The couples ceased their dancing and gathered around as the strains of music faded in uneven increments. Mrs. Morrison hurriedly broke through the crowd and called for a doctor.

"It's too late, my dear," he said. Ignoring his whispered protests, Mrs. Morrison pillowed his head on her lap.

"Fanny." Mr. Morrison grasped Fanny's hand, and she scooted closer. "I'm sorry for the pain I've caused. I have deceived you. That letter wasn't genuine, and I am not your father. I never met your mother. I'm sure . . ." He gasped for a breath of air.

"Someone get a doctor!" Mrs. Morrison called out.

Murmurs filled the room, and Jonas stepped closer. "This is preposterous. He must be delirious."

A number of the guests collectively shushed Jonas while others glared in his direction. Mr. Snodgrass thumped his cane. "When a man's dying, he speaks the truth, Jonas!"

Mr. Morrison's eyes rolled back in his head for a moment; then he regained strength. "I'm certain your mother was a fine woman. Your parents are Winifred and Langley Broadmoor. I wasn't even in the United States during that time. That fact can be verified." He glanced up at his wife. "In my lockbox there's information to prove what I say."

Fanny stroked his face. "Mr. Morrison, please."

His eyelids fluttered. "You are a lovely girl . . . I wish you could have been my daughter. I didn't do this to hurt you. Please believe my sorrow when I tell you it was simply about the money. I couldn't . . ." His voice faded and Fanny bent low, but his final mutterings remained unintelligible.

With one final breath, he was gone. Mrs. Morrison was softly whispering, but Fanny didn't know if she was praying or attempting to talk to her husband. She glanced upward and saw Paul Medford approach.

He bent down. "Let me help you to your feet."

Fanny grasped his hand and attempted to rise to her feet, but the room swirled around her like a whirlpool sucking her into a dark abyss. Somewhere in the distance she heard her uncle Jonas's voice. She detected urgency in his question, but her lips wouldn't move. She was unable to tell him she hadn't heard Mr. Morrison's final utterance.

CHAPTER 32

A cool breeze whispered through the bedroom window, and Fanny heard the murmur of voices. Using what strength she could muster, she opened her eyes.

"You're awake! Finally." Sophie lifted the cool towel from her head. "Aunt Victoria wanted to using smelling salts, but I objected." She grinned. "You can thank me later. I know how you detest the burning sensation."

"Where is . . ."

Amanda moved to the edge of her bed. "There's no one here but Sophie and me. We told Mother we were quite capable of looking after you. With all the commotion, it didn't take long to convince her. She wanted to be certain her party wasn't completely ruined."

"Can't you imagine what the society page is going to say come Monday morning? I can hardly wait to read it: *Man drops dead after dining at the home of Jonas and Victoria Broadmoor.* It's just too delightful." Sophie clasped a hand to her mouth. "Oh, I don't mean it's delightful that Mr. Morrison died, of course. That was horrid. But what kind of man was he, to pretend he was your father?"

Amanda grasped Fanny's hand. "*Enough*, Sophie! Fanny's had a severe trauma this evening, and you're jabbering like a magpie."

Fanny's eyelids fluttered. "Mrs. Morrison? Is she here?"

"Oh no. She left when they took the body—I mean her husband to the . . . well, you know . . . the mortuary. At least I assume that's where they took him. I did hear her say he's to be buried in Syracuse." Sophie hesitated for a moment. "Maybe he's already on the train . . . well, not riding as a passenger, of course, but in the baggage car or something."

"Do stop, Sophie. You're making matters worse by the minute," Amanda scolded.

"How can it be any worse? The man is dead. And deservedly so, I might add. He took advantage of our dear Fanny. I can't imagine what would come over someone to do such a thing." Sophie cupped her chin in one hand. "Do you suppose his wife forged that letter for him? And I thought she was such a nice lady." She wagged a finger back and forth. "So did you, Fanny, and I thought you were an excellent judge of character."

Using her elbows for leverage, Fanny scooted up and propped herself against the pillows. "Mrs. Morrison *is* a wonderful lady, and I think she believed the story, too. Didn't you hear Mr. Morrison tell her there was proof? If she was a part of the hoax, he wouldn't have explained it to her. Like me, I believe she was completely surprised by his confession, and I do want to see her again."

Ever the voice of reason, Amanda recommended Fanny rest now and make her decision regarding Mrs. Morrison in the morning.

"I'm not ill, Amanda. I merely fainted. Come morning, Mrs. Morrison may be gone. I'm certain she'll attempt to leave on the earliest possible train." Fanny glanced at the clock. "You don't think she had time to catch the final train tonight, do you?"

Sophie shook her head. "No. By the time she returned to the hotel for her belongings, the train would have already departed. She'll be required to remain in Rochester tonight."

"Then I shall go and see her this very moment." Before Amanda could protest, Fanny sat up and slid her feet into her shoes. "Please don't be angry, Amanda. If you're overly concerned, one of you can go with me while the other stays here to keep watch. We don't want anyone to discover I've left the house."

"I want to go with you," Sophie squealed.

"Do keep your voice down or someone will hear." Amanda frowned. "I don't like this plan in the least, but if you're determined, I'll remain and keep watch. You can go down the back stairway and through the kitchen. The servants won't question you. I'll do my best to keep your secret, but if Mother comes upstairs to check on you while you're gone . . ." With a beseeching look, she turned her palms upward.

"If your mother comes looking, I don't expect you to lie," Fanny said.

"Tell her I forced Fanny outside for fresh air. That won't be a lie. Just watch as I push her out of here." The three of them giggled while Sophie propelled Fanny out the door and down the hallway.

Once they exited the house, Sophie took charge. Fanny had to admit that her cousin's experience with such escapades was now proving invaluable. Rather than asking one of the Broadmoor drivers to bring a carriage around, they strolled down the driveway, where Sophie hailed a passing cab. "Much less chance of word traveling back to Uncle Jonas as to where we've been," she said.

As long as she had an opportunity to speak with Mrs. Morrison before her departure, Fanny cared little what her uncle might think. However, she appreciated her cousin's concern. They rode in silence until the driver brought the carriage to a stop in front of the hotel.

"Do you want me to wait in the foyer or go up with you?" Sophie asked after instructing the driver to wait for them.

"Sitting in the hotel foyer without benefit of an escort is highly improper," Fanny replied.

Sophie giggled. "You're beginning to sound like Amanda. Let's ask for her room number."

The clerk appeared doubtful he should give them the desired information. Sophie furrowed her brow and leaned forward until they were nearly nose to nose. "If you have ever heard the name *Broadmoor*, my good sir, I suggest you tell me the room number posthaste."

Strangely, the man didn't ask if they were related to the Broadmoors or if they could produce any form of identification before directing them to room 342. Sophie's knack for achieving success astounded Fanny.

"I believe the Broadmoor name frightened him out of his wits. I wonder if he's had a confrontation with Uncle Jonas in the past," Sophie said with a grin.

With her fingers trembling, Fanny formed her hand into a tight fist, knocked on the door, and waited. "Maybe she's asleep."

Sophie shook her head. "I doubt she'll sleep a wink after all that's happened tonight. Knock again."

She lifted her hand again but stopped midair when she heard footsteps. The door opened, and Mrs. Morrison stood in the doorway, pale as a ghost. Fanny opened her mouth to speak, but the words stuck in her throat like a wad of cotton.

Mrs. Morrison grasped her by the hand. "Do come in. I'm very pleased to see you, Fanny."

The night's events appeared to have shriveled Mrs. Morrison's already thin body. She peered at them with eyes that had shrunken into their sockets, and her head bobbled as though she hadn't the strength to hold it upright. Fanny held on to the woman for fear she might collapse before reaching the chairs across the room. Thankfully Sophie remained at a distance and allowed them a modicum of privacy.

"You didn't know, either, did you?" she asked the older woman once they were seated.

"No. I should have questioned him more, but my husband had changed in the final years of our marriage. He remained kind to me, but I knew the financial losses had been extremely painful to bear. He hid many things from me. Men place their value on being able to provide," she said with a faint smile. "I am very sorry for what you've endured. I have spent the last hour attempting to make sense of why my husband would do such a thing, but I have no answer for you.

"If your relatives desire the proof he spoke of, I will make it available to them. I know my husband was genuinely fond of you, Fanny, as am I. Any woman would be proud to claim you as her daughter." A tear rolled down her cheek and dropped onto the gown. She stared at the dark splotch. "I'll send the dress back to you."

"I've no need for the dress, but I would like you to write to me in the future. I will always consider you a dear friend."

The guests had finally departed, and now only the family remained. But the evening had been insufferable. Jonas had expected their guests to immediately leave after Harold's death, but he should have known better. With their curiosity piqued, they had stayed, eager to discuss every detail of the night's ghastly event. Jonas slammed the door to his library and fell into his leather chair. All of his plotting had been for naught. He slammed his fist on his desk and cursed Harold Morrison.

Although most in attendance at tonight's ball had heard of Harold Morrison's initial claim of paternity, Jonas had planned to make an announcement during the evening—unbeknownst to his wife, of course. Victoria would never have approved of such a thing, especially during a party. However, Jonas had viewed the ball as the perfect setting. All of the elite would be in attendance for the formal announcement that Fanny was not a Broadmoor. The men would immediately realize what a financial boon this would be for Jonas, and his status would rise among his peers. Now all of that had been ruined by Harold Morrison's untimely death, and Jonas was once again faced with the dilemma of Fanny's inheritance.

"Here you are!" Quincy strode into the room.

"Have you heard of knocking before entering a room?" Jonas barked.

"My, but you're in a foul mood. I realize the evening was marred by Morrison's death, but I didn't expect to find you in such bad humor." Quincy sat down opposite his brother. "That scoundrel Morrison certainly had you fooled. I daresay I'm surprised, Jonas. You're usually the first one to question the credentials of every one of your business associates, yet this man and his spurious claim slipped by you with surprising ease. How so?"

"What do you mean, how so? If you've something on your mind, speak up, Quincy. I'll not play silly games with you. It's been a long evening."

Quincy rested his forearms on his thighs and stared across the desk at his brother. "We all trusted that you'd checked into this man and his claims. None of us inquired—at least I didn't. For that I blame myself. It never occurred to me that you would be careless."

Jonas jumped to his feet and rested his palms atop the desk. "Careless? Are you implying that I intentionally accepted this man's claims without proper investigation?"

"That's exactly what I'm saying. If you'd properly checked in to the matter, we would have known his claim was false and Fanny would have been saved from this horrid experience." Quincy waved his brother toward his chair. "Sit down, Jonas. I don't believe you meant harm to the girl. I know you're a busy man with many obligations to handle. I blame myself as much as you. In the future, however, we're going to both need to keep a close watch on the girl's affairs and on those who seek to befriend her."

Jonas exhaled a long breath. He needed to remain calm. "I appreciate your concern, Quincy. You're correct. In the future I'll be keeping a close watch. But there's no reason for you to concern yourself with Fanny. I am her legal guardian, and I know you have a myriad of duties requiring your attention at the poorhouse."

"Home for the Friendless, Jonas. It's not the poorhouse."

Jonas snorted. "Same thing, different name. Except your Home for the Friendless has the advantage of Broadmoor money paying the expenses."

"*My* portion of the Broadmoor money. I ask nothing of you, Jonas, and we are digressing from the topic at hand. I believe we must remain vigilant where Fanny is concerned."

"You may rest assured that I will see to doing exactly what is best," Jonas said as he ushered his brother to the door.

Jonas returned to the solitude of his library. He couldn't permit defeat to take hold of him. There must be resolution to this latest dilemma. How could one young girl pose such a problem in his life? He sat in the chair and rested his forehead in his palm, massaging his temples with his fingers and thumb.

Somehow, returning to his earlier plan seemed a form of defeat. But if he was going to succeed in controlling Fanny's inheritance, he must do so. Like it or not he would resume his original plan to find a husband for the girl— a man who could be easily manipulated. In the meantime he must remain vigilant. The girl had likely become even more independent during her stay with the Morrisons.

CHAPTER 33

Monday, October 4, 1897

Jonas had planned to depart for work much earlier in the day. His headache of Saturday night had plagued him throughout the day on Sunday. When the persistent pain continued on Monday morning, he downed his headache powders with a glass of water and returned to bed. Though not completely gone, the pain had subsided, and he'd tired of Victoria popping in and out of the room to check on him every fifteen minutes.

After descending the broad staircase, he picked up the mail that had been stacked on the hallway table and then called for his carriage to be brought around. Jonas riffled through the unusually thick stack but stopped when his fingers came to rest on a letter addressed to Fanny. He tossed the remaining mail onto the table and hurried into his library. His head pounded with a blinding ferocity as he shoved the door closed behind him.

He hurried to his chair and slit open the envelope. He shuffled through the pages until he reached the end, where Michael had neatly written his address. He was in a place called Dyea, Alaska. He returned to the first page of the letter and shook his head as he continued to read the details of Michael's journey in search of gold. Between the paragraphs that spoke of his undying love for Fanny was an optimism that frightened Jonas. There was, of course, no way to know if the young man's accounts were puffery or fact. If what he wrote was true, Michael was doing well and held high expectations for his gold mining. He spoke of teaming up with a man who already had a successful claim near Dawson City. The man assured Michael he could make thousands of dollars by the end of next summer.

"Next summer!" How could it be possible? That young man just seemed to be lucky no matter where he went. The thought only furthered Jonas's frustration. Given Michael Atwell's seeming good fortune, he'd probably find some incredible supply of ore and make hundreds of thousands of dollars.

"I need to remain calm. After all, I must see Fanny married to a man of my choosing before March, when she turns eighteen. After that it will be too late. The property laws in this state will negate any control I might desire to exert," he muttered.

He looked at the letter again. Obviously he couldn't allow Fanny to see it. The last few lines of the letter gave him an idea.

I will soon be bound for Dawson and doubt I will have an opportunity to write again until spring. The mail is difficult to deliver during the winter and questionable at best. So please do not despair if you hear nothing from me until summer.

He smiled. Summer would be too late. Fanny would hear nothing from Michael and believe he had stopped caring about her.

Jonas quickly tucked the letter into his desk drawer and stood. His head throbbed with intensity, but he couldn't yield to the pain. This letter from Michael strengthened his resolve to move quickly. He simply had to force Fanny into a marriage before the young man's return.

He shouldn't have come to the office. He'd accomplished nothing, and the throbbing in his head had grown worse by the minute. Like a possessed man, he paced back and forth in an attempt to find some solution—anything that would gain him access to Fanny's inheritance. Well, not truly Fanny's, he told himself. The money rightfully belonged to him. And to Quincy, he begrudgingly admitted. Of course his brother would squander the additional funds on that homeless charity. It would be truly grand if he could come up with an idea to exclude both Fanny and Quincy, but that seemed impossible.

His clerk tapped on the door and entered the office. "I know you said you didn't want to be disturbed, but Mr. Fillmore is here to see you."

"Vincent or Mortimer?" he growled.

"Mortimer. He said it was important."

Jonas waved for the clerk to send Mortimer into his office. Word had traveled quickly. Neither Vincent nor Mortimer had been at the ball on Saturday night, having sent regrets due to a previous engagement, but there was little doubt Mortimer had heard of Harold Morrison's death.

"Jonas! I got back into the city late last night, and this morning I heard—"

"I'm sure you did. There is such pleasure in being the first to pass along a bit of sensational gossip."

Mortimer sat down and massaged his swollen knuckles. "You have anything to do with his death, Jonas?"

"Of course not. Morrison was my means to the girl's inheritance."

Mortimer grunted. "We'll need to withdraw our motion requesting Fanny be excluded as a beneficiary under your father's will. This puts you back where you started, I suppose. What are your plans?"

"I haven't come up with a solution, but I know I must maintain control of Fanny."

"Or at least her money," Mortimer cackled.

"Instead of your gibes, I need a solution."

"What about those young fellows you had courting her this summer? Any way you could fan the flames of love with an added bonus to one of them?"

Jonas shook his head. "Daniel Irwin stopped by last week. He's in dire need of financial assistance. I told him I didn't have anything available. In addition, forcing Fanny to accept his company would likely prove impossible. I'm at a loss."

Mortimer thumped his cane. "Don't be foolish! This is easily enough solved. Find some way where she is required to be in Irwin's company. And tell that young man he had best prove his ability to pour on the charm, for Fanny will not be easily won. I feel certain you'll be able to convince him with promises of the fortune that awaits him once they are wed." The lawyer withdrew his pocket watch and pushed himself upright. "I must take my leave, Jonas. I promised my wife a month in Europe, and I'm off to make arrangements." He pointed his cane at Jonas. "It's more of a gift to me. A month without listening to her ongoing complaints."

"That's it, Mortimer! Europe! I'll send Fanny, Amanda, and Sophie on a grand tour. Victoria can act as their chaperone. Father had planned on Fanny taking a tour, so the idea won't cause undue suspicion. A stroke of genius. Thank you, my friend."

"Ride along with me and tell me how this is going to solve your problem. I see some deficiencies in the plan."

Jonas grabbed his hat and accompanied the older man outside. He helped Mortimer into the carriage and sat down opposite him. "You're likely wondering how I'm going to marry off Fanny if she's in Europe. Am I right?"

"Exactly."

"I'm going to send Daniel Irwin along. Four women traveling without benefit of a male escort wouldn't be a wise idea. My wife would have far too much difficulty maintaining control over three young women without occasional assistance." His headache had disappeared. He called to the driver to stop the carriage. "I'm going to go and meet with Daniel this very minute. If he agrees to my plan, I'll have this matter settled by day's end."

Uncle Jonas seemed utterly giddy when he returned home later that day. Fanny watched as he joined them in the music room, an uncustomary smile beaming on his face.

"Quincy, I didn't realize you would be here, but I'm glad," he started. "I have a great notion to share."

"I'm sure we can hardly wait," Sophie muttered under her breath. She stepped away from the piano, where Amanda had been entertaining them with a few selections before supper.

"What are you about now, Jonas?" Victoria questioned. "Haven't we had enough surprises for one year? I suppose you'd better sit down and explain, but first let Amanda finish the last movement."

Uncle Jonas remained standing. Fanny knew he didn't have the patience to wait until Amanda completed her piece.

"Never mind the last movement. I have some exciting news. A gift for all of you." He glanced at his daughter. "If you don't mind the interruption."

Amanda turned away from the keyboard and shook her head. "We would be delighted to hear your news, Father."

"I've made arrangements for you three girls and your mother to take a grand tour of Europe. Together—all four of you. You'll depart two weeks from today."

Fanny was stunned. Amanda and Sophie immediately began to object to the idea, while Victoria appeared baffled. Only Uncle Quincy seemed in tune with the proposal.

"Jonas, that must have cost a pretty penny," Quincy declared.

"The cost is irrelevant. It's a gift," he replied. "After all, this family has suffered a great deal because of Mr. Morrison's attempt to steal Fanny's wealth."

Fanny frowned, but it was her aunt who spoke. "Jonas, I cannot possibly just up and leave Rochester. You should have consulted me."

"Truly, Father." Amanda got up from the piano. "I just did a grand tour in the spring. I've no desire to go on another."

"Neither do I," Sophie threw in.

Fanny nodded and folded her hands. "I cannot go, nor will I."

"Ladies, ladies!" Quincy interjected. "You're most ungrateful. Jonas has gone to the trouble and expense of planning a lovely tour for you, and all of you act as though you're being sentenced to a terrible punishment. Where is your spirit of thankfulness?"

The three girls glared at him. Sophie pointed a finger at her father. "I will not go on a grand tour. I have no desire to leave Rochester, nor do Fanny and Amanda."

Aunt Victoria waved for quiet. "Even if I could be readied in time, I'm uncertain I can properly chaperone three young ladies at one time, Jonas. They are all young and beautiful. Their ability to sightsee and attend parties would be limited by my inability to oversee so many activities. I tire of such things after a short time. Besides, Amanda and I have already made her tour. It would be unfair to all concerned."

"I have already thought of that aspect, my dear. Concerns for your safety as well as that of the girls is always foremost in my mind. I wouldn't want you to make the journey without a male escort."

Aunt Victoria relaxed her shoulders. "Oh! If you're planning to join us, then I think this is a splendid idea."

Uncle Jonas smiled. "Then it's settled. I know you don't have the usual amount of time to prepare for the journey, but I'll provide a large allowance so that you may purchase dresses and fabric during the trip."

"I cannot go," Fanny said, standing suddenly. "I will not leave. Michael might return and I want to be here when he does."

Uncle Jonas seemed to consider her words for a moment. "Wait here. I nearly forgot." He dashed from the room and returned only moments later waving a letter in the air. "This arrived earlier for you."

"A letter? From Michael?" Fanny rushed to her uncle and took the note. "Why did you open this? Why didn't you tell me?" She wanted to cry for joy. He had written. He had finally written.

"I accidentally opened it. I thought perhaps it was the correspondence of someone else. I am sorry for not paying closer attention. But as you can see in the letter, Michael has no intention of returning before next summer. You have more than ample time to go on the grand tour. Why, he can't even hope to get you additional letters, as the post is so irregular from that part of the world."

Fanny scanned the letter. It was all true. Michael had written it just as Uncle Jonas said. She supposed there really was no reason not to cooperate. But something in her still rebelled. She didn't want to go abroad. She would much rather return to Broadmoor Island.

"I believe you're going to have an excellent time on board the ship, as well as visiting Paris, Brussels, and Rome," Uncle Jonas began again. "This is the opportunity of a lifetime, and Amanda, we will see to it that you enjoy some new sights along the way."

Amanda folded her arms around her waist. "It seems the adults in our lives never tire of arranging our lives. We are weary of being forced always to yield to what others decide is best for us." She jutted her chin forward. "I know I haven't mentioned this before, but I've applied to begin my college courses and plan to attend medical school. I have no desire to return to Europe."

"Sophie and I don't want to go, either," Fanny said. "I was looking forward to a peaceful time here in Rochester. However, if you must send me somewhere, send me back to Broadmoor Island."

"The plans are made. I will not change them. You are going, and that's all there is to it."

"That's what *you* think," the three of them replied in unison.

Fanny cradled the letter to her chest and left the gathering to let them argue about the trip. She felt a renewed hope in just touching the letter that Michael had penned. Next summer seemed years away, but in truth, she knew it wasn't that long to wait.

"I'll be eighteen by then," she murmured, glancing at the letter once again. She smiled and knew that before Michael returned, she would read this one letter over and over again.

If there was one thing that the events of the summer and the last few weeks had proved to her, it was that nothing mattered as much as the love she held for Michael. She didn't care if they had to live in a tent and grow their own food. She didn't care if society scorned her and rejected her completely. The trials she'd already endured proved to her that she could survive anything— that she was strong.

"Well, I am a Broadmoor, after all," she said with a smile.

AN UNEXPECTED LOVE

Broadmoor Family Tree

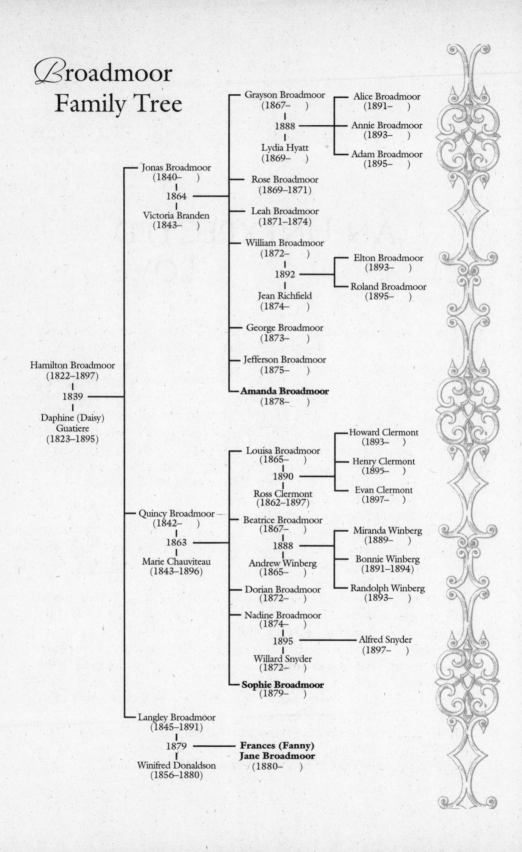

Hamilton Broadmoor
(1822–1897)
|
1839
|
Daphine (Daisy)
Guatiere
(1823–1895)

Jonas Broadmoor
(1840–   )
|
1864
|
Victoria Branden
(1843–   )

Grayson Broadmoor
(1867–   )
|
1888
|
Lydia Hyatt
(1869–   )

Alice Broadmoor
(1891–   )

Annie Broadmoor
(1893–   )

Adam Broadmoor
(1895–   )

Rose Broadmoor
(1869–1871)

Leah Broadmoor
(1871–1874)

William Broadmoor
(1872–   )
|
1892
|
Jean Richfield
(1874–   )

Elton Broadmoor
(1893–   )

Roland Broadmoor
(1895–   )

George Broadmoor
(1873–   )

Jefferson Broadmoor
(1875–   )

Amanda Broadmoor
(1878–   )

Quincy Broadmoor
(1842–   )
|
1863
|
Marie Chauviteau
(1843–1896)

Louisa Broadmoor
(1865–   )
|
1890
|
Ross Clermont
(1862–1897)

Howard Clermont
(1893–   )

Henry Clermont
(1895–   )

Evan Clermont
(1897–   )

Beatrice Broadmoor
(1867–   )
|
1888
|
Andrew Winberg
(1865–   )

Miranda Winberg
(1889–   )

Bonnie Winberg
(1891–1894)

Randolph Winberg
(1893–   )

Dorian Broadmoor
(1872–   )

Nadine Broadmoor
(1874–   )
|
1895
|
Willard Snyder
(1872–   )

Alfred Snyder
(1897–   )

Sophie Broadmoor
(1879–   )

Langley Broadmoor
(1845–1891)
|
1879
|
Winifred Donaldson
(1856–1880)

**Frances (Fanny)
Jane Broadmoor**
(1880–   )

CHAPTER 1

Eighteen-year-old Sophie Broadmoor speared her uncle Jonas with an angry glare. He cocked a brow, clearly surprised by her reaction. Nevertheless, he continued to drum his fingers on the walnut side table as though his impatient behavior would somehow cause his brother Quincy, who was also Sophie's father, to arrive at Broadmoor Mansion's front door. Sophie considered her uncle's conduct annoying in the extreme. He appeared to be holding her accountable for her father's tardy arrival. Well, she had more than enough faults of her own for which she must bear responsibility. She certainly didn't intend to take the blame for her father's breach of etiquette. Uncle Jonas might intimidate his own family, especially his daughter, Amanda, but he didn't frighten her a bit.

Ignoring her uncle's reprimanding stare, Sophie nonchalantly fluffed the lace on her sleeve and turned toward her aunt Victoria. "If you're tired of waiting for Father, I suggest we begin without him. He won't care in the least. You know how he loses all sense of time when he's helping some wayward soul at the Home for the Friendless."

Her aunt cast a quizzical look at her husband. "What do you think, Jonas? Shall we proceed without Quincy? The food will undoubtedly be cold if we wait much longer, and I know how you abhor a ruined meal."

The drumming cadence ceased, and using the chair arms, her uncle pushed himself upright and looked around the room. "Well? Let's proceed to the dining room."

Sophie grasped her cousin Fanny by the arm. "He must believe we're able to read his thoughts," she whispered.

Fanny giggled and offered her agreement. "Sometimes I wish we could. With Uncle Jonas, there's no telling what he's up to from one minute to the next. The ability to read his mind would prove useful, don't you think?"

"Oh yes! And it would drive him quite mad—not that I don't already succeed in that regard."

Amanda tugged on Sophie's sleeve. "Your behavior is decidedly unbecoming. What are you two whispering about?"

The glow of the chandelier cast golden highlights in Sophie's chocolate brown hair. "If it's so unbecoming, why do you want to know, Cousin?" she teased, looping arms with Amanda. "We're talking about reading your dear father's thoughts. Wouldn't that be a treat?"

"I don't know if I'd want to know everything that passes through Father's mind, but it certainly would prove beneficial on some occasions."

The three of them entered the dining room, with Amanda and Fanny flanking Sophie. As usual, both of Amanda's single brothers, George and Jefferson, had managed to avoid the Friday evening dinner. Sophie wished she knew their secret. None of their married siblings living there in Rochester were required to attend these tiresome Friday evening suppers, but Uncle Jonas expected—rather demanded—that his unmarried children, his nieces and nephews, and his brother Quincy, now a widower, all attend. Unless, of course, Uncle Jonas had other plans for himself that might interfere. Sophie always hoped for an interfering event on Friday nights, but she was disappointed more often than not.

As far as Sophie was concerned, her uncle had devised the plan in order to keep his eye on the single women in the family, lest one of them stray and find a suitor he considered undesirable. However, his Friday evening suppers hadn't deterred Fanny. Much to Uncle Jonas's chagrin, she'd fallen in love with Michael Atwell, their former boatswain at Broadmoor Island. But with Michael off in search of gold somewhere in the Yukon and Grandfather's death last year, poor Fanny had been relegated to living under Uncle Jonas's roof until she attained her age of majority. Sophie didn't envy either of her cousins living under this roof. Living in her father's modest home was less than pleasing, but at least she could come and go as she desired. Her father was never around long enough to inquire into her whereabouts.

Sophie feigned a pout and peered down the dining table. "Where are Jefferson and George this evening, Aunt Victoria? I do miss their company."

Her uncle snorted. "You miss their company? Or you wish you, too, could be absent?"

"Jonas! Sophie was making a polite inquiry about her cousins. There's no need to transfer your irritation upon those who are present *and* on time."

Her uncle grunted but didn't apologize. Not that Sophie expected such an unlikely occurrence. Uncle Jonas seldom apologized and certainly never asked forgiveness for a breach of etiquette within his own family. Of late, however, Aunt Victoria had begun to take a more assertive stance with her husband—a fact that pleased Sophie very much.

Jonas snapped his napkin and tucked it beneath his rather large paunch. "Where is supper, Victoria?"

Though he likely hadn't intended to shout, the question was loud enough to bring the servants bustling from the kitchen. They'd obviously been waiting in the wings for Aunt Victoria's signal. One of the servants placed a large serving dish, bearing two perfectly braised ducks garnished with pieces of turnip and carrot, in front of Uncle Jonas.

Her uncle made great fanfare of slicing the duck and then sat down as though he'd accomplished a feat of great importance. He tugged on his vest and motioned for the servants to pass the side dishes. After offering a brief prayer of thanks, he sipped his water and cleared his throat. "I have an announcement to make regarding your voyage to England, ladies."

Sophie audibly sighed. "Please don't tell us you're planning to extend our trip abroad. We've all agreed that England will be the limit of our travels."

Aunt Victoria closed her eyes and shook her head. "Please don't interrupt your uncle. I'd like to hear his announcement." She beamed at her husband. "Do go on, Jonas. What surprise have you planned for us?"

He jabbed a piece of turnip and appeared to be contemplating whether he should speak or eat. Keeping his attention on his food, he said, "I'm afraid it will be impossible for me to escort you ladies to England."

The girls squealed with delight, but Sophie didn't fail to note her aunt's look of dismay. "No need to look so distraught, Aunt Victoria. We'll have a wonderful time here in Rochester. None of us wanted to go to England anyway—not even you."

Her uncle clanked his fork on his plate. "I did not say the voyage was canceled, Sophie. I said that I would be unable to travel with you. Your passage has been booked, and I've arranged for an escort to take my place. You'll be pleased to—"

"But, Jonas, you promised," Victoria interrupted. "The only reason I agreed to the trip was because you promised to make the journey with us. How could you go back on your word?"

"Now, Victoria, there's no need for histrionics over a small change in plans. A business matter of great importance requires my attention, and it will be impossible for me to be away from Rochester on your departure date. Without my attention to the business, there wouldn't be sufficient funds for this family to live in the style to which they've become accustomed." His smile failed to reach his eyes. "Isn't that correct?"

"Correct or not, I'm disappointed that you have broken your promise to me. I've already explained that I don't believe it's wise for me to travel alone with all three of the girls."

"Once my business is concluded here in Rochester, I'll join you in England.

As I attempted to tell you a few moments ago, I have arranged for an escort to take my place," Jonas said.

Sophie could barely contain herself. Whom had Uncle Jonas convinced to make the journey? She waited for Aunt Victoria to inquire, but her aunt remained silent, her lips pressed together in a tight seam. And Uncle Jonas suddenly appeared more concerned with chasing a piece of duck around his plate than divulging the information.

When she could bear the suspense no longer, Sophie blurted, "Well, who is it you've convinced to escort us?"

"Yes, who?" Amanda asked.

Instead of speaking out with his usual pomp and ceremony, Jonas stared at his plate. "Daniel."

Fanny clutched her bodice. "Daniel? *Daniel Irwin?*" She tipped her head to the side until her hair nearly touched her dinner plate. Obviously Fanny was intent upon making eye contact with Uncle Jonas.

Uncle Jonas raised his head and glanced around the table. He appeared to have regained his air of authority. "Do you ladies know any other Daniel?"

Sophie extended her index finger. "I do, but I doubt he's the one."

Her uncle's jaw tightened. "Not if he's one of those men you meet at Brown Square."

Sophie giggled, pleased she'd been able to annoy her uncle yet somewhat surprised by this change in circumstances. Had she been forced to speculate upon whom her uncle had chosen as their escort, Daniel wouldn't have made the list of possibilities. And from all appearances he wouldn't have made Aunt Victoria's list, either. Poor Fanny looked as though she'd suffered a striking blow to the midsection. Only Amanda remained poised and unruffled by the announcement.

"Why in the world would you ask Daniel Irwin?" Fanny croaked the question and immediately took a sip of water. "He's not a member of the family. In fact, he's rather a nuisance, isn't he, Amanda?"

Amanda glanced at Fanny and then her father. Sophie poked her in the ribs, hoping that Amanda would find the courage to take a stand. " 'Tis true he's wearisome, Father. I do think you could have made a better choice."

"Since when do you think you're the one making family decisions, young woman?" He glared down the table, and Amanda visibly shrunk before Sophie's eyes.

"She's merely speaking her opinion, Uncle, and all of us concur. We are permitted an opinion in this family, are we not?"

Jonas shook his head. "Your manners leave much to be improved upon, Sophie. I did not seek any opinions on this decision. Daniel's passage is booked, and I have every confidence he will prove to be a perfect escort."

Sophie planned to argue the point, but before she could wage battle, one of the servants escorted her father into the room, with Paul Medford following close on his heels.

"My apologies, Victoria. I truly lost all track of time." He gestured toward the table. "Please, go on with your supper. Paul and I can wait in the library."

Clearly annoyed, Jonas pointed to one of the empty chairs. "Oh, do sit down, Quincy. You were invited for supper and supper you'll eat." When Paul remained in the doorway, Jonas waved him forward. "You, too, Paul. Sit down and eat."

All concern over Daniel Irwin fled Sophie's mind. Why had her father appeared with Paul Medford in tow? It seemed her father couldn't make an appearance at any family function without his favorite seminary graduate tagging along like a stray mongrel.

Her father offered his profuse apologies until Aunt Victoria finally begged him to cease. "All is forgiven, Quincy. As you can see, we didn't wait for your arrival. Sophie suggested we begin without you."

Her father cast a fleeting smile in Sophie's direction. "I fear she knows me well."

The servants returned with the serving bowls and platters and silently waited while the two men filled their plates. Quincy took several bites of the vegetables and duck. He nodded his approval. "Excellent as usual, Victoria." He downed a gulp of water from his goblet. "I need a favor, Jonas."

Jonas peered over the rim of his coffee cup.

"Paul received word today that his grandmother is quite ill—not expected to live much longer. He believes he should accompany his mother back to England," Quincy said. "I told him it might be possible for you to book passage for the two of them to travel with you and Victoria and the girls. I explained they would be departing on the twenty-third."

Jonas grunted. "Exactly right. I had originally planned the departure for the eighteenth of the month, but Victoria was quick to remind me that most of the luxury liners sail on Saturdays. My wife tends to suffer from motion sickness when she travels on the smaller ships." He patted his wife's hand. "Is that date acceptable for you and your mother, Paul?"

Paul leaned forward on his chair. "Yes, most acceptable. It would help Mother keep her mind off Grandmother's illness if she had someone to visit with other than me. I fear my presence on the ship will serve as a constant reminder of the reason we're crossing the ocean. Your wife and the young ladies could provide a diversion."

Jonas nodded his agreement. "I'll take care of it first thing in the morning." He beamed at his wife. "You see, my dear, this has worked out quite well after all. You'll have someone to keep you company throughout the voyage."

Confusion clouded her father's eyes, and Sophie hastened to relay the news that Uncle Jonas would not accompany them on the voyage.

"What business is it that ties you to Rochester, Jonas? If it's something I could help with, I'd be pleased to lend my assistance. You could then continue with your plan to accompany Victoria."

Jonas vigorously shook his head. "No, nothing you'd be able to assist with, but I do appreciate the offer, Quincy. However, having Paul and his mother along will prove most beneficial, don't you ladies agree?"

Aunt Victoria didn't appear persuaded, and nothing her father or Uncle Jonas said or did would convince Sophie, either. Paul Medford's presence on board the ship would spoil all of her fun!

The three girls escaped the confines of the house the moment they were excused from the dinner table. With a promise to remain on the grounds, they donned their cloaks and strolled to the terrace garden, where privacy awaited them. Even as young girls, they'd enjoyed sitting in the loggia with its towering Greek columns that permitted a view of anyone approaching yet afforded a feeling of privacy—thanks in large part to the grapevines that provided an overhead blanket of leaves and luscious treats when in season.

"I don't know which of our fathers has become the more devious, Amanda." Sophie stood on one of the ornate benches and yanked a withered leaf from one of the sagging vines. "I cannot believe I'll be forced to endure Paul Medford throughout the voyage. You can be certain he'll attempt to quash all our fun. And I can only imagine his mother—a stern and prudish old woman with a constant frown." Sophie shuddered.

The breeze tugged at the corner of Amanda's cape, and she pulled it close to her body. "I believe Paul's circumstances are purely coincidental. Besides, I've never known you to permit anyone to ruin your good time. I predict you'll find some way to avoid him."

"And let's don't forget that Paul's mother will provide company for Aunt Victoria," Fanny added. "However, I do think Daniel Irwin's presence can be attributed to Uncle Jonas and his devious scheming." Fanny squeezed Amanda's arm. "I'm sorry if you find my words harsh, Amanda."

"No need for apologies, Fanny. I've heard much worse. I doubt there's any member of the family who hasn't criticized Father at some point—including me. And, unfortunately, I believe you're correct about Daniel. He is an odd choice. Father barely knows him, and he's not so much older than the three of us. If he merely wanted a young male escort, he could have easily ordered Jefferson or George to come along."

Sophie clapped her hands. "Oh, I do wish he would have done that! The boys are such fun!"

Amanda grinned. "They may still act like boys, but I don't think they'd appreciate your referring to them as such."

"And their youthful behavior is exactly why your father wouldn't choose for them to accompany us." Fanny brushed an auburn curl from her forehead. "We all three know why he chose Daniel Irwin. Uncle Jonas continues to hold out hope that I'll forget Michael and fall madly in love with Daniel. He hasn't fooled me in the least, but his plan will fail. My love for Michael is steadfast. Daniel will never be the recipient of my affections."

Amanda gently tapped her index finger across her pursed lips. "But what if this is Daniel's plan rather than my father's? Have you considered that Daniel may have approached my father and avowed his affection for you?"

"And being Fanny's ever-adoring guardian who wants only the very best for his niece, Uncle Jonas suggested Daniel accompany us on this voyage," Sophie quipped. "Do you truly believe he merely wants to give Fanny an opportunity to discover her one true love?"

"I know you're correct, Sophie, but I thought we should at least give him the benefit of the doubt. He is my father, after all, and I'd not want to misjudge him."

Sophie's rippling laughter echoed through their stone hideaway. "Believe me, dear cousin, you need not worry on that account." A light breeze rippled through the grapevines, and Sophie huddled closer to her cousins. "However, I have decided that we shall have a grand time in spite of the two troublesome fellows who have been foisted upon us." She joined hands with her cousins. "Let's make a pact."

CHAPTER 2

SATURDAY, OCTOBER 23, 1897
ON BOARD THE SS *CITY OF NEW YORK*

The driver maneuvered their carriage onto the pier at breakneck speed and then brought the horses to an abrupt halt that sent members of the Broadmoor family careening inside the conveyance. The driver would likely receive an upbraiding from Uncle Jonas, but Sophie thought the experience quite exciting. An exhilarating beginning to their journey. Granted, Aunt Victoria's hat no longer sat at the same jaunty angle, but the driver had managed to deliver them without any genuine mishap, no small feat for even the most adept of drivers on sailing days in New York City.

Like the Broadmoors, other passengers had arrived more than an hour prior to sailing time, and many were already directing the destination of their trunks and bags while others were ascending the gangway. Livery carriages and private turnouts continued to arrive, dropping off additional travelers on the crowded pier.

Once they'd stepped out of the carriage, Uncle Jonas instructed them to keep a watch for Daniel while he spoke to the driver. Sophie grinned at her cousins. "Perhaps we should hide behind the baggage so Daniel won't see us."

"I doubt that will work. Uncle Jonas would likely discover some method to delay the ship's sailing until Daniel arrives. Unless I can depend upon you two to help me keep Daniel at bay, I fear I'm doomed to spend the entire voyage in his company," Fanny lamented.

"You know I will do my very best," Sophie promised. "The three of us will develop some delicious plans that will bewilder poor Daniel. All we must do is reenact a few of the pranks we've previously used on Jefferson and George."

Amanda didn't appear totally convinced. "We'll do our best to keep him at arm's length whenever possible. But no outrageous pranks."

"That was certainly halfhearted," Sophie whispered. "You could be more supportive."

Aunt Victoria walked toward them just then, waving her handkerchief high in the air. "Wave, girls! There's Daniel, and he doesn't appear to see us." The three of them turned their backs and fumbled in their reticules. Finally Victoria tapped Amanda on the shoulder. "What are you girls doing? I asked you to wave to Daniel."

Amanda nudged Sophie. "We're looking for our handkerchiefs, so he'll more easily see us. However, it appears I've forgotten mine. They must all be packed in my trunk." Sophie batted her lashes and held open her handbag for her aunt's inspection.

Victoria pointed to the piece of lace protruding from the pocket of Sophie's fur-trimmed traveling cloak. "Could that possibly be what you've been searching for?"

Sophie could feel the heat rise up her neck and into her cheeks. "Why, I do believe it is. Thank you, Aunt Victoria." She pulled the lace-edged hankie from her pocket and barely raised her arm. The white square drooped from her hand like a flag at half-mast without a breeze in the offing.

Pushing Sophie's arm upward, Aunt Victoria instructed Amanda and Fanny to make haste. "You girls are not deceiving me in the least. Now, find those handkerchiefs and wave them overhead." She jutted her chin forward in a manner that implied she would not be denied. Had the white linen squares not been produced forthwith, Sophie believed her aunt would have dived right into each of their reticules and retrieved them. The other two girls lifted their handkerchiefs and waved them overhead with little enthusiasm. Unfortunately, their waving provided enough activity to attract Daniel's attention.

"He's seen us," Fanny muttered. "And look! There's Paul." She grasped Sophie's hand. "That must be his mother."

Sophie frowned and shook her head. "No. That woman looks much different than Paul's mother."

"You've never met Paul's mother," Fanny said.

"True," Sophie said. "But I've pictured her in my mind, and that woman looks nothing like her."

"Oh, forevermore, Sophie. You're not making any sense," Amanda said. "She's the only person with him. The woman most certainly must be his mother—she's lovely, don't you think?"

Daniel raced toward them and immediately hastened to Fanny's side while Sophie contemplated the older woman grasping Paul's arm. Very stylish, with an air of dignity and an inviting smile—in truth, quite a lovely woman. Not at all like her son. For in spite of what others said, Sophie thought Paul rather plain. When they'd drawn closer, Sophie noted the similar chestnut brown eyes. Otherwise, there was little resemblance between mother and son.

Mrs. Medford appeared perfectly comfortable, but Paul fumbled over the introductions and was seemingly mortified when he forgot Amanda's name. For some reason, Sophie felt sorry for him and came to his rescue. Perhaps it was a remembrance of times when she'd been thrust into uncomfortable social situations and no one had saved her. Nowadays, she worried little about such things. In fact, she willingly made a spectacle of herself if it provided a modicum of merriment to an otherwise dull gathering.

Mrs. Medford's brown-eyed gaze rested upon Sophie for several moments. "I can see that you have learned to enjoy life, Miss Broadmoor. If laughter is truly good medicine, I would venture to say that you will live a very long life." She tapped Paul's arm with her fan. "You could take a few lessons from this young lady. You are far too serious."

Paul looked heavenward, obviously embarrassed by his mother's assessment. "Now that introductions have been made, I believe we should board the ship, Mother."

"You see? Even though the pier is crowded with other passengers and we have nearly fifty minutes until sailing time, Paul is worried the ship will sail without us." Mrs. Medford patted her son's hand. "We will wait and board with the Broadmoors." Mrs. Medford glanced toward the carriage where Sophie's aunt and uncle were deep in conversation.

Aunt Victoria looked none too happy, but that was to be expected. Although Uncle Jonas continued to promise her that he would meet them in London, Aunt Victoria appeared unconvinced. His refusal to arrive in New York City several days early had not won him favor, either. The Broadmoor women had hoped for at least two days of shopping and an evening at the theater prior to their voyage, but Uncle Jonas had protested, once again citing the burgeoning work that required his attention.

Uncle Jonas grasped his wife's elbow and escorted her toward them as several fancy wagons bearing the names of fashionable New York florists arrived on the pier. Deliverymen hastened to the gangway with ornate floral offerings.

Sophie tipped her head close to Amanda. "Let's hope your father purchased one of those huge bouquets for your mother."

"At this point, I think it would take more than flowers to appease Mother. It appears he is attempting to leave without escorting us on board. If he makes his escape, she'll be incensed. Perhaps I should intervene." Amanda glanced about the group. "If you'll excuse me for a few moments?"

Although Paul tried to engage Sophie in conversation, she maintained a close vigil on Amanda and her parents. Her cousin's assumptions had obviously been correct. The frown on Aunt Victoria's face was enough to wilt an entire bouquet of flowers. When the threesome finished their private conversation and drew near, Uncle Jonas suggested they board the ship.

"Will you be joining us on board, Uncle?" Sophie inquired.

"Yes, of course." Jonas immediately circled the group to greet Daniel. "Glad to see you've safely arrived, my boy."

Her uncle's enthusiastic response surprised Sophie, but she wondered if it had more to do with Daniel than with Aunt Victoria's obvious displeasure. They wended their way through the throngs gathered on the pier. Strains of band music blended with the din of the crowd, while beautifully attired and perfectly coiffed passengers strolled the decks and waved to anyone who turned in their direction. Her uncle continued to fawn over Daniel while he waved the rest of their party forward. His behavior toward the young man was uncharacteristic, even for her uncle, who seemed to change moods as frequently as a chameleon changed its color.

She thought to mention that to Fanny, but Uncle Jonas blocked her way when Sophie prepared to board.

"Fanny, take Daniel's arm. I don't want you to trip on the gangway," he commanded.

Though he carefully paired Fanny and Daniel, he appeared utterly unconcerned whether Sophie or his own daughter might need assistance boarding. Sophie grasped Amanda's arm and exclaimed, "Do permit me to help you aboard, Amanda. I wouldn't want you to trip on the gangway." The remark garnered a hasty look of reproof from her uncle, but Sophie merely tossed her curls and proceeded ahead, with Aunt Victoria and Uncle Jonas following behind.

"I do believe this ship is the finest we've ever sailed on, Jonas. If we must journey without you, we will, at least, have fine accommodations."

Sophie glanced over her shoulder in time to see her uncle bask in the praise. "Let's go into the main salon first. Fanny will want to see the flowers."

Amanda giggled. "And escape from Daniel," she whispered. "An excellent plan, Sophie."

Jonas wagged his index finger at the girls. "There will be no visit to the salon until you ladies have been to your cabin. I want to be certain it meets with your expectations before I return to the pier. You may even discover a surprise."

The remnants of Aunt Victoria's frown evaporated. "Oh, Jonas! We don't need surprises. We'll likely have enough of those on our voyage." She squeezed his hand. "But since you've gone to such an effort, we will do as you wish."

Paul and his mother followed along for only a short distance. Although Uncle Jonas had managed to obtain first-class tickets for Paul and his mother on the *City of New York*, their accommodations were located in the opposite direction, a fact that pleased Sophie.

The Broadmoor traveling bags had been placed outside their cabin, while trunks containing the clothing they would require in England had been secured belowdecks. Once the women completed their tour of the cabin, Veda and Minnie, the two personal maids who had accompanied them from home, would unpack their baggage.

Not one of them could find fault with the cabin. It was a large suite with a sitting room and two large bedrooms—one on either side of the sitting room—along with servants' quarters for the two maids. Flowers had been delivered to their cabin with a note to Aunt Victoria reaffirming that Uncle Jonas would join them in England. It was, however, the silver filigree dresser set that pleased her even more than the flowers. Uncle Jonas had obviously spared no expense on the gift or on their suite.

The opulence of the rooms was far more than Sophie had expected. The walls were paneled in cherrywood, the beds were draped in velvet, and the furniture was upholstered in plush shades of plum and forest green. Aunt Victoria stood in the doorway of one of the bedrooms. "Would you like to share this room with me, Amanda? That way, you girls won't be so crowded."

"Oh, please permit her to stay in the room with Fanny and me, Aunt Victoria. We can make do quite nicely. The rooms are very large, and it won't be nearly so much fun if we're separated from one another."

Amanda stepped to her mother's side. "Do say you don't mind, Mother. You know I enjoy your company, but . . ."

"I understand. I was once young, too, you know." She enveloped her daughter in a fleeting hug.

Jonas waited until the others had disappeared from sight before grasping Daniel by the arm and nodding toward one of the small salons. He must make Daniel understand the depth of his assignment. Fanny had inherited her father's portion of the Broadmoor fortune—a fact that continued to irritate Jonas to no end. His brother Langley had done nothing to add to the family coffers, and it seemed outrageous that his daughter should be given his share.

"He shouldn't even have a share—not after taking his own life," Jonas muttered.

Nevertheless, the situation was quite serious now. If Jonas was to succeed in his plan to gain control of Fanny's inheritance, Daniel must prove reliable and completely in agreement with Jonas's desires. And the journey to England would provide little time for all that Jonas and Daniel must accomplish.

Looking at Daniel now, Jonas began to have second thoughts. The young man was to play an important role in the success of Jonas's plan, a somewhat distressing concept. Though not particularly intelligent, Daniel seemed to be compliant and eager to please. Jonas could only hope those traits would prove sufficient for the task at hand. Had the boy been intellectual rather than greedy, he would have refused the offer at the outset or made more demands for himself. Neither would have worked to Jonas's advantage.

Once they'd located a private spot, Jonas requested two glasses of port. "We must go over the details of my expectations."

When Daniel bobbed his head, several strands of light brown hair fell across his forehead. He pushed the hair back into place and sat down. Only a small round table divided them, and Jonas leaned forward to close the short distance. He didn't want anyone overhearing their conversation.

"I want to be certain you understand what I require of you on this voyage, Daniel. When I arrive in England, I want to hear that Fanny has agreed to marry you. I demand nothing more and nothing less. Is that clear?"

"But what if she rebuffs my advances, Mr. Broadmoor? She attempts to avoid me at every opportunity. You saw that much for yourself a short time ago."

Jonas nodded. "You will be rewarded handsomely if you succeed, Daniel. You must simply remember what is at stake, and you will be able to handle any difficulties that arise."

"I would have more confidence if you were along and I could rely upon you to make certain Fanny didn't evade my attentions." Daniel massaged his forehead with his fingertips. "She does that, you know—keeps a distance between us whenever possible."

The young man's apprehension was of increasing concern. If Jonas couldn't boost Daniel's confidence, he would fail to win Fanny's heart. "Befriend my wife and make her your ally. Convince her of your love for Fanny and your desire to provide a life of comfort with a man of her equal social standing. You need not disparage Michael Atwell. My wife understands the need to marry within the proper social class." Jonas clapped the younger man on the shoulder. "If you win my wife's confidence, she will provide discreet assistance."

After exhaling an audible sigh, Daniel agreed. "I will do my utmost to win Fanny's heart and your wife's respect."

"You must not even consider failure. If all other measures fall short, you must seduce her." Jonas saw the look of surprise in the young man's eyes, but he knew this was his last opportunity to drive home the necessity of Daniel's success. "I hope such behavior will not be necessary, but I want you to understand that I am willing for you to go to whatever lengths are necessary to gain Fanny's agreement to wed. Even if indiscretion is the only means to accomplish that goal. In fact, nothing would please me more than to discover you and Fanny are engaged when I arrive in England."

Jonas withdrew a thick envelope from his jacket and pushed it into Daniel's hand. "I am sending sufficient funds with you to purchase an impressive engagement ring for my niece. I hope to see a ring on her finger rather than money in this envelope. Please don't disappoint me."

Daniel shoved the envelope into his pocket and inhaled deeply. "You can rely upon me, sir." He grasped Jonas by the hand and forced his arm up and down with the enthusiasm of a thirsty man priming a pump.

"We should return to the deck before the ladies wonder at our disappearance," Jonas said. "You'll be pleased to know that your cabin is directly next to theirs. I've done my best to secure you every advantage."

"And I am most appreciative, Mr. Broadmoor."

The men retraced their steps, and even to the most discriminating eye, it appeared neither Jonas nor Daniel had moved away from the railing during the ladies' absence. From his wife's arresting smile upon returning, Jonas knew his gift had pleased her and they would part on good terms.

Victoria softly touched his cheek and thanked him. "The gift is lovely, but I don't believe I've completely forgiven you just yet. If you arrive in England on schedule, then I will consider the slate wiped clean."

The harsh blast of the steamer's whistle preceded the clanging bell alerting visitors to return ashore. "I suppose I must take my leave," Jonas said. He kissed his wife and hoped his ardent display of affection would help to warm her heart. After bidding his nieces farewell, he brushed a kiss on Amanda's cheek. "I expect the three of you to behave in a proper fashion. I don't want to hear any reports that you've caused your mother undue distress during your journey."

Amanda agreed, though Jonas realized it would be Sophie—not his daughter—who would be devising inappropriate plans for the threesome. And asking for Sophie's agreement to behave would be of little consequence.

The final bell clanged, and Jonas turned to Fanny. "I told Daniel you would take a turn on the deck with him once the ship is underway."

Fanny shook her head. "But I don't—"

"No time for argument, Fanny. I've given Daniel my word, and I must go ashore before the gangway is withdrawn. I don't believe I'd have an easy time utilizing the accommodation ladder for my return to the pier." With a final wave, he hurried down the gangway and was soon lost in the crowd of well-wishers.

After a final and prolonged blast of the whistle sounded, the giant propellers churned the dark water, and the steamship slowly moved from her berth. The steward's band struck the chords of "America" while the crowd below hurried to the far end of the pier to shout their final farewells. The passengers remained near the railing, waving until they could no longer distinguish their friends and family.

Careful to keep Fanny in her sights, Sophie attempted to shift her position along the railing, hoping to distance herself from Mrs. Medford and Paul. Mother and son had arrived on the promenade deck after her uncle Jonas had departed, and Paul had managed to squeeze between Amanda and Sophie. Now Mrs. Medford stood beside Aunt Victoria offering profuse apologies. She had seemingly wanted to thank Uncle Jonas for booking their passage. Sophie had not made much progress in getting away from Paul when Daniel insisted Fanny accompany him on a walk about the deck.

"That sounds like a wonderful idea. Amanda and I will come along, too. That way, we'll all become acquainted with the ship." Sophie noted Fanny's look of relief as well as Daniel's glare. "Come along, Amanda," she said, grasping her cousin's arm and taking charge. "We'll lead the way."

"I trust you won't mind if I join you, also," Paul said.

Sophie's heart plummeted. For a moment she considered denying his request, but before she could speak, Amanda agreed he should join them. Sophie had planned to use their stroll to advantage; she viewed it as an opportunity to meet any interesting men who might be on board. Undoubtedly having Paul along would thwart her efforts. At least dear Fanny wouldn't be required to spend the time alone with Daniel.

Sophie raised her parasol and held it to one side, partly to deflect the sun but also to keep Paul at arm's length. She didn't want others to assume he was her escort—let them believe he was keeping company with Amanda. After all, she was the one who had agreed he could join them.

They'd traversed one side of the deck when Sophie spied several young fellows who appeared to be traveling together. One in particular caught her fancy, and nearing his side, she coyly dropped her handkerchief. When the fellow rushed to retrieve it, she batted her lashes, smiled demurely, and thanked him profusely.

"You are most welcome. May I be so bold as to introduce myself?"

Sophie nodded.

"Claymore Fuller of New York City. And you are?"

"Sophie Broadmoor. *Miss* Sophie Broadmoor. I do hope we'll have an opportunity to become further acquainted, Mr. Fuller." Tucking the handkerchief into her pocket, Sophie glanced over her shoulder. Where in the world was Fanny? She silently chastised herself for not keeping a closer watch. Daniel would bear watching. He was obviously more cunning than Sophie had imagined. After a hasty farewell to Mr. Fuller, Sophie hurried to Amanda's side. "We must turn around! Daniel and Fanny are nowhere in sight."

"There's no need for panic. I'm certain they are fine." Paul patted Sophie's arm as though consoling a small child. She jerked away, and he arched his brows. "They have likely stopped in one of the salons for refreshments, Sophie. I truly don't believe there's any need for alarm."

Sophie ignored his remarks and directed a stern look at Amanda. She hoped the look would propel her cousin into action. Fortunately, Amanda didn't hesitate. While the two of them hurriedly retraced their steps, Paul followed behind. "Let's check the main salon; then we'll go to the upper deck," Amanda suggested.

Sophie glanced over her shoulder. "Why don't you go inspect the upper decks, Paul, while we look in the main salon? We'll accomplish more in less time, don't you agree?"

He hesitated, obviously displeased with the plan, but finally turned toward the steps leading to the upper decks.

Sophie sighed. "At least we've managed to free ourselves of him for a while. Now let's locate Fanny. I can't believe Daniel has already lured her away from us."

"Had you not been preoccupied with Mr. Fuller, you likely would have noticed."

Sophie heard the ring of condemnation in Amanda's words. "If that be the case, then why didn't you notice Fanny's absence? Perhaps because you were distracted by Paul Medford's attentions?"

Amanda's lips tightened into a thin seam, and her eyes shone with anger. "Paul is nothing more than a social acquaintance. You very well know I have no interest in him, but we have no time to argue that. We must find Fanny."

"I agree, but you're the one who made the first accusation, Amanda. Let's put aside our differences and—" She grasped Amanda's hand. "There they are in the salon, and it appears Daniel has literally cornered her. She couldn't escape if her life depended upon it."

Amanda peered around Sophie's shoulder. "Dear me! We must rescue her. We should approach from the far side. That way Fanny will see us coming, and Daniel will be none the wiser."

"Excellent plan." Both of them realized Fanny was in no mortal danger. She was, after all, in a large room surrounded by dozens of other passengers. However, Daniel had chosen a small corner table that had been pushed against the wall and blocked Fanny on one side while his chair blocked the other. The arrangement was perfect—for Daniel. Sophie didn't doubt for a minute that he'd been attempting to woo Fanny. Why wouldn't Paul and Daniel content themselves with some other unattached female passengers and permit the Broadmoor women time to enjoy themselves?

Sophie pointed Amanda to the left, and she stepped to the right. They would flank Daniel and, if necessary, push him out of the way. "Fanny! Where have you been? Do move aside, Daniel. Fanny must join us in our cabin immediately. A matter of great importance must be settled." When he didn't move quickly enough, Sophie poked him with her parasol. "Did you not hear me? Move your chair!"

The sharp command caused Daniel to jump to his feet. The chair toppled backwards, and he tripped in his attempt to grab it before it hit the floor. While he struggled to set the chair aright, Sophie waved for Fanny to escape from her position along the wall. The three young women scurried toward the exit, but not quickly enough to elude Daniel. At the sound of his footfalls, Sophie stopped short and turned. Had she been several inches taller, the two of them would have been nose to nose.

"Paul went to the upper decks looking for you and Fanny. Go tell him that all is well and we've gone to our cabin." She spoke with such authority he neither objected nor questioned her instructions.

Sophie waited long enough to be certain Daniel was heading for the upper deck. "Do tell us what happened. One minute you were behind us but the next you had disappeared from sight. Why didn't you call to us?"

The girls hurried to the stairway leading to their cabin. "Daniel intentionally stopped to permit a family with small children to pass in front of us as we neared the main salon. Even if I had called out, you wouldn't have heard me. You were far ahead of us by then, and the music and noise of the passengers would have drowned out my voice. He said we would cross through the salon and meet you on the other side of the ship, but once we were inside, he insisted he didn't feel well and needed to rest."

"Ha! I don't believe that for one minute," Sophie said.

"And you are correct," Fanny said as she opened the cabin door.

After making certain they were alone, Sophie plopped down on the divan. "What happened next?" She could barely wait to hear the rest of Fanny's tale.

"He said he is in love with me and is determined to have me as his wife."

Amanda clasped a hand to her bodice. "Truly? I can't even imagine such a thing. What did you say?"

"I told him that I am betrothed to Michael and he is the man I love." Fanny opened her fan and flicked it back and forth. "I told him he should refrain from making any further advances, but he said my declaration would not deter him. He believes that by journey's end I will return his feelings."

Amanda wagged her head. "He is certainly bold."

"And much too self-assured for my liking," Fanny replied. "He said I am not yet married and he plans to convince me that he is a better match for me."

Sophie leaned back against the cushioned seat and considered Daniel's remark. "He is far too full of himself. I believe he needs a good comeuppance." She giggled. "And no one can do that any better than the three of us. It is, after all, our duty to teach Daniel there are consequences for improper social behavior."

Paul scouted the upper deck looking for Fanny and Daniel. He thought it rather strange that Amanda and Sophie should have worried so much about the couple slipping off for a walk. After all, he had the impression they were intended for each other, and it seemed only natural.

He slipped in and out of the crowd but saw no sign of anyone he recognized. With a sigh he turned back. His thoughts went to Sophie and the way she had flirted with a complete stranger only moments ago. She seemed destined to put herself in harm's way.

It was easy for Paul to see the need in Sophie. His own father had never been all that attentive, and he knew what it was to try desperately hard to gain favor with someone who didn't seem to even remember you existed. His father had always been consumed with work, just as Sophie's father was. Paul had tried to talk to Quincy Broadmoor about his inattention to Sophie on more than one occasion, but his employer's attitude had been that Sophie knew he loved and cared about her, whereas the destitute at his Home for the Friendless had no one else.

"I'm not at all sure that she knows he loves her," Paul muttered. He supposed it was for this reason he held a spot in his heart for the selfish girl. For all the times his mother had assured him of his own father's love, Paul had never been convinced. He couldn't imagine that Sophie was convinced of Quincy's affections, either. Sophie was the kind of woman impressed by actions, not words. Unfortunately, given her current state of affairs and flirtations, the actions she brought upon herself might not be at all beneficial.

CHAPTER 3

Aunt Victoria fluttered into the room late that afternoon. Excitement shone in her eyes, and a faint blush colored her prominent cheekbones. "We've been invited to sit at the captain's table for the evening meal." She sat down beside Amanda, fanned herself, and looked at the three girls with an air of expectancy. "Well? Are you not pleased? This is quite the fait accompli. I don't believe we've ever been invited to sit at the captain's table on our very first night at sea."

Sophie sighed. She would much prefer to sit at a table surrounded by eligible young men who were interested in her. Fawning over the ship's captain held no appeal. Personally, she thought the custom of dining with the captain silly. An invitation to dine at his table was given far too much significance. He was, after all, no more than a man performing his duties; there were men of much greater import aboard the ship. Yet those travelers invited to dine at the captain's table were especially esteemed and envied by the other passengers.

"If it pleases you, Mother, we are delighted," Amanda replied.

Her cousin had chosen to respond in diplomatic fashion, but Sophie cared little about the subtle art of tact. "Must we, Aunt Victoria? I believe the three of us would much prefer to dine somewhere other than the captain's table. However, I'm certain that Daniel, as well as Paul and his mother, would be pleased to accept the captain's invitation."

Her aunt frowned. "I have already sent our acceptance, and I shall expect all three of you to be on your best behavior." She glanced at Amanda and Fanny. "I know I can depend on the two of you." Quickly shifting, she settled a stern look upon Sophie. "Please promise that *you* won't disappoint me, Sophie. I would like to enjoy the evening knowing that you will behave appropriately."

The pointed remark hurt for only a moment, for other than Amanda, Fanny, Jefferson, and George, Sophie knew the entire family considered her a miscreant. Not that she minded. She'd made a genuine effort to overstep the family's boundaries of stuffy social mores. After her mother's death the previous December, Sophie decided she would no longer be restricted by rules of etiquette or family expectations. Of course, there were those who thought she'd been a troublesome daughter prior to her mother's death, but of late she'd given new meaning to the word, and her behavior had been the topic at several family gatherings.

"So long as the three of us have your permission to attend the dance afterward, I promise to be on my very best behavior for our supper with the captain." Sophie was certain her condition would be met with immediate approval. Her aunt wanted to enjoy her meal, and permitting the girls to attend the dance wasn't truly a concession. She would expect the girls to attend the dance.

"Why, of course," Victoria replied.

"By ourselves," Sophie added, "without Daniel or Paul acting as our escorts."

She watched her aunt's smile begin to fade and then quickly return. "Should either of the young men offer to act as an escort, you have my permission to refuse. However, I can't possibly prohibit them from attending the dance. It is open to all properly attired passengers, and I'm certain Mrs. Medford will want to attend for a time. I want to make an appearance myself, especially if the captain plans to escort us into the ballroom."

Sophie would gain nothing further by arguing with her aunt, for she knew the woman would never consider slighting the ship's captain.

"If you girls will excuse me, I'm going to speak with Minnie and Veda. I want them to see that our gowns are in readiness, and you must remember we will need to share their services. I will arrange to have them assist me with my hair and dress, and then they can help you girls."

The minute she left the cabin, Sophie motioned her cousins to draw close. "I have a plan to keep Daniel away from Fanny."

Fanny scooted closer. "I knew I could count on you, Sophie. Tell me."

"We must go to Daniel's cabin. I'm certain he and Paul are still commiserating on the promenade deck. We will go through his belongings and remove all of his formal attire."

Fanny lurched and looked as though she'd been struck by a bolt of lightning. "You're not serious!" She stared at Sophie. "You *are* serious."

"Of course I'm serious. It's a marvelous plan. If he doesn't have the proper attire, he will be refused entry to all of the formal functions throughout the voyage." She brightened. "And in England, too. It will save you a great deal of heartache, dear Fanny. 'Tis a simple plan that will work if we hurry to his stateroom." She took her cousin's hand. "Just think of it! You won't be required to dine or dance with Daniel. That thought alone should stir you to action."

Amanda wagged her finger. "You would be stealing his belongings, Sophie. Such behavior is completely unbefitting a young lady—and it goes against biblical principles, I might add."

"Do stop speaking like a prudish spinster and come guard the passageway. If Daniel approaches, get down on your hands and knees and pretend you've lost your earring and ask for his assistance."

Before her cousins could further object, Sophie grasped Fanny's hand and pulled her to her feet. "Go on," she hissed, giving Amanda a tap on the shoulder when they neared Daniel's door.

Amanda turned and folded her arms around her waist. "I refuse to be involved unless you promise you won't destroy his clothing—or throw it overboard."

"I promise! Now go on before we lose any further time with this prattling."

Sophie waited until Amanda arrived at her position at the end of the passage and turned toward the companionway. "We should knock, just in case he's inside."

"What if his door is locked?" Fanny whispered.

Sophie retrieved a key from her pocket. "I batted my lashes and told one of the porters I'd locked myself out of this cabin. I need only return it after we've completed—"

Before she could finish her explanation, the cabin door swung open, and Sophie gasped. Clearly taken aback, Daniel settled his gaze upon Fanny, and soon a smile played upon his lips. "To what do I owe this extraordinary surprise?"

Rarely at a loss for words, Sophie was struck speechless. She stared at Daniel, her thoughts in a whir. She hadn't expected this turn of events. Granted, she'd momentarily considered the possibility, but she had convinced herself Daniel wouldn't return to his cabin until time to dress for dinner.

Fanny peeked over Sophie's shoulder. "We are in need of an additional glass. They seem to have shorted us. Would you happen to have one we could borrow?"

He grinned. "Of course. Do come in, ladies."

Fanny shook her head. "Oh, we dare not. Aunt Victoria would not approve."

"Of course, of course. I would never want to tarnish your reputation, Fanny."

"Or *mine*?" Sophie inquired, having regained her voice.

Daniel's brows drew together. Her question had apparently befuddled him. He mumbled an unintelligible remark before crossing the room to locate the requested glass. They thanked him profusely and backed away from the doorway. Once certain he'd closed the door, they motioned for Amanda to join them.

Staring at the water glass when she drew near, Amanda asked, "Why do you have that?"

Leaving Fanny to explain what had occurred, Sophie revisited the promenade deck to return the duplicate key. Not wanting to admit defeat after only one attempt to enter Daniel's cabin, Sophie mentioned her enduring forgetfulness to the unsuspecting porter, and he genially offered to assist her in the future should the need arise. She thanked him profusely and then hurried back to their suite. If their encounter with Daniel hadn't completely alarmed Fanny, they could make another attempt tomorrow. Next time, she would insist Amanda or Fanny keep Daniel occupied on an upper deck.

Amanda greeted her with a quick reprimand. "I knew your idea was foolhardy. I'm thankful Fanny was able to devise a clever response. She tells me you were struck speechless when Daniel appeared."

" 'Tis true. I was thankful to have her with me. Tomorrow we will revise our plan."

"Tomorrow?" Amanda's voice echoed throughout the cabin.

Fanny pointed toward the door. "Do keep your voice down, Amanda. We don't want every passerby to overhear our conversation."

"Fine! But I expect further explanation of what you mean by *tomorrow*, Sophie." Amanda folded her arms across her chest and scowled. She looked like an irate mother preparing to reprimand a naughty child.

Hoping to appear nonchalant, Sophie dropped to the sofa beside Fanny and shrugged her shoulders. "With or without your help, I plan to keep my word and help Fanny. I will secure the key again tomorrow, and while one of you keeps Daniel occupied on an upper deck, I will execute my plan." She patted Fanny's hand. "I am exceedingly sorry that you will be forced to abide his presence this evening, but you may rest assured that I will be successful tomorrow."

"I think it's time you lay your plan to rest, Sophie. I'm certain Fanny can avoid Daniel without the necessity of going through his wardrobe and making off with his clothing. I find the idea boorish. We are no longer schoolgirls playing pranks on our childhood friends."

Amanda was trying Sophie's patience. "Think what you will, Amanda, but I would do the same for you."

"What would you do, Sophie?" At the sound of her aunt's voice, Sophie twisted around toward the door.

"I was pledging to help Amanda and Fanny whenever necessary, Aunt Victoria."

"Why in the world would they need help? Is something amiss?" Her eyes clouded with concern.

"No, of course not. We were merely affirming the close kinship the three of us share," Amanda said, beaming a winsome smile at her mother.

"It would appear none of you have paid heed to the clock. If the servants are to have time enough to fashion our hair, we must curtail this idle conversation and begin our preparations for tonight's dinner."

Sophie was first to jump up from the sofa, pleased to be out of earshot and spared further questioning from her aunt.

"I can't decide who is the most stunning among you," Mrs. Medford said when the three young ladies entered the captain's private dining room.

Paul stepped forward, his gaze fixed upon Sophie. She hoped he didn't intend to sit next to her. If so, she would likely fail to keep her promise to Aunt Victoria. In an agile move, she managed to step between Amanda and Aunt Victoria. Though sitting next to her aunt throughout the meal didn't appeal, it would be preferable to forced conversation with Paul. Sophie thought she'd found the perfect resolution until her aunt insisted upon an entirely different seating arrangement.

Victoria wiggled her finger at Paul. "Why don't you sit next to Sophie? I prefer a mixed seating arrangement."

By the time her aunt had rearranged the group, Daniel and Fanny were seated side by side. Due to the uneven numbers, Paul sat to Sophie's left and his mother to her right. She was surrounded by Medfords! Even Fanny's situation didn't seem nearly as bleak as her own.

While Aunt Victoria plied the captain with questions regarding the ship and their route, Mrs. Medford quizzed Sophie about her future plans. The woman appeared momentarily taken aback when Sophie confided she planned to pursue all of the pleasures life had to offer.

While Mrs. Medford was suggesting several different charities that might be of interest to fill Sophie's free hours, they dined on consommé, followed by Blue Point oysters, turbot browned in butter, small entrées of delicious pâtés and mutton chops, and finally turkey and chicken served with asparagus hollandaise. Each dish was more exquisite than the previous, yet Sophie couldn't wait to make her escape. She declined dessert, hoping to be released from the boring conversation that swirled around the table and to be allowed to join the passengers who would be gathering for the dance in the ballroom.

When Sophie discreetly made her wishes known, Aunt Victoria immediately vetoed the idea. Thus far she'd been polite and gracious, but if her aunt planned to hold her hostage for another hour, Sophie would have to break her promise. She absolutely could not bear another hour of the prattle circulating around her. She must find some method to extract herself. Glancing about the table, she decided difficult circumstances sometimes required thorny resolutions. Though she didn't want to mislead Paul, he appeared to be the answer to her dilemma.

She leaned in his direction and, keeping her voice a mere whisper, explained that she would be ever so grateful if he would accompany her to the upper deck for a breath of fresh air. "All of this rich food, combined with the movement of the ship, has me feeling a bit under the weather."

Sympathy emanated from Paul's eyes. He was the epitome of concern. "Perhaps I should escort you to your cabin so you could retire for the night. I'm certain you'll feel much better come morning."

His solution, however, was not what Sophie expected. She faltered only momentarily. "I do believe, once I leave this stuffy room and breathe in the fresh ocean air, I shall feel much better." She lightly touched his arm. "If not, then I shall heed your advice."

Her response appeared to win him over, and his quiet explanation brooked no objection from her aunt. Though she would have preferred to leave with her cousins, her early departure would permit her time to assess the available men attending the dance and to secure a table with excellent access to the dance floor. The music floated up the stairway as they ascended to the promenade deck.

"Let's stand by the railing and see how you feel once you've been in the fresh air for a brief time," Paul suggested.

Sophie agreed and made a great show of inhaling slow, deep breaths. After several breaths, she clasped one hand to her chest. "I feel much better, Paul. Thank you for your concern."

He arched his brows. "I'm surprised you've recovered so quickly."

"Fresh air does wonders for me." She glanced toward the ballroom. "Why don't we go and sit down?"

"Don't you fear the closeness of all the people in the salon will cause a recurrence of your ailment?" The tone of Paul's question matched the question in his eyes.

She'd been too hasty in her desire to join the dancing, and she could see he now wondered if she'd played him the fool. "You are likely correct. However, my legs are feeling a bit wobbly."

Paul's gaze softened. He placed a protective hold around Sophie's waist and walked her to an arrangement of deck chairs. "You'll be able to sit, yet still enjoy the benefits of the fresh air. I believe this is the perfect solution."

Sophie didn't agree, but for once she held her tongue. She must bide her time. In a short while she would convince Paul the breeze had grown too strong for her liking. Hopefully, the wind would cooperate. With Paul sitting beside her, she settled in the chair and waited for the time to pass while couple after couple passed by them on their way to the ballroom. At this rate, all of the tables near the dance floor would soon be filled. When Paul glanced her way, she casually rubbed her arms.

"You're cold! How thoughtless of me. Perhaps we should go inside. The library might be a good choice."

Sophie shook her head. "I believe I'll go into the ballroom. I'll be fine if you'd rather return to the captain's dining room."

Paul rubbed his jaw and stared at her. "I couldn't possibly permit you to enter by yourself—especially since you've not been feeling well. Though I believe you're making a poor choice, I'll go inside with you. But only if you promise that you'll go to your cabin if you feel ill again."

Placing her hand atop his arm, Sophie lowered her eyelids to half-mast and gently squeezed Paul's arm. "I promise."

Undeniably, she shouldn't be taking advantage of Paul's kind nature, but she pushed aside a pang of guilt. Once her cousins arrived, Sophie planned to shed herself of Paul's company and truly enjoy herself. In fact, she hoped the three of them could successfully escape all of the other members of their group. Then they could have a quite marvelous time.

Once inside the doors, Sophie surveyed the ballroom. The band sat on a raised platform that bordered the dance floor. The coffered ceilings were bordered by a delicately carved frieze of mermaids and dolphins, and chairs, covered with beige and green striped silk, framed the round mahogany tables. One unoccupied table remained near the dance floor, and Sophie lost no time claiming it. She and Paul had barely been seated when the others arrived. Even though Fanny attempted to avoid Daniel by taking a chair between Sophie and their aunt, her effort proved futile. It appeared Aunt Victoria was set upon keeping them together, for she insisted upon moving to the other side of the table. With the older woman's blessing, Daniel immediately claimed the vacated chair next to Fanny.

"I'm beginning to wonder if Uncle Jonas convinced our dear aunt to assume the role of a matchmaker on this voyage," Sophie whispered.

Fanny positioned her fan to hide her lips. "I was wondering the very same thing. She appears determined to keep Daniel near me at every opportunity. I do wish both she and Uncle Jonas would turn their attention to Amanda and quit worrying over me. I have, after all, made my future plans known. With or without their blessing, I plan to marry Michael upon his return."

A young man several tables away captured Sophie's fancy, and when he smiled and pointed toward the dance floor, she nodded. He pushed away from his table and approached in record time. "May I have this dance, miss?"

Paul grasped her hand. "Miss Broadmoor is not feeling well this evening. I doubt—"

Sophie yanked her hand free and stood. "I am quite well, Paul, but thank you for your concern." She turned and strode toward the dance floor without a backward glance. No doubt she'd hurt Paul's feelings, but she didn't need his protection, and she certainly didn't want him taking charge of her comings and goings.

The young man was an excellent dance partner, though his vanity soon wore thin, and Sophie requested he introduce her to the other men at his table. Much to her delight, several of the men took turns dancing with her, and soon she found herself in the arms of a roguish fellow who appeared to be at least ten years her senior. His tight embrace held her much too close, but she didn't object, for he proved an impeccable partner. Keeping her eyes closed, Sophie followed his expert lead until he came to an abrupt stop that nearly landed both of them on the floor. While she had been enjoying the dance, Paul had apparently tapped her partner on the shoulder and requested permission to cut in.

Rather than employing the close embrace of her former partner, Paul held her at a proper distance. He didn't laugh or admire her as the other young men had, and she longed to escape his dull company.

"Your behavior is objectionable, Sophie. You need to conduct yourself in a ladylike fashion. You've danced with one stranger after another without any thought for your reputation. Surely you must realize what those men are thinking of you."

She glowered at him. His pompous attitude was enough to set her on edge. For a moment she considered tromping on his foot. "They think I am a lady who enjoys life—when dancing with them. I can't say the same at the moment."

"Am I not holding you closely enough? Is that the problem?"

"No! The problem is that I detest your criticism. I receive enough censure from my elders, and I don't appreciate it from a man who is neither my escort nor a family member." She sighed when the music stopped. "Thankfully, our dance has come to an end."

"Before she returned to her cabin, your aunt requested I escort you back to our table."

"Aunt Victoria has already retired for the night?" A sense of elation filled her soul. At least she'd have one less pair of eyes watching her that evening.

"Your aunt seemed to think the rich meal and the increased movement of the ship contributed to her distress. I imagine she will be fine by morning." He led her to a chair adjacent to his mother.

Sophie dropped beside the older woman with a thud and folded her arms across her waist to emphasize her dissatisfaction. Paul didn't appear to care in the least.

"You seem unhappy, my dear," Mrs. Medford said.

"Your son acts as though I am a child still in need of a parent's guidance." Sophie glared at Paul.

"And you act like a—"

"Paul, I would appreciate something cool to drink. Refreshments are offered at the other end of the room." Mrs. Medford nodded toward the tables laden with sumptuous treats and a punch bowl on either end. "I would greatly appreciate a cup. No doubt Sophie would enjoy one, also."

"No doubt! After dancing with every man in the attendance, I'm certain she's quite thirsty."

"I did not ask for your opinion, Paul. I merely requested two cups of punch."

Sophie grinned, reveling in the moment. It had given her great pleasure to see Paul's mother correct his behavior. And Sophie didn't fail to note that he didn't appear to accept correction any more than she did.

Once Paul had disappeared into the crowd, Mrs. Medford returned her attention to Sophie. "Now, what was it you were telling me, dear?"

"I dislike the way Paul interferes in my life. He thinks I need his guidance." Sophie looked heavenward. "I plan to have fun, and the last thing I want is someone telling me how to behave."

"I know you may not believe me now, but one day you will realize there is much more to life than fun, Sophie." The older woman's eyes shone with kindness, and she patted Sophie's hand. "No matter our age, all of us need guidance from time to time, even an old woman such as me."

Sophie dropped back in her chair. "Your mother still requires you to follow her rules?"

With a gentle laugh, the older woman shook her head. "No, but I do attempt to live by the conventions my parents taught me. More importantly, I do my best to live by the rules God has put in place for all of us." Her tone exuded warmth rather than condemnation.

The topic of God and His rules caused Sophie to squirm a bit. She didn't care to dwell upon what God might think of her behavior, for if it aligned with the thoughts of other authority figures in her life, she'd be considered a heathen.

"As for Paul's behavior, I believe he is simply attempting to protect you from possible harm. Right or wrong, we are judged by our behavior, and Paul appears concerned about your reputation."

"Paul need not worry himself over my reputation. I can—"

"Well, someone needs to, for you're doing nothing to protect your family name or your own character," Paul interjected. He placed two cups of punch on the table.

His words stung, and Sophie pushed away from the table. "If you will excuse me, Mrs. Medford. I don't believe you or your son should be seen in my company." Sophie stood and grasped several folds of her silk gown in one hand before drawing near to Paul. "I wouldn't want to besmirch your fine name, Paul."

She turned on her heel and hastened across the room in search of Amanda and Fanny. Neither was on the dance floor, and she hadn't seen them since much earlier in the evening. While silently chiding herself for not keeping a closer watch, she strolled onto the deck. She'd nearly given up hope of finding them when she heard a hissing whisper.

"Over here, Sophie!"

She strained to see in the darkness and nearly tripped on a deck chair. "Is that you, Fanny?"

"Yes. And Amanda, too."

Sophie peered into the darkened space they'd created for themselves behind several deck chairs and a small table. They had draped a piece of tarp or blanket, she couldn't be certain which, to help conceal their whereabouts. Careful to hold her skirts close to keep the fabric from snagging on one of the wooden deck chairs, Sophie wended her way to their makeshift hideaway. "What are you two doing back here?"

"Fanny is trying to avoid Daniel while I do my best to maintain a proper lookout," Amanda said.

"Do come out of there. I don't want to ruin my dress or my coiffure. Moreover, we shouldn't be required to hide. We're supposed to be having fun." Sophie motioned them toward the railing. The moon cast a shimmering light upon the water as the ship cut through the ocean, leaving a wide trail of white foam in its wake.

"You appear to be annoyed," Amanda said. "Did one of those young men escape without asking you for a dance?"

Sophie flicked her fan on Amanda's arm. "No need for barbed remarks. Paul has already delivered far too many for one evening. That man is a total bore!" She stood on tiptoe, leaned over the railing, peered into the water, and giggled. "Perhaps the two of you could help me toss him overboard."

Amanda's lips parted and formed a wide oval.

"I'm merely jesting. However, I would be most appreciative if you would keep Paul out of my hair for the remainder of the evening."

Amanda glanced back and forth between her cousins. "Fanny wants me to keep Daniel out of her hair; now I'm to keep Paul out of yours. And here I stand with not one man interested in me or my hair." She sighed. "Come along, Cousins. I'll do my best."

Paul's mother smiled and reached out to pat his hand. "I know you are worried about her, but sometimes you have to let matters go."

"She's going to get hurt," he replied.

"That is a great possibility."

He met his mother's sympathetic expression. "I shouldn't care, but I do. Sophie may seem hard and indifferent, but she's hurting."

His mother nodded. "I know, and you are very sensitive to that wound."

"I see the way her father acts around her. He's hurting, too. Losing his wife caused him great grief. Unfortunately, in dealing with it, he's pushed away all his loved ones and focused instead on the Home for the Friendless."

"It's sometimes easier to expend your energy on strangers. You don't come to expect anything from them like you do family. When family disappoints you, it cuts deep. Your Mr. Broadmoor is no doubt afraid of his feelings—even those he has for his daughter."

"I'm sure you're right," Paul said, staring across the room at the blur of dancing couples. "I only hope it doesn't result in causing him even more pain. Sophie is strong willed and daring. There's no telling what she'll do in order to get the love and attention she's so desperate to have. I just feel that in her father's absence, I should do what I can to keep bad things from happening to her."

Mother shook her head. "You cannot keep those you care about from pain. Sometimes it's necessary in order to mature. Sophie may well have to face some bitter trials before she fully understands what life is all about." She squeezed his hand. "You will most likely face them, as well."

CHAPTER 4

MONDAY, NOVEMBER 1, 1897
ROCHESTER, NEW YORK

Jonas shrugged into his topcoat and removed his hat from the walnut hall tree in the corner of his office. He silently chided himself, for he disliked being late. He'd be hard-pressed to make it to the men's club on time today, though he doubted his lawyer, Mortimer Fillmore, would mind the delay. He would likely imbibe a glass or two of port while he waited. Another reason Jonas must hurry! The old lawyer couldn't seem to stop with only one glass. After two or three, he couldn't follow the conversation, and after four, he fell asleep. The behavior was argument enough for Jonas to retain another lawyer, but there was no one he trusted like Mortimer.

Unfortunately, Mortimer's son and law partner, Vincent, held to a higher ethical code than his father. Jonas and Mortimer thought alike—they were cut from the same cloth, so to speak. Both were willing to use any means to achieve personal financial gain. As long as the proposition ended with a hefty increase in their bank accounts, Jonas and Mortimer cared not a whit if others met with monetary ruination. It was, after all, the American way. Each man could be king in his own way if he was willing to take chances and defeat those who would see him cast under. All great fortunes had been made that way, and Jonas could see no reason to alter a course that hundreds of well-bred men had journeyed before him.

Today Jonas needed Mortimer to be sharp-witted because, following their private lunch, the two would meet with Judge Webster, a situation that worried Jonas. On the ride to the men's club he did his best to convince himself all would go well. After all, Mortimer understood the import of today's meeting. The lawyer would not do anything to jeopardize this crucial discussion with the judge. Stepping down from the carriage, Jonas withdrew his pocket watch and snapped open the lid. A full half hour late. The moment he entered the building, he scanned the area for his old friend. It didn't take long to locate him. He had selected a table in close proximity to the bar rather than one in the formal dining room.

Another man sat at the table with his back toward the entrance. Jonas narrowed his eyes and strained to make out the figure. As he approached the table, he shuddered. William Snodgrass! The banker was engrossed in a heated conversation with Mortimer. Jonas must find some way to get rid of him, for they were already pressed for time.

Though the sight of Snodgrass annoyed him, Jonas determined to speak in a cheerful voice. He would accomplish little with anger. "Mortimer! I apologize for my delay. I see you've located someone to help you pass the time while you waited on me." He extended his arm and shook hands with William. "Good to see you, William. I was detained at the office and now find myself late for my meeting with Mortimer."

William pointed to a chair. "Sit down and join us. Mortimer tells me your family is off to England." He jabbed an arthritic finger at Jonas. "I hope they won't further deplete your bank account. Perhaps you should have gone along to ensure they don't spend all your money."

"I plan to join them once I conclude a pressing business matter that holds me in Rochester. In fact, that's why I scheduled this meeting with Mortimer."

William rested his arm on the table. "Then I'm glad I joined Mortimer. I imagine I can be of some help, too." He signaled for a waiter. "Why don't we order something to eat? I always think better on a full stomach."

Jonas glanced across the table. Mortimer had obviously had more than two glasses of port, for his eyelids had dropped to half-mast. If Jonas didn't do something, his lawyer would soon be snoring. Unable to think of any other immediate remedy, Jonas slapped his palm on the table.

The table shook, the glasses rattled, and Mortimer jumped as though he'd been shot. "What's wrong? What happened?" Mortimer rubbed his forehead, clearly dismayed.

"I was expressing my anger over being late. William would like to join us for lunch, but with my late arrival, we don't have sufficient time. I do apologize to both of you." Jonas nudged Mortimer's knee, hoping the lawyer would take his cue. When he failed to respond, Jonas pushed away from the table. "Come along, Mortimer. We don't want to be late for our meeting."

"What? Late?" He looked at the clock and shook his head. "We have plenty of time before we meet with Judge Webster."

William raised a bushy white eyebrow. "Judge Webster?" He leaned a little closer to Jonas. "Have you gone and gotten yourself into some kind of trouble?"

Glances came from several nearby tables, for William's "whispered" words were akin to a shout. Jonas glared at Mortimer, who returned a glassy-eyed stare. "No. This is merely a business meeting regarding some, uh, some investments."

"Right. Investments," Mortimer repeated. "I think I'd like another glass of port."

"There will be no more port. We must be on our way."

William clasped Jonas's wrist with his bony fingers. "Now, wait a moment, Jonas. As your banker, I believe I can add valuable insight about investments. Why don't we order lunch, and the three of us can discuss this matter before you meet with the judge. Who, I might add, has very little business sense. I don't know why you're meeting with him."

"Please keep your voice down, William. I don't want everyone in the club to know my business."

The old banker grinned. "Afraid they'll overhear us and attempt to intrude upon your latest venture?"

Jonas tugged at his collar. "One can never be too careful. You know that."

"Yet you're willing to include Judge Webster in your scheme. Why not the man who's been your banker for years?"

"If our venture succeeds, I promise to deposit a portion of the funds in your bank." Jonas hoped his promise would be enough to hold the banker at bay. Right now Jonas wanted to escape the old man and his prying questions.

William motioned to a waiter. "I still believe we have sufficient time for lunch. And I want to hear more about this new undertaking of yours."

Jonas was losing patience. How could William possibly know if they had sufficient time to dine? He didn't even know when they were due to meet with the judge—unless Mortimer had confided that information, also. "As I said earlier, I'd like nothing more than a quiet lunch. But perhaps later in the week?" Jonas stood and tapped Mortimer on the shoulder.

Snodgrass bobbed his head, causing several tufts of white hair to dance in a slow-motion waltz. "I suggest Wednesday. And I'll expect a full report about this new investment opportunity and what the judge has to say."

Jonas touched his index finger to his pursed lips. "Not so loud, William. I will meet you here at the club on Wednesday. Shall we say one o'clock?" He knew any attempt to depart without setting a time and date would be futile. If need be, Jonas could have his clerk cancel the appointment.

Separating Mortimer from his chair proved nearly as difficult as his own attempt to escape William. Jonas finally braced his hand beneath Mortimer's arm and hoisted him out of the chair. He hoped a dose of brisk autumn air would prove enough to clear Mortimer's mind. The carriage driver approached, but Jonas waved him on. "We'll walk. Please follow. In the event we need you, I'll wave you forward."

"I'd rather ride, Jonas. I'm somewhat weary."

"You've had too much to drink. The walk and fresh air will do you good. You need to regain your senses or this meeting with the judge will be for naught. Now breathe deeply." Jonas held tightly to Mortimer's arm and led him down the street. "And the next time we have a meeting, do *not* indulge in alcoholic beverages beforehand. Do I make myself clear?"

Although Jonas had his doubts the lawyer would keep his word, Mortimer mumbled agreement. If Mortimer muddled today's meeting with the judge, Jonas would have no choice but to discharge him.

"If you hadn't been late, I wouldn't have had my second glass, or my third, or—"

"Don't blame your bad habit on me. Right now we need to concentrate on winning over Judge Webster. If I'm to gain his allegiance, he will want assurance his name and position will be protected. Otherwise, I doubt he'll agree to sign off on the paper work."

The fresh air appeared to have a restorative effect upon Mortimer. "You let me worry about the judge. We go way back, and I don't expect any problem from him. As long as you're willing to line his pockets and keep your lips sealed, he'll agree to whatever I propose. He'll make certain you'll be able to manipulate your niece's inheritance without interference while the records will give every appearance of legality." The lawyer stopped midstep and waved at the carriage driver. "And now, if you have no objection, I would prefer to ride the remainder of the distance to Judge Webster's home."

Jonas followed Mortimer into the carriage, and the two of them rode in silence. Mortimer appeared thankful for the opportunity to rest, so Jonas dwelled upon how he planned to benefit from Fanny's inheritance. He'd invest it, of course, and reap himself a fine profit while doing so—and the foolish girl would be none the wiser. The fact that his father had bequeathed a full one-third of his estate to Fanny continued to rankle Jonas, but knowing he would soon gain complete control of her inheritance helped assuage his anger.

Before long, he could make a large investment in George Fulford's patent medicine business. And along with his previous investment in the company, he would soon be the largest stockholder—next to Fulford himself, of course. If all went according to plan, Jonas would be making a fortune from George Fulford's Pink Pills for Pale People. Of course he'd not limit himself to Fulford. There were many investment opportunities, some safer than others. But he need not spend his nights worrying over poor investments now that he would have Fanny's money. Should he make poor investment choices, he would make certain his records were carefully adjusted to show that it was Fanny who suffered the losses.

ENGLAND

Sophie sighed and stared despondently out the window as they approached Illiff Manor. Despite the grandeur of the limestone manor house, the isolation of the English countryside was far from what Sophie longed for.

"Is it not glorious, girls? Just as I told you?" Amanda's mother questioned. She pressed a gloved hand to her throat. "It is too wondrous for words. We have beautiful estates in America, but there is something captured here in the ancientness of England that speaks to my soul."

"It is charming, Mother."

Sophie frowned. "And ancient."

Fanny tried without luck to suppress a giggle. Victoria seemed not to notice. "The house dates back to the fourteenth or fifteenth century, I can never remember which. It has been in the family for all those generations. There are over eighty rooms and some four hundred acres upon which you'll find terraced gardens, streams, ponds, and wonderful trails for riding."

Sophie sighed louder than she'd meant to. The very sound of such drudgery only served to make her tired.

Her aunt lifted the brim of her hat and studied Sophie. "Whatever is the matter, dear? Are you not feeling well?"

Sophie rested her chin in her palm. "I do wish we would have gone directly to London. Why must we spend time out here in the country, where there is absolutely nothing to occupy our time? We didn't come to England to sit in a garden with our needlework. If Lady Illiff were truly interested in entertaining us, she should have offered her London town house." The carriage came to a stop, but Sophie did not look forward to stepping out, no matter how sore she was after the jostling ride from the train station.

"I truly do not know how to please you, Sophie. Paul's presence on board the ship caused you to grumble and complain, and now that he and his mother have departed, you remain unhappy." Aunt Victoria frowned and shook her head. "I hope that will not be the case indefinitely. Lady Illiff is a dear friend. You may console yourself with the knowledge that we won't be here for long, for she has requested we accompany her to London next week. Lord and Lady Illiff are generously hosting our visit. I trust you will treat them with respect and not embarrass me."

Before Sophie could utter her response, the driver opened the carriage door. In truth, Aunt Victoria was correct: Sophie should have been thankful Paul had taken his leave and gone to tend his ailing grandmother. Mrs. Medford's company had proved to be much more pleasing than that of her son, which was quite a compliment considering Sophie had never been one to enjoy associating with older women.

Daniel maneuvered between Fanny and Aunt Victoria as they ascended the steps of the manor house, and Sophie felt a wave of pity for her cousin. The reminder that Fanny would be forced to tolerate Daniel's unwelcome advances and overbearing manner throughout the remainder of their journey eased her own self-pity for the moment.

"Look at the ivy," Fanny remarked. "I'd love to know more about it. It looks quite delicate yet so very intricate."

Sophie looked at the greenery climbing the manor house walls and shook her head. "Who cares about ivy? I can see ivy at home."

"Yes, but this is English ivy gracing a wealthy English home," Amanda whispered. "Perhaps it is admired by wealthy Englishmen—single men who are enthralled with ivy only because they have no beautiful women with which to occupy their time." She smiled and raised a brow as if to suggest Sophie ponder all the possibilities.

Lady Illiff greeted them in the entry hall and bid the servants deliver the baggage to their rooms. "I am delighted you've arrived. We're going to have a wonderful visit, Victoria." She turned toward Daniel and the girls. "I trust you young people will enjoy yourselves here in the country. Though the gardens aren't quite as lovely as in the springtime, I still believe you'll find them to your liking." She seemed to hardly draw breath.

Sophie thought her reminiscent of a chattering parrot and just as colorful. The woman wore a wide sweeping gown of lavender with shades of blue and green running in a rather disorderly pattern throughout the weave of material. Thick gatherings of yellow and pink lace trimmed the sleeves. It was a riot of color, to be sure.

Lady Illiff turned toward the wide staircase. "I'm certain you'd like to rest before you dress for supper. The servants will show you to your rooms."

Sophie gazed heavenward. It was just as she'd thought: they'd be relegated to sitting in the garden with their needlework. If she was going to spend her time in England visiting gardens, she'd prefer a stroll along the pathways of Kew Gardens near the River Thames. At least she might encounter an eligible man or two along the way.

Lady Illiff's personal maid escorted Aunt Victoria to her bedchamber while another servant led Sophie and her cousins to a connecting suite at the end of the hall. The butler had been charged with escorting Daniel to his room. For Fanny's sake, Sophie hoped his room would be in a different wing of the house. Surely with eighty rooms they could arrange at least a good dozen or more between the two.

However boring, it was evident that Illiff Manor clearly spoke of a wealth and elegance that brought to mind kings and queens. The ceilings were at least thirty feet high. The structure bore intricate plaster work and wood carvings on the banisters, railings, and crown molding, suggesting hundreds of years of labor. Sophie was not blind to the riches displayed for all to see. Nor was she ignorant of the money it would cost to maintain such an estate. She bit her lower lip and tried to remember if the Illiffs had any unmarried sons.

The maid ushered the girls into their room and stood stiffly at the door. "Madam will expect you to dine this evening in formal attire." She said nothing more before turning to go.

The moment the servant took her leave, Sophie plopped into one of the overstuffed chairs in a most unladylike fashion. The rooms were lovely, with a small balcony overlooking Lady Illiff's beloved gardens, yet Sophie longed to be in the city. "I hope madam won't expect us to play a game of charades or whist after the meal."

"Perhaps if she does, you can pretend to be overcome by the closeness of the room," Amanda said with a grin. "After all, it worked on the ship."

"But Paul won't be available to escort you from the room," Fannie added.

"Speaking of which, I don't understand why your mother informed Paul of our traveling plans. I daresay he knows more about where we'll be traveling than the three of us." Sophie barely managed to stifle a yawn. Perhaps a brief rest wasn't such a bad idea.

Amanda sat in front of the dressing table and rearranged several locks of hair. "Do cease your complaints, Sophie. It's quite unbecoming. Mother is doing her best. From what Mother has told me, Paul's grandmother is critically ill. I doubt you need give him further thought."

"I suppose you're right, but it doesn't change the fact that I was required to abide his constant attention on the ship. I would now like the opportunity to enjoy myself."

"You worry overmuch about your own pleasure," Amanda said.

"That's easy enough for you to say, dear cousin. You weren't forced to spend the entire voyage with Paul hovering over your shoulder at every turn. And now that Paul is gone, we're out here in the country with no men at all."

"You succeeded in avoiding Paul much more frequently than I escaped Daniel's unwanted attention," Fanny said. "If you desire an escort, please take Daniel. I would be most thankful."

Sophie shuddered. "No, thank you! Perhaps we should devise a plan to lose him while we're in London. Better yet, we should leave him here. There must be someplace where he could be held hostage until we leave for the city. Or we could bribe one of the servants to keep him locked up!"

"Sophie Broadmoor! What a horrid idea," Amanda declared. "How could you even consider asking the servants to take him prisoner?"

"Then perhaps we could convince Veda and Minnie." Sophie called the two maids, who were busy unpacking their belongings in one of the adjoining bedrooms.

Veda, the younger of the two, peeked into the sitting room, and Sophie motioned her forward. "If we locate a garden shed or some other confined space, would you help us secure Mr. Daniel inside until we've left for London?"

A look of fear registered in the girl's eyes. "Oh no, ma'am, I could never do such a horrid thing as that. Miss Victoria wouldn't approve." She glanced at Amanda. "Would she, Miss Amanda?"

"Go and finish unpacking our trunks, Veda. Miss Sophie is teasing," Amanda said.

The maid peered at Sophie, who nodded her agreement. Once Veda was out of earshot, Sophie folded her arms across her waist. "I still think the plan has merit. I'd wager there is some sort of structure where the gardeners store their tools." She walked to the French doors leading onto the balcony and stared down at the perfectly sculpted hedges and terraced lawns. "Of course, the gardeners would likely discover Daniel before we left."

"I certainly want to rid myself of his company, but I'm not convinced we should do anything to cause him bodily harm," Fanny said. "And I doubt Aunt Victoria would leave for London if Daniel turned up missing."

Sophie shrugged. "We'd simply devise some story and say that he'd become bored with the journey and decided to visit London on his own. Aunt Victoria would believe us if the two of you didn't act suspicious. You must be careful to speak with authority and keep your story straight. My father believes whatever I tell him."

"I'm not at all sure you should be particularly proud of that," Amanda replied. "And I, for one, do not intend to participate in any plan to abduct Daniel."

"Fine!" With her palms on her hips, Sophie turned and was met by Amanda's admonishing look. "I was merely attempting to help Fanny with a solution to her dilemma. Perhaps *you* should be the one to keep Daniel occupied, Amanda, since you're concerned about his welfare."

"Instead of worrying over Daniel, I think we should be more concerned with what we plan to wear to dinner this evening. In less than a half hour Minnie will go to Mother's room to assist her, so if you prefer to have Minnie style your hair, you'd best inform her immediately."

"I thought we were going to have a rest," Sophie muttered.

"And I thought you longed for the excitement and invigorating pace of London," Amanda countered. "Make up your mind. You cannot have it both ways."

Sophie gazed heavenward. Amanda was beginning to act like the grumpy matrons who'd sat on their deck chairs aboard the ship with striped woolen blankets across their legs, books open and frowns tugging at their lips. Occasionally one would look up long enough to issue a curt reprimand to a noisy passerby. Sophie dearly loved her older cousin, but Amanda was growing old far before her time. She needed a beau. Not that Sophie would say so again, for Amanda would simply point out her desire to make a distinctive contribution to mankind. Sophie certainly didn't want to hear such talk—she had listened to enough of that nonsense from both her father and Paul.

While Veda assisted Sophie and Fanny with their dresses, Minnie styled Amanda's hair and then hurried down the hall to assist Aunt Victoria. Veda fashioned Fanny's hair and then Sophie's while Amanda donned her emerald green silk gown.

After Veda had completed styling Sophie's hair, she nodded with approval. "When the three of you stand side by side, you look like an arrangement of autumn flowers."

Sophie laughed, but Veda's assessment was correct. Fanny's gown of rich claret and Sophie's golden topaz resembled the chrysanthemums bordering the garden walkways, while Amanda's deep green matched the foliage that surrounded the blooms.

Fanny stepped to one side of Amanda. "There. We make a perfect bouquet, don't you think, Veda?"

"Indeed you do. You shall make the mistress most proud, ladies," Veda said.

The clock chimed. After a hasty farewell to the maid, the three of them departed their room. Sophie linked arms with her cousins. "We must stay together this evening. Otherwise, I fear we will be bored to tears. I do hope we can escape the old folks soon after supper."

"You mustn't be rude, Sophie. If we're asked to remain downstairs with Lord and Lady Illiff, please don't refuse or feign a headache. Mother will immediately realize what you're up to, and you'll only make matters worse," Amanda warned.

Descending the stairs, Sophie looked into the receiving hall and could barely believe her eyes. There were several other guests. Perhaps this wouldn't be as dull as she'd expected.

Like a hound to the foxes, Daniel besieged Fanny the moment they entered the room. Sophie considered tromping on his foot, but that would only draw unwanted attention from the other guests. While contemplating other possibilities, she surveyed the room, finally locking gazes with a strikingly handsome man. His lips curved in a roguish grin, and then—he winked! At least she thought his wink had been intended for her. She peeked over her shoulder to see if there might be someone else who had captured the attention of the delicious-looking man.

Her heart fluttered a quickstep when she saw him walk toward her with Lady Illiff clinging to his arm, and his dark eyes held her captive as Lady Illiff introduced him. *Wesley Hedrick*. She turned the name over in her mind, enjoying the rhythm.

"Pleased to make your acquaintance, Miss Sophie Broadmoor," he said, surprising her with an American accent. He repeated her name as if committing it to memory.

His memorization would prove unnecessary, for Sophie had already determined Mr. Hedrick would never forget her. Though he was obviously older than her by more than a few years, she thought the combination of his age and good looks enchanting.

"I hope you won't think me forward, but I have asked Lady Illiff to seat me next to you at supper." He hesitated only briefly, his eyes sparkling. "She graciously agreed."

Sophie looked to Lady Illiff and noted her disapproving stare. Though Mr. Hedrick had requested the change, the older woman obviously placed the blame upon Sophie. For a brief moment, Sophie considered saying as much, but then decided she cared little. The evening would be more pleasurable than she had anticipated.

Hours later Sophie decided to ask Wesley to take a walk with her. It was a bold and brazen thing to do, but Sophie figured there was no time like the present to get to know this man better.

"I know," she whispered as the men were adjourning to the library for talk of politics and snifters of brandy, "that you are expected to join the other gentlemen, but I would very much enjoy it if you would accompany me on a stroll around the gardens."

Mr. Hedrick looked rather surprised but then offered her a smile. "I say, such a pastime sounds quite enjoyable. I shall wait for you just outside the front door."

Sophie nodded. She was grateful to find Aunt Victoria and Lady Illiff very much caught up in a conversation about tapestries, while Fanny and Amanda had quickly exited the room to keep Fanny from having to endure Daniel's attention.

Not even bothering to excuse herself, Sophie hurried for the front door. The butler, ever efficient, stood at the ready with her wrap. It appeared to Sophie that Wesley had told the man to anticipate her arrival.

"Thank you," she murmured.

Outside, the air was brisk but not at all unpleasant. She spied Wesley at the bottom of the graveled drive, standing by the path that led into the front gardens.

"I feel like a naughty schoolboy," Wesley said with a grin.

Sophie could clearly make out his features in the glow of light from the house. "I hope you don't think ill of me for suggesting such a thing, but . . . well . . . my mother always taught me to act quickly when an opportunity presented itself."

"And what opportunity is this?" Wesley asked as Sophie led the way to a stone bench.

"The opportunity to better know you, of course. You seem so different from most of the men I've met."

He chuckled and waited for her to sit before answering. "I suppose I should take that as a compliment, but perhaps it is otherwise intended."

"Not at all." Sophie smiled up at him. "I find myself wanting to know everything about you."

He frowned. "Some of my life is not worth addressing."

"I know that you were once married. You needn't speak of it if it causes you pain. I overheard Lady Illiff speak to my aunt about it."

Wesley's expression seemed troubled. Sophie worried that she'd pushed too far and started to comment on the matter when he spoke.

"My wife, Eugenia, was a delicate, fragile woman. Her health was never good, and three years ago she succumbed to a bout of pneumonia."

"I am sorry for your loss but glad to see you have come out of mourning."

"Lady Illiff insisted. She said that three years was more than ample time. She's encouraged me to live life to its fullest, but I can't quite decide how one should go about doing that."

Sophie smiled and patted the seat. With an arched brow that she knew would give her a rather alluring come-hither look, she said, "Well, perhaps I can help you to figure that out."

Though Victoria would have preferred to retire for the evening, she accepted Lord and Lady Illiff's invitation to join them in their luxurious sitting room. She was surprised to see Mr. Hedrick enter the room nearly twenty minutes later. The man had certainly captured Sophie's interest during dinner. Although he was considerably older than her niece, Mr. Hedrick had provided a positive diversion for Sophie throughout dinner. She'd been relieved, however, when the girls had retired to their rooms immediately following the meal. She had feared Sophie would make some sort of scene with Mr. Hedrick.

"Wesley, how good of you to join us," Lady Illiff greeted him. "I was just telling Mrs. Broadmoor how long it has been since you last visited. We are truly blessed to have your company."

"Too true, Wes, old man. I've not had a good hunt since you left," Lord Illiff said. "You must join me on the morrow."

"I believe that would be quite enjoyable."

"We will have to find a diversion for the girls, as well," Lady Illiff suggested, "lest they feel left out."

"Knowing my niece, she will no doubt strive to include herself in the hunt if we do not otherwise occupy her," Victoria said. "In fact I'm surprised that she is not here, affixed to your side, Mr. Hedrick. She seemed to monopolize your conversation throughout dinner."

Mr. Hedrick smiled. "I simply explained I'd made prior arrangements to have a glass of port with Lord Illiff. She is a charming young lady."

"As you say, she *is* young. Unfortunately, her behavior sometimes reflects her youthfulness," Victoria added.

Mr. Hedrick laughed. "Which, I believe, adds to her charm."

Victoria arched her brows. "You might change your mind if you were required to spend much time in her company. I find that those beyond the age of thirty quickly tire of her puckish behavior."

"An interesting observation, Mrs. Broadmoor."

Victoria had hoped to ascertain Mr. Hedrick's age, but he'd carefully avoided being trapped by her question. She didn't believe for a moment that Mr. Hedrick was under the age of thirty. After all, he appeared to be a longtime acquaintance of Lord and Lady Illiff, who were near her own age. She would inquire of Lady Illiff when they were alone.

Lord Illiff took a sip of his port. "I do wish Jonas could have traveled with you, Victoria. The man works far too hard."

"I did my best to convince him, but to no avail. Unless his plans change, he will join us in London, although I believe time in the country would have proved beneficial to rejuvenate him both body and soul."

Wesley leaned toward her, his eyes reflecting concern. "I trust your husband isn't suffering from a medical condition, dear lady."

"No, but I fear that he will soon exhaust himself. Since his father's death, poor Jonas has been forced to take on the added burden of handling the estate as well as the guardianship for his niece. Taking responsibility for the entire financial aspect of such a large estate has caused no end of difficulties."

"I can only imagine," Wesley replied. "Choosing wise investments for family members is a grave responsibility. I'm sure your family is thankful for his skill."

Victoria brushed the folds of her skirt and shook her head. "Until one is faced with the challenge, it is difficult to cope with the conflicts that arise— especially within the family." She sighed. "I must say, I was completely aghast when distant relatives appeared on our doorstep expecting to receive a portion of Hamilton's estate. Their very presence was most distressing."

"I can only imagine," Lady Illiff said. " 'Tis truly sad how someone's death can bring out the worst in people, isn't it?"

Wesley concurred, his eyes filled with sympathy. "Greed. Pure and simple. I can understand your need to come abroad and escape the turmoil."

Victoria sunk back against the cushioned chair, thankful for these friends, both new and old, who understood and willingly offered her peace and solace. If only Jonas could be present to experience the healing effects. He was the one who'd been forced to bear the brunt of hostile relatives and daunting decisions. A wave of guilt assaulted her, for instead of offering her husband the understanding he so richly deserved, she'd acted the shrew when he'd been forced to remain in New York. She silently vowed to beg his forgiveness and offer an understanding spirit in the future.

CHAPTER 5

TUESDAY, NOVEMBER 2, 1897

Per their agreement, Sophie made her way down the long terraced back gardens the next afternoon to locate Wesley. She felt her heart skip a beat when she spied him near the fountain. Just as he said he would be. Goodness, but he was dashing. The dark blue suit hugged his well-formed frame, causing him to appear even more muscular than she'd earlier thought. He turned and smiled at her in such a way that Sophie actually felt faint. She'd never known such excitement from simply being in the presence of a man.

"Good afternoon, Miss Broadmoor," he said and gave a little bow. "I trust that you enjoyed your morning."

"It was boring, to be quite honest."

He chuckled at this. "I must say I appreciate such truthfulness. Whatever did Lady Illiff find to occupy your time?"

"She took us on a carriage ride around the grounds. We visited several of her tenants and learned more about yew trees and their ill effect on livestock than I would ever care to know."

Wesley laughed heartily. "I do not suppose I would have cared for such an adventure, either."

"And what of you? Did you enjoy your morning?"

"I did, although I kept thinking of other things. My mind was not at all on the hunt, and I missed every one of my birds."

Sophie looked up rather innocently. She hoped he had been preoccupied with her but didn't want to appear too eager and say so. "And what, if I might be so bold to ask, stole your thoughts from the hunt? I thought men very much enjoyed such pursuits."

"I enjoy a good hunt," he said with a wicked grin that caused Sophie to tremble. "But it all depends on what I'm hunting."

Friday, November 5, 1897

Sophie pointed to several locks of hair that had escaped their pins. "Veda, please arrange the pins so they will hold the curls in place. I can't meet Wesley . . . ah, Mr. Hedrick with my hair falling in my eyes, now can I? Oh, I've so enjoyed our days here at Illiff Manor. Do you suppose we might stay longer, Amanda?"

Amanda stepped to the dressing table and stood behind Sophie. "I'll do Sophie's hair, Veda. Mother sent word she needs you in her room."

Veda nodded, set down the hairpins, and headed out the door to help Aunt Victoria prepare for afternoon tea.

Amanda looked at Sophie. "I thought you were miserable at the very thought of coming here."

"I've changed my mind. I find it quite appealing."

Their eyes met in the mirror. "He's too old for you, Sophie. I think you should abstain from any further contact." Amanda picked up a pin and began to fashion a curl.

"Don't be ridiculous. Many young women my age marry men far older than Wesley. He is only twenty-eight."

"I wonder if he speaks the truth. He appears much older. His hair has even begun to gray along his temples. Did you not notice?"

Sophie bobbed her head, causing another curl to fall loose and drop forward. "He tells me his father was completely gray by the time he reached the age of thirty-two." She swiped the curl from her forehead. "Are you going to arrange my curls or discuss Wesley's hair?"

Amanda jabbed a pin into Sophie's tresses. "I simply do not understand your attraction to a man his age. And Mother tells me Mr. Hedrick has already been married." She seemed to emphasize the importance of his formal name.

"I know of his past, Amanda. Wesley," Sophie said with equal stress on his given name, "was born in New York and wed Lady Illiff's cousin, Eugenia. She died three years ago. At Lady Illiff's insistence, he has once again begun to attend social functions. Three years is a long time to remain in mourning, especially for a man of Wesley's age."

"Perhaps that's what turned him gray." Fanny clapped her palm across her lips and stifled a giggle.

"I think both of you are jealous. Wesley is a fine man. Lady Illiff tells me he is quite wealthy in his own right. And he exhibits a gracious and generous spirit to everyone he meets."

Amanda arranged another curl. "He didn't display a gracious spirit to me. In fact, he has barely spoken two words to me in all the time we've been here. Then again, I suppose I'm of no import to him."

Fanny quickly added her agreement to Amanda's assessment.

"I don't care what either of you think. He is everything I could ever want in a man. He listens to me and takes me seriously." Sophie thought he was probably the only man who did. He was possibly the only person, male or female, who believed her to show depth of thought and spirit. She knew this because he had told her so. She smiled at the memory and added, "He has shown me every courtesy a woman could expect from a suitor."

"Suitor? Mr. Hedrick isn't your suitor. He's simply a guest here, the same as we are," Amanda said, tugging on a curl. "Do sit up or I'll never finish your hair."

Sophie glared into the mirror, but Amanda didn't look up from the curls she was piling atop her cousin's head. Sophie wouldn't argue with Amanda, but she knew Wesley's interest in her went far beyond that of two guests residing under the same roof. Besides, what did Amanda know of men? She'd never even had a beau.

"Do hurry, Amanda. I would like to speak to Wesley before we join Lady Illiff for tea."

"If Mr. Hedrick is as smitten as you say, I'm sure he will await the very sound of your footsteps on the stairs," Amanda said. She placed her palm on her heart and fluttered her lashes until finally collapsing in a gale of laughter.

Fanny soon joined in, and Sophie pushed away from the dressing table. Her hair would do. "I'm going downstairs."

"I daresay you've lost your sense of humor since taking up with Mr. Hedrick. What happened to the old Sophie, our cousin who enjoyed a good laugh and a practical joke?" Amanda asked as Sophie opened the bedroom door.

Sophie ignored the question and proceeded downstairs in search of Wesley. She peeked in the library but upon finding no one there, went to the parlor, where Lady Illiff and Aunt Victoria had already gathered. Lady Illiff motioned her forward. "Do come in and join us, my dear."

Forcing a smile, Sophie entered the room and sat down beside Lady Illiff, who immediately admired her gown and then spoke of the lovely weather. "I think we will have good fortune in our travels," she said, smoothing the bouncing lace of her neckline. "Lord Illiff wants to discuss the particulars as soon as they return."

"As soon as who returns?" Sophie asked, glancing around the room.

"My husband has taken Mr. Irwin and Wesley riding. I do believe they've the perfect afternoon for a nice long ride, don't you agree?" She leaned to look out the window. "As I was about to tell your aunt, my husband is quite anxious for the city. He has business there, you know." Her refined British accent suggested the business was important.

Sophie nodded, though she began to fret over leaving Wesley. How in the world could she persuade them to remain here at Illiff Manor in the country?

"I hope the ride is not too hard on poor Daniel," Victoria said thoughtfully.

"He isn't much of an equestrian," Sophie commented. She imagined Wesley upon a horse. What a fine figure he would cut. No doubt he was quite masterful at riding. She would have to suggest they take a ride—even if she had to include Fanny and Amanda.

"Lord Illiff will see to him—of this I'm certain. He would never allow a less than experienced rider to suffer. He'll secure a good mount for Mr. Irwin."

Sophie tried to think of how to broach the subject of remaining at Illiff Manor for at least a few more days. She longed to spend as much time as possible with Wesley and to convince him that he should come to see her in America. "I do wish we could remain in the country a while longer." The remark gained her aunt's attention, and Sophie giggled. "I know that might seem out of character for me. Aunt Victoria will tell you that I'm the one who had least wanted to come to the country."

"Indeed! From the moment we disembarked the ship, I heard nothing but complaints."

Lady Illiff smiled. "I would surmise that our Wesley has had something to do with Sophie's change in attitude and her desire to remain in the country. I spied the two of you walking in the gardens yesterday."

"I hope my niece was not acting inappropriately." Victoria's tense tone made it clear that she didn't approve.

"Not at all, my dear. They behaved perfectly well. It actually does my heart good to see Wesley's attention focused on something other than his loss. I think Sophie has been like a balm to him. And obviously she is quite pleased with his company." Lady Illiff gave a deep, throaty laugh. "I would venture to say that Illiff Manor would hold little interest at all for Sophie if Wesley were not in residence."

Amanda concurred with Lady Illiff's assessment as she and Fanny entered the room. "I doubt our dear cousin would care to remain in the country if Mr. Hedrick departed."

"I feel taken for granted," Sophie said, feigning wounded feelings. "I cannot help it if Mr. Hedrick has touched my heart."

"I hope that's all he's touched," Amanda whispered for Sophie's ears only.

Sophie turned to give Amanda a shocked expression, but her cousin had already moved away to take her seat.

"Fortunately, she need not worry on that account," Lady Illiff said, "for Wesley has agreed to accompany us on our return to London."

Had she been alone, Sophie would have shouted with delight. Instead, she offered a demure smile. "That is lovely news. When will we leave?"

Lady Illiff chuckled. "I do believe we should wait at least until we've had our tea, don't you agree?"

Sophie could feel the heat crawl up her neck, but she truly didn't care. All that mattered was that Wesley was going with them to London. Now she must convince him to sail back to New York with them. What a lovely voyage that would be! She could imagine herself sitting on the deck snuggled beneath a blanket, watching the sunset with Wesley by her side. Even better, wrapped in his arms and dancing until the wee hours of the morning. She remained lost in her daydreams until Fanny nudged her in the side.

"Ouch." Sophie rubbed her side and frowned at her cousin.

"Lady Illiff asked if you'd like a cup of tea," Fanny said.

She truly didn't want the tea. She'd prefer to be left alone to think about Wesley. However, she couldn't ignore their hostess. "I would love a cup. Your china is quite exquisite," Sophie declared as she took the tea. "I find the floral pattern charming. I would rather like to have a pattern like this for my own home someday."

"I can put you in touch with a shop that carries an ample supply. The pieces are costly, however," Lady Illiff replied. "Of course, you are an heiress, and as such much will be required in the area of entertaining."

Sophie nodded and sipped her tea. Fanny and Amanda were trying hard to suppress giggles, but she didn't give them so much as a single glance. Let them think what they would.

"Were you able to complete the remodel of your London apartments?" Aunt Victoria questioned.

"Oh yes," Lady Illiff began. "We were uncertain that the third floor could be renovated in time for your visit, but in fact it has been completed. I believe you will find the print for the . . ."

Lady Illiff's droning voice faded from Sophie's mind. While the others discussed the furnishings in London and what they would do once they reached that wondrous city, Sophie retreated into her private thoughts. She couldn't be certain how long she'd been daydreaming when Lord Illiff's shouts startled her back to the present.

Aunt Victoria hurried to the entryway, the other ladies following close on her heels. While Lord Illiff issued orders, the servants hurried to do their master's bidding. A male servant supported Daniel on either side, and in a performance that would have rivaled comedic theater, they half carried, half dragged him up the stairway, Daniel yelping with each step. The ladies had not yet determined exactly what had occurred.

When Daniel was out of earshot, Lord Illiff shook his head. "That boy has little knowledge of horses. Quite obviously Thunderstruck wasn't pleased with the young man's horsemanship and kicked him."

Wide-eyed, Fanny covered her mouth while Sophie stepped forward, anxious to hear all the details. "Your horse kicked Daniel? Where?"

"In the stables after we had dismounted," Lord Illiff replied.

Sophie wondered if the man had taken leave of his senses. "I was inquiring what type of injury he had received."

The older man chuckled. "Forgive me. I misunderstood. He received a kick to the leg. Foolish young fellow walked behind his horse without letting the animal know he was back there. I do believe the horse was more frightened than Daniel. He let out a yelp that would have wakened the dead."

Lady Illiff's lips formed an O. "How absolutely dreadful! Shall I send for a surgeon?"

"I don't believe so. I'll have the servants apply some liniment. I believe he'll be sore, but nothing's broken. All things considered, he's very fortunate."

Sophie listened with interest but maintained a watchful gaze toward the front door, anxious for Wesley's return. When he hadn't appeared by the time Lord Illiff excused himself, Sophie stepped to the older man's side. "I do trust Wesley . . . ah, Mr. Hedrick didn't meet with the same fate."

Lord Illiff chuckled and shook his head. "No, of course not. Wesley is a fine horseman. No need to worry on his account. Being the good fellow that he is, Wesley remained at the stables to help curry the horses."

While the two older women continued to discuss Daniel's condition, Sophie grasped Fanny by the hand. "What good fortune. Perhaps Daniel will be incapacitated for a good long time, and you'll be able to escape his constant pursuit."

"It's unkind to experience pleasure when another is suffering, yet I must admit I'm hoping Daniel won't recover too quickly," Fanny replied, following after her cousin. "Where are you going?"

"I thought I'd take a stroll. It's a lovely day, and I could use some fresh air before dinner."

Fanny brightened. "That does sound lovely. I'll come with you."

Before Sophie could respond, Amanda rounded the corner. "There you two are. I thought you'd completely vanished. One minute I was speaking to mother and Lady Illiff, and the next minute you had both disappeared." She took Fanny by the hand. "Do come upstairs and help me choose a dress for this evening."

Sophie nodded her agreement. "You two go on. I'll be back shortly." She hurried outdoors, thankful that Amanda had appeared and whisked Fanny upstairs. Now she hoped she could locate the stables without difficulty.

Heading off through the west garden, Sophie spied one of the gardeners trimming the hedgerow. She approached the old man and inquired where she might locate the stables. At first he was reluctant, worried that some unforeseen difficulty might befall her if she headed off unaccompanied. Finally he rewarded her persistence and gave her precise directions.

She hiked her skirts and raced toward the stables with unbridled abandon. The erratic rhythm of her pounding feet came to an abrupt halt as she rounded the far end of the stables.

"Whoa!" Wesley grappled to gain his footing as Sophie fell headlong into his arms.

Sophie gazed into his eyes, enjoying the warmth of his arms as he held her close. Her palm rested upon his chest, and she could feel the rapid beat of his heart. Did his heart pound because of her nearness or because she'd nearly sent him toppling to the ground?

"I do hope I didn't harm you," she whispered.

"I fear the only thing you may injure is my heart, dear Sophie. Although I wish I could hold you in my arms forever, I wouldn't want to besmirch your name." He loosened his hold and slowly backed away to hold her at arm's length.

His words filled her with hope that he shared her feelings. "Thank you for your concern. You are a true gentleman."

He brushed straw from his breeches and smiled. "A gentleman in a complete state of disarray, I fear. What brought you to the stables? Surely you're not intending a carriage ride this late in the afternoon."

"No, nothing of the sort. During tea with Lady Illiff, she revealed that you plan to accompany us to London. I wanted to come and tell you that the news gave me great pleasure."

He tucked her hand into the crook of his arm as they started to walk back toward the house. "I'm elated to know my decision pleases you. I had planned to remain at Illiff Manor throughout the winter, but when Lady Illiff informed me you were going to visit London and suggested I come along, I couldn't resist the temptation."

She squeezed his arm. "And which is the greater temptation—London or me?"

He tipped his head back and laughed. "Why you, of course, my dear. London is a marvelous city, but without you to share the sights, I would not have been enticed to return."

She reveled in his words, already certain he was the man who had captured her heart. His statement gave her the courage to add, "And when the time arrives, I hope that I will entice you to return to New York, too."

His smile waned at her suggestion. "And how was young Daniel faring when he returned to the house? He was in a great deal of pain when he was kicked. I feared his leg might be broken."

The abrupt change of topic surprised her, but from Lady Illiff's earlier conversations, Sophie knew Wesley had lived with his wife in New York City and in fact still had a home there. Perhaps the reminder of New York had evoked memories of her death. Sophie hurried to put such grief from his mind.

"I'm afraid Mr. Irwin has made rather a fool of himself. He loves attention, you see. Especially if it involves Fanny. It would not surprise me at all to find out that he planned such a thing just to gain my cousin's sympathy."

"Surely not. He would not risk permanent damage just to impress a young woman."

"It is hard to tell what Mr. Irwin would do to impress. You should have seen him on the ship. He followed Fanny around as if she were his keeper and he a starving pup." She continued describing Daniel's behavior on the trip, exaggerating it until Wesley doubled over in laughter.

"Then to see him come into the manor house, being half carried as though he'd been mortally wounded in battle—a hero being brought back on his shield," Sophie declared with one hand to her forehead. "Well, I'm convinced it was mostly an act for Fanny's benefit." She dropped her pose and grinned.

"We are being most unkind. I'm certain the poor boy has suffered immensely." He wiped a tear from his cheek with the back of his hand. "I must cease this laughter before we go inside the house, or my relatives shall think me quite uncivilized."

Sophie pointed to one of the stone benches that bordered the garden yet remained well hidden from the house. "Perhaps we should wait until you've recovered." Taking the lead, Sophie sat down and then patted the bench with her palm. "Please. Sit with me."

"How could I refuse?"

Wesley's laughter ceased as quickly as it had begun. He looked into her eyes but swiftly turned away. "We must go inside before I say or do something untoward. I wouldn't want to risk . . ." He shook his head. "I'll say no more."

She longed to hear him continue and possibly bare his heart to her, but he would surely think her bold should she tell him so. Taking his arm, she walked with him and considered what she could say. There must be some way to indicate her feelings without overstepping any boundaries that might offend him. "I want you to know that I find your company most desirable, Wesley. You have become . . . well . . . quite dear to me."

Wesley touched his finger to his lips. "Say no more. There are those who might repeat what they hear." He nodded toward several servants standing near the entrance. "I won't risk your reputation, but suffice it to say, I find my feelings for you run quite deep."

The moment she and Wesley parted, Sophie rushed up the stairs. If she was to look her best for him that evening, she must hurry. With luck, both Veda and Minnie would be free to help her get dressed and style her hair.

"Where have you been?" Amanda frowned with the sternness of an angry parent.

Sophie ignored her cousin's question and glanced about the room. "I need Veda and Minnie to help me dress."

The skirt of Fanny's gown swished across the Aubusson rug as she crossed the room to greet Sophie. "They were here first and have gone to assist Aunt Victoria, but we'll be glad to help you, won't we, Amanda?" She helped with the buttons as Sophie pranced nervously.

"Oh, do hurry."

"I wish you'd think of others on occasion, Sophie. You're going to make all of us late for dinner if we don't hurry." Amanda began to pull the pins from Sophie's hair before adding, "Lady Illiff will think all three of us ill-mannered, and Mother will be completely mortified."

"Then we must stop chattering. I plan to wear my midnight-blue gown—I told Veda this morning," Sophie said.

Amanda pointed toward the bedroom. "It is good for you that Veda is dependable. Your dress is ready." The afternoon gown dropped to the floor, and Sophie quickly stepped out of it. Amanda motioned again. "I'll fix your hair while Fanny tightens your stays."

Sophie followed her cousin's instructions, and soon she was sitting in front of the dressing table. Amanda tugged on Sophie's hair, pulling the brush through her tresses with less than gentle strokes and then pinned the curls in place.

"Ouch! You're jabbing those pins into my scalp, Amanda." Sophie reached up and tried to loosen one of the curls. "And I can hardly draw breath. Must you corset me so snug?"

"You've eaten quite enthusiastically on our trip," Fanny said. "The waist of your gown will never close if we do otherwise."

"I shall endeavor to curtail my gluttony," Sophie said, frowning. "I wouldn't want Wesley to think me too plump. That would pain me greatly."

"You may be in far more pain once Mother confronts you," Amanda said.

Fanny slipped the gown over Sophie's head and began to do up the back buttons while Amanda went back to work to fashion a cascade of brown curls around Sophie's shoulders. Fanny sat down on the edge of the bed. "You should confide in us first and tell us where you have been sneaking off to. Every day we've had to make some excuse for you. If you tell us about it, then perhaps you'll be well rehearsed for Aunt Victoria's myriad questions."

Sophie grinned at her younger cousin. "You're not fooling me in the least with that suggestion, but it does hold merit." Her eyes met Amanda's in the mirror. "I've been meeting Wesley, of course. Just now I went out to the stables to locate him and tell him of my pleasure that he would join us in London."

"Oh, how delicious," Fanny replied. "And did you? Find him, that is?"

"Yes. We walked through the garden and then sat on one of the benches. Wesley is everything I could ever want in a man. He treats me with respect, yet I know he cares deeply for me." Sophie tucked one of the curls into place. "And we share a common sense of humor, too. I do believe I've met the man I will marry."

Amanda gasped as she inserted the final pearl pins into Sophie's hair. "Please don't be foolish. You've only just met Mr. Hedrick. Do you realize you're speaking of marriage to a complete stranger?"

"Amanda makes a good point, Sophie. Mr. Hedrick is likely a very nice man, but you should move slowly. And he's older than most of the fellows you've acquainted yourself with in the past. You may find you have little in common once you get to know him better."

Sophie folded her arms across her chest and glared into the mirror. "I know much more than either of you can imagine." She pushed away from the dressing table and surveyed herself in the mirror across the room. The gown fit to perfection, and the pearls in her hair were a lovely touch. She cared little what her cousins or her aunt thought. She and Wesley made a perfect match.

"Wesley sets me on fire. I feel all atingle when I'm near him. My heart races and I can scarcely draw breath."

"Sounds like a state of apoplexy, rather than love," Amanda said, raising a brow in disapproval.

Fanny giggled and got to her feet. "I felt that way once when I fell out of a tree."

Sophie shook her head. "I would have thought that at least *you* would understand, Fanny. You at least suppose yourself to be in love with Michael."

"What is that supposed to mean?" Fanny questioned, sobering. "I do love Michael, and I need not speak as though I'm in need of medical attention to prove it."

"Well, if he doesn't set your heart aflutter and leave you breathless, perhaps you should reconsider Daniel Irwin." With that Sophie stormed off for the door, the blue gown swaying fashionably behind her. "Or better yet—go climb another tree."

CHAPTER 6

Monday, November 8, 1897

Daniel's accident delayed their departure for London, but it gave the girls time to smooth over their differences. Amanda had been first to apologize, and Fanny had quickly followed. Amanda knew there would be little peace in the house if they didn't afford Sophie her dreams. Ever the peacekeeper, Amanda could never stay angry at either of her cousins for long. She supposed being the eldest gave her cause to consider the consequences of delaying apologies.

Even now, knowing that Sophie had once again slipped away to meet Mr. Hedrick in private, Amanda tried to be understanding. She'd never known the feelings Sophie espoused, so how could she remain critical of the matter?

"Obviously Sophie is quite taken with Mr. Hedrick," Fanny said, tossing aside her embroidery. "We shouldn't suppose that her feelings are less than genuine. One cannot always choose whom they will love. I am a perfect example of that."

"Yes, but I do wish she would practice more discretion." Amanda shook her head. "Sophie has been looking to fill the emptiness inside her since her mother passed away."

"It's not just her mother's passing that created the loss," Fanny said. "Losing your father strips away a certain security, too."

"But she's not lost her father."

"In some senses she has," Fanny said thoughtfully. "Uncle Quincy has hardly been taking an active interest in what Sophie does. He seemed quite happy to be rid of her. And her siblings are hardly kind to her. They act as though she's more of a bother than anyone has time for. Then Mr. Hedrick comes into her life and shows her genuine affection and attention."

"I suppose you're right. Still, I would hate to see her suffer additional loss. After all, what will she do when we return to America? I heard Lady Illiff state clearly that Mr. Hedrick intends to remain here in England for some time."

Fanny shrugged. "If he cares for Sophie as much as she believes, then perhaps we'll have yet another man to accompany us on the ship home."

"Well, he is wealthy and a gentleman, so apparently he needn't work for his living. I suppose it wouldn't be a far stretch to imagine he might join us," Amanda agreed. "And it would give us time to better know him."

"Exactly. We may have misjudged the situation. Even if he is older than Sophie, he may very well be the perfect man for her."

"I can hardly imagine you both married. I've not yet met a man who captures my thoughts the way you and Sophie have."

Fanny smiled and reached out to pat Amanda's arm. "He will come in time. Sometimes he's right in front of you, and you never even know it."

"I cannot even begin to see myself with any of the young men I know. None care about the things that interest me. Most are too frivolous with their father's money or lack interest in anything other than increasing their fortunes."

"You speak as though being financially secure is a bad thing," Fanny said. "I'm quite blessed to know that there is money for my use—even if I have to wait until next spring to have say over it. Still it's nice to know that the security is there if I should have need of it."

"But money is hardly a security," Amanda countered. "Our trust is in the Lord."

"True, but the world still demands it. We've known nothing but comfort. We live lives that few people know of."

"My point exactly. There are so many causes—so many people who have needs. I want to use my abilities and fortune to better society." Amanda sighed and put her own embroidery away. "I can't hope to ever convince Father, but Mother seems to understand. I believe she will be my advocate."

"In what way?"

"In allowing me to go to college."

"Are you certain that getting an education is what God would have you do?" Fanny asked.

Amanda shrugged. "I know God would have me help others. I wouldn't feel such a compelling drive to involve myself in such matters if not. Acts of kindness and assistance to the poor are hardly things Satan would desire of me." She smiled. "Nevertheless, pray for me that I might know exactly what I am to do. Obviously I have no love interest to put my attention on as you and Sophie have."

Fanny laughed. "Yes, but you can never tell when that love interest might come into your life. Until we came here, Sophie had no idea of Mr. Hedrick's existence. Your very own Mr. Hedrick might be awaiting you in London."

Amanda shook her head and rolled her eyes to the ceiling. "Goodness, but I hope not. One of us acting like a lovesick ninny is quite enough."

The three Broadmoor girls thought Daniel's injury would give Fanny the peace and solitude she desired. He would, after all, be unable to keep pace with her until his leg completely healed. Unfortunately, Lord Illiff declared the best remedy for the soreness was exercise—particularly walking. Lady Illiff had suggested the gardens as a perfect place for the young man's recuperation and Fanny the perfect person to escort him. And Victoria had concurred.

Sophie glanced up as Fanny rushed into the bedroom and came to a halt in front of Amanda. "Your mother is insisting I go walk with Daniel yet again this afternoon. Do say one of you will come with me. I cannot abide another afternoon of listening to him speak of my lovely tresses or beautiful eyes. He's even begun reading poetry to me—very poorly, I might add."

Sophie rocked back on the bed and collapsed in a fit of giggles. "Daniel reading poetry? I daresay that is something I would truly like to hear."

"Then come with me," Fanny urged.

Sophie shook her head. "I doubt Daniel would recite poetry to you if Amanda or I came along. However, I'm sure I can devise a plan that will prove quite enjoyable for all of us." While rubbing her palms together, Sophie instructed Fanny on what path she should walk with Daniel. "Don't deviate, or we shall never find you among all the twists and turns, and I don't want to miss hearing him."

"You needn't worry. We'll be on the bench by two o'clock. I do hope this works."

Sophie clucked her tongue. "Trust me. After this, Daniel will never again recite a poem to you! And should he fail to bring along his book of verse, you must encourage him to recite from memory."

Once Fanny departed, the two of them secured their bonnets and walked toward the gardens. Amanda admitted she thought the plan fun, but as they descended the stairs, she hastened to remind Sophie she would take no blame for the idea. "If Daniel speaks to Mother, you must confess that you devised this scheme. I doubt she will be pleased to hear we've made him the brunt of a joke."

Sophie was more than willing to take full responsibility for their afternoon of diversion. Other than needlework or reading, there was little else to occupy her time. Wesley had accompanied Lord Illiff to a distant farm to purchase another horse, and they weren't expected to return until evening. Indeed, the opportunity to hear Daniel's poetic reading would be worth any reprimand her aunt could mete out.

Winding around the far end of the garden, Sophie pointed to an opening where they could cut through the hedge. Amanda pursed her lips. "You seem to know your way around these hedges better than Lady Illiff."

Sophie grinned. "It isn't difficult once you understand the design. Wesley made a drawing for me. The arrangement of the flower gardens and hedges is quite easy to navigate once you've seen it mapped on paper."

"It's good to know we need not worry about losing you," Amanda remarked. Though she barely knew him, Amanda had made it abundantly clear she didn't approve of Wesley. However, Sophie remained confident that once Amanda became better acquainted with Wesley, she, too, would think him the perfect match for her.

"This way," Sophie whispered. "Keep your voice low, or he may hear us. We're getting close."

Sophie had chosen the perfect spot. There was a bench on each side of the hedgerow that provided both seating and the ability to hear Fanny and Daniel as they conversed. The two girls tucked their skirts tight to prevent any rustling when they sat down. Amanda leaned close to Sophie's ear. "I don't hear anything," she whispered.

Sophie touched her finger to her lips and leaned against the back of the bench, straining to hear. Perhaps Fanny had misunderstood her instructions. She'd nearly given up when she finally heard Fanny speak to Daniel. "Do come along, Daniel. You're walking much too slow. At this rate you'll never regain strength in your leg."

Daniel loudly complained of his pain and the need to rest.

"I suppose if you can go no farther, we can rest on this bench for a time," Fanny said. "Did you bring your book of poetry?"

Sophie poked Amanda's arm and grinned.

"Not today."

Sophie curled her lip and Amanda shrugged. Unless Fanny could persuade him to recite something from memory, this wouldn't prove to be much fun. Sophie truly doubted Daniel had committed much poetry to memory.

"I'm disappointed. I thought you said you wanted to read to me," Fanny said.

"I do. I've written something especially for you. Something that expresses how I feel about you."

Sophie clapped her hand over her mouth to keep from shrieking with joy. She could barely contain herself. What pure delight—Daniel had prepared a love poem for Fanny, and they would have the pleasure of hearing him recite to her.

"I call this 'Ode to My Love.' " Daniel cleared his throat. "It goes like this:

> "My one true love shall always be,
> A woman who daily walks with me.
> Her auburn hair the breeze does billow,
> And wave before me like a pussy willow.
> Her eyes of brown shimmer in the light,
> To present me with constant delight.
> She moves with practiced grace at dawn,
> Like an elegant, long-necked, gliding swan.
> Her long thin fingers I long to hold;
> Or should I attempt to be so bold?"

"No! You should not be so bold," Fanny shrieked.

Sophie had doubled over and was holding her nose in a valiant attempt to remain quiet while Amanda chortled behind her gloved hand.

"Who is there?" Daniel shouted. Soon he was clubbing the hedgerow with his cane. "Come out of there, or I'll flog you with my cane!"

"Stop, Daniel! It's Amanda and Sophie, and you're going to hurt them."

Sophie moved to one side as the wooden cane sliced through the hedge. When she turned around, Daniel had stuck his head and shoulders through the opening and was peering at her as though she'd grown another head.

"What are the two of you doing eavesdropping on us? Your behavior is unconscionable." A branch flipped back and slapped him in the face, and he withdrew. "Don't either of you attempt to run off. I want to speak to you."

His leg was apparently feeling much better, for he rounded the end of the hedge and hurried toward them at full speed.

"Do be careful, Daniel. We wouldn't want you to further injure your leg," Sophie said.

He pointed his cane at Amanda. "I can believe Sophie would do this, but I'm surprised you would condone such behavior, Amanda. I plan to discuss this conduct with your mother."

Sophie chuckled. "And we plan to discuss *your* conduct with her, also."

"Mine? There is nothing to tell her. I have done nothing untoward." He looked over his shoulder, obviously hoping to receive Fanny's affirmation. When she remained silent, he motioned her forward. "Tell them, Fanny. My behavior has always been that of a gentleman, has it not?"

"I believe it would be best if you said nothing of this incident to my aunt," Fanny said. "I wouldn't want my cousins to be punished for simply enjoying a few moments of laughter."

"At *my* expense." His eyes shone with anger.

Sophie patted his arm. "You do need to learn to control your anger, Daniel. Otherwise you would be a poor choice as a husband, don't you think, Fanny?"

Fanny nodded her head. "No woman wants to wed a man who is easily provoked to anger. Personally, I find a sense of humor an excellent quality."

"An attribute you appear to lack, Daniel. Our family enjoys nothing more than a good prank. You need only ask Jefferson and George the next time you see them." Sophie hesitated a moment. "*If* you see them again." She hoped her words bore the ominous tone she intended.

Daniel leaned on his cane, obviously sensing defeat. "I don't suppose there's any need to discuss this with Mrs. Broadmoor. There's been no real harm done."

Sophie considered telling him that his attempt at poetry had caused great harm. It was, after all, an assault upon the human ear. However, she refrained from further comment. No need to provoke Daniel at the moment, though Sophie wondered what he might think if she recited his poem after supper tonight. She stifled a giggle.

Arrangements had been made: they would leave for London the next morning. A fact that was no longer of great import to Sophie, for she wanted only to be in Wesley's presence. Veda finished lacing a ribbon in Sophie's hair and then gave her an approving nod. "You look quite lovely, miss. I'm certain Mr. Hedrick will approve."

"Thank you, Veda. I do hope so." Accompanying Lady Illiff to visit one of her friends had held little allure for Sophie until she realized Wesley would be in attendance. Last evening she'd first finagled an invitation from Lady Illiff and then convinced Aunt Victoria the outing would be properly chaperoned. In all, the feat had required a great deal of finesse and no small amount of time, but she'd finally received both Lady Illiff's invitation and her aunt's permission. Today, Sophie would enjoy the fruits of her labor.

She descended the stairs, pleased to see Wesley gazing up at her from the entry hall. She accepted his outstretched hand, enjoying the tingle that coursed up her arm. "You look lovely, Sophie," he whispered.

"Thank you," she replied softly. She adjusted her bonnet then took the cloak offered her by the butler. She frowned at the intrusion, but the man moved away quickly to tend Lady Illiff as she descended the stairs.

"I hope we might speak privately today," Sophie told Wesley. "Time seems to be slipping by more quickly than I'd hoped."

"But of course. I would love nothing more than a few stolen moments," he said, smiling. "I truly cannot imagine anything more pleasurable."

Sophie had only seconds to bask in his attention before Lady Illiff swept into the foyer and hurried them out the door to the waiting carriage. Lady Illiff's footman helped her into the carriage then turned to assist Sophie. Lady Illiff patted the cushion beside her. "You shall sit beside me, Sophie. I must say, I am glad for your company. You seem to converse quite easily with your elders, and there is much I would know."

"As the youngest in my family, I've been surrounded by elders all of my life. I have few friends my own age." She said this, throwing a meaningful glance at Wesley. "I have always related better with those my senior rather than my junior. I suppose the only exception would be my cousins, but even then Amanda is older."

"Youth has its merits," Lady Illiff said as the carriage bounced against the rough road. "Enduring lengthy carriage rides for one." She laughed at her own comment, as though feeling extremely witty.

Sophie received only an occasional smile from Wesley as the carriage traversed the winding and rutted road to the country estate of Lord and Lady Wingate. It was Lady Illiff who carried the conversation, plying her with a seemingly endless list of questions. The older woman seemed most interested in Uncle Jonas and his ability to handle her grandfather's estate. Sophie knew little of such matters, but she did her best to respond.

"I give the family financial situation little thought," she told the woman. "My uncle is good to oversee anything of importance. He was well trained by our grandfather."

"It is good that Mr. Broadmoor cares so deeply for his extended family,"

Lady Illiff replied. "So many men would find such tasks tiresome. But, of course, with the deaths you have suffered, it is important that there be at least one level-headed man of means to oversee the family coffers."

"I suppose so," Sophie said, rolling her eyes.

"What of the family estates?"

"I'm not certain what you mean."

"The estates. The family homes. Have they endured? Have they been sold?"

Sophie nodded. "Most have endured. The house I grew up in was sold after my mother's passing. But not for financial reasons," she quickly added. She didn't want Wesley to think her a pauper. "There is still the island castle. It's truly lovely. My grandmother furnished it quite lavishly. She spared no expense to create a palace of sorts."

"And since your grandfather passed on, who now holds possession of the property?"

Sophie was growing bored with the woman's nosy questions. "I suppose we all do."

"All? But who does that reference?" Lady Illiff demanded.

Unfortunately, Lady Illiff appeared to think Sophie's answers less than acceptable, and each reply was followed by yet another question.

The old busybody. She had probably only allowed Sophie to join them so that she could wangle information related to the Broadmoor fortune.

When they finally arrived at Wingate Manor, Sophie sighed with relief. She hoped Lady Wingate would not prove to be so inquisitive.

The Wingates were obviously as wealthy as the Illiffs. The grandeur of the four-story estate reminded Sophie of the Broadmoor Island home. She guessed there to be at least as many rooms, perhaps more.

They were ushered into a palatial sitting room where a white-haired woman sat regally, ready to receive them. The gilded throne chair upon which she sat was some antiquated piece no doubt passed down through the generations.

"Oh, my dears, my dears. How lovely of you to join me. I pray the journey did not overtax you. I have much to speak to you about."

"It was quite exhausting," Lady Illiff declared, "but the good company made up for it. You know my dear Mr. Hedrick, of course, and this is Miss Sophie Broadmoor of America." She leaned down to embrace Lady Wingate and then paused as the woman whispered something in her ear.

Sophie gave a curtsy, uncertain what else to do. She had long ago learned that most adults were offended when younger people spoke without being directly addressed. So she waited rather impatiently to see what might be said. She didn't have to wait long.

Lady Illiff stepped away from her friend and beckoned Sophie and Wesley to her side. "There are several private matters Lady Wingate wishes to discuss with me. She suggested the two of you might enjoy a walk in her gardens."

Sophie's spirit soared at the suggestion, but she forced herself to remain calm and offered no more than a reserved nod. Should she appear overly pleased with the idea, Lady Illiff might withdraw the suggestion.

Wesley escorted her to the garden doors with the formality of a stranger, but once they were a short distance from the house, he grinned. "Can you believe our good fortune? I doubted we would have even a moment to ourselves."

"I told myself I would be content and enjoy your presence, but I had hoped for so much more. I wish to speak to you on a subject of great importance."

He chuckled and patted her hand. "You are a truly winsome young lady, Sophie. I cannot tell you how wonderful it has been spending this time with you. I believe we have been brought together for so much more than mere friendship."

"That is exactly what I wish to speak of. I know it is improper for me to be so bold, but I fear if I do not tell you how I feel, you will think me not interested in what might come of our time together."

"And what might you wish to see come of our time together?" he asked in a low, enticing tone.

Sophie swallowed hard and met his intense gaze. Her spirit soared at his words, and she pushed all restraint aside. "I have never before felt like this, Wesley. I truly do not know what to think."

"Dear Sophie, I understand, for I am overcome by those very same emotions. However, I believe it would be best if we move slowly and see where our hearts take us. I would hate to have your uncle think me taking advantage of one so innocent. He has done much to guard you and keep you from harm. I wouldn't want him to believe me a threat."

She squeezed his hand. "You could never be a threat. Uncle Jonas will find you quite acceptable. You are a gentleman held in high regard by the Illiffs, and therefore you are worthy of his esteem. But we have so little time. I'll be sailing for New York in two weeks. Lady Illiff mentioned that you have considered making England your home." She lowered her gaze. "I don't think I can bear the thought of leaving you. . . ."

He lifted her chin with his finger, and Sophie trembled at his touch. Surely this was true love. No one had ever made her feel like this before.

"Lady Illiff has overstepped her boundaries. Only once have I spoken of permanently remaining in England, and that was shortly after my wife's death. Though I enjoy my visits here, I have no intention of leaving the country of my birth. And now that I know you share my feelings, I hope that you will welcome a visit from me at your home in Rochester."

"Would you consider a visit in the very near future? Perhaps for the Christmas holidays? Our family is rather large, but I know you would receive a cordial welcome—especially from me." She leaned closer, enjoying the scent of him, willing him to say yes.

"How could I possibly refuse such an invitation?" He touched his finger to her cheek. "But you must first make certain your aunt would have no objection. If your uncle were here, I would first seek his approval before accepting your sweet offer."

"Oh, you need not worry over my uncle's approval. Aunt Victoria finds you most charming, and I know she will be in agreement. There is no reason for her to offer an objection."

"You are a true delight, dear Sophie. For so long now, I have wondered if I would ever again feel alive." He placed her palm against his chest. "After I have been so long without feeling, it is you who has caused my heart to beat anew."

Wesley leaned forward as if to brush his lips against her cheek, but Sophie turned to meet his lips with a longing that would not be denied. She wrapped him in an embrace and melted into his arms, feeling as though she'd finally discovered the one place where she belonged.

When their lips finally parted, Wesley stepped back as though he'd been branded by a hot iron. "I apologize for my behavior. Please say you will forgive me, Sophie. I am ashamed of myself, but I fear your beauty and charm have overwhelmed me. Please know that I have never before conducted myself in such an ungentlemanly fashion. I am terribly ashamed."

Placing a palm on either side of his face, Sophie lifted his chin until their eyes met. "You owe me no apology, Wesley. 'Tis I who encouraged your behavior, and I would do the same again. I only hope we will find time to be alone while in London."

CHAPTER 7

Thursday, November 11, 1897
London

Since their arrival in London two days earlier, time had passed at a dizzying tempo. There had been a tour of Kew Gardens, an evening at the theater, and the ritual of teas and socials arranged by Lady Illiff. Victoria had been pleased when Daniel requested a quiet visit with her that afternoon while the three girls accompanied Lady Illiff to several of London's best shops in search of finery. The older woman had insisted no proper young lady could visit London without perusing the latest styles and offerings for next season's gowns, especially since they were not planning to visit Paris on this trip.

Daniel was awaiting her when Victoria entered the sitting room of Lady Illiff's London town house. He jumped to his feet the moment she stepped into the room. Though not the most handsome young man Victoria had ever set eyes upon, Daniel was the epitome of excellent breeding and good manners. And there was no doubt he cared deeply for Fanny. He'd doggedly pursued Fanny since they'd left Rochester—a fact that hadn't escaped Victoria's keen attention throughout their journey. Of late, it appeared Fanny had taken an interest in Daniel, as well. Victoria had observed them together more and more frequently. In most instances, she thought Jonas knew little of the female mind, or even of love, for that matter. However, he'd predicted Fanny would forget Michael once he was out of sight and she had someone of substance to occupy her time. Victoria had thought his claims foolhardy, but now it appeared that her husband had been correct.

Other than Fanny's initial protest of the voyage, the young woman had seemed completely content to have Daniel act as her escort. Although Daniel's dress clothes had mysteriously disappeared three days into the voyage, he'd managed to borrow a suit from another passenger, and he and Fanny had been inseparable, whether on the dance floor or while strolling the decks. The sight of the young couple had, in fact, given Victoria hope, for though she wanted the girls to marry for love, she understood the need to marry a man of substance. Michael was, of course, a fine young man, but he and Fanny shared no commonality.

He had been reared with the strong values of the Atwell family, but his inept social skills would soon prove a burden for any Broadmoor woman. Daniel was the superior choice. And now that Fanny appeared content to leave Michael to the past, Victoria could admit she had taken a genuine liking to Daniel. Throughout their voyage, he had been quick to seek and follow her guidance. The young man had proved quite dependable, too. Indeed, she'd discovered Daniel possessed many fine attributes. And the fact that he continued to seek her advice through these private visits had served to reinforce her fondness for the young man.

He brushed a wave of light brown hair from his forehead. "Thank you for agreeing to visit with me, Mrs. Broadmoor. I've taken the liberty of ordering tea."

"Thank you, Daniel. You are such a thoughtful young man." Victoria glanced toward the enclosed veranda that overlooked the rear garden of the town house.

"Would you prefer to take tea on the veranda?"

His ability to read her cue warmed Victoria's heart. How long had she and

Jonas been married? Over thirty years now, and he still would have failed to realize her preference for the veranda rather than the sitting room.

"You read my thoughts," she replied with a warm smile.

Once they were settled and the maid had delivered their tray, Victoria relaxed with a cup of tea. "I do hope you're enjoying your time here in London."

"Yes, of course, but I have a matter of import that I would like to discuss with you before Fanny returns home."

Victoria patted his hand. "Well, of course, Daniel. You know that I've grown to enjoy our little visits."

He downed his tea in one gulp and clanked the cup onto the saucer. "I love Fanny," he blurted.

Victoria touched her fingers to the white chiffon bow at her neckline. "Your declaration doesn't surprise me overmuch, Daniel. I've not failed to notice a budding romance between you two, and I must say that I am pleased—for both of you."

"Oh, thank you so much, Mrs. Broadmoor. Your approval means a great deal to me."

Though the afternoon remained cool, Daniel removed a linen square from his jacket pocket and daubed his forehead. There was little doubt the young man was a bundle of anxiety. Victoria patted his hand. "I'm surprised to see you appear so concerned. Surely you knew I approved of you, Daniel."

He nervously tapped his fingers atop the table. "No. I wasn't certain. I mean, I know Mr. Broadmoor approves of me, but he indicated you might not think me a good match for Fanny."

Victoria snapped to attention. "Then you've already spoken to my husband regarding your affection for Fanny?"

"Yes. I declared my feelings, for I would never want Mr. Broadmoor to believe I would attempt to win the heart of his niece without first gaining permission to court her."

The revelation surprised Victoria. Jonas hadn't said a word to her of Daniel's declaration, although there had been other more pressing details to discuss prior to their departure. It had likely slipped his mind. Jonas seldom thought matters of the heart deserved much attention. Her husband was no romantic. Perhaps that's why she thought Daniel charming. In his quest to ensure Fanny's happiness, he was willing to set aside his own comfort and seek that which would make her happy.

"Mr. Broadmoor stated that if I was willing to win Fanny's affection, he would offer no objection."

"Well, at least Jonas and I are in agreement on that matter."

Daniel's eyes brightened. "I understand Mr. Broadmoor will arrive in less than two days, but I hoped you might consider helping me choose an engagement ring for Fanny."

"An engagement ring? Oh, Daniel, I would be most pleased to assist you, though I would caution that you continue to woo Fanny and not propose marriage until you are convinced you've won her heart."

Daniel leaned forward. "You will never know the depth of my appreciation, Mrs. Broadmoor. You have been a stalwart friend and confidante throughout this journey, and I hope that our friendship will continue long after we have returned to America."

The young man was a genuine treasure trove of surprises. The fact that he valued her friendship warmed Victoria's heart. "I am certain we will be friends for years to come, Daniel. And I expect the girls will be gone until late this afternoon with their shopping. What do you think? Shall we venture out and begin a search for a ring?"

"Oh yes. I would be very grateful."

Her earlier weariness evaporated, and she looked forward to the excitement of locating the perfect ring for Fanny. She wondered if Wesley would soon be seeking Lady Illiff's help in choosing a ring for Sophie. There was little doubt Sophie had won his heart. Still, Victoria remained uncertain whether Sophie was ready to settle into married life.

For now, however, she would enjoy the pleasure of helping Daniel select the perfect engagement ring. Although her own daughter was the eldest of the three cousins, Amanda remained uninterested in marriage. Despite the fact that Victoria considered her daughter's aspirations toward a career admirable, Jonas would soon expect his daughter to marry. And he would require she marry a man of his choice—one who had attained high social standing and financial affluence.

After retrieving her hat and gloves, Victoria returned to the foyer to join Daniel. "I don't know when I've been more excited."

They were a short distance down the street when Veda came running after them. Victoria opened her mouth to chastise the girl for shouting in such an unladylike fashion until she realized the maid was waving a telegram.

Veda came to a breathless halt and extended the telegram. She took only a moment to gain her breath. "I'm sorry to race down the street shouting like a street vendor, Mrs. Broadmoor, but I didn't know when you would return. This arrived for you earlier in the day, and Lady Illiff's butler forgot to deliver it to you."

Once the maid departed, Victoria motioned Daniel to an out-of-the-way spot. She quickly read the message and then shoved it back inside the envelope. Jonas would not be joining them as scheduled. A combination of anger and frustration assailed her, and she bit her lower lip to stop the trembling. Why must Jonas always disappoint her? He'd given his word, and now there was nothing more than a few words saying business problems prevented his coming. He would have much to explain when they returned to New York.

Sophie very much enjoyed the time spent in London. She found the bustle and excitement of the city stimulated her senses in most every way. Of course, she was constantly overstepping the bounds of etiquette in some manner, but she didn't let that bother her. It concerned her very little that she was to never walk alone in the company of a man without a chaperone. She certainly didn't worry about the scandal caused when a lady danced more than three times with the same partner. So many of the rules were replicated in American society, and Sophie figured that if she didn't pay them any mind at home, she was under no obligation to give them credence abroad.

Throughout their days in London, she'd taken pleasure in Wesley's companionship. He'd regaled her with stories of English history, of kings and queens, grandeur and scandal.

"You'll discover the history of the city quite fascinating," he told her.

"I find the company even more so," she said, smiling.

Fanny, walking ahead of Wesley and Sophie, seemed far less content. Daniel was once again at her side, although he walked with a slight limp. Fanny often glanced over her shoulder at Sophie or looked off to the horizon, as if trying to imagine herself removed from such tiresome company. Sophie felt sorry for her cousin, but not enough to leave Wesley's side to intervene.

"I fear my cousin is less enamored with her own companion. I do wish Amanda hadn't stayed behind to nurse her headache. If she were here, she'd be able to help Fanny." Sophie risked a glance at Wesley. Just the sight of him caused her heart to beat faster and her thoughts to blur. She had found herself stammering and sputtering more than once when his smile or alluring expression sent her thoughts aflutter.

"I could suggest Mr. Irwin join me for a stop at one of the shops. You, in turn, could encourage Fanny to join you elsewhere—say that ladies' shop across the way there." He pointed and Sophie caught sight of a dressmaker.

"I would not wish to be separated from you." She longed to cling to his arm but knew that Aunt Victoria would never allow such a public display.

" 'Twould only be for a matter of minutes. It would give your cousin a brief respite and ease your guilty conscience."

Sophie stopped and frowned. "Who said I had a guilty conscience?"

Wesley smiled. "It's quite obvious to me that you are torn. Would you tell me otherwise?"

"No, I suppose not." Sophie sighed and squared her shoulders. "Very well. Extend your invitation to Mr. Irwin."

"First I shall secure your aunt's permission." He turned to find Victoria and Lady Illiff nearly upon them. "Ladies, I wonder if you would permit me to disengage from our party momentarily. I see a charming ladies' shop across the street and wonder if it would be too much to anticipate your desire to spend a few moments there while Mr. Irwin and I head over there." He pointed to a men's haberdashery and added, "I have need of a new hat and thought perhaps Mr. Irwin might, also."

"I believe that would be perfectly acceptable," Lady Illiff said. "I happen to know they do great work there. The dressmaker is one I had hoped to visit. She carries many handmade pieces that are prepared ahead of time and adjusted for the wearer as she waits. It's quite delightful."

Victoria nodded, much to Sophie's relief. Without waiting, she called out, "Fanny, Daniel, our plans are changing."

Daniel seemed to pout at the announcement that the men were separating from the women, but he nevertheless followed after Wesley while Lady Illiff led the way to the dressmaker's shop.

"I thought I'd never be rid of him," Fanny said as she took Sophie's arm. "What a bore. He cares nothing about anything of interest. I tried to converse with him about the vegetation, the birds, the history of London. He cares naught for any of it. He only wishes to speak of his adoration for me."

Sophie giggled. "Perhaps if you wore some flowers or birds, he might be willing to listen."

Fanny laughed. "I would just as soon keep myself out of the situation altogether. The man will not hear reason. He has hinted at marriage more times than I can count. I fear he will soon propose, and then I shall have to be firm with him."

They followed their elders into the shop and pretended to be interested in an arrangement of shirtwaists while the owner offered the older women refreshments.

"Simply remind him you are already engaged," Sophie replied. She fingered the delicate embroidery of a silky bodice.

"I've tried to speak about Michael more than once. He absolutely refuses to listen. He always changes the subject."

"Then change it back," Sophie asserted. "You mustn't allow him to hold you hostage in a conversation."

"I suppose you are right. I cannot expect you or Amanda to constantly rescue me."

"Certainly not. Besides, if you continue to speak only of Michael, Daniel will surely grow bored and turn his attention elsewhere. Perhaps we should encourage him to give regard to Amanda."

Fanny laughed. "I wouldn't wish that upon our dear cousin for all the world."

The men joined them some time later, and Lady Illiff suggested they stop for lunch. She knew of a wonderful establishment not far from where their carriage awaited them.

Sophie thought it a marvelous idea. She hoped to spend some quiet moments in conversation with Wesley. They wouldn't be much longer in England, and she wanted very much to convince him to sail back with their entourage.

Lady Illiff arranged for them to have a private room where a warm fire blazed in the hearth. The room was obviously fashioned to appeal to the upper class. The oak furnishings were highly polished and decorated with a display of silver and crystal flower dishes, as well as elegant English china.

"What a charming room," Aunt Victoria declared. "So cozy and warm."

"The city is so damp and chilly this time of year," Lady Illiff stated as her attendant came to her aid. The woman removed Lady Illiff's fur-lined cloak then turned and offered to help Victoria, as well. Daniel quickly offered to assist Fanny, while Sophie was mesmerized by Wesley's hands upon her shoulders.

"Allow me," he whispered against her ear.

Sophie couldn't help but shudder as he took the cloak from her. He allowed his hand to trail across her neck, causing Sophie's heart to hammer. She tried to steady her breathing but knew Wesley would understand the effect he had on her. With shaky hands, she focused on removing her gloves but found the button impossible to work.

"Here." Wesley reached for her hand and took it in his. Sophie's gaze fixed on his face as he undressed her hands. "Perhaps you should stand by the fire for a few minutes. You are trembling."

"I doubt the fire would help," she said honestly, knowing he would catch her meaning.

He did and smiled. "Ah, Sophie. Such an innocent treasure."

Victoria watched her niece with growing concern. It seemed Sophie cared little for social proprieties. With Mr. Hedrick in the room, she completely cast aside her upbringing and acted in a most wanton fashion. Still, Hedrick was a man of means and in good standing with the Illiffs. Perhaps this was true love for Sophie and Hedrick.

"What do you think of Mr. Hedrick and my niece?" Victoria asked Lady Illiff quietly.

They were seated near the fire while the younger people were still arranging themselves at the table.

"They make a fine couple." Lady Illiff watched them for a moment then turned her attention to Victoria. "She could do much worse—as could he. I would have liked to have kept him here in England, but I believe you will soon find Mr. Hedrick following you to New York."

Victoria nodded. "I suppose I will have to speak to him on behalf of the family. Extend invitations and such."

"It does my heart good to see Wesley seeking love. He has been alone too long. I told him that I would find him another mate. How fortuitous it was that you should arrive with your nieces and daughter."

They passed a pleasant time dining on roasted beef and Yorkshire pudding. Victoria remained ever mindful of her two nieces. Fanny seemed captivated by Daniel. She was deep in conversation with him, and Victoria felt this a very good sign of their growing closer. Wesley and Sophie were also conversing easily, but then they always did.

"We are seldom in London during this time of year," her friend was saying. "Sometimes we return to the city on Boxing Day after gifting the servants at the manor house. We arrive in time to offer gifts to the servants here, as well. However, it does make it difficult to give them the day off if we are in transit, so we often wait and gift the servants here after the new year."

Victoria smiled and nodded as the woman continued to ramble. "Lord Illiff is always so busy when we return to London. He finds himself caught up with the affairs of the government and such. I seldom see him for days on end. Of course we have a great deal of entertaining to attend to, also. I have a party already scheduled for the day before you depart for America. It's expected, you know, and I couldn't be happier to oblige. It's a fine thing to show off such beautiful young ladies."

"I'm sure we'll enjoy the affair," Victoria murmured. She would have enjoyed it much more had Jonas kept his word and joined them in England, but there was nothing to be done about that now.

Later, as they made their way to the carriage, Victoria happened to glimpse Fanny and Daniel as they walked. Fanny seemed to lean in to hear Daniel's every word. It was a good sign, Victoria thought. She climbed into the carriage and turned in time to see that Daniel had taken a possessive hold of Fanny's arm. She didn't seem to mind in the least.

Oh, this would be quite pleasing to Jonas, to be sure.

"You can let me go now," Fanny told Daniel. "I've quite recovered from my misstep."

"I'd rather see you safely into the carriage," Daniel said, refusing to yield his grip.

Fanny grimaced. "You might at least loosen your hold, or my arm will be black and blue tomorrow. Then I shall have to explain how I came by my bruises."

They waited for Wesley to hand Sophie into the carriage, and Daniel couldn't seem to resist the moment to declare his admiration for Fanny once again. It didn't help that Sophie's gown snagged on the carriage step and Wesley had to work with tedious care to free it.

"Fanny, you know how much I care for you. I cannot imagine my world without you in it every day."

Goodness, but he always seemed to start out the same way. Fanny held up her hand. "Daniel, I must be a very poor communicator."

"Not at all. You speak wonderfully. I enjoy our conversations very much."

"Then why do you not understand that I love another man—that I am engaged to marry and am completely unavailable for your interest in me?"

He looked at her blankly. "You do not even know if your young man will return to you. Mr. Atwell is in the Yukon. Many people fail to return from adventures such as his. The winters in the north are vicious. I've read a great deal about the area."

"As have I," Fanny countered. "I also know that Michael is used to such weather, having lived on Broadmoor Island for many years. He knows how to survive the elements, and I've no doubt he will return to me."

"I have no wish to cause you distress, Fanny dear, but there are circumstances in the north that Mr. Atwell will never have experienced. Wild animals, the desperation of greedy men seeking their own fortunes, not to mention the isolation. I read just the other day of a madness that often overtakes people in the great frozen north."

Sophie was now inside the carriage, and Wesley was waiting for Fanny to move forward and step in. She turned briefly to face Daniel and shook her head. "Michael's strength is in the Lord. I do not fear for his sanity or his safety."

But her words were not as encouraging as Fanny would have liked. Taking her seat beside Sophie and Aunt Victoria, she wished she were back in Rochester. At least there she could receive Michael's letters. Better still, she longed for Broadmoor Island, where Michael's mother and father could offer her hope and she could enjoy the tranquillity of the place. Her grandfather had purchased the island years ago, and though it was smaller than many of the islands that dotted the St. Lawrence River, Fanny thought it perfect. Only two miles in length, the island boasted one of the grandest of the castlelike homes along the river. With its six stories, fifty rooms, and huge turret, the home had been copied by many but never equaled—at least not in Fanny's estimation. However, it wasn't the magnificent home so much as experiencing the beauty of God's creation that Fanny loved. Fishing in the late afternoon with Michael or sitting on the jagged rocks listening to the birds and watching the lapping water—those were the things in which she took true delight.

That night in the quiet of her room, Fanny pulled out the only letter she'd received from Michael. She scanned the words once again, trying to pull additional news from the meager lines. Michael held such hope for their future. He was certain he could secure a fortune by next summer. *Summer.* That seemed an eternity away. She lovingly stroked the paper, knowing that Michael's hands had also touched it. It helped her feel close to him.

I will soon be bound for Dawson, and doubt I will have an opportunity to write again until spring, she read. *The mail is difficult to deliver during the winter and questionable at best. So please do not despair if you hear nothing from me until summer.*

Summer. There was that word again. So much could happen between now and then. As Daniel had said, so much could go wrong. All manner of trouble could befall her beloved, and Fanny had no choice but to wait.

"Oh, it is so hard to wait, my love," she whispered, holding the letter close to her heart. "So hard to endure the months without you."

CHAPTER 8

Sunday, November 21, 1897

Sophie removed her gowns from the wardrobe and piled them atop the bed— her contribution to the packing efforts of Minnie and Veda, who had been diligently folding and arranging the Broadmoor ladies' belongings since the day before. Their ship would sail in the morning, and Sophie would have the pleasure of enjoying Wesley's company on the return voyage. She could barely believe her good fortune. Though Wesley had taken more convincing than she'd anticipated, he'd eventually agreed to abandon his earlier plans to return home in early December and instead sail with the Broadmoors. If her good fortune continued, Sophie might even convince him to accompany her home. Though he'd agreed to a Christmas visit, he'd not yet conceded to the idea of coming any earlier, and Sophie wasn't certain if she should continue to beseech him or to simply accept his refusal. She would, after all, enjoy his company during their luxurious days and evenings aboard ship, and there would be a flurry of activity when they finally arrived home.

Only moments ago Aunt Victoria had expressed concern over entertaining the entire family for a belated Thanksgiving celebration only two days after they were scheduled to arrive home.

"Beatrice likes nothing more than to take charge of everyone. You should have asked her to act as the Thanksgiving hostess this year," Sophie said, while wondering what her older sister would think of Wesley. No doubt, she'd find fault with him, for Beatrice seemed to take delight in dampening Sophie's spirits.

Aunt Victoria motioned for Minnie to gather Amanda's gowns. "Well, it's far too late for Beatrice to take over now. No disrespect, but your sister would complain for years should I even make such a suggestion."

That was certainly true. Even though Beatrice would agree to take on the challenge, she'd act the martyr, and the day would be ruined for all those in attendance. Better that Aunt Victoria summon help from her capable staff than seek help from Beatrice. "Perhaps your housekeeper has already begun to make the arrangements for you," Sophie said.

"I hope so. I'm going downstairs to join Lady Illiff. Don't forget to separate out the gowns you wish to wear on the ship from those that should go to steerage," Victoria reminded them before leaving.

The reminder was enough to send Sophie scurrying into the bedroom to retrieve several gowns from the pile. She hoped to dazzle Wesley on their return to America.

"Surely you don't plan to bring all of those into our room, Sophie. You'll have no need for so many fancy dresses. The weather will be cold enough that we'll need our heavy wraps whenever we venture onto the decks." Amanda rummaged through the pile and withdrew Sophie's woolen coat with the fur collar. "You should fill your traveling trunk with this warm coat and several shawls rather than another satin gown."

Sophie folded her arms across her chest. "I'll have Wesley's embrace to keep me warm should I suffer a chill."

Fanny fell across the bed and giggled. "Oh, do cease your theatrics, Sophie. You sound like one of the actresses in a poor stage production."

Clutching one hand to her bodice, Sophie gazed toward the ceiling and assumed the role of a performing artist. "Oh, dear Fanny, if only you knew the depth of my love and the charm of the man who possesses my heart."

Amanda jabbed Sophie's arm. "Do stop being silly. We need to finish sorting our belongings for the maids."

"You've lost all sense of humor, Amanda. Perhaps you need a man to cheer you. Then we'd see a sunnier disposition from time to time." Sophie opened drawers and began to remove her undergarments and nightclothes. "I, for one, am quite happy that we let Uncle Jonas have his way and send us on this journey. I've had a simply marvelous time and have met the man of my dreams."

"Wesley may well turn into a nightmare once the two of you become better acquainted," Amanda remarked. "I have never seen anyone so easily swayed by men as you."

"And I have never seen a woman so intent upon finding fault with every man she meets," Sophie replied. "Perhaps that's what makes us such good companions. We balance each other."

"I suppose you may be right, although I don't entirely agree that I find fault with all men." Amanda handed Veda her stockings. "I fear poor Fanny has suffered the brunt of it this journey. From all appearances, Daniel is completely smitten with her."

Fanny rested her chin in her palm. "I have done my very best to remain civil with him. Unfortunately, he considers any kindness as an encouragement to continue his amorous advances. Aunt Victoria seems quite taken with him, I must say."

Amanda shook one of her skirts and placed it in the growing heap. "Only last evening Mother said she thought him a fine fellow. I told her you've given your heart to Michael, but she pretended not to hear."

Fanny rolled to her side and rested her head on the stack of pillows. "My attempts to remind Daniel of my affection for Michael have been to no avail. The moment I mention Michael's name, Daniel reminds me of the many dangers of traveling in the Yukon. His comments are beginning to worry me."

"You must continue to pray for Michael. His safety remains in God's hands, and our prayers for him are important." Amanda turned toward Sophie, who was rummaging through the clothing in the chest of drawers. "You, too, Sophie. Have you been praying for Michael's safety?"

Sophie glanced first at Fanny and then permitted her gaze to rest upon Amanda. "Yes, Amanda, I do pray for Michael, but I didn't know you had taken charge of our prayers. If we don't find you a man, you're soon going to become as dour and rigid as my sister Beatrice."

Amanda tossed a scarf at her offending cousin. "How dare you say such a thing! I am not at all like Beatrice. I am planning a career to help the downtrodden, while Beatrice—"

"Enjoys treading on them?" Sophie convulsed into a fit of laughter, and soon her cousins joined her. The maids continued to work as though the girls were not even present in the room with them. How did servants manage to do that, Sophie wondered while swiping at the tears on her cheeks. "You are sworn to secrecy. If you ever tell Beatrice what I said, she'll never be kind to Wesley."

Suddenly serious, Fanny said, "I do hope I'll find a letter from Michael awaiting me when we arrive home. I've read this one so many times, I have it memorized." She removed the tattered envelope from her reticule and pressed it with her hand.

"And I hope that I'll have heard from the medical school to which I wrote." Amanda folded a shirtwaist and placed it in the trunk.

"What?" Sophie shook her head in disbelief. "You actually applied to a medical school? I don't believe you. Does Uncle Jonas know you're serious about this idea? You'll never gain his permission."

"Father knows it's my desire to attend medical school and help the under-privileged. Even though it is too late for me to attend medical school this year, I told Father that unless he gave me permission to begin next year, I wouldn't make this trip to England. He finally relented."

Once again Sophie rocked back against the pillows. "Of course he did. But only because he believes you'll no longer want to attend by next year. He probably plans to have you wed before you can attend college."

"And I'm not certain you'd enjoy medical training, Amanda. You're the one who nearly fainted when I attempted to operate on an injured rabbit a few years ago," Fanny remarked.

"That was an entirely different matter. There was no possible way to save that rabbit. It had been mauled by . . ." Amanda briefly covered her mouth. "I don't even want to discuss the rabbit. My work will be to lend aid and help relieve human suffering."

"What will you do if you come upon some small child who has been—"

"Stop it, Sophie! You're not going to dissuade me with this unpleasant talk of maimed rabbits or injured children. I plan to attend medical school, and Father has said he'll not attempt to thwart my efforts."

"At least not in a manner by which you would become aware," Sophie rebut-ted. There was little doubt her comments had angered Amanda. Though that had not been Sophie's intent, it was time Amanda took stock of her future. She was simply deceiving herself if she thought her father would ever permit such a plan. "Besides, when the right man comes along, you'll be just like me—delighted at the thought of marriage and a husband."

"If and when I ever decide to wed, you can be sure I'll know the man far longer than you've known Mr. Hedrick," Amanda replied. "And what of you, Fanny? What will you do when we return to Rochester? You must find something to occupy your time until Michael returns."

Fanny nodded. "We'll all be busy until the holidays pass. After that, I'm uncertain. I'll come into my inheritance in March when I turn eighteen, and if Michael hasn't yet returned, I shall need to make some decisions. Michael and I discussed purchasing one of the Thousand Islands, but I wouldn't make such a purchase without him. However, I might purchase a house in Rochester that we could live in for a portion of each year—like Grandfather and Grand-mère did."

"Oh, that's an excellent idea," Sophie agreed. "And we could come and visit you."

Amanda jumped to her feet. "Or perhaps the three of us could live together in Grandfather and Grand-mère's house. That would be absolutely perfect." She glanced at Sophie. "If you can put aside the thought of marriage for a time."

"I like that idea very much. We could have great fun, and you should wait at least a year before you decide if you will marry Mr. Hedrick anyway," Fanny said.

Sophie remained silent while her cousins continued to discuss their idea. Had Wesley not entered her life, she would think the idea superb. The cousins living on their own would permit her the freedom and independence she had previously longed for. But now, with Wesley in her life, neither freedom nor independence seemed important. Sophie wanted only to be in his presence. A proposal would soon be in the offing, and she didn't intend to wait until the following fall to wed. No need to say so at the moment, for she'd surely receive another one of Amanda's lengthy lectures.

After bidding Lord and Lady Illiff farewell earlier in the morning, Wesley and Daniel escorted the ladies on board the ship for their return home. Jonas had arranged their passage on the *Kaiser Wilhelm der Grosse,* a recently launched four-stacker that had made her maiden voyage in September. The ship was now being touted as the fastest and most elegant of all the steam liners crossing the Atlantic.

Although the rest of their party had gone to their cabins, Wesley had remained by Sophie's side until the ship was well underway. There had been no one on the docks to bid them farewell; nonetheless, the two of them had remained on deck and joined in the festivities. While Wesley discussed the dimensions of the ship with several other passengers, Sophie surveyed the latest fashions of the female passengers—at least those traveling in first class. There were, of course, those of lesser means who were scuttled off to steerage: emigrants traveling to America, each one hoping to find prosperity in their new homeland. She wondered how many would return disillusioned and brokenhearted.

She pulled her cloak more tightly around her and grasped Wesley's arm. "Let's take a turn about the deck. I heard one of the women say the first-class dining room could seat over five hundred passengers at a single sitting. I do wonder how they manage to cook so much food at one time in such a small space."

"I doubt the galley is as small as you imagine, yet I agree it would be a great feat." He patted her hand. "Fortunately, with your family's wealth, you won't ever be forced to work in a kitchen of any size."

"If my father had his way, I'd cook for the residents of his charity home back in Rochester. He's discovered a few people who share his views but believes we should all carry a burden for the underprivileged."

"It's good for the wealthy to aid the cause of the poor. After all, they can hardly do it for themselves."

Sophie nodded. "It's true, and I do care about their plight. It's just that sometimes I believe my father cares more about their needs than he does mine."

"Well, perhaps you won't need to concern yourself with that much longer."

He didn't elaborate, and Sophie was most vexed by the way he changed the subject.

"Your aunt mentioned a young man named Paul Medford who works with your father. If I recall, she said Mr. Medford had accompanied you on your voyage to England."

Sophie quickly explained the circumstances of Paul's visit. She certainly didn't want Wesley to think she had any interest in Paul, and she had no idea what her aunt might have related to Wesley. "I believe Paul returned to New York last week, but his mother may still be in England." Sophie couldn't remember if that's what her aunt had said or not, for she'd only half listened when Aunt Victoria had mentioned receiving a note from Paul's mother. "I'm afraid the return voyage won't be as pleasurable for my aunt. She found Mrs. Medford's company quite enjoyable." In truth, Sophie worried that her aunt would spend more time acting the proper chaperone—the last thing Sophie desired.

"In that case, we must invite her to join us from time to time. We don't want her to become lonely," Wesley said.

They stepped into one of the sitting rooms, where several elderly passengers were settled on the tufted leather sofas reading newspapers or books. "You need not worry on that account. She has both Amanda and Fanny to keep her company. And she enjoys Daniel's company, as well. I doubt she will feel isolated in the least." Sophie silently chastised herself. She should never have mentioned Mrs. Medford or Aunt Victoria.

Fanny leaned into the cushions of the couch and turned the page of the latest fashion magazine she'd purchased in London. At the click of the door, she glanced up to see her aunt entering the room and immediately returned to her reading.

"Fanny Broadmoor, why are you hiding in this cabin? Daniel has been looking for you. I gave him permission to explore the ship with you, but you were nowhere to be found. It is a lovely day, and you need to get out of this cabin and enjoy the fresh air. If nothing else, go and watch the other passengers while they play quoits or shuffleboard. You can cheer them on."

"I am perfectly content, Aunt Victoria. I don't want to stroll the decks with Daniel or watch a game of quoits, either."

Victoria sat down at the end of the couch and removed her hat. "Why not, Fanny? He is a genuinely sweet and kind young man who appears to be smitten with you. And you seem quite amiable together." Her aunt leaned close. "Daniel would make an excellent match."

"I have attempted over and over to explain to him that I am not interested in anyone other than Michael. I thought you understood that, yet you continue to speak of Daniel's many attributes. If you think him a fine match, perhaps you should direct his attentions toward Amanda."

"That very thought has crossed my mind. However, Daniel has interest in no one but you. I attempted to send him off exploring with Amanda, but he'd have no part of it. Of course, Amanda was unhappy with me, too. She continues to talk about school, and you continue your talk of Michael."

Fanny detected the note of annoyance in her aunt's voice. "You sound as though you disapprove of Michael. I thought you held the Atwells in high regard."

"They are a fine family—not of the same social class but good people. And I have always thought Michael a nice young man. But we are discussing marriage, Fanny. Though I believe a girl should marry for love, she must also seek a man who is a good match."

"I don't—"

Victoria wagged her finger. "Do not interrupt. While Michael is a nice man, he would never fit into our family. He doesn't possess the social graces that are acquired throughout the formative years."

Fanny burst into laughter. "Oh, like the fine manners George and Jefferson possess or their ability to engage in eloquent conversation?"

Her aunt frowned. "They may not act the part when they are around you or other family members, but they know how to conduct themselves when necessary. They have both the education and social mores to impress any critic."

Fanny wouldn't argue the point with her aunt, though she didn't believe either of her cousins could discuss a business venture if their very lives depended on it. "I believe Michael possesses every characteristic I desire in a husband. I have no interest in Daniel and have made every attempt to discourage his advances. I do not wish to hurt his feelings by giving him false hope."

"I think you must carefully consider Michael's circumstances, Fanny. It isn't my intent to cause you fear or distress, but you must be realistic. Many men have failed to return from the Yukon, and those who do are quick to speak of the dangers. Many who have gone in search of gold are unable to withstand the dire conditions in that frozen territory. And there are those who choose to remain. Never satisfied with the gold in their pocket, they continue to search for more and more. Who is to say if you will ever see Michael again?" Her aunt absently traced a finger along the lace edging of her collar. "Daniel presents a fine opportunity for you, whereas Michael will never be accepted socially, no matter his possible wealth."

Her aunt simply would not relent. Fanny had listened to these arguments from Daniel as well as other Broadmoor family members since the day Michael had left. They were always quick to point out every tidbit of bad news that flowed from the Yukon. She would never tell them, but she had worried over some of the issues they had steadfastly drawn to her attention. Though she pretended to read the pages of the magazine, her thoughts remained riveted upon Michael and his circumstances. Perhaps that was the reason Uncle Jonas had so readily agreed to Michael's foray into the Yukon. A shiver coursed down her spine. Did her uncle have some private knowledge that Michael would never return?

CHAPTER 9

Monday, November 22, 1897
Rochester, New York

Jonas had completed a hearty noonday meal of fricasseed chicken and buttered noodles at the men's club before heading off for his final appointment of the day with William Snodgrass. If all went well, he would return home afterwards and relax for the evening. Mortimer's assistance and insight had proved invaluable during the past weeks. He'd overseen the initial meeting with Judge Webster, and the lawyer's predictions had proved to be correct. Once the judge had understood their plan, he'd been pleased to become a silent partner in the scheme.

The jurist's quick agreement had given Jonas pause. He wondered if this was a common practice among the local judges, for all of them appeared to live well beyond their means. Of course, Judge Webster had married a woman of substantial wealth, but rumor had it that the judge's wife closely guarded the family coffers. Jonas absently wondered if frequent conspiracy was how the judge financed his love of fine horses and his gambling habit.

After a return to his office to complete the requisite paper work, Jonas gathered the documents into his case. The weather was brisk, yet the bank wasn't far, and the walk would do him good. Once outside, Jonas inhaled deeply, invigorated by the slight sting of cold air as it filtered into his lungs. There was little doubt Victoria would vent her anger at him when she returned, but he'd accomplished much during her absence. He'd never really planned to join her in England, but convincing her to go without promising to meet them abroad would have proved futile. Considering the inroads he'd made over the past month, he was quite willing to endure a few days of Victoria's wrath. Besides, she'd soon warm to him when he presented her with a diamond bracelet that would rival anything she'd ever seen on the arm of Elizabeth Oosterman or Hattie Pullman.

When he arrived at the bank, one of the clerks escorted him to William's office. He banged loudly. "I'm sorry to knock so loud, but he has trouble . . ." The clerk pointed to one of his own ears.

Jonas nodded. "Yes, I know."

The clerk tried again and then opened the door a crack when they received no response from within. The movement of the door obviously captured William's attention, for he immediately yelled, "Who's there?"

"Your clerk, Mr. Young, sir. And I've brought Mr. Broadmoor. He's here for his scheduled appointment."

The old man waved them forward, his liver-spotted hand trembling overhead. "You should have knocked."

The clerk grinned at Jonas.

"He *did* knock, William!" Jonas shouted. "Where's your ear trumpet?" The old man appeared befuddled by the inquiry. Jonas grabbed the instrument and handed it to the banker. "You should use this!" he hollered.

William grunted. "I can do without it. Most of the time nobody has anything to say that's worth listening to anyway."

Jonas agreed, but today he needed to be certain William understood what he was saying, for he wanted no difficulty with this transaction. The old banker dismissed his clerk and then shuffled through the papers piled atop his desk. "I don't seem to have anything here with your name on it, Jonas. Was I supposed to have some paper work prepared for you?"

"No." Jonas pointed to the ear trumpet and waited until William held the bugle-shaped device to his ear. "I scheduled the appointment because I wanted to go over a confidential matter with you. It will soon become public knowledge, but for the present I'd prefer privacy."

William nodded. "You know you can depend upon me. What is it you need?"

"I'm planning to sell Broadmoor Mansion," Jonas whispered into the ear trumpet.

The old man's jaw went slack, and the metal ear horn dropped to his desk with a clang. "How could you, Jonas? That house was your father's pride and joy."

Once again Jonas handed William the ear trumpet. "My father's will called for liquidation of assets as deemed necessary by the executor. I believe it's for the best, and if the family is upset, I will simply tell them what I've told you—except I won't tell them it was at my discretion. If they believe my father intended for the house to be sold, they'll say nothing."

"Wasn't the will read to the family shortly after his death? Don't you think they'll remember whether there was a stipulation to sell the house?"

Jonas shook his head. "There was chaos at the will reading. Besides, the sale affects only Quincy and me. My brother has no more interest in retaining the mansion here in Rochester than I do."

"In case you've forgotten, the sale of the family home affects Fanny, also," William added. "I believe she will vehemently object."

"What's done is done. I am in charge, not Fanny. That fact aside, she hasn't the wherewithal to maintain the place and can certainly not live there on her own."

"And what of the servants? Have you made arrangements for them? Your parents always employed a fine staff, and I believe they'd want you to look out for their future."

Jonas sighed. He'd come to set up a special account and secure the paper work regarding the house sale. Thus far, he'd done nothing but defend himself to the banker. "I don't think you need worry over the staff members. They will all locate positions without difficulty. I'll send them off with excellent references."

William frowned. "I would hope you'd also give them some type of financial reward for their many years of devoted service."

"Yes, of course. Now if we could discuss the issue of the house sale?" Jonas didn't wait for a response before he removed the paper work from his leather case and spread the pages across William's desk. He pushed the contract across the desk to William. "Read this," he said into the ear trumpet.

After he'd completed his reading, William tapped his finger on the second page. "I assume you want me to set up this account?"

"Yes. That's why I had you read the contract."

He rubbed his jaw and glanced over the top of the spectacles perched on his nose. "Why is this sale being handled outside of the court's oversight? Is that legal? Aren't you required to list this in the inventory of assets?"

"The legalities are not your concern, William. That's why I have a lawyer. Mortimer Fillmore is well versed in estate law, and I have every confidence the sale is being handled properly."

"Don't you think it would be wise to make certain? Mortimer's getting up in years, and he's been known to make a mistake or two in his time."

Jonas wanted to laugh aloud. William was referring to Mortimer as old, yet they were likely the same age. One couldn't hear; the other couldn't stay awake long enough to conduct business. He should replace both of them.

"Mortimer has checked on the legalities and assures me everything is in proper order. If you don't want to open the account, I suppose I could take my business across the street to First National. I doubt they'd turn away my business."

His threat had the desired effect. Jonas knew the prospect of transferring the Broadmoor accounts would be enough to motivate William. The banker dropped his ear trumpet onto the pile of papers and curled his lip. "There's no need to behave like an ill-tempered child, Jonas. I'll make the arrangements, but if any problem arises regarding this matter, remember that I warned you."

Jonas leaned back into his chair. With Judge Webster on his side, there was no need to worry. No one would know about the sale until the transaction had been completed.

AT SEA

Sophie leaned close against Wesley's shoulder and enjoyed the tingle that traced down her arm each time she drew near him. "You fret overmuch. No one will even notice that we've slipped away for a few minutes."

Her words didn't appear to ease Wesley's concerns, for he immediately glanced over his shoulder. "We may have been wiser to wait until later in the evening." He nodded toward a small library that was seldom in use—especially during the evening hours. They stepped inside the dimly lit room, and Wesley led her to a leather couch. "Your charm and beauty have cast a spell upon me, dearest Sophie." He traced his finger along her cheek. "You cannot imagine the depth of despair one feels when hope is lost, but you have renewed my hope and gifted me with the ability to love again."

Her heartbeat quickened at his words. She'd always found pleasure in flitting from one man to another. But now that she'd met Wesley, she was certain no other man could capture her interest for even a second. Strange how Wesley had mesmerized her. And wonder of wonders, she'd seemingly had the same effect upon him. She reveled in his words of endearment and hoped his feelings for her would remain constant once they arrived in New York.

"It's obvious you loved your wife very much. I'm honored that I, of all people, have been the one to renew your optimism for the future." Sophie clasped his hand in her own. "I would enjoy hearing about your wife. What was she like?"

With a faraway look in his eyes, Wesley seemed to consider her question. "She was much different from you—in truth, I'd say you are complete opposites."

Sophie's heart plummeted at the remark. Perhaps she was only a fleeting diversion, and Wesley would soon tire of her. "I see. Then you are generally attracted to staid women who prefer sipping tea and performing charity work."

He tipped his head back and laughed. "No. I've always preferred a woman who has a delightful sense of humor and enjoys life. When we married, I thought my wife to be much like you. And she very much wanted children, but as time passed and children didn't arrive, she became quiet and indifferent to life. Actually, it was quite sad to observe her change from a vivacious young woman to a recluse of sorts. My love for her never swayed, though in the final years of our marriage, I missed her cheerful spirit. You have once again reminded me that life is to be enjoyed."

"That's what I tell Amanda and Fanny all the time. We need to seize the moment and enjoy what life has to offer."

He squeezed her hand and leaned in until only a hairsbreadth separated them. "I love that you dare to speak your mind and show your feelings."

Encouraged by his words, she boldly fell into his arms and savored his closeness. He lifted her chin and looked deep into her eyes. Warmth stirred within and slowly trailed throughout her body until even her fingertips burned with heat. "Wesley." His name was but a whisper on her lips before his head slowly descended and his lips covered hers with a soft, lingering kiss.

"We must restrain ourselves and be careful. If someone should see us, your reputation would suffer, and I would never forgive myself. You are very dear to me, and I would never want to compromise you in any way." He brushed her palm with a kiss. "Your family, as well as the rest of polite society, would consider our present behavior improper."

"Thank you, Wesley. The fact that you are concerned about my reputation touches my heart."

Sophie had spoken with absolute sincerity. Yet why had she always considered such warnings from Paul annoying? She weighed the thought and decided that the answer lay in the way the words were spoken. Wesley's words had been cloaked in an air of protection that both warmed and comforted her. On the other hand, Paul's admonitions always seemed directed with an air of authority and censure, likely due to his religious zeal. Love made all the difference, she decided. Her love for Wesley and, from what he'd indicated, his love for her. Rather than finding Wesley's words harsh and unyielding, she treasured his concern. And though she would have preferred to remain in his arms for the remainder of the evening, Sophie willingly followed him from the room.

Fanny hurried down one of the ship's corridors, certain she'd receive a reprimand from her aunt. Aunt Victoria clearly disliked late arrivals, but this time Fanny's tardiness couldn't be helped. Repairs to her gown and struggling with her uncooperative hair could both be blamed. Minnie had taken ill late in the afternoon, leaving only Veda to assist with her dress. In the maid's haste to press the wrinkles from Fanny's gown, she had torn the lace trim that adorned the bodice. The repair had taken a good half hour. And although

Amanda had attempted to arrange Fanny's hair in a neat pile of curls, they'd easily escaped the hairpins with each movement of her head. Poor Veda had been in tears by the time Fanny finally departed their suite.

Her aunt had been evasive when she'd invited Fanny to the small dinner party—even Amanda, who hadn't been invited, insisted she knew nothing of the event. Fanny hadn't doubted her cousin's word. Amanda had been both intrigued and insulted when Fanny had mentioned the dinner party. Fanny only wished she could have changed places with her cousin. She disliked these formal gatherings, especially when she didn't know what to expect. She'd tried to decline the invitation, but Aunt Victoria would have none of it.

"This is a very special dinner, and you will be amazed by the surprise that awaits you," her aunt had said.

The only surprise Fanny desired was a letter from Michael, but receiving mail on the ship would be impossible. She hoped she would discover a missive or two awaiting her the moment they arrived home. The mere thought of Michael brought a smile to her lips. How she longed to read his words and learn when he would return to her.

She entered the main dining room and was immediately whisked away by one of the white-jacketed waiters. With a wide sweep of his arm, the waiter bid her to enter one of the private dining rooms. The room was dimly lit, and she squinted as she entered. Her eyes soon adjusted to the diffused light, though her smile immediately faded as the figure across the table stood. *Daniel*. Only one table had been arranged in the room—with only two place settings. Surely her aunt hadn't expected her to rejoice over a private dinner with Daniel. Fanny glanced over her shoulder. Surely someone else would join them.

Daniel stepped around the table and stood by the chair. "Do sit down, Fanny."

"Who else will be joining . . ." Her voice faltered. She couldn't speak the word *us*. The implication was more than she could grasp at the moment. "Who else is joining you for dinner?"

He stepped closer and touched her elbow. Her feet moved forward against her will. Within moments they were seated at the table, and Daniel was staring at her. Though she'd never been nose to nose with a fox, the gleam in Daniel's eyes brought that animal to mind. Her chair was positioned on the far side of the table. In order to escape, she'd be forced to pass by Daniel. Once again he'd trapped her in a corner.

Resting his forearms on the table, Daniel reached for Fanny's hand. Surprised by his bold behavior, she yanked away and then watched in horror as the water pitcher tumbled onto its side. Water streamed across the linen tablecloth, soaking and pooling here and there until the final vestiges trickled onto the floor. Too late, she retrieved the pitcher and returned it to an upright position. Only a meager amount of liquid remained at the bottom. Tracing her fingers over the edges, she quickly examined the cut-glass container and offered a quick prayer of thanks when she discovered no chips or cracks.

Daniel hastened to signal the waiter, who politely suggested the couple enjoy a brief turn about the deck while he cleared and reset the table. Though she would have preferred to remain with the waiter or return to her room, Daniel was only too pleased to escort her to the deck. A cool breeze greeted them, and Fanny struggled to lift her lace wrap to her shoulders.

"Let me help," Daniel said, grasping an edge of the fabric. He draped the shawl across her back and permitted his palm to rest lightly on her shoulder.

Fanny shrugged and gave a quick twist of her upper body to jar his hand from her shoulder. "Thank you. I believe my wrap is secure." She sidestepped to place a few inches of distance between them. "You never answered my earlier question. Will anyone else be joining us for dinner?"

The moonlight beamed upon the water and cast a rippling design upon Daniel's face. "We'll be dining alone, but lest you concern yourself over the propriety of our private dinner, be assured that I gained your aunt's permission."

Fanny inhaled a deep breath. Daniel and Aunt Victoria had planned this— the two of them—together. A sense of betrayal knifed its way into her heart. Although her aunt had clearly stated she didn't consider Michael a proper match, Fanny hadn't expected her to aid Daniel in his romantic pursuit. The fact that her aunt had touted the dinner as one that would involve a lovely surprise only served to heighten Fanny's dismay. While Daniel attempted to keep pace with her, Fanny continued along the perimeter of the ship at a mea- sured clip. When they'd circled the deck, she reentered the main dining room and stopped outside the private room Daniel had reserved.

Noting the waiter still at work setting the table, she turned to Daniel. "There's no reason why we couldn't enjoy our meal out here with the other passengers."

Daniel ignored her remark and signaled to the waiter. "How much longer?"

The waiter motioned him forward. "My apologies. I have only to retrieve another pitcher of water. You may be seated if you'd like." He pressed the palm of his hand across the edge of the tablecloth to remove a slight wrinkle.

Daniel stepped to one side and motioned Fanny forward. There was no escape for her. She offered another apology to the waiter before sitting down. "I'll do my best to be more careful."

The waiter tipped his head. "It's my pleasure to be of service."

Fanny doubted he meant it, but she didn't argue. The waiter returned with the water, filled their glasses, and placed the pitcher on a nearby sideboard. He evidently didn't plan on taking any chances. Daniel had ordered their meals in advance, and although Fanny would have preferred making her own choices, she thanked him for his thoughtfulness.

When the waiter later departed to retrieve their dessert, Daniel leaned forward. "You know how much I've grown to care for you, Fanny. From the moment I first set eyes upon you at Broadmoor Island, I knew you were the woman of my dreams."

She giggled. "I'm sorry, Daniel, but I truly don't know how you could consider a complete stranger to be the woman of your dreams. Surely you are interested in more than appearance. I hadn't considered you quite so shallow."

He reared back at the comment. She'd clearly struck a nerve.

"I don't consider myself shallow in the least. 'Tis true that your beauty drew me, but it is your intelligence and sweet spirit that have held me captive ever since."

She bit her lip. Daniel sounded as though he'd been reciting poetry. Had he thought he must find the perfect words to woo her? Obviously he didn't know her. She much preferred a man who would speak straight from his heart. Someone like Michael, who would tell her the truth. "I have no desire to hold you captive, Daniel. Please consider yourself released from any hold you think I may have upon you."

"But can't you see that it is my desire to be your prisoner, Fanny? I want to spend the rest of my life imprisoned by your love."

She stared at him, too dumbfounded to speak. Had her cousins Jefferson and George been aboard the ship, she would have suspected they were playing a joke on her. But neither of them was there.

Now Daniel reached into his pocket and retrieved a jeweler's box. She pushed back in her chair, longing for an escape.

"I love you, Fanny." He lifted the lid of the box and there, encased in velvet, was a massive diamond ring. "With your Aunt Victoria's assistance, I have chosen this ring especially for you, and it is my fervent hope that you will agree to marry me. This diamond reflects the depth of my love for you. Please say you will be my wife."

In one swift gesture she slid her hands from the table. "I couldn't possibly consider your offer. I am already engaged to Michael. You know that."

"And I am begging you to reconsider, for you know that your uncle Jonas would never approve your marriage to someone of Michael's social standing." He squared his shoulders. "I believe your uncle would be pleased to accept me into the family."

"Uncle Jonas has already agreed that I may marry Michael when he returns. We solidified the arrangement before Michael left for the Yukon. Michael will return with his fortune, and my uncle will offer no objection to our marriage."

"And you believe that?" Daniel scoffed. "You are a Broadmoor. Even if

Michael returns a wealthy man, I don't believe your uncle will give his blessing. Money will not give him the social status your uncle requires. He likely
gave his word believing Michael would never return."

"My uncle's blessing will be of little import, for I shall be of age by the time
Michael returns, and I will no longer be forced to adhere to the Broadmoor
rules." She tilted her head and grinned.

"You may be freed from following your uncle's rules, but remember that if
you go against his wishes, you'll be isolated from the rest of the family. Would
you give up your family so easily, Fanny?"

She squared her shoulders. "Amanda and Sophie would never desert me.
We love one another."

"You must remember that your cousins are both dependent upon their
fathers for their well-being. If they are to maintain their social status and eventually make good marriages, they dare not defy the wishes of their fathers."

While Daniel forked a bite of his apple pie, Fanny considered his words. She
feared much of what he said was correct. Although she could help her cousins
financially once she attained legal age, she doubted they would be willing to
sacrifice their families for her. If Uncle Jonas disinherited Amanda, she would
lose her social standing as well as her ability to make a good marriage. And
although Uncle Quincy would never, of his own volition, recommend alienation
of a family member, there was little doubt that he'd abide by Uncle Jonas's
decision. Given Aunt Victoria's willingness to help Daniel arrange this private
dinner as well as assist him in the selection of an engagement ring, her aunt
had obviously come to the conclusion that Fanny would forget Michael and
fall in love with another man.

Tears welled in her eyes, and she pushed away from the table. "You must
excuse me. I'm not feeling well. Thank you for dinner." She avoided Daniel's
outstretched hand as she fled the room. Racing down the corridor, she allowed
her tears to flow with abandon.

CHAPTER 10

SATURDAY, DECEMBER 4, 1897
ROCHESTER, NEW YORK

Sophie strolled toward the punch table, uninterested in the conversation and
dancing that swirled around her; she would have much preferred to remain
at home that evening. Although every eligible bachelor in Rochester was in

attendance, Aunt Victoria's coming-home party held little appeal, and she looked forward to escaping at the earliest opportunity. They'd celebrated with a Thanksgiving dinner only days earlier, and she wasn't interested in any further festivities.

"Am I to assume you are ill this evening?"

Sophie turned from the punch table and discovered herself face-to-face with Paul Medford. She furrowed her brow. "Why would you think I am unwell? Has the pale gray shade of my dress caused me to appear sallow?"

"No. In fact, your gown is quite beautiful, but I am unaccustomed to seeing you stand at a punch bowl. Normally, you can't seem to find enough dance partners, yet tonight I've not seen you dance even once." He pointed to the card that hung from her wrist. "I believe I see a number of vacant lines on your dance card. How can that be? Sophie Broadmoor, the most sought-after dance partner in all of Rochester, not dancing?"

She chose to ignore the gibe. "I'm not interested in dancing with any of the men in attendance." She took a sip of her punch. "How is your grand-mother's health?"

He arched his brows. "I'm surprised you even remembered my grandmother was ill. I must say, you don't act like the same young lady who departed Rochester six weeks ago."

"Perhaps that's because I'm not the same. My life has changed completely." She gazed across the rim of her punch cup.

"I'm intrigued. Exactly what occurred in England to change your life in such a dramatic manner?"

"I have met my one true love, the man who meets my every expectation. If all goes according to plan, I hope to spend the rest of my life with him." She felt a sense of satisfaction as she watched the look of surprise cross his face. "In fact, I expect to be engaged by Christmas."

"Christmas? That's less than a month away. Who is this man? Someone you've known for several years, I would guess."

Sophie shook her head. "Someone I met while in England. We were im-mediately drawn to each other. He's been married previously. His wife died and he'd been somewhat inconsolable until we met. He says that I've given him new purpose in his life."

"So you plan to live in England?"

"Oh, he's not an Englishman. His name is Wesley Hedrick, and he lives in New York City." She set her punch glass on the table. "I'll introduce him when he arrives during the Christmas holidays. Oh, there's Amanda. Do excuse me."

While Sophie expertly wended her way among the visiting guests, Paul maintained a watchful gaze. There was no denying Sophie's behavior had changed dramatically, yet with all the men Sophie had enchanted in her short lifetime, he wondered what she'd found so special in this Wesley Hedrick. And how could she possibly consider marriage to a man she barely knew? Surely her father would not approve of such a match.

As if drawn by his thoughts, Quincy Broadmoor entered the room and strode toward Paul. "I'm glad to see you decided to attend. I dislike these functions as much as the next man, but sometimes we must make the effort—at least that's what the women tell me." He clapped Paul on the shoulder. "You should go in and meet some of the young ladies instead of hovering over the punch bowl."

"I'm not considered much of a dance partner. Unfortunately, I step on the ladies' feet far too frequently, and they are generally pleased when the music stops."

"I can commiserate only too well. You should ask Sophie or one of her cousins to give you a few lessons. I'm certain they'd be pleased to teach you the steps. It seems the women can never get enough of dancing."

"Speaking of Sophie, I enjoyed a cup of punch with her only a short time ago. She mentioned a man named Wesley Hedrick—said she'd met him in England. I don't believe I've ever heard anyone speak of him previously. Have you made his acquaintance?"

"I've not been personally introduced, but Mr. Hedrick has written to me. His letters speak with great enthusiasm regarding the Home for the Friendless. He expresses a genuine interest in paying us a visit at the Home." Quincy tipped his head closer. "He's mentioned that after seeing the work we are doing, he may want to donate a great deal of money to help further our cause. From his letter, I can tell that he's been involved in charitable work for many years. I surmise he is deeply interested in continuing his good deeds."

"That is truly good news. We could use someone with both money and influence to help in our expansion efforts. Does Mr. Hedrick state when he may visit?"

"Sometime before the Christmas holiday. I understand he's been invited to spend Christmas with the family. He's a widower—no children. Having lost my own dear Marie, I can certainly understand his feelings of loneliness. Especially since he has no children or other family nearby. I've told Sophie she should extend a welcome for as long as he can arrange to be with us here in Rochester."

"Since he has just returned from England, I'd think he would need to remain at home and attend to his duties in New York City."

Quincy shrugged. "From what I've been told, he's quite successful. I imagine he has employees who are capable of managing his business ventures. Victoria mentioned that his deceased wife was a cousin of Lady Illiff, though I've never met her, either. Jonas and Victoria know far more people than I. Although my wife was interested in attending occasional social functions, Marie didn't travel abroad like other members of the family do. She much preferred returning to visit her family in Canada." Talk of his deceased wife caused tears to form, and Quincy swiped his hand across his eyes and then nodded toward the door. "Ah, Dr. Carstead has arrived. I should go and greet him."

Paul moved back toward a far corner of the room, suddenly feeling alone in this vast sea of people. He'd attended at Quincy's request, but deep in his heart he knew he'd wanted to see Sophie. Since her return from England, they'd spoken only in passing. She seemed always to be in a hurry nowadays. Her announcement of an impending engagement had come as a complete surprise. Why did he feel as though something had been stolen from beneath his nose?

He'd watched over Sophie's behavior in an attempt to keep her safe and guard her reputation, but these stirrings deep inside were far more than the feelings of brotherly concern for his employer's unruly daughter. When had this change of heart begun?

From his vantage point, he could see Sophie standing near one of the French doors leading to the garden. Was she planning to sneak away and return home now that she'd made her required appearance? To see her ignoring the overtures of each man who drew near reinforced what she'd told him. Yet he didn't want to believe she had so easily fallen in love with some wealthy stranger. He silently reminded himself that he'd been invited by Quincy as an advocate for the Home for the Friendless. Accordingly, his time at this party was expected to yield a few benefactors. Instead, he was leaning in a corner and contemplating Sophie's future. Paul spotted Julius Mansford and forced himself to move from the corner. The owner of the Syracuse Furniture Company could possibly be counted upon for a hefty donation.

Amanda sidled up to Sophie while keeping her attention fixed upon the tall man speaking to her uncle Quincy and a small cluster of people across the room. "You're certain he's a doctor?"

"Yes." Sophie bobbed her head. "I saw him at the Home for the Friendless yesterday. He arrived in town while we were in England. Father convinced him to volunteer his services to the residents one day a week."

"What's his name?" Amanda could barely contain her excitement.

"Carlson, or something like that. I didn't pay much attention."

"I want to meet him! Take me over and introduce me."

"I can't introduce him when I don't remember his name." Sophie wrinkled her nose. "Is all this interest because he's a doctor?"

"Of course. You know how much I want to attend medical school. Perhaps he'll offer some advice." She wanted to take Sophie by the hand and drag her across the room. "Can you honestly not remember his name?"

"I truly don't recall. He's somewhat attractive. Not nearly as handsome as Wesley, of course, but pleasant appearing."

"I care little what he looks like," Amanda said, craning her neck to see beyond the gathering of men with Uncle Quincy. "It's his knowledge that interests me. I'm going to go over and attempt to join in the conversation. Surely someone will introduce me." Amanda squeezed her cousin's hand. "Wish me well."

Sophie grinned. "Always. And if all else fails, go fetch Paul—I'm sure he will introduce you."

After calculating the best way to situate herself among the group, Amanda carefully circled the cluster of guests and stopped near her uncle's elbow. She listened as the men discussed local politics and the new mayor who would soon take office. When several minutes had passed and no one had paid her any notice, she nudged her uncle's elbow.

"Ah, Amanda. How are you, my dear?" he inquired.

"Fine, Uncle Quincy."

"I believe Sophie is across the room."

Amanda nodded. "Yes. I talked with her only moments ago. She mentioned you'd invited a doctor to the party."

"Indeed. A fine man, I might add. He seems most dedicated."

"His name?"

Her uncle rubbed his jaw. "I'm sorry. I should introduce you, shouldn't I?" He waited for a lull in the conversation and then signaled. "Dr. Carstead, I'd like to introduce my niece, Amanda Broadmoor."

Amanda sized him up immediately. Wavy brown hair crowned his head in a barely tamed manner while his dark hazel eyes held a slightly amused glint. He was more than somewhat attractive, but Amanda pushed such thoughts aside.

Dr. Carstead nodded. "Pleased to meet you, Miss Broadmoor."

Amanda didn't give him an opportunity to return to his previous conversation. "And I'm pleased to meet you, Dr. Carstead." When several of the men removed themselves from the group, Amanda stepped closer. "I, too, am interested in a medical career."

"Truly? A midwife perhaps?" He studied her with an assessing glance and tolerant smile.

"No. I plan to attend medical school and become a physician like you."

His grin vanished. "I've heard many young women such as you tell me they are seeking a career in medicine. Once they discover the extent of the medical training they must undergo, I find they are more interested in seeking a husband. Few young ladies understand the depth of knowledge required to hang out a shingle. Even after completing my education, I was required to complete further study to qualify as a surgeon."

Amanda squared her shoulders. "I can assure you that I am not searching for a husband, Dr. Carstead. Quite frankly, I find both your attitude and your tone condescending—and uncalled for, I might add."

Her words were enough to scatter the few remaining members of their group. She folded her arms across her waist and awaited his rebuttal.

"As I said, I've seen many young women think they will become the next Florence Nightingale, but when faced with the reality of sickness, disease, and injury, their plans fly out the window."

"If you know so much about Miss Nightingale, then you know she prefers to focus her attention on nursing. I desire to be a doctor and therefore have no intention of becoming the next Florence Nightingale. I have a sharp mind and good memory. I believe I will make a satisfactory student," Amanda countered.

"You may withstand the educational process, Miss Broadmoor, but you would never survive the daily rigors of medical practice."

"Is that so? Well, *Dr.* Carstead, I will prove you wrong. Permit me to train with you for a time, and I will prove myself."

His eyes shone with amusement as his brow arched. "You? Why, you wouldn't last a week."

It was more than enough challenge for Amanda. "Would you care to place a wager on that, or are you afraid you'd lose?"

"My dear Miss Broadmoor, you surely know that gambling is a bad habit to fall into."

"As are pride and a judgmental attitude, but you appear eager enough to fall into those practices."

He tilted his head and seemed to consider her challenge for a moment. "I know you won't endure a week, but if you do, I'll permit you to train with me for as long as you desire." He grinned. "And you must know how certain that makes me that you will not succeed."

"If you would accompany me, Doctor?" She raised her brows in a question mark. When he offered an affirmative nod, Amanda signaled him forward. "I'd like you to sign an agreement. I'll retrieve a piece of writing paper from my father's desk in the library."

Dr. Carstead reluctantly followed behind her. "Will your family not think it strange that you are slipping into the unoccupied areas of the house with a stranger?"

Amanda pushed open the library door. "Hardly. They know me to be a sensible woman."

He chuckled. "But even sensible women are capable of errors in judgment."

Amanda went to the secretary and opened a drawer. "So are sensible men."

"Are you implying that I have erred in my judgment of you?"

She turned with a sheet of paper in hand. "I'm not implying it. I'm assuring you of it." She lowered the writing table and quickly took up pen and ink. "I believe my abilities will surprise you."

"They already have," he assured. "For I never would have believed I'd find myself in such a position."

She wrote on the paper for several lines, then blew lightly upon the page to dry the ink. Amanda could feel Dr. Carstead's gaze upon her, but she refused to turn and acknowledge him. No doubt he thought her a silly girl with foolish notions. *The next Florence Nightingale indeed!*

"All right," she said, handing him the paper, "I believe this will set things in motion."

He looked the paper over, and although he made one futile attempt to dissuade her, he signed the document and placed it in Amanda's outstretched hand. She would begin after Christmas.

"I hope you know what you're doing, Miss Broadmoor, although I'm certain you have no idea." He grinned and added, "I do believe, however, I will enjoy our little arrangement."

Jonas scanned the room, convinced young Daniel Irwin was attempting to avoid him. When Jonas had met the ship in New York, they'd had no opportunity to talk. And shortly after they'd arrived home, Victoria had informed him that Daniel was away visiting relatives in Syracuse and wouldn't return until the third of December. She'd said the young man had assured her that he would be back in Rochester to attend this evening's welcome-home party. Thus far, however, he hadn't set eyes upon Daniel, and Jonas wanted answers.

He worked his way through the crowd, stopping to say hello and offer a handshake here and there. But when he spotted Daniel talking to a young woman, he postponed any further greetings and picked up his pace. With a forceful hold, he gripped Daniel's shoulder. The young man's knees bent, and he twisted his body to gain release from the painful hold.

"Mr. Broadmoor! Good to see you." Daniel extended his hand and forced a smile, but Jonas could see fear in the young man's eyes, and it pleased him.

"If this lovely young lady will excuse us, I would enjoy the opportunity of visiting with you for a short time in my library."

Jonas could see that Daniel longed to object, but he was smart enough to know he dared not. While the girl assumed a demure pout, Daniel nervously excused himself. From all appearances, Daniel had been wooing her. The thought rankled Jonas. Could he depend upon no one?

Had they been alone, Jonas would have been tempted to grab Daniel by the ear and lead him down the hallway like an errant schoolboy. Instead, he grasped his elbow. At the end of the hall, they made a left turn. Had they not come to an abrupt halt, they would have collided with Amanda and Dr. Carstead.

Jonas frowned and looked from one to the other, puzzled by the twosome. "Were you seeking a book from the library, Amanda?"

"No, Father." She waved a folded sheet of paper back and forth. "I'll explain later." Her gaze shifted to Daniel and then back to her father. "Are the two of you looking for reading material or—"

"I promised to assist Daniel with an investment question. Should your mother be looking for me, tell her I will return very soon." He hoped his response would erase the question he'd noted in her eyes. He had no idea who the man was who accompanied Amanda, but he assumed him to be some lost soul she'd come upon.

Once inside the library, he closed the doors and pointed to one of the leather chairs. "Sit! You have some explaining to do, young man." Jonas pulled a chair closer and sat down. "I don't see an engagement ring on Fanny's finger, yet my wife tells me she helped you choose a lovely ring." Jonas reached into a carved cedar-lined humidor and withdrew a cigar. He clipped the cigar tip and gave Daniel a sideways glance. "Well? What do you have to say for yourself?"

The young man pulled his arms close to his body and appeared to shrink before Jonas's eyes. "I've been doing my very best, but she isn't easily convinced. Each time I attempted to advance my cause, she told me she planned to marry Michael Atwell."

"Of *course* she told you that, but you were supposed to convince her that *you* were a better choice. I made my position clear before you sailed. You knew this would be no easy task, but you promised you could sway her decision." Jonas held a match to his cigar and puffed until the tip glowed with heat. He leaned back into the cushioned chair. "I want further explanation than what you've given."

Daniel squirmed in his chair. "I don't believe Fanny can be convinced. Though I was able to win Mrs. Broadmoor's support for my cause, even her assistance failed to help. Fanny wasn't influenced in the least by my attentions or the beautiful ring. In fact, my overtures seemed to have the opposite effect."

"Did she actually say she considered herself engaged to Michael?"

"Yes—and she said you'd agreed to their marriage prior to his departure for the Yukon." Daniel narrowed his eyes. "A fact you hadn't mentioned to me."

After a deep draw on his cigar, Jonas slowly exhaled. The smoke formed a pattern of curves and ripples as it floated overhead. "I expect you to continue your pursuit of Fanny. Keep away from the other young ladies, both here and at other social gatherings. You are to keep your attention directed only upon her. I expect you to keep our agreement."

"But I don't see . . ."

Jonas clenched his hand into a tight fist. How could one insignificant girl cause him such difficulty? "Just do as you've been instructed. Now go out there and ask Fanny to dance."

Daniel jumped out of the chair as though he'd been shot.

"Close the door behind you," Jonas called after him.

He took another long draw on his cigar and leaned back in his chair. He must find a solution to this situation with Fanny. Michael must never return.

CHAPTER 11

WEDNESDAY, DECEMBER 15, 1897

Fanny unfolded her napkin and tucked it onto her lap while attempting to avoid Daniel's attention. He had arrived moments earlier and had asked to speak to Uncle Jonas. Her aunt had invited him to join them for breakfast. Unfortunately, Aunt Victoria directed him to the chair beside Fanny. No matter how hard she tried, it seemed Fanny could not escape Daniel. She caught Amanda's eye, receiving a sympathetic look in return.

Her uncle offered his usual morning prayer over their food, but Fanny wondered if he truly meant what he said. The prayer seemed little more than hollow words. On the other hand, she ought not to judge her uncle; sometimes her prayers were no more than mechanical recitations. Of late, she'd attempted to make her prayers a conversation with God, which seemed to work much better. Except at night, when she would fall asleep in the midst of her private one-way discussions.

Her uncle motioned for the maid to begin serving, and while the platter of ham and sausage circled the table, Daniel made mention of the light snow that had begun to fall.

Upon hearing his weather report, Aunt Victoria perked to attention. "We need to begin planning the family Christmas celebration. Goodness, but it's only ten days away."

"Oh, must we discuss this over breakfast, Victoria?" Uncle Jonas jabbed a piece of ham and dropped it onto his plate. "You ladies can talk about that later. I don't need to be a part of a Christmas discussion."

"Well, you need to help with the decisions. This will be the first Christmas since your father's death. I thought it would be nice if we hosted the celebration here at our home."

Jonas grunted. "I think of it more as mayhem than a celebration, but if you want to invite the family here, that's fine with me."

Fanny straightened in her chair. "I have an idea."

Her aunt beamed. "Good! What's your idea, Fanny?"

"I think we should celebrate Christmas at Broadmoor Mansion. After all, that has been the family tradition for all these years, and there's no reason we can't continue to do so. It will help us remember Grandfather and Grand-mère, as well as—"

"That is *not* a good idea. We'll host Christmas here." Jonas signaled for the biscuits.

"But Broadmoor Mansion has been my home since I was an infant." Her voice cracked, and she swallowed. "I would truly enjoy it if we could host the event there."

"I see no reason why we couldn't manage the celebration at the mansion," Victoria said as she dabbed her napkin at the corner of her mouth. "After all, the servants are still there to help."

Her uncle gulped the remains of his coffee and cleared his throat. "I'm afraid your plan will not work, Fanny." He shifted in his chair and focused on his plate. "You may find this news a bit discomfiting, but I sold my parents' home." He gave a curt nod. "Broadmoor Mansion no longer belongs to the family."

Fanny's fork slipped from her fingers and clanked on the china plate. "Please tell me you are jesting."

"I'm afraid not. The house sold while you were in England."

"Why? How could you sell Broadmoor Mansion? Other than Grandfather's home on Broadmoor Island, the mansion here in Rochester is the only home I've ever known. Why wasn't I told before this?" Her hands shook as she shouted her questions.

"Now, now, Fanny, do calm yourself. It isn't necessary to shout. I'm certain your uncle will answer all of your questions as well as my own. Won't you, Jonas?" Anger shone in Aunt Victoria's eyes.

"You women need to gain control of your emotions. I had no choice in the matter. Liquidation of some assets was necessary in order to make the partial distribution called for under the terms of Father's will."

The maid refilled her uncle's coffee cup and quickly retreated to her station near the sideboard.

"Why wasn't I advised? I had hoped to purchase the house for myself." The eggs she'd swallowed only moments earlier now roiled in her stomach. How could her uncle do such a thing?

Amanda chimed in and supported Fanny's argument. "You know what you did was improper, Father. You should have first spoken to Fanny."

He shook his head. "The funds were not yet available to her, and the home had to be sold. Telling her would have only caused her greater distress. But if you ladies will permit me a moment without interruption, I think your anger will be assuaged."

Fanny folded her arms tight around her waist. "I don't know what you could say to make this better."

"Before you departed for England, Daniel came to me and professed his love for you, Fanny. I know the house is important to you. It is for that very reason I sold the house to Daniel. Don't you see? This way you can return to your home again."

Daniel's mouth formed an oval. "I don't know . . . well, I'm not . . ."

"I'm terribly sorry to ruin your surprise, Daniel. But as you can see, with all this talk of Christmas, I had no choice but to reveal the truth."

Tears streamed down Fanny's cheeks as she attempted to gain control of her emotions. Amanda rushed to her side and wrapped her in a comforting embrace. "Do take heart, Fanny. If the house is meant to be yours, you will have it one day. I'm certain Father will do everything in his power to help you."

"That's exactly what I've done, Amanda. Why else would I agree to sell the house to Daniel? I thought the two of them . . ."

Fanny glared at her uncle and pushed away from the table. "This is nonsense! You know I plan to marry Michael. Why would you do such a thing?" She wheeled around toward Daniel. "If this is an attempt to coerce me into marriage, it will not work! It's Michael I love. I won't marry Daniel even if he does own Grandfather's house. Even if Michael should die, I wouldn't marry him."

"I was only attempting to help," her uncle called after her.

Fanny stopped in the doorway. "If this is the way you help, then please don't ever help me in the future, Uncle Jonas." Before storming out of the room, she turned toward Daniel. "And I *never* want to see you again!"

The morning quickly dissolved into chaos, but Jonas wasn't the least bit concerned. He motioned Daniel to his office, closed the door, and put the pandemonium from his mind. "I know you're surprised by my announcement regarding the house."

"To say the least, sir."

"I had to do something, and this seemed the best idea. In fact, I don't know why I didn't think of it sooner."

"But, sir, I can't afford to buy Broadmoor Mansion." Daniel looked rather upset at the very idea.

Jonas laughed. "Of course you can't afford it right now, but once you marry my niece, you will have ample funds to purchase it from me. I shall set things in motion for you to be deeded the mansion ahead of time. We can get my attorney to work out the details."

"But won't someone object?"

"Who? My brother? He's too busy with his own affairs, and Fanny is too young to have any say over the matter. Once she calms down, she'll see the sense in this. She loves that house, and I think this might very well be the one thing we needed to get her to focus her attention on you."

"I had rather hoped she'd focus her attention on me, because of . . . well . . . her love for me," Daniel said, sounding like a disappointed little boy.

Jonas rolled his eyes. "We don't always get things the way we'd like them to be. I'm sure in time you can make the girl fall passionately in love with you, if that's your desire. Now leave me. I have to write a letter. Say nothing of this to anyone, and if Fanny speaks to you about it . . . well . . . avoid the details and turn her attention to matters of the heart."

Jonas waited until Daniel had exited the room before sitting down to his desk. While this hadn't been his first plan of action, it did seem to resolve the dilemma nicely. There would be no more discussion of Fanny moving back to the mansion, nor of her trying to force Jonas to let her buy it with her share of the inheritance.

"This will buy me time," he said aloud. He knew there would be a price to pay, but he was more than willing to risk it all for the sake of what he might yet take hold of.

Jonas smiled to himself. "The end will justify my means, to be certain."

Sophie found her emotions a mix of happiness and sorrow. A year ago in December her mother had died without warning. The year since had proven to be harder on Sophie than she liked to admit. She'd filled it with a variety of activities and ambitions, but nothing had given her much comfort. Well, nothing but Wesley, and that's where she cushioned her sorrow with joy. She struggled to contain her excitement. She'd thought this day would never come. Wesley's letter stated he would arrive on the twenty-second of December, and she'd marked off each day on her calendar. Thinking of Wesley had helped her to ignore the anniversary of her mother's passing. Not that her sisters had made it easy. They loved to moan and mourn. On two different occasions, within days of each other, they had invited Sophie and their father to dinner, only to go on and on in tearful conversations about their loss. It had put Father in a dreadful state and hadn't helped Sophie much, either. Still, there was always Wesley's visit to think about.

Now that the day had arrived, her anticipation climbed to new heights. Wondrously, Aunt Victoria had extended an invitation for Wesley to stay in their home. And then she'd offered for Sophie to come and stay with Amanda and Fanny during Wesley's visit. Things couldn't have been planned more perfectly had she made the arrangements herself.

She'd placed all of her gowns on the bed. Thankfully, Aunt Victoria had promised she would send Veda to pack Sophie's clothing and then have the trunks delivered to their house. She simply had no talent when it came to arranging her belongings in bags or trunks. Father had dismissed most of their servants after Mother had died, and it was only at her insistence that he had kept the housekeeper. And just last September he'd added a cook when the housekeeper announced she was unable to keep up with that duty, as well. He hadn't liked the extra expense, but even Sophie's sisters reasoned that it was the only way.

After pinning her hat in place, Sophie scribbled a note to remind her father of her whereabouts. He never remembered what she'd told him from one day to the next, and although she had mentioned Wesley's arrival on several occasions, Sophie doubted he would recall that today was the date she'd been anticipating since arriving back home.

Snow fell in fat, heavy flakes that rapidly covered the deep grooves created by the carriage wheels. The damp cold cut through her heavy cloak, and Sophie shoved her hands deep into her fur muff. In the past, she had always loved the snow, especially at Christmastime, but not now, not today. Not when Wesley was due to arrive. She didn't want anything to impede his arrival. The thought of seeing him sent a lingering warmth through her midsection. "Please don't let anything keep him away," she whispered, snuggling deeper into the cushioned carriage seat.

She'd already purchased and wrapped Christmas gifts for both Fanny and Amanda. Although the family always gathered for Christmas dinner and celebration, gift exchanges were held privately at each home. Years ago someone had declared the family far too large for such an exchange, and the practice had terminated the following year. Sophie was pleased it hadn't ceased while she was a small child, for she'd always looked forward to the pile of gifts each Christmas and thought it unfair to the young children when the tradition was stopped. Sophie had no say in such family decisions, but she, Amanda, and Fanny had vowed they would never stop exchanging gifts at Christmas and on birthdays—and they hadn't. Withdrawing her hand from her muff, she pulled the bag that contained the gifts close to her side. She hadn't entrusted that task to Veda.

Now she must decide what she would give Wesley. She'd been thinking on the matter ever since he had accepted her invitation to spend Christmas in Rochester. Until that morning, she'd had no idea what gift might please him. But when she'd been laying out the items for Veda to pack, her gaze had settled upon the beautifully framed picture of her mother, the one Sophie had kept near her bedside ever since her mother's death. Having the picture near was a comfort to Sophie. Thinking of Wesley, Sophie knew she'd cherish a picture of him and wondered if he would like one of her. With the distance that separated them, she hoped he would enjoy something that would constantly bring her to mind.

Of course, she didn't know if she would have sufficient time to have a picture taken, especially if the snow continued to fall. But she hoped to convince her cousins to accompany her into town. If all else failed, she could at least purchase a frame and write a note telling him she would sit for her photograph and mail it to him. Yes, a photograph of her would be the perfect gift. She would ask her cousins for their opinions. If they rejected her idea, Sophie would require them to furnish her with a spectacular substitute. She doubted they could think of quite so perfect a gift.

After bringing the team of horses to a halt in front of her uncle's home, the carriage driver opened the door. "Careful of your step, miss. It's slippery on this wet snow." Sophie clutched his outstretched hand in a tight hold, but the sole of her leather slipper slid from beneath her the moment her foot touched the ground. The carriage driver tightened his grasp while stretching for her other arm with his free hand. He struggled valiantly to keep her upright, but when she grappled for his free hand, her feet slipped from beneath her, and both of them tumbled into the fallen snow. They were a tangled mix of livery wear and silk gown sprawled across the sidewalk like a hideous Christmas decoration.

The driver managed to disentangle himself and, after several gallant attempts, was able to gain a foothold and maintain an upright position. "I'm so sorry, miss. I do hope your cloak protected your dress to some extent." He forced a smile while assisting her to her feet. "At least the snow is clean, and it permitted us a softer landing."

"True, but it's that very snow that caused our fall." Clinging to the driver's arm, Sophie rescued her fur muff from the snow.

"That was quite a sight, Sophie. Could you do it again? Jefferson missed it the first time." Both George and Jefferson stood on the front porch, doubled in laughter.

She leaned down, scooped up a handful of the wet snow, and deftly formed it between her hands. "Don't let me fall," she commanded the carriage driver before she circled her arm in a wide arc and hurtled the snowball at her cousins. "Perfect!" she cried when the icy sphere made a direct hit on George's leg.

He jumped and squealed in pain as the carriage driver looked back and forth between the young men on the porch and his passenger. "Shall I escort you to the front door?"

Sophie gave a nod. "Both of you go inside the house. This poor carriage driver is afraid to come any closer while you're outside."

She could see a wide grin split George's face. "I'd be pleased to come and help you up the walkway, Sophie." He took several steps toward them, and Sophie pointed a warning finger.

"You best go back into the house, or I'll be forced to report your uncivilized behavior to your father."

Jefferson cackled. "*Our* uncivilized behavior? We merely laughed at you. *You're* the one throwing snowballs."

"Go inside!" Sophie stomped her foot and once again nearly landed on the snow-covered ground. Her cousins chortled with delight while she did a quick shuffle to maintain an upright position. The driver glanced longingly toward his awaiting carriage. No doubt he'd be willing to pay her if he could escape without threat of being pummeled by a snowball.

Her cousins backed slowly toward the front door. When they eventually retreated inside, the driver retrieved Sophie's bag, containing everything except her gowns, from the carriage and then escorted her up the front steps. She handed him an additional coin from her reticule. After enduring a tumble in the snow and braving the possibility of being bombarded by snowballs from her cousins, he deserved even more, but she must save enough to purchase Wesley's gift.

The driver touched a finger to his hat and carefully made his way back to the conveyance. Already fresh snow had filled their tracks. After wiping the remains of wet snow from her coat, Sophie proceeded inside, where George and Jefferson awaited her with gleeful smiles.

"You needn't look so pleased. Both the driver and I could have been injured falling on the sidewalk."

Jefferson snorted. "Perhaps the driver. He did appear somewhat scrawny. But you, my dear cousin, have ample padding to protect you against any such injury."

"*What?*" Hands on hips, Sophie's elbows jutted forward at an angle that invited confrontation. "Are you saying I'm overly plump?"

Eyes gleaming, they shook their heads in unison. Jefferson pointed at her skirts. "I was referring to your skirts and coat, Sophie."

"I don't believe you," she said, shrugging out of her cloak and handing it to the maid, who had apparently heard the flying barbs and come scurrying to the foyer.

"Your coat is quite damp, Miss Sophie. Oh, and your gown, too. Let's go upstairs and get you out of your wet clothes before you catch your death." Minnie, Aunt Victoria's longtime maid, stepped toward the stairway with a determination that caused George and Jefferson to jump out of the way.

Sophie jabbed a finger at Jefferson's chest when she passed by. "We'll finish this discussion later," she hissed.

"Indeed we will," George replied for both of them, rubbing his leg.

Sophie didn't miss his meaning. She'd need to be on the lookout each time she left the house. George and Jefferson would likely be lying in wait with a heaping mound of snowballs. She followed Minnie to the upper hallway and into the bedroom adjacent to Amanda's room.

The maid signaled for Sophie to turn around. "Let me help you out of your gown, and I'll see that it's dried, pressed, and returned this afternoon."

"No." She wagged her head. "I have nothing else to wear. My trunks aren't to be delivered until later, and I must go out."

"You have no choice, Miss Sophie. You can't go out in these wet garments."

Sophie took a backward step. "Where is Amanda? If I force myself into one of her corsets, I should be able to fit into one of her gowns."

"She and Miss Fanny are in the music room. I'll go fetch her."

Once Minnie had gone off in search of her cousin, Sophie paced a circle in front of the fireplace. Perhaps the fire would radiate enough heat to magically dry her gown. Unfortunately, it appeared to be having little effect. How had she managed to get so wet? The carriage driver's uniform must be frozen solid. She shivered at the thought.

"Sophie!" Arms outstretched, Amanda entered the room and enveloped Sophie in a hug.

"We didn't know you'd arrived." Fanny embraced Sophie once Amanda had released her hold. "Minnie tells us you took a tumble in the snow."

"Yes, and I must go shopping before Wesley arrives. Would you fetch me one of your corsets and gowns, Amanda? One that isn't too tight." Sophie turned and stood still while Minnie began unfastening the row of tiny ivory buttons.

"I think my clothing would be the better fit," Fanny said. "Perhaps somewhat shorter than required, but you can wear one of Amanda's long cloaks, and no one will be the wiser." Fanny raced from the room and soon returned with a corset and a pink-and-gray-striped day dress. "This will work, I think."

Once out of her soggy gown, Sophie dismissed Minnie. "My cousins will help me dress. I'm certain you have matters of greater import that need your attention."

The maid draped Sophie's gown over one arm and nodded. "Indeed. Drying and pressing this gown for one. And with Veda gone to pack and fetch your clothing, I must see to her chores, as well." She shook her head and clucked *tsk-tsk* several times before leaving them alone.

While her cousins helped cinch her into the corset, Sophie elicited their opinions. They both agreed that a photograph and frame would be the perfect Christmas gift.

"Will you come with me?"

Amanda glanced out the window. "I don't know if we should go out with it snowing like this."

"This is Rochester, Amanda. Don't act as though we've never been out in the snow before. It will be fun."

Fanny quickly agreed, and soon Sophie had convinced Amanda she should join them. They discovered Maurice, one of the Broadmoor liverymen, in the kitchen enjoying a cup of coffee and a molasses cookie. He appeared none too happy over the prospect of driving them into town for their shopping foray, but they all knew he had little choice in the matter. After a final gulp of his coffee, he agreed to meet them at the front of the house in half an hour. Shoving the remainder of the cookie into his mouth, he headed out the side door toward the carriage house.

"What are the three of you up to?" George called out as they passed the large library Uncle Jonas used as his office.

"We're going—" Amanda started.

Sophie put her finger to her lips and shook her head. "I'll explain later," she whispered. Peeking around the door, she pointed upstairs. "We're going to Amanda's room to choose the dresses we plan to wear this evening."

"Is that all the three of you have to do?" He gazed at the ledgers spread across the desk.

Uncle Jonas thought both of his younger sons far too lazy and had placed George in charge of keeping books for the flour mill, the one remaining business the family still owned. And he'd charged Jefferson with overseeing the mill operation, although Jefferson spent little time at the task. Both of the young men had encouraged their father to sell the mill, but it was an asset Hamilton Broadmoor had required to remain in the family. It was, after all, a symbol of Broadmoor success. It was Grandfather's first business venture—the place that had provided enough income to build the Broadmoor family fortune and to permit future investments. Obviously Uncle Jonas thought work for the Daisy Flour Mill would mature his sons. Sophie doubted her uncle's strategy, but who could say? She had changed since meeting Wesley. Perhaps a bit of work would have a positive effect upon George and Jefferson.

"Where's Jefferson?" Sophie innocently asked George.

"He needed to go down to the mill and decided to go before the weather turned any worse. He should be back in a couple hours if you'd like to continue that snowball fight." He gave her an exaggerated wink.

She offered an apology that she hoped would clear the air. Once Wesley arrived, she certainly didn't want any difficulty with George or Jefferson.

"What was that all about?" Amanda inquired.

Sophie quickly explained the snowball melee. "I don't want him to retaliate," she admitted. "Fortunately Jefferson has left for the mill. I was afraid they would be waiting for us when we walked outdoors."

Maurice arrived with the carriage a short time later. He jumped down and hurried to the front porch to assist them. Thankfully one of the servants had been stationed at the sidewalk and was now keeping the walkway clear of snow. The three young women snuggled close together to ward off the cold.

"You know we think you quite dear," Fanny said. "Otherwise, we would never come out in this weather."

Sophie clasped Fanny's hand. "And you are both dear to me, also. What would we do without one another?"

Amanda grinned. "Remain by the fireside and keep warm?"

Their giggles soon erupted into stomach-clenching bursts of laughter. Had passersby heard them, they likely would have thought they'd all gone completely mad.

They decided they would first stop at the photographer's shop. When the carriage slowed to a stop, they wiped away their tears of laughter and attempted to assume the proper decorum.

Amanda stepped out of the carriage first. "We shouldn't be long, Maurice."

Sophie didn't comment, for she secretly desired to remain inside the shop for quite some time. If possible, she planned to arrange an immediate sitting. At least the snow had subsided, which should allay her cousins' complaints if the owner of the shop had time to photograph her. Although she would have preferred one of her own lovely gowns, Fanny's dress was very pretty, and both her cousins had agreed it was becoming, albeit an inch too short. She'd simply request a picture that wouldn't reveal the hem of her skirt.

A bell jangled above the door when they entered, and moments later a beak-nosed woman peeked around the corner of a back room and held up a finger. "I'll be with you in a moment."

Sophie arched her brows. "Do you think *she's* the photographer?"

"Why not? Women are capable of taking pictures, Sophie."

"I know, I know." Sophie gazed heavenward. She didn't want to hear another one of Amanda's equality speeches. "I merely expected a man would own the business."

Before her cousin could respond, the tall, thin woman returned to the outer room. "How may I help you?" She peered over her spectacles at the three of them.

"Is there any possibility I could sit for a photograph today?" Sophie inquired.

"Today?" Amanda gasped. "You want us to wait, when it's—"

Amanda's diatribe came to a halt when the older woman cleared her throat. "I've completed my scheduled appointments, so I could take you now, if you'd like." The photographer looked at Amanda. "If you're willing to wait?"

Amanda glanced at Fanny, who bobbed her head in agreement. "We've nothing else to do, Amanda. Besides, it's stopped snowing. I'll tell Maurice he can come inside and wait with us."

While her cousins continued to discuss the carriage driver, Sophie followed the woman into an adjacent room. The photographer arranged the room and the lighting to her satisfaction. "So I understand you want several poses. Usually I only do that when numerous family members are involved."

Sophie nodded. "Yes, I need more than one to choose from."

The woman smiled. "Very well." She sounded as though she were indulging a small child.

With each pose, she directed Sophie to smile, tip her chin, or cock her head to the side. Although the photographer didn't appear overly pleased with Sophie's performance during the process, once they'd completed the sitting, she declared the pictures would be excellent.

"You'll have a difficult time deciding exactly which one you want," she remarked when they returned to the outer office.

Maurice stood inside the front door while Fanny and Amanda sat near the front window flipping through a photograph sample book. "If you're ready, we can go shopping for a picture frame," Sophie said.

"If *we're* ready?" Amanda buttoned her double-breasted wool coat and brushed the fox trim into place. She motioned to Maurice, and the four of them returned to the waiting carriage.

"Do you think the pictures will be to your liking?" Fanny excitedly inquired. "I do wish I had a photograph of Michael to keep by my bedside." She stared out the carriage window. "He must be so very cold," she mused before turning back toward Sophie.

Sophie scooted closer to Fanny and grasped her gloved hand. "I'm certain Michael is fine. After years of living on Broadmoor Island through the winter, he's used to cold conditions. Perhaps you should consider having a photograph made of you for Michael."

Fanny shook her head. "My hope is that he will return home and we'll be married by June. I don't even know if a photograph would reach him before he leaves the Yukon. The mail moves slowly and is sometimes lost. I never even know if he's received my letters."

They stopped at the mercantile and assured Maurice they wouldn't be there for long, but Sophie doubted the driver believed them. Their shopping trips sometimes continued for hours.

CHAPTER 12

After several stops to examine the latest fabrics and lace, the three Broadmoor cousins headed off in search of the perfect photograph frame. "I believe silver would be nice, don't you think?" Sophie inquired.

Fanny shrugged; Amanda appeared noncommittal. "I'm not certain. Let's see what they have before you set your mind upon something," her older cousin replied. "Oh, look at these brooches." Amanda picked up one of the pins. "This is quite lovely, don't you think?"

"Personally, I prefer this one."

Amanda wheeled around. "Dr. Carstead!"

He grinned. "Still looking forward to working with me? Or have you decided shopping is more to your liking?"

Amanda's smile vanished. "It appears you, too, enjoy shopping. Does that mean you are neglecting your patients?"

The question appeared to fluster the doctor. His face actually flushed a bit as he stammered to answer. "I . . . ah . . . I never . . . neglect my patients."

Sophie elbowed Amanda and nodded toward the west side of the store. "Fanny and I are going to look at picture frames. Come join us when you've finished visiting with Dr. Carstead."

Without giving her any opportunity to object, the two of them hurried off. Sophie rounded one of the large pilasters, and while Fanny hovered behind her, she peeked around the column and watched her older cousin. She glanced over her shoulder. "They're still talking." Turning back, she continued to observe the twosome. "She's smiling. He is, too," she reported. "I think Amanda may like him more than she's indicated. And he is very nice looking—although he looks to be even older than my Wesley. Still, they'd make a nice couple, don't you think?"

"Do come along. We shouldn't be spying on them." Fanny yanked on her cousin's coat.

"We're not really spying. I mean they're standing right there in the middle of the store. Look at his rich brown hair. It's a perfect contrast to Amanda's blond."

Fanny looked around the pilaster. "He certainly is tall."

"Yes. I think that works well for Amanda. They seem very nicely suited. Of course Uncle Jonas would never approve of her marrying a doctor."

Fanny shook her head. "Enough of this." She pulled Sophie along with her. "No one is talking about marriage. In fact, I don't think Amanda likes him in the least. It's his medical degree that interests her. If she can increase her knowledge before she goes off to school, it will help her immensely. Even though women are admitted to medical school, the instructors still consider female students to be inferior. At least that's what Amanda says." Fanny looped arms with Sophie, and the two of them continued through the store. "Besides, I don't think Amanda is even considering marriage."

"Bah! Every woman considers marriage. Amanda may be consumed with thoughts of this cause or that, but eventually she'll want a husband. After all, you and I will both be married, and it would be awkward if she were to remain single."

"Not necessarily," Fanny said, shaking her head. "Not everyone is meant for marriage."

"Maybe not, but when you look like Amanda, it can't be helped. She'll marry. And why not marry a man who shares the same interest? A doctor would be perfect. He'll always have employment, and if she gets ill, he can fix her with a cure."

Fanny laughed. "Sounds like you've got it all planned out."

Sophie glanced over her shoulder but could no longer see Amanda and the doctor. "I don't have it planned, but it would please me greatly to see Amanda as happy as we are."

Fanny nodded. "Yes. That would please me, too. Maybe we could have a triple wedding when Michael comes home next summer."

"Oh goodness, I don't intend to wait that long," Sophie declared.

"But you must. Even if you break with society and become engaged right away, you have to wait at least that long before marrying. A year, or two would be even better."

Sophie yanked her to a halt and pointed across several glass-topped counters. "Over there. I see picture frames." She didn't give her cousin time to object. This time she was the one tugging on Fanny's sleeve.

"You're purposely trying to change the subject."

Sophie looked at her and smiled. "Yes. Yes I am. Now be a dear and let me. Oh, look at that one." She pointed to a frame that sat nestled in a piece of red velvet inside the glass case. "Isn't it lovely?"

Fanny wrinkled her nose. "Not for a man. These are all much too fancy. Perhaps you should simply purchase a small bronze easel to hold the picture. The photographer will insert the picture in a simple cardboard frame, won't she? I think an easel would prove more practical."

Sophie was making her purchase when Amanda joined them some time later, a faint blush pinking her cheeks. "He's awfully handsome," Sophie said.

"Who?" Amanda asked, arching her brows.

Fanny and Sophie giggled. "You know who!" Sophie nudged Amanda and winked. "Dr. Carstead. I believe you're just like Fanny and me: you're falling in love."

"That's absolutely absurd. He's quite ancient, much too old for me. Not only that, he is arrogant, proud, pigheaded, and lacks civility. In addition, he—"

"I didn't realize you'd made note of all my many attributes, Miss Broadmoor. Now I've completely forgotten what it was I came to say. I suppose it's my old age and all." Dr. Carstead touched his forehead in a mock salute, said, "Good day, ladies," and walked off.

"Why didn't you tell me he was approaching?" Amanda hissed.

"Why should we have warned you?" Fanny asked. "If you don't care for him, what difference does it make?"

"I'll be working with him every day, so it does matter." The clerk was passing Sophie's package across the counter. "If you're done with your shopping, let's go. I've endured enough embarrassment for one day."

Maurice was pacing in front of the mercantile when they stepped outside. He sighed deeply, his breath creating a puff of white air in front of his face. "I thought you would never return." He pointed to the clock that hung above the doorway to the store. "I am supposed to be at the train station to pick up Mr. Hedrick. We must depart now or we will be late."

"But I want to go home," Amanda argued.

Sophie grasped her by the arm and pulled her toward the carriage. "Didn't you hear Maurice? I don't want Wesley to think he isn't welcome. We must all three go to greet him."

They arrived at the station as the passengers were disembarking the train. Her cousins elected to remain behind, but Sophie hurried after Maurice toward the platform. When she finally spotted Wesley, she waved her handkerchief overhead. He didn't appear concerned that no one had been waiting when he stepped down from the train. Then again, she shouldn't have worried. Wesley was accustomed to traveling. If no one had appeared at the station, he would have likely hailed a carriage and come to the house.

Sophie rushed toward him. She'd expected a warm embrace, but when she drew near, he held her at arm's length. When she frowned, he whispered, "I don't want you to be the topic of any gossip." He motioned toward his baggage. With his usual deftness, Maurice grabbed the luggage from one of the heavy wood and metal carts and led them back inside the station. Fanny and Amanda were waiting near the front doors and greeted him warmly, although Sophie thought his return greeting somewhat stiff and formal.

He's likely weary from traveling, she told herself. *Besides, he doesn't know them well and is certain to feel somewhat uncomfortable surrounded by three young ladies.* The carriage ride home was awkward. Although Sophie did her best to act the perfect hostess, the conversation was stilted and lacking. Both of her cousins thought Wesley too old for her. And though Sophie disagreed, she worried Wesley might concur if she didn't impress him with her maturity. She was, however, thankful when the carriage ride ended.

"I do hope you'll find this a memorable Christmas," she whispered as he helped her out of the carriage.

He returned her smile. "I'm sure it will be even more than I could hope for."

Wesley had no more than uttered the words when they were bombarded with a hail of snowballs from the upper balcony of the house. Fanny and Amanda shrieked and hastened toward the house. Forgetting her vow to remain mature throughout Wesley's visit, Sophie grabbed a handful of snow and lobbed a snowball toward George and Jefferson. She knew she'd met with success when Jefferson let out a yelp. Encouraged by her triumph, she grabbed another handful of snow and worked it between her gloved hands.

She'd prepared for her throw when Wesley grasped her arm. "I do enjoy your jovial spirit, Sophie, but snowball fights at your age?" He glanced at the front porch, where her two cousins had taken shelter out of harm's way.

"I don't know what I was thinking," she muttered. She waved her handkerchief in the air. "I give up. We have a guest," she shouted.

George still held a snowball in one hand, but Jefferson shook his head, and the two of them retreated inside while Wesley and Sophie hurried to the front porch.

"And those young men would be?" Wesley asked.

"Amanda's brothers and my cousins, George and Jefferson Broadmoor. They are quite immature for their age."

"I must remember to compliment your aunt on the lovely decorations." Wesley nodded toward the boughs of evergreen tucked along the railings of the upper and lower porches that fronted the house. Under her aunt's direction, the servants had secured the greenery with deep red bows and an occasional cluster of silver bells. A giant evergreen wreath, adorned with matching bows, decorated the front door.

"We'll be decorating the tree on Christmas Eve. I'm so pleased you'll be here to celebrate with me." She tightened her hold on his arm, feeling as though she could never let him leave her side again.

Sophie rolled over in bed and hugged the coverlet close. The bright early morning sunshine reflected off the blanket of snow that covered the porch roof and danced along the frosted bedroom windows. She snuggled deeper beneath the quilted covers until the cobwebs cleared from her mind.

Wesley! She glanced at the clock on the bedroom mantel and immediately wondered if he'd already gone downstairs for breakfast. Though the idea of throwing aside the covers was unappealing, she didn't want to miss even one minute with him. They'd had little time alone since he'd arrived, and today would likely prove no different. There would be great fuss and commotion as each of the Broadmoor relatives arrived to visit and then gather around the festive dining table to partake of the annual Christmas Eve supper. She hoped there'd be none of the usual bickering and arguments that seemed to ensue each time the family congregated. A celebration of Christ's birth or not, the family always managed to find something over which to argue on Christmas Eve. No doubt Wesley would be appalled. The bantering hadn't particularly bothered her in the past: she'd grown up with the familial bickering. In fact, Sophie had contributed her share of it in the past. But this evening would be different, for she'd never before wanted to impress a man.

She rang for Veda. The maid's swift appearance startled her; she must have been nearby helping one of her cousins. "Good morning, Veda. Do you have time to assist me?"

"Of course. I've already helped Miss Amanda with her dress and styled her hair, and Miss Fanny went downstairs an hour ago."

Why was she always the last one to rise? Wesley would think her lazy. She should have asked Veda to awaken her earlier. "And Mr. Hedrick? Have you seen him this morning?"

"Oh yes, Miss Sophie. He was up several hours ago and requested one of the carriages be brought around for him."

Sophie felt as though she'd taken a blow to the midsection. Her stomach lurched and then plummeted. "Did he say where he was going? Did he have his baggage with him? Was he angry? Did some family member offend him?"

Veda stared at her wide-eyed. "I can only answer one question at a time, Miss Sophie, and I don't even remember all that you've asked me. He didn't appear angry. As for his luggage, I don't think so, but I didn't see him depart. What else did you ask?"

"Never mind, Veda. Just help me dress. Quickly!"

Veda didn't have an opportunity to properly fashion her hair, for Sophie wouldn't permit her sufficient time. The maid was still attempting to shove pins into Sophie's hair as she descended the steps. Sophie signaled for her to stop. "Once I discover why and where Mr. Hedrick has gone, you may fashion my hair. In the meantime, please stop jabbing those pins at me. One misstep and I'll have a hairpin stuck in my ear. I don't believe that would prove a pleasant experience for either of us."

The warning carried enough of a threat for the maid to shove the remaining pins into an apron pocket. "Just let me know when you're ready for me, Miss Sophie." Veda disappeared while Sophie continued toward the dining room. Only Amanda and Aunt Victoria remained at the table. They'd finished their breakfast and were making some sort of list.

"Good morning," she greeted them.

"Good morning, dear," her aunt replied. "There's tea and coffee on the sideboard. Ring for Betsy and let her know what you'd like for breakfast."

Sophie poured a cup of tea, but she didn't plan to ring for Betsy or order breakfast until she knew where Wesley had gone. She sat down by her cousin and nodded toward the list. "You two appear busy."

"Just going over the last-minute seating arrangements for dinner this evening." Her aunt glanced over the top of her reading glasses. "We have several extras, and I want to be certain I have everyone on the diagram."

"Do ensure that Wesley is seated next to me," Sophie said.

Her aunt nodded. "Well, of course. And I've seated Dr. Carstead to your left, Sophie, then Amanda—"

"Dr. Carstead? Who invited him?" Amanda reached for the piece of paper.

"Your uncle Quincy. I do think it was a kind gesture on his part. The doctor is alone for the holidays, and Quincy thought it would be a nice way of thanking him for providing medical treatment at the Home for the Friendless."

Sophie scooted to the edge of her chair. Before mother and daughter ventured any further into their discussion of Dr. Carstead, Sophie wanted to gather information regarding Wesley's whereabouts. "Have you seen Wesley this morning?"

"He said he had business to attend to in Rochester but will return in ample time for the evening's festivities."

Sophie wilted. She had hoped to spend the entire day with him. He'd never mentioned any business dealings in Rochester, but then they'd never spoken about such matters. Perhaps he'd gone to purchase her a special gift. She warmed at the thought. That must be it. And he wouldn't want to mention such a thing to Aunt Victoria. Could he have gone shopping for an engagement ring? Last night he'd again spoken of how much he cared for her.

Paul stepped down from the carriage outside the Broadmoor residence. It was nearing four o'clock. His invitation had requested he spend an afternoon of visiting followed by Christmas Eve supper with the Broadmoor family. Although he had hoped to arrive much earlier, the Christmas party at the Home for the Friendless had continued longer than expected. At one o'clock, Paul had insisted Quincy go and join his family. "I'll hail a carriage the minute the party has ended," Paul had said. He'd anticipated a two o'clock departure—at the latest.

The children, however, had been anxious to have him read the books they'd received as Christmas gifts, peel their oranges, or help them pop corn. And he'd been unable to refuse any of their requests. Thankfully the Broadmoor supper wasn't scheduled to begin until seven o'clock. He'd have more than sufficient time to drink eggnog and visit with the family prior to supper.

Another carriage came to a halt in front of the house, and Paul waited a moment, certain he'd know any visitor to the Broadmoor home. He pulled his collar tight around his neck and waited until a man who appeared to be several years his senior approached. He carried a small bag in one hand. If Paul had ever met the man, he couldn't remember. He extended his hand. "I'm Paul Medford. I work with Quincy Broadmoor at the Home for the Friendless."

The man grasped Paul's gloved hand in a firm hold. "Wesley Hedrick, from New York City," he said.

"So you're the man Sophie tells me she met while in England." The two men continued up the walk. "I understand you're considering becoming a benefactor at the Home for the Friendless," he added. "I'm pleased to meet you, Mr. Hedrick."

When they stepped onto the porch, a butler opened the front door before either of them could knock. Paul removed his coat and hat, and handed them to the butler. Mr. Hedrick did the same after tucking the small bag into his pocket. Then the two men stepped into the room, which appeared to be overflowing with women and children.

"Rather large group, isn't it?" Wesley commented.

"Follow me. It may not be quite so crowded or noisy in the other room." Paul threaded through the crowd but discovered the massive sitting room even more congested than the receiving parlor. "Perhaps the library," he said.

There were only a few men in the library, clustered in small groups. Paul located a spot near the fire. "I was hoping we would have some time to talk. I'm anxious to hear about your philanthropic work, Mr. Hedrick. Quincy tells me that you have worked extensively helping the poor and orphaned."

"It's true that I have done my best to help the less fortunate. I find it a genuine thrill to have the resources to lend a helping hand to those in need." Wesley took a sip of the eggnog one of the maids offered. "And please call me Wesley. I feel as though we know each other already. Mr. Broadmoor's letters are filled with accolades for your work."

"That's good to hear. He hasn't told me quite so much about you. I'm anxious to hear exactly what you've done—what has proved successful and what hasn't. I'm always interested to know how others have been able to touch lives and meet both physical and spiritual needs."

"Oh, well . . . uh . . . I'm sure nothing I've done would begin to compare with your work. And I uh . . . um . . . don't think you'd find any of my ideas new. I wouldn't consider anything I've done either new or different. No, not at all."

"You're being much too modest. Quincy did tell me you began your work in New York City. Please elaborate. I'm truly interested in the details."

Wesley gulped the remainder of his eggnog and placed the cup on the silver tray of a passing maid. "I saw much suffering in New York City. There are many destitute sections of the city where immigrants are huddled together in horrid squalor—unbelievable sickness and no medical aid. Very sad."

Paul nodded. "Indeed, very sad. And how is it you helped in that regard? What did you find the most beneficial to aid those suffering folks?"

"Well, my . . . ah . . . background doesn't lend itself to the practical applications of those of someone like yourself. I donated money to several groups attempting to help, but then I was in England a great deal of the time. While I was married to my dear wife, we did our best to help there. Again, mostly financial. Of course, we also had many wealthy friends and encouraged them to give, as well."

Paul studied the man. Mr. Hedrick was likely at least ten years his senior and obviously a man of wealth. Yet he seemed at odds to explain anything of substance regarding his charitable work. Most wealthy men who donated to the Home for the Friendless wanted to know exactly how and where their money was being spent. They wanted to see results and often offered suggestions and direction.

"I'm surprised you never insisted upon any sort of accountability or report regarding your donated funds. How did you measure the success of an organization and decide if you wanted to continue supporting it?"

"I do realize, ah . . . think you're right on that account. I have decided my lack of involvement was a definite shortcoming in the past. Wi-with those other charities," Wesley stammered. "In fact, that's one of the reasons I came to Rochester. I want to be involved in the Home for the Friendless. If I'm going to contribute financial aid, I want to know more about the operation of the Home."

Before Paul could question him further, Sophie arrived and grasped his arm. "And I'm going to need to know more about my future wife, as well," he said only loud enough for Paul to hear. He offered him a wink and a sly smile.

Sophie gazed into his eyes. "What did you say? You two seem to be sharing secrets."

"It was nothing, my dear. Nothing at all."

Paul hadn't liked the man much before, but now he only wished to punch him squarely in the nose. He didn't like feeling this way and quickly offered up a prayer that his spirit might find peace about the matter. There was something, however, that simply didn't set well with him. Hedrick didn't appear to be anything other than what he professed to be, yet Paul couldn't shake the discomfort.

"Maybe it's simply because he's with Sophie—planning a marriage," he murmured. That alone would be enough.

Christmas Eve dinner evolved into the usual chaotic event that they'd all come to expect. Thankfully, there had been no genuine arguments, mostly children crying and siblings bickering with one another throughout the meal. Sophie had hoped Aunt Victoria would wait to decorate the tree until some of the family members had either gone home or retired for the night. Instead, she told the servants to open the boxed ornaments immediately after they had completed their meal. "The children will enjoy helping," she'd said.

The children had enjoyed fighting over every ornament that came out of the boxes. When the task was finally completed, Jonas asked Paul to read the Christmas story from the Bible—since he was a "man of the cloth." In the past, Grandfather Broadmoor had performed the Bible reading, so it seemed odd that someone who was not a member of the family would be given the honor. But Paul had read eloquently; he even managed to maintain the children's interest until the end. And they'd been delighted to participate in his question-and-answer time after he finished reading. Even the smaller children were excited to tell what they knew about the birth of Jesus.

As Paul prepared to leave, Wesley complimented him on his earlier discussion with the children. "Thank you, Wesley. My work at the Home has given me ample opportunity to work with children. By the way, I was wondering if you would like to come and take a tour of the Home on Monday morning."

Wesley nodded. "Yes, of course. I would welcome the opportunity."

Sophie continued to maintain a tight hold on Wesley's arm as he thanked Paul, and the two of them bid him good-night.

"I thought we might find someplace where I could give you my Christmas gift in private," Sophie whispered.

"Where would you suggest?"

Sophie hesitated for a moment. With so many family members staying for the night, locating a place where they could be alone would be nearly impossible. "I know! We can meet in the children's playroom. They've all gone to bed. So long as we leave the door open, there will be no question of impropriety."

He smiled. "Then give me enough time to go upstairs and retrieve your gift."

Her heart beat in quick time. All day she had longed to ask where he'd gone earlier in the day, but she remained silent. Christmas was, after all, a time of secrets, and she didn't want to ruin any surprise Wesley might have planned for her. She hoped he would be delighted with her gift. She had returned to the photographer's the day after her sitting, and they'd reached a monetary agreement. Sophie would present Wesley with both her picture and the easel, and she hoped he would present her with an engagement ring.

The two of them met in the children's playroom a short time later and were careful to keep the door ajar. She eyed the package he held in his hand and was pleased when she noted it was a tiny box. "You first," she said, handing him her gift. He opened the easel first and appeared somewhat confused, although he thanked her profusely. "You'll understand when you open the other package," she explained.

He tore off the paper and smiled broadly. "I couldn't be more pleased," he said. "How did you know?" With a gentle touch, he brushed his lips across her fingertips. "Thank you, Sophie. I shall always cherish this photograph."

He handed her his gift. Slowly she untied the ribbon and then loosened the paper, careful not to rip it. This was his first Christmas gift to her, and she wanted to save both the ribbon and paper. She sighed when she saw the black velvet case resting inside the wrapping paper. Was it? Could it be? Her heart raced in triple time as she lifted the lid.

Sophie bit her lower lip as she stared inside. Tiny diamonds winked at her. "They're lovely." Her voice caught in her throat, and she could say no more. She snapped the lid closed and kept her gaze fixed upon the wrapping paper while she carefully folded it into a minute square.

"Here, let's take them from the box."

"Not now. I'll remove them tomorrow." She jumped to her feet. "I should go upstairs before Amanda or Fanny comes searching for me. Thank you for the lovely gift, Wesley."

He smiled broadly. "I'll expect you to wear them tomorrow." He leaned forward and kissed her forehead. "Good night, dear Sophie. And merry Christmas."

"Merry Christmas to you, too," she replied. Her composure remained intact until she was safely inside the bedroom. She leaned against the bedroom door, and tears flowed down her cheeks. Diamond eardrops rather than an engagement ring. He obviously wasn't yet prepared to marry her.

Fanny sat at the window and watched the snow falling. The house was silent—dawn just minutes away—but it was Christmas Day and everyone would sleep for a time yet.

She touched the frosted glass and thought of Michael. All of her thoughts were of Michael. She couldn't help but wonder where he was and what he might be doing this Christmas morning. Clutching his letter to her breast, Fanny fought back tears as she thought of all that she'd lost over the last year.

Grandfather was gone now, and not only him, but the house. Her home. All her childhood memories were lodged there, and now the estate belonged to Daniel Irwin.

Sighing, Fanny took her hand from the window and touched it to her face. She tried to imagine that Michael, too, might be feeling a chill upon his face.

Somehow holding the letter in one hand and feeling the icy cold upon her face with the other allowed Fanny to believe herself in the Yukon. At least for a fleeting moment.

"Lord, it's so hard to bear this time of waiting. I miss Michael so much. I pray that you allow the time to pass quickly."

Fanny smiled as she remembered times when as soon as Christmas had passed, she would tell her grandparents how she wished that it could instantly be summer.

"Do not wish your life away," Grandfather would tell her. *"None of us know the number of days we are allotted. It would be foolish to discard any of them."*

She sighed again. "I suppose he was right, Lord. Still, I can't help but think that trading this winter and next spring for Michael's return would be worth the loss of time. Even one day spent in his company would be better than a hundred here alone."

CHAPTER 13

MONDAY, DECEMBER 27, 1897

Sophie's father arrived at the front door of Uncle Jonas's home early Monday morning as she and Wesley bundled for the cold. She detected the look of surprise when her father saw her donning her coat. "Where are you off to so early, my dear?"

"Why, I'm coming with you and Wesley. I wouldn't consider remaining here while you take him on a tour of the Home."

Her father tipped his head to the side. She could see confusion register in his eyes.

"But you never—"

"Don't you worry about my time, Father. I truly want to come along with the two of you." She hoped her frown would quell any further discussion of the subject.

He shrugged and waved them forward. "The carriage is waiting."

The snow crunched beneath the carriage wheels as they traveled the snow-blanketed streets, and Sophie scooted closer to Wesley. While the men discussed the assets and liabilities of the Home, the current programs, and the new ideas her father hoped to initiate, Sophie permitted her mind to wander. She had little interest in any of it, yet she wouldn't want to disappoint Wesley. From what she'd learned, he was passionate about aiding the needy and had donated a great deal of money to a variety of charities. She wouldn't begrudge her father a bit of Wesley's time or his fortune. One day she hoped to share in both.

"Here we are," her father announced.

Wesley helped her down from the carriage, and the three of them walked the short distance to the front door of the Home.

"This is the reception area, where we must first gain information from each person who seeks our assistance," her father explained.

The room was small but clean and bright. Crisp curtains hung at the two windows, and chairs were arranged in rows—most of them already occupied by those waiting their turn to receive food or medical care. A young boy sitting on his mother's lap barked a deep croupy cough. The flush of his cheeks resembled the deep shade of summer beets, and Sophie wondered if he might die. She retrieved a handkerchief from her reticule and covered her mouth. Whatever the boy suffered from was likely contagious. Did Amanda truly realize the disease and infection she would encounter in this place? Her cousin wasn't to meet Dr. Carstead here at the Home until tomorrow morning. Sophie would have to warn her against such folly.

They stopped in her father's office long enough to remove their coats and had just begun to make their way out of the room when Paul rushed in. "I'm glad you've finally arrived, Quincy. You're needed across the hall to meet with Mr. Wilfred. Did you forget?"

Quincy slapped his palm to his forehead. "How could I forget? Please forgive me, Wesley, but it's imperative I attend this meeting. I'll rejoin you as soon as possible." He grabbed some papers from the corner of his desk. "I promised Wesley a tour of the Home, Paul. Would you be so kind?"

"Indeed. Take your time. If I can't answer Wesley's questions, we'll make note of them, and you can respond after your meeting." Paul swept back his straight brown hair in a casual manner, then brushed his hand over his brown wool coat. "I'm hardly dressed for a formal presentation, so I ask that you forgive me."

"Nonsense. Your work here is the focus, not your attire," Wesley replied.

"That's right," Sophie said, forcing a smile. Paul met her eyes and pierced her with a stare. She refused to be intimidated and clutched Wesley's arm tightly. "Wesley's nature dictates that he do what he can for the poor and despised. Just as Father does."

"I see," Paul said, his gaze never leaving her face.

Sophie quickly turned away to focus on the room around her. This place had stolen her father's attention and love. It seemed only fitting she learn more about her rival.

The cracked plaster along one edge of the wall caught her eye. She would have preferred to reschedule their visit rather than have Paul conduct the tour.

But the decision had already been made, and to voice a complaint would appear rude. Though she cared little what Paul might think, she wouldn't want Wesley to think her impolite.

They marched down the narrow hall single file. When they entered a large dormitory-style room, Sophie grasped Wesley's arm again. "This is where the women and some of the children sleep at night," she told him. "They also—"

"I didn't realize you were so familiar with the operation, Sophie. Perhaps you'd like to lead the tour, and I'll listen. I'm always prepared to learn something new," Paul said.

Sophie felt the heat rise in her neck. Although her father had talked of nothing else since first opening the doors of the Home for the Friendless, she'd listened little and had seldom been inside the building. She noted the glint in Paul's eye. He was obviously relishing her discomfort. Granted, she'd been acting the know-it-all, but he had no right to embarrass her in front of Wesley.

Regaining her composure, she forced her lips into a demure smile. "Absolutely not, Paul. I've been traveling, and I know you and my father have been working tirelessly. I'm certain there have been many changes."

He shook his head. "No, not really. We haven't had sufficient funding to make the changes we've discussed just yet, so you are welcome to—"

"Please continue. I *insist*." Sophie clenched her jaw until it ached. Paul was definitely enjoying her discomfort. Thankfully, he didn't force her to plead any further. Instead, he took up where she'd ended, going on to describe the housing arrangements for the temporary residents of the Home.

"We have much more we'd like to accomplish. With additional funds, we hope to develop ways to teach new skills and better equip these folks to earn a living. Most of them want to work, but they simply can't find employment or don't have the proper skills or references. Of course, the widows and orphans have special needs of their own."

Sophie sighed with relief when her father returned a short time later and completed the tour. They didn't see Paul again until they were preparing to depart. He stood in one of the side rooms, apparently occupied with helping someone. To Sophie's surprise he was laughing and talking to an older gentleman, all the while helping him button his shirt and secure his tie. Sophie thought at first Paul was rather ill-mannered to ramble on and on, but then she realized something. He was purposefully keeping the old man occupied with his story to keep him from being embarrassed about having to receive help. She was mesmerized by the scene, but for the life of her she couldn't understand why. Not two feet away her father and Wesley were deep in discussion, but Sophie couldn't pull her gaze away from Paul and the old man.

Laughing, Paul reached out and shook the old man's hand. The man smiled and tottered off toward the end of the room. Then Paul turned and caught

Sophie watching him. She felt her cheeks flush as he moved toward her, but he seemed unconcerned that she had observed him.

"Ah, here you are, Paul. Mr. Hedrick and Sophie were just preparing to leave," Sophie's father announced.

"I'm glad I had a chance to say good-bye. I hope you found satisfaction in our establishment," Paul said.

"Very much so," Wesley answered. "I thought it a fine example of what can be offered to the less fortunate."

Paul shook hands with Wesley. "I hope you'll come again."

He escorted them to the reception area, and for a moment, Sophie thought Paul might follow them out the door. He was obviously quite interested in Wesley, for she'd never heard Paul ask so many questions.

Why must he torment me? It's almost as if he hopes to interfere in my time with Wesley. But why? Why must Paul be so—

"I don't believe you heard what Paul said, Sophie." Her father's voice jarred Sophie from her thoughts.

"No, I'm sorry. My mind was on all that we'd just seen."

Her father smiled. "Paul was suggesting that perhaps given your desire to help the poor, you might want to come here more regularly. Maybe run the interview desk."

Sophie looked at Wesley and then at Paul, whose amused expression seemed to challenge her to answer. Sophie was used to dealing with pushy people, however. She could very well handle Paul Medford.

"I think I might be better qualified to encourage the giving of donations from some of our acquaintances and friends, Father. A number of holiday parties are being held, and I believe I can influence our social equals to consider this charity." She smiled sweetly at Paul and even batted her eyelashes just a bit for effect.

"There are many in your family and society who are capable of giving money," Paul countered, "but not so many are willing to give of their time. I thought given your great interest in the Home, you might enjoy working with the people face-to-face." His smile was now more of a smirk.

Sophie started to answer, but it was Wesley who championed her cause. "I hardly think it safe for a lady of Sophie's status to work here in the Home for the Friendless. There are too many . . . well . . . of lesser fortune who might take advantage of her good nature and sweet spirit. I would hate to see her hurt."

"Her father and I would be here to see to her safety."

Wesley shook his head in disapproval. "But that would take you away from the needs of the very poor you seek to aid. It would prove most inefficient—of this I am convinced."

Sophie leaned against Wesley's arm and threw Paul a self-satisfied look. In that moment, she'd never been more in love with Wesley Hedrick. He was truly her knight in shining armor.

A short time later Quincy strolled into Paul's office and dropped into one of the wooden chairs. He rubbed his hands together. "This is altogether exciting, don't you think?"

"Has he given you a commitment of funds?"

"Not yet, but he will." Quincy tapped his foot on the hardwood floor. "He appeared particularly interested in the training program and the addition to the medical facilities he said you'd mentioned earlier."

Paul scooted forward in his chair. "Did he offer any ideas of his own? He seemed somewhat reluctant to divulge much about the organizations he'd worked with in New York and England."

Quincy rubbed his jaw. "We didn't go into details. I don't see the need. Every organization operates differently. Wesley did mention a bit about his dealings in New York City. He tells me the charity that has become dearest to his heart is the Indigent Harbor Society, a group that assists in relocating and assisting homeless widows and children of deceased sailors."

Paul arched his brows. His mother had volunteered at the Indigent Harbor Society for many years. In fact, for the past several years she'd taken charge of the Seafarers' Ball to raise money for the organization. He'd heard her mention the names of many influential men who had donated money to that organization. Strange that his mother had never spoken Mr. Hedrick's name.

"I believe your daughter has become dearest to his heart, as well," Paul said with a frown.

"You sound as if you disapprove." Quincy looked at Paul with a confused expression. "Is there a reason you should find yourself at odds with this man? Has he acted out of line with Sophie?"

"I have no way of knowing. I've not observed anything overly inappropriate, but they have only just met, and already it's said that they are considering marriage."

Quincy shook his head. "Hedrick has not asked for her hand, although he did give her an expensive pair of earrings for Christmas. I know Sophie cares deeply for him, but I believe they are simply exploring each other's company." Quincy turned his attention to the papers on his desk, and Paul knew there would be little else said on the matter.

"Let us hope they show restraint in how well they explore each other," Paul muttered.

"I'm telling you that you're making a mistake." Sophie entered the parlor, shucked her coat, and plopped down beside Amanda in the parlor. "There's time to rethink your decision before morning."

Amanda gave her cousin a sidelong glance. "I have already given it sufficient thought. You know I'm determined to dedicate my life to medicine. Working with Dr. Carstead is an excellent way for me to learn before I attend medical school."

"You cannot believe the illness I saw this morning—why, there was a little boy who sat in the waiting room with the croup, or perhaps it was tuberculosis." Sophie clapped a hand to her mouth. "I covered my mouth as soon as he began to cough. I've been worried ever since. What if he infected me?" She pointed a finger at her cousin. "You'll be around those people all day long—and you won't be able to cover your mouth, either. You're certain to become ill." She shivered.

Amanda patted her cousin on the shoulder. "I appreciate your concern, but you must remember that doctors and nurses have been caring for ill people for many years. Some of the books I've read say that it actually helps build one's immunity when working with the sick on a regular basis."

"Oh, I don't believe such a thing! That is pure nonsense somebody has propagated in order to entice people to care for the sick and infirmed." A curl dropped across Sophie's forehead, and she brushed it aside. "Please reconsider your decision, Amanda. If something should happen to you while you're working at the Home for the Friendless, I don't think I could ever forgive my father."

"My medical training has nothing to do with Uncle Quincy. I doubt he even knows of my arrangement with Dr. Carstead, so you need not concern yourself. Moreover, I have no intention of becoming ill. Now tell me, what did Wesley think of the Home. And where is he?"

Sophie moved the needlepoint cushions to the far end of the divan and scooted closer to her cousin. "Wesley is extremely interested, which is both good and bad."

Curious, Amanda leaned closer and cupped her chin in her palm. "How so?"

"Good, because I think he will spend more time in Rochester, and bad, because I grow weary of hearing about the Home for the Friendless from my father. All who come to visit can speak of nothing else. That's one of the reasons I enjoy being here at your house. I have the benefit of having you and Fanny close at hand. Here, the conversation entails more than the plight of the homeless or the prospect of finding a new donor."

"Right. We discuss weighty issues such as the latest hairstyles or the recent arrival of fabric at Mrs. Needham's Dressmaking Shop." Amanda giggled. "Did Wesley remain at the Home?"

Sophie shook her head. "He said your father invited him to the men's club for a late lunch, and then he had several business matters needing his atten-tion." Sophie tightened her lips into a pout. "I had hoped he would spend the entire day with me."

"You must remember that he's not a college boy home on Christmas vaca-tion. He has obligations to fulfill. Business seems to come first with older men."

Sophie curled her lip. "You make him sound ancient. He's not so old. I think he's quite perfect." She jumped up from the divan and tossed her coat over her arm. "I'm going upstairs to decide what I'll wear for dinner tonight, but do consider what I've told you about caring for those sick people."

"Ah, I was beginning to wonder if you were going to appear, Miss Broadmoor."

Amanda instinctively looked around the reception room of the Home for the Friendless, hoping to locate a clock. Seeing none, she pointed to Dr. Carstead's watch fob. "Please check the time. You said I should arrive at nine o'clock."

He didn't make any attempt to remove the watch from his pocket. "Did I? Hmm. Strange, since I always arrive promptly at eight o'clock. You're certain?" His dark hazel eyes held her captive.

"I, well . . . yes, I distinctly . . ."

"Do you remember or don't you, Miss Broadmoor?" He waved her forward without awaiting her response. "One of the first rules of medicine: be certain before you speak and then don't waver. Indecision breeds fear among patients, and they are already frightened when they seek the aid of a physician. You may hang your coat in my office."

Amanda squared her shoulders and marched into his office. She may have failed Dr. Carstead's first test, but she'd pass any further hurdles placed in her path. He wouldn't be able to fault her attire, for she'd chosen an old frock, knowing her dress might be ruined. He looked up from the paper he'd retrieved from his desk as she withdrew an apron from a bag she'd carried with her.

"I thought it would be wise to have an apron." She pointed to the tapestry bag. "I also brought several books for any of the young children you might need to treat." When he didn't respond, she said, "Their mothers can read to them while they wait, to help pass the time."

He grunted. "The apron was a wise decision. As for the books?" He shrugged. "Most of the people we see in this clinic cannot read."

There was little doubt he was attempting to thwart her enthusiasm. Well, he'd have to do better than a few offhand remarks about tardiness and deci-sion making if he planned to discourage her.

After knotting the apron around her waist, Amanda rested her fists on her hips and looked Dr. Carstead in the eye. "Now what?"

"This way."

He brushed past her, and she followed him to the small room next door. A weatherworn man wearing a frayed shirt and too-short trousers sat on the wooden table. "Mr. Hewitt, this is Miss Broadmoor. She's assisting me today."

Mr. Hewitt bobbed his head and grinned. His smile revealed a row of broken, tobacco-stained teeth. He pointed to his leg. "The doc's gonna take a look at my leg and change the bandage, ain't ya, Doc?"

"That's exactly right." Dr. Carstead motioned Amanda forward. "Mr. Hewitt injured his leg and didn't seek immediate medical treatment. The wound is now badly infected. I'm not so certain you should help."

"If you're not going to permit me to help, I'll never learn a thing. I insist."

With a shrug the doctor proceeded to unwrap Mr. Hewitt's bandages. Amanda took a backward step as greenish yellow pus oozed from the open wound. The smell of rotting flesh assaulted her. Grabbing the corner of her apron, Amanda hastened to cover her nose, but the thin piece of fabric provided little protection against the overpowering stench that permeated the room. The breakfast she'd devoured before leaving home roiled in her stomach, churning to be released. A gag rippled in her throat, and she forced herself to swallow, lest she embarrass herself.

Mr. Hewitt glanced at her and offered a pitying look. "Stinks, don't it?"

Another wave of the putrid stench assailed her as the doctor removed one final bandage, and she could no longer hold down the contents of her stomach. She grabbed an enameled bowl from the nearby table and retched until her stomach ached from the pain. She swiped the perspiration that dotted her upper lip and forehead and returned to the table.

"I apologize, Mr. Hewitt." She unrolled the fresh bandage and cut a length. "Will this do?" she asked the doctor.

He nodded and offered a half smile. "It will. Welcome to the glamorous life of medicine, Miss Broadmoor."

CHAPTER 14

SATURDAY, MARCH 19, 1898

It was unusual for there to be two parties in the month of March, even for members of the Broadmoor family. March was the gloomy month that hung between Rochester's biting winters and the budding flowers of springtime. Save for the St. Patrick's Day parade and Fanny's birthday, little occurred in the month.

Near the end of February, Fanny had requested a small dinner party with only family present to celebrate her March first birthday. Surprising all of them, Aunt Victoria had complied. It wasn't until the Saturday following Fanny's birthday that her aunt surprised Fanny with the huge birthday celebration she had hoped to avoid. With Michael still in the Yukon, Fanny hadn't desired a large party, especially one in her honor. She had been completely taken aback when she'd returned home to find the house overflowing with well-meaning guests prepared to celebrate her eighteenth birthday. For once, Sophie had understood Fanny's dismay. Wesley's inability to attend the birthday party had rendered the evening a failure for her, as well.

This evening's gala would be different. Not for Fanny, of course, since Michael still had not returned. However, Wesley had promised he would be in attendance at this evening's charity event. That alone meant the party would be a success, for her at least.

Both her father and Paul had been hard at work planning the event they hoped would raise enough money to begin work on an addition to the residential portion of the Home for the Friendless. That was Sophie's limited understanding of their plans. Except for choosing a new dress and obtaining confirmation of Wesley's presence at the ball, she'd done her best to avoid any discussion of the ball.

During the past months, Paul had attempted to gain her participation in the planning, but Sophie had redirected him to Aunt Victoria. The older woman was far more knowledgeable in such matters. Besides, Sophie had no desire to spend time with Paul. His conversations focused upon being light and salt in a hurting world, while she much preferred less intimidating topics—ones that didn't cause feelings of guilt each time she desired a new gown or tried on an expensive pair of slippers.

She decided Paul likely donated most of his income to the Home for the Friendless or some other needy cause, for winter was drawing to a close, and he had yet to replace his tattered overcoat. He'd likely wear it to the ball this evening and would be oblivious to the stares he would receive from the finely dressed members of Rochester society. His lack of wealth and social standing seemed unimportant to him.

Shortly after his arrival in Rochester, Sophie had quizzed him regarding his somewhat shabby appearance. He'd shrugged and said that, in the end, only one opinion mattered. Sophie had known what he meant, but she hadn't remarked. Any comment would have opened the door for sermonizing, and she received her fill of preaching on Sunday mornings, thank you very much.

She scurried downstairs, carrying a bag in each hand, and collided with her father as he rounded the corner. His focus settled on the suitcases. "Running away?" A faint smile crossed his lips.

"No, not yet, anyway. I'm going over to join Fanny and Amanda. The three of us will leave for the party from Uncle Jonas's house. One of the maids was to pick up my gown from the dressmaker today, so it should be waiting for me."

Sophie hoped Veda had followed her instructions. No one was to see the gown ahead of time—not even her two cousins.

"And Wesley? I thought he was to act as your escort this evening."

She read concern in his eyes. He cared little if she had an escort to the ball, but he would be greatly disappointed if Wesley didn't attend. She knew her father expected a large pledge of money from Wesley as well as donations from several of his New York City associates who frequently contributed to charitable organizations.

"I'll meet him at the grand ballroom. He'll arrive late this afternoon and is staying at the Powers Hotel. This makes it much simpler."

She'd recited the words Wesley had written in his latest letter as though they'd pleased her when she had first read them. But his decision hadn't pleased her, not in the least. She'd pitched the letter onto the floor and pouted for several days while mulling why he would prefer to meet her at the hotel rather than pick her up at home and escort her to the event. Eventually she had decided the reason was exactly what he'd said—a matter of simplicity.

Now that she'd accepted the idea, it seemed quite perfect. She would enjoy preparing for the ball with her cousins. The excitement and anticipation would increase as they donned their gowns and Veda or Minnie fashioned their hair. She would enter the ballroom and have the pleasure of watching Wesley as he captured his first glimpse of her. Yes, this evening would be great fun indeed.

After grazing her father's cheek with a kiss, she hurried toward the door. "I'll see you this evening. Remember—you're the host. You'll be expected to arrive early," she called over her shoulder.

"I know. Your Aunt Victoria has already warned me against being late."

Sophie opened the door and took a backward step. Paul stood with his hand balled in a tight fist. He obviously had been prepared to knock on the door as she'd flung it wide. "Paul. I didn't realize you were out here."

"Thankfully I didn't hit you. Just think what the Rochester dowagers would say if you appeared at the party with bruises on your face."

"Even worse, think what they would say once they found out it was a man of the cloth who had bruised me. You'd never be permitted to step behind a pulpit again."

He shrugged. "That part wouldn't particularly bother me, for I'm already doing the work God's called me to. But I'd never want anyone to think I'd strike a woman." He stepped to one side and permitted her adequate space to pass by.

She could see the question in his eyes when he spied the suitcases she carried, but he didn't ask. He probably figured she'd tell him it was none of his affair. Instead, he'd likely ask her father, who would be more than happy to share her plans with him. So be it. Right now, she didn't care. Tonight she would be dancing in Wesley's arms.

Preparing for the party was taking far longer than they'd anticipated. Amanda had been indecisive about her gown. She'd decided upon the pink with lace trim, but when she learned that Fanny was wearing a deep pink gown, she instructed Minnie to press her midnight blue.

"Who is it you're planning to impress? Dr. Carstead?" Sophie inquired while Amanda donned the dark blue gown.

"I see Dr. Carstead every day, and if I were trying to impress him, it would be in the examination room, not at a ball. Did I tell you that he permitted me to assist his setting a bone on Tuesday?"

Sophie shivered. "*That* sounds like great fun." She turned toward Fanny and crinkled her nose.

"I can see the two of you," Amanda said. "You may not be interested in anything other than marriage, but my work has proved that I shall have a career in medicine. Even Blake is surprised at how much I've been able to assist him. In fact—"

"*Blake?*" Sophie winked at Fanny.

"Dr. Carstead," Amanda restated.

Her response was far too haughty. This needed further investigation. Sophie scooted to the edge of the bed. "Since when did Dr. Carstead become Bl-a-a-ke?" She intentionally exaggerated his first name, eager to see if Amanda would rise to the bait.

With a quick twist Amanda turned away from the mirror, lost her balance, and had it not been for Minnie's quick reflexes, would have landed on the floor. "For your information, Dr. Carstead said there was no need for formality. We address each other by our first names. It puts the patients at ease."

Sophie giggled. "And I'm certain that's your primary concern."

"Sophie Broadmoor, you just don't know when to stop, do you?" Amanda scowled at her cousin.

This was turning into great fun. Perhaps Amanda's goals weren't as lofty as she claimed. "I think when Michael returns, the three of us should plan a combined wedding: Fanny and Michael, you and Blake, and Wesley and me." She dropped back on the bed and giggled, her petticoat circling around her legs. She'd succeeded in annoying Amanda. "What do you think, Fanny? Wouldn't that be perfect?"

"Just having Michael return and marry me would be perfect. I care little about a fancy wedding."

Amanda waved a hairpin in Sophie's direction. "Exactly what makes you think Wesley is going to marry you? I don't see a ring on your finger. Fanny's the only one who's received a proposal, so I don't think *you* should be discussing wedding arrangements."

There was little doubt she'd pushed Amanda too far. Her older cousin wasn't normally mean spirited, but her words struck a chord. She was right. Wesley hadn't proposed. Although Sophie had been certain she'd receive a ring on Christmas and then on New Year's Eve, there'd been no proposal. When she'd celebrated her birthday in February, she'd held out hope he would arrive with a ring. Instead, he'd sent flowers and an apology, stating business matters prevented him from making the journey to Rochester. She'd been devastated when she received his explanation, yet his letters since then continued to speak of his deep feelings for her. Although she'd said nothing to her cousins, she hoped he would propose tonight. After convincing her father she must have a new gown for an event he was sponsoring, she'd taken great care not to permit anyone a glimpse.

"And when are you going to dress? Fanny and I are nearly ready to depart, and you're still running about in your corset and petticoat."

With Amanda watching her in the dressing mirror, Sophie grinned and stuck out her tongue. "I'm ready except for my gown. I didn't want it to wrinkle." Sophie motioned to Veda, and the two of them stepped into the adjoining bedroom.

Without a word the maid removed the white sheeting and helped Sophie into the dress. Sophie took several turns in front of the mirror, enjoying the dress from every angle. She was certain she'd heard Veda click her tongue and *tsk* while she'd fastened the dress. Now the maid stood at a distance, her frown speaking volumes, but Sophie cared little what Veda thought. It was Wesley she hoped to please.

She turned the doorknob and entered the adjacent room. Amanda gasped, Fanny turned, and Minnie clapped her palm to her mouth.

"What are you thinking?" Amanda was the first to gain her voice.

Sophie smiled and twirled. "Isn't this the most gorgeous fabric you've ever laid eyes upon? It arrived from France, and the dressmaker assured me she wouldn't sell another piece to anyone until after the ball."

"It isn't the fabric that has taken my breath away," Amanda replied. "It's the cut of the bodice. You'll embarrass yourself, Sophie. Do take it off."

She'd known her cousins wouldn't approve, nor would her father. On the other hand, many of the women in attendance would recognize that she had simply chosen the latest fashion: a gown with a revealing décolletage.

"It is the latest fashion and not inappropriate in the least. Besides, I want to make certain Wesley doesn't forget me when he returns to New York City."

"Even if he would forget you, I don't see how he could forget that dress," Fanny said. "I do suppose what you wear is your choice. In any event, there isn't time to change. We're already running dreadfully late."

Amanda handed her a shawl and shook her head. "You'd better take this with you."

"Fanny was correct. We're late," Amanda commented when they entered the hotel. "The guests have already been announced, and it sounds as though the dancing is about to begin."

The musicians were tuning their instruments in preparation for the first dance of the evening. Sophie signaled the man standing guard at the doorway, and he stepped to her side.

"We'd like to be announced, please."

He shook his head. "It is time for the first dance of the evening. We announced the final guest five minutes ago."

"We are members of the Broadmoor family. My father is Quincy Broadmoor, the gentleman hosting this event."

He rubbed his jaw and glanced toward the entrance to the ballroom. "Well, in that case . . ." With a wave of his hand, he motioned them forward and then signaled to the orchestra leader before turning back to Sophie. "Your name?"

"Please announce my cousins. I prefer to enter last." She took a sideways step and ushered Amanda and Fanny forward. After hearing her cousins announced, Wesley would be watching for her entrance.

Standing to the side, Sophie scanned the crowd, hoping to catch a glimpse of him, but to no avail. Amanda had entered the ballroom, and Fanny was now being announced, yet Sophie hadn't yet spotted Wesley. The hotel employee motioned Sophie forward. She straightened her shoulders and tilted her head to one side in what she hoped was a perfect pose. The man announced her name in a loud, crisp tone, and she entered the room still uncertain where she would find Wesley.

Sophie didn't fail to notice the reproachful looks of several women as she passed by and the appreciative glances of their husbands. Her aunt approached and paled at the sight of her dress. She pressed a lace handkerchief into Sophie's hand. "Tuck this into your bodice, young lady," Victoria insisted, waiting until Sophie complied. "You don't want to embarrass your father on such an important evening."

Sophie did as her aunt bid. She could remove the handkerchief later. Right now, she wanted to locate Wesley. While members of the orchestra once again took up their instruments, she continued through the crowd. She circled the entire room. Guests had already taken to the dance floor. Had Wesley not arrived? Her heart plummeted at the idea. Surely he would have sent word.

Someone had invited Daniel Irwin. He had already spotted Fanny, and from all appearances, he was attempting to gain her agreement to dance with him. The young man didn't know when to cease his pursuit. Even after Fanny had made it clear she never wanted to see him again, he continued to send flowers and tried to advance his cause. Dr. Carstead and Amanda were engaged in discussion with Paul. She could go and ask Paul if Wesley had arrived but quickly retracted the thought when she noticed her father. He would be able to tell her.

At the sound of a familiar laugh, she glanced over her shoulder. *Wesley*! She smiled as she worked her way toward him. When she saw a beautiful, unfamiliar woman clutching his arm, Sophie's smile faded. She removed the handkerchief from her bodice as she drew near. "Good evening, Wesley." Sophie stepped around him and grasped his free arm. The woman didn't fail to note the possessive gesture and released her hold. Leaning heavily on Wesley, Sophie nodded to the woman. "I don't believe we've met. I'm Sophie Broadmoor."

The woman surveyed Sophie's dress. "Genevieve Morefield. I see you've been studying the latest fashion designs." She tapped Wesley's arm with her fan. "If you'll excuse me, Wesley, I should mingle. Nice to meet you, Miss Broadmoor."

Wesley patted her hand and leaned close to her ear. "You are stunning. That gown suits you to perfection."

"Who *is* that woman?" Sophie bit her bottom lip as she awaited his reply.

"You're jealous, aren't you?" He circled her waist with one arm and pulled her close to his side. "You need not worry about Genevieve. She's a family friend, nothing more. We've known each other for years. However, I do find your behavior most endearing. It complements how much I have missed you."

Her smile returned and she basked in his praise, yet why hadn't he seen her enter the room? "Did you not hear my name announced when I arrived?"

"No. I thought all of the guests had been announced earlier, so I returned upstairs to my room to retrieve a note for your father from a New York benefactor. You must have entered during that time."

After all her effort to strike the perfect pose, he'd missed her grand entrance. Wesley took her hand and escorted her onto the dance floor, holding her close as they circled the room. She savored each moment and longed for the music to never end.

After the orchestra completed its first set, Sophie's father stepped to the front of the room. "If you'll all find your chairs, I'd like to speak to you about the real reason we've come here this evening."

Without further ado, her father launched into one of his speeches bewailing the plight of the needy. Bored, Sophie leaned back in her chair and surveyed the room while her father thanked those in attendance for their dedication to the troubles of the less fortunate. Sophie finally spotted Amanda and Blake sitting at a table with Daniel and Fanny. Had Dr. Carstead invited Daniel to join them? Poor Fanny looked as though she'd like to bolt and run. When she thought the speech was complete, her father began to unveil his plan for expansion of the Home for the Friendless.

No one would be the wiser if she and Wesley were to sneak out for a carriage ride. And this would be the perfect time to escape. "I was thinking that we might slip away for a short time for a private visit. It's a bit chilly for a stroll, but perhaps a carriage ride?"

He topped her hand with his own, and his touch caused a shiver of delight to settle deep inside. Wiggling his index finger, he beckoned her closer. "I have a better idea," he whispered, his breath tickling her ear and causing another chill to race down her spine. "I have a room here at the hotel. We can slip upstairs, where we won't be interrupted." He glanced around the room. "I fear donning our coats and hailing a carriage might cause undue attention."

Of course. She should have considered the fact that her plan might attract unwelcome notice. Wesley likely thought her foolhardy. Still, he'd suggested he wanted to speak with her in private, where they'd not be interrupted. Her heart raced. Surely this bespoke his plan to propose marriage. Her excitement mounted and then mingled with a hint of fear. Being seen accompanying a man to his hotel room would not prove wise for her reputation. And if her father got wind of such a tête-à-tête in Wesley's hotel room, he would be forced to defend his daughter's honor by rebuffing Wesley—and his financial aid for the Home.

"We'll need to be careful," she whispered.

He nodded. "Of course. You know I wouldn't want to do anything to tarnish your reputation. My room is on the third floor, room thirty-six. Take the stairs at the west end of the lobby. Most people use the main staircase, so you'll have less chance of being detected." He squeezed her hand. "I'll go first; you follow in five minutes."

Her throat was dry, and her affirmative response was no more than a croak. She watched the clock, each sweep of the second hand seeming an eternity. When had it ever taken so long for five minutes to pass? Thankfully no one approached the table. When the clock had finally ticked off the agreed-upon five minutes, she pushed away from the table.

She used the exit near their table, where her departure would go unnoticed. At least that was her hope. Her heels clicked as she crossed the Minton tile in the lobby. One of the clerks glanced up from the front desk but immediately turned back to his ledger. The stairwell wasn't difficult to locate, but by the time she'd ascended the steps, she was thankful Wesley didn't have a room on the fifteenth floor. She hesitated in the stairwell long enough to catch her breath before hesitantly proceeding down the dimly lit, carpeted corridor.

If her cousins had been present to see her trembling hands, it would have dispelled their belief that she was courageous. She stared at the walnut door. The number thirty-six was stenciled in black and outlined with gold. The sound of voices drifted from the stairwell and stirred her to action. She tapped on the door and waited.

The door opened. With hooded eyes and an enticing smile, he reached for her hand. He'd already removed his jacket and tie. The sounds from the stairwell grew louder. She glanced down the shadowy corridor. There was no time to hesitate. Taking a tentative step, she entered the room.

CHAPTER 15

"Where have you been?" Amanda's tone was steeped with accusation. "We've been looking for you everywhere."

Sophie reminded herself to remain calm. She didn't need or want her cousin assuming a parental role. Yet, of late, Amanda seemed to slip into that position more and more frequently. Sophie had hoped to reenter the side door of the ballroom unobserved. Had Amanda not been hovering, she would have succeeded.

"We were beginning to worry." Fanny sighed. "I'm thankful to see you're all right. I was starting to think something terrible had occurred."

"As you can see, I'm perfectly fine." Sophie turned in an exaggerated twirl. "You see? Perfectly fine."

Fanny frowned and pointed to Sophie's hair. "You've rearranged your hair. When did you do that?"

"And *why*?" Amanda retrieved a stray hairpin dangling from a loose strand of hair and handed it to Sophie. "It's a mess and not at all attractive."

"Wesley thinks it's becoming. He prefers my hair this way." She held her breath and hoped one of them wouldn't ask exactly where she'd been while rearranging her hair.

Amanda glanced about the room. "Where is Wesley?"

Sophie could feel the heat rise in her neck and ascend into her cheeks. "I'm not certain. Perhaps he's talking to my father about his large donation to the Home." She focused her attention upon the entrance. If she looked at either of her cousins, they'd know she wasn't telling the truth. "Why don't we go to the punch table? I'm terribly thirsty."

She didn't await an answer before heading off toward the refreshment table that had been set up away from the dance floor. Her cousins were whispering as they followed behind her. Amanda said she was acting strange and something was going on, but she couldn't hear Fanny's reply. Neither of them appeared to believe anything she'd said. She should have taken an extra few minutes arranging her hair before leaving Wesley's room, but there hadn't been time. They'd been away from the festivities far too long as it was.

"I could hear the two of you whispering," Sophie said when they arrived at the punch table.

"We were only saying that you're acting odd, not like yourself," Fanny replied.

Sophie picked up a cup of punch from the lace-and-linen-covered refreshment table. She downed the contents in one swallow, her thirst overshadowing the expected etiquette of tiny sips. Returning the cup to the table with a plunk, she motioned her cousins near. "I'm not going to tell you what it is, but my father is going to be making an important announcement this evening."

"He's been making announcements all night long—and declaring each one of them important," Amanda said.

Sophie shook her head and another curl escaped. "Not as important as this one." She pointed toward the front of the room, where her father had once again taken center stage. "Listen."

Quincy waved a handkerchief overhead in an effort to quiet the crowd. "Ladies and gentlemen. If I could have your attention for one more moment, please."

Sophie grabbed Fanny's hand. "Come on. Let's move closer."

She wanted to hear every word and be close at hand when her father made the announcement. She wanted to hear and see the adulation of the crowd. Her father held a paper in his hand and began to read the names and pledges of those in attendance. With the announcement of each pledge, the crowd erupted in applause. Finally, he silenced them and called Wesley forward to join him.

"Many of you don't know Wesley Hedrick, but before the evening is over, I hope you'll be sure to introduce yourselves." Her father gave a brief summary of Wesley's background and the good works he'd performed in both England and New York City. Murmurs of affirmation could be heard throughout the room. After waiting a few moments, Quincy regained the crowd's attention by waving the list of pledges overhead. "Mr. Hedrick has pledged—" he hesitated, obviously for effect—"ten thousand dollars to the Home for the Friendless."

A stunned silence was immediately followed by a frenzy of shouts and applause that would waken any hotel occupants should they be attempting to sleep—even those on the top floor. The room quaked in an enthusiastic celebration that soon brought the hotel management into the room begging for quiet.

Aunt Victoria and Uncle Jonas had appeared from somewhere in the room and now stood behind Amanda. Her uncle Jonas stroked his hand across the top of his head. "Can you believe this, Victoria? Quincy has found yet another idiot willing to toss away his fortune on the needy. I absolutely do not understand how Quincy convinces these people to pour money into that place of his."

Sophie considered telling her uncle exactly what she thought of his disparaging remark, but her father called her to the stage before she could retaliate. She hurried forward. How she wished her hair looked better for this special moment. She pushed the thought from her mind when she reached Wesley's side.

"I promise this will be my last announcement of the evening." He moved and stood behind Wesley and Sophie, resting a hand on each of their shoulders. "I am pleased to announce the engagement of my daughter, Sophie, to Mr. Wesley Hedrick."

She looked at her cousins. Both were obviously stunned by the declaration, but her attention immediately turned toward the sound of shattering glass. Paul had dropped his cup on the dance floor and was staring at the shards of broken glass lying in a pool of orange liquid. He took a backward step and signaled for one of the waiters before stooping down to pick up some of the broken pieces. He looked up and met her gaze but quickly turned away.

Amanda hurried forward and grasped Sophie's hand as she moved off the stage. "Where's your ring?"

Sophie sighed. "He wanted to be certain my father would raise no objections." She grinned at her cousin. "But I assure you that the ring he chooses for me will be very special."

After the orchestra played the last song of the evening, Sophie slipped out to the lobby to retrieve her wrap. She had rounded the corner and entered the cloakroom when Paul stepped in front of her and blocked her path.

"Where's the man of the evening? I'd think he would be at your side."

"He's speaking with my father, if you must know." She attempted a sidestep, but Paul moved in tandem and prevented her escape. "I'd like to retrieve my coat."

"And I'd like to know what you're doing accepting a marriage proposal from a man you barely know." He tapped his finger to his forehead. "Have you given this thought, Sophie? More importantly, have you considered praying about the direction you're taking?"

Leave it to Paul. He naturally thought every decision in life needed to be prayed over. If she followed that idea, she'd never accomplish anything. The last time she'd asked for divine guidance, she'd waited for nearly two days and still hadn't received a response. As usual, she'd made the decision on her own. She and God didn't work on the same time schedule.

All her life, pious adults had talked about praying before making decisions, but she wondered if they truly received a solution from above. Was she the only one God ignored? Certainly she didn't live a life that would place her on a direct path to God, but she questioned some of those other folks and their claims of answered prayer. Long ago she'd decided God ignored most everyone. She'd also decided the self-righteous were afraid to admit they were just like her: they hadn't received heavenly answers, either.

"I've already made my decision. It's too late for prayer."

He winced. Her offhand remark had obviously set him on edge. Well, he deserved as much. If he'd simply step out of her way, she could leave, but he remained planted in front of her, determined to have his say.

"It's never too late for prayer. Marriage is a serious step. Promise me you'll pray about this matter. Until the wedding, it's not too late to reconsider your decision."

"Promise *you*? Why should I promise you anything?"

"Because I care about you. You're one of God's children," he quickly added.

"I see. And you care about all of God's children."

"Yes, but I care even more about those I know."

"You know my father much better than you know me, and he has given the marriage his blessing. Perhaps you should trust his judgment. Wesley is a wonderful man, and I love him dearly." She tipped her head to one side and several curls cascaded over her shoulder. She glanced at the floor when a hairpin pinged on the Minton tile. "I'd think you would be singing Wesley's praises. You are going to benefit from his generous donation."

Paul stooped down and retrieved the hairpin. "We've not yet seen any of the money he's promised. Even his earlier pledges haven't been forthcoming. Seems he's having difficulty transferring his funds from England, which I find somewhat strange."

"I don't understand your concern. Wesley is extremely wealthy, and these financial difficulties frequently occur."

Paul shook his head. "You're incorrect on that account. Transferring funds is easily accomplished, and a man of Mr. Hedrick's business acumen would be knowledgeable in such matters." He held the hairpin between his thumb and forefinger. "I believe this is yours." She reached to take it. He clasped her hand and turned it over. "Where is your engagement ring? I would think a man of Mr. Hedrick's wealth would have wanted to place a lovely gem on your finger when he proposed."

"Not that it's any of your business, but Wesley wanted to be certain my father approved of our marriage before purchasing a ring. As soon as his funds arrive from England, he plans to choose something very special."

Paul snickered. "Interesting. Seems all of us are waiting upon Mr. Hedrick's transferred funds. Until then, we're left with nothing more than his empty promises."

"Well, I *never!*" Sophie elbowed her way past him and retrieved her wrap. The nerve of Paul Medford. Who did he think he was? All his talk of prayer and God, yet he didn't hesitate to judge Wesley. She considered stomping on his foot but thought it might offer him some perverse satisfaction. With a defiant air, Sophie tipped her chin high into the air. She cringed when two more hairpins escaped her tresses and performed a gentle pirouette before dropping to the floor. Those dreadful hairpins were ruining everything!

CHAPTER 16

Saturday, June 4, 1898
Broadmoor Island

Unlike her cousins, Fanny could hardly wait to arrive in Clayton, New York, and board the boat for Broadmoor Island. She'd been delighted when her uncle Jonas had announced their date of departure. On the other hand, neither he nor the other members of the family had appeared nearly so pleased. But that had come as no surprise to Fanny. Only her grandparents had shared her affection for Broadmoor Island. The rest of the family found no pleasure in visiting the island retreat.

If Grandfather Broadmoor's will hadn't required the family's return each summer, she knew Uncle Jonas would have already sold the island—just as he'd sold her grandparents' home in Rochester. Of course, the sale of the Rochester mansion hadn't bothered most of the family. Only Aunt Victoria, Sophie, and Amanda had also considered the sale a treacherous act. Not because they cared about the house, but because they knew the sale devastated Fanny.

After realizing the sale had destroyed any possible remaining chance with Fanny, Daniel had written her a letter explaining that he would withdraw the contract if her uncle Jonas would permit him to do so. Thus far, her uncle hadn't given him permission—at least that's what Daniel had told her when he attended the charity ball back in March. At first she hadn't believed him, but he'd escorted Uncle Jonas to the table and had him confirm the request had been made.

Predictably, her uncle said it was completely dependent upon what the court decided, and courts were notoriously slow in deciding such issues—especially when it came to the withdrawal of funds from the estate. In addition, he'd explained the house would be sold to someone else if Daniel were permitted to withdraw from the purchase. No one would think it prudent to let a young single woman buy the property—even if she had lived there most of her life.

Given his explanation, Fanny had allowed Daniel to join them at their table at the ball, but she'd made it clear she would never, under any circumstances, permit him to call upon her. She was, after all, eighteen years old now and had given her heart to Michael. Later that evening Fanny had noticed him dancing with several other partners. His wounded heart had obviously healed.

When she stepped off the *DaisyBee* at Broadmoor Island, she experienced the same exhilaration she'd felt since childhood. She would never tire of the fragrant smell of the lush island greenery, the sound of water lapping at the shore, and the prospect of sitting in the kitchen with Mrs. Atwell, inhaling the aromas of freshly baked bread and frying bacon early in the morning.

The older woman had packed many a picnic lunch for her and Michael to take on their frequent treks across the island to fish or to forage for arrowheads in their younger years. Each summer she realized how much Michael's mother had influenced her life. No one could explain God's Word any better than Mrs. Atwell. Not even the preacher at their East Avenue church in Rochester. Today she could barely restrain her anticipation.

Memories of Michael were everywhere. She felt his presence so keenly that she almost expected to see him smiling and waving to her from the boathouse. *Soon. He'll be back soon, and then we need never be parted again. Whether he brings a fortune or not, it no longer matters. I will marry him, and we will be very content whatever our circumstance.*

When they reached the top of the path and entered the house, Fanny started to proceed down the hallway while the rest of the family took to the stairs.

"Fanny!" She turned at the sound of her uncle Jonas's voice. "I'd like to speak with you."

Her shoulders sagged at his request. "But I—"

"This won't take long. The maids will see to unpacking your clothes, and there's nothing that requires your immediate attention." He motioned her back toward the veranda. "Come, let's sit outside, where we can enjoy the breeze from the river."

She wondered if he truly wanted to enjoy the breeze or simply wanted to sit outdoors, where no one would overhear their conversation. Fanny had come to understand her uncle preferred to converse in private. That way no one could prove or disprove anything that he'd either said or denied.

Once outdoors, he dropped into one of the chairs that had already been scrubbed clean in readiness for the family's arrival. She, on the other hand, perched on the veranda railing, prepared to take flight at the earliest possible moment.

"I have good news for you, Fanny. Your investments are doing extremely well. I think it would be wise if you let them stand without any changes. If you like, we could go over the list, and I could show the margin of profit so that you could . . ."

She shook her head. At the moment, the last thing she wanted to do was discuss her portion of Grandfather's estate. "I'm not worried over the investments, Uncle Jonas. Whatever you decide will be fine. You have far more wisdom regarding financial matters than I do."

"Thank you for placing your confidence in me. I will, of course, look after your money as if it were my own." He tapped the bowl of his pipe on the heel of his shoe. "I know all of this has been extremely difficult for you. I'm doing my best to ensure the estate assets are protected."

"I do appreciate that, Uncle. Until Michael returns, I'm certain you are the best man for the job."

The older man frowned. "Of course Michael has little training—"

"Ah, *here* you are, Jonas. I was hoping we could go over your schedule so that I can organize two or three parties this summer." Pencil and paper in hand, Aunt Victoria sat down in the chair beside her husband.

While the older couple discussed dates, Fanny slipped away unnoticed and hurried toward the kitchen. She stood outside the doorway for a moment and watched Mrs. Atwell rolling out a piecrust. A wisp of gray hair had escaped the knot she'd arranged at the nape of her neck. She glanced up and, spying Fanny, dropped the rolling pin on the wooden table, wiped her hands on the dish towel tucked at her waist, and held open her arms.

"I wondered if you were ever going to darken that doorway again," she said with a wink. "How are you, dear Fanny?"

Fanny rushed into the older woman's arms and found comfort in the warmth of the woman's embrace. She had always loved Mrs. Atwell. But now they shared a special kinship: two women who loved and worried over the same young man.

"I would have been here sooner, but Uncle Jonas detained me. I'm fine, although I would be better if Michael would send some word."

"You've not heard from him at all?"

"Only one letter, and that was before I sailed for England in October."

"Frank and I received your beautiful card. It was kind of you to think of us while you were touring the English countryside." She balanced the piecrust over her rolling pin and carefully dropped it into the pie plate. "We've had only one letter, too. From the sound of it, our letter was probably written about the same time as yours."

"Had he written your letter while in Dyea?" Fanny asked.

His mother nodded. "Yes. He said he'd met up with a man named Zeb Stanley and his brother Sherman and was going to be working with them." She formed another ball of dough, patted it flat with the palm of her hand, and began to roll another crust. "He said they're both fine Christian men." She beamed at the final bit of news.

Fanny nodded. "I wish at least one of us would have received a letter with more recent news. I've been doing my best not to worry, but I've heard lots of stories and . . ." A knot formed in her throat, and she permitted her words to trail off without completion. She didn't want to cry in front of Mrs. Atwell. And she need not put troublesome thoughts in the older woman's head. She likely worried about Michael even more than Fanny did.

Mrs. Atwell shook her head while she continued to roll the piecrust. "Worry serves no useful purpose, dear. Use your time wisely and pray for Michael's safe and speedy return. You must remember that he's in God's care."

"I try to remember that, and I do pray for him—all the time, but I'm not certain God hears my prayers."

"Oh, He hears you, Fanny. Never doubt that your prayers are a sweet aroma to God. He wants us to talk to Him."

Fanny tilted her head and grinned. "Talk to Him?"

"Why not? He's my friend, and I talk to Him all the time, just like I'm talking to you. I tell Him what's bothering me. When the flowers begin to bloom, I thank Him for the beauty they provide. If there's ice on the river and Frank has to go to Clayton, I discuss it with the Lord. Just about anything and everything. He's my constant companion."

"I thought you considered Mr. Atwell your best friend and companion. Didn't you tell me that?"

"I did, indeed. But Frank can't always be right here at my side. The Lord is always with me." The older woman arched her brows. "You see?"

"I think so." Fanny knew the Lord was always available to hear her prayers. Mrs. Atwell had told her that before. But the idea of confiding in Him as she would with Amanda or Sophie seemed a bit foreign. If her cousins observed her voicing her innermost thoughts while alone, they would likely think she'd lost her good sense. Besides, she couldn't imagine God having enough time to listen to the jabbering of all the world's inhabitants.

"You don't sound entirely convinced." Mrs. Atwell dumped a bowl of sweetened raspberries into the pie shell. "Why don't you give it a try and see if it helps? Once my older children left home and Michael was the only one here, that's how he overcame his loneliness. I imagine he may be doing the same thing now. It makes me feel closer to God when I have my little chats, but it also makes me feel closer to Michael now that he's away."

"I'll give it a try," she said.

Mrs. Atwell placed the top crust on the pie and sliced the excess dough from around the edges before she expertly crimped the edges. "I am glad that Michael is with men who know the area and can help keep him safe. That thought has given me comfort."

"I'm thinking we should be receiving word from Michael soon. He said the mail could be slowed down or stopped until summer." Mrs. Atwell nodded toward the window. "Well, summer's here. I'm hoping we'll both receive a nice packet of letters. Wouldn't that be a treat?"

Fanny agreed. "Thank you for lifting my spirits. I knew seeing you would help."

Mrs. Atwell beamed at the compliment. "I was sorry to hear about Kate O'Malley's illness. I always look forward to having her here for the summer."

"How did you know?" Mrs. O'Malley had worked for the Broadmoors for many years and had frequently come to the island with them. But the fact that Mrs. Atwell knew of the housekeeper's illness surprised Fanny.

"She wrote me a letter a few weeks back and said she's hoping she'll be well enough to come to the island by the end of the month. I've been praying for her."

"Did Mrs. O'Malley mention my uncle had sold Broadmoor Mansion?"

Mrs. Atwell dropped the knife on her worktable. "Dear me. Mrs. O'Malley didn't say a word. What's to become of her—and the other servants?"

Fanny explained all that had occurred regarding Daniel's purchase of the house. "Needless to say, I was angry with Uncle Jonas. He has assured me the servants will all be taken care of. He'll either find them new positions or keep them employed at his home. I'm not sure I believe him, but I must take him at his word. For now, the servants still remain at the mansion. Uncle Jonas wants it maintained until the new owner takes possession."

"I'm surprised she didn't tell me, but I'm glad to hear the servants won't be left to fend for themselves." Using the tip of her knife, Mrs. Atwell deftly slit a design in the top crust. "She did tell me Theresa had found herself a man and got married." The older woman winked.

Fanny could feel the heat slowly rise up her neck. Theresa O'Malley had proved to be Fanny's arch nemesis last summer when the housekeeper's daughter made an effort to gain Michael's affection. When Theresa had failed in her attempt, she returned to Rochester, and it hadn't taken long for her to gain a marriage proposal from a young man who worked at Sam Gottrey's Carting Company. Fanny had talked with Theresa only once since her marriage, but she had been quite pleased to announce she was expecting a baby before Christmas.

After sliding three pies into the oven, Mrs. Atwell glanced at the clock. "Dear me, I had better keep moving or I'm not going to have supper ready on time. It always takes me several days to become accustomed to cooking for a large crowd after a winter of preparing for only two or three."

"Anything I can do to help?"

"Not on your first day here! You go and enjoy yourself. If I need help, I'll have Mrs. Broadmoor send one of the maids down to help me."

Fanny would have enjoyed a longer visit, but her presence would distract the older woman. After a promise to return later, she brushed a kiss on Mrs. Atwell's cheek and bid her good-bye.

She raced up the stairs and burst into the bedroom. "Mrs. Atwell received a letter from Michael, too. Her letter gave some details that weren't contained in mine. Michael told her . . ." Fanny waved at Sophie, who was sitting near the window overlooking the front lawn. "You're not listening."

"I'm watching for Wesley to arrive." Sophie continued to gaze out the window. "Did Mrs. Atwell say if her husband had returned from Clayton?"

"She didn't mention having seen him. I doubt he'll come up to the house until suppertime, even if he has returned," Fanny said.

During the next several days, Mr. Atwell would shuttle the *DaisyBee* back and forth to Clayton and pick up family members as they arrived on the train. Sophie had told them Wesley would be coming from New York City to join the family. She'd talked of nothing else for several weeks.

Amanda leaned forward and squeezed Fanny's hand. "I'm very pleased for the additional news from Michael."

"Mrs. Atwell believes we'll each receive a packet of letters any time now. I do hope she's correct."

Sophie jumped up from the window seat and brushed the folds from her skirt. "I don't know what's happened to Wesley. I'm going down to the dock to see if he's arrived."

Sophie stopped at the foot of the stairs long enough to check her appearance in the gilt-edged mirror. After straightening the bow at her neck, she hastened outdoors. The *DaisyBee* wasn't moored near the dock, but she couldn't be certain if Mr. Atwell had returned the boat to the boathouse or if he was out on the water. Perhaps he was awaiting the train in Clayton. The trains were known to be late when the rush of summer guests began.

She peeked inside the boathouse and heaved a sigh of relief. Mr. Atwell and the *DaisyBee* were somewhere between Clayton and Broadmoor Island. She returned to the dock and focused her attention upon the river. When she heard the familiar sound of a boat engine, she cupped her palm above her eyes. The *DaisyBee*. She'd know that boat anywhere. She could make out the figures of two men in the boat, and her heart soared. Finally her betrothal would be sealed with an engagement ring.

She struck a pose that would show her summer dress to advantage as the boat came alongside the dock. Keeping her head tilted at a jaunty angle, she turned to greet Wesley.

"Well, this is certainly an unexpected surprise. If I had known you would be on the dock to greet me, I would have arrived even earlier."

Paul! Her mind reeled at the sound of his voice. She dropped her pose and glared. "I wasn't here to meet *you*. I'm awaiting Wesley's arrival. And stay away from me lest you cause me to fall into the water again."

He laughed and shook his head. "Falling into the river was entirely your fault, Sophie."

She wasn't going to argue with him, but she still blamed him for ruining her lovely gold gown last summer during the masquerade ball. If he hadn't surprised her, she would never have taken a misstep and fallen in the water. "Why are you here? I heard no one mention your name as an expected guest."

"Your father asked me to come in his stead. He's busy at the Home and said Wesley had promised to deliver the funds he pledged when he arrived today."

"Well, you can go up to the veranda or sit in the parlor and while away the time because when Wesley arrives, I intend to have him to myself. He'll not have time for you until we've had a long chat and he's had sufficient time to place a ring on my finger." She gave a toss of her curls, hoping for added emphasis.

Paul frowned. "I fear you're acting foolish over this fellow, Sophie."

She tried to turn her back to him, but he moved in front of her and held her arms. "Listen to me. *Please.* Ever since Mr. Hedrick made that huge pledge at the charity ball, I've been attempting to learn more about him. I can find no one who knows anything about him. Even the charitable organizations I contacted know nothing of a Wesley Hedrick."

Sophie tightened her lips and scowled. How dare Paul besmirch Wesley's good name. "I don't believe you."

"If you don't believe me, then believe my mother. She's been involved with the Indigent Harbor Society for years. That's one of the organizations Wesley mentioned as being dear to his heart. My mother has never heard of Mr. Hedrick, and his name isn't listed as either a donor or a volunteer for the organization."

"You have no right to check on Wesley. I'm not interested in anything you or your mother has to say about him. You should mind your own business."

The muscles in his neck tightened. "That's exactly what I was doing, Sophie." He turned on his heel and strode toward the house.

CHAPTER 17

SUNDAY, JUNE 5, 1898

It was nearing ten o'clock the following evening when Sophie saw the lights and heard the sound of the *DaisyBee* arriving at the dock. Except for going inside to eat meals, she'd remained on the veranda all day and throughout the evening. Sophie jumped up from her chair and carefully picked her way along the path to the dock, thankful there was at least a sliver of moonlight to guide her.

She paced the length of the dock until the boat arrived. With a sigh of relief, she rushed to Wesley's arms the moment he stepped out of the boat.

"Careful, Sophie, or you'll knock me into the water, and I'm in no mood to have my suit ruined."

Taking a backward step, she looked into his eyes. "You could at least offer an embrace after all these weeks. I've been terribly worried about your arrival."

He lifted his suitcases several inches higher. "My hands are full. Had I embraced you while holding them, I would have injured you."

She tipped her head to the side. "You could set them down."

He didn't respond, and when she tugged on one of the suitcases, he yanked away. "Let's go up to the house. I'm exhausted."

"But I've been waiting all these weeks to see you. When you didn't appear yesterday, I thought something terrible had occurred. There was no telegram, and . . ."

Wesley circled around her and trudged several steps up the path before glancing over his shoulder. "I'm sorry to have worried you, but there was no need for concern. I'm not a schoolboy. I travel all over the world and am capable of taking care of myself."

Sophie hastened from the dock and came alongside him. "Still, we haven't seen each other in so long that I expected you'd want to spend time with me." They stepped onto the veranda, and she clutched his arm. "If this situation were reversed, I'd want to spend time with you, no matter how tired I might be. I promise you need not rise early in the morning. I'll tell the servants they're not to awaken you. Won't you stay out here for a while?"

Lightning bugs winked in the distance, and a light breeze ruffled the bow at Sophie's neck. How she longed to sit beside him and enjoy his company for a short time. She gently squeezed his arm. "Please? I have something important to tell you."

"You're acting quite childish, my dear." Wesley leaned forward and placed a fatherly kiss on her forehead. "We'll talk in the morning. There's nothing so important that it won't keep until then." Shoving one of the cases under his arm, he opened the door and strode into the house.

One of the servants appeared and retrieved Wesley's bags. Sophie folded her arms across her waist. "You may show Mr. Hedrick to his room."

Without saying good-night, Sophie turned on her heel and marched across the foyer and into the parlor. She hoped Wesley realized the depth of her anger. Although she strained to listen if he would call good-night, she didn't hear another word from him.

"Strange that the man who supposedly loves you doesn't want to remain in your company, especially when the two of you haven't seen each other in weeks."

Sophie spun around in the darkened room. "What are you doing in here, Paul? I don't find eavesdropping becoming." Her eyes acclimated to the darkness of the room, and she saw him shrug.

"I didn't come in here with the intention of eavesdropping, but the windows were open, and I couldn't help overhearing your conversation."

"Fiddlesticks! Who sits in a dark room unless he has some underhanded motive?"

"I do. I was on the porch when I saw the two of you coming up the path. My intention was to give you some privacy and then speak to Mr. Hedrick myself. Obviously, neither of us will be talking to him tonight."

"Wesley was extremely tired. He had a taxing day and needs his rest."

"If that's what you believe, I'll not contradict you, but it's certainly not how I would act if I were in love."

His eyes reflected pity, and she bristled at the idea. She didn't want his sympathy. "Well, what would you know about being in love!"

His jaw twitched. "You'd be surprised." Without another word, he strode from the room and out the front door.

Sophie sighed and stared after him before slowly climbing the stairs. She didn't understand Paul Medford—not in the least.

"Amanda?" Paul squinted in the darkness as a figure rounded the corner. "I didn't realize anyone was out here."

"I'm going up to bed now. Fanny and I were visiting with Mrs. Atwell in the kitchen. Fanny went up the back stairs, but I wanted a breath of fresh air and decided to circle around and sit on the porch for a few minutes. Is something wrong?"

He perched on the rail, hoping she would take his cue and sit down. She glanced toward the door but then sat down in the chair opposite him. "There's something about Wesley Hedrick that makes me think the man is trouble," he said. "If you don't mind my asking, what do you know about him?"

"What makes you think he's trouble?"

He explained exactly what he'd told Sophie earlier then shook his head. "Although Mr. Hedrick speaks of being involved in charitable work, I can find no one in those circles who knows him. That doesn't mean he's a fraud, but I find it highly irregular."

Amanda nodded. "It does seem strange, yet we met him through Lord and Lady Illiff, who both spoke highly of him. He is related to them by marriage—or was. His deceased wife was a cousin to Lady Illiff. I can't imagine that there is anything irregular in his background."

Paul rubbed his forehead. "Probably it's my overactive imagination, but it seems odd that he's had such difficulty transferring his funds from England. People transfer funds all the time, and it doesn't take them months to do so. He's made many promises, yet they've not been fulfilled."

Amanda rested her chin in her palm. "There are instances, though, when difficulties arise with finances. My own father has experienced problems from time to time. He becomes quite irritable with the bankers when his investment transactions are slowed down by their lack of attention to detail. At least that's how he explains it to Mother."

"You could be right, but I'm not convinced it's simply a matter of difficulty with his banker. When he arrived a few moments ago, he didn't even want to spend time with Sophie. He said he was exhausted. Don't you find that strange? A man in love who hasn't seen his betrothed for weeks doesn't want to sit and visit with her for even a short time?"

"Poor Sophie. She must be devastated." Amanda jumped up from her chair. "I'll go upstairs and see if she needs me. I'll visit with you tomorrow, Paul."

"Yes. Tomorrow. Good night, Amanda."

Sophie fidgeted with her breakfast, chasing scrambled eggs around her plate and nibbling on a piece of toast while she watched Wesley from beneath two fans of thick, dark eyelashes. She'd been pleased when he entered the dining room looking well rested only moments ago. After declaring his exhaustion last night, she'd wondered if he would rise in time to join the family for breakfast. He smiled and bid her good morning before greeting the other family members and helping himself to the sausage and eggs arranged on the sideboard. Serving themselves breakfast from silver chafing dishes each morning was the family's nod to summer informality.

"Glad to see you finally arrived, Wesley. You had Sophie worried. She was pacing the veranda long before I went to bed." Jonas sliced open a biscuit and slathered one half with butter and a spoonful of Mrs. Atwell's elderberry jam. "I take it you experienced difficulty departing New York City." His eyebrows arched as he bit into the biscuit.

Wesley sipped his coffee and then nodded. "I'm afraid so. I was detained with last minute details regarding an investment. I know you understand how that can occur."

"Completely. You've got to strike while the iron is hot, or you might lose the perfect opportunity."

Sophie sighed. She disliked talk of investments even more than her father's incessant talk of charitable work. Thankfully Paul hadn't come downstairs, or he'd likely have begun an inquisition about the pledge money he'd come to collect for the Home. If that happened, she'd never get Wesley off to herself. She decided to wait until he finished his breakfast before suggesting that the two of them go for a walk.

Uncle Jonas wiped his lips with the edge of his napkin then placed the linen square on the table. "We should discuss a few of your investments when you've finished breakfast, Wesley. I might have a couple of ideas for you." He winked. "And I hope you might have a few suggestions for me, too."

"I'd be pleased to go over some of my most recent opportunities," Wesley agreed.

Sophie shook her head. "I don't think so. I haven't seen my fiancé for more than two months, and I'd like to have some time alone with him before he begins discussing business with you, Uncle Jonas. That could take the remainder of the week."

Victoria tapped her husband on the arm. "She's correct, Jonas. Let the young people have some time to themselves this morning. You can talk to Wesley later in the day. While you're on the island, I do wish you would cease all this talk of business."

Sophie beamed at her aunt, thankful to have the older woman take her side.

After a final bite of sausage, Wesley downed the remainder of his coffee. "I did promise Sophie we would have time together this morning." He pushed away from the table, his gaze fixed on Jonas. "Perhaps this afternoon?"

Jonas nodded. "This afternoon it is. I shall look forward to visiting with you."

"Shall we go for that walk?" Wesley extended his hand and assisted Sophie from the table.

As they left the house, she grasped his arm in a possessive hold. The two of them strolled in silence until they were well away from the house. "I'm still somewhat unhappy that you didn't want to spend even a little time with me last night," she admitted. She pressed her lips into a moue, hoping her pout would have the desired effect.

"You surely understand that I was tired, Sophie. I don't want to argue again. You heard me tell your uncle I'd had a difficult day. Shall we simply agree that you were disappointed and I was exhausted, and let the matter rest?"

"I suppose, but when you hear what I have to tell you, you'll understand why I didn't want to wait."

"What is it that's so important?"

"Not yet," she teased. She'd waited all night for this time alone; now it was his turn to wait. "Do you know how much I've missed you, Wesley? I've been thinking of you day and night ever since we parted. Have I invaded your thoughts and dreams in the same way?" She peeked at him from beneath the brim of her straw hat.

"Of course. I think of you frequently." He patted her hand and smiled.

Not exactly the eloquent words she'd hoped for, but at least he confirmed that he thought of her often. They approached a grassy spot overlooking the water. "Did you bring my engagement ring with you?" she asked.

Wesley lightly slapped his palm on his forehead. "Oh, Sophie! How could I forget? After spending the better part of three days visiting every jeweler in New York City in order to choose the perfect ring, I went off and left it in my bureau drawer."

"It's all right, I—"

"No. It isn't all right. How foolish. After a late completion of my business meetings yesterday afternoon, I packed in a rush and completely forgot your ring. I should have set it out on top of my bureau so I wouldn't forget it. Now I've caused you further distress. Can you forgive me?"

"Yes, of course." She tamped her disappointment and forced a diminutive smile, the best she could offer at the moment. "I've had occasions when I forgot to pack an item I planned to take with me."

He pulled her into an embrace and whispered another apology. She shivered at the ripple of his breath on her neck while he spoke and reveled in the safety his arms provided. He might be older than many of the men with whom she'd kept company, but Wesley represented permanence and a type of maturity she'd never before longed for in a man. She lifted her lips to him. Unlike his passionate kisses the night of the charity ball, he merely brushed her lips with a fleeting kiss.

"That wasn't the kiss I've been dreaming of all these weeks," she teased, once again tipping her head to receive the kiss she desired. He pressed his lips to hers and tightened his embrace, but still he didn't kiss her with the urgent passion they'd shared at the hotel. "Is something wrong?" She touched her finger to his lips.

"No, of course not. I'm simply distracted by what it is you have to tell me."

"If that's it, then I shall tell you." She pointed toward a large, flat-topped boulder not far away. "Why don't you sit on that rock while I tell you?"

He didn't argue. She followed him, and once he'd settled on the makeshift seat, she stood before him. "I have decided that we should be married right away." He tilted his head back and laughed, the sound echoing on the wind and seeming to mock her.

When she attempted to turn away, he grasped her hand. "I'm sorry, Sophie. I didn't mean to hurt you. It's just that you've caught me completely by surprise. Surely you realize that a girl of your social standing and wealth must have an elaborate wedding. Such an affair takes months and months of planning. You would later regret a hasty marriage." He traced his finger along her cheek. "Besides, I want everyone to admire your beauty as you walk down the aisle of the church in your gorgeous ivory wedding gown."

"That's all well and good, but—"

He stood and cupped her chin in his palm. "Dear, dear Sophie. There is no hurry. After all, the love we share is eternal."

Sophie placed her hand atop his and smiled. "Our love may be eternal, Wesley, but in seven months, everyone is going to know we permitted our passion to precede our marriage vows."

He pulled away as though she'd touched him with a hot poker. "Exactly what are you saying?"

"That I'm expecting our child."

He visibly paled and took a sideways step. "How did *that* happen?"

Sophie rested her hands on her hips. "How do you *suppose* it happened?" She giggled and reached out to him, but he ignored the gesture.

Folding his arms across his chest, he paced along the edge of the overhang. "Now what will we do?" He picked up a small rock and sent it sailing out over the water.

Sophie watched as it landed in the river with a *thunk*; three small rings formed where the rock cut beneath the water's surface. "This isn't so serious, Wesley. We simply get married and no one will be the wiser. After all, we love each other, and our engagement was announced over two months ago."

He continued to pace and wring his hands as her father did when he was faced with some insurmountable problem. Is that what he was thinking? Tears formed in her eyes. "Why are you acting this way?" Her tears overflowed and trickled down her cheeks in slender streams.

"I'm sorry. I didn't mean to upset you." Wesley ceased his pacing and pulled her into his arms. "While you've already had time to adjust to the idea of a baby, this news has come as a complete surprise to me. I've not had time to gain my bearings, but there's no reason to cry. Of course we'll get married. It is, as you say, what we've already planned, but everything must move forward at an accelerated pace."

"Oh, Wesley, you've made me the happiest woman alive." She leaned back and gazed into his eyes. "I suppose we must decide where we'll live. It would likely be much better if I moved into your home in New York City, don't you think? It would be far less embarrassing for my father."

He dropped back onto the rock and stared out over the water. "I don't yet have a house. After my wife's death, I sold our home. I'm living in a hotel."

"But I thought—"

"I've been looking for the perfect place for us to make our home, but I've not found anything I thought would suit us."

She clapped her hands together. "Then we shall find something together. I like that idea much better anyway."

"Good! Then I'm grateful I didn't go ahead without you. We can purchase a house anywhere you would like. After all, with your large inheritance, we won't have financial worries in the least."

"*What?*" Sophie reeled at the remark. "What inheritance are you referring to? I receive a small yearly stipend from my grandfather's estate, but nothing more. My father, Uncle Jonas, and Fanny inherited the bulk of the Broadmoor money. My father has invested most of his money into the Home for the Friendless, and he'll continue to do so until he dies."

The muscles in Wesley's neck constricted, and his lips turned tight and grim. He jumped up from the rock. "You lied to me!"

Sophie stomped her foot, though the grassy carpet muffled any sound. She pointed her finger beneath his nose. "I never told you I was an heiress. Never!" She spat the words across the narrow distance that divided them.

"Your entire family led me to believe you were an heiress, and you never once corrected my assumptions. Now I can see why you've been pursuing me. You were after *my* money. You're no different from any of those other women who've attempted to lure me to the altar."

"That is the most ludicrous statement I've ever heard. You know that I am deeply in love with you. Never once have I given thought to your wealth."

He narrowed his eyes. "Really?"

A slight prick of conscience jabbed her. She *had* expected an extremely large engagement ring—that much was true. But she hadn't pursued Wesley because of his wealth. Social standing and money had never influenced Sophie in her choice of men. He could take a stroll into any of Rochester's diverse neighborhoods and discover she'd attended dances and parties with men who had neither.

"You can be certain that unless I had been in love with you, I would never have permitted the things that happened in your hotel room last March."

He stared at her, anger still evident in his eyes. "I can't talk about this anymore. I need time to think." He turned toward the path they'd followed on their way up the hill and, without another word, stormed back down the hill.

CHAPTER 18

When Wesley hadn't appeared for the noonday meal or returned for the afternoon meeting he'd scheduled, Sophie's uncle approached her. "Where's that fiancé of yours? I've been looking all over for him. He promised to discuss investments."

"I'm not certain. The last I saw him, he wasn't feeling well. He may have taken to his bed to rest for a while."

Her uncle frowned. "I'll send one of the servants up to check on him." Her uncle shoved the tip of an unlit cigar into his mouth.

"He'll ring if he needs anything. If he's asleep, I imagine he'd prefer you not have someone waken him."

"I suppose you're right." He'd repositioned the cigar to one side and talked from the left side of his mouth. "If he comes downstairs, tell him I'll be in the billiard room or out watching George and Jefferson play lawn tennis."

"I didn't know they'd arrived."

Her uncle nodded. "They came in about midmorning, but immediately requested a picnic lunch and headed off for some fishing. They should be back soon. I imagine they'll be challenging one and all to a game of lawn tennis."

Sophie could hear the laughter and chatter of both children and adults outdoors. It appeared additional family members had arrived. Many of them must have requested picnic lunches, for they'd not been in the dining room for the noonday meal.

"If I see Wesley, I'll give him your message, but I'm not feeling quite myself, either. I believe I'm going to take a rest. Tell Aunt Victoria not to be alarmed if I don't join the family for supper."

Her uncle yanked the cigar from his mouth. "Nothing wrong between you and Wesley, is there?"

She glanced toward the stairs, anxious to escape. "I'm merely tired from all the excitement."

"Well, you go up and rest. Your aunt will have a tray sent up if you don't appear for supper. We'll not have you miss your supper—Wesley, either."

Her uncle's kindness puzzled her. She couldn't recall the last time he'd been concerned with her welfare. As she trudged up the steps, she realized his compassion had nothing to do with her. It was Wesley who'd captured his interest: her uncle wanted to be certain he would benefit from Wesley's investment advice.

Sophie felt as though her heart would break. Where had Wesley gone to hide? She'd been to the dock. Mr. Atwell hadn't seen Wesley but promised to advise him of Sophie's concern if he should venture into the boathouse.

Several hours later when Sophie came downstairs for supper, she was surprised to see Wesley sitting on the veranda with her uncle and several of her cousins. She walked outdoors and joined them, but for the remainder of the evening she had no opportunity to speak with him in private. Although she'd attempted to signal him several times, he'd ignored her cues.

While Wesley joked and laughed with the family, Sophie remained in the background, watching, trying to understand exactly what he might be thinking. Well, if he didn't want to be alone with her, so be it. She'd give him the rest of the evening to think on their future and speak to him in the morning.

When one of the maids arrived on the veranda to pick up empty cups and glasses, Sophie stood. "I believe I'll go to bed. If you will excuse me?" She directed her question to Wesley. His dismissive look was enough to tell her he cared little.

"Rather early, Sophie. Still not feeling well?" Her uncle Jonas flicked an ash from his cigar.

"No. I'm having difficulties with my stomach." She pinned Wesley with an icy glare.

An hour later Fanny entered the bedroom, soon followed by Amanda. Sophie sat at the dressing table brushing her hair, still fully dressed.

Fanny plopped down on the fainting couch. "I thought you were going to bed. Didn't you say you weren't feeling well?"

Sophie shrugged and continued to brush her hair.

Amanda pointed to the back of her dress, and Fanny stood to unfasten the row of buttons. "There's a problem between you and Wesley, isn't there? I could sense it by the way the two of you were acting this evening."

Sophie met Amanda's questioning look in the mirror. "He forgot my engagement ring." She turned around on the stool and faced her cousins. "How does someone forget something as important as an engagement ring?"

While her cousins changed into lightweight nainsook nightgowns with fancy bodices finished in tiny pleats and tucks, Sophie explained all that had happened. At least in regard to the ring.

"You're acting like a silly schoolgirl, Sophie. If you plan to wed a mature man, I fear you must grow up and realize that such things happen from time to time. First and foremost, a strong marriage must be built on trust," Amanda said.

"And when did you become an authority on marriage? At last report, you said you weren't interested in marrying," Sophie countered, moving to the bed and sitting down.

"I'm not. I'm simply relating what I've observed between my mother and father throughout the years—and what Mother has told me." Amanda retrieved her hairbrush from atop her chest of drawers and took Sophie's place at the dressing table.

Fanny sat down beside Sophie and removed the pins from her hair. "Amanda's correct. He was obviously in a rush when he departed New York City, and you'll be doubly pleased when you finally receive your ring."

Sophie didn't argue. Her cousins had decided she should forgive Wesley. She slipped into her nightgown without mentioning the true reason they had argued. There would be time enough to tell them of her situation once she and Wesley were married.

Sophie's night had been fraught with bad dreams, and she awakened earlier than usual. Once she'd completed her morning toilette, she hurried down the hall. She hoped for a moment alone with Wesley before they joined the rest of the family for breakfast. His bedroom door was open, and light streamed into the hall from the bedroom window. Gathering her courage, she inhaled a deep breath. She didn't want to argue.

The maid looked up when she stepped inside the doorway. "Oh! I had hoped Mr. Hedrick would escort me downstairs to breakfast, but I see he's already gone down." Sophie pointed toward the bed. "Why are you stripping the sheets from the bed? Mr. Hedrick arrived only the day before yesterday."

"He came downstairs this morning with his suitcases and said that he was going back to New York City. He told me to go ahead and clean his room." Sophie's eyes darted around the room in search of something to disprove the maid's claim. The servant gestured toward the empty chifforobe. "Take a look for yourself. There's nothing here but empty drawers."

Sophie could feel the bile rise in her throat. Surely this was some cruel joke. She raced from the room and down the steps. Keeping to the path, she made her way toward the boathouse taking long, loping strides. She could hear the faint hissing of the boat's engine, and she flung open the door of the boathouse. Maybe Wesley hadn't left yet. The hiss fizzled and died, and Mr. Atwell waved to her after he jumped out of the boat. From across the expanse of the boathouse, she bent forward to gain a view inside the *DaisyBee*. Empty.

"Did you take Mr. Hedrick to Clayton?" She hadn't intended to shout, but she couldn't restrain her rising panic. An invisible band tightened around her chest. While waiting for Mr. Atwell's reply, her heart constricted and pumped a shooting pain through her chest. She thought she might buckle from the pain. Her pain and panic must not be obvious, for Mr. Atwell continued to smile at her.

He touched the bill of his flat navy blue cap in a mock salute. "That I did, Miss Broadmoor. Mr. Hedrick said he wanted to be on the first train leaving the station this morning. Sure is beautiful out there on the water today. A hint of a breeze every now and again, but the St. Lawrence is as smooth as silk." He breathed deeply as though he could inhale some of the calmness into his lungs. Maybe that's what she needed to do.

Sophie forced several gulps of air that seemed to lodge somewhere between her nose and her lungs. The band around her chest constricted more tightly. She leaned against the wall and forced out the air in short panting breaths. Mr. Atwell stared at her as though she'd lost her senses.

"You feeling all right, Miss Broadmoor? I can run and fetch someone if need be."

"Yes. I mean, no." Sophie shook away the cobwebs clouding her thoughts. "Yes, I'm all right, and no, you need not call for help." The poor man had gone pale. She'd likely frightened him out of his wits. "I am merely surprised by your news, Mr. Atwell. I had hoped to speak to Mr. Hedrick this morning."

He reached inside the pocket of the lightweight jacket he'd slung across his arm and withdrew an envelope. "This is for you." He crossed the expanse that separated them. "From Mr. Hedrick. He asked that I give it to you."

Hand trembling, she reached for the missive.

Mr. Atwell's eyebrows knit with obvious concern. "You sure you're all right?"

"Much better now, thank you." She pressed the envelope to her heart. The tight band that constricted her chest slowly released and gently eased the pain.

Mr. Atwell wanted to escort her to the house. Convincing him she was well had required no small amount of effort on her part. He hadn't been sure he should let her out of his sight. Midway up the path, she glanced over her shoulder. Mr. Atwell had taken up watch from the door of the boathouse. Hoping to alleviate his worries, she waved and smiled. He waved in return but remained at his post. When she finally escaped the boatswain's view, she left the path, anxious to be alone while she read Wesley's letter.

Settling beneath one of the ancient conifers, she withdrew the single page of stationery. Her heart tripping, she unfolded the page, surprised to see only a few scribbled lines. The letter contained no flowery salutation. In fact, she doubted it could be considered a letter, for it contained only three curt sentences. *You lied to me, Sophie. This is not my problem, but yours. I cannot marry you. W. Hedrick.*

Not his problem? Once again the band tightened around her chest. She pushed herself to her feet and rubbed her eyes. Surely she must have misread the letter. Forcing her attention back to the page, she once again read his words. How could he? He had said he loved her. She'd given herself to him, a thing she had never before even considered with any man. Though she had done her share of imbibing and even kissed her share of men, she had never before given herself over to a man. Her stomach roiled at the thought of what she'd done. The man she had believed in, the man she had thought loved her completely, now said she had lied to him.

In that moment, staring at the horizon, where the blackness of the water met a cloudless sky, Sophie decided she wanted to die. The weakness of her physical body evaporated, and she raced across the island as though her feet had taken wing. The breeze caught her linen skirt and whipped the fabric about her legs. She raced along the path leading to the distant stone outcropping that hovered high above the water. Pine branches licked at her face and tugged at the lace edging of her shirtwaist. A bramble bush snagged the letter from between her fingers. Uncaring, she let it flutter on the breeze. She didn't need the missive. Wesley's words were seared on her heart.

Paul bent down and picked up a sturdy narrow branch from along the path, deciding it could be fashioned into a beautiful walking stick. Wesley hadn't been at breakfast when he'd come downstairs that morning, but the family members present had been sparse. Last summer he had learned that weekday breakfasts on the island were not a scheduled meal. At times, the table would be quite crowded, and at others, deserted. A game of croquet had begun on the lawn by the time he'd finished eating, but he didn't spot Wesley or Sophie among those playing. When Paul inquired, no one had seen either of them. He had hoped to speak to Wesley, receive his pledge for the Home, and return to Rochester on the afternoon train.

He settled on the veranda, but when neither Sophie nor Wesley had appeared outdoors by nine-thirty, Paul decided the two of them must have been up quite late. In spite of his attempts to squelch the feeling, jealousy invaded his spirit, and he jumped up from his chair. "I believe I'll go for a walk," he told one of Sophie's young nephews who'd been marching back and forth in front of the house. The boy had announced earlier that he was protecting the house from a pirate attack.

"If you see any pirates, be sure to hurry back and tell me," the boy said.

Paul agreed and took off up the path that led to the other end of the island. Broadmoor Island was a beautiful place, and if he must remain another day, he'd at least have the pleasure of enjoying the views before leaving.

By far, the best outlook was at the far end of the island on a high, rocky ledge that provided a spectacular scene. After climbing the hillock, he turned down the path that led to the outcropping. A glimpse of movement caught his eye, and he turned, expecting to see some form of wildlife. Sophie! He opened his mouth to call to her, but something fluttered from her hand and dropped to the ground as she raced away. A handkerchief perhaps? He took off at a mad dash lest the wind carry it away. Bending down to scoop up what appeared to be no more than a piece of paper, he stopped only long enough to read the brief contents. He didn't completely understand the note, but it seemed Wesley Hedrick no longer planned to marry Sophie. Paul couldn't help but wonder what lie she had told him. What could evoke such impassioned behavior? Little wonder she was racing like the wind.

He shoved the paper into his pocket and hurtled onward until, legs aching and breath coming in deep gasps, he stopped short at the sight of her. Arms outstretched as if to embrace the water below, she stood on the edge of the outcropping with her back to him. If he shouted her name, he would startle her. He recalled surprising her on the dock last summer, and how she'd tumbled into the river. Although her dress and her dignity had suffered, she'd not experienced any injury. But if she fell from the cliff, she'd surely die on the rocks below.

Approaching as quietly as possible, he softly called her name. Not a muscle moved. He took another step closer and softly spoke her name again. Still holding her pose, she glanced over her shoulder. Even from a distance, he could see her eyes were red and puffy. No doubt she'd done her share of crying since reading Wesley's letter.

He removed the letter from his pocket and held it in the air. "I know that Wesley has gone. I'm terribly sorry, Sophie."

"If you've come to gloat, you'll not have long to do so. There is nothing in this life I desire. Death is the only answer for me."

Keeping his voice soft and low, Paul stepped closer. "There is always hope, Sophie. Your life is precious to God and to all of us who love you. I know you're hurting, but please believe me when I tell you that in time your heart will mend." He took another step toward her, his eyes locked on hers. "I would guess that by this time next year, you'll have completely forgotten Wesley ever existed."

She shook her head with such violence that Paul worried she would lose her footing. "God can't help me. My life is ruined beyond repair."

"You know that isn't true, Sophie. There is nothing God won't forgive, and nothing in our lives is beyond repair. God's in the business of fixing our messes." He offered up a silent prayer for God's help.

"This is too big, even for God."

He chuckled softly, hoping to assuage her fears. "You know better, Sophie. Maybe you should tell me how anything could be too big for God."

"I'm going to have Wesley's child." She turned back toward the water.

CHAPTER 19

Paul fought to balance rage with compassion. How dare Wesley toy with Sophie's affections, seduce her and steal her innocence, and then walk away? Yes, Sophie had certainly played her part, but Hedrick was older and knew better. If he were there right now, Paul wasn't entirely sure but what he wouldn't push Wesley off the cliff.

Fearful of the consequences if he should draw closer, Paul remained motionless while he carefully considered his response. She truly didn't realize how he felt about her. But if he declared his love, she would think it simply a ploy to get her off the cliff. Watching her stand on the precipice, poised as if ready to fly, he thought his heart would break. He couldn't permit her to give up; somehow, he must save her. "Wesley was a fool, Sophie, but that is no reason you should end your life."

"Easy enough for you to say. I've sinned against God and shamed my family. Everything I had hoped for is in ruins. Everything I believed in is false. Love is nothing more than a fancy. There is no reason for me to live."

Each time she spoke of death, he wanted to rush forward and yank her away from the edge. But he knew he must remain calm, or he would never get her to move away from the cliff. "Sophie, you must think of the child you carry. While it's true you made a bad decision, ending your life and the life of your child won't make things right." He wished for just a moment that Hedrick were there with them. The man should see the damage he'd caused—the life-threatening pain. Sophie was suffering, and Hedrick had just walked away, no doubt to deceive yet another poor girl. Paul squared his shoulders. He had to reach her—to help her see the truth. "Sophie, please."

Sophie dropped her arms to her sides, and he breathed a sigh of relief. Perhaps his words were making a difference. "Don't you see, Paul? There *is* no way to make things right. That's why I'm on this cliff."

His heart pounded with a ferocity that made his head hurt and his ears ring. *Please, God.* "I have an idea for you, if you'll just hear me out. Come away from the edge and sit with me and listen to what I have to say. I think you'll agree it's a good plan." He edged a few steps closer.

She shook her head. "I can stay here while you tell me. There's no need for me to move."

"I can't concentrate with you standing out there, Sophie. It makes me too nervous. One misstep and you could fall. Please, Sophie. I truly have a plan that will work." He took several more steps toward her. "All I'm asking is that you give me a few minutes to tell you my idea. Surely you won't deny me this one request, will you?" He reached to grab her hand.

"I'll listen, but that doesn't mean I'll agree to anything," she whispered.

He nodded, now clutching her tightly. "Come over under the trees, where we can sit in the shade." *And away from the sharp rocks and water that lie beneath the overhang.*

She collapsed onto the ground beside him, her body wracked by unrestrained sobs. Torso folded over bended knees, she buried her face in the layered fabric of her petticoats and skirt. He longed to pull her close and wipe away her tears. Propriety demanded he keep his distance, yet Sophie's pain required compassion and a human touch—his touch. At least that's what Paul wanted to believe. Pushing all decorum aside, he wrapped her in his arms and held her close, wiping away her tears, realizing his own eyes had grown moist. If only he could somehow erase her pain.

When her sobbing finally subsided, he tipped her chin and wiped away a final tear with the pad of his thumb. She attempted a smile but hiccuped instead. With a swipe of her hand, she brushed several loose strands of hair behind her ear. "I must look a mess."

"You look absolutely beautiful. Do you know how much I love you, Sophie?" He hoped the whispered softness of his words would make them acceptable to her ears.

Palm against his chest, she pushed away from him, her eyes shining with disbelief or fear. Or was it anger? Instinctively, he grasped her hand in a firm hold so she couldn't take flight. He had meant to instill hope, not distress, but from all appearances he'd not achieved the desired effect.

"What are you saying? I don't want your pity."

Although she tried to withdraw her hand, he held fast. "This isn't pity, Sophie. I think I've loved you from the first moment I set eyes on you. If not then, I know I was certain that evening last summer when you fell into the water. When we were aboard the ship to England, I wanted to make my feelings known, but I had little time alone with you. It seemed there was always someone else vying for your attention."

"I was intent upon having fun on the voyage," she admitted. "But when I met Wesley, I wanted only to be with him."

He nodded. "I know exactly how you must have felt." He rubbed his thumb across the back of her hand. "Sophie, I want to marry you and give your child a name. Please believe me when I tell you that I love you and want to be your baby's father." He traced his finger along her cheek. "We can be happy. I know we can."

A tear trickled down her cheek. "I can't, Paul. I don't love you."

"I understand, but I still want to take care of you and the baby."

"I've treated you badly since the first day we met. I don't understand why you would want to sacrifice your future for a woman who doesn't love you—doesn't even believe in love anymore."

She was studying him, watching for his reaction, so he would need to choose his words carefully. He must be honest and speak his heart, or he would turn her against him forever. "I love you. Beyond that, I can't tell you with any assurance that I understand any better than you do. But I know it's the right thing to do. I know I will be a good husband to you and a loving father to your child. I hope you will eventually love me, but I'm willing to take that chance, knowing it may never happen." There. That was as much of an answer as he had at the moment, and every word was true. He could only hope she'd heard his sincerity and seen the love with which he'd spoken. He wanted to beg her not to give up on love or on life, but he knew she'd never hear a single word. The pain and betrayal that had become her life were more than she could bear right now. Sophie Broadmoor couldn't accept that good things could still come her way. Only time would prove that true.

The sun peeked through the branches of a towering pine and teased the hem of her skirt. "I don't know if I could ever be a good wife to you, Paul." She stared into the distance.

He turned her chin until their eyes met. "I've told you that I am willing to take that chance. I understand you've been deeply wounded. Unfortunately, there isn't time for your heart to mend before you choose a new path. We must think of the baby."

A soft breeze tugged at the loose strands of hair she'd tucked behind her ear, and she whisked them away from her face. "If you truly believe this is what you want to do, I'll agree to your plan, but I fear you'll later regret your decision."

"Neither of us can say for certain what we may or may not regret, but I believe with God's help, we will have a happy family." He smiled broadly, hoping to lift her spirits. "I believe I should speak to your father before we say anything to the others."

"Can I at least tell Amanda and Fanny?" Sophie touched her palm to her stomach. "I've been holding this secret far too long, and we've always been so close—like sisters." She offered a faint smile. "No. That's not quite correct. My sisters and I aren't at all close. We don't get along in the least. But I do long to confide in Fanny and Amanda. Is that so inadvisable?"

Paul couldn't deny Sophie's request, but he hoped her cousins wouldn't condemn her for a reckless decision that couldn't be changed. Fanny would lend Sophie support, but he wasn't certain of Amanda. He'd seen evidence that the oldest of the three cousins could occasionally react in a strident manner. In Sophie's fragile state, he doubted she could withstand condemnation or rejection by either of them.

He stood and held out his hands to help her to her feet. "If you can trust them and believe they'll tell no one else until the time is right. I wouldn't want any of the other relatives to get wind of this until I've talked to your father."

She nodded her head. "If I ask them to maintain their silence, I know neither will say a thing."

Uncle Jonas was sitting on the front porch with a glass of lemonade perched on the wicker table when she and Paul returned. Her uncle eyed them and waved an unlit cigar in Sophie's direction. "I was looking for Wesley. One of the maids tells me he packed his bags and departed early this morning. What's that all about? We made plans to meet this morning and go over some further investments." He frowned and leaned forward. "Have you been crying? It looks like your eyes are all red and puffy."

"She's not feeling well," Paul replied. "I went for a walk and happened upon her."

Jonas grunted and pointed a thumb toward the door. "Have your aunt send Mrs. Atwell to check on you. If she thinks a doctor's necessary, I'll send Mr. Atwell to fetch the doctor from over in Clayton."

"I think I'll be fine with a little rest. There's no need for a doctor, but thank you for your concern." She cast a glance at Paul. "Thank you for your assistance, Paul. I don't believe I would have made it back home without you. If the two of you will excuse me, I'm going upstairs to lie down."

"You never answered my question. When is Wesley expected to return?"

"He's not."

Sophie hurried inside and fled up the stairs before her uncle could question her further. Spying Veda in the hallway, she motioned the maid close. "I'm not feeling well, Veda, and I'm going to rest. If my cousins inquire, tell them I'd rather not be disturbed."

"You want me to fetch you something, Miss Sophie?" The maid instinctively placed a hand on Sophie's forehead. "You're feeling a might warm. Let me help you out of your clothes, and you crawl into bed."

Sophie didn't argue. She didn't have the energy.

Once Veda had helped her undress, pulled back the covers, and plumped the pillows, Sophie settled on the crisp white linens. "Don't forget to tell the others I don't want to be disturbed." The maid nodded and quietly closed the door behind her. The minute she'd departed, Sophie padded across the floor and locked the door to the hallway as well as the one leading to the adjoining room shared by her cousins. She returned to bed and welcomed the feel of the cool sheets against her skin. Though she'd not felt overly tired before coming upstairs, she soon succumbed to the weariness that silently invaded her body.

She awakened to the sound of light tapping on the adjoining door and Fanny's hushed voice. "Are you awake, Sophie?"

She rolled to her side and was surprised to see the shadows of early evening outside the window. Had she slept the entire day? The tap sounded again, but she remained still. Though she would eventually confide in her cousins, right now she wanted only to sleep. When her mother died, she'd done the same thing. Back then her father had told her that sleeping all the time was a sign of melancholy and hopelessness. He'd been correct. At the loss of her mother, she'd felt a depth of despair that had left a void. Now, she felt as though Wesley's departure had left another hole deep inside that would never be filled. But at least this time she had a vague inkling of hope. Not that Paul would replace Wesley, but at least her baby would have a father. She must cling to that hope, or she would once again return to that precipice.

Another tap. "Sophie? It's nearly suppertime. May I come in?"

Apparently Fanny didn't intend to relent. "Just a moment." Retrieving her lightweight dressing gown from the foot of the bed, Sophie tossed it around her shoulders while crossing the short distance to the door. She opened the door a crack, and Fanny slipped through before Sophie could object.

Fanny studied her for the briefest of moments. "Your color looks good, and I must say you appear refreshed. Did you sleep well?" She plopped down on the bed. "I do hope you'll be able to sleep tonight. Sometimes when I nap during the day, I have difficulty falling asleep at night. Of course, if you're ill, that shouldn't happen. Amanda said Dr. Carstead told her sleep has a genuine healing force in our lives. Isn't that interesting?"

Sophie stared at her cousin, chattering like a magpie from the moment she stepped inside the room. Fanny wasn't acting at all like herself. Perhaps Sophie should inquire into Fanny's well-being. She dropped onto the bed beside her cousin. "Are you . . ." Noting the glisten of a tear, she hesitated. "Fanny, why are you crying? Has something happened while I was sleeping? Please tell me."

Fanny wagged her head. "I've been so worried about you. Even though Veda said you were resting, I came upstairs several times. When the door was locked, I was so worried. Uncle Jonas said that Wesley departed and you didn't seem to know when he might return. I was afraid that maybe you'd done something foolish."

Sophie pulled a fresh handkerchief from the drawer of her chest and handed it to her cousin. "As you can see, I'm fit as a fiddle. There's no need for tears. However, I have no desire to join the entire family for supper."

"I know! I'll ask Mrs. Atwell if I can fix our plates and bring them upstairs before she announces supper. I'll fetch Amanda, and the three of us can eat on the upper veranda. We'll have our own dinner party. Would you enjoy that?"

"That sounds delightful. You're sure you wouldn't mind being away from the rest of the family?"

Fanny hugged her close. "You know I don't enjoy the family dinners. Someone always gets in a snit about some silly matter; then the entire family is off and arguing until Aunt Victoria clinks a spoon on her water glass and calls a halt to the bickering."

Sophie grinned. "Would you tell Paul that you've spoken with me and I'm taking supper upstairs with you and Amanda? I don't want him to worry overmuch."

Fanny's brows knit together in confusion. "I'll be certain to tell him." She glanced over her shoulder when she reached the door. "Should I inform Aunt Victoria, also?"

"Oh yes. Do tell her, as well."

Sophie waited until she heard the click of the door latch and then fell back on the pillows. Mentioning Paul's name rekindled memories of what had happened earlier in the day. She touched a palm to her stomach. Were it not for Paul, both she and the baby would be dead. Even now she wondered if she truly wanted to live. But Paul had been right. The child should not suffer the consequences of her misdeed.

It was a hard reality to face—to realize that the love she thought she'd found had proven false. Wesley had used—seduced—her and convinced her that they were already married, for all intents and purposes. She could still hear his voice against her ear that night.

"We're joined forever in our hearts. Our love will never die."

So much for forever. So much for love.

She would marry Paul and have the child. Then she would decide what she wanted to do with her own life. To live or die—neither seemed all that meaningful.

You'd leave the baby motherless should you ever follow through with your earlier decision.

The thought of her baby without a mother created only a momentary pause in her deliberations. Fanny's mother had died in childbirth, yet Fanny had become a wonderful young woman. In fact, of the three cousins, Sophie thought Fanny the most commendable. Not that Amanda didn't have fine attributes, but she was far too bossy. Fanny was living proof that a child could be reared without a mother and still blossom into a fine adult.

And what of Paul and the sacrifice he is making? Would you leave him alone to raise your child?

She picked at the embroidered stitching that edged the pillowcase. Even though Amanda and Fanny would surely help rear her child, to leave Paul with the responsibility wouldn't be the proper thing. On the other hand, she hadn't forced Paul into his decision; she hadn't even contemplated such an idea. "Paul knows I don't love him," she whispered into the silent room.

But do you love me? You are my creation.

A tear escaped, and she yanked a corner of the bedsheet to her eye. How could she love God or anyone else? Her heart was as cold as stone—dead to the thought of love. She knew her own determination would allow her to make a good show at being content and perhaps even happy at times. But love would never again figure into the matter.

But I am love, Sophie.

She considered this for only a moment. One of the first Bible verses she had learned told her this. She couldn't remember the entire verse from First John, but she knew the part that said *God is love*.

If that was true and love really existed because of God, then why could it not exist for her?

Before she could further contemplate the thought-provoking question, her cousins burst into the room carrying trays that appeared to contain a feast for ten rather than for only three. Veda followed on their heels carrying a pitcher of lemonade and glasses. After moving the wicker table and chairs into a shady spot on the upper balcony, little time was needed to arrange their feast. Veda removed the covers from atop their plates and poured lemonade into the glasses before scurrying back inside.

Sophie had taken only a few bites of her fruit salad when she noticed Amanda watching her every move. "Are you going to eat or merely watch me?" she finally inquired.

"I want to know exactly what is going on with you. Fanny and I agree that you've not been yourself of late. Even before we came to the island, you were more interested in keeping to yourself than usual."

"And sleeping," Fanny added. "Now that Wesley has left with no explanation . . . well, we're worried about you."

Amanda swallowed a sip of lemonade. "Precisely! We've always confided in one another, yet Fanny tells me you've said nothing to her—and I know you've revealed nothing to me. Have you and Wesley had a spat of major proportions?"

"Wesley is no longer a part of my life. That's an absolute certainty."

"But why? Was it because of the family? I don't know how any stranger can endure all the bickering that occurs when we're together." Amanda forked a piece of parsleyed potato and popped it into her mouth.

"No. He made no mention of the family." She stared at her plate and wondered if the words would catch in her throat. "The fact is, I'm pregnant with Wesley's child."

Amanda's fork clattered onto her plate. Her eyes wide with disbelief, she stared at Sophie as though she'd suddenly encountered a stranger. But Fanny immediately grasped her hand. "Whatever are you going to do, Sophie?"

"I plan to marry Paul."

"*What?*" Amanda and Fanny shouted the question in unison.

"You don't even like Paul. What happened between you and Wesley?" Amanda asked, pushing her plate aside.

"When I told him I had conceived a child, he said he wanted no part of me, though I suspect it had more to do with money than the child."

"Whatever are you talking about?" Fanny reached over and touched Sophie's forehead. "Are you running a fever?"

"I'm perfectly well, but the two of you must promise you will not reveal any of this."

Once she'd obtained her cousins' agreement, Sophie related the contents of Wesley's comments, his brief note, and hasty departure. "Not only did he not want the child, but he thought I was in line to receive a large inheritance. When I explained the provisions of Grandfather's will, he decided I was a liar." Sophie watched her cousins, gauging their reaction. "I never once gave him any reason to believe I would ever become an heiress."

"I wonder if he made that assumption based on conversations he'd heard about Fanny's inheritance. I recall conversations when mother and Lady Illiff were discussing Grandfather's will and the family inheritance." Amanda tapped her finger on her chin. "Wesley was present on at least one occasion. Do you suppose he simply assumed you would inherit?"

Sophie shrugged. "I'll never know, but Paul knows about the baby and has asked me to marry him. I agreed, but we want everyone to believe the child is his. Promise you'll *never* tell."

Fanny frowned. "Do you truly believe this is the best way?"

"Given time, the three of us might be able to arrive at a better solution," Amanda said.

"But I don't have time. The baby is due in December. Paul is a good man, and even if I don't love him, he loves me, and I know he'll be a good father to the child."

"I suppose that much is true." Fanny didn't sound convinced but agreed to keep Sophie's secret. "Does your father know?"

"No. Paul went to Clayton to wire him that he needed to come to the island." Sophie tapped Amanda's hand. "You haven't yet given me your word."

Amanda nodded. "I do wish we had time to arrive at another solution, but given the circumstances, it appears marriage to Paul is your only choice. There will be some social stigma for a while, but you're a Broadmoor, and Paul's family is well received in New York City. Society will quickly forgive and forget."

Later that night while Sophie pondered Amanda's response, she realized it wasn't society's forgiveness she needed or desired. God alone had the power to forgive her.

"But why should you, God? I don't deserve it. Everyone tried to warn me that I was being foolish. I knew it was wrong to fall into such temptation with Wesley, yet I allowed it to happen. Why should you care about me now—after my defiance? Why should you love me, when I cannot love anyone in return?" Tears trickled down Sophie's face.

Suddenly another verse from First John floated through her mind. *He that loveth not knoweth not God; for God is love.* That was the Scripture in its fullest part. No wonder she had put aside remembering the first portion. The realization was hard to accept.

"I don't know you."

The emptiness of that truth threatened to completely overcome her. She felt as if she were standing back on that cliff, ready to jump to her death. The isolation and separation she felt were more than she could bear.

She dropped to her knees and sobbed. "God, I cannot bear this alone. I have chosen the wrong way. I have gone against everything I've known to be good and true." She buried her face in her hands. How could God forgive her and love her when she couldn't forgive herself and no longer believed that human love was even possible?

From deep within her memory another portion of Scripture came to mind. *Herein is love, not that we loved God, but that he loved us, and sent his Son to be a propitiation for our sins.*

"What's a pro . . . pish . . . pishiation?" she had asked her father as a little girl.

She could still see his smile as he pulled her onto his lap. *"It means that when you give your life to Jesus, the slate is wiped clean. Jesus takes the blame, and God is appeased through His Son's death on the cross."*

"But why does anyone have to die?" Sophie had asked in her little-girl innocence.

"Because unless we die to sin, we cannot hope to live for God."

The words pierced her heart as nothing else could. She had thought earlier that death was her only hope, and now, in a sense, she could see that she was right. Only this time it was death to herself and to sin. Death to a way of life that held no hope or meaning. Death to that which would forever separate her from God's love—the only true love that would last for all eternity.

CHAPTER 20

THURSDAY, JUNE 9, 1898

Two days later, Mr. Atwell maneuvered the *DaisyBee* into a slip not far from the Clayton depot. Once he'd cut the motor, Paul stepped up out of the boat and onto the dock. The older man motioned to him, and Paul waited until Mr. Atwell made his way to the front of the boat.

"Just wanted to tell you I may not be back here by the time the train arrives," Mr. Atwell started, "but I'll do my best. The missus gave me a list for the grocer as well as the meat cutter, and I need to stop and see Mr. Hungerford at the plumbing shop."

"No hurry. If you're not back when Mr. Broadmoor arrives, we'll go over to the Hub Café and have a cup of coffee." Having time to speak with Quincy prior to arriving at the island might be best anyway, Paul decided.

Mr. Atwell tipped his cap. "Good enough. If you're not at the dock, I'll look for you at the café."

Paul wandered to one of the benches outside the Clayton train depot and dropped onto the hard surface. Burying his face in his hands, he wrestled with his thoughts. A part of him wanted to go after Wesley Hedrick and . . . and . . . what? What would he say or do if he came face-to-face with the man? Paul had never been given to violence, and he certainly didn't want to talk Wesley into going back to make things right with Sophie.

The train whistle howled in the distance, and Paul uttered a prayer that God would give him the exact words he should speak to Quincy. How could he hope to explain to his mentor and friend that he would rather risk his reputation and marry a pregnant woman who didn't love him than live his life without Sophie? Quincy was a man of reason, but he might very well mean to see Sophie sent away to protect the family name. It seemed more likely that this would be the attitude of Jonas Broadmoor rather than Quincy, but one could never tell what the stress of such news might cause a person to do.

Five minutes later, the train chugged into the station. Excited vacationers bounded onto the platform, anxious to board the boats that would take them to their island retreats.

Pushing himself up from the bench, Paul strained to see above the crowd until he spotted Quincy. Yanking his hat from his head, he waved it high in the air. Quincy returned the wave and hoisted his bag overhead while he worked his way through a group of passengers who refused to budge. He sighed when he reached Paul's side.

"The vacationers increase each year. I couldn't even get a seat on yesterday's train." He eyed a young boy pinching his brother's arm until the child howled in pain. Quincy pointed a thumb in their direction. "And none of these travelers seem to have time to look after their children. Can't they see the children are seeking their attention?"

Paul recalled Sophie's telling him that her father never had time for her. That he was too busy with the Home for the Friendless to know she existed. Had she been seeking Quincy's attention with her misdeeds?

Quincy glanced toward the dock. "Where's Mr. Atwell?"

Paul explained that the boatswain had a list of errands and suggested the two of them have a cup of coffee while they waited. After securing Quincy's suitcase in the *DaisyBee,* the two men sauntered across the street to the Hub Café and ordered.

The minute the coffee was set in front of them, Quincy rubbed his hands together and leaned forward. "All right, my boy, you've kept me waiting long enough. I assume this has something to do with Wesley's pledge. I had hoped you would be back home and we'd have the money deposited in the bank by now." He stirred a dollop of cream into his coffee. "What's the problem with the donation?"

Paul ran his thumb along the edge of his coffee cup. "This does have to do with Wesley, but the donation isn't the issue I need to discuss."

"That's a relief. I told the bank I'd be bringing the money and we could sign contracts on the new addition as soon as I returned from the island." Quincy took a gulp of coffee and settled the cup back on the saucer. "So what did you need me for?" He cocked his head to one side.

"First off, I don't have the money. You see—"

"What do you mean you don't have the money? Was Wesley offended I didn't personally come to meet with him?"

"No. He never mentioned that."

Quincy slapped his palm on the table. "Then what's the problem? Why don't you have the money? We're committed to the new addition, and we can't begin without that donation. I'm beginning to lose my patience with you, Paul."

"If you'd quit interrupting and give me an opportunity to explain, I'll be glad to set the record straight." Paul calmed and shook his head. "I'm sorry. That was quite disrespectful of me, but I'm afraid circumstances have changed."

Quincy leaned back in his chair and folded his arms across his chest. "Well, go ahead. I'm listening."

"There will be no donation from Wesley. The man has no money of his own—he apparently lives off the good nature of wealthy friends. At least as far as I can tell. He has left the island and walked out of Sophie's life—for good."

Quincy paled, but he didn't interrupt. While the older man stared into the bottom of his coffee cup, Paul explained all that had occurred since Wesley's arrival. When he'd finished, he reached inside his pocket and retrieved the scribbled note Wesley had written. "This is the manner in which he told Sophie of his decision."

After reading the few lines, Quincy folded the paper and returned it to Paul. "That note should be burned. If anyone else should see it . . ."

Paul nodded. "There's something else."

"*More?* Isn't this enough? My daughter is expecting a child, her fiancé has deserted her, and the addition for the Home is once again delayed." He stared heavenward. "I suppose I have only myself to blame where Sophie is concerned. She made bad choices, but in my heart I know she was seeking my attention."

The waiter returned with more coffee, and Quincy remained silent until the man stepped away from the table.

"Since her mother's death, I've spent little time at home. With her brother and sisters gone, she's had no one. After Marie died, I didn't want to be in the house, and I'm afraid I offered Sophie little attention. How selfish I've been. Now look what my selfishness has done to my daughter."

"I don't think you can blame yourself entirely, Quincy. And blame and guilt won't accomplish anything. Sophie needs a husband, and I have offered to marry her."

Quincy's coffee cup hit the saucer with a clatter. "*What?*"

"And she has accepted. Before you say anything more, let me explain. I have loved Sophie from afar. When I first arrived in Rochester, I thought she was the most stunning young lady I'd ever seen. Of course, she didn't have any interest in me other than when she didn't know my identity at the masquerade ball."

"Ah yes. She was quite surprised to discover who you were, wasn't she? Fell into the river, as I recall."

Paul nodded. "I'm aware Sophie doesn't love me—she's still in love with Wesley. But we have agreed that we will tell no one except you that I am not the father of the child. There is no need for others to know."

"She'll tell her cousins," Quincy replied.

"Yes, but she says she can trust them to keep a confidence. I left that to her discretion. Otherwise, I'd prefer—"

"Are you sure this is what you want to do? You're a young man, and living out your years in a loveless marriage can be a difficult cross to bear. I've heard those who have done so express profound regret."

"Our marriage won't be loveless. I love Sophie, and I'll love her child. I have no doubt the child will love me in return. In time I pray Sophie will come to love me, also. Who can tell what the future will hold? I'm content with my decision."

They'd downed the remains of their coffee and pushed away from the table as Mr. Atwell entered the café.

"Ah, perfect timing, I see. I've loaded the goods on the boat, so if you gentlemen are ready, we can be on our way."

Sophie checked the time before heading down the path to the boathouse. Paul and her father should be returning soon. The smell of the river mingled with the scent of wild flowers that poked through the rocky outcroppings along the water's edge. Sunlight pierced the water in coruscating shafts that created a beauty unlike any other. Little wonder fishermen enjoyed sitting on the quiet banks of the river. Each day they were offered a new panorama of God's handiwork.

Using her cupped palm to shade her eyes, she watched the *DaisyBee* make her approach. Her heart beat more rapidly when she caught sight of her father. If she hadn't been such a coward, she would have accompanied Paul to Clayton and confessed her sordid behavior on her own. But Paul had insisted she think of her health as well as the welfare of the baby she carried. Turmoil couldn't possibly be a good thing for either of them, he'd said. And she had quickly agreed. She hadn't wanted to observe her father's initial disappointment. This way he could absorb the news before seeing her.

She could see the tears in her father's eyes the moment he stepped out of the boat. Her stomach tightened into a hard knot. What must he think of her? Would he even speak her name? She took a backward step, uncertain, but her heart took wing as he spread open his arms. She raced into the comfort of his embrace, her tears flowing like a summer rain.

She buried her face in the shoulder of his jacket. "I'm so sorry. Can you ever forgive me?"

He leaned back and tilted her chin. "Of course I forgive you, Sophie. I realize that I am to blame for much of what has happened since your mother's death. You needed me, but I was so absorbed in my own pain and loss that I ignored you. In some respects, you lost both of your parents when your mother died, a fact that fills me with great remorse."

"We can't change the past, Father. I know I surely would if I could, but . . ."

"You're right. But we can make the future better. No matter what happens, I'll do my best to be at your side, Sophie. I can't promise I'll always meet your expectations, but I will support your marriage with Paul and welcome your child into the family."

"Thank you, Father. I know my behavior reflects on the entire family. I made a terrible decision."

"We've all made bad decisions, Sophie. It's what we learn and how we react once we're faced with the consequences of those decisions that becomes very important. It pleases me that you didn't do anything foolish when Hedrick took off."

Sophie glanced over her shoulder at Paul. One look told her that Paul hadn't revealed that she'd nearly plunged to her death. His compassion continued to amaze her. Why Paul should love her was beyond her comprehension. She truly didn't deserve someone so kind.

Jonas had attempted to gain Quincy's attention ever since he'd arrived earlier in the day, but Quincy seemed uncharacteristically preoccupied with Sophie. Jonas had thought to interrupt at one point but then decided against such action. Perhaps his brother would discover exactly why Wesley had taken his leave. After all, one would think a guest of Mr. Hedrick's social standing would at least offer a word of thanks and a farewell to his host. There was something amiss, and Jonas wanted full details. He had been looking forward to eliciting investment ideas from his departed guest.

Now that dinner was over and most of the family had retreated outdoors to enjoy the evening breeze, Jonas motioned his brother into the library. "We need to talk."

"I was going to suggest that very thing," Quincy agreed.

His brother's immediate consent surprised him. Perhaps there wasn't anything clandestine going on after all. He certainly hoped not, for although Hedrick's departure had breached all rules of etiquette, Jonas would willingly forgive that in exchange for the man's sound investment advice.

Surrounded by shelves of leather-bound books their mother and father had collected for years, the brothers settled in two large upholstered chairs facing the window that overlooked the side yard. Jonas removed a cigar from the humidor. "Exactly what is going on, Quincy? Mr. Hedrick's unexpected departure, your surprising arrival, the girls' twittering among themselves, my wife's avowal that she knows nothing of the circumstances—all of this leaves me utterly confused. Can you enlighten me?"

Quincy nodded. "We are planning a wedding, a very quiet ceremony between Paul and Sophie."

The cigar tumbled from Jonas's fingers and landed on the Axminster carpet. Surely his brother had misspoken. "*Paul?* What of her betrothal to Wesley? That was what I heard you announce at the charity ball, was it not?"

"You heard correctly, but Sophie's engagement to Wesley has been irrevocably broken. She will marry Paul on the fourteenth—with my blessing."

Jonas eyed his brother. There was more to this than he was telling. "And you gave your blessing to Wesley and Sophie, as I recall. What happened?"

"Wesley broke their engagement when he discovered Sophie is expecting a child."

Jonas choked on his cigar smoke. A man of the cloth had taken liberties with his niece? "Why, that fellow should be thrown out of the ministry. I am appalled by such behavior. Are you simply going to let him act as though his behavior is acceptable? He's ruined Sophie's life. She was going to marry a man with a fine career and social standing and now . . . now . . ." he stammered.

"Frankly, this matter is none of your concern, Jonas."

"Of course it is. She's a Broadmoor, and her behavior reflects on the entire family. She's been acting like a trollop ever since Marie's death. Surely you realize Sophie's behavior has been a topic of ongoing gossip among the Rochester dowagers. Her inappropriate conduct is discussed as habitually as they devour their fruited tea cakes. Victoria and I have attempted to speak to you on more than one occasion, but you've turned a deaf ear. Now *this!*"

"I care little about the gossipmongers. Their time would be better spent helping the needy than defaming others. People make mistakes—all of us do. I daresay your life has not been a model of perfection. I seem to recall Father having paid quite a handsome sum to a father in Syracuse when his daughter came into the family way."

"That's entirely different! Nobody knew about that incident, and that girl knew I had no intention of ever marrying her. Besides, she miscarried shortly after Father paid her father off. If he had waited a few more weeks . . ."

"Listen to yourself, Jonas. You speak out of both sides of your mouth. I will not permit any member of this family to speak ill of Paul and Sophie. As for Paul's ministry, I decide whether he is capable of attending to the spiritual needs of the residents at the Home. I do not believe I could locate a man better suited, and I will not discharge him. If benefactors find that a reason to withdraw their support, so be it." Quincy pushed to his feet and strode from the room without a backward glance.

"But what about the fact that Hedrick was to be your benefactor?"

Quincy turned. "Hedrick is a fraud. He hasn't enough funds to sustain his own existence. He was after my daughter's fortune."

"I find that impossible to believe."

Quincy shrugged. "Believe what you will. I really don't care." With that he turned and left.

Slack-jawed, Jonas stared after his brother. Never before had Quincy taken such a stand against him. Of course, Jonas knew the Broadmoor name would withstand Sophie's dalliance. His concern wasn't for the girl or her reputation, or even the family name. His concern was the loss of Wesley Hedrick's financial knowledge.

CHAPTER 21

TUESDAY, JUNE 14, 1898

Sophie clasped her hand to her mouth. "I think I may be sick."

"Don't be silly. You are not going to be sick. There isn't time," Amanda said, checking Sophie's dress. "I do wish we had time to loosen the seam around the waist a little, but it will have to do."

Sophie stared in the mirror. Her cousin was correct. Her waistline wasn't as small as it once had been. The satin fabric now puckered at her waist instead of lying flat. Amanda had warned her against a corset, saying Dr. Carstead didn't recommend tight garments for expectant mothers. But without a corset, the gown wouldn't have fastened at all. Surely for these few additional hours it would make little difference. She'd been wearing a corset up until now.

Amanda stood behind her and stared at Sophie's reflection. "I think your gown is an excellent choice. Paul will be pleased."

"Do you think the family will be shocked? This is far from a traditional wedding gown." An unexpected tear slipped down her cheek. "Of course, this isn't a traditional marriage, either." She wiped away the droplet before it plummeted onto the pale gold silk and left a spot. The idea of a small water mark on the dress caused her to giggle. This gown had been completely saturated when she'd fallen into the river last summer, but Minnie had worked her magic on the dress and restored it to perfection. Sophie had considered discarding the gown, but now she was pleased she hadn't.

"I'm becoming concerned about you. You move from shedding tears to giggling in the same minute. It's rather disconcerting," Amanda said. "Such behavior is common among expectant mothers, but I'd not noticed you having such difficulty until this afternoon."

Sophie nodded. "It hasn't been easy keeping my secret hidden."

Amanda gathered her into a warm embrace. "Oh, Sophie. You should have confided in Fanny and me as soon as you knew. You know you can always rely upon us for support."

Sophie sniffled. "I know. But I wanted Wesley to be the first to know. I had hoped he would be pl-pl-pleased," she stammered. Once again the tears began to flow, and Amanda dabbed a handkerchief to Sophie's cheeks.

"You're going to be red and puffy if you don't cease your crying. Now sit down in front of the dressing table. I have a surprise for you." Amanda opened the doors of her wardrobe and retrieved a beautiful piece of lace. "We'll use this for your veil. When Fanny returns with the wild flowers, I think we can weave them into your hair and the lace."

The lace was a beautiful piece that Sophie immediately recognized. "You purchased this when we were in England. What if it's damaged by hairpins or flower stems?"

"Then it is damaged. The lace will accent your gown to perfection. Now, if only Fanny would—"

"I'm here. I thought I would never find the exact flowers I wanted. I've been all over the island. Then I had to find Veda so she could come and fix your hair." Fanny waved Veda into the room. "Hurry. We don't have much time, and she must look perfect."

The maid appeared confused, but she followed Amanda's instructions while Fanny arranged the remaining flowers into a bouquet and tied them with a wide piece of ivory ribbon she'd removed from one of her dresses. "I need this ribbon back once the ceremony is over, or I'll never be able to wear my dress again," Fanny said with a grin.

"I promise," Sophie replied. She tried to turn and look at the bouquet, but Veda jerked a piece of hair.

"I cannot do this if you continue to fidget, Miss Sophie."

"I'm sorry, Veda. Would you bring the bouquet over here so I may see it, Fanny?" Her cousin appeared by her side and gently placed the bouquet on the dressing table.

"What do you think? Will it do?" Fleabane with its pristine white petals and golden centers, dainty yellow cinquefoil, pink and lavender pincushion flowers, and stems of trefoil the shade of mustard surrounded a cluster of ginger orange daylilies.

"It's absolutely gorgeous. And it will look beautiful with my gown, don't you think?"

Fanny nodded and handed a hairpin to Veda, who inserted the last flower and then inspected her handiwork. "I think it will hold. Turn your head a little, and let's see if it slips." The maid smiled with satisfaction when the veil and flowers remained in place. "You look very beautiful, Miss Sophie. And now if you will excuse me, Minnie said I was to return to assist her as soon as I finished your hair."

"I don't know how I would have gotten this far had it not been for the two of you helping me every step of the way," Sophie said as she stood for her cousins to make one final appraisal of her gown.

A tap sounded at the bedroom door. "Sophie? Are you ready? Paul has returned with the preacher."

"Just one moment, Father." She hugged her cousins in a fleeting embrace. They had agreed there would be no attendants; this was, after all, a simple ceremony. Members of the family had been advised that those who wished to join them in the parlor were welcome, but Sophie did not wish anyone to come out of a sense of duty or obligation. "You two go down and join the others." She hesitated for a moment. "If anyone else is there."

Amanda squeezed her arm. "You know that Mother will be there, as well as George and Jefferson—they love you dearly." She grinned. "And Beatrice will certainly be in attendance wearing her usual frown, but don't let that discourage you. She finds fault with everything and everybody."

"Sophie?" Her father's voice had taken on a tone of urgency. "Paul will think you've changed your mind if we don't go downstairs soon."

After one final inspection, Amanda and Fanny gave their approval and opened the door. "She looks beautiful," Fanny whispered to her uncle.

Sophie stood before her father. He nodded and motioned for her to turn. She performed a small pirouette, and he smiled, his eyes glistening. "I wish your mother were here to see how beautiful you are."

"I'm glad she's not here to suffer this embarrassment."

Her father clasped her shoulders and shook his head. "Like me, she would have been proud to call you her daughter today. You must remember that you are forgiven, Sophie—by me and by your heavenly Father."

She knew he was correct. God had provided her with a husband and a father for her child. One who would love and respect her. If only she could love him in return. Arm in arm, her father escorted her down the wide stairway and into the foyer. Paul stood beside the preacher gazing at her. His eyes revealed a depth of love that both frightened and amazed her. She would surely disappoint him.

When her step faltered, her father looked down with a question in his eye. "All set?"

"I'm not certain I'd ever be completely prepared for this, so we had best keep moving forward."

He grinned. "You're going to do just fine, Sophie. I can feel it in my heart." They stepped into the parlor entrance. "And Paul is going to make you forget you ever met Wesley Hedrick."

Sophie forced a smile. She doubted she could ever forget him. No matter what he'd done, her heart still ached for Wesley. And wouldn't this baby be a constant reminder of him? How could she possibly not remember? How could she marry Paul and pretend to be his wife?

While the thoughts swirled, Amanda struck a piano chord to cue them forward. The soft music continued until her father had relinquished her to Paul's care and the preacher stood before them. Thankfully, Paul hadn't solicited the assistance of Preacher Halsted, who conducted the Sunday worship services at Half Moon Bay. Today, Sophie preferred a stranger, someone who didn't know or wouldn't judge her while conducting the ceremony—someone who wouldn't be prone to mention the marriage to residents of the other islands.

Not that word wouldn't spread quickly enough, but she didn't want an announcement made during the vesper service on Sunday. Of course, if Mrs.

Oosterman got wind of the marriage, she'd be certain to make an announcement on Sunday evening. The woman seemed to enjoy using vesper services to spread gossip. If Sophie had her way, she and Paul wouldn't be attending the service this Sunday.

The preacher opened his Bible. While he was speaking of the sanctity of marriage, Sophie waited for someone to jump up and claim the ceremony a fraud. But all remained silent. While Paul repeated his vows, Sophie silently prayed that God would help her love this man and forget the one who had betrayed her.

Her voice trembled, but she repeated the vows, and when Paul leaned forward to place a chaste kiss on her lips, she didn't pull away. She wouldn't embarrass or humiliate him in front of her family.

Unbeknownst to Sophie, Aunt Victoria had arranged a small reception following the ceremony. Family only, of course, but Mrs. Atwell had prepared tea sandwiches and baked a cake in honor of the occasion. Though Sophie would have preferred to forego a reception, her aunt's thoughtfulness was touching. And Sophie was surprisingly pleased to note that except for her brother, Dorian, who was somewhere in Canada, and her sister Louisa and family, who had sailed for Europe with the Clermont family, the entire family was in attendance.

When Paul hastened to fetch her a cup of punch, her father drew near, his attention focused upon Paul. "I believe you will come to love Paul one day, Sophie."

Sorrow squeezed at her heart. "I don't think I will ever love another man. I'm not even sure I believe human beings capable of love."

"You are young, Sophie. Believe me when I tell you that hearts can heal. Given time, I'm certain yours will mend." He kissed her cheek. "Continue to ask God to bless your marriage, and I will do the same."

"Thank you, Father."

"And, Sophie," he said with a look of adoration, "I love you. That love is very real—even when it seems less than such."

The fireflies danced across the lawn while Sophie sat on the veranda with Fanny and Amanda. Following the day's festivities, Sophie had sought the companionship of her cousins, and Paul hadn't pressed for her company. Instead, he'd remained at a distance. Near enough to hear should she want his company, yet far enough away to provide her privacy. She had noticed that he'd been visiting with her father for the past hour. They always seemed to have much to discuss, though she wondered how it could be possible, since they were around each other nearly every day at the Home.

Thoughts of the Home for the Friendless gave her momentary pause. She and Paul hadn't discussed where they would live once they returned to Rochester. He rented a room at a local boardinghouse, where he took his evening meal when he wasn't preoccupied at the Home. She wondered if her father had told him he could move into the small dwelling the two of them currently occupied. She would ask him when they were alone.

Alone. The thought caused her heart to trip in double time. She grasped Amanda's hand. "Did your mother say anything about . . . later?"

"You mean about your bedroom?" Amanda whispered.

Sophie nodded.

"During the reception, she instructed Minnie and Veda to move your belongings to the bedroom in the west wing of the third floor."

Moments later her aunt joined them on the veranda. "You should go upstairs to your room, Sophie. It's getting late, and I'm sure Paul is wondering why you're continuing to sit here with your cousins." She bent low, her lips brushing Sophie's ear. "You are now a married woman and must begin to think of your husband and his needs," she whispered.

"Well, yes, I suppose I should go upstairs." Though she spoke the words, she couldn't seem to release her hold on the chair arms. "Thank you for seeing to the reception preparations, Aunt Victoria."

"Of course, my dear. And I've had your belongings moved to the bedroom on the third-floor west wing, where you will have the utmost privacy. Don't feel obligated to hurry down in the morning. You should consider the next week as your honeymoon." Her aunt patted her hand. "Go along now and prepare for your groom."

Legs trembling, Sophie pushed herself to her feet. She swallowed hard in an attempt to force down the lump that had risen in her throat and threatened to cut off her air. She cast a beseeching glance at her cousins. The sympathy in their eyes was evident, yet they could offer no assistance. From this point forward, she would be on her own.

Careful to avoid looking at Paul, she quietly retreated into the house. Perhaps he wouldn't notice she'd gone. Plodding up the steps, she wondered if the maids had also moved Paul's suitcase into the room. As Sophie continued the upward climb, she tried to remember the bedroom's design. She hadn't been in the upper west wing for several years. And she'd never slept in any of the third-floor bedrooms. With good fortune it would have a separate sitting room and a private dressing room, too.

She turned the knob and peered inside. Her heart flip-flopped at the sight of only one bed, no sitting room, and only a dressing screen in one corner. Whatever was her aunt thinking? *That you're a married woman.* Sophie ignored that thought. Hadn't her aunt considered that a young woman needed a modicum of privacy? She would go and speak to Aunt Victoria and request her belongings be removed to another, more suitable room.

She turned on her heel and immediately thumped into Paul's chest. He looked even more surprised than she felt. "What are you doing here?"

His brows knit in deep confusion. "I believe this is our bedroom, is it not?"

"Yes. Well, no. Well, it's the one Aunt Victoria gave us," she stammered. "But it will never do. I'm going to ask her what other rooms aren't occupied."

He pushed the door open and peeked over her shoulder. "I see. Could we go inside and discuss this for a moment before you go downstairs and disturb your aunt and uncle?"

Sophie wrapped her arms around her waist and leaned forward. "Has she already gone to her rooms?"

Paul nodded. "She and your uncle came inside immediately after you."

So he'd seen her enter the house. You would think he would have given her more time to get everything arranged. She nearly said as much but decided it would do little to change the situation. He gently steered her inside the room.

She tapped her foot and waited. "Well? What is there to discuss? You can see the problem as clearly as I. There is only one bed. Not even a separate sitting room or a fainting couch for you to sleep on." He sat down as though he planned to take possession of the bed, and she eyed him. "I'm going back down to the second floor with Fanny and Amanda."

He shook his head. "You need not worry. I gave you my word before we married that I would never force myself upon you. Do you judge me a man of my word?"

How did she know? He professed to be a man of God, so he should be a man of his word. On the other hand, she'd thought Wesley to be a man of his word. "I suppose I should trust you until you prove otherwise," she said.

He pointed toward the dressing screen. "Why don't you prepare for bed, and I'll do the same. I'm quite tired, and I'm certain you must be, also."

Slowly, as if being led to the hangman's noose, Sophie went to retrieve her things. She removed a flannel nightgown from the dresser. She'd likely be far too warm, especially in this upstairs bedroom, but she wasn't going to wear one of her delicate nainsook gowns.

It suddenly dawned on Sophie that she would be unable to change her clothes without help. Her gown buttoned up the back, and her corset would have to be loosened. There was no possibility of unfastening it herself. She grimaced and stared at the dresser a moment longer.

"Is something wrong?" Paul asked softly.

Sophie knew she had no choice. To call for Veda would be embarrassing. "I . . . ah . . . my gown." She knew the words made no sense, but she couldn't begin to form a reasonable thought. To her surprise, however, Paul immediately understood.

"With your permission and direction, I will happily help you." He crossed the room and stood behind her. "Tell me what to do."

"The buttons," she whispered.

With painstaking slowness, Paul undid each button while Sophie held her breath. He seemed to understand how uncomfortable the situation was for her and didn't tease or even speak. Had he babbled on about the Home for the Friendless, Sophie actually might have welcomed it.

"There. I believe all of the buttons are unfastened."

Sophie nodded. "Now if you will . . . can you . . ." The words faded. She drew up her courage and straightened her shoulders. "Would you loosen the ties?"

"The ties?" He sounded confused for a moment. "Oh, I see. Yes." He was quicker about this task. It was almost as if he couldn't do the deed fast enough.

Sophie felt the ease of tightness as the corset loosened. She also felt Paul's warm hand glance across her back as he widened the laces.

"Thank you. That will suffice," she murmured and hurried behind the dressing screen. She let the gown drop to the floor then maneuvered out of her corset and shift. Sophie had never changed faster in her life and quickly did up all the buttons on the nightgown.

Although the flannel gown hid her form, Sophie slipped her arms into a dressing gown to further cover herself. She wouldn't want Paul to get the wrong idea.

She inhaled a deep breath. "Are you decent?"

"I am."

She stepped from behind the screen and stopped in her tracks. "Whatever are you doing on the bed?"

He patted the quilts he'd formed into tight rolls and positioned down the center of the bed. "I can assure you that I'll stay on my side of the bed."

"I'm not certain this is . . ."

Paul crooked his finger and pointed to the empty spot. "I truly do not want to sleep on the floor for the remainder of our married life, Sophie. I promise you that I'll remain on my side of the bed so long as you stay on yours." He offered a crooked grin. "But should the time ever arise that you'd like to remove the blanket, I'll be right here waiting for you with open arms."

Sophie flushed and made her way around the bed. "I suppose I have no choice," she whispered. She truly couldn't expect Paul to sleep on the floor, though she wished he would have offered. After positioning her body as close to the edge as possible, Sophie closed her eyes and silently prayed for God's grace to guide her through this loveless marriage. When she completed her prayers, she tucked the sheet beneath her chin and glanced over her shoulder. *I hope he doesn't snore.*

CHAPTER 22

WEDNESDAY, JUNE 15, 1898

Her eyelids were scarcely open, but Sophie already knew she'd remained abed much later than usual. Shafts of sunlight splayed across the bed in giant fingers as if to emphasize the lateness of the morning. Not yet fully awake, she shifted, glanced to her right, bolted upright, and screamed.

"What's wrong?"

"What's *wrong*? You broke your promise." She eyed him suspiciously. "You've been awake for some time now, haven't you?"

He nodded. "You were resting comfortably in my arms, and I didn't want to disturb you. But I didn't break my promise. You're the one who came to me. Please take note that I am still on my side of the bed while you . . . well, you were clearly on my side."

Sophie yanked her dressing gown from the foot of the bed and tossed it around her shoulders, tying it tight around her neck, mortified that her body had betrayed her during the night. "We must figure out some other arrangement. This is not at all acceptable."

Paul grinned. "I thought it most comfortable—and acceptable."

For the briefest of moments, she, too, had enjoyed the safety of Paul's arms, but she immediately forced the thought from her mind. "I'll ask one of the servants to move a couch or cot into the room. That should resolve the problem."

Paul glanced about the room. "I'm not sure where they would fit a large piece of furniture, unless we were to remove the wardrobe. But then your clothing would be out in the hallway or in another room." He frowned. "I don't think that would work. Would you like to remove the changing screen? We could possibly squeeze a small fainting couch over there for you."

"For *me*?"

He smiled. "I couldn't possibly sleep on a fainting couch, Sophie. My legs are far too long. Besides, I have no objection to sleeping in the same bed with you."

She glanced heavenward and continued to pace the short distance between the bed and the wall. Why had Aunt Victoria given them this tiny room? She couldn't have the dressing screen removed. "There must be some solution. Perhaps if we moved the dressing table?"

"That might possibly work if you don't mind being without a dressing table—and if you don't mind the servants gossiping when they move a couch in here."

"I don't care what the servants think. I don't want to risk the possibility of ending up in your arms every morning."

His eyes seemed to darken as he stared at her with such intensity that Sophie actually felt mesmerized. "You're simply afraid that you may learn to love me."

"That's stuff and nonsense," she said, trying unsuccessfully to look away. She'd never really noticed how muscular Paul was. His chest was quite well formed, and she could remember her hands lightly touching the light matting of hair that rested in the center. Goodness, but what man in his right mind slept without a nightshirt to keep him warm? Paul wore little more than some kind of drawstring drawers. That revelation caused Sophie to quickly turn away.

Though she was loath to admit it, Paul was correct. She would not risk her heart again. She wouldn't allow herself to be a fool to another man's pretty words and wooing ways.

"Love has nothing to do with it, Mr. Medford." Gathering her clothes, Sophie tipped her nose in the air and marched to the bedroom door.

"Then you are simply afraid, Mrs. Medford."

The title stopped her in her tracks. She was now Sophie Medford. The thought filled her with awe and perhaps a hint of terror. She looked back at Paul, whose expression seemed to dare her to tell him his statement was false. Her relationship with Wesley had been fraught with lies. If she couldn't give Paul her love, at least she could give him the truth.

"You are right, Mr. Medford. I am afraid." With that she left him. She would dress in the privacy of her cousins' room.

Amanda motioned for the maid to leave the room. "Really, Mother, you do need to calm yourself. The servants are working at a fever pitch in order to meet your demands, but if you continue to bark orders, they'll never accomplish a thing."

"Bark? I do not *bark*, Amanda." Victoria clutched a hand to the collar of her checked silk waist. "What a horrid thing to say about your mother."

"You're correct. My word choice was inappropriate. Please forgive me." She grasped her mother's hand. "But the fact remains that the servants are able to accomplish only one task at a time."

Her mother sighed. "That may be correct, but we must be prepared when our guests arrive this afternoon. In order to do so, I am going to need the full cooperation of both the family and the servants." She rubbed her forehead with her fingertips. "How I could forget we were to host this gathering still escapes me."

A ritual had begun many years ago during which residents of the islands would gather for a time of picnicking and games at the island retreats of one another. At first it had been a monthly event, but soon the social occasions had expanded to an every-other-week affair. Depending upon when they scheduled their arrival at the island, her mother volunteered to host the event at least once and sometimes twice during the summer.

"I suppose since we arrived earlier this year and you had agreed to the date last summer . . ." Amanda's voice trailed off, hoping the excuse would settle her mother.

"And all this upset with an unexpected wedding didn't help, either, I don't suppose. Had I not been worrying over the details of Sophie's reception, I would have likely remembered."

"I don't think you should place the blame on Sophie, Mother. She didn't request a reception. That was *your* idea."

Victoria waved at the silver serving pieces in the cherry cabinet. "We're wasting time. Tell Mrs. Atwell the silver is in need of polishing."

"This is a picnic. We don't need to use the silver, do we? And Mrs. Atwell is busy preparing the food. She doesn't have time to polish silver, and the other maids have been assigned enough duties to keep them busy until the guests arrive."

"What am I to do? We will never be ready in time." Her mother dropped to the dining room chair. "Perhaps I should have Mr. Atwell deliver my regrets to those who are expected to attend." She arched her brows and looked at Amanda. "What do you think?"

"By the time you penned all those notes, I doubt Mr. Atwell would have time to deliver them to each of the islands." Amanda sat down beside her mother. "Everything will be fine, Mother. No one will notice if you serve one less dish than you offered last year. They come to visit and play games, not to judge your food or the house." Although Amanda knew that wasn't entirely true, she hoped the words would soothe her mother's anxiety.

"I should have had Mr. Atwell deliver notes first thing this morning—the moment I remembered. Along with all of these preparations to cause me worry, there's Sophie's marriage. That's bound to cause quite a stir, especially with Elizabeth Oosterman. She'll likely leave early in order to spread the word throughout the entire region."

Amanda giggled. "I believe you are exaggerating just a bit, Mother."

"It might be best if Paul and Sophie went into Clayton for the day. Or perhaps they should go to Canada for a honeymoon. Yes. They could go to Canada for a week or so. If anyone inquires about Sophie's whereabouts, we can say she's gone to Brockville for a brief visit."

"There isn't time for them to pack for a honeymoon. Neither of them has even come downstairs yet. I think you should simply check with Sophie. If she prefers to keep her marriage secret a while longer, you can gather the adults and tell them that there is no need to mention the wedding."

The idea appeared to calm her mother. "Why don't I place you in charge of that task? If Sophie agrees, then the two of you can speak to the family members. Have Fanny help you, too." Victoria pushed away from the table. "Should Sophie be willing to announce the marriage, you might remind her that Mrs. Oosterman will be among the guests. I'm certain Sophie will recall the woman's penchant for unearthing every possible detail and then promptly passing it along."

"I'll remind her. And I'll do my best to keep Mrs. Oosterman otherwise occupied."

"I'm not certain how you'll manage that feat."

"Clara Barton is in the islands this week, and she will surely attend with the Pullmans. I want to find out more about Miss Barton's work with the Red Cross, and I'll do my best to involve Mrs. Oosterman in the conversation. If she attempts to wander off, I will say something that will entice her back to the conversation."

Her mother brushed a kiss on her cheek. "Thank you, Amanda. Don't forget to check with Sophie and advise the family that the wedding topic is taboo." Her mother glanced out the dining room window. "I wonder if some of my grandchildren might be willing to polish silver."

Amanda shook her head and laughed. "I wish you well with that endeavor."

By early afternoon Amanda was standing at her mother's side to welcome their guests. Jonas ushered the men to the side veranda, while the women congregated on the lawn in front of the house and the children scattered to play croquet or tag.

Amanda touched her mother's arm. "Look. Clara Barton is coming up the path with Royal Pullman. I can hardly wait to visit with her." Had it not been a breach of etiquette, Amanda would have run down the path to greet the woman.

"She does look well for a woman of her years," Victoria commented. "I can only hope that I'll be able to climb that path when I'm nearing eighty years."

"Is she truly so old?" Amanda's jaw went slack. The woman appeared no more than sixty.

"So I'm told," her mother said, stepping forward to greet another guest.

The moment Miss Barton drew near, Amanda hurried to greet her. "I do hope you'll have an opportunity to sit and visit with me for a short time while you're here, Miss Barton. I have many questions about your work."

The older woman smiled and glanced at Mr. Pullman. "If you'd like to join the other men, Royal, it appears I've found someone with whom I may converse. I'm certain that if I'm in need of anything, Miss Broadmoor will come to my aid."

Amanda bobbed her head. "I shall see to her every need, Mr. Pullman." Once he'd departed, the two women settled into wicker chairs under a nearby shade tree, away from the noise. "I aspire to enter the medical field, and I'd be grateful to hear anything you believe might assist me in my endeavor."

One of the servants circulated the lawn with a serving tray containing glasses and a pitcher of lemonade. Miss Barton motioned him forward and removed a glass from the tray. "If you want advice on where to attend school and the like, I'm afraid you'll need to get it elsewhere." She swallowed a sip of lemonade. "I started out a teacher, you know."

Amanda sat spellbound and listened while the older woman recounted her past. Miss Barton explained how she'd received her medical training by working alongside doctors during the Civil War. After the war ended, President Lincoln had granted her permission to begin a letter-writing campaign to search for missing Civil War soldiers through the Office of Correspondence.

"How did you conceive the idea of the Red Cross, Miss Barton?"

"Oh, I can't take credit for the idea, my dear. While I was in Europe I learned about the concept. The idea had been outlined in the Treaty of Geneva. Later, I had an opportunity to travel with Red Cross volunteers serving in the Franco-Prussian War. Their good works amazed me, and I knew we needed the same thing in this country. When I returned home, I began to work toward establishing the American Red Cross."

Thrilled by Miss Barton's endeavors, Amanda clung to every word. "You give me hope that I may one day achieve my goals."

Miss Barton offered a wry smile. "You must remember that in order to gain one thing in life, you must sometimes give up another. One day you will be faced with that difficult decision, Miss Broadmoor. Follow your heart and choose wisely."

The guests were beginning to assemble for the afternoon repast, so Amanda assisted the older woman to her feet. "Though I would prefer to continue our chat, I see we are being summoned to join the other guests."

Mr. Pullman rounded the corner, and Miss Barton joined him while Amanda scanned the crowd for her mother. Beatrice had taken charge of the buffet tables and was ordering the servants as to where to place the food. The children scampered nearby, eager to fill their plates. A moment later she spotted her mother with Mrs. Oosterman. Clearly overdressed for a picnic, the woman wore a hat of blue tulle with black chenille dots and peacock feathers that waved in the afternoon breeze.

She hurried toward the women. Her mother would be aghast to know the guests had already begun to fill their plates. As she approached, Amanda detected the distress in her mother's eyes.

"No need to deny what I've been told by several of your nieces and nephews, as well as your grandchildren, Victoria. What I don't understand is exactly how I have offended you." Mrs. Oosterman dabbed her handkerchief to her eyes, although Amanda saw no evidence of tears. "Why weren't Edward and I invited to the wedding?"

Amanda sighed. They should have given the older children explicit instructions, but who would have thought that one of them would even speak to Mrs. Oosterman, much less tell her about Sophie's wedding.

"The guests, Mother," Amanda said, pointing at the veranda. Perhaps she could bring this conversation to an end by diverting Mrs. Oosterman toward the food. Then again, Mrs. Oosterman would likely continue her questions in front of the other guests, and havoc would reign.

"At Sophie's request, the wedding was a private affair. She asked that only family be present," Victoria explained.

"Why would a Broadmoor desire an intimate family wedding? I can think of only one reason why she wouldn't want to celebrate with a huge marriage in Rochester." Mrs. Oosterman raised her brows and snapped open her fan.

Amanda leaned her head close and was attacked by the swirl of peacock feathers. "Sophie isn't given to garish displays, Mrs. Oosterman. Some may find that difficult to understand, but I'm certain a woman of *your* taste and refinement can appreciate the fact that we wanted to honor the bride's wishes."

"I suppose, but I—"

Amanda grasped her mother's elbow. "You truly need to see to our guests, Mother. If you'll excuse us, Mrs. Oosterman?"

"Thank you, my dear," her mother whispered when they were out of earshot. "I doubt that is going to silence Mrs. Oosterman's loose lips, but at least I won't have to endure any more of her questions."

"Mrs. Oosterman will likely talk, but we must simply apply one of Miss Barton's rules of action."

"And what would that be?"

"Unconcern for what cannot be helped." Amanda grinned. "I think it pertains to our circumstance, don't you?"

"I suppose it does. We certainly can't control what Mrs. Ooster-man will or will not do, and there's no need to concern ourselves further. Did Miss Barton have any other rules of action?"

"Control under pressure."

Victoria laughed. "I do believe I could have used that rule earlier this morning."

CHAPTER 23

MONDAY, JULY 4, 1898

Sophie stopped in the hallway outside her cousins' bedroom and listened to snatches of an angry argument floating up the stairway. The voices of her sisters Beatrice and Nadine and Aunt Victoria were easily distinguished, although she couldn't figure out any of the others. From what she could hear, many of them were unhappy, and she was the cause.

Before turning the knob, she tapped on the bedroom door. "Amanda? Fanny?"

Fanny waved her forward. "We're almost ready to go downstairs for breakfast. Have the other family members begun to arrive?"

Sophie shook her head. "I don't think so, but it seems Beatrice, Nadine, and their children are all angry because we're going to remain on Broadmoor Island for our Independence Day celebration. They want to go to either Wellesley or Round Island."

Amanda shoved a hairpin into her golden tresses. "We've celebrated the holiday here on Broadmoor Island several different times. I don't know why you feel you'll be faulted for Mother's decision."

Sophie didn't argue. Once they went downstairs, Amanda would hear the remarks for herself. Sophie knew her older sisters well—especially Beatrice, who would continue to grouse for the remainder of the day. Beatrice loved nothing more than an audience, and she would have a large one today. Except for Dorian and Louisa, all of the family members would be in attendance for the final distribution of Grandfather's estate.

Fanny retrieved several red, white, and blue ribbons from her drawer and waved them at her cousins. "We must keep up the tradition."

The three girls had pinned the ribbons in their hair every Independence Day since they'd been young girls, and Fanny loved the custom. There had been a few years when Sophie or Amanda had offered an objection because the ribbons didn't match their dresses, but tradition had always won out.

With their ribbons in place, the three girls left the quiet of the bedroom. "Let's hope the others have finished their breakfast and we'll have the dining room for ourselves," Fanny said.

Sophie stiffened when she caught sight of Beatrice and Nadine. The children had left, no doubt to go outside and play, but her sisters and Aunt Victoria were still in the dining room. She could tell from the set of Beatrice's jaw that this wasn't going to be a pleasant breakfast.

"Nice to see the three of you have finally managed to dress and come downstairs." Beatrice's disapproving look was followed by a glance at the clock.

Amanda picked up a plate and helped herself to the eggs. "I didn't know we were on a schedule this morning."

Beatrice directed an icy glare at her younger sister. "Perhaps you're not, Amanda, but *married* women generally get up before this time of day."

"I don't know why," Amanda retorted. "We're on holiday." She winked at Sophie before adding a biscuit to her plate.

Sophie filled her plate and sat down opposite Beatrice. "I know you're unhappy that we won't be going to Wellesley Island, Beatrice, and I do apologize. I'm sure you believe the decision to be my fault."

Beatrice cocked a brow. "Well, isn't it? Your hasty wedding has everyone gossiping, and the children will now miss the grand celebration and fireworks at Wellesley."

"I'm certain you are loath to miss the gossip, Beatrice, but if you'll recall, this isn't the first time we've remained on Broadmoor Island to celebrate the holiday. Last year we weren't even on the island in time for Independence Day. We celebrated in Rochester."

"Which is even more reason to enjoy the Wellesley celebration this year," Beatrice said in a smug, haughty tone. "If we don't, the children will be so disappointed."

"I doubt the children will suffer overmuch. There will be fireworks and games and more than enough family members with whom you can discuss my hasty marriage." Sophie plunged her fork into a mound of scrambled eggs and returned her sister's icy glare.

"Besides, Father has ordered fireworks, and unlike that one year, they've arrived early and are ready for use," Amanda added. "So stop whining about the children's disappointment. They will have plenty to keep them occupied."

Aunt Victoria forced a smile. "Now, now, I don't think we need to begin our day with an argument. What time do you think we should eat this evening? Jonas wants to have the distribution this afternoon. Shall we eat immediately following?"

"I think that would be wise, since Beatrice will probably have enough questions and complaints to keep the meeting in progress until well after the supper hour," Sophie said.

"I am not going to dignify that remark with a response." Beatrice pushed away from the table. "I'll be outside if you should need me, Aunt Victoria." Tipping her chin in the air, she marched out of the room with Nadine following close behind.

Fanny giggled. "I do hope it doesn't begin to rain. Poor Beatrice will drown."

Aunt Victoria ignored the remark. "If you girls will excuse me, I need to speak with Mrs. Atwell and some of the other servants."

"Beatrice truly is quite mean. Do you think it's because she's terribly unhappy?" Fanny asked.

Sophie shrugged. "I'm not certain, but I do feel sympathy for poor Andrew. I wonder how he bears to live with my sister's constant tirades. Then again, perhaps she doesn't act this way when she's not around the rest of the family." Sophie was skeptical about the soundness of that idea because her sister had been quick to criticize and gossip from an early age, but she would at least give Beatrice the benefit of the doubt.

"Would you like to do anything special this morning, or shall we go and play croquet with the children?" Amanda asked.

"I don't want to play croquet," Sophie said, "but I'll come and watch if you two want to play. I do feel as though I've ruined the day for both of you. I'm sorry you're going to miss all of the fun at the other islands."

"You seem to forget that it was you who enjoyed those parties, Sophie. Amanda and I went along merely to keep you company. We're happy to remain on the island. We'll have a lovely time."

After finishing their breakfast, the three girls strolled to one of their favorite picnic spots, where they could visit in private and enjoy the view of passing boats.

"When will Paul arrive?" Fanny asked, picking a wild flower and tucking it into her hair.

"He should be here this afternoon. He planned to take some of the children from the Home to the Independence Day parade in Rochester this morning. I don't know if he'll remain there to help with their picnic or not."

"For a recently married man, he's been in Rochester a great deal," Amanda said. "I'm sure Beatrice has been taking note of his absence."

"Most of the men travel back and forth, and everyone knows of Paul's dedication to his work," Fanny offered.

Sophie shrugged. "I'm also certain he's more comfortable in Rochester, where he can sleep in his bed instead of on the floor."

Fanny grasped Sophie's elbow. "On the *floor*?"

Amanda chuckled. "How did you get him to agree to that arrangement?"

"I explained that one of us would be sleeping on the floor. Then I counted on the fact that he was too much of a gentleman to force me from the bed."

Amanda chuckled. "Well, no wonder he's returned to work so soon. Who can blame the poor man?"

"He has been searching for a place for us to live. There's so little room in Father's house, and Paul prefers we have a place of our own before the baby arrives."

Fanny nodded. "I agree. Especially since they work together all day. I wouldn't think he should have difficulty locating a suitable house."

"His ministry work at the Home pays a meager salary, and Father insists they can't afford to pay him more. I spoke to Father privately, and he said the board of directors must approve any increase. He doubts they'll agree, since they've been working to raise enough money for the new addition. And with the loss of that huge pledge Wesley made . . . ."

"Surely there must be something," Amanda said.

Sophie nodded. "Eventually he will locate a place. Even so, it can't be much on his earnings—a room or two in a boardinghouse or a small apartment in one of the tenements near the Home."

Amanda clasped a hand to her bodice. "Dear me! You can't live in one of those tenements. Not long ago Dr. Carstead and I treated an infant who lived in one of those places. A rat had gnawed off part of his ear while he slept."

Sophie covered her ears. "Amanda! Don't speak of such things."

"Well, it's true. You're going to have a baby, and you must consider your living conditions. It would be better to remain cramped in your father's small house than to—"

"One moment!" Fanny waved for their silence. "I have money—lots of money. I will purchase a house for you and Paul."

"Oh, Fanny, what a kind and generous offer. But I don't think Paul would ever agree to such a thing. Like most men, he is proud."

"Then you must let me explain to him that I am doing this because you and Amanda are like sisters to me and the only real family I have. Also, he is a man who preaches God's Word. He should understand that it would bless me to do this for you."

Sophie frowned. "I'm not sure."

"If he does not agree, then I will remind him of the rats," Amanda said.

"Paul is a practical man. I don't think that will be necessary." Fanny took Amanda's hand in her own. "And when you marry, I will purchase a home for you, too."

"Since I have no prospects on the horizon, I doubt you'll have to fulfill the offer. But I do thank you for your kindness, Fanny." Amanda squeezed her cousin's hand. "After visiting with Clara Barton, I think I've decided on a career that will prove fulfilling. And I will come and visit the two of you and spoil your children."

Sophie pointed to the *DaisyBee* making its way toward the island. Even from the hilltop, she could see there were a number of passengers aboard. The house would be brimming with relatives by the time they returned. She glanced at her cousins, thankful they'd had each other through the years. They had bonded as young girls, and though time had tested them on occasion, their friendship and love had remained strong. They had remained a threefold cord that had never been broken. Sophie smiled as she recalled the many times her grandmother had recited a favorite Bible verse to them when they were young: *And if one prevail against him, two shall withstand him;*

and a threefold cord is not quickly broken. "Always remember that verse,"
she'd instructed. And they had.

Sophie had been present on the dock for each of the last three arrivals of
the *DaisyBee*. Not because she had any desire to welcome the influx of relatives, but because she wanted to be present to greet Paul when he arrived. She
cupped her hand to her forehead as Mr. Atwell turned and made the approach
toward the dock. She waved her handkerchief and saw her husband wave in
return. Her heart raced with anticipation as the boat came alongside the dock
and he stepped out to greet her.

She didn't withdraw when he leaned down to place a kiss on her cheek. "I
was beginning to wonder if you'd missed the train."

"It's nice to know you were worried." He squeezed her arm. "I'm delighted
that you came down to meet me."

"I wouldn't shame you. We must keep up appearances."

He frowned. "I had hoped that perhaps you had missed me."

Sophie heard the regret in his voice. "I did miss you. There was no one to
fight with," she said with a grin.

He shook his head and smiled. "I should have known."

"I hope you're not anxious to join the others. Fanny would like to speak
to the two of us alone." Sophie pointed to a spot not far from the boathouse.
"She's waiting for us over there."

"If you're not going to permit me to even take my suitcase up to the house,
this must be important. How can I refuse?"

There was hesitation in his voice, and Sophie smiled, hoping to reassure
him. If he thought something amiss, he'd likely become guarded and unwilling to accept Fanny's offer.

"Tell me about the parade. Did the children enjoy themselves?"

She noted a hint of skepticism in Paul's eyes. "The parade was quite nice.
It lasted for nearly an hour, if you count the time getting everyone lined up.
Some of the children were permitted to march behind the band and carry
small flags, which made them very happy."

"And the picnic? Did you stay for that?"

He shook his head. "I remained long enough to help get the freezers prepared to turn ice cream, and then I left."

"Ice cream? Who provided the cream and sugar for that treat?"

"Mr. Parnell. He even donated the ice and the loan of two freezers. The
boys were lining up to take their turns cranking the handles when I left."

They continued to discuss the children until Fanny stepped forward to
greet Paul. She carefully laid out her plan and then waited for his response.

He shoved his hands into his pockets and stared at the ground. "I can't accept your offer, Fanny. Not that I don't think it's very kind and generous of you, but it's my responsibility to provide a home for Sophie and our baby."

Sophie's heart quickened. He'd said *our baby* as easily as if he'd truly fathered the child she carried.

Fanny leaned against the tree and met Paul's gaze. "I received a full one-third of my grandfather's estate. It's more money than any one person would ever need. If I cannot bless the ones I love, then what good is the money? I have prayed on the matter. I believe God wants me to help you and Sophie so that you may continue your work at the Home. You seek and accept help for others all the time, Paul. Does God not care as much about you as those to whom you minister? If you won't accept this gift for yourself, then accept it because you love Sophie and the baby."

"I suppose I was letting my pride take over. And you're right. It's not proper for me to deny Sophie a decent home."

Fanny beamed and grabbed Paul's hand. "Thank you. I'm going to go speak to Uncle Jonas right this minute. He's preparing for the yearly distribution and will have money on his mind. I'll have him set up a bank account and transfer the money so the funds will be available whenever you find the house you want."

"Thank you," Sophie called as Fanny turned and hurried toward the house. She waved and continued onward. "She's probably afraid to stop for fear you'll change your mind."

"She need not worry. I've given her my word," Paul said. "Tell me, how have things been for you while I've been in Rochester?"

"There has been some gossip, of course, and some members of the family are angry that we're celebrating the holiday here on the island. They blame me, and I suppose they're justified in doing so. I'm certain Aunt Victoria feared the day would be fraught with insensitive questions."

"Don't permit their talk to cause you distress, Sophie."

She tucked a wisp of hair behind her ear. "I'm more concerned about the damage my reputation will do to you than the twittering of gossip that goes on behind my back. What if marrying me means that you must remain on the fringes in places like the Home for the Friendless? My past may prevent you from achieving your goals. Don't you want to pastor a large church some day?"

"I have no idea where God will lead me in the future, Sophie, but if He wants me in a large church, I know it will happen. For now, He wants me exactly where I am, and I'm content." He hesitantly put his arm around her shoulder. "It pleases me to know of your concern, but I weighed the possible consequences of our marriage before I proposed." He winked at her. "Even though I must sleep on the floor, I have no regrets. We'd best be on our way to the house before your aunt sends out a search party."

He continued to hold her close as they walked up the path. "You've been feeling well while I've been away?"

"I've had some occasional pain from time to time, but Aunt Victoria assures me that such twinges are normal."

They'd progressed up the path only a short distance when Sophie came to a sudden halt and placed her palm across her stomach.

Paul stared, his brows knit with worry. "Are you in pain? Should I fetch your aunt or Mrs. Atwell?"

Overwhelmed by a sense of wonder, Sophie looked deeply into Paul's eyes. "The baby. I felt the baby move."

"Truly?" He looked at her as if she'd just accomplished the most remarkable thing.

Sophie smiled and nodded. "I've never known anything like it."

"I'm glad I could be here the first time it happened. I love that we could share this moment," Paul said, placing his hand over hers.

Sophie tried to secure a wall around her heart, but at best it was more of a picket fence. She pulled away. "We should hurry. Uncle Jonas is going to distribute the money as he does every year. I get a small portion, and of course it's yours to do with as you will."

Paul followed behind her as they made their way into the house. He said nothing more, but Sophie could tell he was considering everything that had happened since his arrival on the island.

A half hour later, a very distraught looking Uncle Jonas handed out the yearly disbursements. "As you know," he began, "my father made a stipulation in his will that the summer distributions would continue until Fanny reached her eighteenth summer. That, of course, is this summer. While there will continue to be a very modest amount of money shared each year, we will no longer be forced to meet here on Broadmoor Island."

"Will the island be sold like Grandfather's house?" Beatrice asked.

"No. There are legalities involved that I will not take the time to go into at this moment," Jonas replied. He dabbed sweat from his brow. "I would advise all of you, however, to be wise with this money. The economy has suffered many tests and trials. There is no way of knowing how successful any one investment will continue to be in the years to come. Large purchases could prove foolish." He looked directly at Fanny.

Sophie figured he had protested Fanny's desire to pay for the Medford house, but she didn't care. She certainly couldn't risk the safety of her child.

The grumbling continued for several minutes until finally Jonas stamped a large book against his desk. "Quiet! There is no sense in arguing about the matter. Investment money is dependent upon a variety of issues in our nation."

Sophie shifted uncomfortably. The nagging pain in her back made sitting on the hard chair quite taxing. Paul seemed to understand and stood. "I do apologize, Mr. Broadmoor, but Sophie is feeling a bit tired. With your permission I would like to help her upstairs."

Jonas frowned but nodded. "Very well."

Paul escorted Sophie from the room and led her to the staircase. She put her hand upon his arm as they began to ascend. "Thank you," she told him. "It would seem you are always rescuing me from one situation or another."

"I promise you I do not mind." He smiled. "Your welfare is far more important to me. I would rather you be happy and at peace."

"I am at peace," she admitted, casting a quick glance up at his face. "I managed to give it all over to God. To die, as it were, to my selfish ambitions and sinful nature. At least I am attempting that feat."

Paul paused and gripped her hand. "You needn't struggle alone. God has promised He will never leave us or forsake us. His faithfulness is something you can count on, Sophie. Even when people let you down and disappoint. You might not always understand God's ways. You might even believe He has deserted you, too, but that will never happen. And if I have any say over it—any breath in my body—I, too, will never desert you. I might disappoint, even fail to please, but I pledge to always be with you."

Sophie felt tears come to her eyes. Why was he so good to her? She didn't deserve his kindness or love. How could he love her? She carried another man's child. She mourned the loss of another man's love. How could Paul look beyond all of that and love her?

"Thank you," she barely managed to whisper. Pulling away from him, she took hold of her dress and hurried up the stairs. She didn't want to make a scene, but most of all she didn't want him to question her feelings—feelings she couldn't begin to understand.

CHAPTER 24

FRIDAY, JULY 15, 1898

Fanny heard Mr. Atwell's shouts before she caught sight of him loping up the path from the dock. She squinted into the afternoon sunshine. Michael's father was holding an envelope overhead and waving it in the air.

"A letter for you, Fanny." Hand outstretched, Michael's father bent forward and gasped for air as he reached her side. "From Michael."

She clutched the letter to her chest. "Finally!" She could feel the tears beginning to form. "Did you receive one, too?"

Mr. Atwell shook his head. "No. But you never know. One might arrive tomorrow or the next day." He smiled, and two deep ridges formed in his tanned cheeks and reminded her of Michael. "I'm not going to stand here while you read it. I'm sure you'd like some privacy while you see what Michael has to say. But you might let the missus know how her son is doing when you've a few free minutes—not the personal words, of course."

Mr. Atwell was doing his best to balance their unusual relationship. It was obvious he didn't want to overstep the boundaries of an employee, yet his son was now engaged to Fanny. She knew Michael's parents longed for word of their youngest son.

"I'll go to the kitchen once I've read the letter," she promised.

He tipped his hat and waved before he turned and walked back down the path. A part of her wanted to hold the letter in a loving caress, while the other part longed to rip open the envelope and devour the contents. She traced a finger over the neatly formed letters of her name. She pictured him sitting near a blazing fire as he'd penned the letter to her. How she longed to be with him.

Gazing out across the lawn, Fanny knew there was only one place in all the world where she wanted to read this letter. Her special place. The place her father had loved to go with her mother. The place where she and her father had spent moments so dear to her memory that they often seemed as though they'd only happened yesterday.

She was glad that everyone else seemed occupied. No one called to her in greeting or demanded she join them for games. Fanny slipped across the grassy expanse and made her way north through the trees.

How many times have I made this journey?

Smiling, she knew that for as long as she lived she would come to this place. She hoped one day she might even share it with her children. The thought of children made her think of Sophie and the baby she carried. Her cousin's life was so intricately connected to Fanny. Sophie and Amanda were her best friends, outside of Michael. They had seen her through so many ordeals—deaths, marriages, births. She couldn't imagine not having them in her life, yet she knew from having watched others in the family that life could change very quickly. People married and moved away without giving it another thought. It could happen to them.

The trees thinned and the rocky outcropping came into view, along with the crisp blue of the St. Lawrence River. Fanny went to the tree where she'd found her father's lifeless form so many years ago. She saw the flowers she'd left there as a memorial when they'd first returned to the island in June. They were dry and dead, but the sight did not cause her despair. With Michael's letter in hand, she could face most anything.

She took a seat on the ground and leaned back against the tree. Carefully, she unsealed the envelope and retrieved the pages from inside the paper cocoon. Fingers trembling, she unfolded the pages and began to read, slowly digesting each word.

My dearest Fanny,

I hope this letter reaches you before summer. I heard of a special post going out and paid extra to see if I could get word to you. I will post it to the island, however, in case it is delayed. That way, should it get there before you come, my mother will forward it for me.

She felt her throat tighten. Was something wrong? Why had he been so desperate to get the letter to her? She glanced at the top of the page and realized that he'd written it in February.

The winter is fierce and seems to go on forever. We pass the time in work and darkness. There are few hours of daylight here, and that makes the snow and frigid chill seem even worse. Nevertheless, night and day we work at finding gold. We've been quite successful. Zeb and Sherman are wonderful men of God. They insist on tithing a tenth of everything we find. What a blessing to know such men. We bow our heads not only at meals but at the start of each day. Zeb reads to us from the Bible, and we discuss the meaning of the words. I've learned so much from these simple men. I can hardly wait to see you and tell you all about it.

Fanny sighed. She could imagine Michael and the two rugged mountain men sitting at the breakfast table in a tiny cabin studying the Word of God and praying.

Sherman says that God is interested in every aspect of our lives. I found that quite interesting. I suppose I have always known that I could take everything to God in prayer, but I am beginning to understand more about the idea of praying without ceasing. Here, where gold is worshiped and men can die for little more than stepping on a man's claim, it has been my utmost blessing to share my days with Zeb and Sherman.

I have to tell you about the cabin. Sherman and Zeb were here, you remember, before the rush. Therefore, there were still plenty of trees with which to build. Since then, much of the forest has been cut for the benefit of mining. You wouldn't believe it, but there are towns along the way north that are completely void of trees. Many were used to build boats to float up to Dawson City. Others were used to create buildings for the towns, and much was needed for fuel. Fuel is most critical, as the nights often drop to forty below zero.

Fanny put her hand to her mouth. She couldn't even begin to understand how anyone could live in such temperatures. Why, when it was below freezing in Rochester, she preferred to remain inside, bundled and warm. She turned the page over and found the next line even more shocking.

Many of the folks up here are living in canvas tents. You will hardly believe this, I'm sure, but people have created entire homes by joining their tents together. They use small stoves inside and live quite nicely. Of course the water and food always freeze, but it's that way in the cabin, as well. It makes it easy to store our meat supply, however. Zeb killed a large buck elk a month ago, and we are still eating on him. We have a cache, which is a small storage house built upon stilts. We keep the meat there under lock and key to discourage both four-legged and two-legged animals from taking it.

I'll try to write more about life here in my next letter. The reason I wanted to get this letter to you before summer was to explain that I won't be back until late August or maybe even September or October.

"Why?" Fanny asked, shaking her head. "That's weeks away." She had spent most every day hoping to see Michael walk into the house. She longed for that moment when word would come that he was awaiting transportation to the island. She had already made Mr. Atwell promise to take her along on the trip. If Michael didn't return until September, she'd most likely be back in Rochester. "This is most unfair."

She drew a deep breath and looked at the rest of the letter.

I know that will not please you, but try to understand. Sherman and Zeb would like to make the best of the summer and take out what gold they can, and then sell the claim. They have asked me to stay with them and help them transport their gold back to Seattle. I believe it would be in all of our best interests to travel together. Dangers abound up here, but there's strength in numbers. Don't forget what the Bible says about a threefold cord not being quickly broken.

Fanny smiled, knowing she had just remembered that verse in the course of her time here on the island. She had thought of it as it pertained to her, Amanda, and Sophie and how good they were to support and defend one another. Now Michael was using that thought, as well.

Now lest I leave you with only sad thoughts, I will relate to you a funny story. When Zeb was in town around Christmas, he found a half-starved mongrel and brought him home to our cabin. He joked about how the dog was a Christmas gift for all of us to share. We called the dog Rusty because his coat was the color of a rusted hinge. Rusty immediately became a part of the family, with a particular liking to me. Zeb was rather puzzled by this, as he was the one who found the dog and fed him first. But Rusty would not relent. He follows me everywhere, even to the privy. The other night when Sherman came back from another trip for supplies in Dawson City, he brought a harmonica. Apparently Zeb had always been pretty talented at playing but had lost his harmonica on the trip north and been unable to buy another. Our supplies here are very limited, as you might have guessed.

Fanny flipped to the second page of the letter and smiled.

That night Zeb suggested a concert, and Sherman, being quite capable on the fiddle, agreed he would enjoy that very much. Word soon got out that we were to have a party and folks from up and down the creek came and brought what food and drink they could share. Several benches and chairs were arranged to accommodate the listeners, and to my great surprise, Rusty left my side and went to sit between Zeb and Sherman, as if he were one of the musicians. Zeb commented that perhaps Rusty did care about him as much as he did me and was quite proud that the dog should join them.

Soon the music began and a fine celebration was under way. To everyone's amusement Rusty began to sing. Well, singing is not exactly the word for it. He began to howl. He howled so loud that the music was very nearly drowned out. Everyone began to laugh, and the more we laughed, the more Rusty howled. When Zeb and Sherman finally concluded the song, Rusty stopped, too. The audience applauded, and we thought that to be the end of it because another miner came forward to sing and play a ballad on his guitar. Rusty didn't so much as utter a peep. In fact, he came back to sit at my feet and seemed not to give Zeb or Sherman so much as a glance. That is until they went forward to play once again. When they took their places, Rusty took his, as well. When the music began, Rusty began to howl his own rendition of "Sweet Betsy From Pike."

Fanny giggled at the picture Michael had painted. She could see all the miners gathered and the dog howling to the music.

Every time Zeb and Sherman played, Rusty would have to join them. No matter how hard I tried to keep Rusty at my side, he would not remain so long as those two were entertaining. It vexed Zeb something fierce, but everyone thought it great fun.

Now I must close this letter, or I'll never get it to the post in time. Please tell my folks that I think of them often and miss them very much. I imagine you all there at Broadmoor Island and know there is no place else in the world I'd rather be. I love you, my sweet Fanny. Please don't fret. September is not that far away. Every day I remind myself of that, and know that warmer weather will soon arrive, my days in the north will be spent, and I will come home to you.

Fanny clutched the letter close to her heart. Michael had touched these pages, created the words on them. Michael was even now counting the days until he could return to her.

"I must write to him. I'll spend whatever it takes to see the letter delivered," she said as she scrambled to her feet. First, she knew she needed to share the missive with Michael's parents. They would love hearing from him and knowing that he was safe and well.

She very nearly ran all the way back to the house and slipped breathlessly into the kitchen, where she found Mr. and Mrs. Atwell waiting for her return. "He's doing very well and sends his love," she said, smiling.

"Oh, what a relief. That is good news," Mrs. Atwell said.

Fanny wasn't certain, but she thought there were tears in the woman's eyes. She quickly turned away, however, and made a pretense of checking something in the oven.

Fanny put the letter on the table. "Read it for yourselves. The news is quite good overall. The cold and darkness sound horrible, but Michael himself is in good spirits."

Mrs. Atwell came to her husband's side as he picked up the letter and handed it to her. "You read, Mama. I'm afraid my eyes aren't as good as they used to be."

The woman smiled and took the paper in hand. She sat at the table and began to read. Fanny listened with great pleasure as Michael's words were once again dancing in her thoughts.

"September," Mrs. Atwell murmured, reaching the end of the letter. "That's just a few short weeks."

Fanny laughed. "I thought it sounded like forever, but you clearly have a more optimistic outlook."

"Well, she's right," Mr. Atwell declared. "It's already the middle of July. September will be here before we know it."

"And my family will be returning to Rochester," Fanny said softly. Without warning she spoke the thought uppermost on her mind. "I want to stay here. When the family returns to Rochester, I want to stay behind. I must be here when Michael comes home."

"But of course you can stay. If your uncle will allow it, you are most welcome to be with us," Mrs. Atwell said, and her husband nodded in agreement.

"Uncle Jonas may well not approve, but I am of age now. He cannot keep me from marrying Michael, nor can he put demands upon me that require my residing in Rochester with his family. While it may be more prudent for me to live with them, I would be safe staying here with you."

"Of course you would. You needn't fret one bit about that."

"And you needn't think that I won't be willing to work and help with the chores. I'm not a woman of leisure to sit and do nothing. I want to learn how to make all of Michael's favorite foods. I want to hear all the stories you can remember of when he was young." Fanny smiled. "I want to be a daughter to you both."

Mrs. Atwell got up and smothered her in a fierce embrace. "You have always been like a daughter to me, child. Goodness, but I couldn't be happier that you plan to marry my son."

"Say nothing to Uncle Jonas just yet," Fanny said, pulling away from Mrs. Atwell. "He will make us all quite miserable if he thinks we're plotting behind his back. When the right time comes, I'll speak to him."

"Very well," Mrs. Atwell replied. Mr. Atwell nodded once again and got to his feet. "I'd best get back to work. Someone will want to be taken to Clayton or one of the other islands. If they have to come looking for me, I might well hear about it from Mr. Broadmoor. We'd do well to keep that man happy."

Fanny knew he was right. Uncle Jonas could be such a bear to live with if he thought for even a second that someone else was in charge or making arrangements without his knowledge.

Jonas stepped off the *DaisyBee* and tramped up the path toward the house. He should be in Rochester rather than on the island, but that wouldn't set well with Victoria. She simply did not understand his need to be in Rochester and take care of business. Of course, she didn't realize the current state of their affairs, either. Not that he would ever discuss such matters with her. Women were no help when it came to money or business. Victoria could provide no solutions for him, and even the hint of dwindling bank accounts would likely send her into a frenzy that would only add to his current problems.

He'd been juggling accounts and investments for the past six months and had hoped Wesley Hedrick would prove to be a source of advice. But Sophie had ruined that for him. Women! One could create more havoc with a beguiling smile than a dozen men armed with weapons. Quincy thought the man was nothing more than a fraud, but Jonas couldn't believe that. No one would have the gall to try to impose such deception upon the Broadmoors. No, Hedrick was well off, no doubt, but he would want nothing to do with the family that had given life to such a wanton young woman as Sophie. Now Jonas would have to figure another way to deal with matters at hand.

With the final distribution of funds from his father's estate, he'd been able to realign some of his investments and had paid off a number of debts, but should these new investments fail, there would be no additional Broadmoor money to sustain him. And if the economy took yet another downturn, he could lose everything. He was playing a dangerous game, purchasing stocks while others were selling, yet he believed it would serve him well in the future—if his money held out long enough and the country didn't plummet into a depression. The economic downturn over the past few years had taken its toll, but investing had become Jonas's antidote for boredom and was much easier than the responsibility of actually running a business. Much like a gambler who couldn't stay away from the gaming table, he relished the thrill of investing. He could only hope the stock market wouldn't prove as fickle as a deck of cards.

He caught sight of Fanny sitting on the front veranda. As long as he continued to control her money, he could remain afloat and wait for his investments to begin their upward movement. The girl had caught sight of him and was walking toward him with a determined step. She'd been attempting to discuss some financial matter with him since earlier in the month. Thus far, he'd managed to avoid her. Who could guess what she might want to know. And he certainly didn't want to provide her with an accounting. Like her father before her, Fanny could be headstrong, but so could he—especially when money was involved. He *must* maintain control of her funds.

"Good afternoon, Fanny. A lovely day out here on the island." Jonas continued striding toward the house, and his niece easily kept pace.

"I need a few minutes of your time, Uncle Jonas. Each time I think we can talk, I discover that you've returned to Rochester, or you say you're otherwise involved."

"Could I at least greet your aunt before you insist upon a meeting, Fanny?" He hoped he'd infused her with enough guilt that he could once again escape her questions.

"Certainly."

However, she continued to follow in his wake. Obviously she was not going to be easily dissuaded. Perhaps Victoria would be of some assistance in occupying the girl. He glanced over his shoulder. "Do you know where I might locate your aunt?"

"I believe she took her needlework to the upper balcony."

"Jonas!" His wife descended the stairs and offered him a bright smile. "I saw you coming up the path. I'm pleased you arrived before supper. You do look weary."

Relief assailed him. His wife had offered an escape. "I am completely done in, my dear. It has been an extremely trying week. I trust there will be adequate time for me to rest before supper?"

"Yes, of course. Why don't you go on upstairs, and I'll see that you're not bothered."

Before he could respond, Fanny slipped between them. "Not until I have a few moments of your time, Uncle Jonas. This matter will not wait any longer."

"Surely there isn't anything so important that it won't wait until after supper, Fanny." His wife stepped closer as if to protect him.

"I've been trying to speak with Uncle Jonas for nearly two weeks now."

Jonas patted his wife's hand. He didn't want the tension to escalate. "I'll be fine, my dear. As soon as I speak with Fanny, I'll go upstairs and rest." He waved Fanny forward. "Come into the library and tell me what is of such great importance that it can't wait for another hour or two." He dropped into one of the leather chairs. "Well?"

"I need you to transfer money into an account for Paul and Sophie. I am going to purchase a house for them, and I want the funds to be easily accessible when Paul locates one. He's already begun his search, and I don't want him to miss an opportunity because I haven't arranged the funding." She stared at him a moment while he digested what she'd said. Then with a quick smile, she jumped up from her chair. "That didn't take long, did it? Now you may go upstairs and rest."

"Sit down!" he bellowed. "You want me to transfer funds so that you can purchase a house for Sophie?"

"And Paul," she added. "It's my wedding gift to them."

"Don't be ridiculous. If Sophie has need of a home and Paul can't purchase one, let her father see to it. Quincy inherited as much money as you did. He can well afford to help her."

Fanny folded her hands in her lap. "I appreciate your suggestion, Uncle Jonas, but we both know that Uncle Quincy will use every cent of his inheritance on the Home for the Friendless. He would think it a frivolous waste of money that could be better used to help the needy."

"As do I," Jonas boomed.

"You think I should donate the money to the needy?"

"No, of course not! But I believe purchasing a house for your cousin is a frivolous waste of money."

"Well, I disagree, and it's my money. Amanda and Sophie are closer to me than anyone else in the world. If I want to do this for Sophie, I don't see why you should object. I've already told Amanda I will do the same for her when she marries," Fanny frowned. "Of course, she doesn't think she will ever marry, but—"

"I am not interested in discussing Amanda's marriage prospects. I am certain she will choose a husband who can afford to purchase a house. But we are currently discussing a transfer of funds to benefit Sophie." He wagged his head. "I think this is a tragic error, and I advise against any such—"

"The money is mine. I am of age, and I insist the transfer be made. I've not pressed the issue until now because there seemed to be no reason to do so, but if you will not handle my money in the manner in which I desire, I will simply take full charge of it."

His angry words weren't having the effect he had hoped for. Why was it men cowered at his feet if Jonas so much as raised his voice, but this snippet of a girl stood her ground with ease? If he wasn't careful, he would be sinking in quicksand with no means of rescue. "That won't be necessary, my dear. I'm afraid you just took me by surprise. I'm quite tired and, well, it seemed that your idea was not well thought out. Upon reflection, I see you've considered this for some time. If you insist, I will see to it when I return to Rochester on Monday."

"And you'll send word to Paul the moment the account has been set up?"

He nodded. "I will see to it. What amount do you have in mind?" She told him, and he felt his chest tighten. "Very well." It was the only thing he could say. To speak further would have sent him into a rage.

The moment she exited the room, Jonas pushed himself up from the chair and removed a bottle of bourbon from the enclosed cabinet beneath one of the library shelves. He poured an inch of the amber liquid into a glass. Swallowing the contents in one gulp, he held his breath as the burning sensation coursed down his throat and into his belly. Moments later, he exhaled and poured another glass. This time he sat down in his chair and drank slowly, his level of anxiety now somewhat abated by the liquor.

He didn't know how long he'd been sitting in the chair when Victoria entered the room. Her unexpected appearance startled him.

"I went upstairs looking for you," she said. "I thought you were going to take a nap before supper."

"I was, but I decided I could relax in here just as well. What time is it?"

She sat down in the chair opposite him. "Six o'clock. I told Mrs. Atwell to plan supper for seven. I thought to give you extra time to rest."

"Thank you for your concern, but I'm feeling much better, my dear." He didn't confess it was the alcohol rather than sleep that had helped him to gain his state of relaxation. His wife wouldn't approve.

"How are things in Rochester?" Victoria rang a small bell and, when a servant appeared, requested a pitcher of lemonade.

"Everything is as usual," he said once the servant had disappeared. "Most of your friends are still summering abroad or at their summer cottages. At least that's what their husbands tell me when I see them at the club." He glanced outside. "I am glad most of the family has departed from the island. Now with the final disbursement of money given, I'll be surprised to see any of them for some time. I trust it has been more restful for you, as well."

She nodded. "There's been little happening to speak of. Except for Fanny's letter. But I imagine she mentioned she'd heard from Michael."

Jonas perked to attention. "No, she didn't say a word. What did he have to say for himself?"

The servant returned with the lemonade and glasses arranged on a tray.

Victoria pointed to the small table across from her. She poured her husband a glass of the lemonade and handed it to him. "From his letter, it sounds as though he's been extremely successful in his search for gold."

Jonas snorted. "Well, one can't necessarily believe he's met with such good fortune. He may simply be hoping to keep her waiting by the fireside, so to speak."

"Since he plans to leave the Yukon at the end of August, it would seem his letter must be truthful."

"End of August?" Jonas sputtered and choked on the lemonade. Tears trickled down his cheeks, and he withdrew a handkerchief from his pocket while Victoria clapped him on the back.

When he finally quit coughing and had caught his breath, Victoria returned to her chair. "Goodness, you gave me a fright. Was there a seed in the lemonade?"

He ignored the question. "Did you say Michael is returning the end of August?"

"Or early September. Fanny was hoping he would return even earlier, but it didn't appear he could manage to depart any sooner. She's already planning a wedding for mid-September."

"We can't permit her to marry him, Victoria. It just isn't appropriate. The Atwells are nice enough people, but Michael wouldn't fit in with our people."

"I understand it could make for a difficult marriage, but Fanny is of legal age. If she wants to marry Michael, we can hardly stop her." She poured herself a glass of lemonade. "I've done my best to steer her toward other young men, but Fanny tells me you've given your word, Jonas. The girl has her own fortune, and if Michael has met your requirements, I don't see how you can possibly object. It simply wouldn't be honorable."

"Don't you care if the girl becomes a social outcast?"

Victoria scoffed. "Our social community might treat her coldly for a season, but they would never banish Fanny for the long term. She is a Broadmoor and has inherited a third of her grandfather's estate. And if Michael has made a fortune in the gold fields, his money will gain him acceptance in all the right social circles." She took a sip of her lemonade. "Besides, some things are more important than social status and money. The Broadmoors have always recognized the importance of family."

He stared at his wife, dumbfounded by her last remark. He'd never seen evidence that his relatives, except for his mother and father, cared one whit about family. Instead of encouragement, they provided gossip fodder for one another, each seeming to relish the other's bad news rather than the good. In fact, they would likely be delighted if his investments failed.

CHAPTER 25

SATURDAY, AUGUST 13, 1898

At the sight of the *DaisyBee*, Amanda hurried toward the dock. She kept to the path, her strides long and vigorous. For the past half hour, she'd been waiting for Clara Barton's arrival. The older woman had accepted an invitation to join them for an afternoon on Broadmoor Island, and Amanda planned to use the time to her advantage. Mr. Atwell had departed some time ago. He planned to pick up a few supplies in Clayton, meet her uncle Quincy at the train station, and then stop at Pullman Island for Miss Barton.

Shading her eyes, she peered toward the boat. She could make out two men and one woman. Perhaps Paul had accompanied Uncle Quincy. Sophie would certainly be surprised, for Paul had told her cousin that he would be needed at the Home this weekend. Squinting into the sun, she decided the man wasn't Paul, for the man beside Uncle Quincy was somewhat taller. Royal Pullman may have decided to accompany Miss Barton. Her spirits sagged at the thought, for if so, she wouldn't get as much time with the woman as she'd hoped.

She hastened forward to greet Miss Barton, but when the second man turned toward her, she stopped in her tracks and stared, speechless. *Blake!* Who had invited him to the island? Mr. Atwell assisted Miss Barton from the boat while Amanda wondered if Dr. Carstead had come to meet Miss Barton. With her thoughts skittering helter-skelter, Amanda forced herself to take stock of the situation. Miss Barton was her guest, and she didn't want to make a poor impression. "I trust you had a pleasant boat ride, Miss Barton?"

"Lovely. Too bad it wasn't longer. I told Mr. Atwell that he could take the long way around when he delivers me back to Castle Rest on Mr. Pullman's island. I do enjoy the scenery along the river. Of course, it's always more fun to see a new guest's reaction to the islands." She smiled at Blake. "Dr. Carstead is quite impressed with this little piece of heaven we call the Thousand Islands, aren't you?"

"That I am, Miss Barton. And your enjoyable company has made it all the more appealing." He smiled at Amanda. "You didn't tell me Miss Barton was a frequent visitor to the islands."

A surge of unbidden jealousy caught her by surprise. "I don't believe we ever discussed the islands at all. However, I am surprised to see you here, Dr. Carstead. I didn't realize my mother had invited you."

"Dr. Carstead is *my* guest, Amanda," her uncle replied. His terse tone served to remind her that the island wasn't the sole property of her father. Uncle Quincy and Fanny shared ownership with her father in Broadmoor Island. "Since he so generously donates his time and energy to residents at the Home,

I thought he might enjoy a weekend of relaxation here at the island. A small way of extending my personal thanks."

Miss Barton opened her parasol. "I'm pleased you agreed to accept Quincy's invitation. Time to rejuvenate body and soul is important to those working in the medical profession. The first time Royal Pullman invited me to come for a visit, I nearly refused. I'm thankful he insisted." She chuckled. "Now I invite myself."

Blake pointed toward the house. "It appears there's a game of croquet already in progress."

Amanda nodded. "Most any time of day, you can find someone willing to play lawn tennis or croquet. Shall we sit on the veranda and watch? Or perhaps you'd like to join in, Dr. Carstead? I'm certain they wouldn't object to another player." If he agreed, she would have the time alone with Miss Barton she had hoped for.

"It appears they're already well into their game. I'll join them later if they should decide to play again."

Uncle Quincy bobbed his head. "Absolutely. Sit down and have a glass of lemonade, Blake. I'm sure you and Miss Barton have many things you'd like to discuss."

Amanda considered advising her uncle that Miss Barton was *her* guest, but she knew such behavior would be unseemly. Instead, she inwardly seethed when the doctor positioned himself between Miss Barton and her. Couldn't he at least let her sit next to the woman?

Miss Barton accepted a glass of lemonade and settled back in her chair. "Dr. Carstead tells me you've been quite an asset in the operating room, Amanda."

A smile played at her lips. "He did?" She glanced in his direction, surprised by the revelation.

Blake grunted. "Don't let a few words of praise go to your head. You still have much to learn."

"But you did say she was more adept than some of the physicians you'd trained with, and that she doesn't forget anything once she's been taught."

"He did?" Amanda repeated. She sat up straighter in her chair.

"Yes, but I also mentioned she needs a great deal more training," he added.

Miss Barton tipped her head to one side. "Still, you had the highest of praise for—"

A scream erupted from the yard, and Amanda jumped to her feet. "It's Sophie!" she shouted, racing toward the lawn.

Her cousin was doubled over in pain and was using her croquet mallet to help maintain her balance. Embracing Sophie around the shoulders, Amanda met her cousin's wild-eyed stare. "You are going to be fine, Sophie, but you must tell me what is wrong."

"Terrible pain . . . in my stomach," Sophie sputtered between tearful sobs. "Oh, I cannot bear it."

"We need to get her inside," Blake said. "I'm going to carry you into the house, Sophie. There's no need to worry. Amanda and I are going to take care of you."

The doctor's words seemed to soothe her, but then Amanda's mother arrived from across the lawn and asked, "What's wrong? Is she going to lose the baby?"

Sophie twisted in Dr. Carstead's arms. "Is that what's happening to me?" she wailed. The frantic look reappeared.

"*Mother!*" Amanda pulled her mother aside. "We are trying to calm her. Please guard your words." Without waiting for her mother's reply, Amanda hurried after Dr. Carstead, Miss Barton close on her heels.

"Complete bed rest for a minimum of two weeks," Blake instructed after Sophie's examination had been completed.

"Two weeks? How can I possibly remain in bed with nothing to do for two weeks?" Sophie moaned.

Miss Barton wagged her finger. "No complaining, young lady. I completely concur with the doctor. If you want a healthy baby, you'll do as he's instructed." She tipped her head close to Amanda's ear. "We can count upon you to make certain she follows the doctor's orders, can we not?"

"Yes. I'll keep her in that bed if I have to stand guard over her. Or I'll find some ropes down at the boathouse and tie her in." Amanda smiled at her cousin.

A light tapping sounded at the door. Amanda hurried across the room and opened the door a mere slit. She glanced at Sophie and then at Blake. "Sophie's father would like to see her."

"Oh yes. Do let him come in." Sophie pushed her palms against the mattress and attempted to inch herself into a sitting position.

Dr. Carstead shook his head. "Your father may come in for a brief visit, but no sitting up yet. After your visit, I want you to rest. Understand?"

Sophie didn't appear totally convinced, but the doctor waited until he'd received an affirmative reply before permitting her father into the room. Blake then repeated the instructions to Uncle Quincy and bid Amanda to remain until the visit was complete.

"I'll make certain she's well settled and resting before I leave," Amanda promised as she escorted Dr. Carstead and Miss Barton to the doorway.

Amanda stayed at a distance, observing Sophie with Uncle Quincy. Sophie had mentioned a conversation she'd had with her father after Wesley's hasty departure, yet the obvious affection that had developed between the two of them caught her by surprise. When Uncle Quincy enveloped Sophie in an embrace, he appeared genuinely concerned.

He brushed a lock of damp hair from Sophie's forehead. "I'm going to send a telegram to Paul. He can be here by tomorrow morning."

"That's not necessary. He's needed at the Home, and you're here. It's not as though I don't have family to look after me. Besides, Dr. Carstead says I'll be fine with two weeks of bed rest. There's no reason for Paul to come right away. He's supposed to arrive next Friday."

Her father frowned. "You know how much he loves you, Sophie. I doubt he would forgive me if I didn't send word to him."

"Then you may send him a telegram, but tell him I'm fine." She grabbed his hand. "And tell him if he feels he must come, Monday will be soon enough, that I know he's needed at the Home. Tell him I am well cared for and there's—"

"I'm sending a telegram, not a letter," he said with a chuckle. "I know Paul had special church services planned for Sunday at the Home, so I will tell him you want him to wait to come until Monday."

"Well, he doesn't *have* to come, but if he *wants* to come . . ." Her voice trailed off. "Perhaps I should figure out what to say and write it down for you." She waved to Amanda. "Would you locate a pen and paper for me?"

"No. You need to rest. Your father is quite capable of choosing the proper words to advise your husband."

Uncle Quincy grinned. "Thank you for your confidence, Amanda. Now if you two will excuse me, I'm off to send that telegram." He glanced at his daughter then turned to Amanda. "I hope you have better luck getting her to obey than I did."

Amanda laughed. "I have ways of dealing with patients. I've learned a great deal from Dr. Carstead. Sophie wouldn't dare give me any trouble. Would you, Sophie, dear?"

Sophie rolled her eyes and shook her head. "It seems the odds are already against me. I suppose I have no say in the matter whatsoever."

Amanda heard someone crying and knew that the only person it could be was Fanny. She opened the bedroom door without knocking and called to her cousin. "Fanny? May I come in?"

Fanny sat in shadows by the open window. She sniffed back tears. "Yes, of course."

"What's wrong? I heard you sobbing." Amanda came to where Fanny sat and pulled up a chair to join her.

"It's Sophie. I'm so worried about her. I couldn't bear to lose another member of my family."

"What are you talking about? She just needs bed rest—that's all."

Fanny met Amanda's look of puzzlement. "She could die. My mother did."

Amanda began to understand Fanny's worry. "Oh, Fanny. I'm so sorry.

I didn't think about how that might cause you fear." She scooted her chair closer and put her arm around Fanny's shoulder. "Sophie is strong. I remember hearing that your mother was quite small and not at all hardy in her constitution. You know Sophie—she could run circles around us and not even perspire."

"But childbirth is so hard on women. Many women die for seemingly no reason," Fanny protested. "And now Sophie is suffering pain and has to remain in bed."

"Only for a short time. She'll be fine. She just got too excited and overdid things. We need to be strong for her, Fanny. We'll need to sit with her and keep her entertained; otherwise you know how things will be. She'll want out of bed and argue with us about how bored she is."

Fanny wiped her eyes with her handkerchief. "I want to be strong and helpful to her. I'm sorry for my tears. I suppose sometimes old fears creep in to stir up worry."

"It's all right. Together we will be strong for Sophie, and for each other." Amanda smiled. "Agreed?"

Fanny nodded. "Agreed."

Sophie rolled to her left side and forced her eyes open. Her gaze settled upon a pair of navy blue pants. She rolled to her back, now fully awake. Paul sat beside her bed and smiled down at her.

"Good morning," he said. He softly touched her cheek.

"When did you arrive? I told Father you didn't need to come." Sophie blinked away the cobwebs interfering with her thoughts. She'd lost all sense of time. "What day is it?"

"It's Monday morning. I arrived on the early train, and Captain Visegar offered me a ride on the *New Island Wanderer*. Mr. Atwell didn't know when I'd be arriving, so I accepted the captain's offer. How are you feeling?"

"I'm feeling quite well. The pains have subsided, and I am weary of lying in this bed. But Amanda will brook no nonsense. Those are her words, not mine," Sophie said with a faint smile.

"I'm pleased to hear that she's making you follow the doctor's orders. I spoke with Dr. Carstead last evening after he and your father returned to Rochester."

She detected a hint of concern in Paul's voice and wondered if Dr. Carstead had been completely frank with her. Surely he wouldn't have given her false hope for the baby. "He said we would both be fine, didn't he?" Paul wouldn't lie to her. He was, after all, a man of God. If he affirmed the doctor's report to her, she'd rest easy.

"If you follow his orders, he believes everything will be fine. He said it isn't unusual to have difficulties such as you've experienced. He thinks you simply overdid things."

She sighed and settled back against her pillows, thankful to have someone regale her with stories of the happenings in Rochester. In fact, she was even pleased to hear about Paul's work at the Home, the special Sunday services, and his lengthy report on progress at the new addition—anything to help pass the time. When the maid arrived to tidy the room, Paul requested his meals be delivered to the room.

"You will soon be as bored as I am," she said. "If only I enjoyed reading. I believe Amanda or Fanny would be content with a stack of books at their side." She wrinkled her nose.

Paul jumped to his feet. "I'm going to move your bed so that you have a view of the river and a portion of the lawn. At least you will have something to see other than the walls of this room." He removed his jacket, rolled up his sleeves, and set to work. Bending forward, he lifted one end of the bed and grunted.

Sophie giggled. "It's heavier than you thought, isn't it?"

"It must be the heavy mattress, for my wife weighs no more than a feather."

"Your wife grows larger by the day. If I'm required to stay in this bed, it won't be long until you're unable to move it."

"I like to hear you refer to yourself as my wife," he said, grasping the headboard. "There! I believe that will work. What do you think?"

"Thank you, Paul. This is *much* better. Look." She pointed toward the window. "I can see the boats out on the water." She clapped her hands. "What a smart man you are."

He leaned down and placed a light kiss on her head. "At least I can do one thing to please you."

She frowned but lowered her head so that he couldn't see her. Was that how he felt in her presence? Did he constantly seek to find ways to earn her approval? Or—dare she say the word—love? Sophie pushed the thought aside as Paul was already gazing out the window and seemed to have given it no more thought. Unfortunately Sophie knew it would be on her mind for some time to come.

By midafternoon, Sophie's spirits began to wane. She'd already tired of looking out the window and hearing Paul read to her. She'd dozed for a while, but when she awakened, she longed for something new to fill the hours. Paul suggested a visit from Amanda and Fanny, and Sophie agreed. He squeezed her hand and immediately jumped up to do her bidding. What had she done to deserve such a fine man, she wondered. Paul was everything a woman could desire in a husband. If only her heart would forget Wesley.

Her cousins arrived moments later, both of them looking grim. "The two of you need not look so gloomy. I haven't died just yet."

"That's not humorous in the least," Amanda snapped. "We have been terribly worried about you."

"And the baby," Fanny added. "Paul says you've had no pains since he arrived."

"None. So I don't see why I must remain abed. Couldn't I at least try sitting in one of the chairs for a time? I would truly enjoy going out to sit on the veranda."

"No, no, no." Amanda sounded like a parent chastising a small child. "Must I resort to those ropes I mentioned to Dr. Carstead?"

Sophie giggled. "Attempting to free myself might prove a diversion. I don't think I can possibly do this for two weeks."

Mrs. Atwell entered the room carrying a tray. "Mr. Medford thought you ladies might enjoy tea."

Sophie beamed. "Isn't he the most thoughtful man?"

"He's been terribly worried about you, especially because you've expressed your boredom. He fears you'll get out of bed before the doctor grants permission," Fanny said.

"I can't help that I'm weary of this bed. It's tiresome to be stuck away up here with nothing to occupy my time. Paul has read to me and played cards, but even that becomes wearisome after a time."

Mrs. Atwell settled the tea tray on a table between Amanda and Fanny and poured three cups. She glanced over her shoulder at Sophie. "What about that babe you're carrying, Miss Sophie? You could use this time to make some fine little clothes for the child, don't you think?"

"Oh yes. That's a wonderful idea," Fanny said. "And we'll help you. We can come to your room each afternoon. By the time the baby arrives, we should have a complete layette."

Sophie wasn't so certain. Once she was out of bed, she didn't know how much sewing she'd care to do. After all, domestic duties weren't something she had ever aspired to. However, having her cousins spend the afternoons with her during the next two weeks would help pass the time.

"That's a wonderful idea, Mrs. Atwell. We can make a list and have Mr. Atwell pick up the items over in Clayton."

The older woman agreed. "Why don't you work on your list right now? Frank will be going to pick up supplies in the morning. He can purchase whatever you need at the same time."

While they drank their tea, Amanda jotted several items on a piece of paper. Sophie waved a hand at her cousin. "I don't plan to be in this room for more than two weeks. That list is becoming far too extensive."

"We'll continue on the layette after you've recovered. Instead of fishing when we go on our picnics, I'll sew instead," Fanny promised. "This is going to be great fun."

Sophie agreed, though she wasn't quite so sure. While her cousins were both adept with needle and thread, Sophie's ability as a seamstress lay far below theirs. She pushed aside the thought and suggested Amanda add a yard of fine lace to the list.

"Here, let me help you," Amanda said, taking the piece of soft cambric and examining Sophie's stitches. "Your embroidery is knotting because your thread is much too long."

Sophie curled her lip. "I dislike threading the needle."

"But you see the result?" Amanda picked up her scissors and snipped the thread. "I'll have to cut this and remove the stitches. You'll have to start over."

Sophie sighed and dropped against her pillows. "I don't think I have the necessary talent to embroider."

"Then why don't you stitch one of these gowns that I've cut out, and I'll embroider?"

Sophie agreed, although Fanny's instructions seemed much more difficult than she'd anticipated. They'd been sewing for a week, and she had little to show for her efforts, while her cousins continued to add items each day: tiny embroidered bibs, sacques with lace edging, and a tiny bonnet with silk ribbons. Amanda had permitted one of Sophie's creations into the pile, a bib with ribbon edging. However, Sophie saw that Amanda had ripped out and hemstitched a portion of the edging.

Fanny threaded a needle and handed it to Sophie. "Begin along this side, using tiny stitches."

Sophie dipped her needle into the soft fabric and completed several stitches. Fanny smiled and offered an approving nod before returning to her embroidery work. They worked until suppertime and then set aside their work when Mrs. Atwell knocked at the door. The older woman arranged a tray on Sophie's lap and motioned to her cousins.

"Supper will be served downstairs in ten minutes," she said.

Sophie would have preferred the company of her cousins for the remainder of the evening, but she insisted they go downstairs. They deserved to enjoy themselves with the rest of the family, even if she must remain in bed. Perhaps she could finish the gown this evening and have something more than a bib to add to the layette.

When her cousins arrived the following afternoon, Sophie looked up from her stitching. "I'm almost finished with the gown I began yesterday."

Amanda arched her brows. "So soon? I do hope you've been making tiny stitches."

"I worked on it last evening as well as this morning," she said, tying off the final knot. "There! All done. Such tedious work."

Fanny stepped alongside the bed and quickly examined the stitches. "That's wonderful, Sophie. Let's turn it right side out."

Sophie handed the gown to her cousin, but Fanny's brow soon knit into a frown as she attempted to turn the gown right side out. "What have you done to this?" She placed it atop the coverlet and then giggled.

Amanda leaned forward to examine the gown. "You've sewn the neck and arm holes together."

Sophie grabbed the gown away from her cousin. "I did exactly what Fanny said. I went around the edges with tiny stitches, and now you tell me it's wrong."

"I'm sorry, Sophie. I thought you would understand the need for openings at the neck and sleeves. How did you expect to get it over the baby's head?" Fanny clapped her hand over her mouth and stifled a giggle.

"I believe you should apply your efforts to hemming diapers and blankets," Amanda said.

"Or maybe I should *purchase* the baby's clothes," Sophie declared.

Amanda *tsk*ed and waved her needle back and forth. "You need to remember that you're married to a minister who doesn't command a large salary. Paul's income won't permit frivolous spending."

Sophie sighed and looked out the window. "You're right. I suppose that's my punishment." She grinned at Fanny. "On the other hand, the baby has a wealthy aunt. I'm certain Fanny won't want to see her niece or nephew wearing anything like this." She held the gown in the air, and the three of them giggled.

Paul watched Sophie sleep and wondered if he would ever win her heart. He loved her so dearly that it actually caused an ache deep within. How he longed to hold her in his arms, stroke her hair, kiss her lips.

He shook that thought off as soon as it came. There was no sense in dreaming of such things at this juncture. Sophie was carrying a child and had nearly suffered a miscarriage. He would do nothing to risk her losing the baby. The last thing he wanted her to think was that he cared nothing for the child.

Sophie moaned softly and rolled onto her back. Paul could see the rounding bulge of her abdomen through the light coverlet. He marveled that a child grew inside this petite young woman. He wondered if it was a boy who would favor his father's features. Could Sophie ever truly put Wesley Hedrick behind her if the child looked like his father?

O God, he prayed in silence. *Please help Sophie grow to love me. Help her to let go of the past and all the lies that Hedrick told her.*

"Oh, Paul. I'm glad you're here."

He heard her speak and opened his eyes, certain he'd find her looking at him. But instead, he found she was still asleep. Her words had been whispered in her dreams. He couldn't help but smile. The more he thought about the situation, the broader his smile grew. It wasn't a declaration of love, to be sure, but she wanted him there. At least in her sleep she could admit that much.

Paul felt like shouting. Instead, he thanked God for the glimmer of hope. "All I need is hope," he whispered. "Well, that and a great deal of patience."

CHAPTER 26

MONDAY, AUGUST 29, 1898

The past two weeks had been the longest in Sophie's life. Today she would be permitted to go downstairs for a picnic lunch with her cousins. She didn't want to admit how easily she tired, but her legs were quivering like Mrs. At-well's rhubarb jelly by the time she had completed her toilette. Amanda had warned she must not overtax herself or she'd be returned to bed rest—a fact Sophie didn't favor in the least.

"Miss Amanda said you should wait for her and she'll help you downstairs," Veda said after she'd poked the final hairpins into Sophie's coiffure. "Unless you want me to help you."

Sophie considered the maid's offer. She didn't like the idea of waiting, especially after being abed for two full weeks. On the other hand, she didn't want to get off on the wrong foot with her older cousin. "Thank you, Veda, but I believe I had best wait on my cousin."

The maid tucked one final strand of hair into place and met Sophie's gaze in the mirror. "You might want to pinch your cheeks a little, Miss Sophie. You're still a tad pale." She frowned. "Maybe you should rest in your bed until Miss Amanda comes to get you."

"I'm fine, Veda. You worry nearly as much as Amanda. Go on and take care of your duties. I'll wait here until my cousin arrives."

Amanda had assumed the dual role of parent and doctor, and Sophie would be glad to have her cousin return to being her friend. Rather than having to answer to the probing medical questions Amanda insisted upon asking each time she entered the room, Sophie looked forward to engaging once again in their lively conversation.

There had been few medical changes for Sophie to report throughout the confinement. Other than occasional twinges, Sophie hadn't experienced any further difficulty, and her confidence increased with each passing day. The fluttering movements deep within her body confirmed her baby remained strong and, as if discerning her thoughts, the baby moved. In the past she'd heard women occasionally speak of the wonder of carrying a baby, but such talk had been of little interest to her. Now she wished she could recall every word. Her sister Beatrice would surely be pleased to speak to her of the travails of childbirth and the tragedy of an infant's death, but Sophie didn't want to dwell on those topics. Thankfully, Beatrice had returned home and wouldn't be waiting downstairs to spread gloom.

The bedroom door opened, and Amanda greeted Sophie with a bright smile. "You look wonderful. Fanny is seeing to our picnic. Are you ready to attempt the steps?"

"I'm feeling fine," Sophie said.

However, walking down the stairs proved more exhausting than she had anticipated. By the time they arrived on the veranda, she gladly accepted the chair Amanda pulled toward her and readily accepted Fanny's suggestion to lunch on the veranda rather than walk to one of their favorite island locations. A short time later Fanny and Mrs. Atwell appeared with a tray of assorted sandwiches, strawberry cake, and a pitcher of lemonade.

Sophie selected a roast beef sandwich while still eyeing the cake. "Perhaps I'll try a piece of cake first," she said with a giggle. Fanny winked at her while Amanda lectured upon the fact that medical books now touted proper nutrition as important for the health of both mother and baby.

"I have some news to tell the two of you," Sophie said once her cousins had filled their plates.

"Oh, I do hope it's good news," Fanny replied. "Paul appeared somewhat distracted during his visit this weekend, and I feared something was amiss."

Sophie giggled. "I think he feared he might slip and tell our secret."

"He hasn't accepted a position elsewhere, has he?" Amanda asked, the makings of a frown beginning to crease her brow.

"No, of course not. He's found a house that he thinks will suit us quite well. It's not in the Ruffled Shirt District, of course, but he says it's very nice. It's on King Street or perhaps Madison; I don't remember for certain. He mentioned so many that he'd seen."

"I don't think you should refer to East Avenue as the Ruffled Shirt District,

Sophie—there are already more than enough people who make snide remarks about the area where we live."

Sophie shrugged. "*We* don't live there. My father's house isn't located on East Avenue. Besides, you call the area where the Hollanders live Dutchtown. What's the difference if they refer to an area of town populated by the rich as the Ruffled Shirt District?"

"The name makes those who live there sound ostentatious."

Sophie giggled. "I suppose if it makes you feel better, I can say that Paul didn't look at any homes on East Avenue. He said that as soon as I'm able to return home, he'll take me to see it. He thought you might like to come along, Fanny."

Amanda folded her arms in front of her waist. "Well, what about *me*? Am *I* not invited?"

"Don't be silly. Of course you're invited. But since Fanny is purchasing the house, Paul thought she should see what she is buying."

"I'll be happy to go along, but whatever you choose will be fine with me," Fanny said. "If you and Paul like the house, that's all that's important. I'm delighted he agreed to my plan, and though I may have furnished the funds, it is you and Paul who are buying this home."

Sophie filled her glass with lemonade. "I hope the two of you will help me decorate the house. I have as little expertise decorating as I do stitching baby clothes."

Amanda chuckled. "Then you will certainly need our help. I believe some of Grandfather's furniture is being stored at a warehouse until it can be auctioned. I would guess that you could use some of those items to furnish your house. I'll check with Mother."

"Oh, that's a wonderful idea, Amanda," Fanny said. "I would much prefer your using them than having Uncle Jonas place them in an auction. I'll speak to him when the family returns to Rochester next week."

Summer had slipped by in no more than a wink, yet when Sophie considered all that had happened over the past few months, it seemed far more than a wink. It was strange how time played tricks with one's mind. She was savoring a bite of the strawberry cake when Mr. Atwell approached from the side of the house. He waved and smiled, but his eyes didn't reflect their usual twinkle.

"Sorry to interrupt, Fanny, but Maggie wondered if you could come to the kitchen when you've finished your lunch. She needs a word with you."

Concern edged the older man's words, and Fanny immediately pushed away from the table. "I've finished. I'll come with you now," she said. "Why don't you two wait for me? And say a prayer that it isn't bad news," she whispered to her cousins.

She hurried to keep pace with Mr. Atwell, her nerves beginning to take hold. The roast beef sandwich lurched in her stomach, and she wondered if she might be ill before reaching the kitchen. Silently she chastised herself for expecting the worst.

One look at Mrs. Atwell's face was enough to confirm she wouldn't be hearing good news. She considered backing out the door or covering her ears before the older woman had an opportunity to speak. If something had happened to Michael, Fanny didn't know if she could carry on. She spied a letter on the worktable and pointed to it.

"From Michael?" It was as much as she could manage.

"Yes. There's one for you, too. Why don't you sit down, and I'll fetch you a cup of tea. Or would you prefer something cool?"

"Nothing," Fanny said, dropping into one of the wooden chairs. "He's not injured?" She couldn't bring herself to ask if he was dead. It seemed even to say the word might make it so.

Mrs. Atwell shook her head. "No, nothing like that. But there's been trouble. Both Zeb and Sherman, Michael's two partners, were injured in an accident. Michael wasn't with them at the time."

Fanny sighed, relief washing over her like a spring rain. "Zeb and Sherman will recover?"

"Yes, but they need Michael to stay on with them. They're unable to make it out of the Yukon. If they're to survive, they need his help." Mrs. Atwell forced a smile. "Michael could never leave them."

Fanny nodded. "I know," she whispered, a tear beginning to form in the corner of her eye. "Did he say when . . ."

"Next summer, dear. His letter says there will be no way he can make it back before then." The older woman handed a sealed envelope to her. "I'm sure your letter will say much the same as ours."

No longer able to maintain her brave front, Fanny's tears escaped and cascaded down her cheeks in tiny rivulets. "Each day I've been expecting to see him walk up that path, and now I must wait an entire year," she sobbed.

Mrs. Atwell gathered her into a warm embrace and stroked her hair. "He is in God's hands, Fanny. Michael is young and strong. I understand your disappointment, but the news could be much worse." She lifted Fanny's chin. "Don't you agree?"

"Yes, but that doesn't ease my pain."

"I know, but you'll get through this, and once you and Michael are married, you'll forget this disappointment."

Fanny tucked the letter into her pocket. Mrs. Atwell's words contained wisdom, but it didn't ease her pain. She patted her pocket. "I'll tell you if his letter contains any further information."

Mrs. Atwell kissed her cheeks. "We'd appreciate that, dear." The older woman glanced toward the stove. "I don't want to rush you off, but I must begin the meal preparations. If you want to talk more, come see me after supper."

Fanny pushed herself up from the table and trudged to the door.

"Fanny?"

She turned and looked over her shoulder.

"Don't forget that prayer is the answer. Mr. Atwell and I will continue to pray for both you and Michael."

"Thank you," Fanny whispered. She would need someone else to pray for her right now, for she didn't think God would want to hear what she had to say about this turn of events. She continued around the side of the house, wishing she hadn't asked her cousins to wait for her.

Sophie swiveled around in her chair. "Did you receive a letter from Michael?"

She patted the pocket of her skirt. "He isn't coming home until next summer." After detailing the account, Fanny pulled a handkerchief from her pocket. "I don't know how I will bear to wait another year."

Sophie touched her hand. "I know this is difficult for you. I remember how I felt when I received Wesley's letter. I wanted to die. You feel a hole right in the pit of your stomach."

Fanny touched a hand to her stomach and nodded. "Yes. Right there."

Amanda wagged her finger. "I'm sorry for both of you, but this is no time to sit and commiserate. This kind of talk only makes matters worse. You must focus upon happier thoughts."

"Is that in the medical books, too?" Sophie asked.

"I'm certain it is," Amanda said. "And if it isn't, it should be. With me away at medical school in the fall, it's good, Fanny, that you'll be available to help Sophie. You can assist with the decorating of her house, and when the baby arrives in December, you can help Sophie during her confinement."

"Confinement? I'm not going to be like those women who remain abed for weeks on end."

Amanda waved her cousin into silence. "No matter. Once the baby is born, you'll be glad for all of the assistance Fanny offers you. And, Fanny, you could even move in with Paul and Sophie. Then you'd have an opportunity to spoil the baby at every turn."

Fanny wiped her eyes and tucked the handkerchief back into her pocket. With Sophie's move into a new house and a baby due in the winter, perhaps she could use this time to advantage until Michael's return.

CHAPTER 27

The packing for their journey home now complete, the family gathered in the dining room for breakfast. Aunt Victoria had been in a flurry for several days. No doubt the servants would be happy to return to Rochester and settle back into their normal routine. And Mrs. Atwell would likely be even more delighted when the family stepped foot on the *DaisyBee* for the final time that season.

While Mrs. Atwell poured her a glass of orange juice, Sophie filled her plate with scrambled eggs, toast, and two slices of bacon. Turning toward the table, Sophie suddenly doubled over. Pain spread through her body like fiery splinters, and she stared wide-eyed at Mrs. Atwell. The older woman encircled her waist and eased her into a chair as another pain seared through her belly. She bit down on her lip, and the salty taste of blood assaulted her tongue.

"What's happening?" she asked, her fingers digging into Mrs. Atwell's hand.

"I'm not certain, my dear, but I'm going to send Mr. Atwell to Clayton to fetch Dr. Balch right this minute. Let go of my hand and grab hold of Amanda."

Amanda stepped forward, and the two women exchanged places. Jefferson bounded into the room and took a backward step at the sight of his cousin. Amanda waved him forward. "I need you to carry Sophie upstairs to her bedroom."

Jefferson's jaw went slack. "To the third floor? I don't think—"

"No need to take her up there. Take her to the second-floor room Fanny and I share. Go get George to help you." Amanda calmly called out orders as though she'd been overseeing medical emergencies all of her life.

Fanny knelt down in front of her cousin. "You're going to be fine, Sophie. We'll get you into bed, and you'll be up and about in no time."

Mrs. Atwell scurried back inside. "Mr. Atwell will be back with the doctor before you know it. Any more pains?"

Amanda shook her head. "We're going to move her upstairs to bed. George and Jefferson will carry her. I don't think she should walk."

"Agreed." Mrs. Atwell patted Sophie's shoulder. "Try to breathe regularly, Sophie. Don't hold your breath like that. You and the babe both need oxygen."

"You seem to know a good deal about medicine yourself, Mrs. Atwell," Amanda commented.

"I just listen to what the doctor has to say from time to time." She glanced at the stairs. "Ah, here come your cousins to give you a ride up the stairs."

While George and Jefferson discussed the proper method to carry Sophie, another pain attacked her midsection with a vengeance. Thankfully Amanda interceded and ordered Jefferson to carry her and George to follow in the rear should Jefferson require his assistance.

When her pain had subsided, Sophie frowned at George and Jefferson. "I don't think I'm so heavy that you need to argue over which one of you will carry me." She forced a weak smile, and her cousins joked about how much weight she had gained since becoming an old married woman.

Once she was in bed, the women rallied to her aid. When Dr. Balch arrived a short time later, he stopped in the doorway. "It looks like you're hosting a social in here." Holding his medical bag in front of him, the doctor pressed through the crowded room. "Someone take charge and clear this room. I need only one other person in here with me." He pointed at Mrs. Atwell. "Maggie, you stay. The rest of you, out!"

The doctor conducted his examination and asked innumerable questions. Mrs. Atwell held Sophie's hand, and each time a pain arrived, she mopped the young woman's forehead with a handkerchief. When the doctor looked directly into Sophie's eyes, she knew his message wouldn't please her.

"From the look of things, you folks were planning to leave today. Right?"

Sophie nodded. "Yes. We're going back to Rochester. My husband will arrive this afternoon, and he'll be traveling with me."

The doctor wagged his head. "If you want this baby to survive, you'll be staying right where you are. You need complete bed rest, young lady."

"For how long?" she asked.

"If I had to venture a guess, I'd say you'll need to be on bed rest until you give birth. Not a happy prospect, I suppose, but at least you have no other children that need your attention." He patted her hand. "This isn't an uncommon occurrence, so don't go blaming yourself. It's nothing you've done wrong. Some women just seem to have more trouble than others."

"Once I return to Rochester, I'll go to bed and stay there," she promised.

"You can't make the trip back to Rochester. You'll lose the child for sure if you try. Wiggle down into that bed and make yourself comfortable. We'll hope and pray that the baby stays put until December."

Mrs. Atwell ushered the others into the room, and Dr. Balch delivered the news. "She'll need someone to stay with her, of course. Her husband?"

"I'm going to stay with her," Fanny said, stepping forward. "Her husband must continue his work in Rochester, and I have an entire year I can devote to Sophie's care."

Aunt Victoria touched Fanny's shoulder. "I'm not certain this is a good idea, Fanny. You two young women out here alone."

"We won't be alone. Mr. and Mrs. Atwell are as near as their apartment above the boathouse." Fanny glanced at the older woman.

A tuft of Mrs. Atwell's hair waved in the breeze as she nodded her head in agreement. " 'Tis true that Frank and I would be available to help. If it would make you rest easier, Mrs. Broadmoor, Frank and I could come up here and stay during the night."

Victoria tugged at her lace collar. "I believe I need to discuss this with Jonas. He'll arrive shortly, and we'll decide what must be done."

"You may certainly discuss all you want, Mrs. Broadmoor, but this young woman is to remain in bed. Are my orders clear?"

Seeing Aunt Victoria's frown was enough for Sophie to know the older woman was not at all pleased with the doctor. People, especially those being paid for their services, did not issue commands to Jonas Broadmoor's wife.

Sophie was surprised her aunt permitted the gaffe, but she also ignored the doctor's question.

Jonas rubbed his forehead and waved his wife from the room. Just once he'd like to relax without cares or worries like other members of the family. Since the moment he'd walked in the door, he'd heard nothing but troubles and complaints. Didn't he already have enough to deal with by taking care of the financial problems of the family? The only good news he'd heard was the fact that Michael wouldn't return until next year. He'd breathed a sigh of relief knowing he could maintain complete oversight of Fanny's money for another year. At least he hoped he would. If Fanny should suddenly decide to take an interest in her estate or fund another house purchase, it could cause him financial disaster. He leaned back in his chair and pondered his options. Having her on the island until after Sophie's child was born could prove beneficial. Fanny wouldn't be nosing about asking questions he didn't want to answer. Perhaps this wasn't such bad news, after all.

When the family gathered for lunch a short time later, he announced his decision. Since Fanny didn't respond, he raised his brows. "I thought you would thank me."

"*Thank* you? I'm one-third owner of this island. I'm of legal age, and you continue to manage my financial assets through the guardianship and at my request. I don't believe I need your permission to remain and care for my cousin. It was Aunt Victoria who expressed concern over your agreement, not me."

Jonas cleared his throat and tugged on his necktie. "By law, you don't need my permission, but I am the head of the family."

"Since we all agree, I don't think it's a matter we need to dwell on," Victoria said.

Jonas eyed his niece. It seemed Fanny had turned into quite the independent young woman since her birthday. He'd need to be more careful, but for now she'd be otherwise occupied. "That's true, my dear. How is Sophie faring? No chance she'll lose the baby, is there?"

Victoria passed a plate of sandwiches to her husband. "Who can say? Not even the doctor appeared certain."

Jonas truly hoped Sophie wouldn't lose the child. Not because he cared about Sophie or that whelp she carried. The girl was a disgrace to the Broadmoor name. But if she should miscarry, Sophie and Fanny would return to Rochester that much sooner. He swallowed a gulp of coffee. "You be certain you take good care of Sophie and force her to follow the doctor's directions, even if she doesn't want to. I'm going to visit with the doctor before we catch the train in Clayton. I'll ask him to visit her at least every two weeks."

"How kind you are, Jonas. I know the girls will feel much better if the doctor is checking her progress." Victoria beamed at her husband.

Having dozed off after eating her lunch, Sophie was abruptly awakened by the thump of pounding feet on the stairs. Paul stood in the doorway, his eyes wide with fear. "What has happened?" In three long strides, he was across the room and at her side. He dropped into the chair beside her bed and grasped her hand as though he thought she might take off in flight.

Sophie pushed a strand of hair from her forehead; she must have looked a sight. "I began having those pains again. The doctor has ordered me back to bed." She swallowed, hoping to force down the lump in her throat. "I don't want to stay in bed until December." A tear formed and laced her eyelash. Paul leaned forward to brush it away with a gentle touch.

"It's going to be difficult, but we'll get through this, Sophie. We need to trust God and continue to pray that you and the baby will remain healthy."

"Don't you think God would want our family together? I believe I can make it to Rochester. Uncle Jonas could arrange for a Pullman car, where I could rest for the entire journey."

"Nothing would please me more than to take you home with me, but I couldn't bear to live with myself if anything should happen to you or the baby." He shook his head. "You would be required to ride in the boat to Clayton, and even in a Pullman car there would be jostling. Then there would be the carriage ride from the train station in Rochester to our house."

She perked to attention. "Our house? Did you go ahead and purchase the house you told me about?"

He leaned forward and rested his arms across his knees. "I told Mr. Jefferson, the owner, that we would come by tomorrow with our final decision. Now I'm not certain what I should do. I don't want to purchase a house you won't like."

She thought for a moment and then squeezed his hand. "Ask Fanny and Amanda to come upstairs."

"Now?"

"Yes. I think I have a solution."

Moments later Paul returned with her two cousins, and Sophie explained Paul's dilemma. "When both of you return to Rochester, you can go see if you think the house would suit me. Between the two of you, I'm confident you'd arrive at—"

"I'm staying here with you," Fanny said, "but Amanda could certainly go with Paul. I think she will know if you'd be pleased with the house."

Sophie grinned. "Uncle Jonas agreed you could stay?"

"We arrived at a mutual decision." Fanny glanced over her shoulder at Amanda. "What do you think, Amanda? Will you have time before school begins?"

"Well, of course. I'd be pleased to help. School doesn't begin until mid-September. I may even have time to return here before I leave. If not, we can make a drawing that will show you exactly how the rooms are arranged and mail it to you. Would you like that?"

"Oh yes. That would be splendid, but I hope you'll be able to come and visit before you go off to school."

"I'll do my best. I haven't yet received my letter of accept-ance, but I believe the letter will explain when winter break begins. I'll come to see you then." Amanda leaned down and kissed Sophie's cheek. "Please take care of yourself and do as the doctor instructs. I need to leave now. Mr. Atwell is waiting to take us to Clayton."

Fanny followed Amanda to the door. "We'll leave you and Paul alone to say your good-byes, but I'll return once the family has departed."

Paul sat in the chair near Sophie's bed. "I had so looked forward to your coming home today. This seems completely wrong." He buried his face in his palms. "I don't want to leave you here."

Pain laced his muffled words, and Sophie touched his hands. "I'm going to be fine, Paul. Remember, you're the one who said we must trust God."

He dropped his hands and stroked her cheek with his thumb. "Thank you for the reminder. Why don't we agree upon a time when the two of us will pray at the same time each day? It would make me feel closer to you."

Sophie wasn't sure the arrangement would have the same effect upon her, but she agreed they would pray at nine o'clock each evening. The sound of the *DaisyBee*'s engine drifted through the open window. "You'd better go. They'll be waiting for you," she whispered.

He captured her face between his palms, his eyes seeking permission. When she offered no objection, he leaned forward. Without thought, she lifted her arms and embraced him, her lips returning the warmth of his kiss. Her heart needed the love this man so freely offered.

CHAPTER 28

TUESDAY, SEPTEMBER 6, 1898
ROCHESTER, NEW YORK

Jonas curled his lips and shoved the report across his desk. He'd reviewed the figures several times, but nothing had changed for the better. "How can this be happening to me? Is the economy never going to regain momentum?"

Mortimer picked up the paper and traced a bony finger along the row of figures. "Shame you chose some of these investments, Jonas. You've suffered some terrible losses." He continued to inspect each of the columns. "On the other hand, it appears Fanny's investments are doing very well. Perhaps you shouldn't have placed so much of your money and confidence in George Fulford and his pink pills." The old man cackled.

Jonas slapped his hand on his desk. "If you have nothing to offer except cutting remarks, you may as well go back to your office."

Mortimer folded his liver-spotted hands atop Jonas's desk. "No need to raise such a rumpus. I understand your concern, but nothing positive will be accomplished if you're consumed with anger. We need to think this matter through."

"I've already given it a great deal of thought. We need to transfer a large sum from Fanny's bank account into mine."

"We may be able to transfer some of the funds, but not to the extent you're suggesting. There is no possible way I can accomplish that feat without Fanny's signature on the paper work and presenting it to the court. Could you obtain her signature?"

Jonas shook his head. "She's staying at Broadmoor Island until December. Even if she had returned to Rochester, I doubt I'd be able to convince her without answering a surfeit of questions. Now that she's attained her legal majority, it's become more difficult to manage her."

"I'll transfer what I can, but it won't be near what you need." Mortimer jotted a note on a piece of paper and shoved it into his pocket. Obviously a reminder of what must be done.

Jonas pointed toward the older man's pocket. "You shouldn't be writing down any of this information. Too risky."

"The paper merely says *Jonas* and the word *transfer*. I don't think anyone would find those two words incriminating."

"All the same, I prefer you keep mental notes. If you need a reminder, I'll ask you next week if you've completed the task. Make certain you transfer as much as possible. These losses are creating havoc with my business dealings."

Mortimer removed the paper from his pocket, tore it into tiny pieces, and shoved them across the desk. "I understand. No doubt Amanda's schooling and living expenses are going to create quite an exorbitant expense, as well."

Jonas scooped up the pieces of paper and placed them in a nearby ashtray. He would burn them once Mortimer departed. "Amanda won't be going to school. I contacted the college and told them to deny her admission. She would never accept my refusal, but if the college does not accept her application, she'll have no choice but to remain at home and find a wealthy husband. College is no place for women. It's a complete waste of money. Marriage and children—that's what suits women."

"Well, I wholeheartedly agree, but I must say that I'm surprised you've permitted her to work over at the Home for the Friendless with Dr. Carstead. People do talk, and what I've heard hasn't been good." He furrowed his brow and leaned closer. "Your friends wonder why you would even consider consenting to such an unseemly arrangement."

Jonas forced a laugh. "There would have been no peace under my roof if I had objected. Both Victoria and Amanda were determined. After dealing with financial woes all day, the last thing I wanted was to come home and listen to a harping wife and daughter."

"Back in my day a woman knew her place," Mortimer said.

"Times change, Mortimer. Besides, with Amanda on the island for the summer, I thought she might forget about pursuing a medical career. Unfortunately, she still seems set upon the idea. Having Clara Barton visit the island several times didn't help my cause, either. That woman did nothing but encourage Amanda to follow her dreams. Little wonder Miss Barton remains a spinster. I've never met a woman so set in her ways."

Mortimer removed his pipe from his jacket pocket and filled the bowl with tobacco. "Then you had best put a halt to Amanda's working, or you're going to have your own Clara Barton to deal with."

"I suppose it's time I concentrated on finding a suitable man for her."

Mortimer tamped the tobacco and nodded. "She's far beyond marriageable age. But as you've discovered, this generation tends to dislike arranged marriages. They want to fall in love," he said, patting his palm on his heart.

"Amanda will do as she's told or face the consequences. I expect her to marry someone who will bring something substantial to this family, either name or prosperity—hopefully both. I don't intend to have her marry some irresponsible fellow who's only interested in the Broadmoor wealth."

"Broadmoor wealth?" Mortimer chuckled. "If your investments don't soon see some improvement, such a suitor would be in for quite a surprise."

After offering a fleeting good-bye to her father and mother, Amanda stopped in the foyer and pinned her straw hat into place. The morning mail sat on the walnut pier table, and she stopped to riffle through the envelopes. Her heart quickened at the sight of an ivory envelope with a college seal emblazoned in the upper left corner. *Finally!* She was beginning to think she would never receive her letter of acceptance.

Fingers trembling, she carefully opened the envelope and unfolded the letter. Quickly scanning for the date when classes would begin, her eyes locked upon the words *unacceptable candidate*. Still reading, she stumbled toward the sitting room and dropped to the sofa. This couldn't be possible. There must be some mistake. Surely her qualifications were equal to any other candidate who'd applied for admission—probably better. She traced a finger beneath each sentence. The letter said her application hadn't been received in a timely manner, yet she knew that couldn't be true, for she had mailed it long ago. She would appeal the decision, and they would be forced to accept her.

Surprise soon bowed to anger, and she marched into the dining room, where her parents were finishing their breakfast. Holding the letter by one corner, she waved it in front of them. "Can you believe they are refusing me entry into medical school?"

Her father arched his brows. "I told you that these schools give preferential treatment to men. You shouldn't be surprised."

Amanda slapped the letter beside his plate. "Look at this." She pointed to the sentence that mentioned her late application. "That's impossible. I sent in my application nearly a year ago. How could it be late?"

Her father shook his head. "Who can say what happens with these things, but you should simply consider it a sign that medical school isn't in your future."

"What?" She yanked a chair from beneath the table and sat down next to him. "I plan to appeal their decision. This is unfair."

Her father picked up the letter and quickly scanned the contents. "Many things in life are unfair, but it doesn't mean you can change them." He pointed at a paragraph near the end of the letter. *The admissions board will entertain no further action on your application. This decision is final.* "I believe the matter is settled, Amanda. Even if you send a letter requesting an audience with the board, it appears they'll refuse you."

"And school will likely be in session by the time they would reconsider," her mother said.

"*If* they would even reconsider," her father added. "And from the tenor of this letter, I doubt they will." He sipped his coffee and returned the cup to its saucer. "We need to set aside all of this talk and consider your future."

Amanda couldn't believe her ears. What did her father think this was about if not her future? "Medicine *is* my future, Father. My application to medical college was the first step in that direction."

"I'm discussing your *real* future—marriage, children. We need to find you a husband." He glanced at her mother. "Who was that young man Mrs. Stovall mentioned the other evening? He sounded like an excellent prospect."

Amanda jumped up from the table. "I'm not going to listen to this. Dr. Carstead will be waiting for me at the Home for the Friendless."

Despite her mother's plea to remain and further discuss her future with them, Amanda raced down the hallway and out the front door. It now appeared that her mother was going to join ranks with her father to encourage a proper marriage. Well, that didn't interest Amanda—not in the least. When she'd settled in the carriage, she removed the letter from her pocket and once again read it. Tears wouldn't help the situation, but she hadn't been able to stem the flow. She removed a handkerchief from her pocket and wiped her eyes. She must stop this silly crying. After crumpling the letter, she shoved it into her reticule. Perhaps anger would defeat the overwhelming sadness that had taken up residence in her heart.

As the carriage came to a halt in front of the Home a short time later, she wiped her eyes one final time and inhaled a deep breath. "You may pick me up at the usual time," she called to the driver. With a determined stride she entered the Home and walked down the hall to the area designated for medical treatment.

Dr. Carstead pointed to the time. "I thought you'd decided to remain abed, Miss Broadmoor."

Her shoulders tightened at the remark. She was only two minutes late, and he was already taking her to task. "I would remind you that I am a volunteer, Dr. Carstead. If I am two minutes late, I don't expect to be chastised." Her voice quivered, and he turned to look at her.

"Oh, please don't cry. I didn't think you were one of those weepy ladies who resort to tears when corrected."

She forced herself to think of something pleasant, something happy, anything to keep from actually shedding a tear in front of this pompous man. "I am *not* crying. I am angry."

His hazel eyes narrowed and considered her with great intensity. Then his voice softened with seeming concern. "You may not be crying at this moment, but you have been. What's the matter, Amanda?"

She wasn't certain if it was the gentleness of his final words or the fact that he hadn't addressed her as Miss Broadmoor, but her tears coursed down her cheeks.

He yanked a handkerchief from his jacket pocket and shoved it into her hand. "If you don't dry those tears, we'll have enough water in here to compete with Niagara Falls. Come sit down and tell me what this is all about."

Between hiccups she tried to explain, then finally retrieved the letter from her purse and shoved it toward him. "Read this."

"You're upset because they've denied you admission," he said after perusing the letter. He handed the letter back to her. "So you plan to give up?"

"I wanted to appeal, but—"

He shook his head. "There's no need for such drama, Miss Broadmoor—nor for that medical school. You can work and train with me. Few doctors are privileged enough to attend formal training at a college, but that hardly keeps them from becoming physicians. When I believe you're adequately trained, you may be certified for medical practice." He waved toward the patients waiting in the reception room. "There is no lack of patients here at the Home, and many of the women and children would prefer a woman doctor seeing to their needs."

"You're doing this because you feel sorry for me," she murmured.

Blake laughed. "Miss Broadmoor, I have never felt sorry for you. You live a life of wealth and luxury that few will ever know. You are pampered and spoiled at every turn and are given your way so much of the time that a simple letter telling you no threatens to defeat you in full."

Amanda sobered completely at his words. Gone were her tears and frustration with the school. "How dare you say I'm spoiled? You hardly know me well enough to make such judgments. I have never met a more objectionable man in all my life. All I want to do is learn about healing. I just want to serve my fellow man."

He grinned and crossed his arms casually against his chest. "And I just offered you a way to do both."

"But you said . . . you said that I was pampered and spoiled."

"And you are. Do you deny that you have a new gown whenever you desire? Have you ever gone hungry because there wasn't enough food in the cupboard?" He raised a dark brow and challenged her with his look to reply.

"Well, just because I have clothes and food hardly means I'm spoiled. I care about the people around me. I want to help others. Spoiled people do not seek to help anyone but themselves. They sit around focused on their own needs, and when they do not get their own way, they . . ." Her words trailed off. He was smiling at her, and the truth suddenly began to sink in.

"Yes? You were saying?"

"Oh bother." She whirled on her heel. "There's work to be done, and I'm not going to stand here and argue with you."

"Good. I'm glad you see it my way."

She turned abruptly and crashed against Blake, not realizing he had chosen to follow closely after her. He tried to steady her, but his touch so shocked Amanda that she pushed him away. The action served neither of them in good stead. They both landed on their backsides and could only sit staring at each other in surprise.

Amanda was mortified. She wanted to apologize but at the same time knew it would only bring another round of sarcasm from the good doctor.

Just then her uncle Quincy walked into the room. He looked at them both and grinned. "Are we so poor that we can't afford furnishing chairs upon which you can sit?"

Carstead laughed and jumped to his feet. "Miss Broadmoor was merely showing me the lack of proper cleaning done in this room. No doubt she will wish to scrub the floor quite thoroughly after we tend to the sick."

Amanda clenched her jaw but said nothing. Blake held out his hand in a rather tentative manner.

"If my touch doesn't offend, might I assist you off the floor?"

Amanda looked at her uncle and then at Blake. "Thank you," she managed to say. She took hold of his hand and was quickly on her feet.

"Well, if you two are done with the floor inspection," Uncle Quincy said, "I believe I'll get the papers you said you had for me, Blake."

"Certainly." Blake left Amanda and went to his desk.

"Amanda, should you wish to inspect the floors in my office," Uncle Quincy said with a glance over his shoulder, "I'll leave the door unlocked."

Amanda shook her head and went to the hook by the door for her apron. "Men," she muttered, knowing her uncle wouldn't understand.

"Well, what do you think?" Paul asked when he and Amanda arrived in front of the house.

"The location isn't bad, but let's see what the inside is like before I render a final opinion, shall we?"

When the family had returned to Rochester the last day of August, Paul had anticipated a tour of the house with Amanda the following day and the finalization of the purchase—if it met with her approval. Unfortunately, his plans hadn't coincided with Amanda's. She'd been busy with her duties at the Home, and the Labor Day parade and celebration had interfered, as well.

"I'd begun to worry whether you would have time to visit the house before leaving for college," he told her as they toured the grounds. "Mr. Jefferson has been anxious to sell, and I've been equally worried that he would sell to someone else. I'd hate to disappoint Sophie."

"She would understand if the place was less than perfect for the two of you. But from what I see, it looks quite lovely."

"The yard is nice, but it could use some bushes and flowers," Amanda continued. "I like the large porch. Sophie can sit out here with the baby come springtime. And Fanny will have ideas for plantings. She's the one who is talented with flowers and shrubs. I'm certain she'll suggest lilac bushes along each side of the house."

With paper and pencil in hand, Amanda instructed Paul to measure the rooms while she sketched them on the paper. Mr. Jefferson, the owner of the house, appeared baffled by the procedure, but he led them through the house and answered Amanda's countless questions.

When they finally returned to the foyer, he rested his hands on his hips. "So are you going to buy? I can't wait much longer for my money."

Before Paul could reply, Amanda grasped Paul by the arm. "We need to speak privately for a moment," she told Mr. Jefferson.

The older man heaved a sigh and ambled toward the parlor while Amanda and Paul stepped outside. "Down here," she said, directing Paul toward the yard. "We don't want him to hear what we say."

"You don't like the house?"

"I like it very much, but you should offer him less. He's anxious to sell, and I think he'll take a lower price."

Paul frowned. "But the house is worth what he is asking."

"Yes, but the economy has slowed considerably. Money is tight with many people, and everyone understands the need for compromise and bargaining."

"But—"

"But nothing," Amanda said, hands on hips. "This is the way business is done. I've seen my father at work a hundred times before. Offer less."

"How much less?" he asked.

She sensed his unease. "Let me talk to him."

At Amanda's urging, the owner agreed to lower the price by two hundred and fifty dollars. By afternoon's end, the contract had been signed, money had passed hands, and Amanda's sketches for Sophie were in the mail, along with a promise to add further details when she returned to the island for a visit.

She didn't mention her admission to medical school had been denied. No need to mix bad news with good.

CHAPTER 29

SATURDAY, OCTOBER 15, 1898

The crispness of the fall air brought a smile to Paul's face. He was anxious for Sophie's return to Rochester, and he viewed each passing day as another step toward attaining his goal. His mother used to tell him such thinking was simply wishing one's life away; Sophie had once told him her grandfather used to say the same thing. Apparently older people were more inclined to see it that way, but Paul didn't believe it to be true. He believed his life would truly begin the day Sophie returned from Broadmoor Island.

For today, he would be content to surprise her with a visit. With new construction and additional residents at the Home, there had been little opportunity for him to do so. He and Amanda had made one journey to the island after his purchase of the house had been completed. Both Sophie and Fanny had been filled with excitement as they listened to the many attributes of the home. He grinned, remembering how his heart had swelled with pride when Sophie assured him she would be pleased with whatever he had chosen for them. Since that visit, their contact had been through letters. He'd been diligent in his effort to write, but Sophie's letters had been sporadic. Seclusion on the island didn't provide adequate fodder for letters, or so she said, but he would have been pleased with a daily update on her health.

Paul settled on the train, delighted he'd have the next few days to enjoy time with Sophie. His time at Broadmoor Island would also yield a brief respite for Fanny. Providing daily companionship for Sophie was no small chore, for his wife bored easily. He'd brought along several books for the two women to read, along with some fabric Amanda had sent with sewing instructions. If all of the baby clothes had been completed, Sophie and Fanny were to begin stitching kitchen curtains. He doubted Sophie would be pleased to see additional fabric and thread, yet he didn't mention that fact to Amanda. After all, she'd done her share to put the new house in order.

Amanda had been by his side many evenings, helping to clean and decorate. She'd even enlisted Veda's assistance. Paul wasn't certain if the maid had come willingly, but she'd proved an excellent worker. In addition to her other good deeds, Amanda had convinced her father to release some of the household furnishings placed in storage after her grandfather's death. Though Jonas had argued, he'd finally relented. But not without gaining Quincy's agreement to reimburse him when the remainder of the furniture sold at auction. Paul had been taken aback by Jonas's request, but Quincy had taken the matter in stride.

With his hand clutching the gift he'd purchased for Sophie, he dozed as the train moved from station to station, finally arriving in Clayton by early afternoon.

He smiled when he noticed one of Captain Visegar's boats waiting near the dock. It was late in the season, with few visitors arriving at the islands, and he had wondered if the captain would still be meeting trains arriving at the station. He strode down the aisle carrying his leather Gladstone traveling bag in one hand and a smaller canvas bag filled with the items from Amanda in the other.

Hoping to gain the captain's attention, Paul dropped one of his bags at the end of the platform and waved his hat high overhead. It took but a moment before the captain saw him and motioned him forward. The captain cupped his hands to his mouth. "I'll be leaving in a few minutes. Come aboard." His shout resonated across the wood expanse that separated them.

Paul handed his baggage down to the bearded man before stepping on board. "Glad to see you here. I was worried I might be forced to wait several hours now that the season has passed."

The older man raked his calloused fingers through his mane of graying hair. "Don't you fret, young man. You'll find my boats on the water when most others are in dry dock." He grinned and deep creases formed in his weatherworn cheeks. "You off to see your gal on Broadmoor Island?"

"My wife," Paul corrected.

The captain tipped the brim of his hat. "That's right. I had forgotten you married one of the Broadmoor girls. The dark-haired one that enjoyed the parties and dances over on Wellesley Island. I seem to recall she enjoyed the festivities at Frontenac Hotel, as well."

Paul didn't agree or disagree. Instead, he said, "Sophie. I married Sophie. We're expecting a baby around Christmastime."

"Um-hmm. Doc said she was having some trouble, and he ordered her to stay put on the island until after the young'un was born. I'm guessin' it's a might hard for that gal to stay put. She never was one to let any grass grow under her feet." He chuckled as he slowly maneuvered the boat away from the pier and then headed downriver. When they arrived at the Broadmoor dock a short time later, he once again tipped his hat. "Have a good visit."

Paul clutched a bag in each hand and made his way up the path to the house, his shoulders sagging by the time he finally arrived at the front door. His attempt to open the front door met with failure. Though he was pleased the locked door would prevent intruders, it also prevented his surprise entry. He walked around the perimeter of the house. Perhaps he'd discover the French doors to the library open—or the kitchen door. He rounded the corner to the back, only to give Mrs. Atwell a terrible fright.

The older woman grabbed at thin air before finally steadying herself and planting her feet near a rosebush. "Dear me! What are you doing sneaking around the house like that, Mr. Medford? I may suffer a heart attack if you do that again."

By the time he dropped his bags, she had already regained her composure and her balance. "I'm terribly sorry, Mrs. Atwell. I had hoped to surprise Sophie, but the front door is locked."

"I don't know about Miss Sophie, but you certainly surprised me," she said. "You can come in this way. We keep the other doors locked unless we're *expecting* visitors."

He agreed the practice was an excellent idea before hurrying up the back stairs and down the hall. The sound of his footfalls apparently captured Fanny's attention, for she appeared in the bedroom doorway. He touched his index finger to his lips; she smiled and nodded.

"Who's out there, Fanny?" Sophie called from the bedroom.

"Your husband," Paul said, entering the room.

"Paul!" Sophie glanced back and forth between her cousin and her husband. "Did you know he was coming for a visit, Fanny?"

"I had no idea." Fanny clasped her hand over her heart. "This surprise is Paul's alone."

He grinned and nodded. "She's correct. I didn't tell anyone for fear something would interfere and I might not be able to come. A surprise is much better than disappointment, don't you think?"

"In this case, I would completely agree," Sophie said. "I'm so pleased to see you." She extended her hand and beckoned him forward.

Her response surprised him. Did absence make the heart grow fonder? Or was it purely boredom? Would she have greeted any visitor with the same enthusiasm? He hoped not. When he presented her with his gift, her reaction would prove a better measure of her feelings.

After a few moments Fanny excused herself to allow them privacy. "If you need anything . . ." She pointed to the bell on Sophie's bedside table. "Sophie knows how to gain my attention."

Sophie giggled. "Fanny says she's going to take that bell away from me if I don't quit ringing it every time she goes downstairs."

"Now that your husband has arrived, I'm sure you'll be on your best behavior." Fanny waved and disappeared from sight.

Sophie regaled him with the latest news in the area, though there was little to report now that the summer visitors had departed. "Dr. Balch and Mr. Atwell keep us updated when anything of interest occurs in Clayton or Alexandria Bay, but other than reports of the latest catch of fish or the purchase of a new skiff, they have little to tell us." She scooted up against her pillows. "I hope you're going to have lots of news that will entertain me."

He reached inside his jacket pocket and tightened his fingers around the small box. "I have something for you."

Sophie's eyes sparked with excitement. "You do? Where is it?" She peeked at his bags, which he'd dropped near the door. "Is it something I'll like?"

"I hope so," he said as he withdrew the box from his pocket. Lifting the lid, he presented the box to her and carefully watched her reaction.

"Oh, Paul. Where did you obtain such rings?" She pushed the box back toward him. "These are far too expensive."

He shook his head. "This one," he said, lifting the gold band from the velvet layer, "I purchased for you." He lifted the other ring from the velvet nest—a large diamond surrounded by tiny sapphires. "This one belonged to my grandmother. When my mother returned to New York City after my grandmother's death, she wrote that I was to have it. While I was in Rochester, I sent for it. Now it belongs to you."

Sophie recalled the ailing grandmother—the one Paul and his mother had gone to care for in England. Though Paul had been required to return to Rochester, his mother had remained until his grandmother's death several months later. Sophie shook her head. "I couldn't possibly wear your grandmother's ring. You need to put it away and save it."

"For what? My grandmother bequeathed this ring to me with the specific hope that it would one day belong to my wife. And now that I have a wife, I want this ring to adorn her finger." He gently lifted Sophie's hand. "Please don't disappoint me."

Her hand remained cradled in his palm, and he gently slipped the wedding band onto her finger, followed by his grandmother's ring. "It fits perfectly, and it looks beautiful on your hand." He lifted her hand to his lips and saw a tear slip down her cheek when he looked up. "I had hoped my gift would bring you joy."

She opened her arms to him and kissed his lips, the dampness of her tears brushing his face. "Both of these rings bring me great joy, but I don't feel like I will ever be the wife you deserve. A preacher needs a special woman by his side, and I don't exactly fit that mold." She squeezed his hand. "But I want you to know that I am going to do my very best to make this situation bearable for you."

Paul chuckled. "Bearable? You make my life complete. And once our child is born, I'll be hard-pressed to contain my delight. I don't want you to force your feelings for me. There is no rush. I'll wait a lifetime if that's what it takes. I love you." He lightly touched her bulging stomach. "And I love this baby."

"I fear you are too good for me, but I'll argue no further." She offered him a weak smile. "Now tell me about the house. I've gone over and over the drawings Amanda sent, but you must show me what else has been accomplished since then."

"You'll be pleased to know that she sent along some new drawings as well as some fabric for kitchen curtains. She thought you and Fanny might be in need of another sewing project."

Sophie wrinkled her nose. "Let's look at the drawings. The fabric can wait."

How good it was to see her excited over the prospect of their home. He couldn't wait for the day to arrive when the three of them could begin building a life together in their new home.

Fanny measured the fabric and then retrieved her sewing scissors from her basket. Now that Paul had departed for Rochester, Sophie had agreed at least to look at the material Amanda had chosen for the kitchen curtains.

"I don't think these will take long for us to stitch." Fanny looked up from her basket. "So long as you don't sew the wrong sides together. I don't want any hems turned toward the right side of the fabric."

Sophie giggled. "Is that all I must do to be relieved of the task?"

"Don't you dare," Fanny warned. "I'm not going to sew these by myself."

Sophie's muffled groan captured Fanny's attention, and she hurried to her cousin's bedside. "Are you having pains of some sort?"

"No, but I've gotten so big that each time I shift my weight, I feel like an ocean liner trying to change directions in a washtub." She squeezed Fanny's hand. "You worry overmuch about my health. I'm fine."

Fanny forced a smile and nodded. She'd been attempting to push aside her fears since the first day Sophie had doubled over in pain. The thought that she might die in childbirth haunted Fanny, despite the assurances Amanda had given her. Fanny had revealed her fears to Mrs. Atwell, and the older woman had instructed her to pray and have faith. *"Sophie will be fine. Childbirth is a natural thing. Most women have no difficulty at all,"* she'd said. So Fanny had been praying for a safe delivery of Sophie's baby ever since; but it didn't seem as though her faith had increased.

As the days pressed on, she'd become increasingly consumed with apprehension that Sophie might die. After all, Fanny's mother had died giving birth to her. So whether childbirth was a natural thing or not, it didn't mean Sophie wouldn't die. Each time Sophie grimaced or groaned, Fanny would fret and stew. She'd even moved her bed closer to Sophie's to make certain she could hear her should a pain strike during the night.

"No need to push your bed about the room," Mrs. Atwell had counseled. "You'll have no difficulty hearing Sophie when her pains begin." But the older woman's words had fallen upon deaf ears. Fanny's bed remained in the newly rearranged position. She must be prepared to take action the moment Sophie needed her. If something were to happen to her cousin, Fanny would never forgive herself.

Sophie tried her best to maintain a cheerful disposition as the days passed. All of her life she had been somewhat selfish, and since her mother's death she had become even more self-absorbed. The second anniversary of her mother's passing was soon to be upon them, and all Sophie could think of was how hard it was to be without her at a time like this.

Her mother would have been a great comfort. She would have been able to answer Sophie's questions about childbirth and caring for a baby. Sometimes Sophie's fears overwhelmed her as she thought of being given the charge of another human being. What if she completely failed at the job of motherhood? She already feared she'd be a poor wife to Paul; what if she had no more love to offer her child than she did her husband?

She sighed and gazed out the window to the gray waters of the St. Lawrence. The day was overcast and gloomy. It seemed to fit her mood.

"I don't know what to do, Lord," she prayed awkwardly. "I want to make the best of this situation. I truly do." She shook her head and tried to reason with her worried heart. "Paul deserves better. He deserves a wife who can be madly in love with him. I want to be that woman. I don't want to spend a lifetime in a marriage where there is no love."

"I don't want you to force your feelings for me. There is no rush. I'll wait a lifetime if that's what it takes. I love you," Paul had said when he'd given her the wedding rings.

Sophie looked at her hand and gently touched the pieces. He would wait a lifetime for her. Tears formed in her eyes, and she couldn't help but feel a great sense of regret. Why couldn't she have waited for him? Why had she given herself so foolishly to Wesley?

"He showed me the attention I needed—he made me feel special. I loved him," she whispered, wiping back the tears. Then reality dawned on her. Love had little to do with her relationship with Wesley Hedrick. He certainly had not loved her, and now that time had passed, Sophie could see that she'd never really loved him. She had needed him. She'd found him a substitute for the attention she craved from her father, but love really hadn't figured into it. She'd been a naïve girl with dreams of romance and passion.

And Wesley had mesmerized her. He had fascinated her with the promise of something she'd wanted more than life itself—love to fill the hole in her heart. There had been a great emptiness inside her—an emptiness that only God had been able to fill. The realization was almost more than she could understand. Perhaps she could love Paul. Now that her selfish ambitions were set aside and her heart was set right with both her earthly father and heavenly Father, maybe she could truly come to understand what love was honestly all about. Maybe it wasn't too late. Maybe there was love within her to give not only to Paul but to her unborn child.

CHAPTER 30

Mrs. Atwell closed her Bible, and the three women joined hands and prayed. They'd been following this routine every afternoon since mid-October, when Fanny had divulged her fears to the older woman. And although the prayers centered upon Sophie's condition and a healthy baby, Mrs. Atwell increasingly read Scriptures on trust and faith. Fanny had soon decided the older woman's daily visits were as much for her as they were for Sophie. Although the devotions had lightened Fanny's worries throughout each evening, her fears returned to stalk her during the nighttime hours. Attempts to pray herself to sleep evolved into worrisome thoughts that eventually exploded into overpowering terror. Pictures flashed through her mind: Sophie lying in a coffin with a tiny baby in her arms; Sophie in bed circled by a pool of blood; Michael blinded by a snowstorm; Michael's frozen body lying beside a chunk of gold; Paul holding a baby and weeping. Night after night the images returned, each one an unwelcome reminder of the fears rooted deep in her heart.

Where was her faith? Mr. and Mrs. Atwell loved Michael, yet they appeared content to place his safety in God's hands. Why couldn't she do the same? Even Sophie seemed willing to trust in God's provision for her future. Was she the only one who lived with panic squeezing her heart?

After uttering a soft amen to her prayer, Mrs. Atwell squeezed Fanny's hand. "I have a lovely supper prepared downstairs. It will take me only a few minutes to dish up your meal."

Sophie shifted to her side and beckoned Mrs. Atwell to wait a moment longer. "I have been abiding by the doctor's orders and doing much better, don't you agree?"

"Indeed, I do believe God is hearing our prayers for strength and health," the older woman said.

The instant Mrs. Atwell neared the bedside, Sophie clutched the woman's hand. "I am so *very* weary of lying abed for all these weeks. Do you think I could sit in the chair just long enough to eat my supper? My body aches from constantly being stretched upon this bed."

Sophie's soulful look didn't escape Fanny's notice. Given the opportunity, her cousin could charm the rattlers out of a rattlesnake. Now she was using her wiles to win Mrs. Atwell's agreement to get out of bed. Well, she would put a stop to that plan. "The doctor ordered bed rest." Fanny's ominous tone matched the fear roiling in her stomach. "We can't be too careful."

"Now, now, Fanny. Sophie is correct. Lying abed is wearisome, and she hasn't suffered so much as a twinge for weeks. I don't believe the doctor would object if she sat in the chair for her evening meal." Mrs. Atwell picked up her Bible and tucked it under her arm. "But back to bed once you've finished your supper. Promise?"

Sophie giggled and nodded her head. "I promise. Thank you, Mrs. Atwell."

Fanny followed the older woman into the hall. "I'm still not certain—"

"Have a little faith, my dear. All will be well."

When Mrs. Atwell arrived with their supper tray, Fanny and the older woman helped Sophie up from the bed. Then the three of them slowly made their way across the short expanse to the chair.

Once seated, Sophie beamed at them. "Hard to believe something so simple as sitting in a chair could feel so wonderful."

"Ring that bell if she has the slightest twinge, Fanny. Otherwise, the two of you enjoy your meal. I'll be back up to help you get her back to bed."

Perhaps it was Sophie's excitement over her short time being up, but their meal proved extremely pleasurable. In fact, Sophie didn't even argue to remain in the chair when Fanny and Mrs. Atwell escorted her back to bed. Her only complaint came when Fanny removed the curtain fabric from her sewing basket.

"Not those curtains. Please, Fanny, I don't want to work on those. I've ripped mine until the fabric is frayed."

"I think you do that on purpose so that I'll be forced to complete them. I've packed these away long enough. If we don't finish them, you'll be arriving at your new home with no curtains to hang in the kitchen." She dropped a piece of the material onto the bed. "That one is yours. I've pinned it so that you won't stitch the right sides together again," Fanny said with a grin.

Sophie removed a needle from the pincushion, threaded the eye, and tied a knot. "I do believe Amanda took great pleasure in sending this fabric. Do you notice how she's asked about *my* sewing progress in each of her letters?"

Fanny stabbed her needle into the fabric and readily agreed. There was little doubt Amanda thought it high time Sophie became skilled with a needle and thread. Fanny remained unconvinced Sophie would ever be considered accomplished in the art of handiwork, but at least she was making an attempt.

With one hand resting on her stomach, Sophie beckoned Fanny closer. "Come and feel. The baby is moving."

Fanny lightly touched her palm to Sophie's bulging middle and felt a tiny thump beneath her hand. "He seems quite strong, don't you think?"

"Yes, but I don't think the baby is a boy. I believe I'm carrying a spirited little girl."

Fanny laughed. "Just like her mother!" She knotted her row of stitches and broke the piece of thread. "Have you and Paul talked about names for the baby?"

"If it's a boy, we've decided to name him Hamilton Paul Medford after grandfather and Paul; if it's a girl, her name will be Elizabeth Jane, after you, Amanda, and Paul's grandmother. As it turns out, Paul's grandmother's name, Elizabeth, is the same as Amanda's middle name, so I have coupled it with your middle name, Jane. What do you think?"

"If you have a little girl, I will be honored to have her share my middle name. Thank you, Sophie."

Later that night, Fanny pulled the bedcovers beneath her chin and whispered a prayer that sleep would come without any chilling thoughts or nightmares. She reminded herself that Sophie was doing fine and everything was going along as planned.

"I'm being silly," she said with a sigh.

Four days later, on Thanksgiving, winter arrived with a fury. The temperature took a downward turn and refused to budge. Mr. and Mrs. Atwell joined Fanny in Sophie's room, where they enjoyed a fine meal of roasted chicken and all the trimmings. It was far from the usual Broadmoor affair, with all the noise and more food than could fit the table, but it was good nevertheless. Fanny wished that Michael could have joined them but knew that wishing wouldn't make it so.

By the next morning Fanny could barely see beyond the rooftop. Snow tumbled from the heavens in an unrelenting cascade of pellets and flakes that blanketed the lawn in a pure white carpet. It made her think all the more of her beloved. Were the houses buried in snow up in Dawson? Did Michael awaken each day to sights such as this?

"Isn't it beautiful?" Watching from her bed, Sophie held the curtain away from the window and peered at the unfolding scene.

"Yes, but you need to drop the drapery back in place. It helps keep the cold out of the room. I can feel the draft crossing your bed. I don't want you taking a chill and catching cold."

Sophie grasped her cousin's hand. "Who could ever ask for a better friend than you, Fanny? Michael is fortunate he's going to marry such a fine woman. And the moment he returns, I'm going to tell him so."

While Fanny brushed Sophie's hair and helped her into a fresh gown, Mrs. Atwell arrived with a pile of clean linens. Her Bible rested atop the pile. "We'll change your bed after lunch," she said. "I've a nice pot of stew cooking, and it looks like this is a perfect day for a hearty meal to keep us warm." She pointed to her Bible. "I thought we might have our devotions this morning. I'll begin my ironing this afternoon."

Neither of the girls objected as the older woman sat down in the chair and settled the open Bible on her lap. She had placed tiny pieces of paper between certain pages to mark the Bible passages she planned to read. There were several from Proverbs, but her final reading was from the book of Isaiah. She cleared her throat and placed her index finger beneath the words. "Isaiah 12:2," she began. " 'Behold, God is my salvation; I will trust, and not be afraid: for the Lord Jehovah is my strength and my song; he also is become my salvation.' " She closed the Bible and joined hands with Fanny and Sophie. "Let's thank God for our many blessings and that His Word tells us He is our protector."

Each of them prayed, although Fanny sometimes wondered if God truly wanted to hear from her. While Mrs. Atwell's prayers were words of joy and thanksgiving, Fanny's were filled with fear and misgiving. However, Mrs. Atwell encouraged her, saying God wanted to hear His children's burdens. Once Sophie's baby was born and Michael returned home, then Fanny would be able to utter prayers of thanksgiving—at least that's what she told herself. Surely there could be nothing else in her future that would cause her such fear and distress.

Mrs. Atwell gathered her Bible and, with a promise to prepare their tray, headed toward the door.

"I'll come downstairs and fetch the tray in a few minutes," Fanny said.

"If you're certain you don't mind," the older woman said. "I'll thicken the stew, and the biscuits should be ready in twenty minutes or so."

Once Mrs. Atwell disappeared down the hallway, Fanny dusted the furniture and tidied the room. With the winter days growing shorter, it seemed Mrs. Atwell had less and less time to complete all her duties before nightfall. And the time passed more quickly for Fanny when she busied herself with work.

"Do you think I could sit in the chair for my lunch today?"

Fanny glanced up from her dusting. On almost any other day, she would have immediately refused Sophie's request. But the weather seemed to have created a restlessness in all of them. This was Sophie's first request since she'd been permitted to sit in the chair five days ago, and she'd suffered no ill effects from that episode.

"I think it should be permissible, so long as you don't expect to sit in the chair every day."

Sophie clapped her hands. "Thank you, Fanny. I promise I won't ask again for at least five days."

"I'll assist you to the chair, and then I'll go downstairs and fetch our lunch."

She helped Sophie turn sideways on the bed and, holding her around the waist, supported her until she sat down in the chair. She tucked a blanket around Sophie's legs before pointing toward the door. "I'll be back with our lunch before you have time to miss me. And don't you get out of that chair while I'm gone."

"I promise," Sophie said, her palm facing outward as though taking a pledge.

Fanny hurried down the rear stairs. She hoped Mrs. Atwell wouldn't think her decision regarding Sophie presumptuous. She probably should have obtained the older woman's permission before moving Sophie, but she doubted Mrs. Atwell would have offered an objection.

"It smells wonderful down here." Fanny lifted her nose into the air and inhaled the hearty aromas. Mrs. Atwell had filled two generous bowls with stew and placed them on a tray beside a bread basket covered with a linen napkin.

Fanny lifted the tray but hesitated long enough to tell the older woman of her decision.

"That's fine. We'll get Sophie back to bed when you've finished lunch. Don't linger down here in the kitchen. I don't want either of you eating a cold lunch." Mrs. Atwell shooed her toward the stairs. "Ring the bell when you've finished eating, and I'll come up to help you. We can change the bed while Sophie is still in the chair."

A sigh of relief escaped Fanny's lips as she carefully wielded the tray up the stairs and down the hallway. "I hope you're hungry, because—" The tray fell from her hands. *"Sophie!"* A shrill scream escaped Fanny's lips. Grabbing the bell from Sophie's bedside table, she dropped to her knees beside Sophie's supine body and clanged the instrument over and over. Her gaze traveled the length of Sophie's body, and an unrelenting sob caught in her throat when she spied the blood soaking her cousin's gown. She rocked back and sat on her heels, unaware of anything but the blood-stained nightgown and Sophie's pale complexion.

"Give me that, child." Mrs. Atwell pried the bell from Fanny's hand. "You're going to wake the dead if you don't quit ringing that thing."

Fanny stared up at the woman, and her husband, who was right behind her. "Is she going to die? This is my fault. I shouldn't have given her permission to get out of bed."

The older woman ignored Fanny's utterances and motioned her husband forward to lift Sophie into the bed. Moments later Sophie screamed in pain and clutched the air, holding Fanny's hand in a death grip. "Something is wrong! The pain is unbearable." Wild-eyed, she searched the room until her eyes locked on Mrs. Atwell. "I can't stand this pain. Please! Do something."

"Give me a minute, Sophie. I'm going to check you and see what's happening." She motioned Mr. Atwell out of the room. "Wait in the hall until I see if it's her time, Frank."

"But the baby isn't due until next month," Fanny said.

"Babies don't always come when they're expected," Mrs. Atwell said as she pushed aside Sophie's gown. Moments later she gave an affirmative nod. "The baby's coming. Tell my husband to go and fetch the doctor, Fanny."

Fanny wrenched her hand from Sophie's viselike grip. "I'll be right back," she promised, backing toward the hall. She opened the door and located Mr. Atwell sitting at the top of the stairway. "Mrs. Atwell says we need the doctor."

He offered a mock salute. "I'll see what I can do, but tell her that with this weather, I'm not certain a doctor is in the offing."

"But she has to have—"

He shook his head and pointed a thumb toward the outer wall. "If there's any way to get to Clayton, I'll go, Miss Fanny, but I can't change the weather conditions. There's no need to fret. Maggie's delivered many a babe—just put your trust in the Lord."

There was that *trust* word again. She wondered if her own mother had trusted in the Lord before she died. What good was trusting in God if people still suffered and died? She hurried back to the bedroom. At least Sophie had stopped screaming. Perhaps the baby wouldn't be born, after all.

"Mr. Atwell says the weather may be a factor." Fanny didn't want to alarm Sophie. "Is everything going as expected?"

The older woman nodded. "I think we'll have a baby before nightfall. I'm going downstairs to gather the things we'll need. You stay here with Sophie. You don't need to do anything except remain calm. Prayer would help, too," she whispered.

The moment Mrs. Atwell walked out of the room, Sophie clutched Fanny's hand. "I'm afraid the baby and I are both going to die, Fanny. But if anything happens to me and the baby lives, I want you to promise that you and Amanda will help Paul raise the child."

Sophie continued her sobbing diatribe until Fanny realized she must push aside her own fears and calm her cousin. "Don't talk like that, Sophie. You are going to be absolutely fine, and so is this baby. I don't want to hear another word about dying. You are a strong young woman. You and this baby will live. We're going to pray and trust God to take care of you." She clenched Sophie's hand. "Is that clear?"

"Now, that's what I like to hear," Mrs. Atwell said, coming into the room. She dropped the clean linens at the foot of the bed. "The foul weather is going to prevent my husband from going to Clayton to fetch the doctor, but with God's help, you're going to be holding your fine little baby before long, Sophie."

CHAPTER 31

FRIDAY, NOVEMBER 25, 1898

Tears trickled down Sophie's cheeks as the lusty cries of the tiny baby girl filled the bedroom. Mrs. Atwell gently wrapped the newborn infant in a soft blanket and handed her to Fanny. "Take care of the little one while I tend to Sophie."

Sophie beckoned her cousin to come closer. "Let me have a good look at her." She pushed upward against the pillows to gain a better view until Mrs. Atwell objected. The older woman had raised the baby into the air immediately after she'd delivered her, but Sophie hadn't yet had an opportunity to examine her daughter closely.

Mrs. Atwell motioned her to lie back. "I know you're anxious to see your little one, Sophie, but right now I've got to tend to this bleeding."

Sophie dropped back against the pillows. The older woman's words were enough to send fear spiraling from her throat to the pit of her stomach and back again. Bile clung in her throat, and she swallowed hard, hoping to rid herself of the acrid taste. Perhaps she'd expressed her joy too quickly. Mrs. Atwell's brow had furrowed into a frown. That couldn't be a good sign.

"Am I going to die?" she whispered.

Mrs. Atwell's eyebrows shot upward like two arched cats. "Of course not. You're doing just fine. Every woman bleeds after giving birth, so stop your worrying. As soon as we're finished, you can hold the baby. And before you begin to fret about her, I'll tell you she has all her fingers and toes and looks to be fit as a fiddle. She's tiny, of course, but that's to be expected. We'll need to keep her nice and warm."

Sophie permitted herself to relax while Mrs. Atwell completed her ministrations. "I do wish Paul could have been here to greet his daughter. He's going to be as surprised as we were."

"Mr. Atwell will go to Clayton and send a telegram to Paul once the weather clears. I doubt he'll be able to go before morning." The older woman gave a nod. "That's good. Now let's get this bed changed, and you'll be more comfortable."

As usual, Mrs. Atwell was correct. The clean linens and nightgown did feel much better. Of course, the cessation of her labor pains had provided the greatest relief. And once Sophie felt the warmth of Elizabeth Jane in her arms, all thoughts of the pain were pushed aside.

Mrs. Atwell came to the side of the bed. "I believe we should offer a prayer of thanks for this fine little girl, don't you?"

While the housekeeper led them in prayer, Elizabeth yawned and stretched her body as if to affirm that she was indeed God's special creation. When the prayer ended, her tiny lips pursed into a knot, and her narrow brow creased with a frown.

"She's a bit red, don't you think?" Sophie glanced up at the older woman.

"That's natural," Mrs. Atwell assured. "If you two think you can manage that wee baby for a little while, I'll go downstairs and brew a pot of tea and make some sandwiches." She glanced at Sophie. "I'm sure you're hungry after all that hard work."

Some hours later, Fanny got up and stretched. "If you are feeling all right, I think I'll go get cleaned up and ready for bed."

Sophie looked down at the sleeping babe in her arms. There was the tiniest bit of apprehension in having Fanny go, but she knew it was selfish to keep her cousin any longer. "Go and rest. I'll be fine. Mrs. Atwell plans to come check on me before nine."

Fanny yawned. "All right. I'll hurry back after I wash up."

Sophie waited until Fanny had gone before pulling back the covers to view her daughter. She was so very tiny. Mrs. Atwell had assured her that was normal, but Sophie worried she might hurt the child.

Elizabeth began to fuss. Her mewing cry at first alarmed Sophie, but then something began to change. Something deep in Sophie's heart seemed to awaken. This was her child—her daughter. She drew the baby close to her breast as Mrs. Atwell had shown her earlier. Instinct caused Elizabeth to settle a bit and begin rooting. Sophie guided the baby's mouth to feed and gasped in surprise as Elizabeth latched on with surprising strength.

How natural it all seemed—the way Elizabeth fit in her arms, the way she nursed without coaxing. Sophie relaxed against her pillows in amazement as she continued to watch her daughter. In that moment a love more fierce and complete than anything Sophie had ever known took hold of her. She loved this baby. Despite the mistakes she had made in giving her heart to Wesley and the sorrow that had followed in his betrayal of her trust, Elizabeth was neither a mistake nor a sorrow.

"I want to be a good mother to you," Sophie whispered. "I promise to try my very best. I won't betray your trust. I will never abandon you."

Elizabeth opened her eyes as if to acknowledge her mother's promise. Sophie stared into the deep blue eyes of her daughter and smiled. "I love you, little babe. I don't know what kind of mother I will be, but I want to be a good one."

She thought of Paul and felt the love she held for Elizabeth multiply and overflow until it encompassed him, as well. "I want to be a good wife and mother," she whispered, but then shook her head. "I *will* be a good wife and mother."

Paul clasped Amanda's hand and assisted her down from the train. "Watch that patch of ice," he cautioned as they proceeded into the Clayton train station. "Mr. Atwell should be here any time now." Though patches of ice had formed on the river, boats were still able to traverse the waters of the St. Lawrence. Once the river was completely frozen, sleighs would carry the year-round residents and any visitors to the islands—a thought that struck fear in Paul's heart. He envisioned a weak spot in the ice and a sinking sleigh. Sophie had told him such incidents occurred from time to time, but most folks knew the waters and didn't take chances. He hoped that when the time arrived to take Sophie and the baby back to Rochester, they could leave by boat.

"There's Mr. Atwell," Amanda said as the older man entered the station. He doffed his cap and hurried to their side.

"Sorry to keep you waiting. I had to pick up some items at the store for the ladies." He grinned at Paul. "Congratulations to you, Mr. Medford. You've a fine little daughter waiting for you back at the island."

"Sophie? Is she—"

"Ah, she's doing fine. The birth went well by all accounts, and the missus says the babe is holding her own. She's tiny, for sure, but strong." He winked at Paul. "She's got a lusty cry, so you'll not be able to ignore her when she wakes up during the night."

Paul stepped into the boat and turned up the collar of his heavy wool coat. His excitement continued to build the closer they got to the island. When Mr. Atwell docked the boat, Paul jumped to the pier as though he'd been catapulted from the vessel. He extended his hand to Amanda and helped her out.

Mr. Atwell waved them on. "You go ahead. I'll bring your luggage up to the house later. I'm going to secure the boat inside the boathouse. Don't think we'll need it for the remainder of the day."

The path leading to the house remained covered with the snow and sleet from the earlier storm, and the two of them carefully picked their way along the slick surface. Amanda sighed with relief when they reached the veranda. "Thank goodness. I wondered if I would fall and slide back down to the river."

A rush of warmth greeted them when Paul opened the front door. Before they could remove their coats, Mrs. Atwell scurried down the hall. "There you are. I'm pleased to see you've arrived safe and sound. This weather has been a fright, hasn't it?" She continued to chirp while she brushed and hung their coats. "What would you prefer first? Something warm to drink or a peek at the new baby?"

Paul pointed to the stairs. "I'm not willing to wait a moment longer to see my wife and daughter."

Mrs. Atwell laughed. "Then hurry on up. She's every bit as anxious to see you."

True or not, the older woman's words warmed Paul's heart. During his most recent visits to the island, Sophie had acted as though her feelings for him had grown stronger; he hoped those feelings hadn't changed with the baby's birth. Taking the stairs two at a time, he stopped short outside the bedroom door and tapped lightly. He didn't want to wake the baby if she should be sleeping.

Fanny opened the door and waved him inside. "Where's Amanda?"

"She's following behind," he said, crossing the room in three giant strides. He searched Sophie's eyes, anxious to see if they would reveal pleasure at seeing him.

She extended her hand and pulled him forward. "Aren't you going to reward your wife with a kiss?" she whispered.

He grinned and nodded. "It would be my great pleasure," he said before placing a gentle kiss upon her lips. The baby lay cradled in her right arm, and Paul gazed upon the sight of mother and daughter, both so perfect. "May I hold her?"

"Of course." Sophie gently lifted the babe into his arms.

"She's perfect—just like her mother," he whispered, tears forming in his eyes. "Hello, Elizabeth Jane." He traced a finger along her cheek, and the infant turned her head toward his touch. "If you are only half as wonderful as your mother, you shall be everything a father could dream of."

Sophie laughed. "I do hope she'll prove to be less of a challenge than I've been for my father."

"Well, your father sends his love and is quite excited over the prospect of meeting this new addition to the family."

"Speaking of meeting family members, I'm afraid I've waited as long as I can to see my namesake," Amanda said, crossing the room. Paul laughed and pushed the soft flannel away from the baby's cheeks, but Amanda shook her head. "Why don't you and Sophie visit? I'd like to hold her. I believe Fanny and I can see to Elizabeth Jane's welfare. We won't go but a few paces away."

Paul carefully placed the baby in Amanda's arms and then sat down on the bed beside Sophie. "I wish I could have been here with you for her birth."

"I said the very same thing. It would have given me great comfort to have you close at hand when she was born." Sophie shifted on the pillows. "I've been doing a great deal of thinking over these past weeks. I'm excited at the prospect of going home and beginning our new life together as a family. I know we have a great deal to learn about each other, but I believe God will direct our steps."

Paul tried to hide his private heartache as his thoughts drifted to Sophie's love for another man. He wanted to be strong for her and for their daughter.

He had prayed that God would ease his mind from the one worry that had not ceased to haunt him. His wife loved another man.

"There's something else I want to tell you," Sophie said in a serious tone.

Paul met her gaze. Oh, but she was beautiful. He feared what she might say, but nevertheless said, "I'm listening."

She smiled. "I realized something not long ago, and I thought I should share it with you. You see, when I went to England, I felt so alone and empty. My mother had died, and my father didn't have the time of day to share with me. I had Amanda and Fanny's love, yet it wasn't enough. There was a vast hole in my heart. I wanted only to fill it—to feel whole."

Paul nodded. He wanted her to know he understood. Even if it killed him inside. "Then you found Wesley Hedrick."

Sophie looked at him oddly. "Yes. And I thought he would fill that emptiness. I thought our love would take away my longing for something more."

Paul felt as if he'd been kicked in the stomach but said nothing. He was afraid to even look Sophie in the eye, for fear she'd know his pain.

"But I was wrong."

He felt his breath catch. What was she saying?

"I didn't love Wesley. Not truly. I think I used him as much as he used me. I needed something from him that he could never give."

Paul looked up and shook his head. "What?"

"I needed God. You helped me to see that, Paul. You helped me to know that what I desired wasn't to be found on earth, but rather in heaven. The peace I've had since accepting that—since seeking God's forgiveness and direction—has made all the difference." She reached out and touched his face. "I want you to know that Wesley will never stand between us. He means nothing to me now."

"But what about Elizabeth?" Paul dared to ask. He searched Sophie's face for a sign that she had realized some new truth and changed her mind.

"Elizabeth is your daughter. Yours and mine. Our love will see her through. Our love for her . . . and for each other."

Paul could scarcely draw breath. "What are you saying, Sophie?"

She smiled and drew him closer. "I'm saying that the love you planted in my heart this summer has taken root. I believe with tenderness, honesty, and trust, it will continue to grow."

Paul kissed her passionately, refusing to let her go lest she speak again and take it all back. Her words touched his heart like nothing else could. He'd been praying that she would one day fully accept him as her husband and they could build a life together that would be filled with love and happiness. His prayers had been answered. He silently thanked God for this wondrous gift he'd been given.

From across the room Fanny and Amanda exchanged a glance over the tiny baby. Seeing Sophie and Paul kissing caused them both to smile.

"I do believe everything is going to be all right," Amanda said. "Sophie has Paul, and you have Michael. Perhaps love will even come to me one day."

Sophie surprised her by calling out. "Love often comes from the most unexpected source. I'm confident neither of you will ever be without it. God will send Michael home to Fanny and will no doubt send someone to love you, as well, Amanda. I'm certain of it."

Elizabeth began to fuss, as if protesting that the conversation was no longer about her. Paul laughed and came to take his daughter. Amanda marveled at the tenderness in his eyes. Would she ever see such a look from her own husband as he gazed upon their child?

"I believe it's time to leave these two—excuse me—these *three* to get to know one another better," Amanda said. She looped arms with Fanny and smiled.

"I suppose you are right. We will have plenty of time to fuss over Liza later."

"Beth," Amanda countered.

"Excuse me?" Fanny looked at her oddly as they made their way to the door.

"We aren't going to call her Liza. Liza is too guttural. Too harsh. I think we should call her Beth."

Sophie laughed, causing them both to turn. "Her name," Sophie stated, "is Elizabeth. Not Liza. Not Beth. *Elizabeth*."

Fanny and Amanda exchanged a glance and began to laugh. "It's good to see Sophie feeling like her old bossy self," Amanda declared. "Better be careful, Paul. She's something else when her temper's up."

Paul chuckled and eased into the chair beside the bed. "And well I know it. Talk about something unexpected. I've never seen such a . . ." His words trailed off as he met the quizzical look on Sophie's face.

"Come on, Fanny. I've seen her like this before. We don't want to be around for what's coming."

"You're right," Fanny agreed. "You're so very right."

A Surrendered
Heart

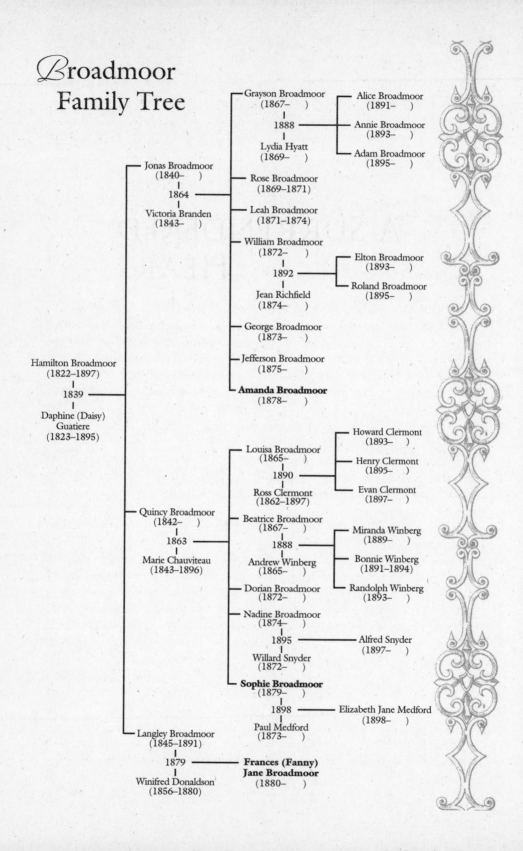

*B*roadmoor Family Tree

Hamilton Broadmoor
(1822–1897)
|
1839
|
Daphine (Daisy)
Guatiere
(1823–1895)

Jonas Broadmoor
(1840–   )
|
1864
|
Victoria Branden
(1843–   )

Grayson Broadmoor
(1867–   )
|
1888
|
Lydia Hyatt
(1869–   )

Alice Broadmoor
(1891–   )

Annie Broadmoor
(1893–   )

Adam Broadmoor
(1895–   )

Rose Broadmoor
(1869–1871)

Leah Broadmoor
(1871–1874)

William Broadmoor
(1872–   )
|
1892
|
Jean Richfield
(1874–   )

Elton Broadmoor
(1893–   )

Roland Broadmoor
(1895–   )

George Broadmoor
(1873–   )

Jefferson Broadmoor
(1875–   )

Amanda Broadmoor
(1878–   )

Quincy Broadmoor
(1842–   )
|
1863
|
Marie Chauviteau
(1843–1896)

Louisa Broadmoor
(1865–   )
|
1890
|
Ross Clermont
(1862–1897)

Howard Clermont
(1893–   )

Henry Clermont
(1895–   )

Evan Clermont
(1897–   )

Beatrice Broadmoor
(1867–   )
|
1888
|
Andrew Winberg
(1865–   )

Miranda Winberg
(1889–   )

Bonnie Winberg
(1891–1894)

Randolph Winberg
(1893–   )

Dorian Broadmoor
(1872–   )

Nadine Broadmoor
(1874–   )
|
1895
|
Willard Snyder
(1872–   )

Alfred Snyder
(1897–   )

Sophie Broadmoor
(1879–   )
|
1898
|
Paul Medford
(1873–   )

Elizabeth Jane Medford
(1898–   )

Langley Broadmoor
(1845–1891)
|
1879
|
Winifred Donaldson
(1856–1880)

**Frances (Fanny)
Jane Broadmoor**
(1880–   )

CHAPTER 1

CHOLERA ON THE RISE! EPIDEMIC ANTICIPATED IN ROCHESTER!

Amanda Broadmoor glanced at the imprudent headline that emblazoned last night's edition of the Rochester *Democrat and Chronicle*. Why must the newspaper exaggerate? People would be frightened into a genuine panic with such ill-advised news reporting. Turning the headline to the inside, she creased the paper and slipped it beneath a stack of mail on the marble-topped table in the lower hallway of her family's fashionable home. Certain this most recent newspaper article would cause yet another family squabble, she had hidden the paper in her bedroom the previous evening.

No doubt the glaring headline had increased sales for the owner of the press. The paper had been quick to report four recent deaths attributed to the dreaded disease, and with an early spring and unrelenting rains, a number of prominent families had already fled the city. After yesterday's report, more would surely follow. And for those who didn't possess the wherewithal to flee, the report would serve no purpose but to heighten their fear.

Of course the Broadmoors were among the social elite of Rochester, New York. Amanda had never known need or want, and when bad things dared to rear their ugly heads, she had been carefully sheltered from the worst of it. All that had changed, however, when she decided to seek a career in medicine.

At twenty-one, Amanda felt she had the right to make her own way in life, but her father and mother hardly saw it that way. Their attitudes reflected those of their peers and the world around them. Women working in the medical field were highly frowned upon, and a woman of Amanda's social standing was reared to marry and produce heirs, not to tend the sick. Especially not those suffering from cholera.

"And Mama can be such an alarmist."

At the first report Amanda's mother had suggested the entire family take refuge at their summer estate located on Broadmoor Island in the St. Lawrence

River. But that idea had been immediately vetoed by her father. Jonas Broad-moor had avowed his work would not permit him to leave Rochester. And Amanda agreed with her father's decision. After devoting much of her time and energy to medical training at Dr. Carstead's side, Amanda couldn't pos-sibly desert her work—not now—not when she was most needed.

Amanda glanced at the clock. Her mother would expect her for breakfast, but remaining any longer would simply ensure a tearful plea for her to cease working with Dr. Carstead. She would then need to offer a lengthy explanation as to why her work was critical, and that in turn would cause a tardy arrival at the Home for the Friendless. Before the matter could be resolved, much valuable time would be wasted, time that could be used to care for those in need of her ministrations. With each newspaper claim, an argument ensued, leaving Amanda to feel she must betray either her mother or Dr. Carstead. She didn't feel up to a quarrel today.

After fastening her cloak, she tucked a strand of blond hair beneath her bonnet and slipped into the kitchen, where the carriage driver was finishing his morning repast. "Do hurry," she said, motioning toward the door. "I'm needed at the Home."

He downed a final gulp of coffee, wiped his mouth with the back of his hand, and nodded. "The carriage is ready and waiting." He quickstepped to the east side of the kitchen and opened the door with a flourish. His broad smile revealed a row of uneven teeth. "You see? Always prepared. That's my motto."

"An excellent motto, though sometimes difficult to achieve," Amanda said, pleased to discover the rain had ceased.

She hurried toward the carriage, the driver close on her heels. Her own at-tempts to be prepared seemed to fall short far too often. Since beginning her study of medicine with Dr. Carstead, she'd made every effort to anticipate his needs, but it seemed he frequently requested an item she'd never before heard of, a medical instrument other than what she offered, or a bandage of a different width. Amanda was certain her in-adequate choices sometimes an-noyed him. However, he held his temper in check—at least most of the time.

"Did you read today's headline?" the driver asked before closing the car-riage door.

Amanda nodded. "Indeed. That's why we must hurry. I'm afraid there will be many at the clinic doors this morning. Sometimes simply hearing about an illness causes people to fear they've contracted it." A sense of exhaustion washed over her just thinking about the work ahead.

The driver grimaced. "I know what you mean, miss. I read the article in the paper and then wondered if I was suffering some of the symptoms myself."

"Have you been having difficulty with your digestive organs?"

At the mention of his digestive organs, the color heightened in the driver's cheeks. He glanced away and shook his head. "No, but I had a bit of a head-ache yesterday, and thought I was a bit thirstier than usual."

"It's likely nothing, but if you begin to experience additional symptoms, be sure to come and see the doctor. Don't wait too long."

Still unable to meet her gaze, he touched his finger to the brim of his hat. "Thank you for your concern, miss. I'll heed your advice."

When they arrived at the Home for the Friendless a short time later, Amanda's prediction proved true. Lines had formed outside the building, and there was little doubt most of those waiting were seeking medical attention. After bidding the driver good day, she hurried around the side of the building and entered through the back door leading into the office Dr. Blake Carstead occupied during his days at the Home.

She stopped short at the sight of the doctor examining a young woman. "You've arrived earlier than usual, I see."

He grunted. "After reading last night's newspaper, I knew we'd have more patients today. I wish someone would place a muzzle on that reporter. He seems to take delight in frightening people. Did you read what he said?"

Amanda removed her cloak and hung it on the peg alongside the doctor's woolen overcoat. "Only the headline," she replied. "I do hope the article was incorrect."

Dr. Carstead continued to examine a cut on his patient's arm. "It was ex-aggerated. There was one death due to cholera, but a colleague tells me the other deaths occurred when a carriage overturned and crushed two passersby. I don't know why the owner of that paper permits such slipshod reporting. If I practiced medicine the way that newspaper reports the news, I'd have a room filled with dead patients."

The patient's eyes widened at the doctor's last remark.

"He truly does a better job than the newspaper," Amanda said, approach-ing the woman's side.

Once the woman's arm had been properly bandaged, Amanda showed her to the door and returned to see how she could best assist Blake that day.

"Honestly, I think the newspaper enjoys putting people in a state of panic," Blake said as he washed his hands.

"Trouble sells papers." Amanda held out a towel.

Blake took it and looked at her oddly for a moment. "You look pale. Are you sleeping and eating right?"

She put her hands on her hips. "I might ask you the same thing. You haven't slept in days."

"I didn't know you were keeping track," he said rather sarcastically. "But I don't have the same privilege of going home to a comfortable meal and bed that you have."

"And whose fault is that?" Amanda countered. "You won't go home, and you won't let me stay."

"It wouldn't be proper."

She huffed. "It won't be proper when you collapse from exhaustion, either, but I'm sure I'll think of something to tell the masses of sick people. 'Oh, we're very sorry, but the doctor is a prideful and arrogant man who believes himself immortal.' Even God rested on the seventh day, Dr. Carstead."

"God wasn't dealing with cholera at the time," Blake replied, unmoved by her comments.

Amanda let out an exasperated breath and went to wipe down the examination table.

It was their last opportunity for private banter, as a steady stream of patients kept them working until well past six that evening.

Exhausted but unwilling to let on to how tired she was, Amanda reached for her coat and suppressed a yawn.

"How are you getting home?" Blake asked.

"I'm certain the driver is waiting for me."

"I'll walk you out and make sure he's there."

Amanda didn't argue. She wanted to ask when he planned to leave but knew it would only stir an argument. She had no energy left to partake of such a silly exchange, and Blake seemed to sense this.

Taking hold of her arm, he escorted her out to the street, where the Broadmoor carriage waited. The driver quickly climbed down and opened the door. His coat revealed that it had been raining much of the time he'd been waiting.

"Try to eat a good meal and take a hot bath," Blake instructed as he helped her into the carriage. "You're no good to me if you get sick."

Amanda shook her head and fixed him with a stare. "I was thinking much the same about you. Besides, you stink and need a shave."

He looked at her soberly for a moment and then broke into a smile. "There you go again. Caring about me."

She reached for the door. "I'm not at all concerned about you, Dr. Carstead, but the friendless and sick are beginning to take up a collection for you. I believe they plan to purchase a bar of soap and a razor."

Amanda pulled the door shut even as she heard Blake roar with laughter. She smiled to herself. It was good to hear him laugh. There had been so little worth laughing about these last days.

THURSDAY, APRIL 27, 1899

"You're late," Blake growled out as Amanda entered the examination room the next day. "I know I told you to rest, but I didn't mean all night and all day."

"Oh, hush. I'm only a few minutes late. The driver was delayed this morning." She hung up her coat and immediately pulled on her apron. She gave Blake a cursory glance. "I see you took my advice. Now at least you won't drive people away in fear."

Blake touched his clean-shaven chin before pointing to the door. "The Rochester Health Board has sent examiners to check us out. I didn't want to look shabby for them."

Amanda dropped to a nearby chair. She gasped as a fleeting pain sliced through her midsection. Once again she had hurried out of the house without breakfast in order to avoid a confrontation with her mother. This time, however, she was certain that had she eaten breakfast, she would have embarrassed herself in front of the good doctor. She swallowed and clasped her open palm tight against her waist. "Has there been any further word regarding the quarantine?"

Dr. Carstead nodded toward the crowd gathered outside his door and touched a finger to his pursed lips. "We don't want to cause undue worry." He leaned forward, his dark hazel eyes radiating concern. "You're not getting sick on me, are you?"

"No, of course not. I experienced a brief moment of discomfort, but I'm feeling fine." She stood and brushed a wrinkle from her faded navy blue skirt. Shortly after beginning her work with Dr. Carstead, she'd acquired a uniform of sorts. The doctor had been quick to advise that if she was serious about learning medicine, she'd best save her expensive silk and satin day dresses for leisure and adopt a more utilitarian form of dress for her days at the clinic. At first she'd been affronted by his remark, but he'd been correct. Even though she had covered her serge skirts and cotton blouses with a canvas apron, the Broadmoor laundress still complained of the stains that required extra scrubbing.

"I'm sure we'll hear of the examiner's decision soon. Why don't you go through the line and separate those who have complaints that suggest they've contracted cholera. Place them in the office at the end of the hallway. When you've completed that, let me know and I'll examine them."

Amanda retrieved a pencil and paper. She preferred keeping notes while she spoke to the patients, especially when there were so many. Otherwise important details could easily be forgotten.

Before exiting the room, Amanda poured a glass of water and quickly downed the contents. The cool liquid slid down her parched throat, but her stomach immediately clenched in a painful spasm. Perhaps she should have eaten breakfast after all. Forcing a smile, she replaced the glass and hurried out of the room with her stomach still violently protesting.

Dr. Carstead waved another patient into his office, and Amanda stopped beside the next person in line. Although the older man appeared disgruntled when she approached, he finally complied when she advised him that he couldn't see the doctor until he'd answered her questions. A brief look at the lump on his head and a view of his scraped knuckles confirmed that today's visit had nothing to do with cholera. After spending too much time at the local tavern last night, he'd challenged another patron to a fight.

Amanda managed to maintain her composure for a while longer but stopped short when she came to the sixth person in the long line. Clutching her stomach, she pointed her finger toward the ceiling. "I'll be back," she promised, then dropped her pencil and paper on a nearby table. Grabbing an enamel basin, she raced into a room at the far end of the hall and divested herself of the water she'd swallowed only minutes earlier. The liquid burned the back of her throat, and her stomach muscles ached in protest, but that was soon forgotten when gripping pains attacked her lower intestines. The intensity sent her running for the bathroom.

When she returned a short time later, Dr. Carstead was waiting. "You're sick. You're as white as a sheet and shaking. Why didn't you tell me earlier? You may have infected all those you came in contact with today."

Amanda clutched her stomach. "You think *I* have cholera?" She shook her head in denial. "I failed to eat breakfast and my stomach is upset—nothing more." Another spasm gripped her midsection, and her knees buckled. Had Blake not held her upright, she would have collapsed at his feet.

Blake Carstead stared at Amanda's pale face while he tucked a heavy blanket over her quivering body. He raked his long fingers through his unruly mass of dark brown hair and turned toward the door. How could he possibly manage without Amanda's help? The crowd continued to increase by the minute.

"Quincy! I need your help," Blake shouted to Amanda's uncle, the proprietor of the Home for the Friendless. If Amanda contracted cholera, her parents would hold him responsible. Neither had encouraged her to pursue medical training. In fact, her father had used every ruse possible to keep her out of medical school. When Blake had suggested she could work with him and receive training, she'd readily accepted.

Amanda stirred and touched his arm. "Water. I'm so thirsty," she whispered.

He offered her only a couple ounces, for he knew what would occur. She clutched the glass and downed the small amount of liquid he offered. Immediately, she pointed to the nearby basin. Fear shone in her eyes as she heaved relentlessly before falling back onto the bed.

Where was Quincy? He rushed to the door and peered into the clamoring crowd of patients. All of them wanted to see a doctor—and none of them wanted to wait in the overflowing room. They all feared the same thing. The person sitting beside them might carry the dreaded disease. When he finally spotted Quincy, he stepped farther into the room and shouted above the din. Two men, neither one appearing particularly happy, stood inside the front entrance. Blake recognized them as officials from the Health Department. They shook their heads, obviously agitated and anxious to be on their way. They pushed a paper into Quincy's hand and hurried from the room.

After Quincy read the paper, he shoved it into his jacket and then cupped his hands to his mouth. "The Home for the Friendless has been placed under quarantine. The authorities have tacked a formal notice to the front gate."

A hum of dissent quickly escalated into angry voices. Quincy retrieved the wrinkled sheet of paper from his pocket and waved it overhead. "This is a letter of explanation. No one is to leave the building."

Blake wasn't surprised when the gathered patients rushed out of the waiting room and onto the streets. They looked like mice fleeing a sinking ship, and there was no one to stop them. Within minutes few remained, and those who did were too infirm to leave under their own power. By the terms of the quarantine, no one should have left the building, but neither Blake nor Quincy possessed the power to hold them prisoner. And the authorities didn't have sufficient time to enforce the orders. They were too busy delivering them.

The behavior of the patients came as no surprise to Dr. Carstead. He'd seen the same reaction in other cities. People understood the need for quarantines, but they refused to be inconvenienced. He'd discovered many were willing to remain within the confines of their own homes, but they didn't want to be held in an unfamiliar institution such as the Home for the Friendless. And he understood their behavior. He, too, would have preferred to be surrounded by the comfort and convenience of his own home, where the downstairs had been converted into a doctor's office with all of the latest equipment to provide care for patients able to afford his medical services.

Recently Blake's volunteer work at the Home was consuming more and more of his time. There was little doubt he would be needed here during the days to come. The living conditions of those who required free medical care made them all the more susceptible to diseases. Besides, there were sufficient doctors within the city of Rochester to care for those patients who could afford to pay for medical treatment.

According to the terms of the notice, they would be quarantined at the Home for the next five days. Further evaluation would be made at that time. And with several patients showing definite signs of cholera, Blake guessed the quarantine would be extended. If they were to stave off the spread of the disease, it would take more than quarantines.

He lifted his gaze upward. "We need you, Lord," he whispered before finally gaining Quincy's attention. When the older man drew near, Blake grasped him by the arm and pulled him closer. "It's Amanda. I'm afraid she's suffering from cholera."

Quincy peered across the threshold. The sight of his niece caused him to pale. "I greeted her when she arrived this morning. She looked fine. When did this . . . How could this . . . Her parents will never forgive me. They'll blame this on me."

"They can't possibly blame you. They—"

Quincy shook his head with a vehemence that caused his hair to settle in unfashionable disarray. "You mark my words. If Amanda doesn't recover, I'll face my brother's wrath for the remainder of my days. Jonas Broadmoor can hold a grudge longer than any man I've ever known."

Both of the men turned when Amanda stirred. "My stomach. I need help," she groaned.

Blake tightened his hold on Quincy's arm. "We must locate a woman to help her. She'll be in further distress if I attempt to assist her while she's in the throes of elimination."

Quincy agreed. They had both assisted one of the men who'd gone through several days of suffering. The poor fellow had died soon thereafter. The episode was an immediate reminder of debilitating scenes of violent vomiting and unrelenting evacuation of the bowels accompanied by gripping pain and spasms that left the victim dehydrated. Nothing good could be said of what lay in store for Amanda.

Blake would oversee her care, but he didn't want to cause her embarrassment. She had been surrounded by wealth all her life. Now she'd be subjected to suffering this terrible illness in pitiable conditions. And all because of him! He should have insisted that she remain at home when the first cases of cholera had been suspected. Instead, he'd encouraged her to continue working alongside him. He'd told himself he was furthering her medical career, while in truth he'd both wanted and needed the caring hands she offered. Only now did he acknowledge his motivation had been borne of selfishness. What had he done?

While Quincy hurried off in search of some willing soul who might lend aid, Blake dragged a wooden screen from across the room and placed it beside Amanda's bed. It would offer a modicum of privacy.

She moaned, and her eyes fluttered open. "Water. Please won't you give me water?"

The result would be the same, but he couldn't refuse. He placed a basin on the table and then poured her a drink.

She'd barely finished drinking when she retched and emptied the contents of her stomach into the basin. Blake brushed the damp strands of hair from her perspiring forehead. Surely she must have had some of these symptoms before she'd come to work this morning. Why hadn't she stayed home where she could be properly cared for?

Before he could ask, Quincy peeked around the screen. "Mrs. Donner has offered to lend a hand."

"But only for a price," the woman said. She tapped her index finger in the opposing palm. "Don't forget you promised to pay me in advance."

Blake met the woman's intense gaze. "You might consider helping for the sake of simply doing good for another, Mrs. Donner."

"Don't you go judging me, Dr. Carstead. If I die from cholera, Miss Broadmoor's father won't take it upon himself to feed my children. I learned a long time ago that God helps them that help themselves."

"If I recall, you and your children have been living in the Home for the Friendless free of charge for well over three months now. Aren't those beds and food worth a speck of charity from you?"

When she shrugged, her tattered shawl slipped from one shoulder, and she yanked it back into place. "You'll not convince me to change my mind. Do you want my help or not?" She turned to face Quincy.

"We want your help."

Blake motioned to a pitcher and water. "You'll need to be careful to wash your hands after you've had contact with Miss Broadmoor." He glanced at the woman's dirt-encrusted fingers. "In fact, I had best teach you the proper method for scrubbing before you begin your new duties."

"Soon as I get my money," she said.

Quincy offered an apologetic look. "She's the only one who would even consider coming back here."

Blake removed several coins from his pocket and placed them in the woman's outstretched hand. "This will have to do for now. We have no way of withdrawing money from the bank. The quarantine, you know."

Her hand remained open. "I'm guessing Mr. Broadmoor can offer a little more."

Quincy withdrew two bills from his pocket and gave them to her.

The older woman grinned and tucked them into her pocket along with the coins. "Now let's have that lesson in hand washing."

While Blake led Mrs. Donner to the washbasin, Quincy followed along, reciting Scripture. " 'And above all these things put on charity, which is the bond of perfectness.' "

Mrs. Donner squared her shoulders and pointed her finger in Quincy's direction. "I don't need you reciting passages about charity. It's easy to be charitable when you got food on your table and money in the bank." Anger flashed in the woman's eyes. "If you want my help, you'll pay me with money and keep your preaching for them that want to hear it."

Blake sent a warning look in Quincy's direction. If he was left to care for Amanda through this undignified illness, she'd never be able to look him in the eye. He didn't want Mrs. Donner to leave him stranded in such a circumstance.

CHAPTER 2

With a mixture of irritation and surprise, Jonas Broadmoor waved Victoria into his office. He was certain his wife had advised him she would be remaining at home all day today. Now here she was distracting him before it was even midmorning. After all these years, Victoria still didn't seem to realize that the business day was exactly that—a time set aside to complete meaningful tasks without interruption.

He dipped his pen into the ink bottle and continued writing in the ledger. "What brings you to the office, Victoria?" A brief glance was enough for him to place the pen in the bronze holder. She was positively pale. "Has something happened?"

Victoria placed her handkerchief to her lips and nodded. "They've quarantined the Home for the Friendless. I sent my maid to pick up that new gown I ordered. The driver passed by the Home, and Veda saw the quarantine sign. She told me they aren't letting anyone in or out of the place."

Jonas shrugged. "I doubt Quincy will be overly inconvenienced. He's at the Home all the time as it is."

Victoria straightened in her chair and slapped her palm on his desk. "Your *daughter* is there, Jonas! Our Amanda is going to be quarantined for five days with those diseased people. Don't you realize what that means?"

Jonas leaned back in his chair. "How does this change anything? I told you months ago I didn't approve of her training with Dr. Carstead. You're the one who agreed with this medical nonsense. You encouraged her when she said she wanted to become a nurse."

"Doctor," Victoria corrected.

Jonas jerked to attention. *"What?"*

"It isn't *nursing* that interests Amanda. She wants to become a *doctor*. There's a vast difference, Jonas."

"Oh, forevermore, Victoria. Why are we quibbling over minute details? Doctor, nurse—it makes little difference. Your decision has subjected Amanda to cholera."

"You know I did everything in my power to stop her from going back to the Home until after the outbreak subsided. If we'd gone to the island as I suggested, she would be safe from harm. Our remaining in Rochester was your doing." She glared across the desk. "And now you dare accuse me of subjecting our daughter to a deadly disease. I'm almost sorry I came here."

"Almost but not quite. Correct?" He arched his brows. They were playing a game of cat and mouse, and he didn't intend to lose. "You expect me to find some way to get her out of that place. That's why you've come here, isn't it?"

Victoria tightened her lips into a thin line and offered only a slight tip of her head. The unanticipated ease of her admission lessened Jonas's thrill of victory. He determined she must be extremely worried—and very likely he should be, too. One of his children had placed herself in danger. He should have insisted that Amanda give up this notion of becoming a doctor. Once he rescued her from his brother's Home for the Friendless, there would be no further discussion. Adult or not, Amanda was going to abide by his rules until she married. And his rules would include the termination of any further medical training with Dr. Carstead!

He closed the ledger and pushed away from his desk. "Before going to the other end of town, let's stop by the house. I do hope Amanda has used her good sense and managed to sneak out after the authorities departed. They're far too busy to guard every home bearing a quarantine notice, and it would be easy enough for her to leave by a back door."

"Jonas! I can't believe you would say such a thing. Those quarantines are in place to help prevent the spread of disease, and Amanda would not ignore such an order."

"She has no difficulty ignoring *my* orders." He shrugged into his black wool topcoat and gathered his hat and cane. "Take us home," he instructed their driver as they exited his office. Victoria didn't argue, and for that he was thankful.

This had been a day he'd set aside to work on his ledgers, and thus far he'd found nothing encouraging in the numbers. His losses appeared even greater than he'd first imagined. The thought was enough to cause perspiration to bead along his forehead in spite of the chilly April breeze. He settled into the thick leather cushion and withdrew his handkerchief from his pocket.

Victoria leaned aside as he swiped his forehead. "Jonas! You're ill. Why didn't you tell me?"

He detected the fear in her eyes. "I don't have cholera, Victoria."

She removed a glove and touched her palm to his forehead. "You feel clammy. That's not a good sign. I've been questioning Amanda regarding the symptoms."

Jonas lightly grasped her hand and lifted it from his forehead. "Please trust me. I am fine."

While keeping her gaze fastened upon him, Victoria worked her fingers back into her glove. "I think your decision to return home before going to check on Amanda is sound. I don't want you going anywhere else if you're ill."

He sighed. No need to argue further. His wife would not heed his words. He dropped back against the seat and stared out the window until the horses came to a halt in front of their East Avenue mansion.

"You sit still, Jonas. I'll have the driver help you down."

Jonas yanked the handle and pushed open the carriage door. "I am not ill, and I do not need assistance out of the carriage. Please stop this foolishness." He extended his hand to help her from inside.

Her furtive glances didn't go unnoticed as they continued up the front steps leading into the house. He wished he'd left his handkerchief in his pocket. "Any word from our daughter?" Jonas inquired of the butler, who helped them with their coats.

"I don't believe so, but you have a visitor waiting in the library, Mr. Broadmoor."

Victoria shot him a warning look. "Do tell whoever it is that we have important business requiring our immediate attention."

Jonas could feel the perspiration beginning to bead across his forehead again, yet he dared not wipe it away. "Please rest easy, my dear. Nothing is going to change regarding the quarantine. We will go there in due time."

Victoria grasped the sleeve of his jacket. "In due time? Amanda needs to be removed from that place as soon as possible. I want her home before nightfall."

"Yes, my dear. And I will see to it that she is." Jonas glanced at the butler, who appeared as rigid and stoic as the statues that adorned their gardens. "I assume you have the name of my visitor?"

With a curt nod the butler retrieved a calling card from the silver tray and handed it to Jonas. He stared at the engraved block letters. *Vincent Fillmore.* The last thing he needed right now was a meeting with his lawyer's son and law partner. And why had Vincent come to the house rather than his office?

"I won't be long," he told his wife before turning down the hallway.

What else could possibly go wrong today? Wasn't it enough that he was suffering these severe financial woes? His stomach clenched into a knot. What if Vincent had come to deliver devastating news regarding a legal issue—something that would send his finances plummeting even further? At the moment he wondered why he'd even gotten out of bed this morning. The day had been filled with enough bad news for at least a month, and it wasn't yet noon!

He opened the library door and motioned for Vincent to remain seated. "What brings you to my home in the middle of the day?" Without waiting for an answer, he dropped to the chair across from the younger man. "Didn't you realize it's a weekday?"

Vincent raked his fingers through his hair. "To be honest, I didn't think at all. My father died just a short time ago."

Jonas gasped. Panic washed over him and seized a tight hold. His mouth went dry.

"Father told me I was to advise you immediately of his death, no matter when it occurred." Vincent slumped forward and shook his head. "I knew this day would arrive, but he'd been feeling better over the past two weeks."

"So it wasn't cholera?"

"No. The doctor said his heart simply gave out. I had feared Father might contract cholera, but the doctor tells me the newspaper reports have been exaggerated."

"Is that so? My wife will be pleased to hear that." Jonas's thoughts whirred as he attempted to maintain his composure. "I am genuinely sorry for your loss, Vincent. Your father was a dear friend and confidant."

"Thank you. He wanted you to say a few words at the gravesite."

"What? Me?" Surely he hadn't heard Vincent correctly. "I think a local preacher would be a better choice, don't you? I mean, it's just not proper. I wouldn't know what to say."

Vincent laced his fingers together. "Whatever you say will be fine. My father was never one to stand on ceremony. You know that better than anyone. He had no use for the church and always thought he'd outwit God. He used to tell me he was going to live like the devil, and at the end he'd ask forgiveness and step into heaven with a smile."

"Let's hope it works that way," Jonas replied. Their conversation was veering off in a strange direction. The last thing he wanted right now was a discussion of right and wrong or of heaven and hell. All he wanted at the moment was to secure his files from Mortimer's office.

He silently chastised himself. He should have transferred his papers to another lawyer long ago. He'd given consideration to the idea several times. Unfortunately, he'd never found anyone else he could trust like he did Mortimer. The two of them had shared the same ideas about making money: There were no rules as long as there was a profit to be made. He had no way of knowing how much of his business and personal information Mortimer had committed to writing. What if he'd maintained files that told of Jonas's business dealings? He couldn't risk anyone discovering such information.

"We must leave immediately and go to your father's office." Jonas pushed up from the chair without giving Vincent an opportunity to disagree.

"What's this?" Victoria entered the room with her coat draping one arm and her hat perched atop her head. "You're not planning on going somewhere other than the Home for the Friendless, are you?"

Jonas stepped forward. "Mortimer passed on this morning. I believe Vincent needs me to assist him with several matters surrounding his father's death."

Victoria hurried to Vincent's side and murmured her condolences. "Exactly how can Jonas be of help at this moment?"

Jonas couldn't hear Vincent's muttered response, but from the hard-edged look in Victoria's eyes, Jonas knew his wife was unhappy.

"Mortimer died this morning and you want to go and retrieve your business files? Jonas Broadmoor! I can't believe you would even *think* of such a thing when Vincent is overcome with grief and mourning the loss of his father." Victoria patted Vincent's arm. "Do let me call for tea."

Vincent shook his head. "No. I really must be on my way. I have much to do."

Jonas forced a smile. "I'm sorry for my lack of tact, Vincent. However, I think you know your father would approve. He was an astute lawyer who always thought of business first." He needed to win Vincent over. Once the younger man departed, there would be little opportunity until after the funeral to retrieve his files. With family members sniffing about, any one of them might go through Mortimer's files. He didn't want to take that chance. "I can have my driver take us to your father's office this very minute. It wouldn't take but a few moments of your time."

The younger man's jaw went slack, and he shook his head. "Not now, Jonas. I must see to the funeral arrangements." Vincent sidestepped around him and strode toward the library door.

"But I truly need those—"

"What you need to do is show some decency and respect," Victoria hissed. "There is nothing that won't keep until after Mortimer is buried." His wife brushed past him and hurried out of the room. "Do keep us advised of the funeral arrangements."

Jonas dropped into a nearby chair and massaged his forehead. The day had gone from bad to worse by the hour. Could anything else possibly go awry this day? If so, he couldn't imagine what it would be.

Paul Medford kissed his daughter's cheek before his wife lifted her from his arms. "Our Elizabeth is the loveliest little girl ever born."

Sophie tucked the soft flannel blanket around her daughter's tiny body. "I couldn't agree more. And she is very fortunate to have you as her papa."

The words warmed him even more than the hearty breakfast Sophie had served him a short time ago. The fact that Wesley Hedrick had forsaken Sophie and his unborn child had proved to be a blessing for Paul. He daily thanked God for the opportunity to call Sophie his wife and claim Elizabeth as his child.

He pushed away from the kitchen table, and Sophie accompanied him to the door. While he shoved his arms into his warm woolen coat, she retrieved his hat. No doubt this day would be busy, but he'd discovered deep satisfaction in his work at the Home for the Friendless.

He lowered his head and kissed Sophie's lips. "I'll be home as early as possible."

Sophie didn't reply. Instead, she lifted on tiptoe and kissed him again. They both knew that he'd do his best but likely wouldn't return until well after dark. The needs at the Home increased daily, especially since the outbreak of cholera. It seemed that anyone having the slightest symptom came to see the doctor. Most simply wanted reassurance they hadn't contracted the disease. Others had genuine problems: a cut that required stitches or a woman laboring to deliver a newborn. And then there were those looking for a safe place of shelter and a warm meal. Most thought God had no use for them, but Paul knew better. And he did his best to show them God's love through his actions.

Unless asked, he didn't offer advice or sermonize to the strangers who came for help. In fact, he could quickly calculate the number of times he'd preached since receiving his divinity degree. Those who found shelter at the Home were encouraged to attend a church of their choosing on Sunday mornings. Residents were sent out the front doors after breakfast and not permitted to return until after twelve-thirty on Sunday afternoon. Whether they actually attended church was between them and God. Sophie's father, Quincy, thought the residents should be permitted to worship in their own manner. He didn't want anyone to think they must adhere to specific religious beliefs in order to be welcomed into the Home.

Paul grinned at the thought. People flocked to theirs doors in overwhelming numbers, and he doubted any would depart if forced to attend a church service on the premises. Most would probably prefer such an arrangement. They wouldn't be required to go outdoors in the cold or rain. But Paul didn't argue with his father-in-law. Nor did he look for another place to serve the Lord. For now, he believed God wanted him to serve at the Home for the Friendless.

He shoved his hands into his gloves and reached for the doorknob.

"Why don't you invite Amanda and Dr. Carstead to join us for supper this evening?" Sophie suggested. "I see my dear cousin far too seldom. And I'm certain Elizabeth misses her aunt Amanda, too."

"I'll do my best to convince them," he said. "There are so many patients that need their attention, I'm not—"

"Tell Amanda that I insist. They both need to take a little time for pleasure. And so do you. I'll expect all three of you no later than six o'clock."

"You're right. An evening of visiting and good food is just what the doctor ordered. Even if the doctor doesn't know it."

The sound of Sophie's laughter followed him down the front steps. As a harsh wind assailed him from the north, he tucked his head low. Paul believed the walk to work each morning helped him maintain his good health. However, he would have gladly exchanged his morning exercise for a ride in a warm carriage on this brisk morning.

Though a cutting chill remained, the wind subsided as he rounded the final corner. He squinted against the sun. Not one soul stood waiting for admission to the Home. Ever since the first frightening case of cholera had been detected, the medical office had been swarmed with daily visitors. And after the recent newspaper headlines, he'd expected an even larger crowd. He strode forward but stopped short at the front gate.

Quarantine! He didn't take time to read the fine print. The one word was enough to explain the absence of the usual morning arrivals.

Paul cupped his hands to his mouth. "Quincy! It's Paul. Can you hear me? Come to the door." He waited a moment and then tried again.

With the windows tightly closed and shuttered against the cold, his voice would never be heard. He glanced at the iron bell used to announce that meals were being served. Without a moment's hesitation, he entered the gate, pulled the worn rope, and waited. The shutters that covered one of the windows in the front of the house opened. Blake! So the doctor had been captured in the quarantine, too.

Paul pointed to the front of the building. "Open the door."

Blake momentarily disappeared before the door opened and he stepped onto the porch. "Didn't you read the notice? You can't come in here, Paul."

"I understand," he said, careful to keep some distance between them. "But what can I do to help?"

Blake rubbed his hands together. "We'll need our food replenished in a couple days. And could you gather medical supplies? Ask John Phillips. He'll help you choose what I need."

Paul had become acquainted with John Phillips when he'd first arrived in Rochester. The man operated a pharmacy nearby. "Anything else?"

Blake stepped down from the porch and drew closer. "Tell Mr. and Mrs. Broadmoor that Amanda has contracted cholera. I'm doing my best for her. She's young and strong, but I can't say with certainty that she'll make it. She's very sick."

Paul grasped the fence and steadied himself. The news would devastate Sophie. And what of Mr. and Mrs. Broadmoor? Amanda's parents would surely blame themselves for permitting her to work at the Home. The thought of delivering this dreadful report left him speechless.

"Paul! Did you hear me?" Blake shouted.

"Yes, yes. I'll tell them. Do you think . . . I mean . . . should I . . . ?"

"Just tell them exactly what I've said. There's no way of knowing what will happen. If they want to speak to me, tell them to do as you have. Ring the bell and I'll come out."

Paul nodded and turned, too dazed to ask any further questions.

"Don't forget the medicine and food," Blake hollered.

Paul waved in recognition of the request. He couldn't find his voice. The possibility had always existed that one of them would contract some fatal disease from one of the patients, but Paul had always believed God's hand of protection was upon them. They were, after all, doing God's work. He rounded the corner and forced such thoughts from his mind. He'd speak to Sophie first. It would be best if she accompanied him to meet with Amanda's parents. Sophie knew them better than he. Perhaps she could lend some advice on how to best approach them. For the second time this day, he wished he hadn't walked to work.

CHAPTER 3

Sophie tied the ribbons of Elizabeth's bonnet beneath the sleeping child's tiny chin while her husband paced in the hallway. Amanda had stitched the bonnet during one of the three cousins' many sewing sessions before Elizabeth's birth. Sophie pictured the three of them—Fanny, Amanda, and herself—sitting in the bedroom at Broadmoor Castle with their sewing baskets and fabric. A smile played at her lips as she remembered her cousins' efforts to help improve her sewing skills. They'd been mostly unsuccessful, and Sophie had accepted the fact that she'd never be an accomplished seamstress—not like Amanda. She traced her finger along the embroidered stems of bluebells with pale green stems and veined leaves that adorned the cap.

The love she held for her cousins was deeper than that which she held for her own siblings. Throughout the years Amanda and Fanny had been her closest friends and confidants. Many had been the occasion when her own sisters had turned away from her in frustration or disgust, but not Amanda and Fanny. They might not always approve of the things she did, but they would never dream of deserting her.

"How can I help?" Paul asked as he continued to pace.

"I'll be just a moment longer. Is the carriage out front?"

"Yes. We really must be on our way."

Sophie turned and frowned at her husband. "I'm doing my best." She lifted Elizabeth from her cradle, careful to keep the blanket tightly tucked around the child. Some said the damp air could cause cholera, and she didn't intend to take her outdoors unless properly protected against the elements. "I want to make certain the baby is warm enough."

"Yes, of course," he replied, shifting his gaze toward the floor.

Her words carried a hint of censure, and Paul had taken note. Sophie immediately regretted her behavior. Paul was worried and needed her support instead of a reprimand. But she was worried, too—about all of them. What if Paul or Elizabeth should fall ill? She couldn't bear the thought of losing either of them.

"I'm sorry for speaking harshly," she said.

Paul smiled and took the baby into his arms. "You're forgiven. We're both worried." He brushed her cheek with a kiss and opened the door.

The carriage ride to her aunt and uncle's home seemed longer than usual, and Sophie fidgeted throughout the ride. Surprisingly, her movement had little effect upon Elizabeth, who continued to sleep. A short time later Paul brought the carriage to a halt in front of her uncle's home, and Elizabeth's eyes popped open. She wriggled in Sophie's arms and whimpered.

"I know. You like riding, but we must stop for a while," she cooed to the baby.

The butler answered the door and, with a nod, bid them enter. He attempted to remain proper, but Sophie noticed his little smile at Elizabeth.

"Are my aunt and uncle at home, Marvin?"

The butler nodded. "I'll inform them that Mr. and Mrs. Medford and baby Elizabeth have come to call."

"Thank you, Marvin." The man was a saint. No wonder her uncle paid him well. "Marvin is the one who helped Amanda, Fanny, and me set up a bucket of whitewash over the kitchen door."

Paul grinned. "I recall your telling me about that incident. I believe it was your uncle Jonas who ended up covered in whitewash rather than Amanda's brothers, Jefferson and George."

Sophie smiled, remembering the sight of her uncle doused in the white concoction. She didn't know who had been more surprised, but she did recall that her uncle's jacket and spectacles had both required a good deal of Marvin's fastidious attention. The entire incident had delighted Jefferson and George, who had promised they'd be on the lookout for any further antics from the three girls.

How the years had changed their circumstances. Sophie missed the times when they would gather at Amanda's or at their grandparents' home to spend the night together. They would giggle and talk late into the night about all their hopes and dreams. Funny how life had taken so many unexpected turns. This was not anything like the dream Sophie once had for herself. Amanda and Fanny had always advised her to marry a wealthy man—for only a man of great resources could keep Sophie in the style she craved. Paul was anything but financially well off.

Elizabeth wriggled in her arms and burst forth with a lusty cry as Marvin returned to the foyer. "Seems your little girl doesn't enjoy waiting. Must take after her mother," he said with a grin. "Your aunt and uncle will see you in the library." He leaned a bit closer. "They were preparing to depart on some business."

"So they're not particularly happy that we've arrived," Sophie replied while Elizabeth continued to cry.

"I believe that would be correct."

Sophie lifted the baby to her shoulder and hoped she could quiet the child while they delivered the news. She glanced at Paul when they arrived at the library door. "I can't seem to quiet her. Perhaps you should go in and deliver the news while I wait out here with the baby."

"No." He shook his head and clasped her elbow. "They'll receive this better if you're along."

Sophie arched her brows. She didn't think her presence would soften the blow, but she didn't argue. Elizabeth released a high-pitched wail as they crossed the threshold and entered the library. Her uncle furrowed his brow and scowled in their direction.

"She has just now awakened from her nap and is a bit fussy," Sophie explained.

"Well, do something to pacify her." Jonas pulled on his earlobe. "I can't tolerate that squealing. It's enough to shatter a mirror."

Sophie edged closer to Paul. "I think I should take Elizabeth to the other room."

"We won't take but a few minutes of your time, sir." Paul grasped Sophie's sleeve when she attempted to move toward the door. "Sophie and I have the task of bringing you a piece of disheartening news."

Before he could say anything more, the baby screeched, and Jonas jumped up from his chair. "Do *something* to make that child happy, Sophie. You are her mother—I would think you'd know how to stop that incessant crying."

"I'm trying," she apologized, swaying back and forth and patting the baby's back.

"Jonas! The baby is likely suffering from colic. Your angry temperament is not going to do a jot of good. You've likely frightened the child even further." Victoria extended her arms. "Let me try, Sophie."

Sophie willingly handed over the baby, though she doubted her aunt would have success. Elizabeth was like the little girl in Longfellow's poem: When she was good, she was very good indeed, but when she was bad, she was horrid. Though Elizabeth lacked the curl in the middle of her forehead, Sophie thought that, too, would appear over time.

Jonas massaged his forehead. "The three of you continue your visit. I have matters that require my attention."

Before her uncle could reach the door, Paul stepped in front of him. "You can't leave, sir."

Jonas straightened his shoulders and extended his chest forward. "What do you mean, I can't leave? How *dare* you tell me what I can or can't do in my own home! Step out of the way before I am forced to have you removed, young man."

Paul directed a beseeching look at Sophie.

Stepping to her husband's side, Sophie said, "Listen to him, Uncle Jonas. This is very important, or we wouldn't have come here."

The baby silenced her wailing, and the room became eerily quiet. Sophie sat down beside her aunt and peeked at Elizabeth. Perhaps she should take the child before Paul announced Amanda's illness. Her aunt could faint and drop the baby. "Let me take her, Aunt Victoria."

Jonas turned on his heel. "Don't touch that child. She'll likely begin to squall if you move her." He shifted around toward Paul. "Now, what is it that's so important?"

"The Home for the Friendless has been placed under quarantine, and—"

"Is that what this is about? We already know that. In fact, if the two of you hadn't interrupted us with your unexpected visit, we'd be on our way over there now. I plan to have Amanda sneak out the rear door and come home immediately."

"You can't do that, sir," Paul said.

"Don't preach to me about what I can and can't do. I'm not going to have my daughter remain in that place with all of those dirty homeless people. They're probably all carriers of the disease. I'm going to bring her home. This doctor nonsense has gone far enough. Amanda is going to remain at home and conduct herself in a proper manner until I find a suitable husband for her."

Sophie shook her head, and her uncle glared at her. "You can't bring Amanda home because she has already contracted cholera, Uncle Jonas. That's what Paul has been trying to tell you." Her aunt's gasp was enough to alert Sophie, and she promptly lifted Elizabeth from the older woman's arms. "Don't fret, Aunt Victoria. Blake will do everything possible for Amanda. She'll have constant care. He won't let her . . ." She couldn't utter the word.

"Die?" Jonas snorted. "Dr. Carstead can't control life and death. Not where cholera is concerned."

"But God can," Paul said. "We must be in constant prayer for Amanda and ask God to remove this plague from our city."

"Why pray? If God has already determined to let my daughter die, your prayers won't change a thing."

The harsh words were meant as a rebuke, but Paul grasped her uncle's shoulder. "You're wrong, Mr. Broadmoor. Prayer doesn't always yield the answer we desire, but God *does* hearken to our prayers. Consider Abraham and his pleas to save Sodom. If we expect God to help, we must communicate the desires of our heart."

When her aunt slumped sideways and fell against Sophie's arm, Sophie placed Elizabeth on the settee. With her free hand she motioned to her husband. "Please ask Marvin to bring a damp cloth."

Jonas tapped his wife's shoulder. "If we're going to go and fetch Amanda, you'll need to muster your strength. This is no time for the faint of heart."

Sophie thought Uncle Jonas an insensitive boor, but his words had the desired effect. Before Marvin arrived with a damp cloth, her aunt's color had returned, and under her own strength she'd managed to return to an upright position.

"You're correct, Jonas. I'll get my hat. We must be on our way."

"She can't be released to your care," Paul insisted. "From what Blake tells me, her condition is grave. Even if permitted, any attempt to move her would prove disastrous. Look at the weather. Would you bring her out in this damp air?"

Victoria stood and steadied herself for a moment before she crossed the room. Pushing aside the curtain, she peered out the window and then turned to her husband. "Paul is correct, Jonas. We can't risk the possibility." Victoria withdrew a handkerchief from her pocket and blotted her eyes. "My dear Amanda. This is my fault. I encouraged her to seek a life of fulfillment."

"Don't blame yourself, Aunt Victoria. Amanda was determined to pursue a medical career. Even if she had remained at home, she might have contracted the disease."

"I doubt that. *We're* all perfectly fine."

" 'Tis true, Aunt Victoria. I'm told Mr. and Mrs. Warford's daughter Jane is one of the recent victims."

Victoria clasped a hand to her throat. "Jane? Oh, her dear mother and father must be distraught. When did you hear this news?"

"Only late last evening. You see, it makes little difference that you granted Amanda permission to work at the Home for the Friendless."

"The Home? I understand it's been placed under quarantine," Fanny said, bursting into the library. She glanced at Paul. "I'm relieved to see that you're not one of those required to remain there. I assume Uncle Quincy has been restricted." She turned to her aunt. "What of Amanda? Where is she?"

Sophie motioned to her cousin. "Come sit down beside me, Fanny." In hushed tones, Sophie related the news of their cousin's illness.

"We must go to her," Fanny said.

"We've already had this discussion. No one is going to go there," Paul said. "Prayer is the answer."

An hour later Fanny and Sophie were the only ones who remained in the library. Paul had helped Jonas get Victoria to bed, hoping a brief nap would help her better cope with the situation, and then had taken Elizabeth for a walk around the house so that Sophie and Fanny might converse in private.

"Do you suppose Amanda is very ill?" Fanny asked.

Sophie shrugged. "She's been exposed to the disease over and over by those she sought to help. I fear she's gravely ill."

"I can't bear it. The very thought of . . . of losing her is more than I can endure. It's bad enough when you expect the death of an older person. I still miss our grandparents terribly."

"I miss my mother," Sophie whispered. "Especially now that I have Elizabeth."

Fanny took hold of her hand. "Of course you do."

"My sisters have never been as dear to me as you and Amanda," Sophie continued, tears in her eyes. "I wish we could be at her side to nurse her." She squeezed Fanny's hand. "I'd just feel better to be near and see for myself that everything possible was being done."

"Or to tell her how much we love her."

Sophie met Fanny's damp eyes. "You do suppose she knows, don't you? I mean, we've often said as much to each other. Haven't we?"

"We certainly could have said it more," Fanny replied. "I don't suppose one ever declares love and admiration for another as much as one should." She paused only a moment before wrapping her arms around Sophie.

"I love you so very much, my dear cousin. You and Amanda are true sisters to me." She sniffed back tears. "I hope you know that I would do anything in my power to help either of you in any way."

Sophie cried softly. "I do know that, Fanny. I feel the same way. I love you and Amanda with all my heart. To lose either of you is . . . well . . . unthinkable."

Blake cradled Amanda's head in the crook of his arm and offered a sip of water. "No," she croaked from between parched lips. She touched her hand to her stomach and he understood. She would only suffer the pain of bringing up the small amount of liquid. He wet a cloth and dampened her lips, hoping it might ease her distress. He'd been by her side as much as possible, doing his best to lend comfort. What good was his medical training when he couldn't do one thing to help this young woman who had willingly sacrificed her own health to help others?

"There are others who need medical attention," Quincy said.

Blake glanced over his shoulder. The older man stood in the doorway, a shaft of light streaming over his shoulder. The sun must have finally made an appearance, but Blake hadn't noticed.

"I'm doing what I can, Quincy. I've worn a path on the floor going back and forth to care for them and Amanda, but I hate to leave Amanda's side." He rested his forehead in his broad palm. "I feel so responsible. I should have forbidden her coming here to work. Instead, I chastised her if she was late and scoffed when she mentioned feeling unwell. What manner of physician does such a thing?" Blake looked at Quincy. "Even worse, what kind of *man* does such a thing?"

"You're being too hard on yourself. These past weeks have been grueling, and you needed all of us to help wherever we could. Amanda understood that. She would never harbor ill feelings toward you. This is where she wanted to be."

"But I knew the risk. I should have protected her."

Quincy clapped him on the shoulder. "Come along. You're needed elsewhere. We've had another death down the hall, and several others are showing symptoms."

Blake nodded. "I'll be there momentarily. You and the others can do as much for the dead as I can."

Quincy didn't argue but instead slipped quietly from the room.

Blake knew his strength would not last much longer. He needed sleep, but he couldn't bring himself to take the time. He rested his elbows on his knees and stared at Amanda. What would he do if she should die? When had she become so important to him? He tried to recall exactly when he'd realized the joy she provided with her quick smile and willing hands. She'd been more help than he'd ever acknowledged. She'd proved to be a bright student, quick to learn, and willing to accept correction and guidance—traits he'd found lacking in any man he'd ever attempted to teach. He should have told her all of these things. Instead, he'd chastised her if she occasionally dropped an instrument or misdiagnosed a patient.

The remembrance of his pomposity shamed him, and he gently lifted Amanda's hand to his lips. "Forgive me," he whispered.

Her eyelids fluttered. She looked at him, her deep brown Broadmoor eyes appearing clear and bright. "For what?" she murmured before slipping back into a semiconscious state.

He wanted her to remain awake so he could ease his feelings of despair. "Selfish man," he muttered. "You should be thankful she's not feeling pain at the moment. Instead you only want to relieve your own guilt."

He released her hand and brushed a damp curl from her forehead. Even in the throes of debilitating illness, she remained lovely. He met with little success as he attempted to recall the first time he'd felt the agonizing ache that occurred when she was absent. She had woven herself into the fabric of his life, and now he couldn't imagine a future without her. He stared at her quiet form and knew without a doubt that he loved her.

"Now what?" he whispered into the silent room. For the first time in his life, he was willing to acknowledge his love for a woman, but he knew she'd likely be dead within a few days—a week at most. He rested his face in his palms and listened to her uneven, rasping breath. "Please spare her, God." He swiped at the tear trickling down his cheek. "I beg of you. Please let her live."

CHAPTER 4

Jonas sighed and shook his head in disbelief when Marvin hurried into the library at a near run. "Mrs. Andrew Winberg and children," he announced, clasping a palm to his chest and inhaling deeply.

Beatrice glared at the butler as she brushed past him to enter the room, Miranda and Randolph at her heels. "I told him I know my way into the library and it isn't necessary to announce family."

The woman's surly tone and pinched features had become her trademark. Yet today she appeared even more agitated than usual. And Jonas had already tolerated his share of distress for one day. Would he never get out of this house? He must find some way to retrieve his papers from Mortimer's office. A wave of guilt assaulted him. His thoughts should be with his suffering daughter rather than the business files. But if any of his underhanded dealings became known, both friends and family would be harmed. He didn't want to dwell on what might happen to him if such a thing should happen. No doubt he'd be faced with the same difficult decision his brother Langley had made years ago. But taking his own life wasn't something he wanted to consider. He wasn't certain if it was that thought or Beatrice's whining voice that sent a chill racing down his spine, but he wanted to rid himself of both.

"If there's a reason you've come to call, you'll need to cease your histrionics, or we'll never understand you," Jonas barked at his niece.

His wife withdrew her handkerchief and waved it in his direction. "There's no need to shout."

"If I'm going to be heard, there is," he retorted.

Beatrice glared at her uncle but curtailed her affected behavior and dropped into one of the overstuffed chairs.

Victoria turned to the children. "Come sit by your great-aunt, children."

"My father has been quarantined at the Home for the Friendless. Something must be done." Beatrice sniffled and cast a woeful look at Jonas.

"I am well aware of the quarantine. You are the third person who has rushed to tell me the ill-fated news. No one could be more concerned than—"

"Than *you*? When have you *ever* been concerned about my father?" Beatrice whipped her fan back and forth with a ferocity that caused her curls to ripple along her forehead like waves lapping at the shoreline.

Jonas sniffed. "I am not going to enter into an argument with you. Suffice it to say, I am very concerned about your father. I am even more concerned about my own daughter, who has contracted the illness."

The fan dropped to her lap. "I didn't know," she whispered.

"Of course you didn't. You never consider others." Jonas felt no sympathy for Beatrice. She had been a cantankerous child, and marriage hadn't softened her. Of course, there were those who would say the same of him. On the other hand, churlish behavior was more acceptable from a man. Women were supposed to be malleable creatures.

Victoria leaned over from the sofa and patted Beatrice's hand. "Don't mind your uncle. He's had a difficult morning. Needless to say, we are most distraught over this recent news, but there is nothing to be done regarding the quarantine. I would like to bring Amanda home and care for her, but we must abide by the order or others may be infected with the disease. Paul has agreed to keep us advised of any changes."

Beatrice straightened her shoulders. "Paul? Isn't he under quarantine, also?"

"No. He hadn't yet arrived at the Home when the authorities delivered the quarantine notice. As soon as Dr. Carstead advised him that Amanda had taken ill, he and Sophie came to tell us. They departed only a short time ago," Victoria explained.

"Isn't that just the way of things? If anyone should suffer, it's my sister Sophie. Instead, all has gone well for her. She has Paul at home, and her baby is well. Meanwhile, dear, sweet Amanda is suffering with cholera. I suppose God has dealt lightly with Sophie because her husband is a preacher." Beatrice sighed and once again lifted her fan.

Jonas frowned. "And is her suffering not as great as your own, Beatrice?"

"There is no good that will come from assessing the individual depth of sorrow or suffering each one of us bear," Victoria said. "We are all family and must care for one another. Our concern is for every member."

"I'm pleased to hear you say that, Aunt Victoria, for I have come to beg your hospitality until this epidemic has passed. Our home is too close to the area most affected by the outbreak, and I believe the children would be safer if we moved in with you."

The children looked wide-eyed from Jonas to Victoria and then to their mother.

"What?" Jonas jumped up from his chair. "Just because you live in close proximity to the area doesn't mean you're in any greater danger than the rest of us. Paul and Sophie don't live all that far from the same area, and they didn't express concern for their circumstances."

"I have heard some discussion that reinforces what Beatrice is saying," Victoria remarked.

Jonas shot a look of irritation in his wife's direction. What was she thinking? Didn't he have enough to contend with in his life? The last thing he wanted was his whining niece and her unruly children underfoot.

He cleared his throat and met Beatrice's beseeching eyes. If he refused her, he'd suffer Victoria's wrath. At the moment he didn't have the energy for an all-out war with his wife. Not now—not with the threat of his personal records being discovered by members of Mortimer's family. He needed a plan.

"Perhaps Beatrice is correct about the threat to family members. I think it would be best if all of you departed for Broadmoor Island as soon as possible."

"What?" Victoria stared at him, her mouth agape. "I suggested we all go to Broadmoor Island weeks ago, but you rejected my suggestion. *Now* you think it's wise?"

"Changes have occurred since that time."

"Indeed they have. Our daughter has been afflicted by the disease, and I'll not leave her in Rochester while I go off to Broadmoor Island. I don't know what you can be thinking, Jonas."

"We need to be practical. There is nothing you can do for Amanda. They won't let you into the Home, and I will keep in touch with Paul regarding her condition. For you to remain and become ill will serve no purpose. And it won't help her."

"But—"

Jonas pointed at his wife. "Hear me out, Victoria. Once Amanda is well enough to be removed from the Home, I will personally accompany her to the island. She'll recuperate more quickly away from the city."

"Oh, do say you'll agree, Aunt Victoria," Beatrice wailed. "It would truly be best for the entire family."

Jonas wouldn't have been surprised if his niece had dropped to her knees and begged. As far as he was concerned, she'd developed into a wretched example of womankind. "Though I am encouraging my wife to take refuge at the island, there is nothing to stop you and your children from going there. Have you discussed that possibility with your husband?"

"I hadn't considered it. I don't think Andrew would object, though I'm certain he'd refuse to accompany us." She nibbled her bottom lip. "I've never been at the island without the family. I don't know the first thing about opening the house. I've never been in charge when we visited."

"I've never noticed you having difficulty issuing orders," Jonas muttered.

Beatrice narrowed her eyes to mere slits. "What did you say, Uncle?"

"Nothing of importance. I'm merely contemplating the family's departure." That much was true. The thought of having the entire family out of the city buoyed his spirits. He'd have ample time to take care of business matters without any interference.

"I'm still not convinced this is what I should do," Victoria argued. "And I know how you are, Jonas. If something arises at work, you'll conveniently forget your promise to bring Amanda to the island."

"You need not worry, Aunt Victoria. I'll remain in Rochester and bring Amanda when she's released from the quarantine," Fanny announced.

Jonas sighed. Fanny had silently retreated to the bay window with her embroidery, and he'd completely forgotten she was present. His intent was for her to go to Broadmoor Island with the others. Now she'd inserted herself in the middle of his argument with Victoria. He had far too many women interfering in his life.

"But you love the island, and it would be an excellent opportunity for you to visit with Michael's parents," Jonas replied.

Beatrice snickered. "Since when are you concerned about that, Uncle Jonas?"

"Don't try my patience, Beatrice. I was speaking to Fanny."

Fanny set aside her stitching. " 'Tis true I'd enjoy seeing Michael's parents, and I do love the island, but not nearly as much as I love Amanda. I would count it a blessing if you'd permit me to remain and accompany her, Aunt Victoria. Even if Uncle Jonas comes with us, I'm certain she will still be weak and need a woman's touch."

"That's likely true." Victoria sniffed and dabbed her teary eyes.

Jonas could see his wife beginning to waver. He must take charge of the family's relocation, or they would all remain in Rochester. And most likely in his house. The idea caused an involuntary shudder. Having only Fanny at the house in Rochester would be the better choice. She'd likely keep to her rooms when he was at home.

"Then it's settled!" Ignoring his wife's obvious trepidation, Jonas voiced the announcement in his most authoritative tone.

Fanny appeared surprised, while Beatrice was giddy with relief. "I'll go home and pack. Do you think we'll be gone for more than three weeks?" She didn't await a reply before rattling on. "I'll leave the children here while I start getting things organized at home; you don't mind, do you? If Andrew insists upon staying in Rochester, I'll advise him he should take refuge here with you, Uncle Jonas."

"No!" Jonas barked. Beatrice's wide-eyed stare and his wife's look of displeasure were enough to warn Jonas that further explanation was in order. "I'm going to send the servants with your aunt, so there will be no one here except for me, Fanny, her personal maid, and my butler, of course. Andrew will be much more comfortable under his own roof."

"But he'll be safer here," Beatrice whined.

Jonas frowned. Like the recent weather, Beatrice offered nothing but gloom. He'd be forced to convince her. "Let me talk to Andrew. I'm certain he isn't nearly so concerned for himself. Once he knows you and the children are safe, he'll settle into his usual routine and won't give cholera another thought. Trust me."

Beatrice offered a halfhearted nod.

Jonas could see she wasn't totally convinced, but he didn't let on. Instead, he patted her shoulder and complimented her insight. "I always knew you were an intelligent young woman."

Beatrice beamed. The lie didn't bother Jonas in the least. Such bold exaggerations were necessary if he was going to make any headway. If left to their own devices, these women would drive him mad before he could arrange for their train tickets.

"I'm not totally convinced I should go," Victoria said. Her taffeta gown swished against his pant leg as she slowly paced across the room.

"Nonsense! It's all settled. Instruct the servants to begin packing immediately. I'm going to the railroad station and will purchase tickets on the first train scheduled for Clayton tomorrow morning." He extended his fingers and began to count. "I'm not certain how many tickets you'll need for the family and servants. We should conduct a head count."

Beatrice quickly came to his aid. After seeking a bit of guidance from Victoria, his niece jotted names on a scrap of paper. When she presented the list to him a short time later, Jonas sighed with relief. He would regain control of his life once he had time to think and calculate his options.

Raindrops plunked into a metal pan that Blake had set beneath a newly discovered leak in the ceiling. They'd patched the roof last fall, but after last winter's harsh snows and the ongoing spring rains, the patches were giving out. The Home needed a new roof. Blake had told Quincy as much, although Quincy had opted to expand the kitchen instead.

"We need to feed the starving," he'd insisted.

When Quincy entered the room, Blake pointed to the pan. "Another leak. If it doesn't quit raining, the cooks won't have any kettles left in the kitchen."

"We'll patch the roof once the weather dries out."

"Patch?" Blake snorted. "A new roof is what's needed. I told you that last year."

"And you were right. But there's nothing that can be done about it until the rain lets up." Quincy stooped down beside Amanda's bed. "Is she faring any better?"

Blake shook his head. "Hard to tell at this point. She hasn't taken in any more liquid, so she's not throwing up. I've given her a dose of morphine. When she awakens, I'll see if she can hold down any fluids."

Quincy grasped his arm. "Until then, you need to come and help me with the others. There are few who are willing to lend a hand."

"I can't blame them. Remember to wash your hands after you touch any of the patients," Blake said as he continued to stroke Amanda's brow.

"I need your help with the others. I know you want to remain with Amanda, but I can't do this without you." Quincy tightened his grasp. "Come along and help me."

Blake shook loose of Quincy's hold. "This is where I need to be right now. Amanda needs me. I'd never forgive myself if she awakened and I weren't here to help her."

"We must find some way to balance this or others are going to die. Amanda is my niece, and I am concerned for her welfare, also, but the other patients deserve your help, too."

"Give me time alone to pray; then I'll join you." Blake waited until the older man exited the room and then buried his face in his hands. He believed in God, but he'd seen few miracles during his medical career. Prayer or not, most everyone with debilitating illnesses died. When medicine failed, he had seen little evidence of God's intervention. But Blake now pushed those thoughts from the forefront of his mind and concentrated on Amanda. He needed a miracle, and he was going to trust that God would find Amanda worthy of healing. Medical science had no answers that would save her.

"Amanda is a fine young lady, Lord." Blake stared at her still form. "You created her, and she's developed into this lovely woman who has a heart to help others. Surely that's reason enough for you to allow her to live awhile longer. You know she's not a selfish person—maybe a little prideful from time to time, but underneath she's a good woman." He gently straightened the sheet and then turned his gaze heavenward. "You know my heart, God. I'm begging you to save this woman. I truly think I love her."

"I do believe it's dangerous when you think for yourself, Dr. Carstead."

He blinked away the tears clouding his eyes, but before he could say a word, Amanda had slipped back into unconsciousness. Even in the throes of cholera, she possessed the determination to banter with him. No doubt remained: This was the woman he desired to wed. If only God would spare her life.

"You absolutely *must* get packed, Sophie. We're departing for Broadmoor Island!"

"Good afternoon to you, too, Aunt Victoria," Sophie said as she motioned her aunt inside.

"There's no time for idle chatter." She yanked off her gloves and tucked them into her reticule. "I do wish your uncle would agree to have one of those telephones in our house. It would save a great deal of time. Come, we must talk."

Sophie didn't mention the fact that a telephone wouldn't help unless the people her aunt wished to call had telephones in their homes, too. And Paul and Sophie certainly couldn't afford such a luxury.

"Did I hear someone at the door?" Paul appeared from the kitchen. "What a pleasant surprise."

The older woman waved him forward. "Oh, good. I'm glad you're here, Paul. I've come to advise Sophie she must hurry and pack. With the cholera spreading, Jonas has decided it's best for the family to take refuge at Broadmoor Island."

Sophie bounced Elizabeth in her arms and shook her head. "We're fine right here. Paul and I aren't fearful of contracting cholera, are we, Paul?" She narrowed her eyes and shot her husband a beseeching look. "There's no need to escape the city."

"Jonas insists it is best for all concerned. Besides, Beatrice is traumatized with worry."

Sophie sat down opposite her aunt and rubbed Elizabeth's back. "Good girl," Sophie cooed when Elizabeth presented them with a loud burp. Sophie lifted the child to her shoulder and met her aunt's steady gaze. "You know Beatrice isn't happy unless she's in the midst of turmoil. My sister enjoys nothing more than drawing others into the center of her turbulence. I can't believe Uncle Jonas has succumbed to her antics."

"This cholera epidemic is more than a silly charade. The disease presents danger to all of us." Her aunt traced her fingers through Elizabeth's fine curls. "I would think you'd be concerned for your daughter."

Sophie's stomach muscles tensed at her aunt's recrimination. "And what of Amanda? Are you going to hurry off to the island and leave *your* daughter behind?"

"Sophie!" Paul chided.

Her aunt flashed Paul a tolerant look. "It's all right, Paul. I'm accustomed to Sophie's truculent behavior."

"Why am I considered quarrelsome when I mention Amanda's needs, yet it's perfectly acceptable for you to intimate that I'm not properly caring for Elizabeth?" Sophie hugged the baby close.

"I am intensely concerned about Amanda's condition, but with the quarantine in place, there is nothing any of us can do for her. I am most thankful Dr. Carstead and your father are present to aid in her recovery. If it were possible, I would tend to her every need, but . . ." Victoria's words trailed into silence.

Sophie noted the tears that had gathered in her aunt's eyes and regret assailed her, yet it didn't change her mind. She didn't want to leave Rochester. "Our homes aren't nearly so close to the area affected. We'll be fine." She glanced at Paul. "Won't we?"

He frowned. "There's no assurance of safety. Perhaps it would be best if you took Elizabeth and went to the island."

She couldn't believe her ears. Paul was going to take her aunt's side. Worse, it sounded as though he intended to send her while he remained in Rochester. That would never do!

Sophie met her husband's intense look with a forced smile. "The minute you've arranged to depart with us, I'll be prepared."

"That's impossible. You know I've promised to deliver food and medical supplies to the Home."

She shrugged. "If you truly think I should leave, then you can arrange for someone else to see to those matters and come with us."

"I have three families who have requested funeral services this week. No doubt there will be others in need during the coming days."

"There are other preachers in Rochester who can bury the dead." Sophie tapped her foot and returned his icy stare.

Paul pushed up from the sofa with a look of determination on his face. "When will the family depart for Broadmoor Island, Aunt Victoria?"

"The servants will call for Sophie's trunks late this afternoon. We'll depart tomorrow morning. Jonas has gone to purchase the tickets." Her aunt retrieved her gloves from her reticule and stood. "I'm relieved you and Elizabeth will be with us, Sophie. We'll have a delightful time." She leaned over and kissed Elizabeth on the cheek. "I look forward to helping you with her."

Sophie's anger bubbled near the surface, but she maintained a calm façade until her aunt departed. The moment the door closed, she turned on her heel and poked Paul in the chest. "How could you take her side against me?" She didn't wait for his response before marching down the hallway. "I suppose having Elizabeth and me out of your way makes life much simpler for you, doesn't it?" she called over her shoulder.

The sound of Paul's heavy footsteps signaled his anger. "I am doing what a man is supposed to do. I'm seeking protection for my family." His eyes shone with anger when she turned to face him. "How can you accuse me of sending you off in order to simplify my life? The only pleasure I gain from your absence is the knowledge that you and Elizabeth are safe. You know that's true, yet you fault me."

"Strange that you didn't express concern for our welfare until Aunt Victoria presented you with this wondrous opportunity to be rid of us."

"I haven't spoken of my fear because I didn't want to worry you. I have prayed for the safety of our family, and I believe this may be God's answer to my prayer. I won't have you remain in Rochester and run any further risk of becoming infected when there is a safe haven available."

Sophie snorted. His argument didn't hold water. "If you prayed for the safety of our family and believe this is an answer to prayer, then you should be coming with us. As the head of our house and a servant of God, surely God would expect you to avail yourself of this opportunity." She tapped her foot and waited. Let her husband find some way to argue *that* point.

He clenched his jaw until the tendons in his neck protruded like taut ropes. "I am a patient man, and you know that since we wed I have given consideration to your wishes. However, I will not argue this matter any further. You and Elizabeth will go to Broadmoor Island tomorrow morning, and I will remain in Rochester."

"When you're unable to provide an argument for your case, you simply cease the debate and issue an order." Sophie wheeled around and stomped toward the stairs. "I'll go to Broadmoor Island, but you'll be sorry, Paul."

She ran up the stairs before he could see the hot tears that formed in her eyes. Her actions were angry and measured as she flung dresses, camisoles, and nightgowns across the bed. She expected Paul would follow and tell her he'd had a change of heart. But he didn't.

CHAPTER 5

Thursday, May 4, 1899

Fanny peeked into the mirror and adjusted the navy blue ribbons that streamed from her straw hat like thick kite strings. When she'd bought the hat in March, Aunt Victoria had declared the chapeau a perfect choice. Fanny hadn't been nearly as convinced. She'd purchased it more to please her aunt than herself. Had there been sufficient time this morning, she would have run upstairs and exchanged it for the one she'd purchased last year. Instead, she collected her parasol and reticule.

"Where are you off to so early this morning?"

Fanny startled at her uncle's booming question. "I thought . . . I'm going . . . it's a lovely day, and I decided . . ."

He waved his hat and continued toward the door. "Oh, never mind. I don't have time."

A sense of relief washed over her once her uncle had descended the front steps. Holding the lace curtain aside, she peeked through the narrow window that framed the front door and watched until his carriage departed.

With a determined step she hurried to the kitchen. "I'll need the spindle-back runabout," she told the stableboy who was helping himself to a cup of coffee. She was thankful her uncle hadn't sent the stablehands to the island. Both the cook and his personal butler had remained, as well. Uncle Jonas had said their services wouldn't be needed at Broadmoor Island. Fanny wondered if Mrs. Atwell concurred and had adjusted to the unexpected arrival of the family. Thoughts of the kindly woman who was the head cook at Broadmoor Island and would eventually become her mother-in-law brought a fleeting sense of remorse that she'd remained in Rochester. She hadn't seen Michael's mother since the family departed the island last year at summer's end. Though Fanny had posted several letters to Mr. and Mrs. Atwell, she'd received only one in return. The missive had been brief. Mrs. Atwell had warned she preferred her kitchen duties to writing letters. She'd certainly spoken the truth on that account.

Fanny inhaled deeply as the driver assisted her into the runabout. The rains had ceased over the last three days, and the air smelled of springtime. The lilac bushes at old Broadmoor Mansion would likely be heavy with blooms. The thought of lilacs served as a reminder of childhood days when she and her cousins had played among the lilac bushes and the grape arbors at their grandparents' Rochester estate. She prayed Amanda would soon be well enough to enjoy the pleasures of the changing season. Dr. Carstead had attempted to assure her that Amanda was making progress, but Fanny remained unconvinced. She leaned back in the carriage. Once her business was completed in town, she'd deliver a bouquet of lilacs to the gate outside the Home for the Friendless. Perhaps the fragrance of lilacs would stimulate Amanda's recovery.

"Where to, Miss Broadmoor?" the driver inquired.

Before leaving home, Fanny had decided against giving the driver her exact destination. If Uncle Jonas discovered she'd taken the carriage, he might question the young man. "The corner of West Main and South Fitzhugh streets."

After climbing to his seat, the driver slapped the reins. The horse slowly clopped down the driveway and turned to head down East Avenue. A variety of colorful flowers dotted patches of green along the way. Rain or not, the gardeners of the wealthy had been hard at work keeping the vast gardens and lawns perfectly manicured.

Had the flowers begun to bloom on Broadmoor Island? She doubted the weather had warmed enough, though a wild flower or two could always force itself from beneath a bed of snow. Winter was slow to disappear in the islands, and dear Sophie would be livid if they remained snowbound and restricted to Broadmoor Castle. Her confinement at the island in the months leading up to Elizabeth's birth had been difficult enough. Though she'd not had opportunity to speak with Paul, Fanny doubted Sophie had easily agreed to be isolated on the island. Epidemic or not, Sophie took pleasure in socializing. The lack of parties, coupled with ongoing interaction with Beatrice and the other family members, would cause Sophie no small measure of suffering. Perhaps a letter advising her to take refuge in the kitchen with Mrs. Atwell would be in order. She would pen her cousin a note this afternoon.

The driver pulled back on the reins, and the carriage came to a halt in front of the Rochester Savings Bank. "Shall I wait while you complete your business, Miss Broadmoor?"

She shook her head. "No. I have several matters that need my attention. You may return for me in two hours. I'll meet you here."

He tipped his hat, hoisted himself up, and slapped the reins. Fanny strolled down Main Street as though she had nothing of import to fill her days. The usually busy streets were nearly void of traffic, and few customers entered the shops along the street. She stopped in front of the narrow brick building on her right. Ebony letters had been outlined in gold leaf to boldly announce the names of the lawyers who occupied the space. She pushed open the door and was greeted by a stern-looking clerk who peered over the rim of his spectacles.

"May I be of assistance?" The man's tone spoke volumes: He thought her an annoying intrusion.

"Miss Frances Broadmoor to see Mr. Rosenblume." She met the clerk's unflinching stare. "He requested a ten o'clock meeting with me."

"You may have a seat. I'll ascertain whether Mr. Rosenblume will see you."

The man's manner was impolite, and she wondered why Mr. Rosenblume tolerated such disrespect from his employees. Then again, perhaps Mr. Rosenblume didn't know. She withdrew the lawyer's note from her reticule. The letter had been personally delivered by a messenger several days ago and asked that she keep the appointment a secret. If either Amanda or Sophie had been available, she would have ignored the request and brought one of them along. The fact that Grandfather Broadmoor's lawyer wanted to meet with her secretly was both intriguing and odd. When Uncle Jonas had hired Mortimer Fillmore to handle her grandfather's estate, Mr. Rosenblume had gracefully bowed out of the picture. Though Mr. Rosenblume would have been Fanny's choice, she'd had no authority in the decision. The judge had approved Mortimer Fillmore.

Perhaps that was why Mr. Rosenblume had summoned her. Another lawyer would be needed now that Mr. Fillmore had died. She had simply assumed Mr.

Fillmore's son and law partner, Vincent, would take charge of the remaining legal details for Uncle Jonas.

Upon his return, the clerk was more congenial. "If you'll follow me, Mr. Rosenblume will see you in his office." With a grand sweeping motion, he waved her forward and opened the door to the adjacent office.

She stopped in the doorway. Mr. Rosenblume sat behind a massive mahogany desk that overpowered his small frame. But it wasn't the sight of Mr. Rosenblume that captured her interest as much as seeing Vincent Fillmore, who stood when she entered the room. Her surprise must have been obvious, for he stepped forward and held a chair for her. "It's good to see you, Miss Broadmoor."

She nodded and sat down. What would have brought these two men together? She glanced back and forth between them. "Have you and Mr. Rosenblume combined your law offices?"

Though his dark eyes appeared dulled by either pain or sadness, the younger lawyer smiled and shook his head. "No, but we have united in an effort to protect you, Miss Broadmoor."

The ominous words were more than enough to capture her undivided attention. "Protect me? Whatever from?"

Mr. Rosenblume shifted in his chair. "We don't want to alarm you, my dear. Your life is not in danger. However, I fear your financial future has been severely compromised."

"By my deceased father and your uncle Jonas," Mr. Fillmore added.

She clasped her hand to her chest. "You must be mistaken. When I spoke with my uncle in February, he assured me that my investments were sound. Had there been any change, I'm certain he would have advised me." Having noted the pitying look the two men exchanged, she hastened to reinforce her position. She didn't want them to think her a complete dolt. "I understand the country continues to suffer with financial woes, but those had begun even before my grandfather's death. Perhaps it would be best if Uncle Jonas attended this meeting with us. He could better explain my—"

"No, it wouldn't be better, my dear." Mr. Rosenblume assumed a grandfatherly tone as he pushed away from his desk. "I know this conversation is going to prove extremely difficult, but I ask that you give us your full attention as we explain what has happened to your inheritance." Mr. Rosenblume circled the desk and held out his hand. "Why don't we move across the room?"

Fanny followed his gaze to the vast library table, where three chairs had been arranged. Neat stacks of paper lined the shiny tabletop. "How long do you anticipate our meeting will take? I have other matters that require my attention, and I told my carriage driver to return for me in two hours." She'd set her mind upon delivering lilacs to Amanda. Thoughts that the spring blooms might aid in her cousin's recovery took precedence over the heaping papers assembled on the table.

"Then we should begin immediately. If necessary, we can schedule a time to meet again tomorrow or next week."

Mr. Rosenblume escorted her across the room and pulled out one of the chairs. She would be seated between the two lawyers. How she wished Michael were here at her side to offer support through what she feared would be an ordeal. She truly didn't want to listen to the facts and figures these men would likely present. Though they'd been nothing but kind, she would feel more comfortable with a family member present—someone who understood finances. Someone like Uncle Jonas. That was why the judge had entrusted him to handle her inheritance.

"Let me begin by telling you that because my own father was involved in this arrangement, it pains me greatly to explain what I've discovered." Mr. Fillmore tapped his fingers on the arm of his chair. "Your uncle and my father share a common bond."

Was Mr. Fillmore going to examine the history of her uncle's friendship with the senior Mr. Fillmore? Fanny understood that the young lawyer was grieving his father's death, but he was using precious time without explaining the details of why she'd been secretly summoned.

"I understand they were dear friends. That's why Uncle Jonas insisted your father handle the estate when Grandfather Broadmoor died. I argued on behalf of Mr. Rosenblume, but because I was only seventeen and a woman, Uncle Jonas wouldn't listen to me."

"And because he wanted to control the money he believed should have been his," Mr. Fillmore added. "He resented the fact that you'd inherited a full third of the estate."

They were covering facts she already knew. Perhaps she should try to move the conversation forward. "But I thought that Uncle Jonas came to accept the terms of Grandfather's will. My financial returns have been excellent. He's told me so. That's why I'm confused by all of this. Why don't you explain." She pointed at the files and papers spread across the table.

"I'm coming to that," Vincent said. "Because both my father and your uncle are devious men who permitted money and power to rule their lives, they devised a plan that would eventually permit your uncle to convert all your assets."

"Convert them into *what*?" This was all very confusing.

Mr. Rosenblume patted her hand. "Convert them to his name, my dear. It appears your uncle and Mortimer Fillmore created a method whereby any financial losses were credited to your portion of the estate and any gains were assigned to your uncle's. It appears to be a complicated accounting scheme that should have been noticed by the court when your uncle filed his financial accounts."

"If you and Mr. Fillmore's son were able to discover what occurred, why didn't the judge?"

Vincent pointed to the table. "These are records and correspondence that my father maintained in his office files, information that wouldn't have been submitted to the judge. However, we have reason to believe my father may have *influenced* the judge to cooperate."

"Influenced? What does that mean?" Fanny looked back and forth between the two men, uncertain which one she should look to for an answer.

"It means the judge may have been bribed to overlook discrepancies in the papers your uncle filed." Mr. Rosenblume hunched his shoulders. "It saddens me to tell you this, but there are occasions when judges succumb to the lure of money, too. Of course, we can't say this is absolute in your case. As Vincent mentioned, we've only completed a cursory review of Mortimer's records."

Fanny turned toward the younger lawyer. "So when you discovered what you thought were discrepancies, you contacted Mr. Rosenblume?"

"Yes." Vincent scooted forward on his chair and rested his forearms across his thighs. He met her gaze with unflinching determination. "Because of my father's involvement in what I believe to be a misrepresentation of your interests, I thought it would be best for you to employ a lawyer who will give you sound legal advice. I believe it would be completely improper for me or any lawyer in my office to represent you. Since Mr. Rosenblume had been your grandfather's attorney, I thought he could lend you the most expertise."

Fanny attempted to digest the scattered information. Was her lack of money the reason Uncle Jonas had argued against the purchase of a home for Sophie and Paul? Although it had taken a bit of prodding, he'd met her request. Had he withdrawn the funds from his own account in order to meet her demand? Would her uncle have stolen from her? Certainly her uncle was a trying and callous man, but she didn't want to believe he'd steal from his own niece.

"So I have no money whatsoever?" she asked.

"Nothing as bleak as that, my dear." Mr. Rosenblume offered her an encouraging smile. "There is some money available. It simply appears your uncle has commingled and transferred many of your financial assets into his own account. Unfortunately, he has made many ill-advised investments and lost a great deal. Once I've gone through all this paper work and discussed the situation with the banks and accountants for the investment companies, I'll have a more substantial answer. That is, if you wish for me to take over as your legal representative."

The need to make an immediate decision left her breathless. If she employed Mr. Rosenblume as her lawyer, what would her uncle say or do? Would he insist she move out of his home? Not that she would mind that idea, of course. She silently prayed for guidance.

"If I should decide to employ Mr. Rosenblume, how would the transfer take place?"

Mr. Fillmore raked his fingers through his thick hair. "You would inform your uncle of employing Mr. Rosenblume as your lawyer. Your uncle has been intent upon removing his files from my office since the day my father died. After a cursory review of the files, I understood his persistence. I immediately removed the files from my office and told your uncle that there is little paper work there." Vincent massaged his furrowed brow. "That much is true. However, he wants to come to the office and review his files."

Fanny was doing her best to digest the information. "Then my uncle doesn't know these records exist?"

Vincent shook his head. "No, not at this time."

"But once I begin to investigate, he will get wind of what is going on," Mr. Rosenblume warned. "It won't take long before he realizes Mortimer left a paper trail and it has fallen into your hands. I must warn you that this could cause no end of trouble for you, Miss Broadmoor. You're the one who must decide if you'll permit your uncle to continue down this path of deceit and thievery. I would strongly urge you not to do so. But you must consider the difficulty this will cause with other family members."

Fanny considered her dear cousins. Sophie would urge her to hire Mr. Rosenblume immediately. But what of Amanda? In spite of his shortcomings, Uncle Jonas was Amanda's father. Once Amanda began to gain her strength, would such news hinder her complete recovery? And what would happen to Aunt Victoria and the rest of the family if proof of his actions came to light? Would they despise her?

Mr. Rosenblume shifted in his chair. "I know this is difficult, Miss Broadmoor, but Mr. Fillmore needs to know what he should do regarding these records."

"Leave the files here. Mr. Rosenblume, I will retain you as my legal representative. At this moment I'm not certain how far I will proceed. I will need time to consider my actions further."

Mr. Fillmore jumped to his feet. The man was obviously delighted to hear her decision and anxious to be on his way. "You have my word that I will cooperate with Mr. Rosenblume in any manner he requests, Miss Broadmoor." He hesitated for a moment. "And I hope I have your word that you won't tell your uncle what I've done."

Fanny nodded. If Uncle Jonas quizzed her at length, she'd simply direct him to speak with Mr. Rosenblume. That was, after all, what lawyers were supposed to do, wasn't it? Moments later, Mr. Fillmore hurried out of the office, leaving her to deal with Mr. Rosenblume and the mountain of paper—a task that didn't appeal to her in the least.

She glanced at the clock on Mr. Rosenblume's mahogany desk. A full forty-five minutes remained until the driver was due to return. Though she understood the importance of the issue at hand, she longed to take her leave and contemplate this unsavory news in private. She longed to walk among the gardens of her grandparents' home and pick lilacs for Amanda.

Before she could excuse herself, Mr. Rosenblume retrieved several papers from one of the files. "There are several things I believe you need to review immediately. Much of this can wait until I've conducted a thorough examination, but this is a matter of import. It appears your uncle has been actively seeking a buyer for the Broadmoor Mansion, and I'm not at all sure you would agree with such a sale."

Fanny frowned. "Broadmoor Mansion has already been sold, Mr. Rosenblume. My uncle sold it without my knowledge. He proposed the sale with the hope I would marry the young man of his choosing. Though I was distraught, the court approved the sale, and there was little I could do. I don't know how he managed the legalities."

"My dear, the entire setup was a sham. Your uncle duped young Daniel. Still, his plan fell short, for he didn't convince you to marry Mr. Irwin, did he?"

Fanny shook her head. The lawyer's knowledge of Daniel Irwin piqued her interest, and she leaned closer to examine the file's contents. "Exactly what makes you think the house is for sale?"

He handed Fanny a note written on her uncle's stationery and dated only a week prior to Mortimer Fillmore's death. The letter confirmed exactly what Mr. Rosenblume had told her. Uncle Jonas blamed Mortimer for not locating a suitable buyer even though they'd lowered the selling price. How could her uncle do such a thing! He knew how much that house meant to her and how much it had meant to his parents. Indignation assailed her as she read the words scrawled at the bottom of the page. *Burn this letter after you have read the contents.*

Mr. Fillmore hadn't followed her uncle's orders. In addition to the letter, there was an unsigned deed made out to Daniel, together with background information that had been gathered on several men, Daniel included. Fanny recognized the names of the others—all of them men her uncle had invited to Broadmoor Island. With each additional detail, her anger mounted.

"Has your review revealed how my uncle gained permission to sell Broadmoor Mansion?"

"The paper work appears to be in order. The judge signed a document approving the sale. You uncle's motion to the court states that cash was needed to meet unexpected debts. He further declared Broadmoor Mansion could be easily sold and the proceeds used to pay those undisclosed debts. Since your uncle has authority to act on your behalf, notification to you wasn't required.

The records reflect your uncle Quincy was notified, but he filed no objection. If he truly received the notice, I doubt he even read the papers. Quincy has never been interested in business matters. I would guess Jonas relied upon that knowledge as well as the fact that Quincy's charity work generally keeps him too busy to worry over issues relating to your grandfather's estate. Like you, Quincy relies upon Jonas."

"Since the court has already granted permission to sell the house, I want to purchase Broadmoor Mansion, Mr. Rosenblume."

Mr. Rosenblume smiled. "I was certain that would be your reaction."

"Can it be arranged without my uncle's knowledge?"

The lawyer hesitated. "I assume your uncle has continued to hold control of your investments and funds even though you've attained your majority?"

"I'm afraid I had little choice. The judge, Mr. Fillmore, and my uncle all advised that it would be imprudent for a woman to attempt managing my vast holdings. The judge indicated he wouldn't approve such an arrangement. Uncle Jonas gives me an allowance each month. Other than that, I don't know if I have access to any of my money or not. I've never made any attempt to withdraw funds. Even when I purchased a house for my cousin, I had my uncle see to the transaction. After what you've told me, I'm doubtful I can access any of the accounts." She silently chided herself for such a grievous error in judgment. "This will ruin my opportunity to purchase Broadmoor Mansion."

"Not necessarily. I could purchase the house for you," Mr. Rosenblume said. "Once we've gained access to your funds, you could repay me."

Fanny stared at the lawyer. No wonder her grandfather had valued Mr. Rosenblume. In addition to his honesty, he was obviously a compassionate man. She didn't want to take advantage of his kindness, but she had little choice. If she didn't agree, Uncle Jonas would continue to seek a buyer for the house. It might be lost to her forever.

"Please do what you can to secure the title for me," she said.

"I know you may find it difficult to trust anyone right now, Miss Broadmoor, but I hope you will remember my years of faithful service to your grandfather. My intent is to help you in any way possible." Mr. Rosenblume gathered the papers and shoved them inside the file folder. "I will make every effort to secure the mansion at the lowest possible price. The fact that Jonas is anxious to sell should work in your favor."

"Let's hope so," she said. "Is there anything else we must address this morning?"

"I do want you to understand that your uncle has commingled funds and it will take time and effort to determine exactly what is yours and what is his. While some of the details are clear-cut, others are clouded."

"If these allegations prove to be true, I want to take every effort to protect my aunt and cousins. They had no part in any of this. It is Uncle Jonas who must answer for his actions."

The lawyer nodded. "I will do what I can to protect both your interests and the family name." He lifted some files from one end of the table. "These files were marked with your name and the word *confidential*. I have not examined their contents." The clock chimed, and he handed her the files. "Take these papers with you. Once you've reviewed them, we can discuss anything you discover that might require my attention."

After bidding Mr. Rosenblume farewell, Fanny tucked the files under her arm and arrived at the Rochester Savings Bank only minutes before the carriage appeared. Instead of stopping to pick lilacs, she instructed the driver to return home. It wouldn't do for Uncle Jonas to be waiting and confront her when she entered the house. What if he spotted the files and inquired? What would she say? Even with the driver's urging, the horse seemed to plod along at an unusually slow pace. She prayed her uncle wouldn't decide to come home for the noonday meal. Since Aunt Victoria's departure, his schedule had become irregular, and Fanny never knew when he might appear. Not that it had mattered much in the past.

Fanny leaned forward and tapped the driver on the shoulder. "Was my uncle at home when you left the house?"

The driver shook his head. "Haven't seen him since early this morning, and he didn't leave any instructions to pick him up until this evening. 'Course you can't never tell about Mr. Jonas. Sometimes he hires a cab to bring him home."

When they neared the house, she once again tapped the driver. "Go around to the back of the house. I'll enter through the kitchen."

The young man glanced over his shoulder and frowned, but he didn't question her. The servants who worked for Jonas Broadmoor knew better.

"Thank you," she said as he helped her down. "After lunch, I'll need you to take me to Broadmoor Mansion and then on to the Home for the Friendless." The driver nodded. Fanny gazed over the driver's shoulder and was pleased to see that her uncle's horses hadn't been hitched to his carriage. She hoped that meant he had remained at his office. The minute she entered the kitchen, she quizzed the cook and was relieved when she heard that her uncle hadn't darkened the doorway.

"When would you like to eat, Miss Fanny?" the cook asked when she continued toward the rear stairway.

"I'll get something a little later. I'm not hungry right now."

The cook nodded. "If you're sure, 'cause I could—"

"I am. I'll be upstairs in my bedroom," she called over her shoulder.

Never before had Fanny locked the bedroom door, but today was different. She placed the files on her bed, removed the key from the top dresser drawer, and slipped it into the lock. One twist of the key and the bolt slipped into place with a soft *clunk.*

Apprehension filled her as she crossed the room and settled in a chair that overlooked the rear garden. She sifted through the papers and then stopped to more closely peruse a letter addressed to Mortimer Fillmore. The missive was written on her uncle's stationery and in his familiar script. More importantly, her inheritance was the subject of the letter.

She clasped her palm to her lips when she read her uncle's directive to falsify the records and deduct his financial losses from her accounts. He set forth a plan that clearly proved what Mr. Rosenblume and Vincent Fillmore had suspected. Her hands shook as she turned to read the final page. *Your fears concerning Fanny are needless. She is a foolish young woman who lacks the intelligence to question her finances. She will never request an examination of the accounts.* He'd signed the letter and added a final caveat instructing Mortimer to burn the letter. Fanny could scarcely believe what she'd read.

She had hoped to find something in the files that would vindicate her uncle. Instead, he had secretly schemed against her. How could someone who professed to love her pledge his loyalty and then betray her? Uncle Jonas had evolved into a Judas Iscariot. She shuddered at the thought.

Amanda struggled to push aside the pile of quilts that enveloped her like a smothering cocoon. Had Blake thought she might freeze to death? She would have inquired, but he appeared to be dozing in a chair near the foot of her bed. The scent of lilacs drifted toward her and momentarily replaced the putrid smells wafting from the bucket by her bed. The quilts landed on the wood floor with a dull thud that immediately startled him awake.

"I'm sorry. I didn't mean to waken you, but I thought I might suffocate under all of these blankets." Amanda forced her dry, cracked lips into a half smile. "I see the rain has stopped." She lifted a shaking hand and pointed to a nearby table. "Lilacs?"

Blake stared at her as though he'd seen a ghost. "Quincy! Quincy! Come in here." He jumped up from his chair and sent it crashing to the floor. Kicking aside the pile of quilts, he rushed to her bed and grasped her hand. "How do you feel?"

"Thirsty, but much better," she said. "May I have a drink?" Her voice was raspy to her ears, and she noted the worried look in his eyes. No doubt he thought she wouldn't manage to keep the liquid down. But the terrible stomach pains had disappeared.

He poured a small amount of water into a glass. Slipping his arm beneath her shoulders, he held her up while she swallowed the contents.

"I must look a wretched sight." She brushed the hair from her forehead.

"Amanda! I can't believe my eyes." Her uncle hurried across the room and positioned himself at the other side of her bed. He touched his hand to his stomach. "Any pain?"

She shook her head while both men stared down at her as though she might disappear if they looked away. "Other than a weak, groggy feeling, I believe I'm fine."

"The weakness is to be expected," Blake said. He squeezed her hand. "I had nearly given up hope."

"I had an excellent doctor caring for me," she whispered.

"My medical ability had nothing to do with your recovery. The fervent prayers of those who love you have been answered."

Those who love me? Did Dr. Carstead count himself among that number? She vaguely remembered his sitting by her bedside and praying, but she couldn't recall what he'd said. Yet he had prayed for her. And he'd said those who loved her had been praying. Could *he* possibly love her? Should she harbor such a thought?

CHAPTER 6

WEDNESDAY, MAY 10, 1899
BROADMOOR ISLAND

Sophie held Elizabeth close and wrapped the soft blanket tightly around the baby's legs. She pointed at two boats passing on the river. "See the boats, Elizabeth?" The baby cooed, but her gaze followed several of her young cousins romping in the yard rather than the boats. She wriggled in her mother's arms and chortled at the children's antics. "It won't be long until you'll be able to run and play, too." Sophie nuzzled the soft folds of the baby's neck until she squealed in delight.

Elizabeth's antics had provided occasional moments of enjoyment, but the days had passed slowly since their arrival on Broadmoor Island. Beatrice had been like fingernails scratching chalkboard since the day they'd set foot on the island. Sophie decided her sister should be awarded a prize for the most annoying person in God's creation. Though there might be someone who was more irritating than Beatrice, Sophie couldn't begin to imagine the possibility. And the fact that she and Paul had parted on less than good terms didn't help, either.

To make matters worse, she hadn't received even one letter from him. Each afternoon when Mr. Atwell brought the mail to the house, Beatrice noted that fact with great pleasure. When Beatrice had made a huge show of the letter she'd received from Andrew yesterday, Sophie had considered throttling her. Hoping to silence her sister, Sophie had defended Paul's inattentive behavior. "While Andrew whiles away his evenings with nothing to do but write letters, Paul is busy seeing to the welfare of others," she'd said. The comment had led to a nasty exchange between the sisters and had heightened Sophie's discontent. Surely there must be some escape from this place. Although she could move about the island at will, she felt as though she'd go mad from the enforced captivity. At least she'd had Fanny to keep her company during the months before Elizabeth's birth.

Veda rounded the corner and waved at Sophie. "Are you ready for me to take Elizabeth upstairs for her nap, Miss Sophie?"

"I suppose it is that time, isn't it?" She kissed Elizabeth's cheek before handing her to the maid. "Make certain you or Minnie remains upstairs while she naps. It's impossible to hear her cry when you're downstairs."

"Yes, Miss Sophie."

Sophie didn't miss the sullen tone. The maid had likely grown weary of hearing the cautionary instruction every day. She wondered if Veda and Minnie hated being tied to the same wearisome duties each day. There must be something good to be said for such a life, but she couldn't think what it might be. It would be similar to living on this island with nothing new or different, each day the same as the last. She tugged at her skirt and sighed. Her tiny waist hadn't returned as quickly as she'd hoped after Elizabeth's birth. Most of her clothing remained snug and uncomfortable. She'd need to either pass on desserts in the future or purchase new gowns. Paul wouldn't be pleased with that option. He hoped to save enough money to reimburse Fanny one day for the cost of their house. Sophie held out little hope for that plan—not with her husband's meager wages.

Perhaps a stroll would lighten her spirits. She downed the last of her tea and meandered along the path that led to the side of the house.

With an old woolen shawl pulled tight around her shoulders, Mrs. Atwell was stooped over, tending a small herb garden. The older woman glanced up as she approached. "Hello, Miss Sophie. Another gorgeous day, don't you think?"

Sophie nodded. "I wouldn't mind a little more warmth to the days. And the company of someone I enjoyed spending them with. Don't you grow lonely during the winter when you and Mr. Atwell are out here by yourselves?"

Mrs. Atwell prodded the ground, pulling a weed here and there as she checked the plants. "Being alone for a time can be a good thing, Sophie. It gives us time to reflect and commune with God. I look forward to each season as it arrives, and I'm never disappointed. I enjoy having your family arrive at the beginning of each summer, but I'm equally pleased to see them depart." She stood and arched her back. "Each year my back protests the gardening chores a bit more."

"Having us arrive so early this year must have taken you by surprise."

Mrs. Atwell shook her head and trudged toward the side of the house. "No, I can't say I was surprised in the least." She picked up an old milking stool from alongside the kitchen door and brought it back to the small patch of garden. "Mr. Atwell had heard that some of the families were fleeing to the islands to escape the cholera epidemic." She sat down on the small stool. Her chin appeared to touch her knees as she bent forward to continue weeding. "I had expected the entire family to come."

Sophie hadn't considered the possibility that no one had explained to Mr. and Mrs. Atwell why some members of the family had remained in Rochester. She should have realized her aunt wouldn't feel the need to provide details. Even though Michael's parents were soon to become members of Fanny's family, they were still Broadmoor servants. And servants weren't entitled to know why. They were simply expected to perform their duties and not ask questions. Mrs. Atwell had probably been beside herself, privately questioning why Fanny hadn't come with them. Yet she dared not inquire.

"You're wondering about Fanny?" Sophie asked.

Mrs. Atwell sat upright on the stool. "Yes. Please tell me she hasn't contracted cholera."

"No. Fanny is fine—at least she was when we left Rochester. It's Amanda who contracted cholera. Fanny asked to remain in Rochester so that she could accompany Amanda here once she's well enough to travel. Although Amanda has shown some slight improvement recently, she is still very ill."

The weeds dropped from Mrs. Atwell's hand and fluttered to the ground. "Dear me, that is sad news. I'm surprised Mrs. Broadmoor didn't stay in Rochester with her daughter."

"She wanted to, but Uncle Jonas insisted all of us come here. Amanda fell ill while working at the Home for the Friendless, and the entire Home was placed under quarantine," Sophie said. "I'm sorry, Mrs. Atwell. I didn't even think—"

Mrs. Atwell waved as if to silence her. "Don't you concern yourself, Miss Sophie. It's not your job to keep me updated on your family. I received a letter from Fanny a week before you arrived. I'm certain she'll be sending another letter soon. Fact is, it's none of my business."

"But it *is* your business. Fanny is soon to be your daughter-in-law—she'll soon be *your* family, too." Sophie settled her gaze on the horizon. "Each day I hope that Amanda and Fanny will be on the train from Rochester. I miss them very much. The island isn't the same without them."

"You girls have been inseparable since you were little," Mrs. Atwell said with a smile. "I always teased that you were three girls sharing one heart."

Sophie smiled. "Yes. I remember." She sighed. "Life would not be the same without them."

"Mr. Atwell and I will be praying for Amanda's speedy recovery and for Fanny's continued good health." The older woman pointed at a boat speeding down the river. "Appears some of the Pullmans have returned to the islands. Mr. Atwell tells me that folks have been arriving every day. Some say they'll not be going home before the end of summer. Others say they'll go home the end of May and then return the end of June."

Sophie perked to attention. "Has he heard if any socials have been scheduled at the Frontenac Hotel?" She didn't await an answer. "Do you have a copy of the paper? In the summertime they list the parties on the society page. With folks returning early, perhaps they've already begun."

"The paper should be in that stack near the kitchen door. To tell you the truth, I don't look at the social page, so I don't know what they've listed in there."

Sophie bounded off toward the kitchen and shuffled through the papers until she located the latest edition. She spread it on the worktable and quickly turned the pages of the meager weekly offering. The social news had dwindled from the full page of last year's summertime news to half a column of winter offerings. Disappointed, she flapped the pages together and was about to shove the paper back in place when she noticed a small article on the front page.

"Wonderful!" she whispered. A party had been scheduled for Saturday evening at the Frontenac Hotel. All who were seeking refuge in the islands were invited to attend.

Of course, those who read the article knew not *everyone* was invited. The party was being hosted by Mr. and Mrs. Edward Oosterman. Certainly they weren't Sophie's favorite host and hostess, for they generally catered to an older crowd. All the same, it was a party. Perhaps Georgie and Sanger Pullman would be there to add some fun. Both Jefferson and George, Amanda's unmarried brothers, had booked passage for Europe when threatened with banishment to the island for several months. Not that Sophie blamed them, but she was jealous of the freedom and wealth that permitted them such an escape.

She hastened back outdoors. Mrs. Atwell had disappeared, but Sophie didn't bother to seek her out. Right now she was more concerned about what she would wear to the party. The better question was what *could* she wear? Stones skittered beneath her slippers as she quickened her step and returned to the house. She'd packed several gowns, but none of them fit. The green silk might have adequate fabric to release the seams. Yet even if the alterations permitted an extra half inch, she'd need her corset laced as tight as possible.

Minnie would be the best choice to alter the dress, but Veda was far superior at squeezing her into a tight corset.

Veda looked up from her sewing when Sophie entered the nursery. She crooked her finger at the maid. "Come here," she whispered.

The maid tiptoed across the room and followed Sophie into the hallway. "I have need of a dress that will fit me for a party Saturday evening. Where is Minnie?"

"Minnie doesn't have a party dress," Veda replied.

Sophie sighed. Sometimes Veda didn't have the sense God gave a goose. "I don't want to *borrow* a dress from Minnie. I want her to *alter* one of mine."

"Oh, I see." Veda's head bobbled like a worn-out spring. "You might look in the servants' quarters. She was going to—"

With a brief wave Sophie turned and hurried off. Veda had a way of explaining things that took forever, and Sophie didn't have forever. She had only a few short days. The thick hallway carpet muffled her footsteps—and those of her aunt Victoria, as well. They had a near collision when Sophie rounded the corner.

Her aunt gasped and took a backward step. "Where are you off to in such a hurry?"

"Oh, Aunt Victoria, you startled me. I was going to look for Minnie."

"Whatever for? Isn't Veda looking after Elizabeth?"

"Yes, but I wanted to see if Minnie had time to alter one of my gowns. There's going to be a dance at the Frontenac Hotel on Saturday evening."

"I've heard nothing of a party. Did you receive an invitation?"

Sophie did her best to remain patient while she described the article in the paper. "I knew you'd approve since Mr. and Mrs. Oosterman are hosting the event."

Her aunt frowned. "I'm not certain you should be attending unescorted. I wonder if Andrew will be coming to see Beatrice and the children this weekend. If Beatrice wants to attend, you could accompany them."

The thought of Beatrice and Andrew acting as her chaperones was enough to cause Sophie to rethink her plan. If she had to spend the evening under Beatrice's watchful eye, she didn't want to attend. "Wouldn't *you* like to go? Mrs. Oosterman will be disappointed if you don't attend, and you could act as my chaperone if you truly think I am in need of one. Since I'm now married, an escort shouldn't be required, but I'd be delighted to attend with you."

"Being married doesn't permit you to overlook the proper rules of etiquette, Sophie. I realize many of you young married women have decided you can attend formal gatherings without a proper escort. However, you'll find such behavior is still frowned upon." Her aunt looped arms with her. "Let's see what Minnie can do about altering your dress; then we'll decide upon the matter of an escort."

Escort, chaperone, someone to watch over her behavior—how was she to have any fun? Aunt Victoria wouldn't have blinked an eye if Beatrice had divulged plans to attend the dance without Andrew. Of course, Beatrice wouldn't want to attend the party with or without Andrew, especially if she knew that remaining at home would prevent Sophie from attending.

They discovered Minnie polishing silver in the dining room, and Sophie presented her idea. The maid shrugged while she continued to polish a silver platter. "Until I look at the seams and measure you, I can't say it will work. Even so, such refashioning will take time."

"Then let's be off," Sophie said. "I'll have Veda finish polishing the silver when Elizabeth wakens."

Once they'd arrived in Sophie's bedroom, Minnie made a cursory examination of the seams before Sophie wriggled into the dress. "Turn," Minnie commanded while she poked and prodded the fabric.

Her aunt maintained a watchful eye throughout the process. While Sophie removed the dress, her aunt nudged Minnie. "What do you think? Can you make it work?"

"If her corset is tightly laced, it should fit. I could use lace overlays to hide the fact that the seams have been let out," Minnie suggested.

Sophie clapped her hands. "That is a wonderful idea, Minnie. You have saved my life."

"I don't believe refashioning a dress constitutes a lifesaving event," her aunt said. "And there is still the matter of an escort."

"Do say you'll come with me, Aunt Victoria. You know Beatrice won't want to attend."

Her aunt tapped her fingers on the dresser. "I would enjoy visiting with the Oostermans. . . ."

"Then it's settled." Sophie hugged her aunt around the shoulders. "I can't thank you enough."

SATURDAY, MAY 13, 1899

After numerous fittings and hours of stitching, Minnie completed the alterations to Sophie's satisfaction. "It looks lovely," her aunt remarked as the two of them descended the stairs Saturday evening. "No one would ever guess that your dress has been refashioned. You look absolutely lovely."

"I would think you'd consider it more important to remain here and care for Elizabeth than go off to a party without your husband," Beatrice said. She was sitting in the front parlor where she had a view of the staircase, obviously lying in wait.

Sophie forced a smile. "My daughter is being well cared for, and I don't believe I asked for your opinion. If you prefer to sit at home, I don't question your choice. I would appreciate the same courtesy."

"Marriage to a fine man and the birth of a healthy baby girl would be enough to satisfy most women, but you're never happy. You can't wait to go to the hotel ballroom and become the center of attention. What would Paul think of your behavior?"

Sophie clenched her hands into tight fists. "My behavior is beyond reproach. It's your evil thoughts that make this anything more than an evening with friends."

"I want the two of you to cease your bickering." Victoria pointed her fan toward Beatrice. "I would not escort your sister on this outing if I believed our attendance overstepped proper etiquette or protocol. Whether it was your intent or not, you've also insulted me, Beatrice."

Sophie grinned at her older sister as Beatrice hastened to offer an apology to their aunt. Though she had doubts, Sophie wondered if the reprimand would put an end to Beatrice's constant criticism.

"Is this the final menu for the weekend meals, Mrs. Broadmoor?" Mrs. Atwell asked as she hurried toward them waving a piece of paper in one hand.

While her aunt and Mrs. Atwell stepped aside, Beatrice drew near to Sophie. "You don't fool me, Sophie. You were an unruly child, and you've grown into an ill-behaved woman. Though you won't admit it, we both know your intentions aren't to sip punch and visit with the old dowagers. You plan to flirt with the men and pretend you're a young debutante."

"You have no idea what I plan to do this evening," Sophie hissed.

An evil glint shone in Beatrice's dark eyes. "Perhaps I shall spend my evening penning a letter to your husband. Does that prospect remove the smirk from your lips?"

"Do what you will, Beatrice. A letter to my husband doesn't concern me in the least." Sophie hoped the response sounded more assured than she felt, for there was no telling what Paul would think if he received such a letter from Beatrice.

She took a deep breath as she and her aunt walked onto the veranda and down the path to the boat. Let Beatrice write her letter if she wanted. Paul had insisted she come out here against her wishes. She'd pleaded to remain in Rochester; it was Paul who had pushed her away. She had wanted to stay by his side, not on this horrid island with nothing to do but miss him. Instead of honoring her wishes, he'd given her no say. She wanted a husband who would listen as well as talk, one who would truly consider her wishes before issuing ultimatums. Perhaps Paul needed to learn a lesson.

CHAPTER 7

Monday, May 15, 1899
Rochester, New York

"Vincent! This is a surprise. I was beginning to wonder if you were ever going to meet with me. But I had hoped to meet in your office so that I could examine my files."

Mortimer's son patted his leather satchel and a box he'd placed on the floor. "They're right here. I apologize for the delay, but as I explained on several occasions, it was necessary for me to address issues with all of my father's clients."

"As his dear friend, client, and business associate, I think he would have wanted you to attend to *my* files first," Jonas said. "And wouldn't it have been easier for me to go there to review the contents?"

Vincent shook his head. "I've delivered your files to you because I have come to the conclusion that you need a lawyer who can devote a great deal of time to your legal matters—much more time than I can spare."

"Don't be ridiculous, Vincent. Your father was a much busier man than you, and he found ample time to represent my interests. Once you have a better understanding of my files and investments, you'll discover you can complete them with ease. I'll lend you the assistance you need to gain that understanding."

"That won't be necessary, Mr. Broadmoor. You see, I've conducted a cursory review of the files myself. It didn't take long to realize that you and my father went beyond the boundaries of the law in handling many of your business matters." Vincent reached into his leather satchel and withdrew a stack of files. "I can't be a part of this." The files landed on Jonas's desk with a dull thud.

Jonas massaged his forehead. "I don't know what you're talking about, Vincent. If your father and I hadn't been dear friends, I would throw you out of my office for making such an appalling accusation." Though his stomach roiled at Vincent's revelation, Jonas hoped the young lawyer would believe his feigned indignation and surprise. "How can you stand here and disparage your dear deceased father? What a disappointment you must be to the rest of your family."

"You need not concern yourself with how my family will react to this news,

Mr. Broadmoor. You have more than enough right here to worry about."
Vincent tapped the files. "Once you review these files as well as those in the
box, you'll clearly understand why I have adopted this position."

Jonas leaned back in his chair, his mind suddenly reeling at what the files
might contain. Surely Mortimer had followed his orders and burned all the
incriminating documents. The man wouldn't have been foolish enough to retain
records of their misdeeds. Mortimer knew any leak of their actions would
ruin both their power and reputations among their peers—not to mention
the possibility of criminal proceedings. Of course, Mortimer didn't need to
worry about any of that now. But Jonas did. Fingers trembling, he reached
across the desk and glanced at the folders.

"Put that box up on my desk," he commanded.

Vincent lifted the box and slid it across the desk. "I have other things that
require my attention this morning." He picked up his coat and hat while Jonas
riffled through the box of files.

"I don't see any files regarding my niece. Did you locate any files with the
name Frances Jane Broadmoor?"

"Indeed, there were a number of files with her name. They have been delivered to her," Vincent replied. "Good day, Mr. Broadmoor."

Jonas didn't look up. There was little doubt Vincent would detect his fear.
He wanted to flail the man for giving any of the files to Fanny, but he dared
not object. Besides, it wouldn't change anything. The files were already in
her possession.

He removed the files from the box. One by one he opened the folders, each
one revealing far more information than the last. Information that Mortimer
had been instructed to destroy. And what if Vincent had retained some of
the incriminating records? How would Jonas know until it was too late? He
couldn't recall even a portion of the paper work he had passed along to his
lawyer. He could burn the records, but the thought gave Jonas no reassurance.
Vincent could have shown the files to someone before turning them over.

He silently chastised himself. In spite of Vincent's protests, Jonas should
have insisted upon retrieving his files the day Mortimer died. In his younger
years, Jonas never would have permitted anyone to hold him at bay. Now he
would suffer for his kindness. For that's what his agreement had been: a simple
act of kindness. What a fool he'd become in his old age!

Strange how he'd believed that Mortimer had begun to lose his edge and
bordered on senility. Under his façade of memory lapses, Mortimer had been
intensely shrewd. There was little doubt he'd saved all these documents as
insurance against any attempt at betrayal. The old man had safely maintained
every record that could implicate Jonas and prove that he'd been the one to
initiate the plan to use Fanny's money. *Use.* Jonas liked the word *use* much

better than *steal* or *convert* or *embezzle*. *Use* didn't sound as though he'd intended any real harm to his niece or her assets. And if his financial hunches had been solid, her accounts wouldn't have suffered. At least that's what he told himself.

Now Mortimer was dead, and Jonas was left to wrestle through this treachery. He would be the one who would suffer the loss of reputation, power, and money. Well, he wouldn't give up easily. The Broadmoors weren't among those who had only recently become rich. They were old money. That fact alone granted immense power and prestige. Power and prestige that Jonas wouldn't relinquish—no matter the cost.

For now, he must direct his attention to Fanny and those records Vincent had given her. How much did those files contain, and did she go through them? Surely Mortimer had heeded the instructions to destroy those incriminating records. But given what he'd found thus far, his doubts continued to rise. If Fanny had discovered his less-than-legitimate handling of her affairs, he needed the assurance of available cash to set things aright. Or at least to appease her until he could develop some story to convince her that none of this had been his doing. He yanked his coat from the chair where he'd tossed it earlier that morning. A visit with Jonathan Canby at the Profit Loan Association bank was in order.

Jonas wasn't going to beg, but he'd certainly remind Jonathan of the loyalty and preference he'd given his bank since it had opened its doors for business. Had it not been for Jonas, their father would have never considered moving his accounts from the Rochester Savings Bank. Jonas had argued at great length with his father, but he'd finally won his confidence. When his father had made the change, many of his business associates eventually followed. Once the transfers had been completed, Jonathan had shown his appreciation with any number of loans at lowered interest rates or without proper security. Of late, the banker hadn't been as agreeable when Jonas had requested financial aid. There was no way to know whether Jonathan would be amenable to this request. But Jonas was prepared to remind the banker of past favors. He had no choice. He needed help, a fact he didn't like to admit, even to himself.

Head bowed against a stiff wind, Jonas didn't notice the bulky white-thatched man until they collided near the front door of the bank. He mumbled a quick apology, but the thick fingers digging into his upper arms caused him to look up and twist away from the hold.

"Jonas! It *is* you, isn't it? Jonas Broadmoor. How long has it been?"

Jonas stared into the intense blue eyes for a moment before realization slowly washed over him. "Ellert Jackson. Where did you come from?"

Ellert clapped him on the back and, with a hearty laugh, pointed over his shoulder. "The hotel. I'm here for only a few more hours. I was going to have lunch at the men's club. Do you have time to join me?"

"Of course, of course," Jonas replied. "I was going to take care of some banking business, but it can wait. Friends are more important than work."

Ellert gave him a sideways glance. "Since when?" He guffawed and nudged Jonas in the ribs. "If you've changed that much, it may take more than one lunch to hear what's been happening in your life."

From time to time Jonas had heard mention of Ellert's continued success in New York City, but the two men hadn't seen each other in years. While living in Rochester, Ellert and Jonas had invested in several of the same business enterprises, though they'd never been close friends. Ellert had never been accepted in fashionable social circles. He'd belonged to the gentlemen's club, of course, but his name failed to be included on the Rochester social register. When Ellert later joined forces with some foreign investors and moved to New York City, the two men lost contact. Some years ago Victoria had mentioned reading an obituary for Ellert's wife. Or had one of his wife's gossipy friends mentioned the death? He couldn't remember, but he did recall there had been no children born to the union. Jonas had expected Ellert to meet with failure and return home, but that hadn't occurred.

They walked side by side the short distance to the club. "It appears life has treated you well in spite of the country's bleak economy," Jonas said.

Ellert smiled and nodded. "I can't complain. Life has been good since moving to New York City."

Ellert's words seeped into Jonas's consciousness like a soothing balm. His old acquaintance who could access financial resources had appeared after years of absence. Was this simply a fortuitous encounter, or was God looking out for him? Jonas smiled at the thought. Even though he attended church services on Sunday mornings, it had been a long time since he'd truly considered the possibility that God might be interested in his life.

Mr. Rosenblume welcomed Fanny with a kind smile. Perhaps because he had been her grandfather's trusted lawyer for years, Fanny felt a sense of comfort whenever she entered his office. He escorted her to the library table, where he'd arranged papers for her review.

Fanny handed him the private files he'd given her at their last meeting. "I thought I should bring these back to you for safekeeping."

He nodded and accepted the folders from her, setting them aside. "It is probably for the best. I hope the information was useful to you." He offered her a seat. "I wanted to go over a few details regarding the purchase of your grandparents' home."

Fanny's pulse quickened as she settled into one of the leather chairs. "So I still have an opportunity to purchase it?"

The old lawyer nodded.

"I was afraid my uncle had located a buyer and hadn't passed along the details to Mr. Fillmore." She clasped her palm to her bodice. "I can't begin to tell you my relief."

"I've been using another party, one I trust, as an intermediary in this transaction. I don't want to tip our hand and have Jonas discover you're involved. I've been told that your uncle is desperate for a quick sale. He's apparently in need of cash, but real estate sales are nearly nonexistent at this time. To my knowledge he's not had any offers. We can't be absolutely certain, but I believe that if we offer him less than the asking price, he'll accept out of desperation."

This talk of finances and sales gave rise to an important question. "Have you examined the records closely enough to know if there are any funds maintained solely in my name? I'd prefer to pay for the house myself rather than rely upon your personal funds."

"I haven't visited the bank, as I didn't want to alert Jonas. However, in going through the papers, it appears there are some funds that he hasn't attached." The lawyer tugged at his starched collar. "But I fear if you attempt to withdraw any of it, the bank will notify your uncle. Since you've never before attempted to access your inheritance, the bank would feel obligated to make an inquiry."

"Even though I've attained legal age?"

The lawyer offered a sympathetic nod. "You've never notified the bank to withdraw his authority to act as your representative, have you?"

"No," Fanny murmured. Mr. Rosenblume was likely correct. The bank officers wouldn't permit her to withdraw money without notifying her uncle. "If you pay for the house from your own funds, how can my name be placed on the deed?"

"If you trust me, I have a proposal for you."

Fanny gave the old lawyer her full attention. "I'm willing to listen to any idea you have."

"The intermediary will act as our agent to purchase the house. Jonas will be told that the purchaser wishes to remain anonymous. He won't care, as long as he gets his money," Mr. Rosenblume explained. "I will pay for the house. You and I will enter into a contract. Once we manage to release any of your inheritance that your uncle hasn't converted to his own use, you can reimburse me and the house will be yours."

"But what if there isn't enough . . . ?" She couldn't bring herself to say the words.

Mr. Rosenblume patted her hand. "There will be enough. From all appearances he didn't commingle all of the funds. He and Mr. Fillmore had a fairly detailed plan."

"So you've completed your review of the files?"

"All but a stack of personal notes. Still, additional time will be needed to complete my findings." He retrieved a stack of papers and pushed them toward Fanny. "If you have time, you could review these in the adjacent office before you leave."

"Of course." She followed Mr. Rosenblume into a small office that adjoined his. She wondered if this was where he escaped when he didn't want to be bothered by the worries of the world. Though the room contained a small desk, it was the overstuffed brocade chair that captured Fanny's attention. Situated alongside a large window that offered excellent light, it provided a perfect place to read a book. She strode toward the chair. "I believe I'll sit here."

"An excellent choice." He padded back across the thick carpet, and a click of the door announced his departure.

Fanny settled into the chair, the bright rays of afternoon sun warming her as she sifted through the papers. An ivory envelope with a gold and blue seal in the corner captured her attention. Holding the corner between her finger and thumb, she gently pulled it from the center of the stack. The envelope was addressed to her uncle Jonas, but one glance revealed the fact that it was from the medical school where Amanda had applied for training. She withdrew the letter and scanned the contents.

"How *could* he?" She tried to grasp the full impact of what she'd read. Her uncle had bargained with the president of the school and had gotten what he wanted. In return for a letter rejecting Amanda's admittance, Uncle Jonas had donated money. Lies and betrayal. Was there no end to what the man would do in order to have his way? In spite of the sun's warmth, an unexpected shiver coursed through her body. She tucked the letter into her skirt pocket and hurried out of the room.

Mr. Rosenblume looked up from his desk. "Done so soon?"

"I'm suddenly not feeling well and believe I had best go home and rest. I'll finish going through the papers tomorrow or the next day."

He pushed to his feet and came to her side. "You are pale, my dear. I'll have my driver bring the carriage around and take you home."

She apologized for her early departure, thanked Mr. Rosenblume for the use of his carriage, and bid him good-bye. Her thoughts raced in circles during the ride home. Even though Uncle Jonas had voiced his disapproval of Amanda's medical training, Fanny had never considered he would go to such lengths. And if he would commit such an odious act against his own daughter, how much more might he do to her?

Jonas paced in front of the library fireplace considering where his niece might be. No one seemed to know where Fanny had gone. Neither her personal maid nor the cook could offer a scrap of information. He'd used the last hour to advantage and searched her room, but to no avail. Either she'd hidden the files somewhere else in the house, or she'd taken them and gone in search of a lawyer. It was the latter thought that caused his head to ache. If those files contained incriminating information, his life would be ruined. He attempted to calm himself with the thought that she wouldn't be interested in the contents of the files. Or that a woman wouldn't understand what they contained.

The familiar click of footsteps on the hallway tile brought his pacing to an immediate halt. Fanny was home. He hurried out of the room. Had his niece not stopped midstep, they would have collided. "I'm sorry. I didn't realize you were right outside my door." Her complexion was pale. "Where have you been, my dear? You don't look well."

"Since when have you concerned yourself over my health, Uncle Jonas?"

He took a backward step. Clearly, she was upset—and suspicious. If he was going to gain any information, he needed to adopt his usual attitude or she'd become even more guarded. "Vincent Fillmore mentioned that he had given you some files regarding your grandfather's estate. Poor fellow is simply too busy with his other work to handle anything as large as the Broadmoor estate." He straightened his shoulders and hoped he was exuding an air of confidence. "And now he's burdened you with a portion of the files. I'm uncertain of his reasoning, but I wanted to assure you that you can depend upon me to continue handling all matters regarding your inheritance."

"Truly?" She folded her arms across her chest.

"Indeed. Why don't you tell me where you've stored the files, and I'll see to them this very minute."

"That won't be necessary, Uncle Jonas. I have already employed a lawyer. Mr. Rosenblume has agreed to act as my legal representative and ease me of the *burden*."

His stomach clenched in a tight knot. Under any other circumstance, he would have been tempted to throttle the girl. But not now—not today. He must maintain his decorum and continue to try to win her over. "Mr. Rosenblume will understand if you advise him you've changed your mind. Women are permitted that concession."

"I feel quite confident that Mr. Rosenblume will be a perfect representative for my interests. After all, Grandfather thought him to be the best lawyer in all of Rochester."

She flashed a smile, though her complexion remained pale. How much did she know, he wondered. "In that case, I'd be more than willing to deliver the files to Mr. Rosenblume. I can drop them off tomorrow morning."

"That won't be necessary. They're already in his office."

His head throbbed as she headed off toward the kitchen without a backward glance. He touched his fingers to his temples. This encounter had not gone at all as he had hoped. If he didn't devise a plan, his life would be a shambles. While Mortimer lay cold in his grave, Jonas could be prosecuted for their criminal actions. To the world it would appear otherwise, but Jonas decided he had drawn the short straw. Death would have been easier than facing disgrace.

He dropped into his chair and continued to massage his temples while misery threatened a tighter hold. "I'm alone, with no one who would understand," he whispered.

Had his brother Langley felt this same sense of despair and loneliness during the ten years following Winifred's death? Had the possibility of a future filled with pain and solitude provided the impetus for Langley to take his own life? A vision of his brother slumped beneath a tree on Broadmoor Island flashed through his mind. When Jonas had arrived on the scene that day, he'd discovered the empty bottle of laudanum and a grief-stricken young Fanny. Jonas had thought Langley a coward—a man afraid to face life. Now he wondered if he might sink to that same depth of hopelessness.

"No," he muttered, silently vowing to save himself at all cost.

Ellert hadn't planned to see Jonas Broadmoor. In fact, he hadn't thought about him in years. Even his journey back to Rochester hadn't brought his former acquaintance to mind. Had they not run into each other outside the bank, Ellert would have left town that same afternoon. Jonas hadn't been himself during their luncheon. At first Ellert thought it simply the span of time between visits. But as their conversation continued, he knew there was more to it. His years of dealing with shrewd businessmen had instilled an ability to know when something was amiss, and something was very wrong with Jonas Broadmoor.

It hadn't taken much time or effort to discover that Jonas had recently suffered some significant financial losses, although he managed to keep the details to himself. The most Ellert could gather was vague information about Jonas's investments. Since the entire country was suffering through a financial downturn, perhaps that was the sum total of his old acquaintance's problem. But Ellert sensed there was something more than bad investments. Jonas had been far too careful with his answers during lunch. And although Jonas had alluded to the possibility of needing to locate financial backing, Ellert hadn't responded. First, he'd wanted to conduct his own research.

The two men had parted outside the men's club, but Ellert returned a short time later. Discovering exactly what had happened with Jonas's finances had proved a costly endeavor. Ellert had crossed the palms of more greedy men than he cared to recall, but the end result had been worth the effort—and the money. Mortimer's clerk had been easily persuaded. On the other hand, Judge Webster had turned out to be the most difficult piece of the puzzle—and the most expensive. But in the end Ellert had succeeded. Money spoke volumes to men at the top of the ladder, and even more so to those like Judge Webster, who teetered near the bottom rung with only a powerful position to make him acceptable. The judge had upped the ante, and Ellert had complied. The information he'd gained had been more than he could have ever hoped for—enough to bring Jonas Broadmoor to his knees.

A feeling of self-satisfaction washed over him. He would be more than pleased to speak with Jonas about a loan or investment. After the many social snubs he'd endured from the entire Broadmoor family, nothing would give him more satisfaction than to bring Jonas to ruin. There had also been the incident when Ellert had wanted to invest in a silver mine. He'd attempted to secure a loan through every means possible before he'd gone to Jonas Broadmoor. After a great deal of cajoling, Jonas had finally agreed—but at a huge cost to Ellert. He had repaid the loan and the exorbitant interest, but Jonas never knew that it was the silver mine that had set Ellert on his path toward financial security.

He raked his fingers through his thick white hair. Indeed, he would be very pleased to offer Jonas help in his time of need—the same way Jonas had helped him—at a very dear price.

CHAPTER 8

FRIDAY, MAY 19, 1899

"What are you doing out of bed?"

Amanda whirled around. Seized by a bout of dizziness, she dropped to the side of the bed. "You startled me!" She pressed her fingertips to her temples in a futile attempt to ward off the sickening feeling. Would she never regain her strength?

While the room continued to swirl in a tilting motion, Blake drew near. "What must I do? Shall I be forced to tie you to that bed in order to keep you there?"

"Don't you dare think such a thing!" She shouldn't have shouted. The dizziness returned with a vengeance, and she was forced to lie back on her pillow. Exactly what Blake wanted. He stood peering down at her. "Are you happy now?" she whispered.

"I'm not pleased if you're feeling worse, but it's good to see you back in bed." He placed his palm across her forehead. "No fever. That's good."

"I know I don't have a fever. And I wouldn't have experienced the dizziness if you hadn't startled me."

He chuckled. "So my voice alone is enough to cause you to swoon. Is that what you're saying, Miss Broadmoor?"

"I didn't *swoon*. I am not one of those young women who swoon in order to gain a man's attention. And I see no reason why I must remain abed. Only yesterday you said I was much improved. Can I not trust your medical opinion, Dr. Carstead?"

"I'm ashamed of you, Miss Broadmoor. You are twisting my words in order to achieve what you want. However, your little game is not going to work. I said you were coming along nicely. I did *not* say you could or should be out of bed."

Now that she was lying down, the dizziness had subsided, and she continued to wage her argument. "You obviously need my help. Do you not think I know how many patients are in those adjoining rooms? Uncle Quincy is worn to a frazzle, and you look like you haven't slept or taken a razor to your face in days," she said, pointing at the several days' growth that covered his jawline. Though she'd never reveal such a thought, Amanda found his unshaven appearance somewhat appealing. "I am bored with nothing to do but stare at the paint chipping from the ceiling."

Blake looked up and then grinned. "The ceiling does appear to need some repair, doesn't it? I'll mention that to your uncle. I'm certain he'll want to have it repainted once—"

"Don't attempt to turn this conversation into a discussion of building repairs. We are discussing the fact that I am well enough to help you with the patients."

"You are having a memory lapse, my dear. We were discussing the fact that you need to remain in bed."

My dear? Had she heard him correctly? She'd not mentioned the memory that had lingered since the turning point in her recovery when she'd rallied and been awake for nearly five minutes. Even now the picture of Blake sitting at her beside and declaring his love remained vivid. As she'd continued her period of recuperation, she'd thought the memory genuine. During those first days, Blake had been nothing but attentive and kind. But as she had continued to gain strength, he'd been provoking her at every turn. The remembrance of his declaration couldn't be real. If he loved her, he wouldn't be such a disagreeable boor now.

She could only assume that the words *my dear* had been nothing more than a calculated plan. Clearly he hoped she would embrace his decision. Well, it would take more than a few words of endearment to convince her that she should remain abed while others suffered without proper care. "I suggest we strike a bargain. If I am able to carry out my normal duties for the remainder of the day, then you will admit that I am well and permit my return to work. I assume you will prove you have confidence in your medical opinion by agreeing to my terms." She pushed herself upright and held her breath. Her words had been full of false bravado. She could only hope he would take the bait she'd dangled in front of him.

"I'm not one to pass up a wager so easily won." He gestured for her to remain still a moment longer. "Your duties will be what I assign. I don't want you fainting atop one of the patients."

"I see. You plan to wear me down scrubbing floors and emptying pails of—"

"I will not assign any duties you didn't perform before you contracted cholera. Do you still wish to bargain with me?"

"Indeed." A quick nod created another wave of dizziness, but she forced herself to remain upright and smile. If she was to win this contest of wills, she must remember to make all movements in a slow and determined fashion.

"Come along, then. And remember that when I win this wager, you must follow my orders without question. I have a great need for bandages. You can tear and roll the old sheets in between your other duties. Fortunately for you, the sheets have already been laundered." His lopsided grin was enough to lend added resolve.

"If they weren't, I'm sure I could accomplish the task," she countered.

His hazel eyes sparkled from beneath thick dark brows. "Then you should have no difficulty preparing the necessary medicines for my patients. You may place the individual doses on the trays, and I'll deliver them. Don't hesitate to call me if you have any questions or need any assistance."

The patronizing offer set her teeth on edge, but Amanda resisted the urge to tell him so. He might withdraw his proposition and send her back to bed. Blake followed her into the small room adjacent to his office and pointed at the cabinet lined with jars of medicinal remedies. She opened one of the glass doors and peered inside. There was little evidence of powders or liquids in the bottles. "How could you permit the supply to fall so low? I trust we'll receive more today."

"Let me refresh your memory, Amanda. There has been sickness throughout the city. Even though the entire city has not been placed on quarantine, many people fear doing business in Rochester. Supplies of every variety are in high demand. I have placed orders with all three pharmacies. They bring what they have to the front gate."

"Then I suppose we must make do." She looked about the small room. "Where is the chair?"

"In the women's quarters. We're housing more people than usual, and they had need of additional seating." He narrowed his eyes. "Are you feeling too weak to stand and complete the task?"

"Not at all. I was merely inquiring." She waved him from the room. "I don't require supervision."

He returned to his office but reappeared minutes later with a small brass bell. "Ring this if you need me." The clapper bounced against the bell with a soft *clunk* when he set it on the table. "Don't let your pride get in the way of your good sense, Amanda."

Before she could reply, he strode out of the room. She heard his soft footfalls on the carpet and then the louder click of his shoes on the wooden floor of the hallway. She peeked into his office to make certain he was gone before she scanned the room for a chair. Blake's large chair remained, but she couldn't possibly move it from behind the desk and through the small entrance to the adjacent room.

After reading the names of the patients and the list of medications, she began the process. She placed the powders on tiny squares of paper until only two names remained. The jar of medicine she needed was nowhere to be found. Could Blake have used the last and forgotten? Resting her hands on her hips, she stepped back and surveyed the cabinet one final time. *There!* On the bottom shelf at the very back, a dark blue bottle—exactly what she'd been searching for.

Bending at the waist, she leaned forward and immediately knew she'd made a mistake. "I should have crouched down instead," she whispered as she lunged for the brass bell.

The bell was the last thing she remembered until she forced her eyes open to stare into Blake's frowning face. "You are a stubborn woman, Amanda Broadmoor. Why didn't you ring the bell?"

"I couldn't reach it," she whispered.

He gently lifted her into his arms and carried her back to bed. "I believe we had an agreement. You will remain here until I declare you well enough to be up and about."

"But what am I to do? Can you not understand my boredom?" Thoughts of Sophie during her months of confinement came to mind. No wonder she had complained so arduously about remaining abed for all that time. "At least bring me something to read and some paper so that I may write to my family."

"If all of my patients were as demanding as you, I'd accomplish very little," he called over his shoulder as he strode back toward his office.

Moments later he returned with an article he'd clipped from a medical journal. "Read this. I found it quite interesting."

"This won't keep me busy for long," she grumbled.

He ignored her complaint, not even offering so much as a good-bye before leaving the room.

She propped herself up in bed, slapped the article on the small table beside her bed, and stared across the room. She must regain her strength and get out of this bed or she'd go mad.

"What's this I hear about my niece being a difficult patient?" Her uncle entered the room carrying a tray laden with two plates and two cups. "I thought a bit of company while you ate your lunch might be in order."

"I would be delighted to have lunch with you. I am starving for both food and civil conversation."

Quincy laughed and set the tray atop the small table. "Are you implying that Dr. Carstead is boring?"

"He does nothing but issue the same orders over and over. I'm to remain in bed until he deems me fit to return to my duties. Surely you would agree I'm strong enough to be of some help around here."

"I'm not a physician, so I can't offer any opinion about your recovery, but I can offer you some chicken and dumplings that smell quite delectable." He handed her a napkin. "I thought you might be interested in hearing about the family. Your father received a letter from your mother, and it seems all is going well at the island. She included this note for you." He handed her the paper, and she tucked it under her pillow.

"I'll read it after I finish my lunch." Amanda swallowed a bite of chicken and sighed with approval. "This is as good as it smells." She poured a cup of tea for each of them. "Has Sophie adjusted to being on the island without Fanny or me? I'm certain she must be lonely."

He patted her arm. "She knows it's best for Elizabeth that they remain out of the city, and I imagine caring for the baby fills most of her waking hours. Your mother mentioned some of the other families have also escaped to the islands."

"Others who live in Rochester?"

"Yes, but also families from other cities. I think most of them thought it prudent to escape earlier than usual, although I think the idea rather silly. Mr. and Mrs. Oosterman are there and have already hosted a gathering at the Frontenac Hotel."

Amanda ate the final bite of her lunch and wiped her mouth. "I can't say I'm surprised. Mrs. Oosterman wouldn't be happy without some sort of soirée where she can gather the latest gossip."

"That seems a bit harsh. I think she's lonely when she's in the islands, and social gatherings are her way of helping pass the time."

Amanda didn't argue. Let her uncle think what he would. But he wouldn't convince her that Mrs. Oosterman simply wanted to while away the hours. As far as Amanda was concerned, Mrs. Oosterman had more interest in the lives of others than in her own.

Her uncle returned her plate and utensils to the tray. "I could bring you some writing paper and a pen if you'd like to post a letter to Sophie. I'm certain she'd enjoy hearing from you, and it would help pass the time."

She nodded. "I asked Dr. Carstead to bring me writing supplies, but he hasn't done so. I would be most appreciative."

He kissed her cheek, and after a promise to return with paper and pen later in the day, he left. She withdrew her mother's letter from beneath her pillow and perused the contents. Except for a few additional details regarding the Oostermans' party, there was little more than what Uncle Quincy had related. She tucked the letter back into the envelope. Now what?

She folded her arms across her chest and then remembered the article Blake had given her a short time ago. She took it from the bedside table and read the headline. *Infant Mortality Rate Approaches Twenty-Five Percent in Largest Cities in the United States.* Amanda immediately considered little Elizabeth and was thankful Sophie had taken her to Broadmoor Island. The article commended some progress where tent cities had been erected for infants during the summer months.

Amanda was familiar with the concept. Though she'd never visited any of the facilities, she'd heard about the Infant Summer Hospital near Rochester. It had been established along the shores of Lake Ontario several years ago. The doctors professed that lake breezes blowing through the tent community were believed to be healthful for the babies during the hot summer months. They also quoted statistics showing a reduced number of deaths among those children afforded the opportunity to spend their days in such an environment.

She was nearing the end of the article when Blake arrived and dropped a stack of books, newspapers, and magazines onto her bed. "What's all of this? Do you expect me to complete a research project?"

"You said the article wouldn't occupy you for long, so I located a few more items to keep you busy for the remainder of the day."

"Are they all medical books? If so, you may find I'm more knowledgeable than you by the time I return to my duties."

He reached for one of the publications and held up a copy of the *Delineator.* "I believe this should keep you from learning enough to take over my medical practice."

"Did you wish to discuss the article regarding the Infant Summer Hospital?" He shook his head. "I haven't time to stay."

"I'm willing to help you," she called after him, but he didn't acknowledge her offer. At least now she had some excellent reading material to help pass the time.

She finished reading the article on the Infant Summer Hospital and then thumbed through the newspapers. She wondered where Blake had found such a variety. Surely he didn't subscribe to all these newspapers. Many of them were several months old, but she continued her quick review. Out-of-date news was better than no news at all. She snapped open a copy of the *New York Journal* and turned to the social columns. She scanned the page but stopped short when she saw Wesley Hedrick's name.

The article stated that Wesley Hedrick had been the host at a number of grand parties attended by many dignitaries. Wesley was described as the sole beneficiary of Lord and Lady Illiff, who had been lost at sea when their ship went down off the coast of France. The newspaper fluttered to her lap. How could this be possible? The man who had fathered Sophie's child and then run off like a thief in the night had inherited a vast fortune and was dividing his time between London and New York City.

What if he should decide to reenter Sophie's life? Surely he wouldn't do such a thing. He'd have far too much to explain. Should she tell Sophie? Would it be best to prepare her cousin for such a happenstance, or would such a revelation only open old wounds and create more pain? She considered writing Fanny to seek her advice, but there was the possibility the letter would be seen by someone other than Fanny. She best not take such a chance. If only they would lift the quarantine, she could talk with Fanny. Together they could come to a sound decision. She looked to the bedside table for scissors but seeing none decided to simply tear the article from the paper. It might come in handy later when she tried to explain her concerns.

Fanny stood outside the gate at the Home for the Friendless and pulled the rope attached to the metal bell. She hoped the noise wouldn't disturb any patients who might be resting. Her uncle waved from the doorway and then hurried down the path to greet her. "Fanny!" he said, stopping a few feet from her. "I do hope you've brought some of the supplies from the pharmacy."

She nodded and set the basket down in front of her. "Yes, but not the amount requested by Dr. Carstead. The pharmacist said to tell him that he's running low on supplies but expects another shipment next week."

"Next week? Some of our patients can't wait that long. Perhaps Paul could take the train to Syracuse. Surely he could purchase drugs at one of the pharmacies there."

"I'll give him your message and tell him it's important he leave as soon as possible." She dug her toe in the dirt. "I brought these things for Amanda. There's also a note for her," she added.

"Why so downcast? Is something amiss?"

"Nothing that can be easily remedied, and nothing that I can't learn to accept, I suppose."

Her uncle frowned. "Are you ill?"

"No, but I do feel pain."

"What kind of pain? In your stomach? You should see a doctor immediately. We don't want you coming down with cholera."

She shook her head. "My pain isn't caused by illness. Have you ever felt betrayed by someone you care about? Someone you trusted and thought loved you and cared for you?"

"Does this have something to do with Michael? Has he written and said he no longer intends to marry you?"

Tears welled in her eyes. "No. I haven't had a letter from Michael in months."

"Tell me what's happened, Fanny. I'll help in any way I can."

She longed to tell him that Uncle Jonas had betrayed her trust and deceived Amanda. Yet she didn't want to be the cause of another rift between the two brothers. There had been enough harsh words among family members in the past. Better to remain silent than say something that couldn't be taken back. What was the Bible verse that Michael's mother had quoted to her? It was from Proverbs. Something about the tongue and power. "The tongue has the power of life and death, and they that love it will eat the fruit," she muttered. That was close, anyway. Better to keep Uncle Jonas's name out of the conversation. "I'm simply disappointed because someone I thought I could trust has let me down."

His brow furrowed. "What has Jonas done now?"

CHAPTER 9

MONDAY, JUNE 12, 1899

Amanda folded her hands in her lap. "This is entirely unfair. My parents can't continue to order me from pillar to post because it suits their whims. I'm no longer a child."

"They are doing what they believe is best for your full recovery. Besides, it's June and the weather is quite lovely. In times past we would already be at the island for our annual summer stay. And when your mother departed, I promised I would escort you to the island." Fanny had been trying to reason with her cousin for well over an hour before Dr. Carstead and Uncle Quincy joined them.

"In the future, you should refrain from making promises you can't keep." Amanda tightened her lips into a sullen pout.

After more than six weeks the quarantine had finally been lifted the preceding day. Immediately after breakfast Fanny had arrived at the Home and announced she planned to escort Amanda to Broadmoor Island. Amanda had promptly refused. She planned to remain in Rochester and work at the Home. Though their train would leave the station in only two hours, Amanda continued to wage a battle.

"Tell my cousin that I am needed here to assist you with your duties," Amanda said, waving Blake forward.

"I'll do no such thing. I plan to escort you to the train station and make certain you board the train." He sat down in a vacant chair beside her. "In fact, I'm going to wait until the train leaves the station to make sure you don't attempt an escape."

His chuckle didn't ward off her feelings of betrayal. How *could* he? Until stricken with cholera, she'd worked alongside him without complaint. There had been days when her back ached and she longed for a few minutes' rest, but she'd continued to do his bidding. Now he sided against her. "So this is my reward? What did my father promise you in order to gain your complicity in this plan?"

Blake's jaw twitched. "I have not had contact with your father, and I have not sided against you. But I am intent upon seeing you attain a full recovery."

"I *am* well. Why don't you offer me that wager again, and we shall see who will win this time?"

He shook his head. "That kind of talk is exactly why you must leave Rochester. If you stayed here, you'd work too hard. No matter what you say, I will not change my mind."

"You don't control me, Blake Carstead. If I want to remain in Rochester, you can't force me to go to Broadmoor Island."

He shrugged. "You're right. But if you don't go, I'll no longer teach you. If you want to continue with your medical career, you'll have to enroll in medical college or find another physician willing to train you."

Amanda extended her neck. "Do you have a collar and leash you'd like to place around my neck so you may control my every step?"

Fanny nudged Amanda and shook her head. "What has come over you?"

"Nothing has come over me. I'm simply weary of others controlling my life."

Blake leaned forward and rested his forearms across his thighs. "You're exaggerating in an attempt to gain a toehold in this argument. You know that your plans to remain in Rochester are faulty." Blake raked his fingers through his unruly dark hair. "I don't want to part on unpleasant terms. Surely you know that my concern for you is well founded and has nothing to do with any edict you've received from your parents. You have my word that you can continue your training with me once your family returns. I hope you'll get plenty of rest and avail yourself of the fresh air."

"I'll have little choice, will I?" Her behavior was no better than that of a petulant child, but Amanda didn't care. "And we'll see whether I'm still interested in working with you when I return." She shrugged her shoulders. "I may very well decide to move to Syracuse or New York City. I'm certain I'll find a physician who will be pleased to continue my training there."

"Please give that matter considerable thought, Amanda." He stood and held out his hand. "I believe we should be on our way. I assume you'd like to stop at home and put some things in a trunk before we head to the depot."

Amanda huffed but took his hand nevertheless.

"We'd better make haste. I don't want you ladies to miss your train."

Throughout the ride to the train station, Amanda stared out the carriage window. Fanny and Blake discussed the cathartic effect the fresh air at Broadmoor Island would have upon Amanda during the next weeks, but she steadfastly ignored their conversation. Let them attempt to win her over by expounding upon the beneficial and invigorating effects she would experience while languishing in the fresh air and strolling along the St. Lawrence River—she'd not be swayed by their talk.

Blake didn't budge from the strategy he'd laid out to her. He accompanied them through the station and out the heavy wooden door that led to the platform. "Once Amanda ceases her pouting, you might ask her to tell you about the healing effects of fresh air upon infants who have been transported to live near the water during the heat of summer. She read a lengthy article on the topic, didn't you, Amanda?"

Amanda decided against breaking her silence, but she did offer a slight nod.

Fanny grasped her arm. "Oh, I do hope you'll tell me all about what you've learned. It sounds fascinating."

The hissing and clanging of the arriving train mixed with shouts from the porters, crying children, and passengers bidding their loved ones farewell. Amanda was thankful the noise prevented further conversation. While Blake assisted Fanny up the steps to the train, Amanda stared longingly at the door leading back inside the station. She could make a run for it—but to where and for what purpose? She'd still be unable to tend to the ill. Blake would make certain of that. No need to dwell on thoughts of escape.

"Come along, Amanda," Blake said.

The toe of her shoe caught on a heavy baggage cart as she stepped toward the train. Like a bird attempting to take flight, her arms spread and flapped while she lunged to gain her footing.

Blake charged toward her and captured her in his arms. "Are you all right?" His dark hazel eyes glistened with concern.

Her pulse quickened as she stared into his eyes. "I th-think so," she stammered.

He pulled her close to his chest. "I was so worried. I thought you were going to fall and injure yourself."

She took a backward step. "Did you worry for my safety, or was your concern that if I suffered injury you wouldn't be able to send me off to Broadmoor Island?"

His eyes turned darker. "Think what you will, Amanda. Whether you wish to believe me or not, my concern is for your welfare."

"Are you injured, Amanda?" Concern edged Fanny's voice.

Her cousin's words were enough to bring her back to the present. One glance at his hands resting on her hips was enough for Blake to release his hold. He escorted her to the train and bid her a formal good-bye. As promised, he waited on the platform while their train departed the station.

Once the train had begun to gain speed, Fanny nudged her. "I believe Dr. Carstead cares for you."

"I had thought the same thing. But what man who truly cares does everything in his power to rid himself of the woman he loves?" Amanda settled against the dark green upholstered seat. "Now let us speak of something else. I don't wish to dwell upon Dr. Carstead."

"As you wish, but I'm not convinced you're correct." Fanny adjusted her skirts around her. "Do tell me about the report you read on the infant hospitals."

At Fanny's mention of the article, Amanda's thoughts returned to the piece she'd seen in the paper regarding Wesley Hedrick. "I'll tell you about the summer hospitals later. First I must tell you about something else I read while I was in confinement." She reached into her reticule and handed the now neatly trimmed piece of newspaper to Fanny.

Fanny quickly scanned the piece and looked up in disbelief. "Instead of simply a ne'er-do-well, Wesley has become a wealthy ne'er-do-well. I cannot imagine why Lord and Lady Illiff would leave their vast fortune to the likes of Wesley Hedrick." She handed the article back to Amanda.

Amanda shrugged and slipped the paper between the pages of a book she'd brought along. "They had no other family."

"He wasn't a blood relative. I'm not certain he was married to Lady Illiff's cousin for more than a few years before she died. I would think they could have found someone more deserving of their wealth. A charity would have been a better choice. I can only imagine the women who must be flocking around him."

"Like hens scratching for feed." Amanda giggled, then stopped short and clapped her hand to her lips. "I shouldn't be making light of the situation, for this bit of news could upset Sophie. What if someone should read the news and mention it to her? I have been weighing whether to tell her since the day I picked up that newspaper. What do you think?"

"I don't believe it would serve any good purpose to tell her. And few people were acquainted with Wesley."

"Few people? Do you forget that Uncle Quincy announced at the Home for the Friendless fund-raising event that Wesley had pledged a huge donation? I would think those who attended would remember his name."

"You give the local gossips far too much credit, Amanda. They would have discovered more recent fodder long ago." Fanny tapped her finger on the armrest. "On the other hand, a wealthy eligible man does stir up a great deal of interest. How long ago was the piece in the newspaper?"

"I don't remember the exact date, but all the out-of-town papers were at least three months old."

Fanny gave an affirmative nod. "You see? No one gave notice to the news. If anyone had remembered Wesley, we would have heard something by now. I don't think we should mention any of this to Sophie. Wesley is but a bad memory in her life."

"I suppose you're correct, but Uncle Quincy told me Mr. and Mrs. Oosterman have arrived at the islands. And you know Mrs. Oosterman doesn't forget even the tiniest morsel of information. What if she's heard something? I would rather Sophie hear the news from us than from someone such as Mrs. Oosterman." Amanda scooted sideways in her seat. "And what if Sophie should discover we knew and didn't tell her. Would she think we'd betrayed her?"

"You worry overmuch about something that isn't likely to occur. Even if she should find out, Sophie would understand our reticence to tell her. She would know our decision was made with her best interests in mind. Unlike others, the three of us would never intentionally hurt one another." Fanny turned and stared out the train window.

"I suppose you're correct," Amanda replied.

Her cousin appeared lost in thought. Amanda studied Fanny and decided that she hadn't been herself since they'd boarded the train. No. It was before that. Even back when Fanny had first arrived at the Home, she hadn't had much to say. Not that she'd been rude. Fanny would never be impolite. But she'd barely entered into the conversation before their departure. Of course, Fanny had been polite to Blake during the carriage ride, but that was likely to offset her own ill-mannered behavior.

Amanda tapped her cousin on the arm. "Are you feeling unwell, Fanny?"

"I'm fine," she said without turning away from the window.

"We've been separated for weeks with only a few letters exchanged between us, yet you have nothing of interest to tell me? Come now, Cousin, what ails you?"

"Truly, I am fine. Don't worry yourself over me."

Amanda slapped her gloves on the leather seat. "You are not fooling me in the least. I know you as well as I know anyone in this world, and I can certainly tell when something is amiss. You may as well tell me, for I'll not give you a minute's peace until you do."

"Ever the persistent one, aren't you! Sometimes it's best to let sleeping dogs lie. I can't talk about what is bothering me just yet."

"I *knew* it! You're keeping a secret from me. We've never kept secrets, Fanny."

Fanny arched her brows. "We're going to keep a secret from Sophie."

"Because it's for her own good."

"Then you must consider this the same thing. If and when the time is right, I will tell you. For now, you must trust my decision to remain silent." Fanny squeezed Amanda's hand.

Though she longed to know what bothered her cousin, Amanda said no more. They conversed little during the remainder of the journey. Fanny appeared lost in her own thoughts while Amanda contemplated whether Dr. Carstead might hire someone to help at the Home during her convalescence. Although she knew he needed help, the very thought annoyed her.

"Wake up, we're here." Fanny's words were followed by a gentle nudge.

Amanda forced herself awake as the train hissed and jarred to a stop in the Clayton train station. "I didn't realize I was so tired."

Fanny smiled. "Dr. Carstead would say that you've proved his point and that you've not fully recuperated."

"Well, he would be incorrect. I didn't sleep well last night." Amanda peered out the train window. "I suppose Father notified Mr. Atwell to come and meet us." She glanced over her shoulder. "Or did you write to Michael's parents?"

"I believe your father sent our arrival information to the Clayton telegraph office. He said Mr. Broomfield would pass along the information."

Amanda didn't doubt Mr. Broomfield would do exactly as her father wished. Years ago the old telegrapher had forgotten to deliver a message that her father had wired from Rochester for delivery to his father on Broadmoor Island. Mr. Broomfield had suffered the wrath of Jonas Broadmoor and had never again made the same mistake. She imagined if necessary, the poor man would row to the island to ensure that the message arrived.

A stiff breeze greeted them when they stepped down from the train. Amanda grasped her hat with one hand and pointed to the *DaisyBee* with the other. "There's the boat. Mr. Atwell must be inside."

Fanny locked arms with her cousin, and the two of them bowed their heads against the wind as they hurried inside the train station.

"Fanny! Amanda!" Sophie rushed forward and grabbed them around the shoulders in a giant hug. "I am so excited to see you. Now that the two of you have arrived, it's going to be just like old times."

Amanda took a backward step and glanced around the station. "Where's the baby? I'm anxious to see how much she's grown."

"Elizabeth is with her nanny. Aunt Victoria found a wonderful lady who lives here in Clayton, and she's come to stay at the island to take care of Elizabeth. Both Veda and Minnie complained they had too many other chores to accomplish now that there are so many parties taking place." Sophie glanced outside and then motioned to her cousins. "Mr. Atwell has your trunks loaded. You're both going to think it's the height of the summer season once you get settled at the island. It is absolutely amazing how many dinner parties and dances have taken place since shortly after we arrived." She winked at Amanda. "There are several fine bachelors among the attendees, and all of them are capable dance partners."

Amanda shot a glance at Fanny. In the past Sophie had been unwilling to leave Elizabeth in the care of anyone but Paul or one of them. Now it appeared she'd relegated the baby's care to a stranger. The change seemed inexplicable, but before Amanda could gauge Fanny's reaction, Sophie stepped between them. She continued to regale them with the details of a dinner party she'd attended Saturday while they walked across the train tracks to the dock and boarded the *DaisyBee*.

When Sophie finally stopped long enough to take a breath, Amanda leaned forward. "What do you hear from Paul?"

"He says he's busy helping several churches that are without preachers. He doesn't know when he'll be coming to the island for a visit." Sophie shrugged. "I don't mind in the least. There have been more than enough social gatherings to keep me occupied, and there are even more in the offing. Now that the two of you have arrived, it's going to be completely grand."

"I brought only two gowns that would be appropriate for such festivities," Amanda said. "And you were complaining before you departed Rochester that you hadn't been able to fit into your gowns since Elizabeth's birth. Exactly what have you been wearing to all of these galas?"

"Your mother has been ever so kind in that regard. Once she realized the state of my wardrobe, she enlisted the help of a seamstress in Clayton. Thankfully, the woman has several others who work in the shop with her. Minnie and Veda have been called upon to lend occasional help, as well." Sophie's eyes sparkled with excitement as she told them of the various fabrics she'd chosen for her dresses.

"And with a nanny to care for Elizabeth, that leaves you free to attend as many parties as you desire," Amanda remarked.

Sophie's smile disappeared. "You disapprove?"

Amanda nodded. "I can't comprehend the change that has taken place since I last saw you. Back in Rochester you were content with your life and found joy in your marriage to Paul and caring for Elizabeth. There was no mention of parties or fancy dresses. What has come over you?"

Sophie glared at Amanda. "You're always finding fault with me—isn't she, Fanny?"

"I don't think that's true. Unfortunately, what Amanda says is true. You do seem like a different person."

"I don't want to talk about this anymore. You've only just arrived, and we shouldn't have an argument before we even arrive at the island."

Before Fanny could respond, Mr. Atwell waved an envelope overhead and smiled. "Would you be interested in what arrived just yesterday, Fanny?" he called.

Fanny clasped her hand over her heart. "A letter! From Michael?" She jumped to her feet and dropped back down as the boat lurched through the choppy water.

"Stay there," he called. "I'll bring it to you."

With the ease of a practiced sea captain, Mr. Atwell arrived at her side and handed her the missive. "This one was tucked inside the letter he sent to us." He pointed to the seal and grinned down at her. "As you can see, we didn't open it."

Fanny nodded. "He's doing well?"

"I think you'll be pleased to hear his news." He tipped his hat and returned to his post.

She slipped her finger beneath the seal and carefully opened the envelope. She was now sandwiched between her cousins, who were peering over her shoulders as she withdrew the pages. Fanny waved them away. "Do move back a little. I promise to tell you what he says, but I'd like to read it first."

Amanda leaned back, though she wasn't certain Sophie paid heed to Fanny's request. She waited what seemed an eternity before nudging her cousin. "Well, what does he say?"

The pages crackled as she held them to her bodice. "He's coming home in June, and he says to plan the wedding." Her broad smile seemed to stretch from ear to ear. "Finally! Can you believe it?"

Amanda shook her head. "No! He obviously doesn't realize how long it takes to prepare for a wedding. We'll need to begin immediately. I do think we should enlist Mother's help, too."

"You must choose the perfect wedding gown, Fanny. With all your money you'll be able to afford the finest wedding Rochester has ever seen," Sophie said.

"Michael and I plan to be married on Broadmoor Island," Fanny told them. "Still, there will be much to accomplish before we are wed, and I will need help from both of you."

"You know you can depend upon us," Amanda said. She extended her fingers and the three of them joined hands. "Together always."

"Together always," the three repeated in unison.

Jonas folded his hands atop his desk and did his best to remain calm. Ellert Jackson was a shrewd man, and he'd sniff out any hint of fear. Several days earlier Ellert had confirmed he would stop by and discuss the possibility of a loan. Jonas had expected him to appear that very day. When he hadn't arrived by the next morning, Jonas had gone to the hotel and discovered Jackson had checked out. The news had rendered him despondent. But today his spirits had buoyed.

He'd received word that Ellert had returned to Rochester. And when the man had entered Jonas's office only a few minutes ago, his heart had pounded with renewed hope. Ellert could help him escape from his financial woes, but Jonas must play his hand with finesse.

"I'm surprised to see you back in Rochester," Jonas said.

Ellert guffawed. "You're *relieved* to see me. Isn't that what you truly mean, Jonas?" He didn't await a reply. "They tell me at the hotel that you came looking for me after I'd checked out the last time I was in town."

Jonas silently chided himself. He should have tipped the hotel clerk and told him to keep his mouth shut. Too late now. Ellert had gained first advantage in this game of cat and mouse. "Yes. I stopped by to extend an invitation to supper."

Ellert tapped his walking stick on the floor. "You came to the hotel because you were worried I had forgotten about your loan." He stared across the desk, his eyes unwavering.

There was no doubt Ellert expected Jonas to acknowledge his assessment was correct. Jonas could read it in his eyes. Though he longed to remain silent, Jonas didn't hold the advantage. He gave a half nod. "Because I wanted to invite you to join me for supper and discuss the loan."

Like a cat preparing to pounce on its prey, Ellert leaned across the desk. "You are in no position to play games with me, Jonas. I know what you've been up to with your niece's inheritance."

Jonas willed himself to remain calm, but perspiration covered his palms and a sudden weakness assailed him. He'd never fainted in his life. Was this how women felt when they swooned? He fought to bolster himself with a deep breath—and then another. How could Ellert possibly know what he'd done?

"I don't know what you're—"

"Stop!" Ellert slapped his palm on the desk. "I will not play games with you. The only way you will receive a loan from me is on my terms. I know you are in dire financial straits. And my terms require a full disclosure of your finances and those of your niece." He removed a sheet of paper from his pocket and pushed it across the desk. "This is only a small portion of what I know. If you want my help, you'll tell me the rest—all of it."

Jonas scanned the page and felt the blood rush from his head. Ellert had been digging, and he'd excavated far more information than Jonas would have thought possible.

"How did you come by this knowledge?"

Ellert smiled and crossed his arms casually against his chest. "Come now, Jonas. You above all men should know what a well-placed dollar or two can do for a man. I have my sources—friends, if you will. Surely you wouldn't expect me to divulge such information."

Jonas forced himself to concentrate. Who would have had access to the records? Possibly one of the clerks in Mortimer's office had snooped in the files before his death. That had to be it. If only Mortimer would have done as instructed and kept no written documentation of their dealings. If only he would have realized the harm it could cause in the days to come.

Jonas dropped back against his chair and stared into Ellert's gleaming eyes. The man was taking great pleasure in seeing him squirm. "It appears I have little choice," Jonas said.

Ellert had won—at least this round.

CHAPTER 10

Thursday, June 15, 1899

Jonas sighed at the sight of his brother entering the outer office. He should have closed his door and told Mr. Fryer to send any visitors on their way. Though he truly couldn't afford the services of an office clerk any longer, Jonas couldn't imagine his office without Mr. Fryer. The man had worked for him for nearly twenty years and could be trusted to do Jonas's bidding without question, a trait that had long ago endeared the man to Jonas.

His brother nodded at Mr. Fryer but continued past the clerk's desk and strode into Jonas's office. "We need to talk." He closed the door and dropped his hat atop Jonas's massive desk before sitting down.

Jonas straightened in his chair. Without the slightest show of manners or greeting, his brother had entered his office and made himself quite comfortable. "Good morning to you, too, Quincy."

"Good morning!" Quincy shot back.

Jonas didn't miss the irritation in Quincy's voice. "Looks as though we're going to have some nice weather today."

"I didn't come here to discuss the weather. I came here to ask what you've done to aggrieve Fanny. I spoke with her shortly before she and Amanda departed for Broadmoor Island, and she wasn't herself."

"You know women. Their moods are as changeable as the weather—perhaps even more so." He chuckled, though he gripped the arms of his chair in a fierce hold. What had Fanny been up to now? How much had she divulged to Quincy? His brother didn't act as though he knew anything, but he'd not fall into a trap. "I have no idea why Fanny is upset. Did you not inquire yourself?"

"Yes, of course, but she wasn't as forthcoming as I had hoped. She simply said someone had betrayed her."

Jonas rubbed his jaw. "Probably that useless Michael Atwell. Let's hope he's found another woman and doesn't plan to marry Fanny."

"No. I specifically asked her about Michael. She denied he was the cause of her despair. Naturally I could only think something had gone amiss in regard to her inheritance." Quincy arched his brows and waited.

Jonas shook his head and feigned ignorance for a moment before acting as though he'd had a sudden flash of genius. "She must be unhappy over the sale of Broadmoor Mansion—that must be what has caused her despondency."

"What are you talking about? You sold the mansion to Daniel Irwin long ago." Quincy frowned. "I'm beginning to worry about your memory, Jonas."

"I did sell it to Daniel, but once Fanny refused to marry him, he no longer wanted the house. He petitioned the court to withdraw from the agreement and was granted permission."

"Why didn't I know anything about this?"

"If you'll recall, you told me that unless the Home for the Friendless would be adversely impacted, you didn't want to be bothered with matters related to the estate."

"That's true," Quincy mumbled. "So you've sold the mansion to another purchaser?"

"Yes, but at a loss. The maintenance expense on the place was costing us more and more, so it was better to sell at a loss than continue the upkeep. The court agreed. Unfortunately, I think Fanny felt betrayed by my action."

"Because she wanted to buy it for herself?"

"Yes, but I couldn't permit a young single woman to live alone in that place. It wouldn't be prudent or proper. I was looking out for her best interests, but you know how young people are—they simply want their way in everything." Jonas loosened his grip on the chair arms. From all appearances, his efforts to convince Quincy were meeting with success.

"I wonder why she didn't mention that. Selling the house doesn't seem like something she'd be reluctant to tell me."

There was a question lurking in his brother's comment. Had he misjudged him? Did Quincy know more than he'd revealed? His confidence waned. Best to meet the situation with a direct question of his own. "Did Fanny mention me specifically or any problem she's had with me?"

"No, but I assumed that since she's been living in your house, you would be the cause of her unhappiness—or at least know what the problem might be."

"Your assumptions are unfounded on both accounts. Fanny and I have had little contact over the last weeks. We didn't take our meals together, and I saw her only in passing on one or two occasions. She didn't appear unhappy or troubled on those brief encounters. And now that she's left for Broadmoor Island with Amanda, I'm certain she's in good spirits."

Quincy leaned back in his chair and stared out the window as if contemplating the explanation. "No," he said, shaking his head. "I believe something of greater import than a change of mood has occurred with our Fanny."

Our Fanny. Jonas winced at the affectionate expression. When had Quincy become so worried about the girl's welfare? And why? Normally he couldn't be pried away from the Home for the Friendless long enough for a family gathering. Suddenly he sounded like a protective father rather than a disengaged uncle. Jonas needed to shift his brother's focus.

"What do you hear from Sophie and Beatrice? In her most recent letter, Victoria mentioned that Beatrice seems to be out of sorts most of the time. Strange, don't you think, since she was the one most interested in fleeing the city? Perhaps she's suffering from some mental ailment and should see a physician."

Quincy scooted to the edge of his chair. "Is that what Victoria thinks? If so, I shall ask Dr. Carstead if there's a doctor he can recommend. Of course, Beatrice has always been somewhat antagonistic. I believe she bears a good deal of anger and jealousy, though I don't know why."

Jonas guffawed. "Truly? Perhaps because you devote all your time to everyone except your immediate family."

"That's not true. I've done my best since Marie's death. Besides, Marie encouraged my work with the underprivileged."

Pleased that he'd managed to redirect their conversation, Jonas didn't retreat. "No one would disagree that Marie offered her support to your work. I never quite understood why, for it surely placed an undue burden upon your family, though there are many things I don't profess to understand."

Using the desk for leverage, Quincy pushed up from his chair. "I promised Dr. Carstead I would stop at the pharmacy. He's likely wondering what happened to me."

"Don't let me keep you from your duties." Jonas tapped the stack of papers on his desk. "I have many matters needing my attention, as well."

Without further comment, Quincy picked up his hat and strode to the door. He waved his walking stick in a farewell gesture as he departed.

Jonas exhaled a low whistle and leaned back in his chair. By the time Quincy had exited the office, he'd clearly forgotten why he'd come calling. Jonas reached into his humidor and removed one of the two remaining cigars. He'd given up purchasing the expensive Cubans—a self-imposed punishment for being lax and overlooking details in his business dealings with Mortimer. He passed the roll of thick brown tobacco beneath his nose and inhaled the fragrant odor before returning it to the box. There wasn't time to indulge at the moment.

He stood and looked down to the street below. Quincy was nowhere in sight. He'd likely departed by carriage. Jonas removed his hat from the hook by the door and stepped through the doorway. "I have errands to complete, Mr. Fryer. I'm not certain what time I'll return."

The clerk glanced up from his journal. "I'll lock up if you haven't returned by six o'clock, sir."

Jonas could always depend upon Mr. Fryer. No matter the task, Mr. Fryer never asked questions. He faithfully appeared each morning and disappeared like a vapor ten hours later. Jonas had no idea if the man had a wife or family. They never discussed anything unrelated to business. Yet another reason Jonas was grateful for Mr. Fryer.

Jonas walked the four-block distance to the courthouse. By the time he rounded the side of the brick structure, he was puffing for air. He entered a side door that would take him through a private corridor that led directly to each of the judges' chambers. It was Mortimer who had originally shown Jonas the entrance used by the lawyers to conduct business with the judges. The side door provided easy access. And if one was fortunate, one could slip in and out without ever being seen. Jonas hoped he could accomplish such an entrance and exit today.

Before rapping on the door, he glanced over his shoulder. Not a soul in sight. He sighed with relief and tapped on the door where the name *Harlan G. Webster, Probate Judge* had been painted in black. Proper etiquette dictated he await a response, but Jonas wouldn't chance being seen, so he turned the knob and stepped inside. The clerk's desk was empty. "Judge Webster?" Jonas called.

"Who's there?" A drawer slammed. "Make yourself known!"

"It's Jonas Broadmoor." He crossed the room at a near run and stood in the doorway to the judge's inner sanctum.

The judge traced his finger down a list on his desk. "I don't have you on my calendar for today."

"I don't have an appointment, but it's urgent that we talk. Can you spare me a few minutes right now?" Jonas felt like a sniveling child. Judges! They took absolute delight in wielding their power. A year or two ago, Jonas could have bought and sold every judge in the state. Now he was relegated to begging for a few minutes of this pompous man's time.

Judge Webster waved at one of the threadbare upholstered chairs. "Sit down, but don't get comfortable. I have another appointment in half an hour."

Don't get comfortable? How did the foolish man think anyone could find a scrap of comfort in this shabby office? "There have been some problems since Mortimer's death."

"And?" The judge arched his bushy brows.

"Mortimer maintained far too many records of our business dealings regarding my father's estate." In a rush of words, Jonas detailed the plethora of events that had unfolded since his lawyer's death. Judge Webster stared out the window, seemingly bored by the tale. When he had revealed all of the facts, Jonas edged forward on the chair. "Well, what do you think I should do?"

The judge shrugged his bony shoulders. "I suggest you get your books in order and hire an excellent lawyer to represent you." His glasses slipped down on his nose as he leaned across the desk. "Mr. Rosenblume has already been here to meet with me on behalf of his client. He has expressed a deep concern for what he considers inappropriate handling of estate funds."

Jonas grasped the judge's thin arm. "You're a part of this. You must help me."

With a steely glare, the judge nodded toward his arm. "Remove your hold."

"Yes, of course. I didn't mean to—"

"Now, you listen carefully, Jonas. I am no longer a party to this. This plan was developed by you and Mortimer. I will deny any knowledge of what has transpired. I've already told Mr. Rosenblume I am shocked and appalled by the very idea that Mortimer, a lawyer sworn to uphold the law, may have presented falsified records to the court."

Jonas slapped the desk with his palm. "That's it! We can blame all of this on Mortimer, and both of us will be free from any liability. Frankly, it does appear Mortimer didn't keep me completely apprised of matters, and my financial condition is much worse than even I had imagined."

The judge didn't appear completely convinced. Jonas would be forced to use his trump card. "I thought you might be interested to know that when I was reviewing the files, I came upon a note you wrote to Mortimer."

The judge wrinkled his forehead in a frown. "I don't have the slightest idea what you're talking about."

So the judge wanted to play coy and see if Jonas was bluffing. Well, he could certainly understand that tack. Hadn't he done the same thing countless times? Jonas couldn't fault the man for being suspicious.

Jonas tapped his pocket. "Your note tells Mortimer to deposit funds into an account at a Syracuse bank prior to the date of our hearing regarding the estate inventory and appraisal. Does that help jog your memory?"

The judge narrowed his eyes. "Mortimer told me all correspondence between us would be destroyed."

Jonas took a modicum of pleasure watching the judge squirm. The old man didn't appear quite so supercilious at the moment. "Obviously Mortimer lied to both of us."

"I suppose there is merit to joining forces and placing all of the blame on Mortimer. If we both disavow knowledge of what he was doing, we should be able to avoid being drawn into the fray. The fact that your finances are in worse condition than you thought will help substantiate our claims to lack any knowledge regarding Mortimer's wrongdoing." The judge leaned back in his chair and stared into the distance. "Yes. This is perfect. Who will doubt us?"

"Then if we've agreed, I'll be on my way. I don't want to further interfere with your busy schedule."

The judge pointed to Jonas's pocket. "I would be grateful if you'd give me that note I wrote to Mortimer."

Jonas withdrew an envelope from his coat pocket. "Oh, *this*? This is a letter from my wife. Surely you didn't think I would carry your note on my person."

The judge gripped his pencil with a fury that caused it to snap. He stared at the two pieces of wood as though he couldn't determine how they'd come into his possession. "You may bring it to me the next time you pay me a visit."

Jonas forced a smile. "Of course." If the judge thought he would gain possession of that note before all of the legal proceedings had been completed, he was a fool. And Jonas didn't think the man a fool. "I do hope the rest of your day passes without interruption."

The judge's obvious irritation created a warm feeling of self-satisfaction that lasted until he returned to his office. He settled at his desk and reviewed the ledgers and bank accounts. Their plan would cause little difficulty for the judge. But Jonas realized he would be faced with an onslaught of questions from both Quincy and Fanny. They would make prying inquiries that would require both precise and consistent responses. Before any of their questions arose, he must be prepared with answers that would nip any thought of wrongdoing in the bud. If he was to succeed in his ploy, he must appear shocked and surprised by Mortimer's mishandling of the estate.

Jonas hoped the files Vincent had given to Fanny held nothing that would incriminate him.

CHAPTER 11

MONDAY, JUNE 19, 1899

As the train came to a hissing, jerking stop at the Rochester train station, the three cousins stood and then edged down the aisle. Sophie grasped Amanda's arm when they stepped onto the platform. "Do you think Dr. Carstead will be surprised to see you?"

"I imagine he will. And what of Paul? Did you tell him that we were coming to Rochester to shop for Fanny's wedding gown?"

The fashionable feathers on Sophie's hat waved back and forth as she shook her head. "No. He would have insisted I bring Elizabeth with me. Had the baby accompanied us, we would get little shopping completed."

"I wouldn't have minded in the least. She's a good baby, and I'm sure Paul would have been willing to look after her while we shopped," Fanny said.

Sophie stopped in the middle of the depot and planted her hands on her hips. "Whose side are you on, Fanny? I came along to help you, and you are taking Paul's side against me."

Fanny sighed. "I'm not taking sides, but I imagine Paul misses the baby and will be sad that you didn't bring her."

"From his lack of attention, I doubt he misses either of us overmuch. He hasn't yet come to Broadmoor Island for a visit." Sophie tipped her head to the side as if to challenge anyone who might defy her. "Here's a cab. Come along."

"But ever since you wrote to him, he's been writing with regularity. And you said he was needed to help with several of the churches in town, didn't you?" Fanny truly couldn't understand Sophie's recent behavior. The only things that now evoked any excitement in her cousin were the mention of shopping or the latest invitation to a dinner dance at one of the island hotels. She was acting like a silly debutante seeking a husband instead of a married woman with a delightful infant daughter.

Sophie shrugged. "If his work is of greater import than his family, so be it. He's become much like my father, tending to the needs of others instead of his own family. I'm capable of being occupied without him." She clasped Fanny's arm. "I do need to stop by the house and retrieve a piece of jewelry that I forgot to pack."

"Your mother's necklace?" Fanny asked.

"Yes. The amber stones match my gold satin gown. And now that Aunt Victoria has had it altered for me—"

"You'll suffer Beatrice's wrath if you wear the necklace in her presence," Amanda said.

"I don't care if she becomes angry. Father gave the necklace to me, and

Beatrice can complain all she likes. Jewelry shouldn't be stored away; it should be worn. Don't you agree?"

Amanda peeked around Fanny's flower-bedecked hat. "Why don't the two of you go to Sophie's house while I stop by the Home for the Friendless? Blake is always there on Monday, and I'd like to speak to him. Then we can begin our shopping in earnest."

Fanny hesitated. "I suppose that would be acceptable, but we do want to reserve enough time to choose fabric and flowers."

"We will not leave Rochester until we've made the perfect selections for you. Even if we must remain several days." Amanda tapped on the window and gave the driver Sophie's address.

Sophie shook her head. "We need to complete our shopping by Friday at the very latest. The Armbrusters are hosting a party at the Crossman House on Alexandria Bay. I do enjoy parties at the Crossman, don't you?"

Amanda made a *tsk*ing sound and shook her head. "I should think you'd refrain from attending *all* of the parties, Sophie. It gives the wrong impression."

"Oh, do cease your chiding, Amanda. I'll begin to think Beatrice is at my side rather than one of my favorite cousins. Besides, your mother has given her approval to every party I've attended."

"That's because she doesn't know that you disengage yourself from the couples she's arranged to act as your escorts."

Sophie giggled. "Well, you had best not tell your mother, or I'll be slow to forgive you. I've done nothing improper. A few dances and a bit of conversation with a gentleman or two mean absolutely nothing."

Fanny didn't wish to enter into the fray between Sophie and Amanda, but Sophie's comment was a sudden reminder of how easily she had been enchanted by Wesley Hedrick not so long ago. There was little doubt Sophie could be easily swayed by the charms of a smooth-talking man. But surely she'd never do anything to threaten her marriage to Paul.

Worry loomed in Fanny's mind as their carriage came to a halt in front of Sophie's house. Fanny and Sophie stepped down. "Once you've seen Dr. Carstead," Fanny said to Amanda, "why don't you return and then we'll go shopping." Fanny drew close to the carriage window and lowered her voice. "If Paul is at the Home, you might tell him Sophie is here."

Sophie nudged her cousin in the side. "I can take care of arrangements for meeting my own husband, Fanny. Didn't you say you wanted to allow ample time for shopping?"

Amanda leaned forward and pointed at the runabout sitting near the side entrance to Sophie's house. "I think you two may stop arguing. I'll return shortly."

The carriage driver slapped the leather reins against the horse's backside.

Once the carriage had pulled away, Fanny turned her attention to Sophie. "I didn't mean to anger you, but I do find your lack of concern toward Paul disturbing. You *do* love him, don't you?"

Sophie frowned, her displeasure obvious. "Of course I love him, but he's the one who banished me to the island. I wanted to remain in Rochester, and he wouldn't even consider my wishes. I could have been a great deal of help to him. That's what I wanted to do—assist him with his work. It is Paul who decided on this separation." She strutted toward the front door as though she'd sufficiently defended her behavior.

Fanny quickened her pace and came alongside her cousin. "He didn't want you or Elizabeth to contract cholera. And I believe he hasn't come to visit because he didn't want to take the chance he might carry the disease to any of us. Neither your father nor Uncle Jonas has set foot on the island, either."

"And none of them have become infected with cholera. There was no reason to send Elizabeth and me to the island."

"I disagree, but now I realize that you're behaving badly to teach Paul a lesson." Fanny tugged on her cousin's arm. "I'm correct, aren't I?"

"That was my intent at first, but now I'm simply enjoying the parties. And I'm *not* behaving badly."

"By whose standards?" Fanny followed her cousin up the porch steps.

Sophie glanced over her shoulder as she turned the doorknob. "Do stop these tiresome questions. You're beginning to sound like Amanda." She stepped across the threshold. "Paul! Are you here?"

From the kitchen the sound of a chair scraping across the floor preceded Paul's appearance. He stepped into the hallway, his eyes wide with surprise. "Sophie! I can't believe you're here. Why didn't you tell me you were coming? And where's Elizabeth?"

"She's at Broadmoor Island, of course. If you're disappointed she isn't with me, I suppose you can blame yourself for sending us away—or you can blame Fanny, if you prefer. We've come to shop for her wedding gown, and it would have been difficult to bring Elizabeth along when we have so much to accomplish. And I thought you would be busy with your many charitable duties."

Fanny didn't miss the sarcasm in Sophie's curt response or the pain that shone in Paul's eyes. She longed to remove herself from this awkward situation.

Amanda's stomach tightened into a knot when she caught sight of the Home for the Friendless. She clasped a hand to her midsection, hoping to ease her anxiety. Would Blake be pleased to see her? She hoped he would regard her unexpected visit a welcome surprise.

The carriage driver assisted her down. "Please wait for me. I shouldn't be more than fifteen minutes."

He nodded his agreement, and Amanda inhaled a deep breath as she approached the front gate. It seemed an eternity since she'd departed. How she had missed caring for the ill. Perhaps Blake would reconsider and permit her to stay. Before entering the gate, she pinched her cheeks. If she hoped to convince him that she should remain and work, she'd need to look like the picture of health. She hoped a rosy complexion would help. After a quick adjustment to her hat, she entered the front door and tiptoed down the hallway to the medical office.

She instantly smiled at the sight. Blake sat at his desk hunched over a medical book. He didn't even know she was around. "Could you spare a few minutes for someone who isn't ill?"

Blake snapped to attention. Instead of the bright smile she'd expected, he pinned her with an icy look that immediately wilted her resolve.

"Amanda! What are you doing here? I gave you explicit medical orders. You of all people should be willing to follow orders. Surely you realize you're risking your recovery."

She folded her arms across her waist. "May I say that it's a genuine pleasure to see you, too, Dr. Carstead."

He pushed away from the desk. "No need to mock me. I doubt you thought I'd be pleased to see you here."

"Frankly, that's exactly what I thought," she said, before dropping to one of the chairs opposite his desk. "I do believe you are the man who made declarations of love while I lay dying." She touched her index finger to her lips. "Or was that some other doctor who ventured in and sat vigil by my bedside?" She settled in her chair and smiled. How she had missed bantering with Blake. He always had an excellent riposte for her.

"No other doctors were in the infirmary during your illness, but I fear you were suffering from delusions if you believe I declared my love for you, Miss Broadmoor."

"You're not fooling me in the least. I know what I heard. You're simply unwilling to declare the truth to me because you fear rejection."

"Rejection? Whatever are you talking about? Perhaps I should take your temperature. I fear you are once again suffering from hallucinations."

Amanda chuckled. "You fear my only interest in you is your medical knowledge and that if you declare your love, I will surely reject you." She held up her hand to ward off his reply. "I haven't time to sit and argue the depth of your affection for me, Doctor. I've come to Rochester to assist my cousin in her choice of a wedding gown."

"Michael has returned?" Blake asked as he rounded the desk.

"No, but she received a letter. He'll be back soon, and he's instructed her to begin preparations for a summer wedding at Broadmoor Island. *Some* men are anxious to declare their love and marry," she teased while he walked alongside her to the front door.

"And some *women* are far too anxious to hear a man declare his love and then move along to another. I believe some refer to it as the excitement of the conquest."

"I believe you're the one suffering from hallucinations, Dr. Carstead. It's men who enjoy the conquest and then move along to another woman." Amanda chuckled as she slipped her hands into her lace gloves.

Blake joined in her laughter, but as the front door opened, his smile was replaced by a look of utter disbelief. "Julia," he whispered.

A striking dark-haired woman clothed in the latest fashion brushed by Amanda and pulled Blake into an embrace. "I've come to say yes, my darling."

"Yes to *what*?" Blake attempted a backward step, but the woman held him close.

"Yes, I will marry you, dear boy."

Marry? Amanda turned on her heel and rushed from the room.

Jonas waved his brother into the library. "I thought you would be here hours ago. It's nearly one o'clock."

"There was work at the Home that needed my attention, and then I decided to partake of my noonday meal. You weren't expecting me for lunch, were you?"

"No. I was expecting you *before* the noonday meal. My note said I had an urgent matter to discuss with you. I thought you would realize that *urgent* meant you should arrive as early as possible."

Quincy nodded. "I understand the meaning of the word, Jonas. And I came as quickly as possible. Your sense of urgency doesn't always align with my own."

"Oh, do sit down. We don't have time to quibble over such nonsense." His voice held a sharp tone, and Jonas silently reminded himself he didn't want to alienate Quincy. "I apologize for my impatience, but I find myself involved in a tumultuous situation."

"Does this have something to do with Sophie, Amanda, and Fanny returning to Rochester today?"

"What? I didn't know any of them had returned home. For what purpose?" A burning sensation crept from the pit of his stomach and deposited hot bile in the back of his throat. He swallowed hard. Why had Fanny returned to Rochester? Had she discovered something and come to talk to Quincy? Worse yet, had Mr. Rosenblume summoned her back to Rochester?

"Fanny received a letter from Michael. He is returning to Broadmoor Island and has told her to make plans for a summer wedding. The girls are in Rochester to help her choose a wedding gown." Quincy scratched his head. "At least that's what Sophie told me. I saw the three of them only briefly. Amanda stopped by the Home to speak with Blake. I assumed Amanda and Fanny would be staying here overnight."

"I know nothing of their plans." Jonas could barely gather his thoughts. He needed to convey his concerns to Quincy before the girls walked in on them. But before he could regain his momentum, Quincy interrupted.

"I was surprised Victoria wasn't with the girls. Amanda said you'd written Victoria that you planned to come for a visit next week. Your wife decided to remain at the island to ensure you kept your word." Quincy appeared somewhat bemused. "I didn't know you'd made arrangements for a trip to the island."

Jonas sighed. "You don't know my plans because we seldom see each other. If we could get back to the matter at hand, I have an issue of greater concern than a visit to Broadmoor Island or the purchase of a wedding gown." He leaned across the desk. "I've been in meetings with Judge Webster regarding the estate, and we have combed through all of Mortimer's records."

"I'm sure that proved to be terribly boring."

"Quite the contrary. We discovered that Mortimer had deceived me and falsified the records he presented to the court as true and factual documents." Jonas didn't need to force himself to appear distressed. He worried that the girls would walk in the house at any minute, and he wasn't prepared to include Fanny in their discussion just yet.

Quincy frowned and shook his head. "How is that possible? Did you give Mortimer free rein? You're the man who prides himself upon keeping abreast of details. How did this slip by you?"

The questions and comments were not what Jonas had expected. He'd thought Quincy would simply acknowledge the oversight and ask for financial details. Instead, his brother appeared unconvinced that Mortimer could have accomplished such a feat without his knowledge.

"You may recall that I have had my own business matters to handle. I didn't have time to oversee all of the issues surrounding the estate. That's what a lawyer is hired to do. Rest assured that if I'd been checking on Mortimer, I wouldn't have suffered such huge losses myself. His actions have created problems for all of us."

With the revelation that Jonas had been financially affected, his brother appeared at least partially convinced. "Exactly how did Mortimer commit these transgressions?"

"From what the judge and I have unraveled thus far, it appears Mortimer commingled the money and skimmed a healthy portion off the top for himself."

"Why would he commingle the funds?"

"To make his crime more difficult to discover. It appears he'd been converting assets for his personal use for some time. Now that he's dead, we're unable to locate any of those funds. This is a financial disaster. And to think that I trusted Mortimer!"

Quincy visibly paled as he digested the unwelcome news. "This affects all of Father's estate? *All* of the Broadmoor holdings?"

"I won't be able to say with absolute certainty until we've completed our audit of all the records, but I assure you that Judge Webster has been assisting me with a plan to secure the estate from further losses."

"This is tragic news." Quincy massaged his forehead. "We ought not to tell Fanny just yet. There's no need to upset the girl with this news when she's in the midst of making plans for her wedding. However, I do hope that you've retained a reputable lawyer to help you work through this muddle."

"I haven't had sufficient time to decide upon a lawyer. I thought my first obligation was to talk to you."

"I appreciate that, Jonas. But now that we've talked, I think you must make your priority hiring a lawyer who will protect all of our interests. If you'd like me to assist you in finding someone, I'd be happy to request references from several of my acquaintances."

"No, no—that's not necessary. You're busy enough with your duties at the Home. I can make inquiries at the men's club. I'm sure one of the businessmen there can offer an excellent recommendation."

Quincy appeared shaken by the revelation, but at least he'd accepted Jonas's explanation that it was Mortimer who was at fault.

"I suppose you're correct. The men at the club could furnish an excellent recommendation."

"You do understand none of this is my fault, don't you? I hope I can count on your support."

Quincy nodded. "I know you would never intentionally do anything that would cause the family to lose any of our assets. We'll get this all worked out. Who knows, perhaps something good will come from all of this."

Jonas arched his brows. How like his brother to think something good could come from having his inheritance stolen from beneath his nose. He wanted to tell his brother he was a fool. But he remained silent. For now, Jonas needed Quincy as his ally.

"I know you'll manage to find the proper attorney to help us through this maze. You have my every confidence," Quincy continued as the men walked toward the front door.

"And we're agreed that we'll say nothing of this to anyone else," Jonas said.

"Yes. I would especially urge you to remain silent where Fanny is concerned. We don't want her unduly upset."

"You need not worry yourself in that regard. I'll not say a word."

CHAPTER 12

While still in the arms of the carriage driver, Amanda glanced over her shoulder to make certain no one had observed her. She'd let out a high-pitched yelp that should have wakened the dead. But from all appearances, no one had noticed. Or if they had, they obviously weren't concerned over her distress. In her haste to escape Blake and his beautiful visitor, she'd forgotten to lift her skirts and had snagged her hem on the toe of her shoe. Had the carriage driver not been standing nearby, she would have been thrown headlong into the front wheel of his cab.

After righting herself, she showered the driver with profuse thanks. Unfortunately she'd likely overdone it, for the poor man's face had turned the shade of a ripe tomato by the time he closed the carriage door. Once they were on their way, Amanda leaned forward and lifted the edge of her skirt to examine the stitching. She hadn't torn the fabric, but the hem would require repair before she went shopping with her cousins. Otherwise she would likely once again become tangled in the hem and end up flat on the sidewalk before day's end. A disgusted sigh escaped her lips as she dropped her skirt back into place. What had begun as an enjoyable few minutes of banter with Blake had ended in disaster.

She stared out the window and tried to convince herself she'd gone to the Home to check on the progress of ailing patients. In truth, she'd wanted to know how Blake was faring without her. She had hoped Blake would tell her he'd been rendered useless without her and beg her to remain at his side. Before going to bed last night, she'd played the scene over and over in her mind. But instead of being implored to stay, Amanda had been forced to witness a strange woman rushing into Blake's arms and accepting his marriage proposal. Tears pooled in the corners of her eyes. She batted her lashes, but to no avail. The tears trickled down her cheeks. No wonder Blake had disavowed he'd ever proclaimed his love for her. He was engaged to marry. What a fool she'd made of herself!

When they arrived at the small house belonging to Paul and Sophie, the driver jumped down and opened the door. Amanda withdrew a coin from her reticule. "For your excellent service," she said, placing the coin in his hand.

He tipped his hat. "Thank you and a good day to you, ma'am."

"I don't think it can get any worse," Amanda muttered, holding her skirts high. She climbed the front steps to Sophie's house and tapped on the door.

Within moments Sophie opened the front door. "What has happened? You look like a thundercloud about to burst."

"*I'm* not the thundercloud, but you're right about one thing. A dark cloud arrived in Rochester, and it has dumped a bucketful of cold water on my entire future." Amanda brushed past Sophie and strode into the parlor while still holding her skirt above her ankles.

"Was that Amanda I heard?" Fanny brightened when she entered the room. "I'm so pleased you've returned. We do need to be on our way."

"We can't go anywhere until I st-stitch my . . ." She waved the hem of her skirt in the air and broke into heaving sobs.

Amanda sat down and both Fanny and Sophie rushed forward. The two of them surrounded Amanda, and Fanny gathered her into a warm embrace. "Do tell us what has happened. Did you fall and injure yourself?"

"N-n-no," she sniffled. "It's B-b-blake." She accepted the handkerchief Sophie offered and wiped her eyes.

"Take a deep breath and then tell us," Fanny instructed.

After several restorative breaths, Amanda gave an affirming nod. "I think I'm better now." In between occasional sniffles, she related the unexpected and harrowing events. "Then, as I rushed down the path and through the gate, I caught my hem on the toe of my shoe and lost my balance."

Sophie straightened her shoulders. "Exactly who is this Julia woman?"

"I've told you everything I know. Blake has never mentioned her to me, but from all appearances they are very well acquainted."

Sophie's eyebrows pinched together in a frown. "Who does this Julia think she is, coming to Rochester and interfering with the man you want to marry? I've half a mind to go over there and have a long talk with her. I could set matters aright in no time."

"Sophie Medford, you'll do no such thing! Remember, you're a lady." Fanny tapped Amanda on the arm. "When did you decide you wanted to marry Dr. Carstead? The last I recall hearing, you said you wanted only to become a doctor and that he was too old for you."

"I never said he was too old." How could Fanny say such a thing? Amanda had always considered Blake quite perfect—his age, at least—if not his actions. "He is less than ten years my senior."

"If he's not ten years older, then he's nine and three-quarters," Fanny replied. "I care little about his age. It is you who took issue with his age when he first arrived."

"I don't recall any such thing. Sophie, do you remember me ever saying Dr. Carstead was too old for me to consider a suitor?"

Sophie shrugged. "As I recall, you've never wanted a suitor, no matter his age."

Amanda sighed. Their conversation was hardly relevant. It seemed Blake Carstead was a fraud. He'd never so much as hinted that he already had plans to marry. She sniffled and wiped her eyes.

"I'm sorry, Amanda. Instead of showing you proper sympathy, I've been busy asking questions." Fanny grasped Amanda's hand. "Please forgive me for my insensitivity. I think we should put aside today's shopping expedition and wait until tomorrow. The two of us should take our bags and get settled at your house, Amanda."

"I want to come along, too," Sophie put in.

Amanda blinked away her tears and glanced toward the kitchen. "What about Paul? Don't you want to remain here with him?"

"He's not very happy with me," Sophie whispered.

"All the more reason you should stay," Amanda replied. "If Paul must return to work later, you can come and join us at the house. We promise that we'll not do anything fun without you."

"I doubt the two of you would ever do anything fun or exciting if you didn't have me to urge you along." Sophie grinned. "I suppose you're correct. I'd best stay here for a while."

Fanny leaned close to Sophie's ear. "See what you can do to resolve your difficulties with Paul."

Sophie turned her gaze toward the staircase. "I will."

A sense of relief washed over Fanny once they arrived at Broadmoor Mansion and the butler informed them the master of the house had departed only a few minutes earlier. "A shame that you missed him, for he'll likely be out the remainder of the afternoon."

Fanny hoped that would be the case. The one thing she'd dreaded about this trip back to Rochester was seeing her uncle and living under his roof. If she had her way, she'd spend the majority of her time at Broadmoor Island until Michael returned. Of course, legal matters with Mr. Rosenblume might require a return to Rochester, but she hoped any such legal proceedings could be conducted without her.

"Shall we have tea prepared?" Amanda inquired.

The question pulled Fanny from her thoughts. "Yes, of course. Tea would be lovely. After today's events, we would both benefit from refreshments. I'll go to the kitchen and ask to have tea served in half an hour. That way we can go upstairs and freshen up beforehand."

"An excellent idea," Amanda said as she peered into the mirror above the mantel. "My hair is a fright and my eyes are puffy."

Fanny chuckled. "Your eyes are not puffy. You didn't cry enough to cause puffy eyes. Go on—I'll join you upstairs shortly."

The two of them parted in the foyer, Amanda turning toward the front staircase and Fanny toward the kitchen. Once Fanny had greeted the cook, she requested tea and hurried up the back staircase to her bedroom. The maid had already unpacked the few belongings she'd brought along. She had hoped they would need to stay under Uncle Jonas's roof only one night, but with Amanda's tears and the angry exchange between Paul and Sophie, they would likely be here longer than expected. She removed a dark brown gored skirt and fawn silk blouse from the wardrobe. These would do nicely for a quiet afternoon.

She was adjusting the last pin in her hair when Amanda tapped on the bedroom door and called, "Are you ready for tea?"

With a determined push, she stuck the pin into her hair, took one final look in the mirror, and hurried to the door. "I am refreshed and eager to have a cup of tea." She looped arms with her cousin. "I do hope the cook put a few of her wonderful lemon cookies on the tray. I saw she'd been baking earlier in the day."

Amanda chuckled. "If she didn't, we'll have to go in and demand our fair share."

Fanny had poured tea in both of their cups when the front doorbell rang. Marvin hastened through the hallway, and moments later Sophie appeared in the parlor doorway. "I see my timing is impeccable. I'm just in time for tea."

"Sophie! I thought you were going to spend the afternoon with Paul." Amanda set her cup and saucer on the marble-topped table and leaned forward to peek around Fanny.

"That was my intention, but soon after you departed, he told me he had an appointment at one of the local churches and then was needed at the Home for the Friendless." She took a seat across from her two cousins. "Once he left, I decided to join you two."

Paul couldn't have been at home for long, as Sophie had refashioned her hair and changed into a different dress, one that appeared brand-new. "Was Paul in good humor when you two parted?" Fanny asked.

"I believe he was rather preoccupied. He said he would call for me when he had completed his duties." Sophie helped herself to one of the lemon cookies. "If he forgets, then I may spend the night here. Are you feeling better, Amanda?"

"I suppose, but I am shocked by this secret life Blake has been leading."

"I wouldn't make any hasty judgments," Fanny cautioned. "There may be an explanation."

Sophie chortled. "An explanation? How does a man explain a woman rushing into his arms and accepting his marriage proposal? Amanda's already told us that Blake knew her. After all, he said her name, did he not?"

"I suppose there's some merit to what you're saying, but—"

"Then you do think he's an ill-bred cad," Amanda cried as she removed a handkerchief from her skirt pocket and dabbed her eyes.

"I don't think I would consider him ill bred, but perhaps a cad," Fanny said. "Of course, I knew nothing of this romance you indicate existed between the two of you, so I find it difficult to judge the man or his actions."

"Indicate? He said he loved me. I heard him when I was lying on my sickbed near death. He was praying. I know what I heard."

"This discussion is doing nothing but causing distress. I suggest we formulate our plans for tomorrow's shopping," Fanny said. "I think if we begin—"

"Good afternoon, Mr. Broadmoor." At the sound of the butler's greeting, the three cousins turned toward the foyer. "Your daughter and two of your nieces are taking tea in the front parlor."

When Jonas appeared in the doorway, Fanny met her uncle's intense stare with what she hoped was a hard look. She was determined that he would be the one to turn away first. Silly, perhaps, but she didn't want her uncle to think he frightened her. Let him worry that his disloyal behavior would cause him no end of difficulty.

"I had heard the three of you were in Rochester. I do hope you don't plan to remain here for any length of time." He set his gaze on Amanda. "I have much I need to accomplish before going to the island to visit your mother and don't need any added inconvenience."

He turned and walked off before any of them could respond to his curt announcement.

"That was certainly a fine welcome for his daughter and nieces," Fanny said. "Your father appears to have set aside all civility and love of family since your mother has departed." She glared after her uncle. "In fact, long before Aunt Victoria departed."

"There's no need for harsh words, Fanny. Father is preoccupied with his business. From what Mother tells me, he worries overmuch since the financial downturn. He doesn't want the family to suffer any losses."

Fanny attempted to shake off her feelings of disgust. The only person her uncle worried about was himself. Yet she couldn't say that to his daughter. What would Amanda think if she knew her father had thwarted her plans to attend medical school? Fanny doubted Amanda would think him such a fine patriarch if she knew he had no more character than a rotted turnip.

Jonas closed the door to his library and removed a bottle of scotch from the bottom drawer of his desk. Of late he'd taken to drinking during the afternoon, especially when he couldn't control the circumstances of his life. And that lack of control seemed to occur more and more frequently. Of all days, why had his nieces and daughter appeared in Rochester today?

He glanced at the clock. Ellert Jackson would be arriving for dinner, and he didn't want anything to go amiss. Just as the return of his daughter and nieces had come as an unwelcome surprise, Ellert's arrival in town had managed to catch him off guard. Though there should be no cause for worry, the very fact that Ellert wanted to see him caused a sense of apprehension. The liquor would quiet the demons that danced in his mind nowadays.

He tipped the glass against his lower lip and then savored the burning sensation the amber liquid created as it slid over his tongue and trickled down his throat. He finished the glass and then poured another. What could Ellert want? Their agreement had been completed, the papers had been signed, and Ellert's bank draft had been deposited in Jonas's bank account. Did Ellert call upon all the men who owed him money? Jonas attempted to quiet his fears with some simple explanation. Perhaps Ellert had other business in Rochester that required his attention. Yes, that must be it. He was paying a simple social call since he was in the city. Jonas threw back the contents of his glass and swallowed hard before returning the bottle to its hiding place. Instead of worrying, he should be pleased that Ellert had requested a social appointment.

There was nothing to fear. He had five years before his note to Ellert would come due. Granted, he had no formal plan for how he would repay the funds, but Jonas had to trust that eventually everything would work out for the best. The liquor warmed his belly, and his hands relaxed as he leaned his head against the leather chair. Everything would be fine.

Jonas didn't know how long he'd been napping in his chair when sounds of an argument interrupted his sleep. He strained to listen but couldn't hear well enough to discern the voices. He pushed away from the desk, raked his fingers through his hair, and plodded to the door.

"What's all the commotion out here?" he called. Was it Sophie? "Yes, of course," he muttered. That girl was always creating havoc. When no one responded, he used the noisy sounds to direct him. He came to a halt outside the parlor doors. Paul and Sophie were in the midst of a disagreement, and it seemed Fanny and Amanda were spectators for the event. "Exactly *what* is going on in here?"

Sophie turned on her uncle and sent an icy glare in his direction. "This has nothing to do with you, Uncle Jonas. I am having a discussion with my husband."

"If you don't want my interference, I suggest you keep your voices down. I would think you could control your wife, Paul."

"*Control* his wife?" Sophie fired. "I am not a servant that is employed to do his bidding, Uncle Jonas. I am a woman with a mind of my own."

"Yes, we all realize you insist upon making your own choices, even when they're to your own detriment."

"I believe I can deal with Sophie without your interference, Jonas."

"Deal with me?" Sophie stomped her foot and glared at Paul. "What is that—"

The doorbell rang and interrupted Sophie's response. Jonas waved at his relatives. "If we could please maintain a modicum of dignity, it would be appreciated. Before I knew all of you would be here this evening, I invited a business associate and old friend to join me for supper."

Paul beckoned to Sophie. "Perhaps we should leave. We can continue this discussion at home."

"There is nothing to discuss. If you want to see Elizabeth, you can come to the island."

Jonas sighed. He had better things to worry over than where Paul would visit his child. "Answer the door!" Jonas called to the butler when the doorbell rang for the second time. "And I expect all of you to be on your best behavior. Amanda, you can act as hostess since your mother is absent." Jonas didn't fail to note Fanny and Sophie glaring at him before he exited the room to greet Ellert.

Jonas hastened to explain as he led Ellert into the parlor. "Some members of my family arrived home unexpectedly earlier today. I'm certain you'll enjoy the pleasure of their company while we dine."

"Why, I'd be delighted. During the years I lived in Rochester, I don't believe I ever had the pleasure of meeting any members of your family. This is a genuine pleasure."

An undeniable hint of satisfaction shone in his guest's eyes as Jonas introduced him. Though Jonas couldn't guess why, Ellert appeared inordinately interested in chatting with Paul as well as the three young women. Thankfully, the butler entered and announced dinner before any of them made an inappropriate remark. Now, if they would simply eat their meal in silence, all would go well. The effects of his scotch had worn off, and his nerves were on edge. He could have downed another drink before Ellert's arrival if Sophie hadn't been in the parlor squabbling like a fishwife.

"And where did you purchase yet another new gown?" Paul inquired as they prepared to exit the parlor.

"You need not worry. I didn't spend any of your money," Sophie rebutted.

While Mr. Jackson escorted Amanda into the dining room, Jonas stepped between Paul and Sophie. "Would the two of you *please* cease this bickering for the duration of the meal? I care little what you do once you are out of my house. But I am entertaining a guest and expect your cooperation. Now, go in there and act like civilized adults."

"I'll not say a word," Sophie hissed in return.

Jonas tugged on the corner of his vest as he made his way to the head of the dining table. Amanda was seated to the right of Jonas; Paul took the seat to his left. Sophie sat between Paul and Fanny. Mr. Jackson had taken the chair beside Amanda and was making an unsuccessful attempt to engage her in conversation.

The silence around the table was deafening. Jonas was accustomed to his wife leading the dinner conversation while he simply enjoyed the food. Tonight, however, it appeared he'd be required to perform this social duty. "Do tell us what brings you to Rochester, Ellert."

"I had a few business matters that required my attention, but let's not discuss business during this fine meal." He smiled at Amanda. "Perhaps your daughter could regale us with a story or two. Won't you tell me about your plans, Miss Broadmoor?" His gaze settled on Amanda's left ring finger. "I don't see any evidence that an immediate wedding is in your future."

Amanda stiffened. "I have no interest in discussing that particular topic, Mr. Jackson."

Jonas chuckled, hoping his laughter would lessen the impact of his daughter's strident response. "Amanda envisions becoming a doctor." Jonas grinned. "Her application for medical school wasn't approved, so she's been helping one of the local doctors at the Home for the Friendless."

Ellert shook his head as if in disbelief. "Why, I would think any university would be pleased, even proud, to have such a beautiful and intelligent woman in their numbers."

"I'm certain the school would have been delighted to have such a brilliant student if her application had been received in a timely manner." Fanny leaned forward and flashed a look of hatred at her uncle.

Jonas flinched at his niece's tone and her angry stare. Did she have knowledge about what he'd done? Foolish thought! He'd burned that letter from the school. Hadn't he? He attempted to recall exactly what he'd done with that missive.

Ellert's attention remained fixed upon Amanda. "So you're training with another doctor, but you'd prefer medical school. Is that correct?"

"I don't wish to discuss my education at the moment, Mr. Jackson. You and my father must have far more interesting topics you'd like to discuss."

"My daughter and nieces have been at Broadmoor Island. They left during the cholera epidemic and have returned to Rochester for a shopping trip. They'll be leaving in a day or two. Isn't that correct, Amanda?"

"That's correct. However, the outbreak of cholera here wasn't a true epidemic, Father. In truth, Rochester lost few lives. There is no comparison to the epidemic of 1852. Uncle Quincy said that epidemic was a genuine tragedy. If the city would enforce the sanitation codes, we'd have far fewer worries of disease."

Mr. Jackson chuckled. "You have a daughter who is intelligent beyond her years." He turned toward Amanda. "I will tell you why those codes aren't enforced, Miss Broadmoor. It is because high-powered men are willing to grease the palms of those in authority in order to bypass the rules."

Amanda arched her brows. "Men such as yourself, Mr. Jackson?"

Mr. Jackson placed his palm against his chest. "*Me?* No, Miss Broadmoor. I don't even own property in Rochester. But your father could affirm that I speak the truth. Couldn't you, Jonas?"

Jonas shifted in his chair, annoyed by Ellert's snide remark and irritated that the conversation had taken a turn he didn't like. "I'm sure there is truth in Mr. Jackson's comment. However, I don't believe I could produce a list for you, Amanda. Now, if we could discuss something of greater interest to all of us, I think that would be wise."

"There's always the weather," Fanny remarked while feigning a yawn.

A stifling quiet hovered over the dining room like the stillness before a storm. With each bite, Jonas worried that Amanda or Fanny would say something to irritate Ellert. Fortunately, Sophie had maintained her vow of silence—out of anger either at Paul or at him. Jonas cared little as long as she didn't speak.

The moment they'd completed their final course, Jonas pushed away from the table and suggested Ellert join him in the library for brandy and a cigar. The sooner he could get Jackson away from family members, the better. Although Ellert gave only a nod to the other guests at the table, he kissed the back of Amanda's hand and said he hoped they'd soon meet again. He couldn't hear his daughter's response or the rest of what was said, but Ellert chuckled when he finally stood and followed Jonas from the room. Jonas hoped his laughter was a good sign and that Amanda hadn't offended the man. She certainly hadn't been herself at supper this evening. He'd need to speak to Victoria. Obviously their daughter needed further training in proper etiquette.

After Ellert lit his cigar, Jonas poured two snifters of brandy and handed one to his guest, who sat down in one of the leather chairs near the library fireplace. Jonas held a match to his cigar and puffed until the tip fired bright orange. "I do hope you enjoyed dinner. My family can sometimes be . . . shall we say, less than affable."

"No need to apologize, Jonas. I'm not easily offended by the social set. You'll recollect I was generally snubbed by Rochester society during the years I lived here."

"Were you? I don't seem to recall." Jonas took a sip of his brandy and hoped it would calm his nerves. "So have you come to Rochester to invest in a new business?"

"No. Merely checking on a few of my holdings, and I thought I'd see if you were taking steps toward repayment of your loan by Christmas."

Jonas startled and met Ellert's intense gaze. "Christmas? When we discussed the contract, we both agreed that it would be five years from this Christmas— Christmas of 1904 was what we said."

"You're right. We did mention a date that was in 1904, but if you'll read your contract, I believe you'll see that your loan comes due this Christmas."

"That's impossible!" Jonas said, jumping to his feet. He set his brandy on the corner of his desk. With his cigar clenched between his teeth, Jonas pulled open his desk drawer and retrieved a file. With trembling fingers, he dropped the file onto his desk and riffled through the papers. When he'd finally located the contract, he pulled it from the pile and waved the white pages in the air. "Here it is!" He dropped to the large leather chair behind his desk and traced his index finger down the page.

When he reached the middle of the second page, Jonas ceased reading and looked up. A gleam of satisfaction shone in Ellert's eyes. How had this happened? In the past, Mortimer had reviewed Jonas's contracts. But Mortimer was dead, and Jonas had quickly perused the pages. He'd had no reason to doubt the terms would be exactly as they'd discussed.

"But you knew I thought it said 1904," Jonas croaked. "What would you have done if I'd noticed the incorrect date?"

Ellert shrugged. "If you'd objected or if you'd had a lawyer read the terms and protested the provision, I would have been required to reassess the terms. However, you didn't, and the contract is valid."

"I can't possibly pay you by Christmas. Why, I won't even have the issues surrounding Fanny's inheritance settled by Christmas. Be reasonable, Jackson."

"You owe the money, and I intend to collect in a timely manner and according to the terms of the contract."

"Surely you understand I'm in an extremely difficult place right now."

"Indeed, I do. I understand difficult situations better than most, Jonas. You played a large part in one of the most harrowing times in my life."

Jonas picked up the glass of brandy and downed the contents before returning to the chair beside Ellert. "I don't know what you're talking about." He waited for the brandy to quiet his fears.

"Don't you?" Ellert took a puff on his cigar and blew a smoke ring into the air. "Then it was completely insignificant to you that I was forced to sell my family home in order to repay a debt I owed you years ago?"

Jonas raked his fingers through his hair and forced himself to think back to the loan he'd made to Ellert, but he couldn't recall ever forcing any man to sell his home in order to repay a loan. He shook his head. "You have me confused with someone else."

"No. It was *you*, Jonas. I sold my family's home to pay your debt."

"But I didn't force you to sell. I didn't know—"

"Of course you didn't. I wasn't about to let you know!" He sipped the brandy and placed the glass on the table between them. "Selling my family's home caused me a great deal of pain, Jonas. I believe it is only fair that you suffer the way I have suffered. You'll have to part with something you love in order to meet your obligation to me."

"But I can't let anyone know the details of the situation," Jonas protested. "Not only that, but I can't touch any of my properties."

"What of the Broadmoor Island estate?"

"It's bound by legal terms to remain in the family. Currently there are other members who hold shares in the property, but none of whom could afford to buy out my portion."

"And what of your home—your business affairs?"

"As I stated, I cannot let anyone know what has happened, or my reputation will be ruined and there will be no hope of me reclaiming my fortune. I can't even suggest selling this place for a smaller home without my wife and sons questioning me. Besides, you know full well it wouldn't come close to paying off what I owe you."

Ellert smiled in a smug manner. "I suppose it wouldn't, but mark my words, Jonas. I care little for your reputation or good standing with your family. You owe me, and you will pay me."

"But I can't do it by Christmas. Surely it is in your own best interest to give me an extension. That way at least you will receive regular payments and eventually the entire note will be redeemed."

"Father?" Jonas turned to see Amanda standing in the library doorway.

He waved her forward, glad for the momentary reprieve. "What is it, my dear?"

"I've had a tiresome day, and tomorrow will be filled with shopping. If you have no need of me, I'm going to retire for the night."

"Of course. You go upstairs, and I'll see you at breakfast."

She leaned down and placed a kiss on his cheek and then glanced toward her father's guest. "Good night, Mr. Jackson. I trust you'll have an enjoyable visit in Rochester."

He smiled broadly. "I already have. I had the pleasure of meeting *you*, Miss Broadmoor." Ellert stared after Jonas's daughter and then shifted in his chair. "Now what was it we were talking about? Oh yes, an extension. Perhaps if you had something of value to offer me, I might be convinced that extending your note terms would be of benefit to us both."

Jonas shook his head. "I have nothing."

Ellert glanced at the door through which Amanda had just exited. "I believe you have something of great value, Jonas. Something you can give me that will cause me to reconsider the terms of our agreement."

Amanda's shoes clicked on the tile and echoed through the hallway as she strode toward the staircase. When she neared the foyer, a knock at the front door surprised her. The butler had gone upstairs to turn down her father's bed. "Who could that be?" she muttered.

She opened the door and took a backward step. Hat in hand, Blake Carstead stood in front of her. Before she could close the door, he stepped over the threshold. "We need to talk. From your hasty departure earlier today, I fear you formed some incorrect assumptions."

"I made some assumptions, but I doubt they are incorrect, Dr. Carstead."

He pointed toward the parlor. "Could we sit down and talk for just a moment? I can explain if you'll only give me the opportunity."

Although she desperately wanted to hear how he could possibly explain this afternoon's happenings, she didn't want him to think her overly interested. Nor did she want him to know how deeply he'd hurt her. She'd not let that happen again. "I was preparing to go upstairs to bed. I've already bid my father good-night."

"I promise to be brief. Please?"

In spite of her best intentions, there was a longing in his voice she couldn't deny. "We can't go into the parlor. My father has a business associate meeting with him in the library. Their visit may end shortly, and I wouldn't want my father to find you with me this late at night and without a proper chaperone. Whatever you have to say must be said right here." Blake didn't argue. He was probably surprised that she'd even speak to him. And after what she'd observed, he should be!

"I know you were both surprised and shocked when Julia appeared this afternoon. However, your surprise can't begin to match my own."

Amanda tapped her foot. "I don't intend to argue about which of us was more surprised. Go on with your story."

He pressed the brim of his hat between his fingers. "When I was living in California, I met Julia. She was an important part of my life. I fell deeply in love with her and asked her to be my wife."

Amanda sucked in a breath of air. *So Julia* was *his fiancée!*

"Julia said yes, but a few weeks later, she told me she'd chosen to marry someone else. A man who'd be able to provide for her in much better fashion than a doctor could. After she gave me her decision, I left California." He took a step closer. "Now, after nearly two years, she has shown up to tell me that she made the wrong decision and that she loves me and wants to marry me."

"I don't know why you're telling me all of this. You don't owe *me* any explanation. Go ahead and marry Julia. I don't care one bit."

She turned on her heel and started toward the stairs, but before she had taken more than a step, Blake grasped her by the hand, pulled her into his arms, and captured her lips in a passionate kiss.

Amanda melted into Blake's arms and felt her lips form perfectly to his. Her heart pounded an erratic beat, and his kiss sent shivers of excitement racing through her body. She'd never experienced such a feeling.

She drew even closer, but he pulled away from her and looked deep into her eyes. "*Now* tell me that you don't care." Without another word, he released her and walked out the door.

CHAPTER 13

MONDAY, JUNE 26, 1899
BROADMOOR ISLAND

A few days after the cousins returned to Broadmoor Island, the door to Amanda's room creaked open, startling her. She clasped a hand over her heart. "Sophie! You should knock before you enter."

"I'm sorry. I shouldn't laugh, but the look on your face . . ." She clapped her hand over her mouth and burst into a fit of giggles. Tears rolled down her cheeks as she crossed the room and dropped into a chair near the window.

"I don't believe I looked *that* funny." Amanda yanked a handkerchief from the top drawer of her chest and tossed it at her cousin. "Did you come here for a purpose or simply to see if you could frighten me?"

Sophie wiped her eyes. "I'm sorry. I shouldn't have laughed." A loud snort followed the apology, and she clapped a hand over her mouth again.

"Somehow it's difficult to believe you're truly sorry when your words are laced with laughter." Amanda dropped to the edge of the bed. "Are you enjoying Paul's visit?"

Amanda hoped her cousin would answer in the affirmative, for Sophie had been less than pleased when Paul had unexpectedly arrived at the island with Amanda's father Friday evening. The tension between the young couple was obvious.

"Enjoying? Haven't you noticed how he's put a damper on every suggestion

I make? I was so looking forward to the party at the Frontenac Hotel, but Paul won't even consider attending." She shook her head and a hairpin dropped to the floor. A rich coffee-colored tress fell across her forehead.

"No doubt he simply desires time alone with you and Elizabeth. After being away from you and the baby, you can understand his feelings." Amanda arched her brows, hoping for a positive response from her cousin. It seemed the young couple had been quarreling ever since Paul's arrival. Amanda hoped she could somehow smooth the waters.

"Oh, *pshaw*! Quit defending him, Amanda. You've done nothing but come to his defense since he set foot on the island. He's the one who banished me to this place, but now that I'm enjoying myself, he thinks I should return home."

"And you disagreed?" Amanda couldn't withhold her alarm. "You need to reconsider, Sophie."

"We're in the midst of planning Fanny's wedding. I can't possibly go back to Rochester while the two of you are here. Absolutely not! I told Paul that once we've completed all of the arrangements, I'll return." She picked up the hairpin and walked to the mirror. "Of course, that may not be until after Fanny's wedding." With a deft hand, she refashioned the fallen tress and jabbed the hairpin into the wayward curl. "There! That should hold it in place."

"I'm not certain your decision is wise."

Sophie shrugged. "And I don't believe your assessment of Paul's reasoning is correct. Elizabeth was in bed for the night long before we would have left Broadmoor Island to attend the party." Sophie returned to the chair and picked up one of Amanda's books from the small table. "He said he was too tired from all his work these past weeks. You may recall that while we were playing charades, he retired early Saturday night. Is that the picture of a man who desires his wife's company?"

The question brought a vision of Blake's unabashed kiss to mind. Amanda felt the heat rise in her cheeks as she remembered how thoroughly she had enjoyed the feel of his body next to her own and the surprising softness of his lips as they'd taken command over hers. Yet she dared not think of a future with Blake. He'd stunned her with his kiss and walked out the door without a word.

Even though Blake had told her of his past with Julia, he hadn't admitted he no longer loved the woman. Why, he'd not even asked her to remain in Rochester. She had hoped he would send word or reappear and tell her of his love, but he hadn't. Now she decided the best thing was to erase any feelings for Blake Carstead from her mind and concentrate on Fanny's wedding plans.

Amanda forced her thoughts back to the present. "Perhaps you should reconsider your decision and tell Paul you'll return to Rochester. You've helped choose the fabric for our dresses and Fanny's gown, and I believe Fanny would concur that you belong at home with Paul." Amanda turned toward her cousin. "Did you hear what—"

Sophie dangled a newspaper clipping between her index finger and thumb. "Exactly *when* did you plan to tell me about this?"

"What?" Amanda paled as she focused upon the news clipping. Her stomach lurched as she attempted to gather her thoughts.

Sophie held the clipping at arm's length and waved it back and forth as she walked toward Amanda. "How long have you been hiding this from me?"

"Hiding? I wasn't hiding it from you. Frankly, I didn't believe it was anything that would be of interest now that you're happily married with a family." Amanda fervently hoped the word *happily* still applied to her cousin's marriage.

"If you didn't think it was important, why did you cut it out of the newspaper? And how long have you known about Wesley's inheritance?"

"I can't recall exactly." Choosing her words carefully, Amanda explained how she'd happened upon the item in one of the many stacks of reading material Blake had given her to read while she was recuperating. "I was surprised by the information and cut it out. I wish I'd never seen it, yet I don't see how it should matter in the least."

"Not matter? Wesley Hedrick has inherited a vast fortune and you think I wouldn't be interested?"

"Tell me, Sophie, exactly *why* would news of Wesley interest you?" Amanda walked to the window. "Look down there at your husband playing with Elizabeth." She grasped Sophie by the arm. "Come here. Look at them and tell me why you should care about Wesley Hedrick or his inheritance."

Sophie jerked free and turned on her heel. Her shoes pounded across the carpet. She yanked open the door and then slammed it behind her, the bedroom window rattling in the quake.

When had life become so complicated? Back when Amanda and her cousins had been young girls, life had been so simple and problem free. Now it seemed there was upheaval at every turn.

Amanda opened her bedroom door, and as if on cue, she heard her parents arguing. Was there no peace to be found anywhere in this house? She did a quick turnaround and proceeded to the rear stairway, where she could avoid the possibility of being drawn into the dissension. Careful to avoid Paul and the other relatives on the front lawn, she took the path leading from the rear door to the north end of the island. Only a short distance down the path, she heard the crackle of branches and looked overhead. The wind had picked up, but the sky remained a cloudless azure blue. No storm in sight. Not unless she counted the storms that raged among her relatives.

She turned toward a rustling of leaves, took a backward step, and inhaled a deep breath. "Fanny! I didn't know you were out here."

"I was at the outcropping overlooking the water. I find it a good place to gather my thoughts."

"You're not having second thoughts about the wedding, are you?"

"No, of course not. I love Michael with all my heart and can't wait for his return. I only wish he were here now."

"Be careful what you wish for. We've not yet completed your wedding preparations." Amanda observed the brooding look in Fanny's eyes. Even *she* was unhappy. "Do tell me what's wrong. You don't seem yourself. Ever since Father and Paul arrived, you've distanced yourself from the rest of us."

"To be honest, I don't want to be around your father."

"Whyever not? I know he can be brusque and unapproachable at times, but—"

"I don't think we should discuss this any further. I don't want to say anything that will cause a rift between us."

"You know that could never occur. No matter what happens, you and Sophie will always remain dear to me. I believe I could tell you anything and you would understand. I only wish you felt the same way about me." Amanda didn't know which she found more distressing: the fact that Fanny wouldn't confide in her or the idea that her cousin believed there was something that could cause a breach in their relationship. "I *want* you to tell me what's wrong. I promise whatever you have to say will not change how I feel about you."

Fanny sighed. "I truly need to talk to someone, if you're certain you want to hear. But be forewarned, what I say about him will not be pleasant to hear."

"My mother has probably said worse. Don't you recall her anger when Father didn't accompany us on our voyage to England?"

"I believe this goes far beyond anything any member of your family might imagine." Fanny paused and gave another sigh. "I don't want to go into all of the details, but I have ample proof that you father has cheated me out of a great deal of my inheritance. Your father betrayed me. I shouldn't have given him the authority to continue managing my inheritance." Fanny reached forward and grasped Amanda's arm. "I'm sorry to tell you this, but now you know why I find it difficult to be in his presence."

Amanda swallowed the lump that had quickly formed in her throat. How could her father do such a thing? Didn't he have enough money without stealing from Fanny? It seemed his greed knew no boundaries. "Have you confronted him? How did this come to light?"

"When his lawyer died, the situation was brought to my attention. Your father is aware of the fact that I have hired Grandfather's former attorney, Mr. Rosenblume, to act on my behalf."

Amanda dropped to the ground and stared across the grassy expanse toward the distant horizon, where water and sky met in melding shades of blue. She wondered if her mother knew of her father's treacherous behavior. Was this the cause of the argument she'd heard when she departed the house?

Jonas placed a firm hand along the center of his wife's back and moved her toward the parlor. "I don't believe we should be having this discussion in the foyer. If you want to talk, I suggest we go into the other room."

Once they'd entered the parlor, Jonas closed the pocket doors. Of late, Victoria seemed determined to discuss everything in detail. He sighed. No wonder he stayed in Rochester as much as possible when the family was on the island. He didn't want to hear trivial details about the fabric for Fanny's wedding dress or the fact that Victoria didn't like the china or glassware Fanny had chosen. He'd done his best to avoid any wedding talk, but Victoria had been insistent they must talk. Thus far, it seemed Amanda, Sophie, and Fanny were his wife's favored topics.

"I am concerned about all three of the girls. Sophie and Paul appear to be having a disagreement, Amanda has been despondent since her return from Rochester, and Fanny has avoided the entire family since you and Paul arrived."

"First of all, they are not *girls*, Victoria. All three of them are young women, and you should cease your ongoing attempts to coddle them."

"Coddle them? I'm doing no such thing. I'm simply attempting to find out what is causing all the discord among the family of late."

"Of late? When has there been anything but dissension in this family?" Jonas glanced about the room. With a grunt he sat down on the divan. "Why isn't there one comfortable chair in this parlor?" He felt like an oversized bird perched on a fragile branch.

"I'm especially concerned about Amanda. Something happened with Dr. Carstead while she was in Rochester, but that's as much as I've been able to learn from her. When I've pressed her for more information, she refuses to confide in me."

While his entire financial world was tumbling down around his ears and his contractual obligations to Ellert Jackson were resulting in disaster, Victoria was worried about nothing more important than Amanda's preoccupied state of mind. What would Victoria do if she were faced with a genuine problem? He felt the perspiration bead along his forehead. No doubt he would soon discover the answer to that question.

"Did you hear me, Jonas? I believe she's in love with him, and they had a spat while she was in Rochester. Did you notice anything while she was at home?"

Jonas pulled his handkerchief from his pocket and wiped his forehead. "No, Victoria. I had concerns of greater import that required my attention."

"I'm sure it was something that had to do with business—that seems to be the only thing of importance to you anymore. I want you to speak with Dr. Carstead and see if—"

"Whether or not she's had an argument with Dr. Carstead does not matter. Amanda has no future with him."

"Please, Jonas. Don't bring up the topic of an arranged marriage again. You know that I truly do not approve. Dr. Carstead is a fine man, and even though he isn't wealthy, he is well educated and is esteemed in the community. I believe he would make a fine husband for Amanda."

Jonas pushed himself up from his uncomfortable perch and began pacing the carpet. "Another man has requested Amanda's hand in marriage."

For a moment Jonas thought his wife had been struck dumb. But then she jumped up, grabbed the sleeve of his jacket, and shouted, "*Whaaat*? That's impossible. Amanda hasn't had a gentleman caller of any sort. Who could be asking for her hand?"

Jonas led her to the divan. "Do sit down. You look as though you may faint."

She permitted him to assist her to the couch, but she pulled on his sleeve until he sat down beside her. "Tell me this is your attempt at humor, Jonas."

"I'm afraid not, my dear. The truth is, Ellert Jackson has professed his love for Amanda and has requested permission to marry her."

The color returned to Victoria's cheeks. "Amanda doesn't even know him. It's inconceivable that you would mention his name as a possible suitor for our daughter. Even if Amanda loved him, I would expect you to refuse his offer of marriage. And the fact that you would force her to consider such a marriage is beyond my belief. Why, they would have little in common."

"He's a successful businessman who respects Amanda's interests in medicine. He would be a good match."

"A good match? She doesn't know him. That fact aside, he's nearly your age, Jonas. He's far too old for Amanda. She's young and vibrant and deserves a husband her own age. Amanda doesn't want to marry someone who reminds her of her father."

"Nonsense. Ellert's hair has turned prematurely white. He is only forty-five, which is an acceptable age for Amanda."

"No! I will not allow it. If you attempt to proceed with this ridiculous match, I'll do everything in my power to stop you, Jonas. I want our daughter to marry for love, and I am certain she loves Dr. Carstead."

Pain shot up the tendons at the base of his skull, and Jonas massaged his neck. He had foolishly hoped that Victoria would easily acquiesce to this arrangement and he wouldn't be forced to lay out the brutal facts of their finances. He'd known that he'd be required to admit the truth to Victoria eventually, for there was no doubt Ellert would be quick to tell Amanda that she had been given in marriage as payment of her father's debt. The words sounded harsh, but Jonas salved his conscience with the fact that such marriage arrangements had been an accepted practice for many years. Amanda would be happy once she reconciled herself to the idea.

Victoria rose to her feet and folded her arms across her waist. "I mean what I say, Jonas. I will not agree."

"Sit down, Victoria." She had left him no choice: He must tell her. "I want you to listen to me carefully. This is not a decision I have made lightly. However, it is a decision that must be followed. We are in dire financial straits. I don't mean that we are suffering a slight problem, Victoria. I owe Ellert Jackson a great deal of money. If Amanda does not marry him, everything we own will be at risk. *Everything!* Do I make myself clear?"

CHAPTER 14

SATURDAY, JULY 1, 1899

Amanda picked her way along the path following Fanny's footsteps. The sunshine filtered through the trees, creating a splotchy patchwork along the trail. The day was beautiful, but she couldn't put aside thoughts of what her father had done to Fanny—to all of them. How could he be so deceiving?

"This shortcut will take us directly to the kitchen," Fanny called over her shoulder. They'd been finishing their picnic lunch when Fanny announced that she needed to return to talk with Mrs. Atwell.

"I do wish you would have told me you'd made plans for this afternoon before we arranged for our picnic. I had hoped to spend the entire afternoon away from the house. I told Mother we wouldn't return until supper."

"I'm sorry, but you're welcome to join me. I promised to discuss some of the wedding plans with Michael's mother. I don't want her to feel excluded. She's insisting on preparing much of the food, and she's going to bake our wedding cake." Fanny's eyes sparkled with excitement.

"I don't know how you can just go on as if nothing has happened. Fanny, I can't even begin to understand what my father has done."

Fanny stopped and took hold of Amanda's hands. "It cuts me deeply to know the pain I've caused you in revealing the truth. I should never have said anything."

"No. You were right to tell me everything. I can't help but wonder how many other lies have been told."

Fanny frowned and looked away. "I've been praying about such things. I know that nothing can be gained by dwelling on the bad. We must think of the good." She smiled. "That's why I choose to think of Michael and how much I love him. When I think of him and that we'll be married very shortly, nothing else seems as important."

The feelings of envy that filled Amanda's heart surprised her. She loved Fanny and wanted Michael to return and marry her cousin. There was nothing she desired any more than to see Fanny and Michael happily wed—or was there? The sudden stab of jealousy stopped her in her tracks. She forced herself to trudge onward. She didn't want Fanny to question her. Not now. Not when she couldn't understand these strange, unwelcome feelings.

Amanda spotted Mrs. Atwell's skirt and shoes below the line of damp clothes hanging on the line. As they drew closer, the older woman leaned down, lifted a towel from the basket, and flipped it in the air with a loud snap. A bright smile creased her face the moment she spotted them. "Just in time for tea," she called.

"Don't tell her we've just finished our picnic," Fanny whispered.

"I'm not a dolt. I wouldn't refuse her hospitality." There was a sharpness to her words that she hadn't intended.

Fanny spun around. "I've hurt your feelings. I'm so sorry. That wasn't my intent."

A rush of guilt washed over Amanda. "No need to apologize. I'm the one who was short with you. Forgive me. I want to choose better things to dwell on, but my father's actions have grieved me in a way I cannot explain. He has wronged you, Fanny. I would rather he had wronged me a hundred times than to have hurt you."

"Don't say such things," Fanny said, shaking her head. "There is pain enough to go around."

"But I needn't add to it. I'm sorry."

Fanny smiled and grasped Amanda's hand. "Then all is well. I'm so thankful to have you. Life wouldn't be the same without you and Sophie."

Mrs. Atwell gathered up the empty clothes basket and joined them. "Come along, you two. I have the tea brewing, and I've made some special tea cakes." Her gaze settled on the picnic basket dangling from Amanda's arm. "You're probably not hungry right now, but if you come down later, I'll be sure and save some for you."

While Fanny followed the older woman inside, Amanda set the picnic basket beside the back door and then joined them. Mrs. Atwell scooted close to Fanny with a list of items she'd already prepared for Fanny's review.

"I believe the wedding cake should be the bride's choice, so you tell me what you have in mind."

"Both Michael and I have a special fondness for your lemon pound cake. Do you think that would be appropriate?"

Mrs. Atwell beamed. "I don't know. You two know far more about fancy weddings than I do. What do you think, Amanda?"

"I'm not certain—"

Before she could complete her reply, Fanny jabbed her elbow into Amanda's side. "But that's exactly why we're having the wedding here at Broadmoor Island. We don't want to conform to what everyone else does. We want a wedding that is special and meaningful to both of us. And I think a lemon pound cake will be perfect." Fanny patted the older woman's work-worn hand. "If it will make you feel better, we'll ask Michael. He should be home any day now."

"That's fine by me," the older woman said. "We'll have time to decide once he's home."

"What if he doesn't come home?" The words had slipped from Amanda's thoughts to her lips, and now it was too late to take them back. Both Fanny and Mrs. Atwell stared at her, gape-mouthed. You would have thought she'd uttered a sacrilege. "That is a possibility, isn't it? After all, he didn't come home last year when he was expected. And now it's July and he said he'd be home in June. . . . He could be delayed again."

"I have faith he'll be home," Mrs. Atwood replied. "Mr. Atwood, Fanny, and I have been fervently praying that nothing will stand in the way of his expected return. We're trusting God will bring Michael home to us."

Amanda didn't argue. Perhaps God would answer their prayers. Yet she remembered Fanny's praying for that same thing last year, and God hadn't seen fit to send Michael back to her then. "I believe I'll go and see if there are any plans being made for this evening."

She thought Fanny would protest her departure, but when she didn't, Amanda slipped out of the room unnoticed. All this talk of weddings served as an ongoing reminder of Blake and Julia. Had the woman remained in Rochester and managed to convince Blake that she would be the perfect wife for him? Since she'd heard nothing from him, Amanda could only assume they had resumed their relationship. A woman wouldn't come all the way from California and then give up easily. Especially not a woman as forward as Julia. Why, she was probably planning their wedding this very minute.

"*There* you are!" Her father's voice boomed from the lower porch. Startled, Amanda looked up to see him waving her forward. "Come into the house. I need to talk with you."

She couldn't imagine why her father would want to talk to her. He seldom said more than a few words in passing, and now knowing what he had done to Fanny, she really didn't want to speak to him at all. "Is something wrong? Mother hasn't taken ill, has she?"

He shook his head. "Your mother is fine. She's waiting for us in the library."

What possible reason could her parents have to join together and speak to her? Her heart skipped a beat. Had her mother managed to convince her father to use his influence so that she could be enrolled in medical school during the next year? Surely not. He'd been adamant that he'd never agree. What then? Had Blake spoken to her father and asked permission to court her? The very thought caused her mouth to go dry. That must be it! Why else would they want to speak with her?

Hurrying her step, she followed behind her father like a small child expecting a treat. She stopped short at the sight of her mother. From her mother's appearance, this would not be a pleasant conversation. Her complexion was pale, and her red puffy eyes were evidence she'd been crying.

Amanda rushed over to her mother's side. "What's happened?"

The question was enough to release a floodgate of tears. They spilled down her mother's cheeks unchecked. She pointed to Amanda's father. "Y-y-your f-father will t-t-tell you. I ca-ca-can't." Her mother dabbed her eyes and then pinned Amanda's father with any icy stare.

"All these tears are frightening me. Exactly what is this about?" In spite of the warmness of the room, Amanda's hands were now trembling. A part of her was afraid to hear, while another part of her felt an urgent need to know exactly what had caused her mother's tears.

"Sit down, Amanda." Her father closed the library door. He waited until she had taken a seat beside her mother. "Our family has a critical problem, and you are the only one who can resolve it for us."

She thought of the things Fanny had told her. Was there something more to this than her cousin had confessed? "I can hardly believe there is anything I can do or say to help in matters so desperate that my mother is left in tears."

"Just hear me out," her father replied. "You'll understand soon enough."

Amanda sat in stunned silence while her father told her of the plan that would save the entire family from financial ruin. When he finished, he stared at her with an intensity that made her look away.

"Well? Will you do it? Will you marry Ellert Jackson?"

"Surely you don't expect an answer this very minute, Father. You've only just told me of a plan—your plan—that will completely alter my life, and you want me to give it no thought?"

His eyes burned her like hot coals. "You realize I could have agreed to the arrangement without speaking to you. However, I wanted you to understand the seriousness of our financial situation."

"I do understand, but that doesn't change the fact that I need time to make my decision. I don't even know Mr. Jackson, and he's old enough to be my father. He's not a man I would choose to marry under normal circumstances, so please permit me time to weigh a decision that will affect the remainder of my life."

"She's right, Jonas. Go along upstairs, Amanda. I'll be up shortly, and we'll talk."

She bolted from her chair and hurried out of the room without giving her father the opportunity to object. Once inside the sanctuary of her room, she threw herself across the bed and considered what her father had done in light of what Fanny had already told her. There had been a brief moment when she'd considered confronting her father, but what purpose would it serve? Her mother was already devastated beyond belief. No need to create further havoc.

Her thoughts raced back to the supper shared with Ellert Jackson at her home. Had the idea of marriage been discussed in her father's library that evening in Rochester? She forced herself to recall every detail of that meeting. Mr. Jackson had done his best to draw her into conversation during supper, but she'd been preoccupied with thoughts of Blake and Julia. She hadn't given the man any indication that she held any interest in him. Instead, she'd been rather rude. In retrospect, she recalled his lingering gaze when she had entered the library to bid her father good-night. He seemed pleasant enough, but the idea of courtship had never even been discussed. How could she possibly consider marriage to the man? Did Ellert Jackson truly hold regard for her after one simple meeting?

"People often marry without being in love," her father had told her at one point in their conversation that evening.

Amanda thought of Blake and the pain she felt in misunderstanding his feelings for her. Maybe emotional love was not at all what she had believed it to be. Perhaps her father's idea of an arranged marriage truly merited consideration. After all, letting her heart choose for her had done Amanda little good.

JULY 4, 1899

Amanda descended the staircase carrying three thin ribbons between her fingers. She was determined to put aside her sorrow and concerns and enjoy the Independence Day celebration. Spotting Fanny and Sophie on the front porch, she walked outside and waved the red, white, and blue strands overhead. "Look what I've found. Now Elizabeth can join our Fourth of July tradition and wear ribbons that match ours."

Sophie ran her fingers through the baby's thin fluff of hair and giggled. "I don't believe she has enough hair to keep the ribbons in place."

Undeterred, Amanda twisted the ribbons together and tied them around Elizabeth's waist. "There! That will do. Everyone will know she's one of us." She stood back and gave an approving nod.

Fanny waved toward the dock. "There's Mr. Atwell. Come on, Sophie."

"Where are you two going?"

"Your mother volunteered Sophie and me to greet guests as they arrive at Round Island for the celebration. We're supposed to be there early to receive our instructions," Fanny said. "Mrs. Oosterman's orders."

There would be no Fourth of July celebration on Broadmoor Island this year. The family would attend the huge gala being hosted by the Oostermans on Round Island. Amanda's father had announced it would be a nice change for the family, but Amanda wondered if it was his way of avoiding the expense of their usual festivities.

"Wait a moment and I'll go with you," Amanda said.

Sophie shook her head. "Your mother wants you to go with them."

"But why?"

"I'm sure I don't know, but she was insistent you remain here." Sophie nuzzled Elizabeth's neck until the baby chortled with delight. "Would you mind taking Elizabeth upstairs to her nanny? Paul said he would bring her with him. We have a long day ahead of us, and she'll be in better humor if she has a nap."

Amanda lifted Elizabeth from Sophie's arms and watched her cousins stroll down the path to the dock, still uncertain why her mother should want her to remain behind. She kissed Elizabeth's plump cheek and carried her inside. "Let's go upstairs. As soon as you take your nap, you can go on the boat and have fun." The baby gurgled and smiled. How simple life was for babies. No cares or worries. They had only to cry and their needs were met. "Your life will become more difficult with each passing day, dear girl. You had better enjoy this simple life while you can."

After leaving the baby with her nanny, Amanda went in search of her mother. She made a stop on each floor of the house and inquired of the servants, but none of them were any help. Even her father seemed to have disappeared. When she wanted to speak to her parents, they were nowhere in sight. After a half hour of searching, she gave up. She'd return to the front porch and wait.

"Uncle Quincy! When did you get here?" Her uncle was sitting on the lower veranda watching Beatrice's children play a game of croquet.

He looked up and smiled. "I arrived only a few minutes ago. Managed to jump on board with Captain Visegar and save Mr. Atwell a trip to Clayton."

"Mr. Atwell's off to Round Island at the moment." She pulled a chair close. "I'm glad to have a few moments alone with you. I wanted to know how work is faring at the Home since I've been gone. Have you been able to meet all of the necessary needs?"

He shook his head. "I doubt we'd ever be able to do that, my dear. However, I will tell you that it has been much more difficult without you. I didn't realize what a load you must have been carrying. And now . . ." His voice trailed off as he stared at the river.

"Now what? I pray there hasn't been any further outbreak of the cholera."

"No, but there are always those in need of medical attention. And with no one to care for them . . ." Once again his sentence remained incomplete.

"What do you mean no one to care for them? Dr. Carstead is capable. He managed quite well before I came to train with him."

"He managed. Though not as well as when he had you working by his side. But now that Blake is gone, it leaves us without anyone to tend to the needy."

"Gone?" She hadn't meant to shout. "Where? Why? I don't understand."

"I can't give you many answers. I only know that he left town with a young woman. I don't know where they went or if they're ever coming back."

Amanda wasn't certain if it was fear or fury that propelled her out of her chair. "Why didn't you ask him?"

Her uncle raised his brows, obviously startled by her brusque behavior. "If I'd had an opportunity, I would have done so. He left a note. I've told you everything he wrote in his message."

"That's it? *Dear Mr. Broadmoor, I'm leaving town with Julia?*" Amanda couldn't believe he wouldn't say something more.

"Well, something like that. He did apologize for his abrupt departure."

As her anger dissipated into an overpowering sadness, she dropped back into her chair. How could Blake leave without a word? Then again, why would he feel the need to tell her? He'd obviously decided he still loved Julia. The two of them were likely married and settling into a beautiful home in California. Her lips trembled as she struggled to keep her tears in check. Perhaps she *had* only imagined those words of love being whispered by her bedside. There was no hope for a marriage filled with love and laughter in her future.

As if on cue, her father stepped onto the veranda. "There you are. Look who's come for a visit."

Amanda swiveled around and looked directly into the eyes of Ellert Jackson. This was the reason she'd been told to remain on Broadmoor Island. Her parents had invited Mr. Jackson.

Her stomach churned at the sight of him.

Though he offered a smile, Amanda was unable to clearly gauge his mood. His expression seemed almost guarded, but his words were affable. "It's a pleasure once again to be in your company, Miss Broadmoor. Or may I address you as Amanda?"

Her father patted Mr. Jackson's shoulder. "Of course you may. You'd welcome that, wouldn't you, Amanda?"

Her throat felt as though it had been stuffed with cotton. Her lips moved, but not a word came out.

Mr. Jackson chuckled. "I do believe she's so overcome with joy at the sight of me that she can't even speak." He pulled a chair close and sat down beside her. "I hope you will be pleased to know that your father especially invited me to be your escort to the festivities at Round Island." Resting his left ankle across his right knee, he tapped his finger on the arm of her chair. "I trust that bit of news is agreeable."

Her father stood behind Mr. Jackson's chair with a beseeching look in his eyes. He appeared to be holding his breath. She cleared her throat. "I accept your invitation, Mr. Jackson." Her brief acceptance would have to suffice, for she couldn't bring herself to say the idea of spending the afternoon and evening in Mr. Jackson's company gave her any joy. "If you gentlemen will excuse me, I believe I'll go upstairs and fetch my hat."

"Don't be long," her father called after her. "The boat is leaving in fifteen minutes."

Chin tucked, she raced up the steps and into her bedroom. Slamming the door behind her, she leaned against the cool wood and wrapped her arms around her waist. For a short time her breath heaved in short rapid bursts and then slowed to a more normal rate. Her dreams of love collided with the reality of Ellert Jackson, and she wondered if she could possibly marry him. Perhaps he would be willing to wait until they gained a better understanding of each other. If she didn't love him, she would at least want to become better acquainted prior to their marriage. She pressed her knuckles to her mouth at the thought of marriage to someone so old—a complete stranger. They would have nothing in common.

A knock sounded on the door, and she jumped in surprise. "Who is it?" The quiver in her voice was obvious.

"It's your mother. May I come in?" Her mother didn't wait for a response. Instead, she was across the threshold and into the room before Amanda could object. "I know this is more than you should be required to bear, and I'm so very sorry." She wrapped Amanda in a warm embrace and then stepped back and looked her directly in the eyes. "Not all marriages that begin as arrangements are unhappy. If you work at pleasing Ellert, I believe he will treat you with kindness and generosity. After our talk the other night, I had hoped you had begun to accept the arrangement. Who can say? You may even grow to love him."

"Mother! How can you ever imagine I could love that old man? We have nothing in common. I won't even have the comfort of my family close at hand, for you know he won't want to live in Rochester."

"Your father tells me he admires your interest in medicine. Perhaps he would allow you to get the proper education you desire. Maybe in time the age difference won't seem that great."

"But I had hoped to marry for love. To truly desire to spend my life with my husband has always been my dream."

Her mother held up her palm. "You know I have never liked this idea of arranged marriages. In the past I've opposed your father on every front. But I fear I can be of little help to you now. Too much hangs in the balance for your father—for all of us." She clasped Amanda's hand within her own. "Spend some time with Ellert and give him a chance to woo you. A spark may unexpectedly ignite if you give yourself over to the idea that you could care for him."

There was nothing to say. She wouldn't argue with her mother, but she couldn't deny the foreboding weight that had settled in her heart.

Ellert Jackson waited impatiently for Amanda's return. She was as beautiful as he remembered her, and he desired to be in her presence. He desired something infinitely more intimate but knew that would have to wait.

He smiled to himself. How marvelous that things should have worked out so well in his favor. Not only was Jonas Broadmoor in his debt, but he was in a most desperate bind that left the simpleton forced to barter his own daughter to keep out of the poorhouse. The man's social standing and financial reputation were still the only things that mattered to him.

"And people believe me to be the cold and calculating one," Ellert mused.

"Mr. Jackson, it was a pleasant surprise to hear of your arrival."

He looked up to find Victoria Broadmoor standing before him. He gave a polite bow and beamed a smile. "The pleasure, I assure you, is mine. Why, this island is positively blooming with beauty."

She blushed. "I wonder if I might speak frankly."

"But of course. I would have it no other way."

"My husband has told me of your desire to marry our daughter."

Ellert nodded. "It was love at first sight. Your Amanda is the most radiant and beautiful woman I have ever laid eyes upon. Her intelligence and charm far surpass all others."

Victoria looked at him oddly for a moment. "You love her?"

"But of course. Would a man propose marriage for any other reason?"

"I thought . . . well, that is . . . I presumed this was a type of financial arrangement," Victoria replied.

"My dear woman, I know there are those who would consider such an arrangement acceptable, but I cannot be counted among their numbers. My heart's desire is to marry your daughter and give her the love she deserves."

Victoria's expression seemed to change almost in an instant. The worried countenance softened to a look of pleasant surprise. "I must say, hearing you say that does my heart good."

"I'm so glad I could assuage your fears, madam. I would hate for us to get off on the wrong foot. Especially if you are to become my mother-in-law, although with such a youthful and beautiful woman as yourself, we would be better considered siblings than mother and son."

She laughed nervously at the comment, as Ellert had hoped she would. Women of her ilk were so easily persuaded by a few flattering words. He would charm her and win her over. While Jonas might know the truth of his choosing Amanda to wed, Ellert believed the man would never confide such a thing to his wife. To tell her he'd all but sold their daughter to save his hide and beloved reputation would surely have killed Jonas Broadmoor.

CHAPTER 15

Mr. Jackson didn't appear pleased when Amanda lifted Elizabeth from Paul's arms and carried her to the boat.

"I believe the baby would be happier with her father or her nanny," he said when Amanda settled Elizabeth on her lap.

"She's perfectly content right here," Amanda said, clutching the child closer. She had hoped the baby's presence would deter him, but Mr. Jackson sat down beside her.

"I'm pleased to see you are fond of children, Amanda. I hope to have a son—perhaps by this time next year." He winked and slid closer. "Of course, I wouldn't want it to interfere with your passion for medicine. But with my money, we could afford the best help. I believe it would be entirely possible for you and me to have a family, even while you completed your medical training."

Amanda didn't know quite what to say. Ellert Jackson was clearly indicating his approval of her interest in medicine. "Your comment surprises me, sir."

He leaned close. "And why is that?"

His breath tickled her ear, and she drew away. "Most men would not desire their wives to seek employment, much less to take an interest in something so controversial as medicine."

He straightened and squared his shoulders. "You will learn quickly that I am unlike most men. I respect intelligence, and I equally desire a family."

"You were married before, were you not? Did you not desire children then?"

"My wife suffered certain . . ." He hesitated a moment before continuing. "Difficulties. She suffered difficulties throughout her life that prevented her from bearing children."

Heat rose in Amanda cheeks. She shouldn't have pursued such a delicate subject.

"I'm sure you'll have no such problems, my dear Amanda." He patted her hand. "I hope I have not embarrassed you, my dear. I would like to think we could speak openly about anything."

Amanda looked up and nodded. He was clearly doing his best to be kind and considerate of her feelings. Perhaps she could bear this arrangement better than she'd originally thought. Still, there was something about the man that made her uneasy. Maybe it was her inexperience in courtship and matters of the heart. Mr. Jackson had been married before and knew what it was to share such intimacy. That might have explained why he seemed rather . . . possessive. Yes, that was it. He seemed as if he already knew what her answer to his proposal would be. His confidence in the situation made Amanda feel very uncomfortable.

The water churned alongside the boat as they pulled up to the dock. When Paul extended his arms to Elizabeth, the baby chortled and lurched forward. Amanda watched Paul step onto the dock with Elizabeth in his arms. Silly, but she felt as though she'd lost a semblance of security when she'd handed the infant over to her father. Now there would be no escaping Mr. Jackson.

"Do you plan to remain on the boat, Amanda?" Mr. Jackson stood in front of her and offered his arm.

She shook her head. "I was lost in thought."

With a firm stance, he offered his arm when she approached his side. Amanda ignored his authoritarian attitude and tucked her hand inside the crook of his arm but was taken aback when he placed his hand atop hers in a far too possessive manner.

With a jerk she attempted to withdraw from his grasp. He squeezed her hand tight against his arm. "The ground here is quite rocky. I would not want you to fall, dear Amanda."

She forced herself to relax. "You are very kind."

"I can be kind in many ways," he said in a low husky voice. "I can hardly wait to show you."

"It's very inappropriate for you to whisper, Mr. Jackson. I wouldn't want others to get the wrong idea."

He laughed. "But we are engaged. Surely they will understand."

Amanda frowned and looked away. She hadn't agreed to marry him, but already Ellert Jackson presumed everything was settled. "Oh, there are my brothers. I'd like to say hello."

She tried again to pull away, but he would not release her. "I would be happy to meet your brothers. Why don't you introduce us?"

Just then the boys linked arms with their companions and headed toward the hotel. "We should hurry or we'll never catch up with them. I don't want to lose them in the crowd."

"It appears they are engaged with a group of their friends. Why don't you wait until later when they aren't otherwise occupied."

The tight grasp he maintained was enough to alert her that his remark was a command rather than a suggestion. A command he meant for her to heed. There was no need to argue. She could see from the set of his jaw that she'd not win.

When amplified bullhorns announced the horse races would soon begin, Ellert said, "Come along. I have a horse and rider participating in the race. I want to place a wager with some of the owners."

"You wager on the horses?"

Ellert guffawed. "Yes, my dear. So does your father, as well as every other wealthy businessman who attends or has a horse in the running. I'd guess that your brothers have even been known to place a wager or two on an animal. A well-placed wager has proved an enormous help to many a man."

"And an enormous loss to others, I would guess," Amanda said. "I don't think the risk is worthwhile. And I've been told it can become addictive—just like strong spirits."

Once again he laughed. "Forgive me. I forget your youth and how much you have to learn." He pulled her close to his side. "I will take great pleasure in teaching you how to become a woman."

"I *am* a woman," Amanda said.

"According to the year of your birth, but you are not a woman in the true sense of the word. Not yet." When they neared the edge of the racing track, Ellert said, "Wait here while I go and speak to my rider and place my wager."

A shiver ran up her spine. What manner of man was this that he would speak so intimately of things proper people never discussed in public? She thought to leave, to go in search of her brothers, but knew it wouldn't please Ellert. She supposed there was no sense in appearing unkind or disrespectful, so she remained in her assigned spot and watched the horses prancing and snorting while their riders led them toward track. The animals held their heads high, seeming to anticipate the attention that would soon be centered upon them.

"Here you are!"

Before Amanda could turn around, she was being hauled into the air. She twisted and stretched her toes toward the ground. "Jefferson! You look so much older."

He set her on her feet and then held her at arm's length. "And you look far too thin. Your bout with cholera has taken a toll on you, sister. I think an extra portion at each meal is called for."

"Enough about how I look. Do tell me when you arrived home." She peered over his shoulder. "And where is George?"

"He'll be here soon." Her brother chuckled and leaned closer. "He's gone to place a wager on a horse. He's hoping to help save the family from complete financial disaster, although I've been advised that you have been charged with that duty."

She took a backward step. "Who told you?"

"Mother. She's none too happy over the turn of events, but she tells me she holds out hope that all will be well, since your suitor is quite smitten with you. George and I arrived only a short time ago, and we didn't have time for a long talk with her."

"And why did I not know of your return?"

"We wanted it to be a surprise. Our way of adding to the holiday celebration. We haven't even been home to Rochester yet. We came directly to Clayton, where Mr. Atwell met us at the train station and brought us directly here. He'd been sworn to secrecy."

Amanda grasped his arm. "Well, having you and George home has certainly added pleasure to my holiday. Otherwise I would find this day totally gloomy."

"What? When you're here with a man who adores you and has asked for your hand?" He nodded toward a clump of trees not far away. "The shade of those trees would be preferable to standing out here in the sun." He grinned. "I don't have the protection of a parasol."

After quickly scanning the area and seeing no sign of Ellert, Amanda agreed. "Based upon your earlier remark, I assume you've learned that Father is headed for financial ruin. At least that's what he and Mother have told me."

"Frankly, George and I had knowledge of the difficulties before we sailed. Father had us look into some possible investments overseas, but once we'd located a few high-yielding prospects, he couldn't raise sufficient capital." They located an unoccupied bench, which Jefferson swiped with his handkerchief. "I don't want to see that lovely dress ruined."

She stared at him for a moment, remembering the mischievous young brother who had taken pleasure in teasing her throughout the years. When had he evolved into this considerate young man their father now trusted for investment advice? How had she missed the transformation?

Jefferson sat down beside her and peered into the distance. "Of course we didn't realize the depth of Father's difficulty." He covered her hand with his own. "Father speaks highly of this man you are to marry. I hope he will prove to be deserving of you." He smiled and the dimple in his left cheek appeared.

She reached up and touched the small indention. "There's that dimple I love," she said.

He laughed. "As I recall, you always took great pleasure in teasing me because of that dimple. Now tell me about this man of yours. Mother says we've never met him—that he lived in Rochester some years ago."

"Many years ago would be a more accurate statement. His first wife is deceased and—"

"Amanda! I thought we agreed you would remain near the race track? And who is this?" Ellert asked, focusing upon her brother.

Jefferson stood and extended his hand. "I am Jefferson Broadmoor, Amanda's brother. And *you* are?"

Amanda stood up and grasped Jefferson's arm. "This is Ellert Jackson. The man to whom Father has pledged me in marriage."

Jefferson let out a snort. "Do cease your teasing, Amanda."

"I do not consider our betrothal a matter of jest, Mr. Broadmoor. Perhaps you could enlighten me as to why you find our engagement so astonishing."

The gleam in Jefferson's eyes faded, and his smile disappeared. "Forgive me, Mr. Jackson. I merely expected Amanda's suitor would be a man who was not so, so . . . A man closer to her own age."

"I believe Amanda is convinced the advantages of marrying a mature man far outweigh any benefit of marriage to someone her own age. Isn't that correct, my dear?" Ellert turned sideways and edged between Amanda and her brother. "Nice to meet you, Jefferson. If you'll excuse us, we're going over to the races."

"I'm sure Jefferson would be pleased to join us," Amanda said.

"On the contrary, my dear. I imagine your brother would be much more comfortable with his *young* friends—boys with whom he has more in common." Ellert grasped her elbow with a force that caused her to flinch and propelled her forward. "Do come along. We don't want to miss the first race."

In spite of Ellert's remark, Amanda hoped her beseeching look would persuade Jefferson to join them. But as they walked away, her brother remained near the bench, staring at them. While she hastened to keep pace with Ellert, she glanced over her shoulder at Jefferson. They locked gazes, and he mouthed the word *later*. Her spirits soared. He understood she needed him.

The remainder of the afternoon passed in a blur. The races, the polo matches, games of horseshoes and lawn tennis. Ellert kept her close by his side but refused to participate in any of the fun. "Games are for children," he'd said, and she didn't argue. Since losing wagers on the races earlier in the afternoon, he'd become a bit ill-tempered. She supposed it was to be expected, but she didn't want to provoke him further. He thwarted her efforts to visit with friends or family at every turn. Even during the picnic supper, he'd arranged for them to maintain a distance, insisting to her mother that they needed time to become better acquainted without family interference. He gained her mother's approval with honey-laced words and an engaging smile.

Amanda supposed he was right. They didn't know each other at all, and it would benefit their arrangement to spend time together. Still, there was a side of Ellert Jackson that Amanda couldn't quite explain or understand. It was as if just beneath the exterior of his charm and wit, a monster was waiting to be unleashed.

Ellert maintained his hold on her arm as the musicians began to play for the first dance of the evening. Jefferson was working his way through the crowd, but before he could approach, Ellert insisted they take to the dance floor.

The second dance had begun when Jefferson tapped Ellert on the shoulder. "I'd like to cut in, Mr. Jackson." Ellert frowned as he stepped back and handed her over to Jefferson.

"I believe I've angered him," Jefferson said, grasping her around the waist.

"I'm confident he will recover," Amanda said with a grin.

The dance ended all too soon, and before she knew it, Ellert reappeared to claim her. "I wonder if you wouldn't enjoy a walk with me. I would like very much to discuss our plans."

Amanda thought to reply in the negative but changed her mind. Given all that had happened—the things her father had done to Fanny and others in the family, she really needed to do her best to make this work. "Of course."

Leaving the dance behind, Ellert led Amanda down to the river walk.

"I've decided that we will be married immediately."

His words startled Amanda. She looked at him and found his fixed expression betrayed determination. "But that's impossible. The family is in the midst of making arrangements for Fanny's wedding, and that must come first."

His eyes shone with lust. "Unless her wedding is to take place in the immediate future, I'll not wait. I have my needs and desires, and I plan to have them met—by you."

Fanny spread a blanket a short distance from where Paul and Sophie had settled. Under most circumstances she would have joined them, but they'd been in a state of disagreement for most of the evening. Paul had protested when he discovered Elizabeth had returned to Broadmoor Island with her nanny. Although Sophie explained that the damp night air would have worsened the baby's case of the sniffles, Paul dismissed the explanation as an excuse for his wife to be free of any responsibility. Their voices drifted across the short expanse, and Fanny wanted to chide them for their behavior. Neither was completely correct.

The band struck up a lively march, and the young children paraded across the grass, keeping time to the music. When Paul stood and started wending his way through the young marchers, Sophie scooted over to Fanny's blanket.

"Can you believe the way he's acting?" Sophie asked.

"I think I can."

"What? You're taking *his* side?" Anger flashed in Sophie's dark eyes. "You know the night air doesn't agree with Elizabeth."

"I'm not taking sides. I think you are both wrong. Paul is jealous because you've been attracting a lot of interest from the single men. He believes you've sent Elizabeth back home so that you will have total freedom to do as you please without the hindrance of a baby or her nanny. And you, dear Cousin, still want to punish him for sending you to Broadmoor Island when you wanted to remain in Rochester."

Sophie peeked from beneath the brim of her straw hat. "When did you become so wise?"

"I'm not wise. I can be objective because I'm not involved. I do think you're both squandering time that could be put to better use." Fanny looked toward the sun setting on the distant horizon. An edge of the orange globe touched the water and sent rays of light shimmering across the dark ripples. "You love each other. Why not replace your childish anger with joy and thankfulness that you have the pleasure of his company? I'm sure you'll find that Paul will respond with the same spirit."

Sophie appeared lost in thoughtful consideration for several moments. "You're right," she finally said, grinning. "But it's difficult to be the first to extend the olive branch, don't you think?"

"Yes, but it appears Paul is trying, too."

Sophie followed Fanny's gaze across the lawn, where she spotted Paul returning with two tall glasses of lemonade. "Thank you," Sophie whispered as she brushed a quick kiss against Fanny's cheek. "Why don't you move your blanket and sit with us. You look far too lonely over here by yourself."

"I'm quite content. You need to be alone with Paul. I think Amanda may join me a little later."

Sophie wrinkled her nose. "If she can get away from Mr. Jackson. I can't imagine why she accepted his invitation to escort her."

"I'm uncertain, as well, but there isn't enough time for us to discuss her reasons right now. You'd better return to your spot or Paul will think you've deserted him."

As the sky began to darken, Fanny leaned against the trunk of a giant pine tree and waited for the first explosion of color in the sky. How she longed for Michael's return. He'd promised a June return, but June had now turned to July. Each morning she and Mrs. Atwell prayed for Michael's safe and speedy return. And when their spirits waned, they did their best to encourage each other. Now that the last day of June had passed, keeping faith that Michael would soon return proved increasingly difficult. This was the Fourth of July celebration that she and Michael should be attending together—at least that had been Fanny's dream. Now she simply longed to know he would return before summer's end.

Seeing the many couples happily settled on the blankets that dotted the grass did little to keep her jealousy in check. "Be happy for them," she muttered in an effort to tamp down her feelings of envy. The first explosion boomed overhead, and a proliferation of color streaked the sky in a showy display. The crowd responded with thunderous applause and appreciative *oohs* and *ahs*.

When the second blast exploded and the overhead illumination offered a silhouette of Paul and Sophie locked in a warm embrace, she could feel her resolve begin to vanish. "Why hasn't he returned? I'm trying to trust, but . . ." Words failed her. She did want to believe all would be well. But how did one continue to cling to hope in spite of disappointment?

"May I join you?"

The grass had muffled the sound of approaching footsteps, and Fanny twisted around. She jumped to her feet, unable to believe her eyes. "Michael!" She was certain her squeal of delight could be heard above the sound of the fireworks, but she didn't care in the least. "When did you arrive? Let me look at you! Have you been back to the island yet? Are you well? I can't believe it's you!" She clasped his face between her hands to assure herself he was truly standing before her.

He pulled her into a warm embrace and tipped her chin with his finger. "Before I have the strength to answer all of those questions, I believe I need a kiss." He claimed her lips with a long and passionate kiss that set her heart racing. "I love you, Fanny, and I promise I'll never leave you again. Tell me that the wedding plans have been made and we'll be married soon."

"We can be married in only a few days from now." She breathed his name and returned his kiss with reckless abandon.

CHAPTER 16

WEDNESDAY, JULY 5, 1899

After removing a cigar from the humidor, Jonas settled into the leather chair situated behind the desk in the library of Broadmoor Castle. He was never quite comfortable at this desk—probably because the chair had been a better fit for his father's lanky frame. Jonas was required to stuff his portly figure into the chair at an angle. "Most uncomfortable chair in the house," he mumbled while he clipped the end from his cigar. Not a Cuban cigar, but a cheaper, less aromatic replacement.

Michael's return during yesterday's Fourth of July celebration had caught

Jonas unaware. He first thought Fanny had withheld information regarding the young man's return, but apparently she had been as surprised as the rest of the family. Now Jonas was eager to discover the profitability of Michael's sojourn to the Yukon. He'd set up an appointment to meet with Michael at one o'clock, and the clock had struck the hour several minutes earlier. Jonas puffed on his cigar, growing more annoyed as each minute ticked by. Who did Michael Atwell think he was to exhibit such disrespect? His time in the North had apparently numbed his good manners.

When a knock sounded at the library door, Jonas first looked at the clock before calling, "Come in." The moment the door cracked open, Jonas leaned across the desk. "You're late, Michael."

"Yes, I know. Fanny and I were discussing our wedding plans."

Jonas couldn't believe his ears. No apology or request to be forgiven for his breach of etiquette? Not only had Michael forgotten his manners, he'd also forgotten his place in this household. "I'm accustomed to servants following orders."

Michael met his gaze with an air of indifference. "So you are, but I am no longer your servant, Mr. Broadmoor. I have been providing for myself since my departure to the Klondike."

"Technically that's correct. But let's don't forget that your parents are dependent upon me for their positions in my household." The comment didn't have the desired effect, for the young man had developed an air of confidence he'd lacked prior to his departure. "Sit down, Michael. We need to talk." Jonas took a long draw on the cigar. "I'm sure you recall we had an agreement before you departed."

"How could I forget."

The statement dripped with sarcasm, and Jonas arched his brows. Michael had best watch his tongue or he'd find himself off the island and out of Fanny's life before nightfall. "Since you've already made yourself comfortable, why don't you tell me about your travels. I'm anxious to learn of your success—or failure, whichever the case may be."

"I suppose you could say I experienced some of both. I was blessed with the friendship of two men and joined with them in prospecting. I think Zeb and Sherman were the greatest blessing I received. Their friendship and what I learned from them are more valuable than the gold we discovered."

Jonas perked to attention. "What could be more valuable than gold? What is it they told you about? If you've come upon some other discovery, you must permit me the opportunity to invest."

Michael laughed and shook his head. "What they taught me is free, Mr. Broadmoor. While I was with them, I experienced the love that Jesus taught about. They shared with me as though I were their brother, and they willingly made me a partner in their claim. Best of all, they taught me what it means to be a true follower of Christ."

Jonas pushed away from the desk and flicked his ashes into the fireplace. "I don't want a Bible lesson, boy. I want an accounting of your finances. We had an agreement that if you attained enough wealth that I could be certain you weren't after Fanny's inheritance, I'd permit the two of you to wed."

"You can demand whatever you wish, but Fanny and I intend to be married in three days. I doubt I could ever offer an accounting that would convince you Fanny's wealth isn't of importance to me."

Jonas narrowed his eyes, convinced Michael was toying with him. The younger man didn't want to divulge the depth of his fortune, or lack thereof, and Jonas wasn't enjoying their game of cat and mouse. "You owe me repayment of the funds that I advanced for your journey. Are you able to pay me?"

Michael withdrew a leather pouch from his pocket and dropped it in front of Jonas. "I believe this will cover my obligation to you."

"There's interest due on the loan."

Michael nodded. "If you look inside, you'll find that your interest has been included with my payment."

Jonas picked up the bag and arched his brows. He'd expected the bag to be heavy with gold nuggets. Instead, it felt empty. He tossed the bag at Michael. "Is this a joke?"

With a swipe of his hand, Michael grabbed the bag and yanked open the top. He withdrew a bank draft and pushed it across the desk to Jonas. "I believe a bank draft is still considered negotiable tender."

Jonas lifted the draft and examined the amount. "This will do, but there's still the issue of how well you fared financially while you were gone. You have a responsibility to convince me, as Fanny's guardian, that you can care for her in a proper fashion."

"I'm not required to convince you of anything, Mr. Broadmoor. You're no longer Fanny's legal guardian, and we intend to be married—with or without your blessing."

"Don't you raise your voice at me, Michael! You're nothing but—"

"Jonas! What is going on in here?" Victoria pushed open the library door and stepped inside. "I could hear the two of you the moment I entered the hallway." She continued to stare at him. "Well? What seems to be the problem?"

"Michael is unwilling or unable to fulfill an agreement we made before he went to the Yukon. Therefore, I've told him it will be impossible for him to marry Fanny."

"Oh, pshaw! Cease your nonsense, Jonas. Fanny and Michael will be married on Saturday. The plans are made." She smiled at Michael. "You and Fanny have our blessing, Michael. We will be pleased to welcome you into the family."

She patted the young man's hand. "Now, if you will excuse us, I need to speak with my husband privately for a few moments."

"Yes, of course. Thank you, Mrs. Broadmoor." He stood and nodded at Jonas. "Good day, Mr. Broadmoor."

The moment Michael had exited the room and closed the door, Victoria wagged her finger at him. "Refrain from any further meddling in this wedding, Jonas. They will be married on Saturday, and we will be happy for them or you will suffer the consequences."

His anger mounted, and Jonas tugged at the starched white collar that surrounded his thick neck. "I have tolerated your outbursts from time to time, Victoria, but I do not like being threatened."

"And I do not like having my daughter forced to marry for other than love." She stepped closer, her face contorted by pain. "Mr. Jackson may be a fine man, and indeed he has proven himself to be of the best manners and expression; however, Amanda should be allowed to choose her own husband, and I cannot abide that we are forcing her to do otherwise. If I can't, I will at least see Fanny happily wed. And if you can't wish her well in this marriage, you had best appear genuinely pleased to walk her down the aisle and offer her hand to Michael on Saturday. Otherwise you may not find the consequences to your liking."

His wife didn't present him with an opportunity to respond. Not that he had the words to put Victoria in her place without forcing her hand. He couldn't risk the possibility that she would find some way to destroy the marriage arrangement with Ellert. Women! If only the world could exist without them. He leaned to the right and pulled open the bottom drawer of the desk. He needed a drink.

Fanny worried that it might rain but proceeded down the path nevertheless. She had received a note from Michael suggesting they meet in one of their favorite secluded spots. It was a place where they often enjoyed fishing and whiling away an afternoon, and Fanny thrilled at the thought of once again sharing it with her beloved.

"I thought you might not come."

Fanny looked through the dark shadows of the trees but couldn't see Michael. "Where are you?"

He laughed. "I'm right here." He moved forward into the fading light.

Fanny rushed into his arms. "I can't believe you've really come home. I've longed for this more than words can say."

"I know," he replied, combing back her unruly curls with his fingers. "There were so many times when I thought I might never see you again."

She touched his cheek. "I tried to imagine you up in your frozen North. I read everything I could find about the area. There really isn't much to be had."

He laughed. "I don't doubt it. There weren't many folks up that way prior to the rush—at least not folks who might want to write a book about it. There were some very interesting native people in the area. I found their culture and ways so different from ours."

"Tell me about them," Fanny urged.

"I'd rather talk about us—about you."

He kissed her gently and then hugged her close. "Every time I lit a fire, I'd see your hair in the dancing flames." He kissed her ear. "I thought of you every night before I went to sleep." He kissed her neck, letting his lips linger for just a moment.

Fanny melted against him. She had no words for what she was experiencing, but at last her heart felt as though she'd truly come home.

"Every morning I woke up with thoughts of you. I could see your smiling face and very nearly hear your voice. It was all that got me through our time apart—that and the Lord. God gave me a comfort that compared to nothing else."

"I know. He gave it to me, as well. All the times Uncle Jonas tried to marry me off to someone else, God was there to sustain me with memories of you."

The light was gone from the sky, but overhead the stars glittered like diamonds. Michael took hold of Fanny's hand and led her to a clearing. "Look, see there? It's the North Star. Remember how we used to wish upon it when you were a little girl?"

Fanny nodded, but she wasn't sure Michael could see her. "When you were gone, I'd find it and think of you. I imagined that it shone right over the place where you were living. I made so many wishes on that star." She stopped and put her head on his shoulder. "And they've all come true."

He held her close and sighed. "I love you, Fanny."

She snuggled against him and smiled. "I love you, Michael. I will always love only you."

SATURDAY, JULY 8, 1899

Although clouds had loomed overhead Friday evening, Saturday dawned without a hint of rain in the offing. Both Amanda and Sophie had come to assist Fanny with her gown and veil. Amanda fastened the final button on the gown. "You are an absolutely beautiful bride. Michael is fortunate to have you."

"I am the one who is fortunate. Had I searched the world, I know I could never have found a man who loves me any more than Michael does. He is a perfect match for me. We place importance on the same things."

"Like what?" Sophie asked as she wound a strand of Fanny's hair and tamed her curls.

"We both love the islands. Don't tell anyone, but he's purchased one of the islands for me as a wedding gift." She grinned with excitement. "He didn't want to wait to see if we'd be able to buy Broadmoor Island."

"I'd be willing to sell you any share I might have in this place," Sophie said. "Unfortunately, I don't think I have any, but perhaps I can convince my father to sign over his share and then Amanda can talk to Uncle Jonas."

"I doubt my father would listen to anything I'd ask. I have little sway over what he decides. If so, I wouldn't be—" Amanda clamped her lips. No need to ruin Fanny's wedding day with her own problems.

"I do hope that Ellert Jackson isn't going to act as your escort," Sophie said. "I don't like him in the least. The way he clings to you and won't let you out of his sight is most annoying. Why, he wouldn't let any of us near you at the Fourth of July festivities. You need to tell your father that you want another suitor."

"I don't think that's possible, Sophie. Father believes Ellert would be a perfect husband for me."

Sophie clasped her bodice and dropped to the nearby rocking chair. "You jest! Surely you haven't agreed to the match."

"I have no say. It has been arranged. In fact, we will be wed very soon. Had it not been for Fanny's wedding, I'd already be his wife. I managed to convince him we had to wait until after her marriage." She locked eyes with Fanny. "Forgive me, Cousin, but I had hoped Michael wouldn't return until August. I thought I might be able to convince Ellert that he didn't want to marry me. He can be pleasant enough, but there is something quite demanding about him."

Fanny swiveled around on the chair. "Oh, Amanda. You need not apologize. I understand how you must feel. When your father was trying to force me to wed Daniel or one of those other young men he thought to be perfect, I became panic-stricken. I understand your plight. There must be something Sophie and I can do to help."

"It's best neither of you interfere. Father and Ellert would be angered, and it would do no good. We won't be making our home in Rochester, and my one hope is that I'll be permitted to return and visit with both of you from time to time. If Ellert thinks you've done anything to hinder his plans, I fear he won't allow me to come back to visit."

Her mother entered the room before her cousins could respond, but Amanda didn't fail to see the pity in their eyes. Even though Sophie hadn't been in love with Paul when they married, his kindness and love had won her heart. Both of her cousins were in love with their husbands, but Amanda doubted she could ever love Ellert. Her heart had room for only one love, and that, unfortunately, was Blake Carstead. If only she could have realized it in time, she might have been willing to fight for his affection. She had considered telling Ellert about Blake, but something told her it wouldn't change his mind. He wouldn't care that she loved another.

"Do hurry along, Fanny. Few though they be, your guests are waiting."

Fanny stood and twirled in front of the mirror, examining her gown from all angles. "We wanted only close friends and family to attend. And Uncle Jonas seemed relieved when I told him I wouldn't need a large sum to prepare for the wedding."

Amanda stepped aside as her mother reached to smooth the folds of Fanny's veil. "There, that's perfect. I'm sure your uncle Jonas would have agreed to a large wedding at the church in Rochester if that's what you'd asked for, dear. Personally, I would have preferred a church rather than sitting in chairs out on the lawn, but it's your wedding." She handed Fanny a lace handkerchief. "This is the handkerchief your grandmother carried at her wedding. I know she would be pleased to have you carry it. Now, come along. I'll go down and take my seat. Listen to the music and come out on cue."

Along with the help of two servants, Jefferson and George had managed to move the piano to the veranda earlier in the day. "I do wish you had contacted the pianist from the church in Clayton," Fanny whispered to Amanda. "I hadn't even planned to *invite* Mr. and Mrs. Oosterman, much less have her play the piano."

"I know, but Mother asked her before I had an opportunity to go into Clayton. I believe Mother invited several other guests who weren't on your list, too. She didn't want me to tell you, but I think it's better if you're prepared."

Fanny's veil fluttered as she spun around to face Amanda. "Why would she do such a thing?"

"You know how Mother is. She didn't want anyone to feel slighted or to do anything that might give rise to gossip." The reply was Amanda's best guess. She couldn't be absolutely certain of her mother's motivation. Perhaps it was her father who had insisted that the social set be invited. She could never be completely sure what prompted her parents' decisions.

Fanny pulled aside the lace curtain and peeked outside. "This isn't what I expected. Your mother said my *few* guests had arrived, when all the while she knew—"

A crescendo of three piano chords interrupted, and Amanda stepped to the door. "We can discuss this later. That's my signal."

Fanny shot her a look of frustration.

Amanda glanced over the crowd that had gathered to witness the couple's nuptials. More than a verdant aisle separated the attendees. The Broadmoor guests were clothed in fine attire and bore looks of disdain for the guests who sat on the other side of the grassy division. This would be quite an afternoon and evening—an integration of social classes. She uttered a prayer that this day wouldn't turn into a disaster for Fanny.

Throughout the ceremony Ellert's gaze felt like a hot poker boring through to her soul. Amanda had hoped he wouldn't appear, that some business or personal matter would keep him away from the wedding so that she could enjoy this time with her family. But he had arrived. And he'd taken possession of her from the very first moment he set foot on the island. He'd even voiced an objection when she'd excused herself to prepare for the ceremony. Amanda had prayed this day would create many happy memories for Fanny. However, Ellert's presence affirmed that her own recollections of this day wouldn't be so pleasant.

She knew he could be charming, but his lustful nature frightened her. He seemed to think it completely appropriate to discuss topics of a most intimate nature. He alluded to the things they would experience together—some appropriate subjects for discussion and others quite inappropriate.

But she really had no choice in the matter, Amanda realized. She had talked at length with her mother and father, and the situation was quite grave. Every idea for helping the family had failed to move her father toward a change of mind. All he would say was that this was the best solution to the situation if their family was to maintain its position in society. When they had been alone, her father had told her quite simply that it would kill her mother if they were to lose their home and standing. Amanda was starting to believe that he was right. Her mother had always loved her status among Rochester's elite. To take that from her now would be cruel.

Once the ceremony ended, Ellert pulled her aside. "I've been lonely for your company," he whispered. "Hearing your cousin repeat her vows pleased me, for I knew you would soon be promising to love and obey me. You can't imagine how much I'm going to enjoy being loved and obeyed."

She didn't want to discuss Ellert's marital expectations. The thought caused her stomach to lurch. "Why don't we go and join the other guests? Fanny may need my help."

"*I* need you far more than Fanny does. She has a husband who can assist her if she has need of help. I haven't had a tour of the island, and this would be a perfect time for you to show me about."

"You want me to escort you around the island? *Now?*"

"Now!"

"But the wedding guests—"

"If I didn't know better, I'd think you were attempting to avoid me, my dear." Ellert pulled her close. "Come along and show me the wonders of Broadmoor Island. Who knows? I may find that the seclusion of island living appeals to me."

Amanda cast a glance toward the crowd. She had hoped to locate someone who would save her from Ellert, but no one came to her rescue. They walked to the rear of the house and continued along the path leading to the north side of the island. When they reached a small grove below the overhanging rocks, Amanda said, "The view of the water is excellent from this vantage point, but if you'd care to climb the rocks, you'll need to continue on your own. My shoes won't withstand the jagged rocks."

"I find the view from here quite lovely," he said, pulling her into his arms.

Without further warning, he crushed her lips in a bruising kiss. She pushed against his chest, but her attempt to escape his hold only spurred him on. He pulled her to the ground, his hands now groping her body. Frightened, she clawed at his back, but his jacket offered him too much protection. His cruel laughter mocked her, and she yanked at his hair. "Stop or I shall refuse to honor the agreement you made with my father."

His hands stilled and he stared into her eyes.

"I mean it, Mr. Jackson. If you take advantage before we wed, I will *never* be your wife. I am of legal age and care little if my father disowns me."

His anger was evident for only a moment before his expression turned contrite. "I apologize, my dear Amanda. It's just that your beauty—your very presence—is intoxicating. I could not help myself. I desire you more than anything else."

Amanda thought his apology less than sincere, but she couldn't for the life of her explain why. He helped her up and quickly let go his hold. She dusted off her dress, hoping there would be no grass or dirt stains to reveal her shame to others.

"You are so innocent of the power you have over a man," he said, his voice seductive and low. "I promise you will enjoy our wedding night. I only insist that it come very soon. I cannot say that I will be able to control my desires for you much longer. Do you understand?"

Amanda swallowed the lump in her throat. "We can announce the engagement next week. If my parents' reputation is to be protected, we must follow the rules of propriety."

Ellert chuckled. "A few minutes ago, you didn't care if your father disowned you, but now you worry over his reputation?" Wedging her chin between his thumb and forefinger, he tipped her head upward. "The wedding will take place before the end of August. Agreed?"

"You have my word." Her voice quivered, and he smiled.

He traced his fingers down the nape of her neck and then leaned close as his fingers returned to her cheek. "You'll soon learn not to refuse me anything."

CHAPTER 17

SATURDAY, JULY 15, 1899

Blake bounded up the steps of the Home for the Friendless, glad to be back in Rochester and the life he'd come to enjoy. The contentment and challenges he'd found in this community had come as a surprise to him, but he now felt at home in Rochester. He'd stopped at home only long enough to clean up after his journey. Now he was anxious to see his patients and visit with Quincy and Paul. He hoped all had gone well during his absence.

He yanked open the door and nearly collided headlong with Paul. "Whoa! Sorry, Paul. I didn't see you." He grinned.

"No apology needed. I'm running late and wasn't watching where I was going. It's good to see you've returned, Blake. We were afraid you might not come back."

Blake laughed. "You'll not get rid of me quite so easily." He cocked his head to one side. "Where are you rushing off to?"

"I have to catch the train. I was supposed to be at Broadmoor Island by noon. If I don't board the next train, I'll miss Amanda's party, and Sophie will never forgive me." He chuckled. "I'm certain she's going to be unhappy when I don't arrive by noon, so I had better be there by the time the festivities begin."

Blake stood in the doorway, blocking Paul's exit. "What kind of party are they having for Amanda? I know it's not her birthday."

"Oh, I forgot. You don't know. While you were gone, Amanda was betrothed. The engagement party is this afternoon at Broadmoor Island. I fear you'll need to find a new medical assistant. Amanda and her husband won't be living in Rochester. Although I have heard it said he intends to send her to university for proper medical training."

Blake leaned against the doorjamb to maintain his balance. He felt as though Paul had plunged a two-by-four into his midsection. "Did you say Amanda is engaged?"

"Exactly. Now, if you'll step aside, I need to be on my way."

Blake grabbed the sleeve of Paul's dark suit jacket and jerked him to a halt. "Wait! Could I . . . Is there any way . . . What I'm trying to say is that

Amanda and I are . . . were close friends. I'd like to go to the party if you think it wouldn't be overstepping proper etiquette to show up."

Paul smoothed his hair into place before donning his hat. "I don't know why anyone would *want* to go to one of these things, but I imagine the family would be happy to have you attend." He clapped Blake on the shoulder. "Having you there will be a nice surprise for Amanda."

Obviously Amanda hadn't been overly distressed by his disappearance. Otherwise Paul would have refused his request. Blake didn't know whether to be pleased or displeased that Paul had so readily agreed, but there would be time enough for questions later.

"Will your wife be joining us?" Paul asked.

Blake shook his head. "Whatever gave you the idea that I was married?"

"I suppose it was something Sophie said."

Blake let out an exasperated breath. Maybe that was the reason for Amanda's sudden engagement. If she thought he'd left to marry Julia . . . "Come on, let's hurry," he said, pushing the thought aside.

After a hasty carriage ride during which the carriage came far too close to colliding with several pedestrians, the two men stepped down, paid the cab driver, and hurried inside the train station. "That was exciting," Paul called over his shoulder while racing toward the ticket counter.

Determined to keep pace, Blake ran to catch up with him. The train was slowly chugging out of the station even before they'd arrived at their seats. "I'd say we didn't have a minute to spare," Blake said, settling into the upholstered seat of the Pullman car. "At least we'll travel in comfort."

"Let's hope the train remains on schedule. I'd rather not have an argument with Sophie the minute I set foot on the island." He chuckled. "You don't have to worry about such things, but one day . . ."

Blake forced a smile. "Yes, one day." He turned to look out the window. How had all of this happened so quickly? Amanda had never mentioned another man. She'd given every indication that she cared for him. He'd expected her to be angry over the incident with Julia and his sudden disappearance, but marriage to another man? The idea was beyond his comprehension. Perhaps it was a man she'd known for years.

When Blake knew he could make no sense of it without help, he turned to Paul. "Who is this man that Amanda plans to marry?"

Paul glanced up from his magazine. "Who? Oh, his name is Ellert Jackson. I can't tell you much about him except that he seems an odd match for Amanda. He's much older. From what I've gathered, Jonas is the only one who is well acquainted with the man. They had business dealings of some sort years ago when Mr. Jackson lived in Rochester."

"And this man suddenly appeared in Rochester and he's already proposed to Amanda? How much older?"

Paul shrugged. "I'd say he's near Jonas's age. Could be a few years younger."

Blake's jaw went slack. He couldn't believe his ears. "Did Amanda consent to this marriage?"

"I imagine she agreed, don't you? She is of legal age. I know her father can be overbearing, but Amanda is a strong-willed young lady. When I consider how she defied her father in order to learn medicine, I find it difficult to believe she would have accepted Mr. Jackson's proposal unless she wanted to marry him." Paul closed his magazine and placed it on the seat. "I hope you won't think me intrusive, but I'd be interested in hearing about your hasty departure. Sophie told me you left town to marry someone named Julia."

"I don't want to offend you, Paul, but I think I should first discuss that matter with Amanda. I assure you, it's not what it might have seemed."

"Of late, nothing in this family is what it seems," Paul said, shaking his head.

"This engagement is a mistake, Amanda. I think you should march downstairs and tell your parents that you've decided you aren't going to marry Ellert Jackson." Sophie folded her arms and gave a single nod for emphasis. She and Fanny had been doing their best to prevent the party, but thus far they'd met with failure.

"Sophie's right. It's clear that you don't have anything in common."

"He's not even as nice as he was at first" Sophie added. "He doesn't seem to care what people think of him."

"You don't understand, and I'm not at liberty to explain," Amanda said, her expression clearly one of distress.

"Why are you being so stubborn? You've made it quite clear to us that you love Dr. Carstead, so why are you permitting your parents to announce your engagement to someone else?"

Fanny sat down on the bed beside Sophie. "She's right, Amanda. You're old enough to refuse your father's demands in this matter. You can come and live with Michael and me. I know he would understand and welcome you."

Amanda sighed. "You and Michael won't be living in Rochester. I want to continue with my medical training, and I can't do that if I'm living out here on an island."

"You can't do that if you're married to Mr. Jackson, either. You'll not be living in Rochester, where you can return to your work at the Home for the Friendless," Sophie put in. "Even if you are able to locate a doctor who will agree to continue your training, do you think Ellert is going to tolerate such an idea?"

"He said he would."

"And you believed him?" Sophie asked. "I can't see that man allowing you to go to a party, much less become a doctor."

"I can't, either. Amanda, he doesn't at all seem the type to want a wife working for any reason. He's much too controlling. Surely you see that."

"But if I prove to be a loving wife, perhaps he will allow me to do the things that are important to me."

Sophie clucked her tongue. "You don't really believe that, do you? Men like Uncle Jonas and Ellert Jackson don't change their attitudes when they take a wife. After you're married, he'll have no more respect for you than he does now."

"Probably less," Fanny said. "Once you're married, there will be no opportunity to refuse his decisions for you. He'll make you miserable, and there will be no escape. You know you couldn't divorce him."

Her cousin appeared to be wavering, and Sophie stepped closer. She knelt down beside Amanda and clasped her hand. "Don't do this, Amanda. There are other choices available. I know you're grieving the loss of Blake, but this man is no replacement for him. From my observations, the man has no admirable qualities. Save for your father, it seems no one I've talked to has anything good to say about the man."

Minnie knocked on the open door. She held Amanda's freshly pressed gown draped across her arms. Ellert had purchased the dress, and although it had been a poor fit, he'd insisted she wear the gown. Minnie had devoted painstaking hours to ripping out seams and restitching the garment. "I hope it will please you, Miss Amanda," she said.

"Has my husband arrived, Minnie?" Sophie stepped to the window overlooking the lawn.

"I haven't seen him. Mr. Atwell picked up a number of guests at the train station two hours ago, but there haven't been any arrivals since that time."

"Thank you, Minnie." The party would begin at two, and Paul had promised to arrive by noon. Her father had conveyed the message when he'd arrived last evening. Had something happened at the Home or at one of the churches he was serving? Surely he would tell them he had a family commitment that required his attention. "When does the last train arrive?"

The flounces of yellow taffeta rustled as Minnie walked across the room and placed the gown atop the bed. "I believe Mr. Atwell said he would make one final pickup in Clayton at one o'clock. Everyone should be here by then," she said.

"Paul will be here. Don't fret," Fanny said. "He probably lost track of time and had to rush to catch a later train."

"You're right. He likely became preoccupied."

"You've done an excellent job, Minnie. Thank you for all your hard work.

I know you've been stitching until very late each night to make certain the dress was ready. I appreciate your help," Amanda said.

A blush of color tinged Minnie's cheeks. "Thank you, ma'am. I wish you every happiness in your future."

The moment the maid exited the room, Sophie jumped to her feet. "Did you see the look in Minnie's eyes? Even she knows this isn't a good idea."

"Oh, forevermore." Amanda gazed heavenward. "Minnie didn't appear any different than she normally does. You're simply looking for evidence."

"Don't fool yourself. The servants see and hear things, Amanda. You know that's true. And they talk about us, too. They know as much about what's going on in this house as we do—probably more." Sophie paced back and forth. "Why don't you go and ask Mrs. Atwell what she's heard." She stopped in her tracks. "Better yet, why don't all three of us go downstairs and have a chat with her. She won't lie to us."

"There isn't time for a conversation with Mrs. Atwell." Amanda picked up the gown and motioned to Fanny. She was thankful her cousin had delayed her wedding trip until after Amanda's wedding. Even though Fanny disapproved of her marriage to Ellert, her presence remained a comfort. "Will you help me with my dress?"

"So you're going to ignore my suggestion? Sometimes I do know what's best, even if the two of you don't think so."

Dropping the dress back onto the bed, Amanda turned to Sophie. "You're correct. I don't love him. But not everyone has the privilege of marrying for love. I'm truly happy that you and Fanny have married honorable men who love you. If circumstances were different, I'd refuse to marry Ellert. But this is something I must do. The future of my family hinges upon this decision."

Fanny slipped the dress over Amanda's head. "Your father is the one who created all of this financial difficulty. Shouldn't he be the one to find a resolution to his problem?"

"He has found a solution; it's me."

"That's not what I meant," Fanny said. "I know I can't make your decision for you, but I think this idea is deplorable and you should refuse to go through with it."

Sophie peered out the window and shook her head. "Look at him down there. Puffed up like a rooster with the run of the barnyard."

"Who?" Fanny and Amanda asked in unison.

"Mr. Jackson. He's strutting around smoking his cigar." She turned and shuddered. "How can you possibly think about marriage to that man?"

"Do stop, Sophie. All this talk has become wearisome and changes nothing."

"Then let's make a plan!" Unable to bridle her enthusiasm, Sophie hastened across the room and pulled a sheet of paper from Amanda's writing desk. "I'll write down our ideas."

Amanda followed her cousin across the room and removed the sheet of paper from her hand. "I've told you that I must marry Ellert. Please stop trying to find a way out for me."

Amanda gathered the taffeta skirt in her hand and descended the staircase. Sophie and Fanny followed. Even with all of Minnie's hard work, they all three agreed the dress was ugly. Styles had changed, but evidently Ellert's taste in women's fashion had not. The color washed out Amanda's complexion. Even with extra color on her cheeks, she looked far too pale. The topaz and diamond necklace and earrings Ellert insisted that she wear were gaudy. The color of the large topaz stones didn't match the dress and made her appear garish. She'd mentioned the differing shades of yellow didn't complement each other, but Ellert had been insistent.

She stepped onto the porch and was immediately besieged by Mrs. Oosterman. The old woman frowned and tsked several times. She leaned close to Amanda's ear. "What were you thinking when you chose that gown? This isn't a costume party, is it?" She touched a bent finger to the necklace. "Although I'm certain this necklace was costly, it looks frightful with your gown. What's come over you, my dear? You have impeccable taste."

"Oh, it's not Amanda who has flawless taste, Mrs. Oosterman. It's me." Ellert had silently approached and obviously had heard only Mrs. Oosterman's final statement. "I chose her gown and jewelry. I'm pleased to hear you approve. Amanda wasn't quite so convinced." There was reproach in his voice.

"To be honest, Mr. Jackson, the ensemble doesn't enhance Amanda's beauty. It might work for someone else, but her complexion is far too pale for this color. She should be wearing a vivid color. I was, in fact, chiding her for this choice when you interrupted our conversation."

Ellert appeared momentarily taken aback but quickly regained his poise. "In the future I shall listen more closely to Amanda's suggestions," he said. He'd managed to keep an even tone, but his fingers were now digging into the folds of Amanda's dress. There was little doubt the woman had angered him.

"I do believe I see Mrs. Pullman across the way," Mrs. Oosterman said. "If you two will excuse me, I want to say hello."

"By all means." Ellert glared after the older woman. The moment she was out of earshot, he said, "I detest that old woman. She has a wagging tongue and an evil heart."

"Truly? I'm surprised then that you didn't put her in her place." Everything had changed between Amanda and Ellert after his attack on her. Amanda no longer even tried to pretend she was happy with their arrangement.

"I was not born into wealth, Amanda. Therefore, I lie in wait for people who either take advantage or treat me with disdain. Eventually I have the pleasure of turning the tables, and it always gives me great satisfaction." His eyes turned dark with hatred. "One day Mrs. Oosterman will be sorry. She doesn't realize that through my silent partnership in many companies, I control many of her husband's assets. If she isn't careful, she may soon discover her husband isn't nearly as wealthy as she thinks."

Amanda sucked in a breath of air. How could one man harbor such deep hatred and disdain? Instead of banning Sophie's idea, perhaps they should have used that final half hour upstairs to formulate a plan to prevent her engagement and marriage to this despicable man.

"I've frightened you. I can see it in your eyes." He pulled her close. "I enjoy the look of fear. It arouses me," he whispered in a hoarse voice.

Her mother caught sight of them and crossed the lawn at a near sprint. She grasped Amanda's hand. "The two of you are supposed to be over here to greet your guests," she said. There was concern in her eyes, but she maintained a smile. "Come along."

"I'd rather have you to myself," Ellert whispered. "I shouldn't have agreed to this large party. None of these people like me."

"An astute observation," Amanda murmured while weaving through the throng of guests.

CHAPTER 18

While Amanda and Ellert greeted their guests, Sophie returned to the quiet of her upstairs bedroom. The window from her room would provide a good vantage point to watch for the return of the *DaisyBee*. Mr. Atwell had departed over an hour ago to pick up the final guests due to arrive at the Clayton depot. He should have returned before now. Sophie sat down in the floral upholstered chair beside the window. With no sign of the boat, a knot of fear formed in her stomach. Could something have happened? A train wreck or some other mishap back in Rochester before Paul departed? Perspiration formed on her palms, and she uttered a prayer for Paul's safety. Observing Mr. Jackson's behavior over the past days had served to deepen Sophie's love for Paul and his gentle, caring manner.

Only moments before returning upstairs, Sophie had stood in the shadows of the veranda and overheard Ellert issuing angry orders to Amanda. Sophie hadn't heard the content of his commands, but from his tone of voice and contorted features, there had been little doubt he was enraged. She shivered at the thought of being married to such a man. Although she'd tested Paul's patience on several occasions, he had never been cruel or unkind. He had steadfastly loved her and Elizabeth. From the moment the babe had been born, Paul had accepted her as his own.

"Elizabeth is his child," she murmured. "Perhaps not by blood, but in every other way. Wesley Hedrick was never Elizabeth's father." She removed the clipping she'd shoved inside the book on her bedside table. All of Wesley's wealth could never make him a good man or a good father. Having a man like Paul was worth more than all the money Wesley Hedrick could ever offer.

Shading her eyes against the bright afternoon sun that streamed through the window, Sophie recognized the *DaisyBee* cutting across the water toward the dock. Her heart skipped a beat at the thought of seeing Paul. She dropped the newspaper clipping to the table and rushed down the stairs. "Paul has arrived," she called to Fanny while running down the path leading to the dock. Her shoes thumped against the hard dirt, and she slowed her pace a modicum when she neared the steepest portion of the path.

Paul waved his hat overhead as she reached the dock. The moment he stepped off the boat, she rushed to embrace him. "Oh, Paul, I have missed you so much." She raised on tiptoe to kiss him.

He chuckled and cocked his head to one side. "And here I expected you to be angry with me for my late arrival. What a wonderful greeting." Pulling her close, he covered her lips with a warm kiss.

"I've missed you, and I love you very much," she replied. "I don't tell you often enough."

"Thank you, my dear. Here I have been dreading this engagement party, but you've already made my journey worthwhile."

She took a backward step and stared at the boat. "Is that Blake Carstead?"

"Yes. As a matter of fact it is."

"What's he doing here?"

Paul shrugged. "He appeared at the Home just as I was leaving. I told him about Amanda's engagement party, and he asked if he could come along."

"Hello!" Blake called while stepping onto the dock.

Sophie tapped her foot on the wood planks. "*Now* you return!" She glanced around to see if anyone was within earshot. "What's wrong with you, taking off like that? And where's that Julia woman? Did you marry her?" Her calm demeanor had evaporated at the sight of Dr. Carstead. "Don't you realize Amanda is about to marry a man she doesn't love, and it's all because of you!" She wanted to shake him until his teeth fell out.

Blake ignored her and looked at Paul. "It appears your wife is somewhat disturbed by my arrival."

"Don't you take a condescending attitude with me, Doctor. I am *disturbed* because you've ruined Amanda's life. She is going to marry Ellert Jackson. A man she clearly does not love."

"If she doesn't love Mr. Jackson, why has she agreed to marry him?"

"She refuses to give me all of the details, but it has something to do with the family. I can't believe you ran out of town to marry that other woman. You are a disappointment, and had my husband known all of these details, you can be sure he wouldn't have invited you to join us. Did you not consider Amanda's feelings? While her father announces her engagement to a man she doesn't love, you reappear—now a happily married man."

"*Sophie*, do mind your manners," Paul whispered. "Dr. Carstead is here at my invitation."

Sophie didn't know who appeared more perplexed by her behavior, Paul or Blake. But at the moment she didn't care if she'd offended the fine doctor. She wanted him to suffer for his abrupt departure with that other woman.

Blake was the first to regain his composure. "Where is Amanda? I need to speak to her."

"I wish you well with that prospect. I'm not certain of her whereabouts, but you can be sure that if you locate her, Ellert Jackson won't be far from her side."

Once Blake was out of earshot, Sophie turned to her husband. "I truly do not understand Amanda's agreement to marry Mr. Jackson. She seemingly feels a sense of obligation to marry him, but he's a dreadful man. You should hear the way he speaks to her. He treats her as though she's a servant who must do his bidding." Sophie grasped Paul's arm as the two of them meandered up the path.

Paul frowned. "If what you say is true, something must be done."

Sophie shook her head. "There's nothing we can do. Fanny and I have exhausted all possibilities. Even when I attempted to develop a plan, Amanda wouldn't join in. She said she must marry him or the family will suffer—whatever that means. I'm certain Uncle Jonas is behind all of this. Aunt Victoria doesn't appear overly pleased by the match, but if Uncle Jonas has made the decision, she'll have no say in the matter."

"Then we must hope that Blake will be able to sway her."

"Why would his words count for anything? He never told me if he married that woman. Did you inquire?"

"I did, but he said he didn't want to discuss it until he'd first talked to Amanda."

"You should have insisted." She yanked him to a stop. "Did you see her?"

"See who?"

"Julia!" How could men be so blind to the important things in life? "Was Julia with him?"

"No, but he did mention he had stopped at home to refresh himself before coming to the Home. Perhaps Julia is at his house."

"Or perhaps he isn't married at all." Would a recently married man return to his home and immediately depart to see another woman? "Did he stop at home before the two of you departed Rochester?"

"No. He didn't mention the need to do so. Even if he'd wanted to, there wouldn't have been time. As it was, we had to travel at breakneck speed to arrive at the depot before the train pulled out."

Sophie weighed the possibilities and then steered Paul toward a secluded grove of trees a short distance off the path. "I think we should pray for Amanda and her future. I don't believe God would want her to marry a man she doesn't love."

Paul cupped her chin in his palm. "You're absolutely correct. We must pray about Amanda's future."

Amanda's cheeks ached from forcing herself to smile for the past hour. If only she could escape this madness. Ellert had maintained a tight hold on her elbow while they worked their way through the crowd. She didn't fail to note the women staring at her. Nor did Ellert. He was pleased by the attention, for he thought their stares were in admiration of her dress.

"Look at them. They're jealous," Ellert said with obvious delight.

But Amanda knew the unsightly flounces of yellow taffeta had elicited looks of horror rather than envy. The hideous frock had created fodder that would fuel the gossip mill for weeks to come, but she permitted him to gloat over a dress that made her look like a wilted dandelion.

She managed to free herself from Ellert for a moment and glanced over the crowd, hoping to spot Fanny or Sophie. "Blake," she whispered, her gaze settling on him as he made his way through the crowd and headed in her direction. She glanced over her shoulder. Although Ellert wasn't far off, Mr. Oosterman had engaged him in conversation. Perhaps he wouldn't notice if she slipped away. Fear and panic mixed to form a knot in her stomach. Her temples throbbed like beating drums. She must speak to Blake but not where Ellert might overhear.

Taking several determined strides, she reached Ellert's side and touched his arm. "If you'll excuse me, I'm going inside to powder my nose."

"Don't be long or I'll be forced to come looking for you." He glanced at Mr. Oosterman. "She's a beauty, isn't she?"

His remark annoyed her, and Amanda didn't wait to hear Mr. Oosterman's response. Turning, she hurried toward the house. She could feel Ellert's burning stare until she rounded the corner and was out of sight. Moments later, a strong hand clamped her arm in a tight hold and she let out a gasp. "Ell— Blake!" She swallowed hard in an attempt to remain calm. Instead of Ellert's cold stare, she was now looking into Blake's questioning eyes.

"Exactly what is going on, Amanda?"

The sharpness in his voice surprised her, and she took a backward step. "Good afternoon, Blake. I don't recall having seen your name on the guest list. Aunt Victoria must have added it after I perused it." She fought to maintain her composure. "I must say that I'm surprised to see you here. I heard that you'd left town with Julia and the two of you wed."

"I don't know how you could have heard such a thing because there's not an ounce of truth in anything you've said."

She arched her brows. "So you didn't leave town?"

"Yes. I left town, but—"

"Amanda!" Ellert's voice boomed from alongside the house. Before he could observe Blake at her side, she hurried off. Better to have her questions go unanswered than have Ellert discover she'd been engaged in a private conversation with Dr. Carstead. No matter what explanation she gave, he'd believe the worst. She didn't want Ellert creating havoc in Blake's life. Her betrothed had already wreaked enough devastation for a lifetime.

Paul cradled Elizabeth in his arms and carried her upstairs to the bedroom. She'd been awake for most of the afternoon's festivities, and he'd marveled at her sweet disposition as she'd been cuddled and fawned over by so many strangers. He nuzzled her neck and silently thanked God for bringing Sophie and Elizabeth into his life. Although he'd felt complete in his service to God before he met Sophie, she and Elizabeth had added a whole new dimension that continued to amaze him.

Elizabeth wiggled in his arms. He sat on the edge of the bed, holding her until she once again settled into a peaceful sleep. Carefully he stood and then laid her down in the cradle. Her tiny lips formed a moue. Her whisper-soft snoring caused him to smile. With a gentle touch, he placed the delicate white cover across her tiny form. So young and innocent she was, and he'd been charged with the privilege of helping to shape her into a fine young woman. He touched a finger to her soft cap of hair. "I'll do my best for you, sweet Elizabeth."

He straightened, walked to the window, and peered down at the milling guests. The party consisted of the usual food, beverages, and boring conversation. Given a choice, he'd remain up here with Elizabeth. He looked longingly at the bed. A nap would be wonderful, but propriety wouldn't permit such a luxury. As he turned back toward the window, a newspaper clipping lying atop the nearby table captured his attention.

At first glance the clipping appeared to be no more than the report of social gatherings in New York City, but as he continued to read, his lungs deflated, and a whoosh of air escaped his lips. Wesley Hedrick was the sole beneficiary of Lord and Lady Illiff, who had been lost at sea when a ship went down off the coast of France. There were words of praise for the magnificent parties he'd recently hosted at his home in New York City.

Could Sophie still be in love with Wesley? Paul dropped to the chair. Certainly Wesley could now provide a better life for Sophie and Elizabeth. Yet Sophie had greeted Paul with great warmth and affection only a few hours ago. Had her loving kiss been merely the expected behavior of a dutiful wife? Surely not. But during her months on the island without him, Sophie had certainly proved she missed the parties as well as the expensive clothing that he could never afford to purchase for her. Had her earlier behavior been no more than an attempt to ease her guilt? Without warning, his joy and contentment evaporated like the morning mist.

CHAPTER 19

Amanda maintained a watchful eye the remainder of the afternoon. She had hoped for an opportunity to steal away and speak privately with Blake, but Ellert had not given her a moment of solitude. At every turn he was at her side, clasping her elbow or placing a proprietary hold along the small of her back. She edged away every time she had a chance, but he wouldn't be deterred. He appeared to find her attempts to withdraw amusing, and that further annoyed her. When she noticed Blake stop and speak to Paul and then head off toward the dock with a group of departing guests, her spirits plummeted.

A short time ago the guests had congregated to hear the formal announcement of her engagement to Ellert and had offered congratulations, but Blake had remained at a distance. Though she'd hoped at least to discern his reaction to the announcement, there had been little opportunity. The crowd had gathered around and blocked her view. How she longed for a few minutes alone with him to ask why he had appeared at her engagement party. Even more, she had hoped to discover why he'd left Rochester without a word.

"Ellert!" Her father strode toward them with a satisfied look on his face. "Some of the men wondered if you'd like to join us in the library." He managed to make himself understood while holding his cigar clamped between his teeth, a practice Amanda thought disgusting.

For the first time since she'd come downstairs, Ellert appeared to weigh the idea of leaving her alone for a time. She momentarily considered encouraging him to join the men but then thought better of the idea. It would be wiser to remain silent and let him think his decision was of little interest to her.

"Do you think you can survive without me for a short time, my dear?" His eyes shone with perverse delight.

"I'll do my best," she said, forcing herself to maintain an even tone lest he think her overly anxious to be rid of him.

The moment Ellert entered the house with the other men, Amanda waved to Paul as he returned from the docks. At the very least, Paul should be able to provide some insight into Blake's reappearance. She hastened down the sloping lawn. "Finally I have a few minutes to myself." She glanced over her shoulder. "Ellert has joined my father and some of the men inside. I was wondering if you could tell me when Blake returned to Rochester and who invited him to the party."

Paul gave her a sheepish grin as he described Blake's surprise return to the Home for the Friendless. "I do hope you're not angry. He asked to come along, and I thought—"

"It's quite all right, Paul. I did want to talk to him, but except for a very few minutes, we had little opportunity. And now he's departed without answering the questions I had for him."

Paul gazed toward the river. "Unless he changed his plans, he's not far away. He told me he was going to stay at the Frontenac Hotel tonight, since he'd missed the last train to Rochester."

"I see." Amanda considered this news for a moment, but Paul interrupted her thoughts.

"Might I ask you something?"

Amanda nodded, hoping it wasn't a question about her feelings for Blake. "What would you like to know?"

"It's . . . well . . . Sophie. Do you think she's happy? I mean I know she didn't want to come here, but do you think she's otherwise happy?"

Amanda looked at Paul and considered his sad countenance. "I believe she is content. She loves being a mother and wife. I think this is probably the happiest I've seen her in years. Why do you ask?"

He shook his head. "I don't know. I suppose I just worry that she . . . well . . . perhaps regrets marrying a poor preacher."

Amanda smiled. "You two might have married under strained circumstances, but I honestly think Sophie is happy. I don't think she'd change anything even if she could."

"Amanda! Oh, Paul!" Sophie called as she made her way down the path. "Good, you're both here. I didn't know where you'd gotten off to."

"I was just asking Paul about Blake. I wanted to talk to him."

"Where is he?" Sophie asked, looking around.

"He's gone to the Frontenac Hotel," Paul replied.

Before Amanda could say a word, Sophie eagerly spouted, "You must go and talk with him before you go through with these wedding plans, Amanda. Paul and I would be happy to accompany you, wouldn't we, Paul?" Sophie tugged on Paul's sleeve, her eyes dancing with excitement.

"I wouldn't want you to enter into a marriage to Mr. Jackson if you harbor feelings for another man, Amanda." Paul's voice held a hint of melancholy. "Such a marriage would eventually prove painful for both of you."

"Well, the only feeling she has for Mr. Jackson is a deep loathing, so I believe a visit to Dr. Carstead is in order," Sophie said without missing a beat. "This will be such an exciting adventure. Do you think we should ask Fanny and Michael to come along, too?"

Apparently Sophie hadn't perceived her husband's dejected tone. Or perhaps Amanda had misinterpreted. Sophie surely would be aware of a change in Paul's demeanor, wouldn't she?

"I think it may be wise to keep the number of people to a minimum. I wouldn't want to attract unwanted attention."

"Oh, of course," Sophie giggled. "I do enjoy plotting clandestine meetings."

Paul looked at his wife. "And how many have you planned recently?"

Sophie batted her lashes. "I'll never tell."

"Truly?" Without waiting for a response, he motioned toward the house. "I believe I'll go and see if there's any of that punch left from the party."

"Wait a minute, Paul. We need to decide the details of—"

He glanced over his shoulder and appeared even sadder to Amanda. "I'll leave the plans to you, Sophie."

"But you will come with us?" she called after him.

He nodded and waved. "You can furnish me the details later."

"I don't know what's wrong with Paul. We were having such a wonderful time earlier in the day, but he suddenly seems despondent." Sophie glanced at Amanda. "Did you notice?"

Amanda nodded, thinking about Paul's question as to whether or not Sophie was happy. Perhaps that question had come about because Paul wasn't happy. Amanda prayed that wasn't the reason. "He didn't seem quite himself. Do you suppose he's tired?"

Sophie bobbed her head. "That's likely all it is. Now, let's decide on the arrangements. When do you think we should go to Round Island? This evening or tomorrow?"

"I can't possibly escape Ellert this evening. I think early tomorrow morning would be my best opportunity. If no one sees us depart, Ellert will think I've decided to sleep late."

"And if he sees us return, I'll tell him we awakened early and decided to try our hand at fishing. We can toss in our fishing lines along the way so we won't be telling him a lie." Sophie clasped her hand over her mouth. "This is such fun. Just like when we were young. Remember those detailed schemes we used to make in order to annoy Jefferson and George?"

"I remember. But tomorrow will be different. I won't be laughing if Ellert discovers I've gone to talk to another man. We need to be very careful," Amanda said.

Sophie nodded and looped arms with her. "No need to worry. Ellert will never know."

SUNDAY, JULY 16, 1899

As the sun peeked over the horizon the following morning, Sophie tiptoed to Amanda's bedroom and lightly tapped on the door before entering. She grinned when she saw the mound of pillows tucked beneath the coverlet. "Hoping the servants will report you are still sleeping, I see."

"Hoping to keep Ellert fooled for as long as possible," Amanda whispered.

Carrying their shoes in their hands, they silently padded across the carpeted hall and down the back stairs. After slipping outdoors, they sat down and put on their shoes. Neither spoke a word until they were secluded in the trees alongside the house.

"Where is Paul?" Amanda hissed.

Sophie pointed at the river. "Follow me," she whispered.

The sun hadn't yet forced its way through the heavy pines, and once they'd taken to the woods, they clasped hands to keep from becoming separated in the dim light. Pinecones and tree branches spiked with pine needles crunched beneath their feet. Sophie waved Amanda to a halt several times in order to stop and listen for footsteps. They didn't want to arrive at the river and discover they'd been followed. When they reached the clearing, Sophie could see Paul waiting in one of the skiffs from the boathouse.

"How did he manage to get the skiff without alerting Mr. Atwell?"

"He went down to the boathouse last evening and told Mr. Atwell he wanted to take a boat out early this morning. When Mr. Atwell told Paul that he would get up early and meet him, Paul refused. He suggested they tie the boat to the lower dock last evening. Mr. Atwell assumed Paul was going fishing this morning. He even put fishing poles and bait in the boat before they took it to the dock."

A blanket of dew glistened across the sloping grass leading down to the dock. "Careful you don't slip," Sophie warned.

She smiled broadly and waved to Paul. He lifted his cap to signal he'd seen her, but there was only a faint smile in return. He'd brooded all last evening, avoiding her at every turn. She had hoped a good night's sleep would improve his disposition. Thus far it didn't appear it had helped. What in the world had caused such a mood?

After assisting Amanda into the skiff, Paul offered his hand to Sophie. Holding tightly to his hand, she carefully stepped into the bobbing skiff.

When he didn't offer even the slightest acknowledgment, she leaned forward and kissed his cheek. "Thank you," she whispered.

He didn't acknowledge the kiss or her thanks. Not so much as a smile or a twinkle in his eyes. What was wrong with him! "Did you have any problems when you left the house this morning?" she asked.

Paul shook his head. "I think it's best if we remain silent. There's fog, and you never know who might be out here fishing. We don't want to draw attention to ourselves."

Sophie could feel the heat rise in her cheeks. She didn't believe Paul's admonition had anything to do with other fishermen overhearing her comment. He simply did not want to talk to her. She'd done everything in her power to prove she was sorry for acting badly when he'd sent her to Broadmoor Island, yet he now ignored her and spoke in an abrupt, hurtful manner. Was he attempting to show her how deeply she'd wounded him? She had hoped this would be a time of mending their differences. Instead, it seemed he was unwilling to forgive her.

Paul manned the oars with remarkable ease, and their silent journey soon ended with the three of them stepping onto the pier at Round Island. Several fishermen sat on the dock in their collapsible chairs, tossing their lines into the water. Paul stopped long enough to exchange a few words with one of the men before they proceeded to the hotel.

"Do you know that man?" Sophie inquired.

Paul shook his head. "No. I told him to spread the word that if they caught any fish they didn't want, I would purchase them when we returned."

Sophie patted his arm. "An excellent idea. I should have thought of that! I'm usually the one who comes up with the best way to make our schemes work."

"Indeed," Paul replied.

Normally Sophie would have considered the remark a compliment, but Paul's frown canceled that thought. When they arrived at the steps to the veranda that surrounded the hotel, Paul stopped. "Sophie and I will have coffee at one of the tables here on the veranda, Amanda. You go inside and have a message delivered to Blake's room that you'd like to meet with him in the lobby." He offered her a gentle smile. "There will be no appearance of impropriety if you remain in public view while you speak to him."

"Thank you, Paul. Say a prayer that all goes well."

"I will," he said.

"*We* will," Sophie added. She waited until Amanda disappeared from sight and then followed Paul to one of the tables that lined the veranda. Once they were seated, a waiter hurried to take their order.

"Just coffee," Paul said.

Sophie glanced across the table, but Paul had turned away from her and was staring into the distance. He hadn't even asked if she'd like something to eat. Not that she was hungry, but he could have at least inquired.

The waiter returned with their coffee and disappeared as silently as he'd arrived. Sophie poured a dollop of cream into her coffee and stirred with a vengeance. "Exactly what is wrong with you, Paul? You've been in a foul humor since late yesterday afternoon. Have I offended you?"

"Have you done something that should offend me?" he asked in a manner that seemed guarded yet hostile.

Sophie looked at him intently. "I know I was awful in the way I acted about coming to the island during the epidemic, but surely you have accepted my apology and we can let that be behind us."

"Are you happy with me?"

"What a silly question," Sophie said, trying to make light of the matter. "Of course I'm happy with you."

He swiveled around in his chair. "When did you plan to tell me about this?" He slapped the newspaper clipping onto the table.

Confusion combined with fear to form a tight knot in her stomach. She should have told him about the article. "Is that clipping the reason you've been so irritable?"

"I have been both confused and concerned. I can never provide you and Elizabeth with the way of life you deserve, but it appears Wesley Hedrick can now do so." Paul slapped his palm on the table and sent the piece of paper floating to the wood floor of the veranda.

Sophie reached to clasp his hand, but he withdrew it. There was a time when his actions would have made her angry, but this time was different. Sophie could see the doubt and fear in his eyes. She softened her voice. "Surely you know better than that, Paul. I love you dearly. You are all that I desire."

He shifted in his chair and leaned down to pick up the clipping. Crumpling it in his hand, he stared at her. "Am I? I can't give you expensive things. I can't buy you new gowns and furnish our home with beautiful furniture. I'm a simple man of God. I'll never be wealthy."

"That isn't important to me." Sophie realized the depth of just how true that statement was. It was freeing to know that she loved and cherished her husband far more than the things money could buy.

"I couldn't help but wonder if you would consider taking Elizabeth and running off to be with Wesley."

She could see the sadness in his eyes. "I would never do such a thing, Paul. You have been a loving husband and father. I have no desire for anyone except you."

"I want to believe you, but . . ."

Disbelief shone in his eyes. How could she convince him of her love? "I know I exhibited dreadful behavior when I first arrived at Broadmoor Island. And I won't deny that I was quickly wooed by the new gowns and parties. I was lured back into my old habits far too easily. I admit that. But after seeing the barrier it created between the two of us, I understood that what I truly wanted was a life with you and Elizabeth."

He unclenched his fist. The balled-up clipping rested in his palm, a silent accusation. "Then why do you have this?"

"Amanda read the article in a New York newspaper while she was recuperating from the cholera. She clipped it out and wasn't even going to tell me about it, but I found it when I was looking at one of her books." She wanted to hold his hand but feared he would again withdraw, so she folded her hands in her lap. "In truth, reading that piece helped me to see that money wasn't as important as I'd previously thought. I realize that even though Wesley may have enough money to buy gowns and jewels, he would never cherish or love me as you do. I understand that money is not a key to happiness. In fact, it seems frequently to have quite the opposite effect. It is you I love, Paul, and I am most content to be your wife, even if I never have another new dress."

"Yet you failed to mention Wesley or the newspaper article to me," he murmured.

"Because Wesley Hedrick is of no importance to me." She cupped his jaw in her palm. "I realize how blessed I am to have you as my husband. You are a good man, and I will always be thankful that you came to my rescue. Without you, I would have thrown myself from those rocks and taken Elizabeth with me." Her voice cracked at the remembrance that she'd been only minutes away from destroying her own life and that of her unborn child. Only Paul's gentle, pleading words had saved her from a crushing death upon those jagged rocks below. "Recently I've acted badly, and I apologize for my churlish behavior. I know that you have our best interests and protection in mind whenever you make a decision."

With the tip of his finger, Paul raised her chin and stared into her eyes. "I'm thankful for your kind words, but I know it was my uncompromising decision to send you and Elizabeth to Broadmoor Island that caused you such unhappiness."

Sophie lifted his hand to her lips and kissed his palm. "That's true enough. Yet I never doubted your love. In my heart I knew you made that decision in order to protect us. Now, seeing the distress Amanda has suffered since agreeing to marry Mr. Jackson, I truly realize how fortunate I am to be married to the man I love."

"And I to the only woman I could ever love." He leaned down and captured her lips in a lingering kiss.

Sophie pulled away. "Let's never allow these kind of things to come between us again. I love you, and that will never change. I do not want Wesley and his money. I want you and your love."

Amanda paced the length of the lobby while she waited for Blake. The bellboy had delivered her message and returned to say Blake would join her in a moment and to please wait. The gossamer curtains that shaded the lobby windows fluttered in the morning breeze and made her long to run outside. She shouldn't have come here. What if Ellert should discover she'd left the house? And what if Blake told her he'd been joking and he and Julia were husband and wife? Worse yet, what if Julia descended the staircase at his side?

There was still time to escape. She turned. "Blake," she gasped.

Obviously perplexed, he tipped his head to the side and arched his brows. "You did ask me to meet you in the lobby, didn't you?" He held her note between his fingers.

"Yes, of course." She cleared her throat, hoping to quiet the tremor in her voice.

"Shall we go for a walk?"

She recalled Paul's earlier comment about proper decorum, but the lobby was filled with guests and who could know what might be overheard. Any number of people might recognize her. She had no idea if any of their other guests had elected to remain in the islands throughout the weekend. What if one of them told Ellert he'd seen her in the hotel lobby visiting with a young man? Without further consideration, she nodded to a door leading to the east side of the veranda. Their departure wouldn't be visible to Paul and Sophie.

"It's good to see you. I had hoped we'd have another opportunity to visit before I left your en-en-gagement party, but Mr. Jackson seemed to be constantly keeping you by his side."

Amanda noted that Blake had stumbled over the word *engagement*. "Mr. Jackson tends to be somewhat possessive," she replied.

"I'm surprised you would choose such a man, since you are such an independent young woman. But I suppose you know what type of man appeals to you."

Amanda led him toward the river, choosing a spot where guests couldn't see them from the veranda. "I don't have time for banter or stilted conversation. I can't be away from Broadmoor Island much longer before I'll be missed. I came here to ask exactly what happened between you and Julia."

"Absolutely nothing happened between us. It's true that I had proposed to Julia before I moved to Rochester. I thought we loved each other, and I asked her to be my wife. As I told you before, she accepted the engagement ring but returned it a short time later. She'd found another prospect more appealing—or so she told me. But things didn't work out with him, so she came to Rochester thinking I would be delighted to pick up where we'd left off."

"But you weren't?"

He cupped her chin in his palm. "No, I wasn't. When I told her I wouldn't marry her, she begged me to accompany her back to California to explain to her parents that I was in love with someone else. She said they would never believe her. I offered to write a letter, but she cried until I finally agreed."

"So that's why you departed in such a hurry?"

"Yes. I knew my explanation wouldn't sound plausible. But I've known Julia for years. Even though she'd broken our engagement to be with another man, I felt an obligation to her and to her parents."

"She probably wanted the time with you, hoping to change your mind."

"You may be correct, but I knew that wouldn't happen. After you left that day, I realized the feelings I'd had for Julia were nothing compared to my love for you. I admired her and considered her a friend, but it's you I desire to have by my side for the rest of my life. I never experienced that intense desire for Julia—only for you."

His words made it difficult for Amanda to breathe. "You truly love me?"

"You know I do. I don't want you to marry Ellert Jackson. You belong with me. Surely you know that's true."

"But that can't happen. The future of my family depends upon my marriage to Ellert."

"I don't understand. How can a family's future depend upon a marriage?"

"My father owes Mr. Jackson a great deal of money. If I refuse to marry him, our family will lose what's left of our assets, not to mention the loss of social position. I am not aware of all the details or arrangements Ellert made with my father, but I do know that my family will be ruined if I don't go through with the wedding."

"But you don't love him. Knowing you'll be subjecting yourself to a life of misery in a loveless marriage, how can you agree?"

"Love doesn't matter. This marriage is required of me."

Blake pulled her into his arms and covered her lips with a fierce and passionate kiss and then pulled away from her. "Tell me again that it doesn't matter." Before she could gain enough breath to speak, he devoured her with another fervent and unyielding kiss. "Tell me you don't love me."

"What I feel isn't important," Amanda said, tears blurring her sight.

Blake wiped one tear away and placed his hand against her cheek. "It's important to me." He lifted her chin, forcing her eyes to meet his. "Tell me that you don't love me, and I will go away and leave you alone."

Amanda did her best to stifle a sob. "I'm already alone, Blake. I will be for the rest of my life."

Ellert had quietly inquired about the young man who'd been speaking to Amanda near the back door yesterday afternoon. In all likelihood Amanda didn't think he'd observed her little tête-à-tête, but she'd soon learn very little escaped his scrutiny. The clueless girl didn't understand that it took only a few coins placed in the proper hand to loosen tongues.

He wasn't all that comfortable around the water, but he was thankful for the rowing experience he'd acquired in his younger years. His muscles would ache by evening, but it would be worth it. If the fisherman who'd watched the threesome depart from the dock a short time ago was correct, he'd locate Amanda at Round Island. Instead of rowing toward the dock where guests might see him and wonder at the sight of Ellert Jackson rowing himself to the island, he approached from the other side. If necessary, he should be able to pull the skiff onto dry land without much difficulty.

He spotted a young couple near the water's edge—young lovers clinging to each other in a passionate kiss. There was something oddly familiar about the woman. He lifted a pair of binoculars to his eyes. Amanda!

She clung to the man—the same man he'd seen her talking to the day before. How comfortable she appeared in his arms. The man touched her face with such familiarity that Ellert wanted to shout across the water and demand he release her. She certainly had never allowed him such liberties.

Ellert shoved the binoculars into the leather case and turned the boat back toward Broadmoor Island. The tightness in his chest caused his breath to come in a strained pant. How dare Amanda toy with him this way? She knew what was at stake. Ellert gripped the handles of the oars until he felt the muscles in his arms spasm in protest. She would pay dearly for this indiscretion. They both would pay.

CHAPTER 20

TUESDAY, JULY 18, 1899

"You are the most beautiful woman in the world," Michael whispered against Fanny's ear.

Fanny opened her eyes to find Michael watching her while she slept. She smiled and reached out for him. "I still can't quite get used to your being here."

He pulled her into his arms and kissed her soundly. "I dreamed of this every night while in the Yukon."

"Was it horrible?" Fanny asked.

"Dreaming of you?" He looked at her oddly. "What would make you think such a thing?"

"No, silly, I meant the Yukon. I heard such horrible stories. The newspapers were full of accounts of tragedy and death. You've hardly told me anything about it."

"It was some of the most beautiful and deadly country I've ever experienced. You would like it there, I'm quite sure. The mountains are incredible, and the vast size of the country is unbelievable." He kissed her again. "But right now I'd rather talk about how much I love you."

Fanny sighed and put her arms around his neck. "And right now I'd love to hear you tell me how much you love me."

"Oh, I nearly forgot," he said, pulling away slightly. "The paper work arrived. We now have the deed to our own island."

"How wonderful. How soon can we move there?"

He laughed. "Well, there's hardly more than a shack on it at present. We'll need to build a better house first."

"I suppose in the meantime we can live here or at Broadmoor Mansion in Rochester."

"I'm so glad you were able to lay claim to it. I know how much your grandparents' place meant to you. I fear, however, there would be very little I'd be able to do in Rochester to make a living."

"Between the gold you mined in the Yukon and whatever I have left of my fortune, we hardly need to be so concerned about that."

"I can't sit idle," Michael countered. "At least out here I can work with the boats. On our little island I plan to set up the finest shop to make and repair boats."

"And I shall cook and clean for you and raise our beautiful children."

He kissed her and pulled her close again. "I really don't care where we live, my sweet wife, so long as you are by my side."

"I feel the same way, Michael. I pray God never allows us to be separated again."

Later that morning Fanny bid Michael good-bye as he headed out to help his father in the boathouse. The house seemed strangely quiet until Fanny recalled that some of the family had departed for Canada earlier in the day. Her cousin Beatrice had decided a trip to Brockville would provide an opportunity for all of the young children to become better acquainted with their Canadian ancestry. Fanny thought Beatrice simply wanted an excuse to go shopping, for she'd made certain that nannies were included among those slated for the daylong adventure.

If all went according to plan, Fanny would locate Uncle Jonas in the library. For some time she'd waited for an opportunity to speak with him in private. She inhaled a deep breath before tapping on the door. When her uncle responded, she opened the door while offering a quick prayer for strength.

"Good morning, Uncle Jonas. I'm glad to find you alone."

"Why?" He didn't look up.

She continued into the room and stood directly in front of the expansive mahogany desk. "Because we need to talk."

"I'm not aware of anything that requires my attention," he said, dipping his pen into the ink.

Not once did he make eye contact, yet she refused to be deterred by his boorish behavior. "Why don't we discuss Amanda's betrothal to a man she doesn't love, a man who bears a terrible reputation and is known throughout Rochester as cruel and heartless. And then why don't you explain to me why you would force your daughter to marry such a man."

Finally her uncle looked up. His angry stare seared like a hot poker, and she took a backward step.

"My daughter and her marriage are none of your business, but I know that Ellert loves her. You are like so many foolish women who harbor a romantic notion that you must be in love with a man before you wed. Love can grow after marriage. You will see. Once Amanda is married to Ellert, she will learn to love him. Your aunt Victoria didn't profess to love me before we married."

Fanny wondered if her aunt had *ever* professed to love this cold and uncaring man, but she dared not ask such a personal question. "Even if one sets aside the age difference between Mr. Jackson and Amanda, it is obvious they have nothing in common. How can she possibly build a life with him?"

"You have nothing in common with a boatswain, yet you profess to love him. Tell me, how is this different?"

"You would dare to compare Michael to the likes of Ellert Jackson? Unlike your Mr. Jackson, Michael is a kind and generous man." Anger welled within her, and she pointed at her uncle. "Mark my words: I will not stand by and watch you force Amanda into a loveless marriage with that despicable man."

Her uncle scratched the nib of his pen across the writing paper. "I find it amazing that you think you have the ability to influence decisions regarding *my* daughter." He lifted the pen into the air and aimed it at the door. "Go on with you. I have work that requires my attention."

"I will not leave this room!" Fanny considered stomping her foot but decided her uncle would laugh at such behavior. Instead, she folded her arms tight against her chest, hoping the defiant stance underscored her determination. One look proved she'd failed. Her uncle appeared unmoved.

"Suit yourself, but I've given my final word on the matter." Her uncle stood up. "If you won't leave the room, then I will."

She had hoped it wouldn't come to this, but he'd given her no choice. "I think not, Uncle Jonas." Before he could step from behind the desk, she said, "If you don't release Amanda from this preposterous arrangement, I shall be forced to tell everyone that you stole a great deal of my inheritance, and I will also make it known that Amanda's rejection to medical college was due to your interference. I know that you sent money to the school in exchange for a letter rejecting her application."

He collapsed into the large leather chair. His complexion turned as gray as yesterday's ashes. "None of what you tell Amanda or other members of the family can change the arrangement that I've made with Ellert."

"Your bluff won't work."

"This is no bluff." A shadow of defeat darkened his eyes.

Fanny maintained a steely look. She'd seen her uncle manipulate far too many people in the past. He'd not make a fool of her again—not after stealing her inheritance and lying to Amanda. Uncle Jonas wouldn't win her trust so easily this time. "If you expect me to believe what you say, then I need further explanation."

He closed his eyes and leaned his head against the back of the chair. "Sit down, Fanny. This will take a while."

With her hands clenched into tight knots, she followed his instruction and waited for him to begin. It seemed an eternity before he finally struggled through the first sentence. She considered his words before stopping him. "I don't know what you mean when you say Mr. Jackson bailed you out and you owe him. You owe him *what*? Amanda? Is that what you're saying? You used your own flesh and blood as a guarantee for money?"

Her uncle sighed and hung his head forward. "Mr. Rosenblume is an excellent lawyer. I knew it would be only a matter of time before he pieced together all that had happened. He's obviously revealed many details to you." He shook his head in dismay. "Mortimer was instructed to destroy all of those incriminating papers. Since his death, it's given me pause to wonder if there's any man who can be trusted."

"I had hoped you would say that these circumstances have caused you to reflect upon your own deceitful behavior and you have begged God's forgiveness. Instead, you place blame on a dead man because he maintained a record of your misdeeds."

"He was a partner in my transgressions. They were his misdeeds, as well. Keeping such records was stupidity."

"Was it? I think Mr. Fillmore may have been protecting himself. He likely feared you would attempt to place all of the blame on him if accusations arose in regard to handling the estate. Maintaining the records provided him with proof that you were involved." She shook her head in disgust. "The bards of old wrote that there is no honor among thieves. You and Mr. Fillmore certainly followed that dictate."

"Have you no pity? Had I not been faced with financial ruin, I wouldn't have touched your inheritance. I needed to save the family from disaster. My plan was to borrow from your funds and repay you when my investments improved." His voice faltered.

"But they didn't improve," she said. "And when you could think of nothing else to save the Broadmoor financial empire, you decided Amanda could be sacrificed."

"You make it sound so . . . so . . ."

"Cold and calculating?" She unfolded her hands and leaned forward. "That's exactly what it is, Uncle Jonas. You care little if Amanda spends the rest of her life with a man who is cruel and uncaring. I daresay, he's a man not unlike yourself."

"No! I could never be as ruthless as Ellert Jackson," he defended.

Fanny shook her head in disbelief. "You've just now admitted you know Mr. Jackson to be a heartless man, yet earlier you professed him to be a man Amanda could someday love. How is that possible? You think only of yourself, Uncle Jonas."

"That's not true. I was seeking a way to cover my wrongdoings—that much is correct. But my actions were to protect the family. I knew how they would suffer if the truth came out. Ellert's proposition was my only recourse. Unfortunately, he now holds all the cards. There is nothing I can do to change things."

Her uncle appeared to be telling the truth, yet one could never be certain with him. Had he truly explored every possible option? Fanny tapped her finger atop the desk until an idea occurred. With newfound energy, she jumped up from the chair. "I know! I'll pay Ellert's loan with what remains of my inheritance. Then you'll be free to break your agreement with him." She folded her arms across her chest, pleased with her solution.

Her smile faded as he guffawed and waved away her suggestion. "Don't you think that if there had been enough money remaining in *either* of our accounts I would have used it to save the family?"

"Michael has money now. Perhaps if we pool our efforts."

Desperate to find an answer to Amanda's dilemma, Fanny sat down. She peered across the desk at her uncle. "Do you think Uncle Quincy saved any of his inheritance? Surely he hasn't placed all of it in the Home for the Friendless. With his share he could have built a much more lavish place. If you ask him, perhaps you'll discover that he's invested some of his funds."

"Quincy? He'll be no help. I'm sure he used most of his fortune to pay past debts. You'll recall that Wesley Hedrick's huge pledge never came through as promised. When pledges failed to be paid, I imagine he used his inheritance to cover his losses. No doubt he's given a good deal to several other charities. He never could give his money away quickly enough."

"I'll sell Broadmoor Mansion. Combined with what is left of my inheritance, there should be adequate funds, shouldn't there?"

His brow furrowed, and he swiped at the air as if to brush away her question. "You own Broadmoor Mansion? How is that possible?"

"Mr. Rosenblume handled the details for me. I'm not certain what transpired, but he received permission from the judge before making the acquisition." She took a modicum of pleasure seeing him pale. He was momentarily struck speechless by what she'd accomplished without his knowledge.

He massaged his temples. "Even if you sold the house, there would be insufficient funds to pay off Ellert, and he will agree to nothing less than what he is owed, plus interest. You may take my word for that or ask him yourself. He is set upon this marriage. Believe me, I tried to change his mind." Her uncle laced his fingers together and bowed his head. "You can tell Amanda about the college situation if that's your desire. But I believe hearing such information will only cause her undue anguish. There's no way I can alter the past."

Were Amanda not the one who would suffer, Fanny knew she would shout her uncle's selfish offenses from the rooftop. She cared little if the revelation would embarrass Uncle Jonas, but Fanny would not inflict further pain upon her cousin. "At the moment there is no good that can come from telling her," Fanny said. "Tell me, was Broadmoor Island included in your bargain with Mr. Jackson, or does it still belong to the family?"

"It remains with the family by the dictates of my father's will. Please understand, Fanny. Ellert Jackson knows too much—he can ruin our family even if I had a way to pay him back. At least this way, he will forgive a portion of my loan and grant me an extension to repay the remainder. This will allow your aunt to go on in society as she has before and will see that my sons' good names continue to be respected. Their futures are at stake as much as Amanda's. I've done nothing but cause pain and misfortune to all those I love."

Uncle Jonas covered his face with the palms of his hands and turned away from her. He made no sound, but his quaking shoulders were proof he'd finally been touched by remorse. Fanny stood and quietly crossed the room. After a quick glance over her shoulder, she pulled the door closed behind her. She had no desire to watch her uncle collapse in defeat. Though he'd brought this upon himself, it was Ellert Jackson who now controlled all of their lives. How could Mr. Jackson so easily take advantage of her uncle when he was in dire circumstances? Then again, Uncle Jonas had done the same thing to Ellert years ago. Though two wrongs would not set things aright, Fanny knew Ellert would take great pleasure in watching her uncle suffer.

A tear trickled down her cheek, and she swiped it away with the back of her hand. If only she could think of some way to help Amanda. Keeping to the path leading from the front of the house, she followed the trail until she neared the water's edge. Gathering her skirts in one hand, she picked her way toward a large flat rock, where she could stare at the water and contemplate a solution. Although she normally did her best thinking while near the river, her remedy didn't work today. Not one single idea came to mind. She longed to help Amanda escape before it was too late. But how?

Fanny now understood why her cousin had agreed to marry Ellert, but that wouldn't save Amanda from a lifetime of cruelty. Why did Amanda feel compelled to save the family? Had Uncle Jonas presented such an idea to George or Jefferson, they would have laughed at him. Neither of the young men would willingly agree to such an arrangement. Amanda deserved to make her own choice. It seemed Fanny's marital happiness only served to underscore Amanda's tragic plight all the more. Her tears flowed unchecked as she stared across the water.

"Here you are!"

Fanny swiped at her eyes before turning to look up at Michael.

"What's happened? Why are you crying?" Concern shone in his eyes as he dropped down beside her. He reached around her waist and pulled her close. "Tell me what has made you cry, my love."

She rested her head against his chest and described the exchange with her uncle. "I cannot bear to think of Amanda spending her life with a man like Ellert Jackson. There must be something we can do. I've been sitting here for well over an hour trying to devise a plan, but I can think of nothing." She straightened and looked into Michael's eyes. "Have you any idea how we can help?"

Michael gently wiped away her tears. "No matter what, I believe things will work out for Amanda. We must pray that God will protect her from both her father and from Ellert Jackson." Michael tipped her chin upward until their eyes met. "God knows what's happening. None of this has taken Him by surprise. Right now we don't understand, but I believe good will prevail."

"I know you're right, but it appears it will take nothing short of a miracle to save Amanda from being sentenced to a lifetime of misery with Ellert Jackson."

"Then you must pray for that miracle, dear Fanny, and I will do the same."

CHAPTER 21

SATURDAY, JULY 22, 1899

After a final look in the mirror, Amanda walked to the bedroom window and glanced outside. The sight of Ellert standing near a large pine in the front yard was enough to send her scurrying toward the bedroom door. He appeared none too happy. She hoped that during their tour of the island today she could summon up some sort of feelings, something other than intense distaste, for the man she would soon wed. Ellert could be nice enough when he wanted to gain favor, but he could also be demanding. His passion and lust frightened Amanda more than she could say. Blake's kisses had stirred feelings of desire within her heart, but when Ellert so much as touched her, she wanted to run.

"Amanda! Where are you rushing off to?" Fanny asked. "I told Sophie we would join her for a picnic today."

Amanda glanced over her shoulder. "I can't. I'm late meeting Ellert. I promised him a walk around the island." She could hear Fanny's muffled footsteps on the carpeted hallway and knew her cousin was hurrying after her. She twisted around at the top of the stairs and waved her cousin to a halt. "I'm sorry, but I simply cannot go with you."

"I don't understand why you want to spend time with that despicable man. If we don't find a solution, you'll be tied to him for the rest of your life. I'd think you would want to stay away from him while you can."

"There isn't going to be any miraculous solution, Fanny. If I spend time with Ellert, I may find that he actually possesses a few redeeming qualities—that we are compatible. At least that's my hope."

Fanny sighed. "I don't think you'll be successful, but I wish you well. We'll miss having you with us."

Amanda pulled her cousin into a fleeting embrace. "And I shall miss being at the picnic. More than you can imagine." She released her hold and nodded toward the door. "I must be on my way."

"Do promise to give me a full report later today. I'll want to hear if you discover any admirable qualities in the man."

With a sense of foreboding Amanda ran down the steps and out the front door. Like her cousin, she doubted Ellert would exhibit any admirable qualities. But refusing his request for a full tour of the island had been impossible. The thought of being alone with him caused a tremor. His cruel assault during their previous excursion remained a frightening memory. She slowed to a ladylike gait as she crossed the lower veranda and strolled to Ellert's side. "I do hope I haven't kept you waiting long."

He tapped his watch pocket. "As I recall, we agreed to meet at ten o'clock."

She offered what she hoped was a demure smile. "That's correct."

"You're seven minutes late. I don't tolerate tardiness. Don't let it happen again." Then he smiled and extended his arm. "Tardiness causes so many problems in life. If I sound harsh, it's because I know the damage that can be done in not dealing with matters in a timely manner."

Her stomach lurched, but she managed to maintain her smile. "I'm generally not late, so rest assured I'll give heed to your desires for promptness."

He smiled. "See. It's not all that difficult to please me."

Amanda nodded. "I'll do my very best. Shall we begin our tour?" He offered his arm, and though she accepted, she would have preferred to maintain a greater distance between them. Mr. Jackson's angry, immediate rebuke had increased both her fear and dislike of the older man. "The house sits two-thirds of the way between the furthermost tips of the island. Do you have a preference for which way we begin?"

"I thought you were in charge of this tour. Surely you know which way is best to proceed, don't you? I thought you wanted to be an independent thinker."

She looked at him rather confused. "I do enjoy that privilege, but you've made it clear to me that you would have it otherwise."

"My dear Amanda, there are things I will not tolerate in our marriage, be certain of that." He narrowed his eyes. "Betrayal of my trust in any form will be punished swiftly and without mercy."

She frowned. "But doesn't everyone deserve mercy? Surely you are a godly man. Does not Jesus ask us to practice mercy and forgiveness, even to those who do not deserve it?"

Ellert laughed. "I am amused that you presume me to care one ounce what godly men might think or do. I serve no master but myself." He looked around. "Now are we to take that walk, or would you prefer to further discuss my supposed shortcomings where spiritual matters are concerned?"

The man was rude, but she'd already known that. "We'll take the path leading south," she said.

Mr. Jackson made no comment on the beauty of the island or the amazing views of the river as they headed southward. Instead, he maintained a downward focus. Perhaps he feared tripping on a branch or a rock. She did her best to draw him into conversation, but it seemed he had no interest in the magnificence of the island. Her attempt to provide him with a brief history had been met with a quick silencing glare.

Curling his fingers into his palm and using his thumb to point back toward the island mansion, he asked, "Who owns the house and this island? The entire family? Your father? Who?"

She hesitated, uncertain why he would ask and not sure she had an answer. "My grandparents owned this island. I'm not sure what distribution has been made since my grandfather's death. I believe there was some stipulation in the will that it remain in the family. Why do you ask?"

"Because I want to know."

His curt response annoyed her. "There are several islands currently for sale. Several have homes even larger than—"

"I don't want to buy an island. And if I did want to purchase property, I *wouldn't* seek the *advice* of a *woman*."

He emphasized the final words as though he intended each one to deliver a fatal blow. And they had—to her ego. If she didn't change the topic, she might tell him exactly what she thought of him.

"I've been completing the wedding plans and thought you might want to offer some suggestions. Other than insisting the wedding take place at the church on Round Island, you've not indicated your preferences."

"I don't care a whit about the wedding plans. The wedding is simply something I will abide for your sake. I agreed to a formal wedding only to satisfy your father's need to pander to the social crowd."

"I believe he was thinking of you, also," Amanda said. "Without a gala affair, gossip would run rampant. I doubt such talk would serve you well."

He laughed. "I have never worried what others thought of me. I don't need their approval. Your entire family concerns itself far too much with the wagging tongues of Rochester society. I have succeeded in spite of them. And you, my dear, will learn they are of little import once we are married. Let them attend the wedding, but that shall be the end of such nonsense."

She wanted to ask if he planned to keep her away from her family, but she feared his response. "Then I may continue to make all of the arrangements without seeking your approval?"

He pulled her close. His dark eyes bore down on her like a vulture prepared to attack. "The only thing that interests me is our wedding night. Make certain you prepare for that event."

Amanda squared her shoulders but didn't fight his hold. "You know that I am an innocent woman. Why must you speak to me in such a manner? I may be trained in various medical procedures, but I have never been with a man." She surprised them both with her bold statement.

His harsh laughter cut through the morning breeze and echoed through the treetops. In spite of her best effort to remain calm, she shuddered. Ellert pinched her chin between his thumb and forefinger. "I'm pleased to hear that you are innocent, but in truth your fear already betrayed that fact. And I find it exciting. Fear enhances everything, don't you think?"

"Don't you mean *desire* enhances everything? Shouldn't both a man and a woman look forward to their wedding and their life together? Fear has such a negative connotation. I fear things I don't understand—destructive, mean, evil things." She raised a brow. "Surely you would not have me think thus of you. Are there not more benefits—more loyalty and respect—if I should honestly and completely love you?"

He looked at her for a moment. It was clear he was taken off guard by her comment. He softened his hold and let his fingers skim her cheek. Amanda took the opportunity to continue.

"I know the arrangement you've made with my father. Whatever hard feelings and ill will that lay between you two needn't come between us. I am willing to help my family in the demanded manner, despite the fact that my loved ones and friends think me mad. However, I would much rather have a husband to whom I could look up to and respect, love, and obey, as you once mentioned, with a glad and willing heart."

He pulled back as if her skin had suddenly burned him. Ellert looked at her oddly for a moment, and then his features hardened. "I thought you a woman of intelligence, but I can see you hold the same nonsensical beliefs as the rest of your gender. I care nothing about your desires or love. I demand your respect and obedience, and I find that fear is often the best way to get both. You will learn quickly just how cruel and hard I can be, both in public and private, when I am crossed or otherwise made to look the fool."

His words and behavior appalled Amanda, but she fought to remain calm. She must attempt to find some common ground with this man if she was to spend the rest of her life with him. Perhaps it would help if she could discover his interests. Amanda forced herself to take hold of his arm. "Let us continue our walk. Tell me of your business ventures. What interests you the most?"

"Anything that will make me money. I don't give in to the whims of what I might like or dislike. If it is a venture that will add to my holdings, I am interested. Although I abhor the boorish stupidity and the silly games played by social elitists, I do enjoy the many comforts money can buy. And I'm not opposed to purchasing occasional trinkets for myself or for those who show me loyalty."

Amanda was quite certain he didn't frown upon worldly possessions, at least for himself. The servants had been quick to tell her that Mr. Jackson had arrived with seven huge trunks filled with tailor-made suits and more shoes than had been brought by any other guest who'd ever visited Broadmoor Island—male or female. Amanda had been keeping a close watch, and as yet she hadn't seen him wear the same pair of shoes more than once. No doubt he was a man who would take a great deal of understanding, but becoming better acquainted with Ellert Jackson was proving most difficult.

She watched a boat pass by carrying a group of sightseers pointing at various islands. They appeared carefree and happy. She wondered if they'd enjoy a picnic lunch later in the day. Ellert remained a short distance from the edge of the bluff, and she turned to wave him forward. "There is a particularly lovely view from this vantage point."

"I've never been overly fond of the water. The view is fine from here."

His words affirmed his earlier comment. If he didn't enjoy the water, he would never buy one of the islands. She had hoped he might consider a summer home so that she could visit with Fanny and Sophie each year. Of course, he'd not yet said where they would make their permanent home. The thought of life without her cousins close by spurred her to ask, "Where we will make our home once we are married?"

"In New York City. I purchased an estate when I first moved to the city. It was constructed more than a century ago, but it has been well maintained and has been furnished with all of the modern amenities found in your Rochester mansion. I believe it is far superior to any home in Rochester." He crooked his finger and beckoned her to his side.

Though she would have preferred to maintain the distance between them, she did as he bid. If she hoped to persuade him to change his mind, she'd need to appear malleable. "I had hoped we might live in Rochester, at least part of the year. I've always been surrounded by family members. I'm sure you understand my desire to remain close to them."

"If you remain near your home and family, you'll never become reliant upon me." He pulled her close in an ironlike grip. "I don't want your family involved in my life—only you, dear Amanda." He chuckled at her frown. "You'd be rushing home to cry on your mother's shoulder every time you were unhappy. Then your father would pay me a visit and plead with me to behave like a good husband." Ellert shook his head. "I don't want interference in my business ventures or in my home."

"But they won't interfere. I wouldn't allow for it."

"Don't whine at me. I've seen some of the things you're capable of, my dear. I know now that I must put you fully in your place or we might never know a moment's peace." His face contorted, and it was almost as if he became someone else. "I won't tolerate you putting others between us."

"I would never do such a thing if only you will agree to live in Rochester. I can't bear to think of losing the companionship of my cousins. I have lived in Rochester my entire life, and my family is of great importance to me. Won't you please reconsider?" When he didn't respond, she decided to plead her case a bit further. "You are aware I've been working with the impoverished in Rochester, and I truly desire to continue my work. I have begun my training to become a physician and realize it is my life's calling. I love medicine and want to continue. You have often commented that I might do exactly that and—"

He yanked her forward and pushed her against a nearby tree with a ferocity that knocked the wind from her lungs. His transformation from gentleman to monster was complete. Unable to speak, Amanda stared at him in disbelief. He bared his teeth like a mad dog.

"I know exactly how much you love medicine—I saw you along the shore of Round Island with Dr. Carstead. Tell me, what medical procedure was he teaching you when I saw you locked in his embrace?"

She cowered as he leaned even closer, his hot breath on her face. With his free hand he yanked her hair until her head tipped back against the tree.

"Look at me when I speak to you!"

Hands trembling, she forced herself to meet his hardened stare. "I'm sorry," she whispered.

"*Sorry?* If you know what is good for you, you will heed my words. In the future there will be severe consequences for such behavior. As I said, I will not tolerate being made the fool, and I will punish betrayal. If our wedding were not close at hand, I'd show you what punishment you can expect in the future. You can count yourself fortunate that I don't want you marked up for our *blessed nuptials*."

Her scalp throbbed with pain when he finally released her hair, but she didn't want to give him the satisfaction of seeing her massage her head. She thought he'd finished with her, but when she attempted to take a sideward step, he pushed her back.

"You will move when I tell you to move! Your life with me will be as I direct. The only decision you will make is to follow my instruction. You will not come or go without my approval, and you will see no one unless I've given my consent. On the other hand, you will likely hear the servants whisper about consorts who will visit my bedchamber from time to time. I tire of women easily, and I'm certain you'll be no different than any other. You should prepare yourself to become accustomed to my habits."

"Then why marry me?" The question slipped from her mouth before she'd given thought to his reaction.

He drew back his hand as if to slap her and then stopped only inches from her face. "You are slow to learn, aren't you? I am the one who asks the questions." A cruel smirk played on his lips. "However, this one time I shall answer you because you are a silly woman with naïve beliefs about men and women. My marriage to you is nothing more than a means of repaying your father for the cruelty he heaped upon me when I was a young man. I must admit there is the added benefit of causing other members of your family a great deal of pain." He shrugged. "Besides, the marriage will require nothing of me. I will continue to live in the same fashion I've always enjoyed, but I shall have a pretty young wife on my arm and in my bed whenever I choose. And she's a Broadmoor. All of society will bow at my feet for the chance to share such an auspicious connection." He pinched her cheek until she was afraid it had turned bloodred. "I have told you how I enjoy inflicting pain, haven't I?"

She didn't know if she should answer, but when he arched his brows, she said, "Yes, you've told me several times."

"Good. I'm pleased to see there's something you remember. I can play whatever part I need to in order to accomplish what I desire. If you dare to tell anyone of this encounter, I will merely appear as gentle as a lamb, with such tenderness and concern for you that your friends and family will immediately believe you mad. You would do well to hone your own acting skills and portray in public the obedient and desirable little wife that I intend you to be." He let her go, and Amanda immediately put her hand to her cheek.

"Don't worry, it won't bruise. But please remember this. Should you do anything more to betray me—should you mention this incident—should you so much as tell your father that you do not wish to be married, I will find a way to hurt you more deeply than you can possibly imagine. It wouldn't be all that hard to create an accident for your dear Dr. Carstead."

"No!" Amanda couldn't even try to pretend his threat hadn't hit her hard. "Don't hurt him."

He grinned at her coldly. "I see it must be true love for you to react in such a near hysterical manner. At least we both know now exactly how to keep you in line."

Amanda didn't respond. There was no need. Finding any hint of goodness in this man would be impossible. Life as she had known it would end on the nineteenth day of August.

Blake ignored the knock at his front door. He was unable to offer aid to anyone at the moment. Since his return to Rochester, he'd been rendered completely useless. Each day had been consumed with endless thoughts of how he could rescue Amanda from Ellert Jackson. He didn't consider himself a poor man, yet he was far from wealthy. There was no way he could raise enough money to save Amanda. With only his small house and his medical instruments for collateral, any banker would laugh at a request for a sizable loan. His thoughts continued to race to and fro as the incessant knocking continued.

"Blake! Answer the door. It's Paul Medford. I need to speak to you."

"I can't see any patients today."

"I haven't come about a patient. We need to talk. I'm willing to shout through the window, but I don't think you want the entire neighborhood listening to our conversation, do you?"

Blake raked his fingers through his uncombed hair and plodded across the kitchen and through the parlor to the front hallway. Twisting the key, he unlocked the door and pulled it open. He met Paul's startled expression. "Well, what is it that's so important?"

"You look like death itself, Blake. Have you had any sleep or considered some hot water and a razor?"

Blake rubbed his palm across the stubble on his jaw. "Ever since my return from the island, I've been consumed with—"

"Helping Amanda. I told Quincy I assumed that was the case. But locking yourself in the house is not going to help. Quincy wants to speak with you. Perhaps the three of us can put our heads together and come up with an idea. Besides, you look like you could use a good meal."

Blake took a backward step and shook his head. "I don't want to be around anyone right now. I'm in no condition to lend aid to the sick. I can't even help myself right now."

"Please come with me, Blake. We don't expect you to care for anyone. Just come and talk with us. You need some fresh air and a different perspective." Paul clasped Blake's shoulder and pulled him forward. "Come along. You'll feel better. I promise."

Blake considered shoving Paul out the door and retreating back into the kitchen, but he knew such an idea was foolhardy. He could see the determination in Paul's eyes. The man would not be deterred. "I won't stay long."

Paul didn't argue or say much of anything except to comment on the warm weather until they'd arrived at the Home and were settled in Quincy's office. "It's just as I thought. He's dejected over Amanda's approaching marriage."

Quincy frowned. "You don't look good, Blake. I know you love Amanda and had hoped to convince her to set aside her marriage plans, but you can't permit her rejection to ruin your life. You have your work, and there are many eligible young ladies who would be delighted to have you as a suitor. Believe me, I know whereof I speak. Isn't that true, Paul?"

Paul nodded his agreement. "He's absolutely correct. Only yesterday Lila Harkness was asking about you. I believe she's hoping that you'll come calling."

Blake massaged his forehead. What were these men thinking? "I don't believe you understand my dilemma."

"Of course we do, my boy." Quincy patted his shoulder. "We've all gone through the ups and downs of love and rejection. If Amanda has decided she wants to marry Ellert Jackson, then you must determine to move forward with your own life. It's simply the way of things."

"But she didn't reject me," Blake said. Before either of the men could interrupt him again, he explained what had occurred when Amanda had come to Round Island. "We love each other, but her father is forcing her to marry Ellert in order to save himself from financial ruin."

Mouth agape, Quincy sat up straight. "Jonas has bargained away his own daughter? How could he?"

"I'm sure you know him better than I do, but it seems that money and social status are the driving force behind his decision. I've tried to come up with a solution that would resolve this entire matter, but money is the only answer. And I don't have access to enough money to be of assistance."

Quincy hunched forward and rested his arms across his thighs. "I don't want to believe my brother would lower himself to such an arrangement, but I don't doubt your word, Blake. There is nothing left but for me to do but return to the island and speak to Jonas. I knew he had business dealings with Ellert years ago, but I didn't know they'd recently entered into any business contracts. Then again, Jonas seldom confides in me. I must find out exactly what agreement he's made with Ellert." He shook his head. "None of this makes sense."

"When will you go?" Blake asked.

Quincy appeared dazed when he looked up. "I think I should catch the next train to Clayton. If things are as you say, we will need as much time as possible to get this all straightened out."

For the first time since he'd talked to Amanda, Blake felt a glimmer of hope. "If you have no objection, Quincy, I'd like to accompany you to Broadmoor Island."

CHAPTER 22

Broadmoor Island

Quincy could barely wait for the boat to pull alongside the dock before he stepped onto the wooden pier. He extended his hand to Blake. "You may not be welcome, you know."

Blake nodded. "I understand, but even if your brother orders me off the island, I had to come."

Quincy grinned. "The last I knew, I still owned a portion of this island, so I don't think he has the authority to order you to leave. On the other hand, your presence may lead to an uncomfortable confrontation, and I'd like to speak to Ellert and my brother before they're overly displeased with me." He nodded toward the boathouse. "I see Fanny and Michael are over at the boathouse. Why don't you ask Fanny if she can arrange a meeting between you and Amanda while I go up to the house?"

Blake sighed. "That sounds like an excellent plan. I was afraid I might be forced to return home without an opportunity to speak to Amanda. I'm certain Fanny will help."

Quincy patted the young man's shoulder and then turned to the path that led to the house. Both his brother and Ellert appeared surprised to see him when he topped the hill and neared the veranda. He offered an affable greeting to them, but if their frowns were a gauge of their feelings, neither was particularly pleased to see him.

Nearing his brother's chair, he said, "I'd like to speak to you and Mr. Jackson in the library." Without giving them an opportunity to object, Quincy continued into the house. He'd never been assertive with his older brother, and he hoped curiosity would force the two men away from their game of cards.

He sat down in one of the leather chairs. When several minutes passed without the arrival of either man, Quincy drummed his fingers atop the massive desk in nervous fashion. Finally he heard the faint creak of the screen door as it opened and closed. He ceased drumming and folded his hands in his lap. He wanted to appear calm and composed when he spoke to his brother and Mr. Jackson.

"If this turns out to be another one of your brother's woeful tales that he needs money to help the poor and ailing, I'll walk out."

Quincy clenched his folded hands as the comment drifted into the library. "Don't concern yourself, Ellert. I can handle my brother."

He felt a momentary sense of satisfaction that today's meeting would have nothing to do with requests for his charitable organizations. Both of these men would learn a thing or two today. They thought him lacking in business acumen, but today they would discover he wasn't quite so laughable.

Quincy remained seated when Jonas and Ellert entered the room. "Thank you for accepting my invitation," he said.

"Invitation?" Ellert said with a frown. "It sounded like a command to me. And for future reference, Quincy, I do not take orders. I give them. Had Jonas not persuaded me to humor you, I'd still be on the veranda playing cards."

Quincy gritted his teeth. He'd be dealing with two pompous men, not an easy task under the best of circumstances, and what he had to say would likely make matters even more difficult. He waited until they had settled in their chairs.

Jonas rested his arms across his wide girth. "Well, speak up. We didn't come in here to sit and stare at one another. What is so important that you've arrived unexpectedly and called us away from a private discussion?"

"Discussion? I thought you were playing cards." His brother scowled and Quincy turned serious. "I have recently been informed of the ill-conceived plan the two of you have entered into, and I have come here in the hope that we can set things aright before it is too late."

Ellert chuckled. "Ill-conceived plan? I don't know what you're talking about. And how *you* think you could possibly help me with anything is beyond my imagination."

"Let's don't mince words, gentlemen. I know that Amanda is being forced to marry Mr. Jackson in exchange for a sum of money. It's a bargain I find unconscionable."

Ellert's eyes turned dark, and he shook his head. "Who told you this? Amanda? You've been misinformed, Quincy. To be sure, the marriage has been arranged by your brother and me, but I did not pay for Amanda's hand in marriage. I loaned your brother some money, which he will be required to repay even though Amanda and I will be husband and wife."

Quincy straightened and threw a glance at Jonas. "Amanda said nothing to me, but I can see that the situation is as I've been led to believe. I can read it on my brother's face."

"So Jonas has been complaining of his situation? Is that it?"

"I've said nothing, Jackson. You know full well that I wouldn't."

"Then where has your brother gotten such ideas?" Ellert shot Jonas a hard look.

"Look, I know how to do business as well as you do."

"Ha! If that were the case, you would never have found yourself in such a bind," Ellert countered.

Jonas and Ellert continued to spar until they realized Quincy knew what had transpired between them. When the truth was finally spread out before them, Quincy leaned toward his brother. "Why didn't you come and speak to me, Jonas?"

"For what reason? So you could revel in the news that your brother has made a mess of the family finances?"

"Is that what you think of me? That I would gloat over your misfortune? Surely you know me better than that. Did you think I wouldn't offer aid?"

Jonas sneered. "What aid? I needed money, Quincy. You're the one who has spent these past years begging and pleading with others to give *you* money for your charities. What would you have done? Arranged another benefit and asked for pledges to pay your brother's debts?"

The sarcasm dripped from Jonas's words. His brother held him in greater disdain than he'd imagined. "If that's what it took. I have friends who would no doubt help."

Jonas jerked away as if Quincy had slapped him. "And let the entire world know that the Broadmoors were in financial crisis? We would be the laughing-stock of Rochester. Society would turn its back and never allow a Broadmoor to darken its doorstep." He shook his head. "You would quickly find that we have no friends."

Ellert guffawed and pointed an unlit cigar at Quincy. "You have no idea the sum of money I've loaned your brother. Your miserable friends and their donations wouldn't be enough to sway me in the least."

Quincy scooted forward on his chair. "Can we come to an agreement, Mr. Jackson? Surely you do not want to impose marriage on an innocent young woman. She had nothing to do with causing the bad feelings between you and Jonas."

Ellert slammed his hand on the desk. "The only agreement I'm willing to make is the one I have already secured. I want your brother to suffer as much as I did. I want to take the only thing away from him that truly matters—his family's respect."

The remark caused a stab of pain, and Quincy gave his brother a sideward glance before returning his attention to Ellert.

"But it's unfair to punish Amanda for her father's offenses."

"Members of my family were hurt by your brother. That was unfair, also." Ellert shrugged. "I've learned that life isn't fair, and therefore I seek my own methods in order to repay those who have wronged me."

" 'Avenge not yourselves, but rather give place unto wrath: for it is written, Vengeance is mine; I will repay, saith the Lord.' Romans 12:19."

"No need to quote the Bible to me, Quincy. I have no interest in what your Lord has to say about those who have wronged me or how I choose to retaliate. I don't look to God for help, and I don't plan to wait on Him to mete out His vengeance. I prefer my own methods."

Quincy bowed his head and considered a response. He couldn't permit El-lert's statement to go unchallenged, yet he didn't want the man to storm out of the room before they'd arrived at a better solution. He looked up at the man. His features had hardened into an angry sneer. "None of us is perfect, Ellert. We've all sinned and come short of the glory of God. You, me, Jonas—everyone who has ever lived. And we've all been hurt by others. But freedom from the pain of injustice doesn't come by inflicting misery upon others. You may feel some fleeting pleasure when you force Amanda into marriage, but you'll gain no permanent relief by hurting her. Forgiveness is what heals wounds. Just as Jesus forgives our sins, we must forgive one another."

Ellert held out his palm as if to stave off the words. "Enough! I said I don't want to hear your Bible verses, and I don't want a sermon, either. I have no desire to forgive or forget. My wounds are as fresh as the day your brother inflicted them, and that's exactly the way I want them. Pain is what makes people remember they are alive."

Quincy shuddered. "Surely you do not truly believe what you're saying. It is love and kindness that—"

"If you will not heed my admonition, this meeting is over."

"Wait." Quincy reached for Ellert's arm. "I promise I'll say nothing more about forgiveness or the Bible, but please remain a few moments longer."

Fearful he might be detected before he could speak with Amanda, Blake silently followed Fanny up a steep path she'd declared safer than the main trail. She waved him to a halt as they neared the top. "Wait beside this tree and watch for me to wave you forward," she instructed. "Many of the windows are open, and I want to be sure no one will see you and call your name."

Blake nodded and stationed himself between two half-grown fir trees that would keep him well hidden. He inhaled shallow breaths while he awaited her signal. When he heard a faint whistle, he stepped out of his hiding place and topped the hill.

"This way," she said, waving him close to the house. "Keep low so you're not spotted if someone should look out one of the windows."

He was surprised by Fanny's stealthy maneuvers until he recalled the stories Amanda had told him of the three cousins and their escapades around the island as well as in the city of Rochester that still remained a secret. They'd obviously learned many useful tricks. He wondered what any family members might think if they should see the two of them creeping beneath the window ledges as they circled the house. He pushed aside the thought. Fanny would likely tell them it was a game they were playing with her cousins. And they just might believe her.

As they edged toward the rear of the house, Blake could hear an angry exchange taking place inside. He recognized Quincy's voice and then heard a heated response. What if Mr. Jackson stormed out of the meeting before Blake could speak to Amanda? His mouth went dry at the thought, and he pushed Fanny forward.

"Hurry. I think the meeting is going to end."

Fanny turned and placed her index finger against her pursed lips. Her searing look was enough to silence him. She motioned for him to remain hidden behind a small bush while she checked the kitchen. A moment later she waved him forward and pointed to the rear stairs. They crossed the kitchen on tiptoe and then hurried up the steps. After passing several bedrooms, she lightly tapped on a closed door and turned the knob, not waiting for an answer. With her free hand she grasped Blake's wrist and yanked him into the room.

Shock registered in Amanda's eyes when she looked up. The book she'd been reading clattered to the floor, and Fanny lunged forward and clapped her palm against Amanda's lips. "Remain quiet and I'll remove my hand."

Amanda bobbed her head, and Fanny slowly released her hold. "You two don't have long to talk. I'll wait outside the door and keep watch."

"It might be best if the door remains ajar. I don't want any accusations of impropriety," Blake replied.

The moment Fanny stepped outside the door, Blake clasped Amanda's hands in a firm grip. "I have wonderful news." He stroked the back of her hand while he explained Quincy's hopes to put an end to the forced wedding. "Quincy believes he can solicit the help of old family friends and raise enough money to see this matter dealt with. I can't imagine Mr. Jackson will refuse. I believe he loves money above all else, don't you?"

Amanda bowed her head. "No."

"No? You believe he truly loves you?"

"No, of course not. But Ellert will not agree to take the money. He has already told me that his greatest pleasure is inflicting pain upon others. No matter what Uncle Quincy offers, he'll never agree." She withdrew her hand from Blake's grasp and caressed his face in her palm. "You will never know how grateful I am that you are attempting to help, but neither you nor my uncle Quincy will convince Ellert to change his mind. He is cruel and evil. His deepest desire is to punish both my father and me."

"I don't understand why he would want to punish you. The financial transaction took place when you were a young girl. You had nothing to do with it."

A tear slipped down her cheek. "He saw us," she whispered.

"What do you mean?"

"At Round Island—he saw us kissing. He was in a skiff out on the river— he'd come looking for me."

She shivered, and he longed to pull her into his arms.

"He has threatened to harm me if I ever disobey him or if he should receive a report of me seeing any other man."

"I'll not stand for this. How dare he threaten you! I'm going downstairs and confront him. I'll not stand for—"

Amanda clutched his arm. "No, please. You'll only make everything worse. He means to harm . . ." She fell silent. "There truly is no means of escape for me. I've resigned myself to a future as his wife. Ellert has been clear—my life will be lived according to his dictates." She released her hold on his sleeve and looked deeply into his eyes. "You must not continue these attempts to save me from Ellert, but please remember that no matter what happens, I will always love you. That must be enough."

"Until you are his wife, I will not accept this arrangement your father has made. Somehow, we must find a way." He leaned forward to kiss her, but she took a backward step.

"I can't . . ." she whispered.

Blake turned on his heel and trudged across the room with the weight of defeat hanging over him like a shroud. He hoped that Quincy had met with greater success than he had. Fanny was sitting outside the door at her self-appointed post. She smiled up at him as he offered his hand to pull her to her feet.

"You don't appear very happy," she whispered. "Didn't your talk go well?"

"She has resigned herself to the marriage." He shook his head. "She seems to have no will to fight against it. Even though she's asked me to make no further attempt to save her from the marriage, I refuse to give up. Perhaps you can talk some sense into her."

Fanny glanced toward the room. "Wait here and give me a few minutes. Then we'll return to the boathouse."

Blake took up Fanny's position outside the door, and from his vantage point he watched Jonas and Quincy walk through the front foyer and exit the house. He glanced at the bedroom door. Fanny might be in there for some time. His curiosity attacked him with an intensity that wouldn't be stilled. He hadn't heard anyone downstairs since the men departed. With one final glance at the bedroom door, he walked down the front steps.

Ellert stared at the library ceiling while he finished his cigar. He'd felt a sense of relief when Jonas and Quincy left. Let the two of them wander around their island and commiserate over their misfortune and wallow in their sorrow. The thought gave him great pleasure. In fact, the entire meeting had provided a great deal of entertainment. Simply watching Jonas go pale at Quincy's suggestion that they employ the help of old friends had been quite amusing. Jonas couldn't bear falling into social obscurity. He knew it would forever damage any hopes for business dealings—at least lucrative ones.

Ellert chuckled. In time Jonas would come to realize that his position as a reigning leader of Rochester had come to an end. He could only imagine what Quincy and Jonas would do and say now that they were alone. Quincy was likely quoting Scripture to Jonas. Ellert grinned. Perhaps Jonas and his pretentious wife could take up residence in Quincy's Home for the Friendless when all was said and done. He chuckled at the idea.

With the same harshness that permeated his thoughts, Ellert stubbed out his cigar and blew one final puff of smoke into the room. The air had grown warm and dank. He looked out the far windows. A bank of clouds had turned dark and appeared to be rolling in toward the island. The breeze would surely prove cooler outdoors. He pushed himself up from the chair and ambled toward the library door. He'd made his way only a short distance down the hallway when he heard muffled footfalls on the carpeted stairs. He stopped midstep. *Blake Carstead!*

With his fingers curled into his palms, he formed two tight fists and remained motionless until Blake disappeared into the darkness. Only then did he take four long strides and look up toward the second-floor balcony. Amanda stood looking down at the front door. Anger welled in his chest until he thought it might explode. No one had mentioned Blake had come to the island. When and how had he gotten here? *Quincy*. He must have arrived on the boat with Quincy. He clenched his jaw. The entire time the three of them had been meeting in the library, Blake had been upstairs dallying with Amanda. How *dare* he? How dare *she*?

A fire raged in Ellert's belly. "That young man will pay for this. Something must happen to him—and soon," he hissed from between clenched teeth.

CHAPTER 23

Friday, August 4, 1899

Victoria sat at her dressing table pulling the brush through her hair, the gray streaks more noticeable with each passing day—or so she thought. She lifted the top layer of hair and examined the strands that lay beneath and then leaned closer to the mirror. The roots were definitely gray. She'd be completely gray before long. And little wonder. Few women would have survived a marriage to Jonas without turning completely gray long ago. Unfortunately, the mere thought of her husband had seemed all that was necessary to propel him into their bedroom.

He crossed the room and dropped into one of the upholstered chairs that flanked the double door leading from their bedroom to the upper veranda. While Victoria continued to brush her hair, he sighed and leaned back to rest his head against the soft upholstery. "This has been a most trying day."

Victoria remained silent.

A few moments later, he said, "There was something or someone to create disharmony at every turn."

If Jonas expected her pity and comfort, he would be sadly mistaken. She stared at her own reflection and continued her ministrations. She could feel his stare boring through her until she finally turned to meet his annoyed look in the mirror. Yet she said nothing. Her piercing look should be enough to speak volumes.

"I will not tolerate this silent treatment of yours any longer, Victoria. I had no choice but to agree to Ellert Jackson's terms." He hunched forward in his chair and continued to stare at her in the mirror. "That's what this is about, isn't it? I wouldn't want to misinterpret what has caused your ire."

Victoria gathered her dressing gown in one hand and twisted around on the chair. She gave a slight nod before turning back to the mirror to braid her faded hair.

"Nothing will be resolved between us if you refuse to speak to me."

The single braid swung forward when she lurched from the chair and bent toward him, anger flashing in her eyes. "Nothing was resolved when we *were* speaking. I have told you over and over again that I do not want my daughter relegated to a loveless marriage. She is precious to me—she deserves more, even if you don't think so. I've come to realize that none of us means as much to you as your bank account."

"Don't you judge me, Victoria. When there is no money to purchase new gowns or pay servants' wages, you'll think the money every bit as important as I do. Worse still, when society turns its back on you and all the doors close to those glorious homes you frequent, you'll certainly begin to understand. I have made it abundantly clear that I had no other choice. Everyone else has accepted the arrangement. Even Amanda has come to terms with the wedding. I don't know why you can't do the same."

Victoria seized her brush from the dressing table and pointed it at her husband. "*Why?* I'll tell you why, Jonas. Ellert is a deceptive man who will do harm to our daughter, and yet you insist that she marry him. I was momentarily charmed by him, but after spending time with him here on the island, it's become apparent that he's far more than he pretends to be. You found a means to settle your mistakes, and Amanda is the one who will suffer. You made the wrong choices, yet you expect someone else to pay the price." No doubt she'd overstepped proper boundaries, for Jonas appeared stunned into silence.

Soon, however, he regained his former pomp. "What happened to my prim and proper wife who vowed to obey her husband?"

"I believe she went the way of her husband, who vowed to love and honor his wife and family." The fact that Jonas continued to deflect all wrongdoing from himself only fueled Victoria's anger. She'd not sit back and watch Amanda's life destroyed without a fight. "What would your father think of what you are doing?" She clasped a palm to her bodice. "Worse yet, what would your mother think? Family—not society—was the centerpiece of their lives. Not only did they teach you that principle, but they also lived it. How can you so easily discard what they've taught you?"

Sadness invaded her spirit. "If you permit this marriage, I don't know how you can ever again hold your head high. Besides ruining your daughter's life, your behavior shames the entire family."

Her husband's jaw twitched. Instead of softening his heart, she'd angered him further.

"I will not listen to—"

Dropping her hairbrush atop the vanity, Victoria jumped to her feet. "No need." Before Jonas could say another word she rushed from the room. Now what? As she glanced down the hallway, her focus settled on Amanda's bedroom door. Hastening to the door, she tapped lightly and waited only a moment before turning the knob. She didn't want Jonas coming into the hallway and creating a scene that would be whispered about among the servants come morning.

She glanced over her shoulder to be certain all remained quiet before she closed the door behind her. Moonlight shone through the window and splashed across the room. Amanda pushed herself upward and leaned against the pillows. "Mother! What are you doing here at this time of night? Are you ill?"

"I'm fine—at least physically. However, I cannot say the same regarding my mental state." She sat down on the edge of the bed and clutched Amanda's hand within her own. "I simply cannot bear the idea of having you wed to Ellert Jackson. I have spoken to your father at length, but he refuses to listen." Victoria continued to pour out her heart. Above all, she wanted to save Amanda from this horrid mistake.

"You can do nothing, Mother." Amanda held her mother's hand against her cheek. "There is nothing any of us can do. The agreement has been made. Ellert won't hesitate to use every means available to ruin the family."

"Let the family suffer financial ruination. I love you far too much to stand by while your father signs away your future." Victoria scooted closer. "I have a plan," she whispered.

Amanda fixed her with a wide-eyed stare. "Truly?" Amanda drew her legs to her chest and leaned forward until her chin rested upon her bended knees. "Tell me!"

"We will run away. If we dress now and hurry, Mr. Atwell can deliver us to Clayton. We can board the first train of the morning before anyone misses us. Once we're in Rochester, we'll gather the remainder of our belongings, take the train to New York City, purchase passage on the first available vessel, and sail for Europe. We can make our home abroad."

When Amanda didn't immediately answer, Victoria continued. "My plan will work. I know it will. We have friends enough in England and France who will help us once they learn of our need."

"I'll admit the idea is tempting, but too many people would suffer in the wake of such a decision." Amanda shook her head. "No. I couldn't. What about George and Jefferson? And what of William and Grayson and their families? And what about Father? I know you are angry with him, but he is your husband. What if he did harm to himself because of our decision to leave? Neither of us could ever forgive ourselves if such a thing would happen."

Victoria hadn't considered Jonas taking his life. He loved himself far too much to do such a thing—didn't he? Yet her daughter's questions haunted her. Could she bear the thought of alienating the rest of her family? What if none of them ever wanted to see her again? Unbidden tears rolled down Victoria's cheeks, and Amanda pulled her into an embrace.

They clung together until Victoria's tears were spent. She dabbed her eyes one final time and then glanced toward the door. "Your father is likely asleep by now. I should probably go back to our bedroom."

Amanda nodded. "Thank you for your deep concern and love. We must not lose hope."

Victoria smiled and kissed Amanda's cheek. The young woman had maturity far beyond her years.

Once her mother left the room, Amanda leaned back against the pillows. Strange that she should be betrothed to a man who possessed money enough to ease the suffering of many. Yet he chose to hoard and increase his own finances while those around him suffered. "He's completely oblivious to anyone's needs or wants except his own," Amanda muttered. She plumped the pillow behind her and reached for her Bible. How is it that the Lord blessed the likes of Ellert Jackson? she wondered. Shouldn't God Almighty strike him down instead? It seemed that Ellert's life was one of charmed existence. At least it had been for many years. Granted, he'd likely suffered in his early life, but shouldn't that give him more reason to help those in need?

There was little doubt she'd be married to one of the wealthiest men in the country. Some said his fortune rivaled John D. Rockefeller, though Amanda found such assertions difficult to believe. Would a man of such wealth bother with the petty rivalry that he had displayed over the past months? Surely not. At any rate, Ellert's finances would be of little concern to her. He was not a man who would be convinced to turn loose of his money unless he could even a score or gain a profit. Helping the poor wouldn't qualify on either account. She hugged the Bible to her chest and closed her eyes. "You must help me, Lord, for there is no one else who will be with me. I earnestly pray that I won't be forced to marry him, but if there is no other way, I pray that you will grant me peace and acceptance."

Still holding the Bible in a firm grip, she closed her eyes and drifted to sleep.

CHAPTER 24

Saturday, August 5, 1899

Walking downstairs the following morning, Amanda clenched her fingers into a tight fist. Ellert awaited her at the bottom of the steps. "I was beginning to wonder if you were ever going to come down for breakfast." He offered his arm and escorted her to the dining room. "You'll not be remaining abed so late once you're my wife. If I must be up and earning money, I expect every member of the household to do likewise."

"And how shall I earn money, sir?"

He scowled at her flippant reply. "You will earn your keep by properly running my estate and by warming my bed at night." He pulled a dining chair away from the table and bid her sit down. Once she was seated, he leaned close to her ear. "Be advised that I intend to take my pleasure with you quite often."

His hot breath on her neck caused an involuntary shudder. She didn't want to think about Ellert Jackson in such a way. She didn't want to think of him at all. Ignoring his salacious remark, she signaled the servant to pour her coffee. "I have to go into Rochester with my cousins today for the final fitting of my wedding gown and their dresses." She hoped he hadn't detected her trepidation. "Please pass the cream," she added, hoping to relieve the tension. How she wished another family member would join them at the table, but they'd probably eaten earlier. She silently chided herself for remaining upstairs until this late hour.

He handed her the silver cream pitcher. "I think not."

She turned to face him. "A final fitting is required, or the gown will not be completed in time for the wedding. I can only imagine what the social column would say. *Ellert Jackson marries Amanda Blake on August 19. The bride's gown was an ill-fitting dress of white satin with an unfinished hem and wide sleeves that drooped beyond the bride's fingertips.*" She stabbed a piece of ham and dropped it onto her plate.

"Do you think I truly care what the newspaper writes about me—or you, for that matter? What I do or say is not controlled by newspapers or the old dowagers who consider themselves authorities on proper social etiquette. However, I do want you beautifully clothed when we are married, for I look forward to removing every article that you will wear."

She felt dirty beneath his leering stare and turned away. "If you want my gown completed, I must go to Rochester."

"And I said that you will not. Do you truly believe I would permit you to go to Rochester and visit your wonderful Dr. Carstead?" He pinched her chin between his thumb and forefinger. "Do you think I'm so stupid that I don't realize your true intent? You don't care about your wedding gown or your cousins' dresses. The only thing you care about is another secret meeting with that doctor."

She twisted her head and freed herself from Ellert's grasp. "Believe what you wish, but my only reason for going to Rochester is to keep my appointment with the seamstress."

"I'll send word to the owner of the shop. They can send seamstresses here to the island. I doubt the owner will refuse the amount of money I offer for special services."

Amanda didn't argue. It would be of little use. "Then I suppose you'd best send your message soon, or there won't be sufficient time." She pushed away from the table. "If you'll excuse me, I've lost my appetite."

Amanda had expected Ellert would bark an objection when she hastened from the room, but he surprised her and remained silent. She breathed a sigh of relief once she'd made it outdoors.

Fanny rounded the side of the house with a carefree spring to her step and waved at Amanda. "There you are. We missed you at breakfast. I was going to come and waken you, but your mother said I should permit you the extra sleep." She drew closer, her eyebrows furrowed in concern. "Are you not feeling well?"

Before she could respond, Sophie bustled out the door and joined them. "Elizabeth is taking her morning nap. What time are we to leave for Rochester?"

Amanda shook her head. "We're not going. Ellert has decreed that he will make arrangements with the shop owner to have seamstresses delivered to the island to fit my gown." She hesitated a moment. "To fit all of our dresses."

"But why?" Sophie demanded. "This is our final fitting, and it has been scheduled since the very first day you ordered our dresses. Why did you agree? Tell him you're withdrawing your consent, and we are going to Rochester."

Amanda struggled to keep her tears at bay. "I can't. Ellert has made it clear that it would be in my best interest to do as he says."

"He has made you his prisoner, and you're not yet wed to him." Sophie cupped Amanda's face between her palms and stared into her eyes. "Listen to me—you cannot marry this man. Do you not realize what your life will be like?"

At the sound of footsteps approaching the door, Amanda freed herself from Sophie's hold. If Ellert was watching them, she'd be quizzed about the conversation. "Why don't the three of us walk down to the boathouse, where we can speak freely?" She hurried toward the path without awaiting a response from either of her cousins.

Once they were on the path, Sophie came alongside Amanda and grasped her hand. "I am at a complete loss, dear Cousin. At first I thought you'd agreed to this marriage simply to create some jealousy on Blake's part. It's obvious you've succeeded on that account, yet you still continue with your plans to marry this dreadful man. I know it cannot be Mr. Jackson's wealth, for you know your father would never let you suffer from want."

An unbidden frantic laughter escaped Amanda's throat. She clasped a hand to her mouth to hold back the hysterical sounds that echoed through the trees.

Wide-eyed, Sophie grasped Amanda by the shoulders. "What has come over you?"

"She'll explain once we're at the boathouse," Fanny said. She turned to Amanda. "You should tell Sophie."

"That's not fair. The two of you have been keeping secrets from me." Sophie came to a halt and glared at them like a petulant child.

"Do cease your prickly behavior, Sophie. This is much more important than your bruised feelings. Once you hear the full extent of what has happened, your sympathies will be directed toward Amanda rather than yourself. Come along, now," Fanny said, grasping Sophie's hand and pulling her forward.

Although the door to the boathouse creaked in protest, the river's familiar scent seemed to bid them come inside. Water slapped along the sides of the moored boats and swayed them in a peaceful rhythm that created a calming effect. Fanny pointed to the wooden chairs along the back wall.

"Let's move them close to the window that overlooks the path. We want to be able to see anyone who might be coming in this direction," Fanny said.

They formed the chairs in a semicircle. Once they'd each taken a seat, Sophie folded her hands in her lap and arched her brows. "I'm waiting."

Amanda smiled at her cousin. Dear, dear Sophie. She was obviously doing her best to overcome her wounded feelings, but her tone of voice indicated she'd met with little success. "My intent was never to hurt your feelings by withholding information from you, Sophie. But my time alone with you has been limited since Ellert's arrival on the island. And you are busy with Elizabeth and Paul. That is as it should be," she quickly added.

Although relating the details of all that had occurred proved more taxing than Amanda had contemplated, she explained the agreement her father and Ellert had devised, as well as the fact that he had observed her with Blake when they'd gone to Round Island.

Sophie clasped her palm to her mouth at the revelation. "You mean while Paul and I were sitting on the porch of the Frontenac Hotel, Ellert was in a skiff on the river?"

Amanda nodded. "Yes. He saw us kiss, and though I can't be certain, I believe he knows Blake visited with me upstairs in my room after he arrived with Uncle Quincy."

"Blake visited you in your bedroom?" Sophie giggled. "I can't believe my prim and proper cousin would entertain a man in her bedroom. I can only imagine what occurred during that visit."

"Sophie!" Fanny's scolding tone was enough to halt Sophie's laughter. "I can attest to the fact that nothing happened. The door was left ajar, and I sat outside until he departed."

"It's all right, Fanny. I know Sophie was merely jesting. Because Ellert believes I'll go and visit Blake, he won't permit me to leave the island. To make matters worse, he insists we must live in New York City. I doubt he'll grant me permission to visit you, but I'm hopeful that he will become more lenient with me once we are married."

"I wouldn't count on him loosening his stranglehold on you. I fear he'll become even more possessive once you're locked into your marriage vows," Sophie replied.

"We should be offering Amanda encouragement," Fanny said.

Sophie shrugged. "I believe it's best to be honest with her. She needs to find some way out of this wedding, for she'll never escape Mr. Jackson once they are wed."

"I know you're right, Sophie, but there is no way out." While her cousins kept a mindful watch on the path, Amanda recounted her mother's visit the previous evening.

Sophie inched forward on her chair. "What if we helped you escape without your mother? Surely Fanny and Michael have enough money to pay for your passage to Europe." Sophie looked at Fanny for confirmation.

"We do, and I know Michael would agree to give Amanda sufficient funds, but that doesn't resolve the problem."

Amanda nodded. "She's right, Sophie. Ellert has threatened to harm too many people if I refuse to go through with the marriage." She didn't feel she could share the threat Ellert had made on Blake's life, so she continued from a different angle. "My escape would leave the family in financial ruination. Although Mother thinks she could survive such a disaster, I know she could not. And though my father has brought this upon himself, I believe he would take his own life rather than face the social ostracism that would follow public knowledge of his financial ruination."

She met Fanny's surprised expression. "I know he said your father was weak and pitiable for such an action years ago, but that was before my father faced his own personal demons. I think he has amassed more insight at this point in his life and more fully understands the depth of despair that can overwhelm the mind."

"I hope he will never meet such an end, for there is always hope when we look to the Lord for guidance. Mrs. Atwell has helped me to understand that there is no problem that cannot be conquered with God's help."

Sophie nibbled her lip. "Then why don't we have an answer for Amanda's dilemma?"

Fanny sighed. "I'm not certain, but I continue to pray and trust that when the time is right, she will be delivered from this situation. To that end we must all remain diligent in our prayers."

"Agreed," Amanda replied.

Fanny and Amanda stared at Sophie.

"Agreed," Sophie muttered. "But God had better hurry up, or you're going to be in New York City before the end of the month."

Not only did a seamstress and helper arrive at the island, but Mrs. Smithfield, the owner of the dress shop, came along to oversee the fittings. Though Amanda couldn't be certain, she guessed that Ellert had paid dearly for the service. Much to Amanda's relief, Mrs. Smithfield insisted he remain far away from the upstairs guest room that the servants had converted into a fitting room. The furniture had been moved to one side of the room or shoved into the hallway to provide adequate space for the seamstresses to complete their assigned tasks.

The time with her cousins proved to be a mixture of joy and sorrow. They laughed and reminisced about their very first grown-up dresses and many of the dresses they'd worn since that time. Yet beneath the laughter remained the foreboding that this might be last time they would be permitted to enjoy the company of one another. When Mrs. Smithfield finally announced that their task had been completed and she would return with the finished gowns the day before the wedding, Amanda longed to summon her back and insist upon one more fitting. Anything to prolong this time with her cousins and away from Ellert's watchful eye.

Amanda remained in the room while the seamstresses followed Mrs. Smithfield like chicks scurrying after a mother hen. How she wished she could follow them to Rochester and go back to her work at the Home for the Friendless and to the warmth of Blake's arms.

A short time later she trudged down the rear stairs, through the kitchen, down the hallway, and into the library in search of a book that might take her mind off of the approaching wedding and her future with Ellert. Slowly she traced her fingers along the leather spines, hoping one of the titles would capture her interest.

The sound of the approaching footsteps caused her to glance over her shoulder. "Good afternoon, Father. I'm looking for a book."

"I've been looking for you ever since the seamstresses departed. Please come and sit down." He closed the door and drew a deep breath.

Her father's somber appearance and the fact that he had closed the door weren't good signs. Had he been seeking her out to deliver additional bad news? She truly didn't know if she could withstand anything further, yet it appeared there was little choice but to hear him out. She trudged toward the chair, her feet growing heavier with each step.

He waved her onward with a waning smile. When she'd dropped into the chair beside him, he leaned toward her. "I owe you a deep apology for what I've done to you, and I want you to know how much I regret the decision I made with Ellert Jackson. If I could withdraw from my contract with him, I would do so. I truly never meant for things to come to this. My greed and desire for power have proved to be my undoing and created a tragic circumstance for the entire family—but more than any other, I have inflicted tragedy upon you."

She was taken aback by the sight of tears forming in his eyes. Never had she seen her father cry. The idea that he could feel such sadness disarmed her. "Father, I . . ."

He shook his head. "Let me finish while I have the courage." It seemed he could not look at her. Instead, he stared at his highly polished shoes. "Throughout my life, I have prided myself in the fact that I could control every situation. Now I find myself up against something that surpasses my own abilities. I can find no way out of this disaster I've created."

She spied a single teardrop on his shoe. If he noticed, he made no move to wipe it away. How had their lives come to this? Her father weak and defeated—the rest of the family suffering the pain of his decisions. This was a time that should be filled with joy and happiness. Instead, they were all overcome by grief and despair. She reached out and rested her hand on her father's thick arm. "Please don't continue to berate yourself. Although I doubt I will ever be happy with Ellert Jackson, I am resigned to my role as his wife, and I forgive you for what you've done. I pray you will never consider committing such a misdeed again, but I cannot leave home holding this against you."

He reached forward and cupped her face between his palms, then kissed her on the forehead. "I am forever grateful and overwhelmed by your compassion. I don't deserve such a daughter as you."

CHAPTER 25

Friday, August 18, 1899

Amanda stood on the dock holding Ellert's arm while members of the wedding party boarded the *New Island Wanderer* for their brief journey to Round Island for the wedding rehearsal. Ellert had chartered Captain Visegar's boat for the entire weekend. It was a silly and unnecessary expense, as far as Amanda was concerned. She hoped Mr. Atwell hadn't been offended by Ellert's arrangement, for the *DaisyBee* would have proved more than adequate for their needs throughout the weekend.

"I believe that's everyone," Ellert said.

"No," Amanda replied, pulling from his hold. "Sophie and Paul haven't arrived." As if on cue, Sophie scuttled down the path, her skirts hiked above her ankles.

Ellert curled his lip in a look of disgust. "Your cousin will be late to her own funeral."

"She has a baby who requires her time and attention. Besides, she's not late. She's exactly on time." Amanda didn't give Ellert an opportunity to refute the comment before she hastened to greet Sophie.

"I'm sorry if I've kept you waiting. Elizabeth sensed I was leaving her with the nanny and continued clinging to me. Paul is going to stay with her until she goes to sleep; then he'll have Mr. Atwell bring him over on the *DaisyBee*."

"No apology necessary, Sophie. Come sit by me." Amanda noted Ellert's glare when she sat down between Fanny and Sophie. He'd expected her to remain at his side. For a man who boasted he didn't care what others thought, he certainly appeared intent upon making an impression throughout the weekend.

"A wedding in Rochester would have proved much simpler," Sophie whispered.

"Indeed. However, the plans are made, and there's no need lamenting what is past," Amanda replied.

Sophie leaned closer. "Are you speaking of the wedding location or the fact that you are going to marry this man? Fanny and I can still help you escape."

"I do appreciate your loyalty, dear Sophie. But I have accepted that this marriage is going to take place and my future is with Ellert in New York City."

"And I have continued to pray that a miracle will occur and he will release you from the marriage. I fear you will be completely miserable with him, and once he moves you to New York, we'll never see you again."

"I'm determined that won't happen. We are family, and somehow I will find a way to visit you and Fanny. You must write me often and tell me about Elizabeth and her achievements."

After clanging the bell of the *New Island Wanderer*, Captain Visegar maneuvered the boat away from the dock. The water churned in seeming protest, but moments later the engine prevailed. Soon they were on their way.

Ellert signaled for her to join him, but Amanda averted her gaze and remained between her cousins. She'd likely hear of his displeasure later in the day, but for now she'd enjoy her cousins' company. Once they were well under way, she managed a glance at Ellert. He'd taken a seat beside her father, and the two of them were in the midst of a discussion. She hoped their conversation revolved around something other than her.

When the boat docked at Round Island a short time later, Amanda's father jumped to his feet and darted to her side. "Ellert is displeased that you chose to sit with your cousins rather than with him. He's known to exhibit an unpleasant temper, Amanda. I understand your desire to visit with Fanny and Sophie, but I wouldn't intentionally provoke him."

One look at Ellert was enough to confirm he had prompted the admonition. Amanda stepped forward and grasped his arm. "Do lead the way, Mr. Jackson."

"My pleasure, Amanda. Once we're married, you'll follow only my lead." He leaned close, and his lips brushed her ear.

She attempted to stifle the involuntary shudder that coursed through her body at the touch of his lips. How could she ever learn to love this loathsome man? Stepping into the waiting carriage, she determined to remain silent throughout the short journey to the church. She had nothing to say to him. Ellert seemed impervious to her silence, for he stared out the carriage window and made no attempt to engage her.

Smiling broadly, the preacher stood in the doorway of the steepled church and waved them forward upon their arrival. He appeared to be the only one who bore some semblance of joy. He held his Bible in one hand and shook hands with each of the men before directing them to their respective positions inside the church. "You ladies will use this room off the foyer," he said, walking with them into the room, "so that you may enter the church without being observed prior to the ceremony."

Amanda smiled and nodded as the preacher offered each directive. She cared little if Ellert saw her before she walked down the aisle. The entire marriage was a charade, yet there was no way the solemn minister could know. She covered her mouth to withhold a sudden burst of laughter, but it escaped her lips like an overflowing brook. Soon she slipped into a fit of uncontrollable laughter. Tears blurred her vision when she finally caught sight of the preacher, who appeared confounded by the situation. She did her best to stop, but each attempt proved a miserable failure.

"I believe you may have developed a case of nervous agitation, Miss Broadmoor. This sometimes happens prior to marriage. If you'll breathe deeply and exhale slowly, I'll fetch you a glass of water." He hesitated. "If that doesn't work, perhaps we should seek medical assistance for you."

Amanda giggled and shook her head. "No. I don't think a doctor will be necessary."

"Unless you could arrange for a doctor from Rochester," Sophie whispered.

She nudged Sophie in the side, but the reminder of Blake proved enough to turn Amanda's convulsive laughter to tears.

Mouth agape, the minister pushed a chair behind her. "Sit down, Miss Broadmoor. I believe you've moved from nervous agitation to wedding hysteria. I will see if I can locate smelling salts."

Those unwelcome words were enough to stop both her laughter and her tears. Amanda straightened in her chair and pointed at the man. "Don't you dare try to treat me with smelling salts." The preacher took a backward step. "I apologize for my sharp retort, but I cannot abide the use of smelling salts." She took his timid smile and nod as his agreement. "I will be fine if you'll give me a moment to compose myself."

"We will begin when you are ready," he said.

After several slow breaths, Amanda gave a slight nod. If she waited until she was truly ready, they would never begin. Soon after the minister's departure, the three of them exited the small room. In the foyer they were greeted by her father and her two older brothers, Grayson and William. Her younger brothers, Jefferson and George, stood near the doors to the sanctuary. They would act as ushers. Both had privately stated they'd prefer to take a beating rather than see her marry Ellert Jackson. She'd refrained from revealing the details of the arranged marriage to either Jefferson or George, and she wondered if they'd feel the same way if they knew the truth. Would they be willing to give up their lives of affluence and social standing for her sake? Perhaps. However, her older brothers and their wives wouldn't be so sympathetic. None of them would want their lives disrupted in any manner. Jefferson and George had attended college, and although they enjoyed living well, Amanda didn't think her younger brothers were interested in hard work—or *any* work, for that matter.

The chords of the piano sounded, and Fanny glanced over her shoulder. "An organ would have been better, don't you think?"

"Or a piano that had been tuned," Sophie suggested with a giggle.

Amanda clung to her father's arm as they walked down the aisle. After he turned her over to Ellert and retreated to her mother's side in one of the front pews, the remainder of the rehearsal proceeded in a blur. Once they'd practiced to the minister's satisfaction, they were dismissed with final instructions for the following day.

"This wedding is going to be the highlight of the summer." The preacher propelled Ellert's arm up and down as though priming a pump. "Thank you for choosing our little church for this magnificent event."

"If Amanda has not already offered an invitation," Ellert told the preacher, "you and your wife are invited to join us at the Frontenac Hotel this evening, where we'll be enjoying dinner and an evening of festivities beginning at seven o'clock." Ellert attempted to wrest himself free of the man's hold.

Amanda nearly laughed at the remark. An evening of festivities? More likely an evening of mourning. This would be her last evening to enjoy with her cousins and family before she became Ellert's wife.

Ellert remained close to Amanda throughout the day and didn't even consider leaving her alone until they'd finished dinner at the hotel.

"I'm going out on the veranda for a cigar. I'm certain you'd prefer to remain inside with your cousins."

"I would."

He nodded. "I'll return before the dancing begins. Do not permit anyone to sign your dance card. Do I make myself clear?"

"Abundantly."

His eyes narrowed. "I sincerely hope so."

The warm August air was heavy with the scent of rain, and Ellert glanced at the sky as he bounded down the front steps of the hotel and strode toward a distant stand of trees. Amanda's clamoring friends and relatives were enough to send a sane man into turmoil. He much preferred solitude. This wedding was enough to reinforce his plans to avoid Amanda's family once they were married. Until after the wedding ceremony, she could believe that he'd permit occasional visits to Rochester or that he'd extend an invitation for her family to come to New York on holiday. Tomorrow, he'd abruptly put an end to those fantasies.

He struck a match to the tip of his cigar, leaned against the tree, and stared at the moonlight reflecting upon the water. Everything was falling into place just as he had planned. By tomorrow he'd be married to Amanda Broadmoor, and the Broadmoor family would be at his mercy. He took a deep draw on the cigar and considered the many possibilities.

"Strange that a prospective bridegroom would be hiding out here by himself."

Ellert wheeled around. Anger seized him as he came face-to-face with Dr. Carstead. "What are you doing here? I know your name isn't on the invitation list."

Blake shrugged. "This is a public hotel. I am a paying guest and am here to enjoy the pleasure of a weekend in the Thousand Islands. To my knowledge, an invitation is not necessary."

Ellert fought to gain control of his seething rage. How dare Blake Carstead come here and cause trouble. "We both know the only reason you're here is to interfere with my marriage to Amanda. You have no reason to be here." He spewed the words from between clenched teeth.

"Quite the contrary. You know that Amanda doesn't love you, and I don't believe you love her, either. I've come here to see if we can reach an agreement so that Amanda is free to marry me."

The young man had courage—Ellert would give him that much. And he obviously loved Amanda, or he wouldn't continue his attempts to interfere. Love truly was for fools—for those willing to step outside the realm of reasonable contemplation. He was glad he would never have to count himself among such foolish people.

"If you know what is good for you, you'll go back to Rochester and forget Amanda. I'm certain any number of young ladies would be pleased to become your wife." He gripped Blake's shoulder in a tight hold. "The circumstances surrounding my marriage to Amanda are none of your business. And they are far beyond your understanding, Dr. Carstead."

Blake twisted free of Ellert's hold and pinned him with a defiant glare. "You're wrong. I know exactly what has transpired between you and Jonas Broadmoor."

Ellert inwardly raged while he listened to Blake recount detailed information of his agreement with Jonas. Obviously Amanda and the young doctor had been doing more than kissing the morning he spotted them together on this very island. Like one of those old dowagers who whiled away the afternoon with tea and gossip, Amanda had passed along her arsenal of information. Just like her father! A genuine fool. She'd take more training than he'd thought.

When Blake had finally completed his onslaught, Ellert tossed his cigar to the ground and crushed it with the sole of his shoe. "I've heard enough." He took a step closer and grasped Blake's arm. "Now, you listen to me, Dr. Carstead. Either you put aside any thought of marriage to Amanda and forget all of what you've been told, or I'll have to see that your handsome face receives a bit of damage. Those pretty girls in Rochester might not be nearly as interested in you once you've met with an *accident*. Do I make myself clear?"

"You don't frighten me." Eyes flashing with anger, Blake pulled free from his grasp. "I can take care of myself."

"I might not frighten you, but I do frighten Amanda." He smiled. "The fact is, you cannot take care of yourself. Not against the men that I will send to pay you a visit. And if a beating doesn't do the trick, it is easy enough to have you killed." Ellert snapped his thumb and forefinger together. "It takes only money and the snap of a finger."

"You can try whatever you like, but I'll not be deterred by your threats. If I can't have Amanda, it matters little what you or your bullies do to me."

Ellert studied the young man for a moment. Blake's words rang with sincerity, and that fact alone was enough to stir Ellert to action. He straightened his shoulders and looked directly into Blake's eyes. "You listen to me, and you listen very carefully. I don't doubt what you've just said. You would likely die for your lady fair, so you leave me no alternative."

"What is that supposed to mean?" Blake curled his fingers into tight fists.

Ellert knew the young doctor longed to punch him between the eyes. He'd likely take great pleasure in pummeling him to death. But Ellert knew that wouldn't happen. Blake was a doctor. A man dedicated to saving lives, not taking them.

"I mean that unless you return to Rochester and forget Amanda, I'll be required to punish *her* rather than you. If you take any action to stop this wedding, you may rest assured that she will suffer dearly—all because of you."

Blake raised a fist and punched the air. "Only a coward would do such a thing. I cannot believe you would hide behind Amanda's skirts."

"Don't be foolish. I'm not hiding behind anyone. I'm simply telling you what will happen: You either disappear from Amanda's life or know that she will suffer for your refusal. It is your choice, dear boy." Ellert turned and walked away. He would leave the young doctor to dwell upon his choices.

BROADMOOR ISLAND

The boat ride back to Broadmoor Island was done in silence. Amanda sat rigidly beside Ellert but said nothing, and he seemed just as glad for her lack of words. When they disembarked and everyone went their separate ways, Ellert didn't attempt to control Amanda. She found it strange but was greatly relieved to make her exit.

Amanda had just begun to change for bed when, without warning, Fanny and Sophie bounded into her room. Veda continued to unbutton Amanda's dress as Sophie dropped onto the bed. Fanny stepped forward. "I'll do that, Veda. You can go on to bed."

The maid frowned and shook her head. "I know what will happen if I leave. The three of you will stay up late talking, and Miss Amanda will be all puffy-eyed for her wedding. She needs a good night of sleep before her wedding day."

Amanda smiled at the servant. "I promise we won't stay up much longer, Veda. You go ahead. Fanny will help me out of my dress." When Veda didn't make a move, Amanda lightly touched her shoulder. "You have my word."

The maid trudged toward the bedroom door, her reluctant steps evidence she wasn't completely convinced. With one final warning look, she closed the door behind her. The three girls sighed in unison and then giggled.

"Goodness, but she's become the protective mother hen these past few days," Sophie said. "We're either sidestepping Ellert for a few minutes of your time or staving off the servants with promises of proper behavior. What happened to those days when we used to gather in our rooms and talk for hours on end? Nobody cared in the least back then."

Fanny laughed as she unfastened the final button. "They were pleased to have us contained in one room instead of carrying out one of our many pranks. I do believe we were a greater threat than Jefferson and George." She met Amanda's brown-eyed gaze in the mirror. "Don't you agree?"

"Absolutely! Those two were never our match, though they still remind me of the whitewash incident."

"I can still see your father covered with that pail of whitewash. I'm not certain who was more surprised." Sophie rolled back on the bed and convulsed in laughter.

"It is a pleasant memory," Amanda admitted.

"Oh, and do you recall the first time we attended a dance at the Frontenac Hotel?" Fanny glanced over her shoulder while she carried Amanda's dress across the room to the wardrobe. "The three of us in our party dresses thinking the young fellows would die for an opportunity to dance with each one of us." She hung up the dress and turned around. "As I recall, they did flock around the two of you. I was the only one left standing by the punch bowl."

"I received my first real kiss that night," Sophie recalled.

"You *didn't*!" Fanny joined them on the bed. "You never told us." She looked at Amanda. "Did she tell you?"

"No! You've been keeping secrets from us!" Amanda pointed at Sophie. "What else do you need to confess?"

"Nothing. I promise," Sophie said, turning serious. "We shall miss you,

Amanda. You must remember that though we are separated by distance, you will always be in our hearts and in our prayers."

"Yes, always," Fanny added. "And if you should need us, you must send word, and we'll hurry to your aid. Promise that you will write us the truth of how you are faring so that we may know how to pray for you."

"You have my word that I will do everything in my power to visit and to write as often as possible. We may be apart, but our love and our memories will keep us together always."

"Agreed," Fanny said. "I suppose we'd best leave. I don't want Veda to hold us accountable if Amanda should have puffy eyes for the wedding." She leaned forward and kissed Amanda's cheek. "Good night, dear Amanda. I hope you are able to sleep well."

Sophie added her wishes for a peaceful night before embracing Amanda and bidding her good-night. "We'll be with you through every step tomorrow."

"Thank you both. I don't know how I would have managed throughout these past weeks without the two of you." Amanda stood at her bedroom door for a moment and watched her cousins walk hand in hand down the hallway.

After crossing the room, Amanda slipped into bed. How she would miss Fanny and Sophie. Once she departed for New York, the opportunity for friendship with other women would likely disappear. She feared everything she held dear would vanish once she married Ellert Jackson. As a tear slipped down her cheek, she uttered a silent prayer for strength to face the unknown fearful future that lay ahead of her. She must remain strong.

SATURDAY, AUGUST 19, 1899

"Miss Amanda, come on now and wake up." Veda's appeal was soon followed by a tug on the sheet. "No time to dawdle. This is going to be the most hectic day of your life."

Amanda rolled over and sat up on the edge of the bed. It had been close to dawn before she'd fallen asleep, and even that brief time had been filled with ghoulish nightmares.

"Look at those eyes. I knew you three wouldn't keep your promise," Veda said as she strode across the room and opened the windows.

A damp breeze wafted into the room, and Amanda glanced out the window. The dismal overcast skies predicted an impending storm—a perfect reflection of the dismal future awaiting her.

CHAPTER 26

The sky was still dark and foreboding by the time Captain Visegar docked the *New Island Wanderer* at the Broadmoor boathouse. He would provide transportation to Round Island for all the family and friends attending the wedding. He and Ellert had detailed the plans for pickup of wedding guests from several of the many islands.

Ellert had also reserved the rooms at the Frontenac Hotel without Amanda's knowledge or consent. However, she was now grateful for a place where she could prepare for the ceremony and avoid contact with Ellert until time for the wedding. These final hours before the exchange of vows would be the last when she could at least partially consider herself a free woman. Certainly she'd always been subject to the dictates of her father, but life under Mr. Jackson's roof would undoubtedly prove much more restrictive. She closed her eyes and inhaled a deep breath. How she longed to lift her eyelids and discover this was merely a bad dream. Unfortunately, the pitching boat and the mist that dampened her cheeks were enough to prove this nightmare was real.

Once they arrived at Round Island and she and her cousins were alone in the small suite of rooms, Amanda beckoned Sophie forward. "I'd prefer to eat lunch here in the room by ourselves rather than go downstairs and join the others. Do you think you could convince the chef to have our meal sent upstairs?"

Sophie winked. "Of course. You can count on me. I'll even go downstairs shortly before lunch and explain to Ellert that you won't be joining him. He probably won't be happy, but you can count on me to explain."

After her cousin left the room, Amanda signaled Fanny closer. "I have questions . . . about the wedding night. Mother has avoided all talk of what I might expect, and Sophie would likely laugh at me for asking. As you can expect, my knowledge is nonexistent. Would you be willing to enlighten me as to what I should anticipate?"

A faint blush colored Fanny's cheeks as she drew near and sat down beside Amanda. "I can only tell you that for me, the wedding night was very special because of the deep love Michael and I share. From my observation of Mr. Jackson, I fear he may not be kind or gentle with you."

Amanda swallowed hard and forced back the threatening tears. "Whatever shall I do? Many of his comments make me believe he won't be easily deterred. I had thought to feign a headache or stomach ailment if I couldn't abide his attentions, but . . ." She shrugged her shoulders and looked to Fanny for an alternative suggestion.

"He will undoubtedly take any attempt to discourage his advances as an affront. You don't want to anger him. I do fear Mr. Jackson would become unduly cruel if incensed. Perhaps you should simply plead the truth: You are a woman of virtue and would appreciate that he show patience with you."

Amanda removed her handkerchief from her pocket and dabbed a tear from her eye and nodded agreement. "I'll try what you've suggested." She forced a smile. There was no need for further discussion, for neither of them had an answer. She knew that pleading her virtue would have little impact upon Ellert. He cared only about himself and probably would take great pleasure in causing her pain. Hadn't he said as much in the past weeks?

Before Fanny could respond, Amanda's mother bustled into the room with two of the servants and several trunks in tow. She pointed and issued directions and then shooed the servants from the room. "Send Veda up here immediately," she called after them.

"I don't need Veda yet, Mother. I'm not going to dress this early in the day."

Wagging her finger as a warning, Amanda's mother continued across the room. "Nonsense. You must dress for the luncheon. Ellert has arranged a lovely affair—or so the chef tells me."

Amanda grimaced. "I plan to eat here in my rooms. I want to reserve all of my energy for the wedding festivities. Besides, Ellert and his guests will want time to visit prior to the wedding. What better time than at the luncheon he has arranged?"

"Ellert tells me that he will have only one guest attending the wedding. His lawyer, Leighton Craig, has arrived."

Fanny arched her brows. "None of his friends or family responded?"

Her aunt grimaced. "He has no family—at least none that he invited. His friends were either otherwise obligated or out of the city. This is, after all, August. Many of them are traveling abroad or enjoying themselves at their summer homes." As if to indicate such an occurrence was a normal and expected happenstance, her aunt gave an affirmative nod.

"Still, it would seem he would have at least a few friends and business acquaintances who would be willing to return for such an important event," Fanny said. "Many of the Broadmoor family friends are returning from their—"

"Mr. Jackson is aware his guests are unable to attend, and he appears quite content with the arrangement. He is the one who insisted upon an August wedding," her aunt replied. "If I'd had my way, this wedding would not even—"

Amanda reached forward and grasped her mother's hand. "Mother, please. There's no need to fret. Sophie is going to make my excuses to Ellert. He can visit with Father and Uncle Quincy."

Her mother squeezed her hand. "Of course. You girls enjoy this final bit of time together. I'll preside over the luncheon and do my best to assure El-lert you are using the additional time to make certain you are prepared for the ceremony."

Amanda leaned forward and kissed her mother on the cheek. "Thank you."

"It's the least I can do. I fear I'm sending you into a lion's den without any form of defense," she whispered into Amanda's ear.

"I'll be fine. You worry overmuch."

Her mother's eyes had turned as dull as the gray skies. "I pray you're correct."

"That's what we must all do," Fanny said, drawing near her aunt and cousin. "We must pray that God will keep Amanda in His constant care and protection."

"Yes. You're correct, Fanny. We must pray for Amanda without fail. And we should begin at this very moment."

With their heads bowed, Amanda's mother prayed for her well-being and for God's direction. Though Amanda was thankful for her mother's prayer, the somber plea did little to alleviate her fear.

After the men had been transported to the church, the carriage returned to the Frontenac Hotel for the ladies. Preceded by Fanny and Sophie, Amanda descended the wide staircase of the hotel with Minnie clucking orders and draping the flowing train over one arm. Veda followed close behind with the veil and headpiece while Amanda's mother directed them outside.

"Do hurry before it begins to rain. I think you should have dressed at the church, Amanda. Your gown will be ruined if—"

Amanda touched a finger to her lips. Thankfully, her mother took the cue. The gown was of little concern. Even if she walked down the aisle soaking wet, Ellert wouldn't be deterred. He was determined to punish the Broadmoor family, and he would soon achieve his goal.

The ride to the church was over much too soon. Veda and Minnie whisked Amanda into the small anteroom, arranged her headpiece and veil, and pronounced her beautiful. The minute the two maids had completed their ministrations, Sophie and Fanny entered the room and added their enthusiastic approval. The gown was of the finest quality. Ellert had paid the seamstresses well, and they'd produced a gown befitting royalty. Embellished with seed pearls and imported lace, the softly pleated bodice fit snug around Amanda's waist and flowed into an overstated train that had been delicately edged with the same pearls and lace. Had she been walking down the aisle to marry Blake, she would have been delighted with the overall effect of the gown and headpiece. Instead, she cared not a whit.

The piano chords sounded like a death knell as she followed Fanny and Sophie from the room. Attired in a frock coat, double-breasted vest, and striped trousers, her father paced the narrow vestibule like a caged animal. Careful to avoid tripping on the hem of her gown, Amanda stepped to her father's side. She reached up and straightened his tie.

"You look beautiful," he whispered. "I'm so sorry this mus—"

"No more apologies, Father." She grasped his arm, and the two of them stood just beyond the sanctuary doors while Fanny and Sophie preceded them down the aisle.

At the minister's nod her father patted her hand. Together they walked toward the front of the church, where Ellert stood waiting. She shivered at the sight of him and wondered what he would do if she broke loose and ran from the church. Would he run after her, or would he simply announce to all of those present that her father was a thief and a scoundrel of the worst possible sort? She heightened her resolve and took the final halting steps toward her ill-fated marriage.

The minister's words echoed in the distance. Though she heard everything being said, she remained oddly detached. She heard Ellert repeat his vows and affirm that he wished to take her as his wife. Now the minister was staring at her, waiting for her corresponding response. Ellert grasped her fingers and squeezed until she flinched in pain.

"I do," she croaked, her hoarse whisper barely audible.

"Louder," Ellert hissed.

"I do." This time the words were crisp, clear, and loud enough to be heard by the congregation of family and friends.

At the preacher's signal Ellert crushed her mouth in a possessive and bruising kiss. When he finally released her, their guests appeared shocked or embarrassed; Amanda couldn't be sure which. But of one thing she was absolutely certain: Her life would never be the same.

CHAPTER 27

A soft rain began to fall shortly after the wedding guests returned to the hotel. The light showers continued as their soup was served, but the storm that had threatened throughout the day struck with a vengeance during the main course. Although thunder clapped overhead and lightning streaked the skies, the wedding guests appeared unconcerned. They ate their fill, made several toasts, and applauded when Ellert and Amanda cut their wedding cake.

A short time later the guests followed the couple into the huge dance hall. At Ellert's signal, the musicians began the promenade march and then followed with a waltz. The moment the waltz began, Ellert crushed himself against his bride. "Look at me and smile."

Although Amanda considered ignoring his command, he tightened his hold until she thought her ribs would break. She looked up at him and forced a smile. "You've already succeeded in making me your wife. You say you care little what others think, so why must I appear to be happy?"

He leaned down until his lips were nearly touching her own. "Because I dislike dour women. Women were created to please men, and it pleases me to see you smile. Therefore, you will smile in my presence. Is that clear?"

She broadened her smile in response. He didn't appear to detect the anger that raged beneath her smile. If he had, he likely would have snapped her in two. The thought was enough to keep the smile frozen on her lips for the remainder of the dance.

Following the waltz, the musicians began to play a gallop, and Ellert shook his head. "I don't enjoy gallops or polkas." He grasped her arm and nodded toward the outer edge of the room. "You are not to dance with anyone without my approval. Is that clear?"

"Not even my father or my brothers?"

"Your father and brothers, but no one else. Do you understand?"

"Completely."

He reached forward and positioned his thumb and index finger on either side of her lips. He pushed upward, forcing her lips into a more pleasant expression. "Smile!" When she complied, he approved. "That's much better. I'm going to join my lawyer for a short visit. Make certain you behave like a good wife." He grasped her cheek in a bruising pinch before he strode off to speak with Mr. Craig.

With a sigh of relief Amanda dropped down onto one of the nearby chairs and withdrew her fan. If Ellert remained in the company of his lawyer for the rest of the evening, she would be more than pleased. Yet thoughts of the night that lay ahead wouldn't desist. What had seemed no more than a knot in her stomach during supper now felt like a boulder.

"May I have the pleasure of this dance, Mrs. Jackson?"

Amanda looked up into the dark brown eyes of her older brother Grayson. The fact that he'd addressed her as Mrs. Jackson annoyed her. Neither Jefferson nor George would have done such a thing. She stood and took his arm. "Am I now to address you as Mr. Broadmoor rather than Grayson?"

He appeared baffled. "Of course not. Why would you ask such a silly question?" He glanced heavenward. "Oh, you mean because I addressed you as Mrs. Jackson?" He chuckled. "Since the quest of every woman is to wed, I thought you would enjoy being addressed by the coveted title."

Was her brother truly so dense? Probably so, she decided. After all, his wife, Lydia, had tirelessly pursued him until he proposed marriage. And Amanda doubted her father had taken Grayson into his confidence and told him of his financial misdeeds. Yet how Grayson could think she would desire marriage to Ellert was beyond her imagination. She had never been close to Grayson, but for him to think she'd pursue such a marriage truly emphasized the lack of understanding between them.

"I don't care to be addressed as Mrs. Jackson today—or ever. And especially not by members of my own family. Don't hesitate to inform Lydia of my wishes. I'm certain she'll see that word circulates."

Grayson leaned back as they continued to circle the dance floor. "Are you saying my wife is a gossip?"

Amanda arched her brows. "Call it what you will. I'm simply saying your wife keeps little information to herself."

She'd obviously affronted her brother, for he remained silent throughout the dance. When the music stopped, he escorted her to her chair and then crossed the room and spoke to his wife. There was no doubt he'd related their conversation. Lydia looked over Grayson's shoulder with an angry glare.

The rest of the evening passed in a blur. Amanda danced with her father and brothers, as well as with Ellert and his lawyer. As Ellert's only guest, Mr. Craig had received special dispensation to dance with her. However, the podgy man had been able to circle the floor only twice before gasping for air. They'd been forced to make a prompt return to the punch table, and Mr. Craig stayed near the refreshments for the remainder of the evening.

Ellert was leading her to the dance floor when Captain Visegar approached. "Sorry to interrupt the party, Mr. Jackson, but the storm has calmed a bit. I do think it would be wise to head back to Broadmoor Island as soon as possible. There's no telling how long we'll have before the storm will strike again."

"Then again, perhaps the weather has cleared for the evening," Ellert said.

The old sailor shook his head. "No chance of that. I know the skies and the river. We're in for more bad weather this night."

"I'll go upstairs and change while you inform our guests," Amanda said. When Ellert didn't object, Amanda signaled to Fanny. "Would you come upstairs and help me with my dress? Captain Visegar says we should return to Broadmoor Castle as soon as possible."

"Of course. Go along upstairs, and I'll tell Michael to wait for me while I assist you."

Hiking her gown off the floor, Amanda hurried up the stairs and into the suite. Her embroidered peach gown lay across the bed in readiness, but she took no pleasure in the beauty of the dress. She removed her headpiece and veil and wondered if she would ever again find joy in anything.

The door opened and Fanny hurried across the room. "Let me help you with those buttons," she said. Without awaiting a response, her fingers moved deftly down the row. "Remember that I will be praying for you all night long," Fanny said as she gathered the yards of satin skirt into her arms. "Hold on to the bedpost and step to your left. That way you won't step on the dress."

Amanda did as instructed, though she cared not at all if she stepped on the gown; the dress was a symbol of a marriage that was no more than a mockery. Before she could express her opinion, the door burst open and Ellert entered the room.

Fanny gasped. "You should knock before entering a lady's dressing room, Mr. Jackson."

Ellert glared at her. "Get out of here." When Fanny didn't move, he leaned toward her. "Now," he growled in a menacing voice.

Amanda touched her cousin's arm. "Go on," she urged. "I'll be fine."

Fanny dropped the wedding gown across the bed and scurried toward the door. She edged around Ellert, careful to give him a wide berth.

Amanda reached for her robe, but Ellert slapped her hand. "I prefer you uncovered," he said. "Turn around so I may admire your beauty."

She did as he said, but when she'd completed the pirouette, he clenched her cheeks. "I told you to *smile*. You have a short memory, Amanda. It seems you're going to need to be punished. Perhaps then you'll remember to do as you're told."

She forced a smile to her puckered lips, and he finally released his hold. "I promise I'll remember in the future," she whispered.

He pulled her closer. "I'm starting to think we should remain here at the hotel and let the others return to Broadmoor Island. You are, after all, nearly undressed."

"I beg of you, please let me return to Broadmoor for this one final night. I won't request any other concessions during our wedding trip, and I'll do as I'm told. I promise." Her lips remained fixed in a tight smile.

"We'll return to Broadmoor Castle, but not because of your pleading. I have papers at the house, and I'll need them before we depart in the morning."

She didn't mention that a servant could secure the items and bring them to the hotel. Ellert was surely aware of that fact. Most likely he didn't trust the Broadmoor servants with his business papers. That was fine with her. At least she'd spend one final night on the island. She lifted her dress from the bed and stepped into the folds of the peach silk. He motioned for her to turn around and, to her surprise, buttoned the dress with ease.

"I will take much more pleasure in removing your dress this evening," he whispered before touching his lips to her neck. She wanted to pull away but feared Ellert would renege on his agreement. She clenched her hands into tight fists and didn't move a muscle. She even remembered to keep a smile on her lips while he continued to press his lips along her shoulder. He growled when a knock sounded at the door.

"Shall I respond?" she whispered.

He lifted his head and turned toward the door. "Who is it?"

"Jonas."

Ellert stalked across the room and yanked open the door. "What is it?" he barked.

"The others have all boarded the boat. Captain Visegar is anxious to cast off. I asked him to wait for Amanda. You and I can remain behind to complete financial matters with the hotel and the orchestra. We can take a smaller boat back to the island once we've finished."

Ellert hesitated only briefly. "Give me a moment alone with my wife, and then we'll join you downstairs. You can tell the captain that Amanda will return with him."

The moment her father was gone, Ellert seized Amanda's arm in a viselike grip. "I expect you to be ready and waiting for me when I arrive. And make certain I'm not greeted by either of your cousins. Do you understand?"

"I understand," she said, careful to maintain her smile.

The moment the captain spotted the couple on the hotel steps with Jonas, he waved Amanda onward. "Hurry!" he shouted from the walkway leading to the dock. "The storm may not hold off much longer."

Although she wanted to run as fast as her feet would carry her, Amanda waited until Ellert kissed her farewell. When he finally released her, he said, "You may join the others."

Captain Visegar joined her on the path and hurried her along. She didn't need the old captain's encouragement. Short though it may be, she was thankful for this reprieve and the distance it placed between her and Ellert.

The two men stood on the hotel veranda and watched as the boat left the pier. Ellert gazed toward the horizon and shook his head. "I don't think there's any worry over another storm. There appear to be some stars in the distance. Had I noticed the clearing skies, I wouldn't have consented to Amanda's departure."

"The captain is known to be cautious. He doesn't want to jeopardize the lives of his passengers," Jonas said.

"I'd guess he's more concerned with himself than his passengers. If the skies clear, he'll have time to return to Clayton and take a group of summer visitors for a midnight cruise. He's likely thinking of the additional money he'll earn by returning the wedding guests earlier than anticipated."

Jonas shrugged. "I suppose one can never be certain." He walked alongside Ellert back into the hotel lobby. "There is another matter I wish to discuss. Why don't we sit down for a moment?"

What did Jonas want now? At every turn it seemed there was something Jonas needed to discuss. "No need to sit down. What is it you want?"

Jonas glanced over his shoulder. "You'll recall that we agreed you would sign off on part of the loan once you and Amanda had exchanged your vows. I'd like to complete that portion of our agreement before we leave the island."

"*Now?* We can transact that portion of our business when we return to Broadmoor Island."

"No. I prefer we take care of it immediately. The minister is still here, and he's agreed to act as a witness."

"You told the preacher of our arrangement?"

"No. I merely told him we needed a witness to our signatures on a contract. He need not know the content of what he witnesses." Jonas pointed toward the far end of the lobby. "He's waiting over there, and I have the papers right here."

Ellert extended his hand. "Let me look at the papers. Unlike you, Jonas, I read everything before signing my name." Once Ellert had reviewed the document, he grunted. "Although I believe this could have waited until later, I'm willing to sign now."

Both men signed the document, and the preacher added his signature without question. He'd likely been pleased with the generous sum Ellert had paid him to perform the wedding ceremony.

"Any further requests?" Ellert asked once the minister was out of earshot.

"No, I believe that's all."

Jonas had obviously failed to detect the sarcasm in Ellert's question. "I'm going to pay the orchestra leader. Why don't you make certain the hotel manager has my account prepared so we aren't unduly detained." Although Jonas immediately bustled off toward the manager's office, the accounting was not completed when Ellert arrived a short time later. In fact, Jonas was the only person in the office. "What is the problem?"

Jonas shrugged. "The man said it would take only a few moments to compile the figures, but he hasn't returned."

Ellert paced back and forth for several minutes. "I'm going to find the manager. Should he return during my absence, tell him to wait here." He leaned down and looked into Jonas's eyes. "Do you understand?"

"No need for acerbic behavior, Ellert. I was conducting business long before you closed your first contract."

"If that remark is intended to assure me of your competency, it falls short. One need only look at your dismal financial condition to realize you are a poor businessman." Ellert turned on his heel and strode toward the front desk. He stopped short when he spotted the manager entering the front door. Waving the man forward, Ellert pointed his thumb toward the office. "Mr. Broadmoor and I are waiting for a final accounting, and you are doing what, sir? Enjoying the evening breeze? I'm certain the owners of the establishment wouldn't approve of your shoddy practices."

"My apologies, Mr. Jackson, but there's another storm moving in. I wanted to ensure that all of our guests were informed."

Ellert frowned. "I would think you could dispatch other employees for such a mundane task, but I'll not argue the point. I'm anxious to pay my account and depart."

"I don't think you want to consider leaving—"

"If I want your advice, I'll ask." Ellert nodded toward the manager's office. "Now, I'd like to conclude our business." He clenched his jaw and followed the manager. No wonder businesses failed nowadays. How could any establishment be expected to succeed when the hired help required constant supervision? Another affirmation that strict control must always be maintained—both in his business and personal life. He shook his head in disgust. No one could be trusted.

After examining the account in detail, Ellert pointed out several discrepancies. "You've charged me for an extra night on one suite of rooms and sixteen extra dinners. You'll need to adjust the account, and then we'll be on our way."

The manager opened his mouth as though he might object, but Ellert pinned him with a deadly stare. He knew he was correct, and he didn't intend to argue with a sniveling hotel manager. Ellert leaned back in his chair while the man drew a line through the objectionable charges and recalculated the balance. The manager pushed the paper across the desk. Ellert gave a curt approval and paid the sum in full.

The man stood and extended his hand. "Thank you for doing business with us, Mr. Jackson. I hope you were pleased with our services."

A clap of thunder rumbled overhead, and Ellert pushed away from the desk. "Come on, Jonas. It sounds as though we need to be on our way."

"I do hope you'll reconsider your decision." The manager glanced at Jonas. "Surely you're aware these waters can be difficult to navigate once a storm moves in, Mr. Broadmoor."

"Yes, of course, but I've been around this river for years. I can handle a skiff better than most of the young fellows who navigate the river." Jonas puffed his chest and strutted across the room.

Such nonsense! Jonas was wavering on the brink of financial disaster, yet he still felt the need to impress a simple hotel employee. Ellert would never understand these men born to wealth. If they'd had to suffer poverty early in life, they'd be better equipped to handle their inherited wealth. Instead, they made poor decisions and worried over their social status.

The doorman offered them an umbrella, but Ellert refused. With the surging wind, an umbrella would provide little protection. A bolt of lightning illuminated the churning water as he and Jonas neared the river. He'd never been particularly fond of water, and the sight of whitecaps gave him pause.

Jonas cupped his hands to his mouth and shouted to a young man near the water's edge. With his head bowed against the wind and holding his raincoat between clenched fingers, the boy scurried to meet them on the dock.

"What can I do for you, Mr. Broadmoor?"

Jonas pointed to a boat alongside the dock. "I want to take that skiff to Broadmoor Island." He dug in his pocket and retrieved several coins. "I'll see that it's returned tomorrow morning."

The young man maintained a tight hold on his raincoat. "I don't think it's safe to go out in a skiff, Mr. Broadmoor. The winds are—" A rumble of thunder drowned out the rest of the young man's sentence.

Jonas stepped closer to Ellert. "What's your preference? I'm willing to take to the river if you are."

Although the journey didn't hold much appeal, thoughts of Amanda prevailed. "Let's go before it gets any worse. I don't want to keep my bride waiting."

Jonas shoved the coins into the young man's hand with instructions to untie the skiff once they were onboard. The boy shrugged. "Don't say I didn't warn ya. You're gonna be in for the ride of your life if this keeps up."

Ignoring the young man's warning, Jonas and Ellert stepped into the boat and shoved off. For a short time the winds diminished, and Jonas rowed with the vigor of a young man. They were halfway to Broadmoor Island when a low rumble sounded in the distance as if to announce impending danger. The skies had turned as black as pitch, and the wind howled with a fury that struck fear in Ellert's pounding heart. The river swelled with angry waves, pummeling the boat like hammering fists. Lightning split the heavens, and Ellert trembled at the sight of the billowing waves. A sudden shriek of wind sent the boat in a frenzied turn, and it lurched to one side.

"We're taking on water," Ellert shouted. Though he couldn't be certain Jonas heard him, he was too frightened to move. He clung to the wooden seat and hoped Jonas was in control of the boat.

The winds briefly subsided, and Ellert felt a wooden object hit his hand. "Use this and start bailing water out of the boat," Jonas hollered.

Ellert clutched the bucket in one hand while continuing to maintain a hold on his seat with the other. The rising water had reached his ankles, and he cursed the ruination of his expensive shoes.

"I'd be worried about more than my shoes if I were you," Jonas shouted in reply. "This storm is besting me, and you're no help."

"You're the one who said you could handle a boat in any weather," Ellert screamed. "Now I see that you are an incompetent fool in more than business matters."

Jonas heaved the oars but made no headway in the churning waves. "This has nothing to do with incompetence, Ellert. I believe this is God's retribution upon both of us for the wrongs we've committed."

Though Ellert wanted to tell Jonas he was a fool, there wasn't opportunity. The wind regained its fury, and a massive wave whipped the boat onto its side and the men into a swirling caldron of angry water. Waves and rain lashed Ellert from all sides. He grabbed for Jonas but couldn't reach him. Clinging to the side of the skiff, he gasped for air as the wind ripped the wooden support from his hands. Amid the crushing waves, he thrashed at the water and fought to remain afloat. He must breathe. He must live. Amanda was waiting for him.

CHAPTER 28

Sunday, August 20, 1899
Broadmoor Island

Early the next morning, bright shards of sunshine splayed across the carpeted bedroom. A splinter of light danced across Amanda's fingers and settled on the shiny rings that now adorned her left hand. One glimpse and she sat upright in her bed. The wedding hadn't been a bad dream. She was truly married to Ellert Jackson. With a slight jerk she checked the opposite side of the bed. The covers remained undisturbed. Ellert hadn't come to her during the night. Had he returned late and gone to one of the upstairs bedrooms so as not to disturb her? Not likely.

Throwing back the covers, she slid her feet into a pair of soft slippers and padded across the room. Quietly turning the knob, she opened the door and peeked down the hallway. All was quiet. Not surprising considering the excitement of yesterday's festivities and the storm that had continued throughout most of the night. Her nieces and nephews had likely been unable to sleep. After retrieving her robe, Amanda tiptoed downstairs to the kitchen.

Mrs. Atwell looked up from the flour-sprinkled board where she was preparing morning biscuits. "Good morning, my dear. I trust you had a pleasant night."

"I slept well, thank you, but I was wondering if you've seen my father or Mr. Jackson this morning."

The older woman removed the lump of dough from the crock and shaped it into a circle. "No. You're the first family member I've seen today. I suppose you're anxious to begin your wedding trip to Europe. Fanny mentioned you'd be taking the train to New York City and then sailing for a month-long tour. Sounds as though you'll have a lovely time." Using her forearm, Mrs. Atwell brushed a strand of gray hair from her forehead. "Veda said she finished packing your trunks last night, so you have nothing to worry about. There's plenty of time for a good breakfast before you and Mr. Jackson depart for the train station in Clayton."

Amanda didn't argue. "I'm going back upstairs, Mrs. Atwell. If Mr. Jackson should appear, would you tell him I'd like a word?"

"Of course, my dear. You go on up and get dressed. Breakfast will be ready when you are."

Amanda didn't take time to explain that locating Ellert and her father was of greater import than eating breakfast. She rushed up two flights of stairs and down the hallway to her parents' bedroom.

After tapping on the door and receiving no response, she turned the knob and entered the sitting room. "Mother, may I come in?"

The swish of bedcovers in the adjacent room was followed by her mother's muffled permission. "Goodness, what time is it? I must have overslept. Why didn't Minnie waken me?"

"It's not yet eight o'clock."

Concern shone in her mother's eyes. "I do hope your wedding night wasn't dreadful." She glanced at the other side of the bed and suddenly appeared wide awake. "Your father must not have come home."

"That's why I'm here. I've not seen Ellert since we left Round Island yesterday. Do you think he and Father decided to remain at the Frontenac Hotel and wait out the storm?"

"That must be exactly what happened. We need to hurry and dress. We can have Mr. Atwell take us to Round Island and join your father and Mr. Jackson there. Then the two of you can go directly to Clayton."

Her mother rang for Minnie before she hurried across the room and pulled open the door of the wardrobe. "Let me see, what shall I wear?" She glanced over her shoulder and motioned toward the door. "Hurry along, Amanda, or you'll miss the train in Clayton. From what you've told me of Mr. Jackson, I doubt he'll be happy if that should occur."

Her mother was correct. She didn't want to suffer Ellert's wrath. He'd do more than pinch her cheek. "I'll meet you downstairs as soon as I'm dressed."

"I'll send Veda to assist you."

Before nine o'clock Amanda was dressed and downstairs, her trunks had been loaded onto the *DaisyBee*, and Mr. Atwell was waiting at the dock. Both Fanny and Sophie had joined her to bid their final farewells.

Upon receiving the news that Ellert hadn't returned to Broadmoor Island the previous night, Sophie grinned. "At least you were given a small reprieve. I do wish we could go with you, but I don't think either our husbands or Ellert would grant us permission."

Fanny giggled. "When has a lack of your husband's permission ever stopped you?"

Sophie folded her arms across her waist and tipped her head to the side. "Paul will tell you that I have become a comforting and dutiful wife. I'm doing my best to show him how much I love him."

Amanda leaned forward and kissed Sophie's cheek. "I'm very proud of the changes you're making. Paul's a wonderful man. And so is Michael," she quickly added. "Both of you are most fortunate, and I pray that God will continue to bless your marriages." She swallowed hard to keep her emotions in check. She didn't want a tearful final good-bye. "Pray that Ellert will permit me the opportunity to come home for a visit very soon. If I don't—"

"Come along, Amanda. We don't have time to tarry," her mother said as she descended the stairs. "I trust Mr. Atwell is waiting for us."

"Yes." Amanda motioned for her cousins to accompany her, but her mother shook her head. "I'm sorry, but we don't have time for prolonged good-byes. It's better if Sophie and Fanny remain behind."

"We'll be praying," Fanny whispered. "Please write."

"I promise."

After Amanda hugged Sophie one final time, her mother grasped Amanda's elbow. "Come along, dear."

Amanda sat at the rear of the boat and watched until Broadmoor Island disappeared from sight. A tight knot formed in her stomach. Would she ever see this place again? She had taken her life of privilege for granted. So often she had thought herself wise and savvy to the needs of others and the miseries of the world, but there'd always been the comfort of home to ease her mind. Now that was lost to her. Just as Blake was lost to her.

While Mr. Atwell steered their course toward Round Island, she stared into the clouded water. The roiling waters appeared to have turned the riverbed upside down, leaving a murky brown waterway teeming with unwanted debris in its wake. "Much like my own life," she muttered. Ellert had stormed into her world and turned it upside down. Was the unsightly river a reflection of her future? She shivered at the thought.

Mr. Atwell cut the engine, guided the boat alongside the Frontenac Hotel's dock, and tossed a line to a young man working at the pier.

Tying off the boat, the lad offered a quick salute. "Good morning, Mr. Atwell. Anything special I can do for you today?"

"Morning, Chester. We've come for Mr. Broadmoor and Mr. Jackson. I believe they must have stayed overnight at the hotel."

The young man rubbed his jaw. "Nope. They took a skiff and left last night. Against my advice, I might add. I told 'em both they was making a mistake, but Mr. Broadmoor said he could handle the storm. I ain't seen hide nor hair of either one of 'em since they left in that skiff."

"You let them leave here in a skiff? During that storm?"

"I warned the both of 'em, but they wouldn't listen. Nobody's seen either one of them since last night?"

Mr. Atwell shook his head. "Sound the bell."

Chester hurried across the wooden planks and yanked on the rope that hung from a large warning bell at the end of the dock. The bell clanged and echoed across the island, tolling a plea for help. The response was swift. Hotel staff and guests hastened toward the dock, but it was Blake Carstead who captured Amanda's attention. Where had *he* come from? Had he been at the hotel during the reception last evening?

A group of men gathered around Mr. Atwell while he explained the need to form search parties. "Neither Jonas Broadmoor nor Ellert Jackson has been seen since they left this dock in a skiff during last night's storm. We can only guess that the boat capsized, but the men may still be alive and waiting to be rescued on one of the uninhabited islands. We need to make haste and keep a sharp lookout."

"Were they headed toward Broadmoor Island?" one of the men shouted.

"Yes, but in the storm they may have been blown off course. The Broadmoor family will greatly appreciate your assistance in the search. I plan to return Mrs. Broadmoor and her daughter to their home, and then I will join you in the search."

While Mr. Atwell continued to organize the men, Amanda edged through the crowd until she was at Blake's side. "I'm surprised to see you here. Were you here during the . . ."

He shook his head. "I was here on the island but stayed away from your wedding. I couldn't have endured watching Ellert Jackson claim you as his wife. I wanted to discuss a matter with your uncle Quincy. Because of last night's storm, I thought he'd be at the Frontenac, but the manager informed me the family had returned home during a lull in the storm."

"All except my father and Ellert," she said. "They remained to conclude some business matters and were to follow later. Mother and I thought . . ."

Her mother hastened toward them and grasped Blake's arm. "Dr. Carstead. Thank goodness you're here. Jonas may need medical attention. I fear he'll be suffering from exhaustion. He doesn't exercise much, and I'm certain the rowing was strenuous. You will come with us, won't you?"

"Yes, of course. I'll return to Broadmoor Island with you and make sure they haven't returned, then go out with Mr. Atwell to help in the search."

The hours moved slowly while the family awaited word of the two missing men. Amanda's four brothers, as well as Paul and Michael, had gone out with search teams and all had now returned. Jefferson had discovered an oar and several pieces of wood floating in shallow water not far from Broadmoor Island, but they couldn't be sure the items were from the skiff that had carried Jonas and Ellert.

"I simply refuse to believe your father isn't safe and sound," Victoria told the family. "He's probably pacing back and forth on one of the islands, wondering when he's going to be rescued. I can just see him fussing and fuming, can't you?"

Amanda watched her mother search for some sign of agreement from the family. When no one responded, Amanda reached forward and grasped her mother's hand. "Why don't we go upstairs? I'll ask Minnie to bring tea to your sitting room. Afterward you can rest."

"Absolutely not. I'm going to be right here when your father walks into the house. I couldn't possibly sleep until he's home."

"Then I'll have Mrs. Atwell bring tea into the library. I don't think Father would object if you had a cup of tea."

Before she could step out of the room, her mother perked to attention. "Did I hear the front door?" Victoria jumped to her feet. "Yes! I hear voices. You see, your father *has* returned. I told you he'd be home for supper, didn't I?" She hurried to the library door but stopped mid-step when Blake and Mr. Atwell stepped into the library. "Where is my husband?"

Blake's eyes shone with sympathy. "I'm sorry, Mrs. Broadmoor, your husband has been gravely wounded. He might not live through the day. We have him on the boat and are preparing to take him to Clayton. I thought you might wish to accompany us."

After a wailing denial, her mother dashed for the door. "Mr. Atwell, take me to my husband."

Amanda looked at Blake. "Did they . . . ? What of . . . ?" She couldn't bring herself to ask.

"Ellert Jackson is dead. We found his body. We wrapped him in a blanket and are preparing to take him to the undertaker in Clayton."

Ellert was dead. Her father might well die, too. Chaos swirled around her, yet Amanda couldn't move. It was as if her feet were permanently affixed to the spot where she stood. Except for remaining frozen in place, she felt perfectly calm. Amid their concerns for her father's survival, several family members stepped forward and offered condolences for the loss of her new husband.

"Such a pity to be a widow a day after your wedding," someone said.

"You're young; you'll marry again," another remarked.

Amanda couldn't seem to comprehend all that had happened in the past twenty-four hours. It seemed like a dream.

"We need to get your father to Clayton. Come on," Blake said, pulling Amanda along.

She felt a gentle tap on her shoulder. Ellert's lawyer, Mr. Craig, stood beside her. He had accompanied the family to Broadmoor Island to await news of Ellert.

"I'll come with you."

"You don't need to do that," she replied.

He offered a sympathetic smile. "I'm afraid I must. We need to discuss how you would like to handle your husband's funeral arrangements, Mrs. Jackson."

CHAPTER 29

Monday, August 21, 1899
Rochester, New York

The return journey to Rochester proved more exhausting than Amanda had expected, but she'd done her best to remain calm in the wake of her many decisions. Her choice to have Ellert laid to rest beside his deceased wife in Rochester hadn't taken long. But Mr. Craig didn't approve. He thought New York City a better place, but Amanda remained steadfast in her decision. Mr. Craig likely thought her uncaring and selfish, but no matter the location of the services, she doubted any of Ellert's business associates would appear. With the exception of Mr. Craig, none of them had been there for the wedding. Why would they attend his funeral?

"I do wish you would reconsider. I think Ellert would have preferred New York City as his final resting place," Mr. Craig said once they'd entered the Rochester depot.

Amanda stopped and met the man's pleading look. "His final home is either heaven or hell, Mr. Craig. What truly matters is not where we bury his bodily remains but where he spends eternity. If Ellert didn't make his peace with God before he died, I imagine we both know where he is." She didn't want to seem unduly harsh, but arguing was useless. She patted the man's arm. "Besides, Ellert never mentioned a specific desire to be buried in New York City—at least not to me."

"I'm sure he didn't. Ellert thought he was indestructible."

"Then he was a foolish man. My decision stands, Mr. Craig."

"Very well. I will abide by your wishes, Mrs. Jackson. If you'd like me to accompany you to the mortuary, I would be willing to do so."

"You are most kind. I'd be pleased for your assistance. I know Ellert trusted your judgment." She would never be able to refer to Ellert as her husband, and she certainly didn't feel like a grieving widow. "If you will advise one of the porters to have the body delivered to the Ambrose Funeral Home, we can go directly there and meet with Mr. Ambrose."

Mr. Craig arched his bushy brows. "Now? Don't you think you should rest? You've been subjected to a great deal of distress. I fear the strain will be too great."

"Thank you for your concern, but I need to see the arrangements completed. After that, I will make my way to the hospital and check on my father's progress."

He shrugged. "I'm truly glad that he is recovering. I was relieved to hear they were able to bring him directly to Rochester from Clayton."

"I appreciate your concern about my father," Amanda said with a smile. "Dr. Carstead took care of everything. Father's body was quite battered by the storm, and the doctors fear he's developed pneumonia. However, the Rochester hospital is quite good. Now if you'll excuse me."

"But of course. Again, you have my condolences."

While Mr. Craig strode off to locate a porter, Amanda motioned to her cousins. Both Fanny and Sophie hurried to her side. "I'm going to the funeral home to arrange for Ellert's burial. Would you be kind enough to go to the hospital and check on Mother? Let her know that I will head over there afterwards to see Father."

"And Blake?" Sophie questioned with a slight grin. "He has been most attentive to care for your father, as I've heard Paul tell it. I suppose he hopes to charm Uncle Jonas so that he will allow you to marry him. Not that Uncle Jonas will have that much to say this time."

"Sophie!" Fanny chided.

"Well, it's true. We all know Amanda didn't love Ellert Jackson. Now she's free to marry Blake." She offered Amanda a consoling look. "I'm ever so sorry about your father nearly dying, but isn't it grand that your future isn't tied to that nasty Mr. Jackson?"

"I didn't wish Ellert dead, but I am most thankful that I am no longer his wife."

"Your next wedding will be a much happier occasion," Sophie said.

"Talk of another marriage is highly inappropriate while I'm in the midst of Ellert's funeral arrangements, but should I marry again, you may be assured it will be for love and not for money."

Fanny signaled toward the door leading to the train platform. "We'll see to your mother. You will come home directly after the hospital, won't you?"

"Yes." She kissed each of her cousins on the cheek. "Tell Mother I'll come to the hospital as soon as I make these arrangements."

"I doubt we'll be at the mortuary for more than an hour," Mr. Craig added as he approached and offered his arm.

Once they were settled inside the coach, Mr. Craig leaned forward and clasped his hands together. "We will need to meet during the next weeks to discuss your future, Mrs. Jackson."

"My future? What do you mean?"

"You will need to advise me how you wish to proceed regarding your financial assets."

"Financial assets?"

"You are now a very wealthy woman, Mrs. Jackson. I'm not certain you know the full extent of your husband's vast holdings, but you are his only heir, and many decisions will be required." He rubbed his hands together. "I represented Ellert for many years and would be willing to act as your legal advisor. I know how difficult it is for women to understand the complexities of business matters."

"Many of us are not as obtuse as you may believe, Mr. Craig. I am willing to meet with you and review all of the documents concerning Ellert's assets. I will then decide how I wish to proceed." She hoped she had spoken with enough authority to convince Mr. Craig that she'd not be cheated. Her entire family had suffered due to the corruption and greed of lawyers and learned businessmen, her own father among them. She'd not traverse that same path. The money she received would be put to good use helping those truly in need. She would begin by using some of Ellert's money to finance a multitude of infant summer hospitals.

Bright sunlight slanted across the crisp white sheet on Jonas's hospital bed. Ellert would still be alive if there had been weather such as this on Amanda's wedding day. Or would he? *Is it true that we have an appointed time to die?* Jonas wondered. Was that why he had survived and Ellert had died? Or was it merely because he'd grown up around the water, knew how to swim, and hadn't panicked?

What if he had been the one to die and Ellert had lived? The thought gave him pause. His family's suffering would have been extreme. Ellert would have produced their contract and taken delight in seeing every Broadmoor possession sold. Victoria would have been left destitute, and Amanda would have lived the remainder of her life in a loveless marriage. He shuddered at the thought of such a legacy.

His life had been spared. What legacy would he create for his family with this second chance he'd been given? Jonas rested his arm across his forehead, and for the first time in many years, he wept. Sorrow enveloped him more tightly than the sheet the nurse had tucked around his body.

"Forgive me, Lord," he whispered. "I know I don't deserve forgiveness from you or from my family, but I beg you to hear my prayer. Teach me what I must do to make amends and heal the wounds I've caused. Amen."

He couldn't recall the last time he'd prayed. The plea hadn't eased the agonizing pain; the gnawing remorse remained lodged deep in his heart. He'd hoped to experience immediate relief, but he knew that wasn't going to happen. His decisions had cut too deeply, and that would be too easy. God's forgiveness was immediate, but a simple prayer wouldn't set things aright with his family. From this point forward, his actions must speak for him. His family would test him and expect to see changes in his life. He massaged his forehead. Could he truly change his ways? Would God help him restore his place as head of his family? Did he even deserve such a chance?

The family would likely be better off if he had drowned along with Ellert. But death hadn't come, and he must be man enough to face the consequences of his wrongdoings. "It won't be easy," he muttered before sleep once again overtook him.

Amanda slipped into her father's hospital room and marveled at how small and unimposing he looked lying there in the bed. His eyes were closed, and for a moment Amanda feared he might have passed on, but stepping closer she could hear his even breathing.

As if sensing her presence, Jonas opened his eyes and stared at her for a moment. "Amanda."

She smiled. "Hello, Father. The doctors tell me you are doing much better. That is good news."

He gave a feeble smile. "Your mother says God has given me a second chance."

Amanda nodded. "He's given all of us a second chance."

Her father's eyes filled with tears. "I . . . never meant . . . I know it was . . ."

"Hush, don't worry yourself. Everything is resolved."

"No. There is a great deal of business to attend to once I recover. I wronged so many that it's difficult to know where and how to begin making amends."

"I'm certain those you've mistreated will come to forgive you in time," Amanda said.

Jonas extended his hand, and she took hold of it. "I've done so much wrong. Money—accruing it—has ruled my life. I have asked for God's forgiveness and prayed that our family be restored. Do you think that's possible?"

Amanda could hear the desperation in his voice. She had never seen her father like this before. She smiled and patted his hand with her gloved fingers. "If there is one thing I have learned in all of this—it's that God can do anything."

"I pray you're right."

"I am. But remember that forgiveness doesn't mean there won't be consequences. People will still have to deal with their wounds, and because of that, you will also have to deal with them."

"I will take whatever punishment I must. I deserve to be ostracized by the entire family. I can't expect everyone to simply understand and accept what I've done. I hope I can prove to them that I've become a better man. I may be required to face time in jail for what I've done." He pressed the back of his hand across his lips.

"I don't think—"

He shook his head. "I've stolen and lied, and that's merely the beginning. Those I've harmed will think it only fair that I pay the penalty for my crimes. And they're correct. It is the just and fair thing."

"This isn't about being fair," Amanda replied. "It's about grace. God has extended it to us, and we ought to extend it to one another." She leaned down and kissed him on the forehead. "I must go now. You need to rest."

Nothing she could say would ease his guilt. Even with the promise of God's forgiveness and the reassurance that she'd forgiven him, Amanda knew it would take much longer before her father was free of his own shame. Each time he looked at his family members, he would be reminded of the tragedy he'd caused among those he claimed to love the most. She prayed her father would discover that the love of God and family would eventually heal all of them.

"The doctors tell me I might return home in another few days," her father said.

Amanda smiled. "We shall all anticipate it with joy."

She walked down the hospital corridor, the smile still on her face. Amanda knew that God had completely touched her heart where her father was concerned. She held him no ill will or malice for the things he'd done, and to her surprise she found not only comfort but liberty in that knowledge.

I'm free, she thought. *Free of the pain and sorrow. Free from the worry of whom to blame for what. Free to forgive. I'm free, and now I can make my own choices about the future.*

She looked at the sterile hall and glanced into the rooms as she passed. The hospital had always intrigued her, even as a child, but more so now as she considered how she might reenter her training to become a doctor. Maybe even a surgeon. Now, there was a challenge.

"I hope I'm not interrupting. You seem to be daydreaming about something very pleasant."

"Blake." She whispered his name with great love.

"When did you return?"

"Just a short time ago. I escorted Ellert's body to the funeral home and arranged for his service. It won't be much. He has no friends or family. I imagine it will simply be the lawyer and me in attendance."

"I can be there if you want me."

She shook her head. "Thank you, but no. I want to lay this part of my life to rest and be done with it forever. It seems best to do that on my own."

Blake opened the door to a small room. "Come sit with me for a moment. This room will afford us a little privacy."

Amanda entered the room, took a chair, and sat rather primly on the edge. "I appreciate all of the help you've given us," she said, feeling awkward as Blake closed the door.

"It was the least I could do." He looked at her and seemed tongue-tied.

"How are things at the Home?" She disliked the silence that hung between them.

"Good. Quincy has obtained several new investors." Blake picked at a piece of lint on his trousers. "I think we'll finally get those ceilings replastered and painted."

Amanda smiled and then giggled. She relaxed and leaned toward Blake to whisper, "There are three hundred and twenty-seven places where the paint and plaster has fallen away in my recovery room."

Blake grinned. "Counted them, did you?"

"I had nothing else to do. I had the cruelest of physicians. He wouldn't let me do anything at all."

"Sounds like a very wise man."

"He wasn't acting out of wisdom."

Blake raised a brow. "Do tell."

"He was lovesick. He was mooning over me like a schoolboy. That's the only reason he wouldn't let me out of bed."

"Perhaps you were just delusional—hallucinating. Cholera can do that to a person." Blake gave her a look that suggested she challenge his comment.

Amanda got to her feet, and Blake quickly did likewise.

She shrugged. "I had considered that. I'm still not completely certain that I didn't just imagine it all."

He grabbed her unexpectedly. It was nothing like the harsh, painful manner in which Ellert had taken hold of her.

"Maybe you're just imagining this, as well." He kissed her passionately, pulling her tightly against him.

Amanda couldn't help but sigh.

"I didn't mean to lose control," he whispered against her ear. "I honestly didn't come here to impose myself upon you. I know it's the worst possible time."

"We both know I didn't love Ellert Jackson. He meant nothing but pain and sorrow to me. It sounds callous, but his death only served to remind me of how sin can corrupt a man to death."

Blake shook his head. "I was so afraid for you—for us. I couldn't bear to think of him touching you, holding you." He shuddered.

"Then don't think of that," Amanda countered. She touched his cheek with her hand. "Think only of us."

He put his hand over hers. "I know I should probably wait, but I can't permit you to slip away from me again. I can't bear the thought of losing you." He inhaled a deep breath and stared into her eyes.

"Exactly what are you saying, Blake?" She pulled away slightly, but Blake refused to let her go far.

"I'm saying that I need you beside me for the rest of my life. I'm saying that I love you and want you to be my wife."

She arched her brows and grinned. "Are you certain you're not merely looking for someone to help with your medical practice? Uncle Quincy said you have been rather grumpy of late."

"My grumpiness was due to losing the woman I love," he said. "That's not to say I don't miss your help with my patients, too. And I'm more than willing for you to complete your medical training if that's your wish."

She gazed into his eyes, and when he lowered his head, she willingly accepted his kiss.

"There are many things I want to teach you," he said before pulling her close again. He covered her lips with a lingering kiss that caused her to tremble.

"I'd be pleased to learn whatever you'd like to teach me, Dr. Carstead," she whispered.

He tucked a wayward strand of her hair behind her ear while he continued to hold her close. "I know we'll have to wait until your mourning period has ended, but I don't want any misunderstanding between us. I love you and want you to be my wife. Say you'll marry me."

"Of course I'll marry you. You are the desire of my heart, and I long only for us to be together always."

CHAPTER 30

WEDNESDAY, JULY 4, 1900
BROADMOOR ISLAND

"I now pronounce you man and wife," the pastor declared. "You may kiss your bride."

Blake looked at Amanda and leaned forward. "We're well practiced at this, eh, Mrs. Carstead?" He covered her mouth with his before she could answer.

A cheer went up from the crowd of observers. Amanda cherished the moment. It drove out all memories of her wedding the previous year. Ellert Jackson was nothing more than a bad dream pushed aside in the light of a hopeful new day. As Blake let go his hold on her, Amanda caught sight of her mother and father. They offered her a broad smile before a swarm of well-wishers surrounded them.

"Congratulations!" Michael and Fanny were the first to reach them. Fanny pulled Amanda away from Blake's embrace and hugged her close.

"I'm so happy for you, Amanda. I feel like I've been waiting forever for this day to come."

"You're telling me," Blake said, laughing. He received Michael's embrace and then Fanny's as other members of the family began to gather around them on the lawn of the Broadmoor Island estate.

"You treat my cousin right," Fanny admonished, "or you'll have to answer to me."

"And me," Sophie said, tapping Blake's shoulder.

Amanda laughed at their stern expressions. "We Broadmoor ladies know how to take care of our own," she reminded him.

"I can vouch for that," Paul admitted. He reached down to pick up their year-and-a-half-old daughter. Elizabeth held out several flowers she'd picked.

Amanda took the flowers and pretended to sniff their scent. "Oh, how pretty."

"Pre-ey," Elizabeth mimicked, and everyone laughed.

"I'm sorry for the interruption, Mrs. Atwell," Veda announced, bringing Fanny a bundle. "But I believe Miss Carrie is hungry."

Fanny blushed and took her whimpering daughter. "Carrie Winifred Atwell, do you not realize this is your cousin Amanda's day?"

"Oh, she is so beautiful, Fanny," Amanda declared, gently touching the baby's cheek. This only served to cause the infant to begin rooting. Carrie quickly latched on to Amanda's finger.

"Oh my!" Amanda gasped in surprise. Everyone laughed while Fanny carefully pried her daughter's mouth away.

"Come, little one. We'll give you something a bit more substantial."

"You realize, Amanda," Sophie began, "that you'll have to have a baby girl next year in order to continue the line of stair-step cousins. We're counting on you."

Amanda hadn't expected this announcement and felt her cheeks grow hot. Blake leaned down and furthered her embarrassment. "I know I shall do my part to see that legacy continued."

The wedding party lasted well into the evening, with fireworks crowning the events of the day. Amanda and Blake slipped away from the crowd, anxious to escape the noise and festivities.

"I feared at times this day would never come."

Amanda nodded. She looked at her husband in the soft glow of lanterns and fireworks. She trembled at his touch, but not for the same reasons Ellert had caused her to tremble. "I'm so happy. I never thought to marry. Not really. I never felt the pressure to wed, as many women do. At least not until that disaster last year."

He put his finger to her lips. "I never want to speak of that time again."

She kissed his finger. "I feel the same. I just want you to know that you completely changed my mind about love and marriage. I truly thought I'd seek my fulfillment in being a doctor."

"And you've changed your mind now?"

She looked up at him and shook her head. "Not at all. I intend to seek it there, as well. I plan to be the best doctor in all of Rochester."

"Second best," he countered.

She pulled back and put her hands on her hips. "I beg your pardon. Are you suggesting that I can't surpass your knowledge and become an even better doctor than you?"

He laughed. "You are so competitive. Everything you know about medicine, I've taught you. Now you want to throw it back at me and suggest that you can best me?"

"How arrogant and prideful you are, Dr. Carstead. I'm not at all certain this arrangement is going to work out," she said, feigning concern. She started to walk away, but he easily caught her and lifted her in his arms.

"I can see I will have to work hard to teach you to appreciate me," he said, nuzzling her neck with a kiss.

Amanda didn't feel like challenging him any longer. "I doubt you'll have to work that hard, Dr. Carstead."

Blake laughed and headed for Broadmoor Castle. "I'm not ever going to take any chances where you're concerned. I've learned my lesson. One has to act fast when a Broadmoor is involved."

Amanda giggled and clasped her hands around Blake's neck. "I'm a Carstead now. That means I get to act obstinate, ill-tempered, and smugly superior."

He stopped mid-step and looked toward the river. "It wouldn't be hard to toss you into the water to cool off that opinionated little mouth of yours."

She tightened her grasp on him and laughed. "Where I go, you go."

He pulled her close and sighed. "That's the first reasonable thing you've said all evening. And it's a promise I give you. If I have anything to say about it, we'll be together always. Now and forever."

TRACIE PETERSON is the bestselling, award-winning author of more than 80 novels. Tracie also teaches writing workshops at a variety of conferences on subjects such as inspirational romance and historical research. She and her family live in Belgrade, Montana.

JUDITH MILLER is a bestselling author whose avid research and love of history are reflected in every book she writes. Judy makes her home in Topeka, Kansas.

For more information on Tracie and Judy and their books, please visit

www.traciepeterson.com
www.judithmccoymiller.com